ONE THOUSAND
Inspirational Things

Compiled by
AUDREY STONE MORRIS

Published by
SPENCER PRESS
Distributed by
HAWTHORN BOOKS, INC.
NEW YORK

THE COMPILER AND PUBLISHERS *wish to thank the following agents and publishers for granting permission to reprint in the United States, its possessions and Canada these copyrighted selections:*

THE AMERICAN MAGAZINE and the author for permission to reprint *David's Star of Bethlehem* by Christine Whiting Parmenter.

. APPLETON-CENTURY COMPANY, INC., for permission to reprint *The Deep-Sea Doctor,* from "Heroes of Today," by Mary R. Parkman, copyright, 1916, 1917, by the Century Company, 1945, by Lawrence Koenigsberger and Cornelia Whitney; *Our Lady of the Red Cross: Clara Barton,* from "Heroines of Service," by Mary R. Parkman, copyright, 1916, 1917, by the Century Company, 1945, by Lawrence Koenigsberger and Cornelia Whitney.

BASIL BLACKWELL & MOTT, LTD., Oxford, for permission to reprint *Wanderlust* by Gerald Gould.

BRANDT & BRANDT for permission to reprint *The Grand March of the United States of America* by Dana Burnet, from Collier's, The National Weekly. Copyright, 1947, by Dana Burnet; *Afternoon on a Hill,* from "Renascence and Other Poems," by Edna St. Vincent Millay, published by Harper & Brothers. Copyright, 1917, by Edna St. Vincent Millay; *On Hearing a Symphony of Beethoven,* from "The Buck in the Snow," by Edna St. Vincent Millay, published by Harper & Brothers. Copyright, 1928, by Edna St. Vincent Millay.

JACQUES CHAMBRUN, INC., for permission to reprint *A Word to Youth* by André Maurois.

CHICAGO TRIBUNE-NEW YORK NEWS SYNDICATE, INC., for permission to reprint *On the Subject of Courage* by Ed Sullivan.

CHILDRENS PRESS, INC., for permission to reprint *The Littlest Angel* by Charles Tazewell.

COWARD-MCCANN, INC., for permission to reprint *Happy Land* by MacKinlay Kantor, copyright, 1942, by The Curtis Publishing Company; 1943 by MacKinlay Kantor.

CURTIS BROWN, LTD., for permission to reprint *Grandpa and the Miracle Grindstone* by Joe David Brown, copyright 1946 by The Curtis Publishing Company, reprinted by permission of the author; *Holiness* by John Drinkwater, copyright 1919 by John Drinkwater, reprinted by permission of the author's estate; *I Remember the Frandsens* by Kathryn Forbes, copyright 1946 by The Reader's Digest Association, Inc., reprinted by permission of the author.

JAMES A. DECKER for permission to reprint *Reach Me Your Hand,* from "Forty Shillings," by Ruth Crary.

DODD, MEAD & COMPANY for permission to reprint *The Joys of the Road* by Bliss Carman from "Last Songs from Vagabondia," by Bliss Carman and Richard Hovey, copyright, 1900, 1927, by Bliss Carman and Julian Hovey; *Roadside Flowers,* from "Bliss Carman Poems," by Bliss Carman; *At the Crossroads* by Richard Hovey from "Last Songs from Vagabondia," by Bliss Carman and Richard Hovey, copyright, 1900, 1927, by Bliss Carman and Julian Hovey; *Unmanifest Destiny* by Richard Hovey; *The Passing of the Third Floor Back* by Jerome K. Jerome, copyright, 1908, by Dodd, Mead & Company; *The Song of Life,* from "Faraway Stories," by William J. Locke, copyright, 1919, by William J. Locke; *Work,* from "The Hour Has Struck," by Angela Morgan, copyright, 1914, by Angela Morgan; *Death Is a Door,* from "Star in a Well," by Nancy Byrd Turner, copyright, 1935, by Dodd, Mead & Company, Inc.

DOUBLEDAY, DORAN & COMPANY, INC., for permission to reprint *Louis Pasteur and Lengthened Human Life* by Otis W. Caldwell, from "Science Remaking the World," by Otis W. Caldwell and Edwin E. Slosson, copyright, 1922, 1923, by Doubleday & Company, Inc.; *The Dreamers,* from "The Dreamers and Other Poems," by Theodosia Garrison, copyright, 1917, by Doubleday & Company, Inc.; from *Great Possessions* by David Grayson, copyright, 1917, by Doubleday & Company, Inc.; *A Retrieved Reformation,* from "Roads of Destiny," by O. Henry, copyright, 1903, by Doubleday & Company, Inc.; from *Let Us Have Faith* by Helen Keller, copyright, 1940, by Helen Keller; *Roofs,* from "Main Street and Other Poems," by Joyce Kilmer, copyright, 1917, by Doubleday & Company, Inc.; from *The Moon and Sixpence* by W. Somerset Maugham, copyright, 1919, by W. Somerset Maugham.

E. P. DUTTON & CO., INC., for permission to reprint *In the Hospital,* from "Death and General Putnam and 101 Other Poems," by Arthur Guiterman, copyright 1935 by E. P. Dutton & Co., Inc.; *Jenny,* from "Man with a Bull-Tongue Plow," by Jesse Stuart, copyright, 1934, by E. P. Dutton & Co., Inc.; *Log Shacks and Lonesome Waters,* from "Head O' W-Hollow," by Jesse Stuart, copyright, 1936, by E. P. Dutton & Co., Inc.

THE EMPORIA GAZETTE for permission to reprint *To an Anxious Friend* by William Allen White.

HARCOURT, BRACE AND COMPANY, INC., for permission to reprint *"Listen! The Wind Is Rising,"* from "Listen! The Wind," by Anne Morrow Lindbergh, copyright, 1938, by Anne Morrow Lindbergh; *A God for You,* from "Once in a Blue Moon," by Marion Strobel, copyright, 1925, by Harcourt, Brace and Company, Inc.; *Three Stockings,* from "Mrs. Miniver," by Jan Struther, copyright, 1940, by Jan Struther.

HENRY HOLT AND COMPANY, INC., for permission to reprint *Testament,* from "Address to the Living," by John Holmes, copyright, 1937, by Henry Holt and Company, Inc.; *Baby Face,* from "Cornhuskers," by Carl Sandburg, copyright, 1918, by Henry Holt and Company, copyright, 1945, by Carl Sandburg; *God Is at the Anvil* and *Refuge,* from "Many, Many Moons," by Lew Sarett, copyright, 1920, by Henry Holt and Company; *Old House,* from "The Shape of Memory," by Winifred Welles, copyright, 1944, by Henry Holt and Company.

HOUGHTON MIFFLIN COMPANY for permission to reprint *My Mother's Words*, from "Songs for My Mother," by Anna Hempstead Branch; *Lost Road*, from "These Acres," by Frances Frost; *Lilacs*, from "What's O' Clock," by Amy Lowell; *We Were on That Raft—A Hundred Million of Us—*, from "The Great Answer," by Margaret Lee Runbeck; *A Religion That Does Things*, from "Forty Years for Labrador," by Wilfred Grenfell.

THE JOURNAL OF THE NATIONAL EDUCATION ASSOCIATION OF THE UNITED STATES for permission to reprint *The Hope of Tomorrow* by Joy Elmer Morgan.

ALFRED A. KNOPF, INC., for permission to reprint *In the Night*, from "The Collected Poems of Stephen Crane," copyright, 1926, by Alfred A. Knopf, Inc.; *Sundown*, from "A Penny Whistle," by Bert Leston Taylor (B.L.T.), copyright, 1921, by Alfred A. Knopf, Inc.; *Old Friendship*, from "Leaves in Windy Weather," by Eunice Tietjens, copyright, 1929, by Alfred A. Knopf, Inc.

LITTLE, BROWN & COMPANY and THE ATLANTIC MONTHLY PRESS for permission to reprint from *Good-bye, Mr. Chips* by James Hilton, copyright, 1934, by James Hilton; from *The Story of Dr. Wassell* by James Hilton, copyright, 1943, by James Hilton.

LOTHROP, LEE AND SHEPARD CO. for permission to reprint *The House by the Side of the Road*, from "Dreams in Homespun," by Sam Walter Foss, copyright, 1897.

THE MACMILLAN COMPANY for permission to reprint *The Pines*, from "Strange Holiness," by Robert P. Tristram Coffin and *Winter Morning*, from "Collected Poems," by Robert P. Tristram Coffin; *I Want a Pasture*, from "Branches Green," by Rachel Field; *General William Booth Enters into Heaven*, from "Collected Poems," by Vachel Lindsay; *Tomorrow*, from "Poems," by John Masefield; *Flammonde*, from "Collected Poems," by Edwin Arlington Robinson; *Alchemy*, *April*, *Song*, and *Stars*, from "Collected Poems," by Sara Teasdale.

THE MACMILLAN COMPANY OF CANADA, LTD., for Canadian permission to reprint, in this anthology, from *The Story of Doctor Wassell* by James Hilton and *The Ballad of East and West* by Rudyard Kipling.

ROBERT M. MCBRIDE & COMPANY for permission to reprint *The Book That Converted Its Author*, from "The Story Behind Great Books," by Elizabeth Rider Montgomery.

MCCLELLAND AND STEWART, LTD., for Canadian permission to reprint, in this anthology, *Joys of the Road* and *Roadside Flowers* by Bliss Carman.

HAROLD MATSON for permission to reprint *Before Gabriel Blows His Horn* by James Street, taken from Cosmopolitan, July, 1941.

NATURAL HISTORY for permission to reprint *Every Man His Own Naturalist* by Donald Culross Peattie as condensed in The Reader's Digest.

THE NEW YORK SUN for permission to reprint *An Epic of the North* by Frank M. O'Brien.

THE NEW YORK TIMES and the author for permission to reprint *Just Passing By* by Glenn Ward Dresbach.

NOBLE AND NOBLE for permission to reprint *Possibilities* by Mary Elizabeth Bain, from Boone's "New Declamations."

THE PHILADELPHIA BULLETIN and the author for permission to reprint *When the Wise Man Appeared* by William Ashley Anderson.

POETRY (Chicago) and the author for permission to reprint *Lost* by Maurice Lesemann.

THE READER'S DIGEST and the author for permission to reprint *Like Summer's Cloud—the Gossamer Dreams of Boyhood* by Merle Crowell.

THE REILLY & LEE CO. for permission to reprint *The House at Peace* and *My Creed*, from "Collected Verse," by Edgar A. Guest, copyright, 1934, by Edgar A. Guest.

PAUL R. REYNOLDS & SON for permission to reprint *We Just Live* by Dorothy Canfield.

SYDNEY A. SANDERS and the author for permission to reprint *Poetry* by Lord Dunsany.

THE SCIENTIFIC MONTHLY for permission to reprint *Mother of Comptons* by Milton S. Mayer.

CHARLES SCRIBNER'S SONS for permission to reprint from *Courage* by James M. Barrie, copyright, 1922, by Charles Scribner's Sons; *A Mother in Mannville*, from "When the Whippoorwill," by Marjorie Kinnan Rawlings, copyright, 1931, 1940, by Marjorie Kinnan Rawlings; *A Handful of Clay*, from "The Blue Flower," by Henry van Dyke, copyright, 1902, by Charles Scribner's Sons, 1930, by Henry van Dyke; *Song*, from "The House of Rimmon," by Henry van Dyke, copyright, 1907, by Henry van Dyke, 1935, by Tertius van Dyke; *The Things I Prize*, from Part VII of "God of the Open Air," from "Music and Other Poems," by Henry van Dyke, copyright, 1904, by Charles Scribner's Sons, 1932, by Henry van Dyke; *Work*, from "Music and Other Poems," by Henry van Dyke, copyright, 1904, by Charles Scribner's Sons, 1932, by Henry van Dyke.

RALPH FLETCHER SEYMOUR and the author for permission to reprint *Immortality*, from "Immortality and Other Poems," by Francesca Falk Miller.

SIMON AND SCHUSTER, INC., for permission to reprint from *Peace of Mind* by Joshua Loth Liebman, copyright, 1946, by Joshua Loth Liebman; from *Bambi* by Felix Salten, copyright, 1928, by Simon and Schuster, Inc.

THE SOCIETY OF AUTHORS as the Literary Representatives of the Estate of the late Jerome K. Jerome for Canadian permission to reprint, in this anthology, *The Passing of the Third Floor Back*, by Jerome K. Jerome.

THE STAR WEEKLY for Canadian permission to reprint, in this anthology, *Last Day on Earth* by Cynthia Hope and Frances Ancker.

THIS WEEK MAGAZINE for permission to reprint *How To Stay Young*, copyright, 1945, by the United Newspapers Magazine Corporation; *Last Day on Earth* by Cynthia Hope and Frances Ancker.

TURNER COMPANY for permission to reprint *Morning Song*, from "Dreamers on Horseback," by Karle Wilson Baker.

THE UNIVERSITY OF NORTH CAROLINA PRESS for permission to reprint *The Need for God in an Age of Science*, from "The Human Meaning of Science," by Arthur H. Compton. Copyright, 1940, by The University of North Carolina Press.

THE VIKING PRESS, INC., for permission to reprint *Father Duffy*, from "The Portable Woollcott," by Alexander Woollcott, copyright, 1934, by Alexander Woollcott, 1946, by The Viking Press, Inc., New York.

A. P. WATT & SON for permission to reprint *The Ballad of East and West*, from "Barrack Room Ballads," by Rudyard Kipling.

YALE UNIVERSITY PRESS for permission to reprint *Creeds and Thrushes*, from "Blue Smoke," by Karle Wilson Baker; *Ballade of the Dreamland Rose*, from "Poems," by Brian Hooker; and *Earth Lover*, from "White April," by Harold Vinal.

WE ALSO WISH TO THANK the following authors for permission to reprint their selections in this book: George Matthew Adams, Frances Ancker, Preston Bradley, Gail Brook Burket, Thomas Curtis Clark, Ruth Crary, Grace Noll Crowell, Louise Driscoll, Clara Edmunds-Hemingway, Fannie Stearns Davis Gifford, Hermann Hagedorn, Cynthia Hope, Ethel Jacobson, Elias Lieberman, Adelaide Love, Archibald MacLeish, Annabelle Merrifield, David Morton, Joseph Fort Newton, S. Alicia Poole, Laura Lee Randall, Margaret E. Sangster, Hester Suthers, Adele Jordan Tarr, Charles Hanson Towne, Nancy Byrd Turner, A. Warren, and Margaret Widdemer.

Poems or stories by Keene Abbott, Elbert Hubbard, Edwin Markham, Mildred Plew Meigs, Cale Young Rice, Damon Runyon and Ida M. Tarbell

(*Work* taken from Cosmopolitan, December, 1936), reprinted by special permission of the copyright owners.

Great pains have been taken to obtain permission from the owners to reprint material which is in copyright. Any errors that may possibly have been made are unintentional and will gladly be corrected in future printings if notification is sent to Consolidated Book Publishers.

The compiler is deeply grateful for the help she has received from the editorial staff of this publishing house, and Walter R. Barrows, Barbara Clyne, Herbert H. Hewitt, William E. Hill, S. Alicia Poole, Laura Lee Randall, Mary Reardon and Adele Jordan Tarr.

To my sister

BETTY STONE MORRIS

whose life always will be a

great inspiration to those

who knew her

Publisher's Foreword

*H*ere is a collection of great stories of the human spirit, of soul-searching essays, of beautiful, inspired poems and of stirring thoughts by outstanding thinkers and doers.

Surely every home has need for such a volume— a volume to give us a lift when a lift is needed and to bring forth in all of us "diviner feelings kindred with the skies."

May the selections by the great writers in this book help us all better "to live in pulses stirred to generosity, in deeds of daring rectitude, in scorn for miserable aims that end with self, in thoughts sublime that...urge man's search to vaster issues."

ONE THOUSAND

Inspirational
Things

HOLD FAST YOUR DREAMS
Louise Driscoll

Hold fast your dreams!
Within your heart
Keep one still, secret spot
Where dreams may go,
And, sheltered so,
May thrive and grow
Where doubt and fear are not.
O keep a place apart,
Within your heart,
For little dreams to go!

Think still of lovely things that are not true.
Let wish and magic work at will in you.
Be sometimes blind to sorrow. Make believe!
Forget the calm that lies
In disillusioned eyes.
Though we all know that we must die,
Yet you and I
May walk like gods and be
Even now at home in immortality.

We see so many ugly things—
Deceits and wrongs and quarrelings;
We know, alas! we know
How quickly fade
The color in the west,
The bloom upon the flower,
The bloom upon the breast
And youth's blind hour.
Yet keep within your heart
A place apart
Where little dreams may go,
May thrive and grow.
Hold fast—hold fast your dreams!

THE COMMON TASKS
GRACE NOLL CROWELL

The common tasks are beautiful if we
Have eyes to see their shining ministry.
The plowman with his share deep in the loam;
The carpenter whose skilled hands build a home;
The gardener working with reluctant sod,
Faithful to his partnership with God—
These are the artisans of life. And, oh,
A woman with her eyes and cheeks aglow,
Watching a kettle, tending a scarlet flame,
Guarding a little child—there is no name
For this great ministry. But eyes are dull
That do not see that it is beautiful;
That do not see within the common tasks
The simple answer to the thing God asks
Of any child, a pride within His breast:
That at our given work we do our best.

2

THE PINES

ROBERT P. TRISTRAM COFFIN

Behind the barn was mystery,
The pine trees there were like the sea
When wind was up; but it was more
Than waves upon an unseen shore
That made the boy's heart burn and sing.
He knew well there was a thing
In that spot which bound in one
All splendid things from sun to sun—
Amber jewels of roosters' eyes,
The floating beads of golden flies,
The rainbow's lintel of brief light
Arched across the door of night,
A duck's white feather like a flower
On a pool left by a shower,
The hot sound, steady, small, and keen,
Of August mowing by machine.
The cool sound of a scythe. The small
Madness of the cricket's call,
The sudden smell of apples in
October twilight from a bin,
The pleasure, lonely and immense,
Of the hearth-cat's confidence.
The pines behind the barn somehow
Joined the lowing of a cow
To the moon that marched through crowds
Of angels of fair-weather clouds.
The pines possessed the ancient right
Of opening doorways in the night
To let the day and cockcrow through,
They built a fire in the dew,
Laid the hand of East in West's,
Filled the eggs in robins' nests
With thunder rolling deep below
The earth at night. They mingled snow
Of Junetime daisies with December's,
And built the roses in the embers.

It took a boy of ten to see
Such a tremendous unity.

3

Grandpa and the
Miracle Grindstone

By JOE DAVID BROWN

*W*OMEN WERE STILL WEEPING over the graves at Gettysburg when my grandpa came to Walesburg. Nobody ever quite figured out where he came from or why he came. He just showed up one night in a blue-serge store-bought suit and eased his way into Jere Higham's place.

Grandpa walked quietly to the end of the bar and put down his Bible. He didn't have to call for silence, because it followed him through the long smoky room like a hound dog.

Grandpa cleared his throat and began to speak. "Boys, I'm your new preacher," he said, "and I aim to give my first sermon right here."

A couple of General Lee's men, still in uniform, began to laugh. Grandpa didn't even glance that way. He just reached under his long coat and pulled up two long-barreled cavalry pistols and slapped them on the bar.

"Either I speak," he said, "or these do!"

Nobody ever crossed my grandpa after that, except old Jed Isbell. But then, it took a miracle to convince Old Jed. Grandpa's first sermon was the golden rule, and for forty years he preached that same sermon with variations. Later on, when the legends began to grow, folks used to say that the sermon grandpa gave in Jere Higham's that night was the first one he had ever preached. These folks said grandpa had been a member of Quantrill's guerrillas and that he decided to be a preacher when he left Missouri.

I never knew, because grandpa had grown mellow and soft-spoken by the time I got big enough to run along by his side. He always wore black, my grandpa did; and he stood tall and erect. He had white hair, and it curled down around his collar. He wore black string ties and big, broad-brimmed hats. As far as I know, he never raised his voice, and I saw him angry only once. A salesman was beating a livery-stable horse down by the covered bridge one day. My grandpa's face flushed and his jaw muscles stood out like knobs. He reached up and took the whip from the fat little salesman's hand.

"Stranger," he said, "that's a good hoss. He don't balk for nothing. You better go in that bridge and find out what's wrong."

The salesman started to say something, but grandpa looked at him with those hard blue eyes of his, and he thought better of it. He eased down out of the buggy and waddled into the covered bridge. A few seconds later we heard his frightened yelp. His face was purple when he came out, panting.

"Rattler!" he gasped. "Bigger'n my leg!"

4

My grandpa swished the whip. "Stranger, I could drive you back in there."

The sweating man looked startled, then frightened. "No, no!" he said.

Grandpa looked at him coldly for a full minute. Then he walked into the bridge and with one slash of the whip cut off the rattler's head. He came back and handed the salesman seven rattles and a button.

"Stranger, keep these in your pocket, and whenever you hear them rattle, remember: do unto others as you would have them do unto you." He walked away a few steps, with me churning my little fat legs to keep up and almost splitting with adoration. Then he turned for a parting shot at the uneasy little salesman. "And that means hosses and dogs . . . and all God's creatures."

Grandpa's church was the biggest building in Walesburg. The people gave it to him after he had been there for three years, preaching around in saloons and houses, and, on occasions, even barns. The church sat on a little rise over by Brown Springs, and the people loved it because it was part of them —part of their lives and built with their sweat.

If ever a church was put together with loving hands, that one was. Times were hard then. Nails cost a dollar apiece, and the only dollars around Walesburg were signed by President Jeff Davis. All of them together wouldn't buy a single nail. Labor wasn't cheap either. It couldn't be bought at any price. But it was the most plentiful commodity around Walesburg. Sweat and calluses were the dollars and cents that paid for grandpa's church.

The men cut down the straight young pines in the bottom lands for flooring. They sent up into the hills for the biggest oaks for joists and beams. And the nails—that was the difficult part. The women and children made them—shaped them lovingly and carefully out of pieces of hard ash and oak.

Right behind the church site, Old Gene Caldwell started building a windmill. Work went sort of slow because Old Gene had lost an arm at Bull Run, but he was too proud of that windmill to let anybody help him. It was a mighty good monument to Old Gene's faith when it was finished, because it was high as any in the valley and it could pick up a breeze that wouldn't even ripple the surface in Edward's pond.

Nearly everybody in Walesburg had a hand in building that church. Even old Granny Gailbraith, who lived in George Washington's time, had her split-cane-bottomed chair moved down amid the hammering and sawing. Her gnarled old hands whittled out the last wooden nail. It was carried up to grandpa, and he drove it into the base of the block supporting the cross on the steeple. Then the folks moved into the church. It still smelled of pine and oak and cedar. They prayed and grandpa preached. I asked him once what he said.

"I can't rightly remember," he answered, "but it was to do with using God's property. I told them that we had taken a part of God's land and the things which grew on that land to build a monument to

5

Him." He mused a moment. "Just an ordinary sort of sermon, I guess. Just a plain 'thank you, God.' There wasn't any use going into a long-winded spiel on why we were thankful. God could look at our sweaty clothes and blistered hands and know that."

Other churches were built in Walesburg after that. They built them out of stone and bricks. They brought in polished pews from Louisville, and the Baptist church had a big stained-glass window which came all the way from St. Louis. Somehow, though, they never rivaled grandpa's church for beauty.

City folks used to call it "quaint," and once a circuit-rider preacher who had gone to Harvard College came by and wrote it up in the *Southern Methodist Magazine.* Grandpa used to carry the clipping in his big black wallet. But that was before the miracle of the grindstone. After that, I guess nobody could keep count of all the stories. Even Miss Gussie ·Lou Hamilton down at the library gave up after filling two composition books.

Old Man Jed Isbell caused the miracle. He came down into the valley around '85 or thereabouts. He worked hard and kept his mouth shut, Old Man Isbell did. He took forty acres of flinty land and a mule, and built up one of the nicest farms around Walesburg. Grandpa tried for twenty years to get Old Man Isbell to come to church, but it was no use. Old Man Isbell just claimed he didn't believe in the Gospel. He was almost as tall as grandpa and he would speak right up to him.

Old Man Isbell had carried a Minié ball in his right leg ever since the Battle of Chattanooga. I guess I had been to the Isbell place, out on the edge of town, with grandpa, a hundred times, and it was always the same. We would always drive up in grandpa's buggy, and Old Man Isbell always saw us before we reached the frame house sitting under the two big oaks. He would always limp out to meet us.

"Howdy, parson," he'd say, "light down and have some of the best well water in the county."

Grandpa's first words always were, "How's that game leg of yours, Jed?"

For as long as I can remember, the answer was always the same, "Jes tol'ble, parson. Jes tol'ble."

I sometimes used to think that grandpa thought more of Old Jed Isbell than he did of some of his regular psalm singers, but I never could be sure. Especially after we used to leave Old Jed's farm, because grandpa would mutter, "That dadburned Jed Isbell, that stubborn pigheaded rebel."

It was always the same. After we'd had some of Jed's iron water and he and grandpa had discussed crops and the price of cotton, grandpa would ask, "When you comin' to church, Jed?"

Jed's eyes would get shrewd under his ragged brows. "Jes as soon as you can git God to plow the bottom land for me, parson."

With that, grandpa would sigh and climb up into the buggy. "Good-bye, Jed. Be callin'," and off we'd go.

I was knee-high to a good squirrel gun when the pay-off came. It was a hot August afternoon and grandpa had been cranky all day. The Gailbraith cow had stomped down our vegetable garden, Uncle

Henry Wallace said the church roof couldn't be patched no more, and a fox had killed grandpa's favorite bantam rooster. I guess grandpa had reasons to feel bad.

We stopped by John McCollough's place to buy some steel traps. Grandpa said he'd get that dadburned fox or bust. There was a big crowd in the store and in the middle of it all was Old Man Isbell, riding sidesaddle on the first store-bought grindstone I had ever seen. I heard it cost Old Man Isbell thirty dollars.

Grandpa couldn't take his eyes off that grindstone. He just glanced absently at Old Man Isbell. "Howdy, Jed. How's that game leg of yours?"

"Jes tol'ble, parson. Jes tol'ble," said Jed. You could see he was as pleased as a partridge at all the commotion he was causing. "Give her a try, parson," he said, sort of showoffish.

Grandpa climbed on the seat and spun the grindstone real fast. Then he got off and looked it over carefully.

"Yessir, Jed," he said, "that's a real piece of machinery."

Grandpa jawed awhile and then he told Jed good-bye like he usually did. It was automatic, I guess. "When you comin' to church, Jed?"

Old Man Isbell got that shrewd look in his eyes, and he lowered his head and looked at grandpa through his bushy brows and sort of grinned. "When the Lord starts turnin' this heah grindstone for me, parson."

Grandpa had already started away, but he turned back and made that store a pulpit just by drawing himself up to his full height. "Jed Isbell, you mean that after all the Lord has done for you, you would have to see Him turn that grindstone before you'll believe in Him?"

You could see Old Man Isbell was embarrassed, but he wasn't giving ground. "I guess that's jes about the size of it, parson."

Grandpa studied Old Man Isbell's stubborn face a minute, and I could feel my little old heart pounding away.

Then grandpa spoke quietly, "Hitch up your wagon and take that grindstone up to my church, Jed. Then you come to service tomorrow night and I'll see what the Lord will do for you."

That was Saturday. By nightfall, everybody in town had heard the story. Down at Jere Higham's place there was all sorts of talk about grandpa's offer. There was a lot of speech-making about bets and odds. But, of course, there weren't any bets made. The only people who would have taken grandpa's side just weren't the kind of people who gamble.

Along about sundown, grandpa left the house and was gone for a long time. When he came home, I asked him where he had been. He sort of smiled.

"Just meditatin' with the Lord, son—just meditatin' with the Lord."

Not since Granny Gailbraith's funeral had I seen as many people as came to grandpa's church that Sunday. It was a flat, calm night and the katydids sounded loud as thunder. Folks came from as far away as Gadsden. I suppose nobody showed up at the other churches in Walesburg. The Baptists and Presbyterians kept off to one side, but you could see they wouldn't have missed it for anything. Even Jere Higham showed up. Guess it was the first time he had ever been in church.

When people came into the church, their eyes just naturally went to that big, bright grindstone. It stood right in front of grandpa's pulpit, and if old Satan himself had been standing there, I guess he couldn't have attracted more attention.

Old Jed Isbell and his family drove up in a wagon. Mrs. Isbell and the girls were sitting in chairs, but Old Jed's oldest son, Rufe, sat on the tail gate. Everybody was looking at the Isbells out of the corners of their eyes, and Old Jed was turkey-red in the face. But his face was determined when he and his family walked down the main aisle of grandpa's church. There was a lot of neck craning and glancing going on in that church, but I guess everybody was sort of breathless. I know I was.

Grandpa came down off his pulpit to shake Old Jed's hand. Jed's family sat with the Wheelers, but there wasn't room for him, so he walked down to squeeze into the pew beside me.

I watched grandpa while the choir sang "Rock of Ages." Then Gussie Lou Hamilton did a solo, "In the Garden." I knew grandpa was nervous, too, because he usually sat quietly during the singing, nodding in time to the music and fanning himself with his big old palmetto-leaf fan. But tonight he sat still with the fan held against his chest.

Then grandpa got up and explained that the church needed a new roof, and the stewards passed the collection plates while the choir sang softly. Brother Patton made sure he didn't pass up the Baptists and Presbyterians with his plate, and everybody's eyes just about popped out when Jere Higham put a dollar bill on top of all the coins.

I can't rightly remember what grandpa preached about, and I doubt if anybody else can. That big old shiny grindstone just claimed all our attention. Grandpa paid it no mind. Finally he pulled out his watch, and I knew it was about time for him to stop. He leaned forward over his pulpit with his big hands gripping the edge.

"Friends and neighbors, many of you have come here today to see if God will manifest Himself. Many of you would have come anyway. You always do, and you don't need any signs to believe in Him and in His works."

I could just feel that crowd tensing. Old Man Jed's Adam's apple was bouncing, he was swallowing that hard. And it was so quiet you could hear the Adams' dog barking way down by the river.

Grandpa went on, "I've never been much for callin' on the Lord for miracles. I've been laborin' in His vineyard for forty years now, and I've always wanted to help the Lord 'stead of Him helpin' me. But now I'm goin' to ask for a hand." Then grandpa threw back his head and said, "Let us pray."

I'd heard grandpa pray a lot of times, but never like that day. I've heard him pray until it seemed like thunder and lightning were blazing around the room. I've heard him pray so softly and simply that everybody wept.

But this was a different sort of prayer, sort of strange, as if grandpa was asking for forgiveness. While his strong old voice rolled out over that packed church, I got that

8

puffed-up feeling of pride I always felt whenever grandpa did something especially grand. I knew then that I didn't care whether that red-and-gold grindstone ever turned or not. I knew then that even if God didn't stand by grandpa, those people would. You could almost hear their prayers rising. It was that quiet and still, and I wasn't afraid any more.

"You sent me a call to go out over this land and preach Your gospel, Lord," grandpa said, "and I will always try to do that. If You can't help me, I know You will be at my side. I will always be helpin' You."

Grandpa stood there with his head thrown back. There wasn't a sound in that church. More than a hundred pairs of eyes followed his finger as he slowly pointed it straight at that old grindstone. We watched, fascinated. Nobody stirred. I could hardly breathe. With every heart thump I prayed, "Lord . . . let . . . it . . . happen . . . Lord . . . let . . . it . . . happen."

A light breeze swept through the church. It made little chills run down my back, sort of like somebody I couldn't see was walking down the aisle of that church.

Then suddenly I thought I saw the far treadle on the grindstone move . . . ever so slow . . . but move! For a second I thought I was mistaken. I blinked my eyes. But then I knew I wasn't wrong. Somebody else had seen it too! I heard a gasp. Then several. The treadle was moving now for certain, slowly, but picking up all the time. The round stone went around, barely moving . . . then faster . . . faster . . . faster.

Somebody sort of sobbed. Some-body else whispered, "My God," but it was a prayer.

That stone still turned. Our throats were dry and our mouths hung open. We were scared. Goose pimples stood out all over me. The stone turned, turned, turned. It was going almost as fast as a full-grown man could pump it.

For some reason I'll never know, I looked from the grindstone to grandpa. Everybody else had their eyes glued to the turning wheel. Grandpa was sitting in his chair, looking like he was seeing a vision, and his eyes were brimming with tears. I looked for just a second, because there was a loud bang and a thump. I looked back to the grindstone. It was flat on the floor. It had been going too fast to stay on its shiny legs.

Nobody moved for a full minute. They just looked at that grindstone like a ground squirrel stands frozen-still when a rattler pins him with his eyes. Then the people began to move like they were just waking up. Awe made most of them sit still with their mouths hanging. But there was a lot of low sobbing, and I heard later that the youngest Wheeler girl had fainted.

Somebody in one of the front pews—one of the Lokey boys, I think—started toward the grindstone.

Grandpa's voice stopped him. "Let it alone," he said. "Leave it there."

Then grandpa fixed his eyes on Old Jed Isbell, who was as white-faced and stary-eyed as any of us.

"Jed Isbell," he said, and his voice was soft and not a bit braggy, "are you satisfied?"

Then grandpa stepped down from his pulpit and looked at the

9

grindstone a long time. He sort of smiled, and everybody just waited, sitting quiet like in a dream. Grandpa finally looked up and swept his eyes across that big crowd until they came to Old Jed. Then his mouth sort of crinkled at the edges. "Jed Isbell," he said softly, "you're a fool." He said it like a blessing. He nudged the fallen grindstone with his foot. "You're a fool, Jed Isbell, because you let a little red and gold paint and an armful of wood and stone convince you that God loves you. Look into your soul, man. What do you see? Do you see Lookout Mountain and the grapeshot buzzin' around like hornets? There were a lot of good men with you there, Jed—Ned Mc-David, Jeb Ware and your brother Tom. They stayed there, Jed, stone cold and not breathin' God's blessed air. But you—you came off that mountain, and life was good and sweet." Then grandpa lowered his voice, "Think, man, think! Which is more important—this machine turnin' or God's gift of life? And do you remember when Rufe got sick when he was a baby, Jed? How could you forget it? That little baby turnin' and twistin' in pain. Remember how you cried, Jed—cried like a man in hell when the city doctor told you that little boy would never walk again? What do you think now, Jed, when he works in the fields with you—when you see the muscles workin' in his strong young body? Tell me, if you dare, man, that this—this machine spinnin' is more important than that."

Grandpa looked down at the grindstone like it was a cottonmouth. Then he leaned forward and looked Old Jed in the eye again.

"And tell me this, Jed Isbell: What do you think when you drop seeds in the ground, and cotton and corn pop up? Your sweat and your achin' back can't help them. But they grow . . . and you know they will. That's all faith is, Jed—trust in something you can't do for yourself. You never questioned a seed, did you, Jed?"

Grandpa's voice was so soft now that people leaned forward in their seats to hear him. He was speaking directly to Jed.

"What do you think when you sit down to a full table and look about you into the faces of your wife and children? What is more important —what you see then or what you saw here today? The Lord has been good to you, man, mighty, mighty good!"

I heard a sort of choking sound next to me. I looked at Jed. Big tears were running down his weather-beaten old cheeks. Old hard-boiled Jed Isbell was crying!

But grandpa wasn't through yet. He let his words sink in a minute. "All your life, Jed Isbell, you've been askin' the Lord to give you something—to show you a sign that He was by your side. All the time He was there so constantly, so close that you took His help as your just due. When people pray, Jed, the first thing they should do when they get up off their knees is to roll up their sleeves and start answering those prayers."

Grandpa stepped back, and I could tell by his face that he had some sort of surprise.

"Friends," he said, talking to everybody now, "when you came into this church tonight there wasn't a breeze stirrin'. There is now. I prayed for that breeze. The Lord

10

answered my prayer. Now I'll show you why."

Grandpa reached down and fumbled around the right treadle of the fallen grindstone.

When he straightened up, he had a long piece of black fishline in his hand. He had the string up high. The string went down into a crack in the floor.

"The far end of this string is tied to our windmill," grandpa said. "This end was hooked to this grindstone. The wind blew. The grindstone turned. God caused that wind to blow. I don't think it's important that this grindstone turned. If we are to give thanks, let's get down on our knees because the breeze turned windmills all up and down this valley. The breeze pumped water for our stock. It may bring rain for our corn crops. God and I together turned the grindstone. I had no right to shoulder off the whole load on God."

Grandpa looked at Old Jed and smiled sort of sadly. "Here's the miracle, Jed—this string, my two hands . . . and God!"

I had been sitting open-mouthed while grandpa spoke. I was almost afraid to look at Old Jed. But I just had to do it. I turned slowly. Old Jed had that mild smile on his face now. He was looking at grandpa through his bushy brows, but his eyes didn't have that shrewd look in them.

Old Jed stood up slowly. While we all watched, almost scared to breathe, he walked straight toward the pulpit. When Jed reached grandpa, he stood right in front of him, almost shoulder to shoulder, almost eye to eye, every bit as tall as he was. Then Jed poked out his calloused old hand and grandpa took it.

Grandpa smiled. Jed smiled. And God in his high heaven must have been smiling too. The breeze blew so hard it rattled the windows in grandpa's church.

CREEDS

Karle Wilson Baker

Friend, you are grieved that I should go
Unhoused, unsheltered, gaunt and free,
My cloak for armor—for my tent
The roadside tree;

And I—I know not how you bear
A roof betwixt you and the blue.
Brother, the creed would stifle me
That shelters you.

Yet, that same light that floods at dawn
Your cloistered room, your cryptic stair,
Wakes me, too—sleeping by the hedge—
To morning prayer!

11

GOD'S PROTECTION is man's hope.—*Vladimir II*

THE FRIENDSHIP of a great man is a favor of the gods.
—*Napoleon*

HE BIDS FAIR to grow wise who has discovered that he is not so.
—*Syrus*

THE GREAT MAN is he that does not lose his child's heart.—*Mencius*

THE WISE MAN guards against the future as if it were the present.—*Syrus*

To KNOW the mighty works of God; to comprehend His wisdom and majesty and power; to appreciate, in degree, the wonderful working of His laws, surely all this must be a pleasing and acceptable mode of worship to the Most High to whom ignorance can not be more grateful than knowledge.
—*Copernicus*

HONEST MEN esteem and value nothing so much in this world as a real friend. Such a one is as it were another self, to whom we impart our most secret thoughts, who partakes of our joy, and comforts us in our affliction; add to this, that his company is an everlasting pleasure to us.—*Pilpay*

A PROVERB is a short sentence based on long experience.—*Cervantes*

I BEG YOU take courage; the brave soul can mend even disaster.
—*Catherine of Russia*

"HE PREACHES WELL that lives well," quoth Sancho, "that's all the divinity I can understand."—*Cervantes*

BOOKS make up no small part of human happiness.
—*Frederick the Great*

ALL THINGS proclaim the existence of a God.—*Napoleon*

12

THE AGES

To DO two things at once is to do neither.—*Syrus*

HE THAT plants thorns must never expect to gather roses.
—*Pilpay*

HE IS STRONG who conquers others; he who conquers himself is
mighty.—*Lao-tse*

A MAN that seeks truth and loves it must be reckoned precious to any
human society.—*Frederick the Great*

YOU CANNOT step twice into the same stream. For as you are stepping
in, other and yet other waters flow on.—*Heraclitus*

WASHINGTON is dead! This great man fought against Tyranny; he established
the liberty of his country. His memory will always be dear to the French
people, as it will be to all free men of the two worlds; and especially to
French soldiers, who, like him and the American soldiers, have combated
for liberty and equality.—*Napoleon*

DO NOT SUPPOSE, my dearest sons, that when I have left you I shall be
nowhere and no one. Even when I was with you, you did not see my
soul, but knew that it was in this body of mine from what I did. Believe
then that it is still the same, even though you see it not.—*Cyrus the Great*

WE OUGHT to do our neighbour all the good we can. If you do good,
good will be done to you.—*Pilpay*

HE CONQUERS TWICE who conquers himself in victory.—*Syrus*

ONE should never despair too soon.—*Frederick the Great*

UNLESS you make allowances for your friend's foibles,
you betray your own.—*Syrus*

EVERY ONE is responsible for his own acts.—*Cervantes*

13

The Grand March of the United States of America

By DANA BURNET

He HAD COME at evening because it seemed the best time to find them at home, but the blackness of the stairs was a physical shock. It was as if he had been plunged back once more into the gloom of Europe's rubble heaps. There was no light above the entrance hall, and as he groped his way upward, Captain Hammond had an uncomfortable feeling that he was lost.

He reached out and grasped the stair rail. It was loose and shaky under his hand, but at least it served to remind him that he was mounting the steps of a tenement on 113th Street near Lenox Avenue in Harlem, in the City of New York, in the United States of America.

David Hammond knew that he had come on a doubtful pilgrimage. But long months ago he had promised himself to make this call, and while that promise had grown vague with the passage of time, it had reasserted itself sharply since his return to the States. He'd been home a week, and this was the first chance he'd had to carry out his self-imposed mission.

He climbed steadily to the fourth floor. A scrawled card on the mailbox in the entry had informed him that the Taylor family lived in Apartment 4-A. He took out his cigarette lighter and by its meager light found the right door. Behind it he heard radio music. He snapped shut the lighter, and instantly, as its small flame died, the darkness overwhelmed him like a wave.

He stood helpless, incapable of movement, afraid not of this actual dark but of its likeness flooding his own mind. Captain Hammond wore on his left breast, among other decorations, the ribbon of the Silver Star for gallantry in action; and yet he was afraid, and knew it— and knew that his fear was of the shadow he had seen in men's eyes, on their faces, wherever his duty on the Continent had taken him.

It was the shadow of an all-pervading doubt, an uncertainty that clouded everything, from the course of his own life to the future of that postwar world which he had observed, for almost a year and a half, at its clinical worst.

He had seen too much uncertainty. Too many people who weren't sure of their next meal, or their next breath. Too many faces lifted to the sky, not in hope but in grim wonder whether the sun would rise tomorrow.

Thinking of tomorrow reminded him of the ordeal he would have to face in the morning. It was nothing more than a routine physical examination, but Captain Hammond dreaded it. The medical men would find him organically sound ... but those damned phychiatrists! They'd

14

prod and pry into the state of his mind, the state of his spirit, till they found that doubt which had partially paralyzed his will.

For some time past, it had cost him an effort to make even the least decision, or issue the slightest order. If the psycho boys discovered that weakness it would mean the end of the only career for which he had been trained. It would mean goodbye to the Army in which he had served with honor, even with distinction. His own future would tumble silently around him, and he would be lost indeed.

The sound of radio music came insistently to his ears through that door in front of him, and somehow its measured beat brought him back to present reality. He lifted his hand and knocked on the panel he could not see.

The music stopped. Someone came with quick steps to the door and opened it. David Hammond, a tall man, found himself looking down at a young woman whose upturned brown face startled him with its unmistakable familiarity. He was astonished not so much by this recognition as by the fact that he remembered so clearly the original—the face of the boy he had last seen alive many months ago, and of which the young woman's face was a true but softer copy. Over her shoulder he saw three vague figures sitting motionless in a dimly lighted room.

"Are you—?" he began, then changed his question. "Is this the Taylors' apartment?"

"I'm Lucy Taylor," the girl said. Her eyes moved in swift appraisal of this stranger, this white man who wore the cloth, if not the manner, of authority. For the first time in years, David was conscious of his uniform.

"My name's Hammond. Captain Hammond. I've come—"

"Lucy," a woman's voice broke in calmly, "if he's from the station house, I already bought my ticket to the police benefit."

"Mama, this gentleman's an Army officer."

The pause that followed was curiously disturbing. David had again that sense of helplessness, as though the whole scene, and his purpose within it, were dissolving into illusion. The figures in the room were shadows, the girl scarcely more substantial except for the imprint of her face recalling that other face in his mind. He said, "You must be Buddy Taylor's sister"—and felt like a man who had smashed his way out of a dream.

"Buddy?" the girl said. "Why, yes. I—" Then he heard her catch her breath. "Buddy?"

"I knew him," David said. "He was in charge of a platoon of engineers attached to our headquarters near Pilsen, in Czechoslovakia. That was in May, '45."

Lucy Taylor spoke in a low tone that had the resonance of an organ note. "Come in, please."

He stepped into the room. It was lighted by a single lamp with a pleated, brown paper shade that stood on a card table near an overstuffed sofa whose springs dragged on the floor. On the sofa sat two women; a dark-skinned girl, with a baby asleep in her arms, and a big-bosomed, gray-haired matriarch in a black dress, with a proud black face that seemed to Captain Hammond wonderful in the lamplight. The only other person in the room was an old man wearing a stocking

15

cap and a shabby, brown dressing gown tied with a string around his waist, like a monk's robe. He sat erect in a straight-backed chair at the window and stared out into the mild autumn night.

David had heard the door click shut behind him and now Lucy was standing at his side.

"Mama, this is Captain—" She glanced up at him quickly. "I'm sorry I didn't catch your name."

He repeated it for her.

"Captain Hammond," the girl said to her mother.

The gray-haired woman inclined her head but did not speak. David waited till the proud, challenging eyes again met his.

"Mrs. Taylor, I hope you won't think this is an intrusion. I've been looking forward for a long time to meeting you and your family. I got your address from the Army chaplain who wrote you about your son."

The eyes flickered momentarily. "I heard you say you knew Buddy." Then the matriarch resumed her impenetrable mask. "Lucy," she said, "introduce the captain to your sister and grandpa."

Lucy's sister was the girl with the baby. Her name was Mrs. Williams. The grandfather was the old man by the window. When Lucy introduced him he got up and bowed gravely to the visitor in uniform.

"Lost my son in the first World War and my gran'son in this one," Grandpa Taylor said, in a thin, sweet, wandering voice. "I was at El Caney in Cuba in '98, but I don't study 'bout war no more." He sat down again, and turned his wrinkled, leathery face to the night. "I

got no comfort but my Jesus now," he said.

"Lucy," Mrs. Taylor said, "get a chair for the captain."

There was only one other chair in the room. Lucy pulled it into the circle of lamplight, then sat down on the sofa between her mother and sister. Facing them, David was conscious of a blurred symphony of noises coming up from the street and through the floor. But here was a stillness that would defeat him unless he overcame it. He said to Mrs. Taylor, "I've come to ask a favor—or rather to try to find something that may not even exist. It has to do with your son, and I—"

"My son is dead, isn't he?" the mother said.

"Yes."

"Killed after the war was over and done."

"Yes."

"Over and done," she said, with a finality beyond lament, beyond even bitterness. "I don't ask why. I got over asking why Buddy had to do that terrible work, whatever they call it—"

"Demolition."

"Whatever big name they call it, he was doing what the gov'ment told him. Gov'ment took him the way it took his father in '17. Carried him across the ocean, and Buddy hated it and was proud of it, too. Got blown up by a German bomb"—(It was a mine, David thought mechanically)—"a week after peace had come, and they buried him in foreign ground. What more does the gov'ment want of him? Why does it come bothering 'bout him now?"

David was puzzled. "The gov-

16

ernment?" he said. Then he understood. "I'm not representing the government."

"You said you wanted to find out something."

"I said *find*, not *find out*."

"Well, that sound like gov'ment." It would have been funny if it had not been so completely and profoundly the reverse. He said, "I'm here for a purely personal reason."

"You wearing the uniform, so I thought—"

"I'm an officer in the Regular Army. I've just got back from four years' service overseas, including a seventeen months' tour of occupation duty. At present I'm stationed on Governors Island." He gave her these facts deliberately, and with still more deliberation added, "The last thing I did before I left Pilsen was to visit your son's grave. I wanted to pay my respects to a man I met only once, but will never forget."

The three women simply stared at him—only Lucy's wide brown eyes seemed at all responsive—and David went on talking against the stillness. "He was buried in the Corps cemetery just outside the city in a green and quiet place. At least it was green when I was there. The grave was well cared for and—"

"Yes," Mrs. Taylor said without evident emotion, "the chaplain sent us a picture of it. Shows Buddy's name plain on the cross." Her look was remote. "He was baptized 'Buddy.' I was afraid they wouldn't put that on the cross."

"They did."

The mother nodded. She said, "We never called him anything else from the day he was born."

Grandpa Taylor's reedy voice came waveringly across the room, "The Lord gave, and the Lord taken away. Blessed be the name of the Lord."

Mrs. Williams' baby stirred and whimpered with a tiny animal noise. She patted it till it slept quietly again. Lucy said to David, "Just what is it that you came here to find, Captain Hammond?"

He looked at her with sudden relief. "Your brother was a musician," he said.

"Why, yes, he played piano."

"He was also a composer, wasn't he?"

"Why," Lucy said, "he was always making up tunes and playing them. But I don't know that you'd call him a composer."

"I would," David said. "But maybe I'd better tell you my whole story. It starts with a party we gave for the Russians at our regimental headquarters in Czechoslovakia. I know the chaplain didn't write you about that because he wasn't there. It was May 13, 1945."

Lucy glanced at her mother, then at David. "The day before Buddy was killed," she said.

"The night before, yes." He tried to speak as factually as possible. "We had captured Pilsen on the sixth, the war ended on the seventh and on the tenth a group of Russian officers, the staff of one of their units opposite us, asked some of us to a celebration on their side of the line. Everyone was busy celebrating right after the victory, and three days later Colonel Grace, my commanding officer, returned the compliment. He invited the Russians to dinner at our headquarters."

The faces of his listeners showed

17

only a faint and puzzled curiosity. He hurried on: "The line between the two zones of occupation ran about ten kilometers east of Pilsen and we were living in a country villa not far from the line. The villa had been used during the war by a German *Luftwaffe* officer who had got out without doing any damage. It had belonged originally to a Czech official of the big Skoda works in Pilsen and was handsomely furnished. There was a grand piano in the drawing room."

He paused, aware that he had struck a spark between the women's memories and his own. He said to Lucy, "I first saw your brother sitting at that piano. He wasn't playing anything. He just sat there with his hands resting on the keyboard and his head turned as if he were listening to something inside the instrument."

"I know!" the girl said. "I can just see—" She did not finish the sentence.

"We'd come in from the dining room after the longest and most tiresome dinner I've ever sat through." He was telling it as he would have told it at the Officers' Club on the Post; any attempt to embellish or dramatize it for their benefit would have been an inexcusable condescension. "We couldn't get to first base with the Russians. They'd been good hosts at their own party, but now they acted as if they were afraid or suspicious of any friendliness. We'd had a lot of toasts—there was plenty to drink, including vodka in honor of our guests—but nobody seemed to loosen up, and the whole thing dragged like a bad movie.

"They were combat men, just as we were—some of them wore the Stalingrad medal—and we admired them and made half a dozen speeches saying so. They made speeches, too, but I got the impression that they thought our contribution to the victory was mostly technical and mechanical. On the human side, we and our Soviet friends were a long way apart.

"A couple of them spoke a little English, but they were cautious about using it in front of their fellow officers, so almost every word had to be translated by interpreters. It struck me as a kind of stupid practical joke that we should all be eating the same food and drinking the same drinks, that we had all fought the same war for the same reasons, yet couldn't speak the same language."

The old man at the window, in spite of his assumed indifference, must have heard every word, for now he said in his piping quaver, "It all go back to the time of Babel. The Lord mix up the language then, and it stay mix up till yet."

The women paid no attention to this interruption, and David said to Mrs. Taylor, "As it turned out, your son had the only language that was worth anything. His music saved the evening. It did something more. It spoke for us Americans as we never could have spoken for ourselves."

For the first time Mrs. Williams, the young woman with the baby, broke her curious, dreamlike silence. "How come Buddy was there?"

David said, "He'd appeared at a victory concert in the Pilsen Municipal Theater a couple of nights before. His playing had stopped the show. Colonel Grace heard of it— news like that travels fast in

18

the Army, especially a halted Army —and he asked Sergeant Taylor to come to the villa. I happen to know the invitation was a request, not an order."

Lucy said, "Buddy would play for anybody, any time, anywhere he could get his hands on a piano."

"Yes," Mrs. Taylor said, and suddenly her great bosom heaved. "Oh, yes, Lord! He was born with a misery of music in him!" There was a kind of anger in her eyes. "Why, when he was just a little skinny boy, I'd miss him and go looking for him and find him in the corner saloon, in the back room where they had the piano." She shook her head in still-smoldering resentment. "Be sitting up there on the stool screwed as high as he could get it, fooling with his chords."

"The chords come natural to him," Mrs. Williams said.

"Natural or unnatural," Mrs. Taylor said, sighing, "Buddy grew up with his head full of tunes and his fingers fixed to play them. Taught himself by working in bars or dance halls or any place they would let him practice. Every new piece he heard he was possessed to learn it. But it was his own tunes that really deviled him."

David leaned forward. "Did he ever write them down?"

The blank look came back to the matriarch's face. He turned to Lucy. "Did your brother ever write down the tunes he played? I mean his original compositions?"

"No. At least I don't think so." Then, aware of his eagerness, she said, "Why do you ask, Captain Hammond?"

"Because I heard him play something, on the night we entertained

the Russians, that I'd hate to think was lost. I'd hate to think it was one more fine thing lost—"

His voice was too loud. He controlled it and went on quietly: "The party was almost over—I remember the windows of the room were getting gray—when Buddy stood up to make an announcement.

"He said to Colonel Grace, 'Sir, now I'd like to play something special for this occasion. It's a piece I've been carrying around in my head for a long time. I call it The Grand March of the United States of America.' "

It was strange how the rhythm of the words brought back to David Hammond the exact look and mood of that scene in the villa. He remembered the gray-green landscape taking shape beyond the windows and the lights in the room turning pale. He could see the Soviet officers in their dress uniforms, their blouses covered with medals and their shoulder boards giving them a stiff, square look. He could see their faces as Sergeant Taylor's long title was translated to them. Their expressions showed that they expected an outburst of musical boasting. Then Buddy began to play. . . .

Captain Hammond said to Mrs. Taylor, "I'm a professional soldier. I know little about music, except that I'm fond of it. So I'm not competent to judge whether your son's concerto, if that's the right name for it, was as great as it seemed to me. All I can tell you is that when he'd finished—he must have played for an hour—our colonel got up and went to him and shook hands with him. The rest of us followed, and so did the Russians. They kept shouting 'Bravo! Bravo!' and I saw

19

one of them unpin a medal from his blouse and shove it into Buddy's hands. They had heard something that really moved them, something they understood and respected."

He stopped, conscious of values beyond his power to project. He had told it as well as he could in terms of fact; but there was no way, he could convey to them either the quality of Buddy's music, or the kind of truth it had let loose in the room, a truth deeper and stronger than words, that had broken the tension between the two groups as a thunderstorm clears the air on a stifling summer day.

Only the music itself could bear witness to that truth, and now David Hammond turned again to the girl whose face in the lamplight was a link between the living and the dead.

He said bluntly, "I came here hoping to find the manuscript of your brother's composition."

"Manuscript?"

"A score, if that's what it's called. Or at least some notes—?" His bluntness had become a kind of pleading.

"I see," Lucy said. And then, "Do you have any reason to believe there ever was such a manuscript?"

"Only that Buddy said he'd been thinking about his Grand March for a long time. Then, too, it seems incredible that he could have improvised such a complicated thing. He played it as though he knew it by heart."

Lucy said gently, "He probably did, but I don't think he ever put anything on paper. I don't think he could." She looked sidelong at her mother. "Mama, was there anything like a music manuscript in the package the chaplain sent us?"

"No," Mrs. Taylor said. "It was just my letters to Buddy and his watch and a medal and some little things."

"What about the box he tied up before he left? That cardboard box on the shelf in his closet?"

"I don't know," Mrs. Taylor said. "I never opened it or bothered it, except to dust it. I don't know what's in it."

Lucy looked at David Hammond. Then she got up and walked quickly out of the room.

From his chair by the window Grandpa Taylor spoke his ancient mind. "The Book say, when the dead is at rest, let his remembrance rest."

It was a ghostly warning, empty as an echo; yet David was grateful when the old man's protest was overborne by the fretting of Mrs. Williams' baby. "You better put that child to bed," Mrs. Taylor told her daughter.

"In a minute," Mrs. Williams said.

Lucy came back into the room. She was carrying a shoe box tied with a white string. She sat down on the sofa and held out the box to her mother, but Mrs. Taylor folded her hands in her lap.

"You thought of it. You open it, Lucy."

The girl tried to loosen the knot, then broke the string and removed the lid from the box.

David drew his chair closer, and Mrs. Williams, mechanically patting her baby, craned her neck to see.

"I don't know why you had to break the string," Mrs. Taylor said.

No one answered. David watched Lucy's slow brown hand as it lifted and then replaced, one by one, the objects in the box.

There was a spinning-top, painted yellow with a red stripe and cracked down one side; a soiled cheesecloth marble bag; a wad of tin foil; a Christmas tree ornament in the shape of a swan; a slingshot; a small metal airplane; a jackknife with a broken horn handle; a greenish copper penny; a homemade baseball—the kind boys make by winding tar-tape around a hard rubber core; a mouth organ; and a small American flag furled on its slender stick. That was all.

Except for the mouth organ, there was no hint of Buddy Taylor's musical life, which apparently he had lived without record or visible symbol. . . .

"I'm sorry, Captain Hammond," Lucy said.

For an instant David was tempted to resist defeat, to continue his questions, his search for the manuscript he had pictured, so conveniently, in his mind. But now he knew, by the very tone of the girl's voice, that he had been cherishing an illusion on which she had pronounced a final judgment.

He stood up, not trying to hide his disappointment. "I'm sorry, too," he said.

Mrs. Williams gathered up her baby and rose from the sofa. With that gesture she seemed to recapture her air of detachment, to withdraw into a world that included only herself and her child. "Well, time to say good night," she murmured, and walked with easy languid grace from the room.

Mrs. Taylor got up and stood facing David.

"It was kind of you," she said, "to come and tell us about Buddy."

"No," he said, "it wasn't kindness. It was just—it was something that seemed important to me." But he could not tell her why. You could never explain the really important things, and yet he felt he must say something more. "You see, I'd counted a good deal on hearing your son's music again."

"I would rather hear his voice again," the mother said, "but I got to wait till the Judgment Day."

She said it calmly, without grieving or complaint; but the dark face, the dark stately figure seemed to Captain Hammond the personification of bereavement. He thought of the thousands of her sisters he'd seen in other lands, the shadowy ones to whom suffering had brought the final equality.

He thought of the great democracy of sorrow that made no distinction of kind or color in the faces it set its seal upon; and in himself he felt the fear that had nothing to do with cowardice, but was rather despair of a world unable to make the one distinction that counted—the simple, vital difference between man and man-beast. . . .

He felt the fear in his belly, and pity like a hand at his throat; and he turned away, and saw the old grandfather in his monklike robe getting up from his chair by the window.

"Ain't so long to wait till the Judgment," Grandpa Taylor said. He began a slow, stooping advance toward the sofa. "Anybody study Scripture know the first sign already been fulfilled. Like it say in the Book, hail and fire mix with blood going to be cast down upon the earth—and it sure been cast down!" He came into the lamplight, stopped and lifted his arms. They were like charred branches thrusting from the sleeves of his dressing gown. "Then the sun going to turn black, and the stars fall, and all us poor sinners going to hide from the wrath of the Lamb. For the great day of His wrath is come—" The frail voice gasped and broke, the scarecrow body drooped in sudden impotence, bent double by a twitch of pain.

"There now you see!" Mrs. Taylor said. She went to the old man quickly and put her arm around him.

"Crick in my back. Lord, Lord—!" His hand fumbled for the place.

"Yes, all right, Papa Taylor, you come with me. I'll rub it with the liniment."

One moment he was the inspired prophet, uttering solemn portents of doom; the next, he was a shriveled child being helped by a woman to the humiliation of his bed.

"Can I help?" David asked.

"No, but you will have to excuse us, Captain, please."

The old man was making the most of his infirmity. As she led him away he kept groaning and calling on the Lord and saying that the liniment was no good. Then the door closed on them, and David was alone in the room with Lucy Taylor.

He had a queer notion that she had not seen or heard anything that had happened since she last spoke to him. She sat in a kind of trance, staring down at the shoe box on her lap.

"I'm afraid I've upset you all," he said.

"No. . . . No, I'm glad you came. It makes me feel better about my brother." She didn't raise her head. "I miss him. . . . We were twins. I guess twins are specially close—" Her speech blurred, became clear again. "Now I can think of him always in that room, sitting at the piano the way you told it, the way I used to see him—"

"Well—" David said.

He had put his cap on the table under the lamp and now he moved to get the cap. But the girl spoke again, and he heard in her voice the deep, resonant organ note.

"You said it was *important* to you, Captain."

"My coming here? Yes." He turned back abruptly, almost blundering into the chair opposite the sofa. "I've been telling myself it was my duty to make this call—to try to salvage a work of genius. But that was just an excuse."

"An excuse?"

"The truth is I was looking for something I seem to have lost. Something I had once—a feeling— a conviction—" His hands went out and gripped the back of the chair. He was like a blind man reaching for some tangible support. "Anyway, I think I should tell you that my reason for coming here was a selfish one."

She looked up at him then; and he wondered confusedly why the faces of saints were always painted white or ivory or rose. He had never seen anything saintlier or more compassionate than this autumnal face lifted toward him in the lamplight.

Lucy said, "Selfish people don't talk about their selfishness, Captain Hammond. You seem more like somebody seeking."

"Seeking?"

"It's a word Grandpa Taylor uses

22

sometimes. It means somebody seeking salvation. Seeking faith."

David said slowly, "I guess that's the word for me."

She said, "When you were talking about Buddy, I thought there was something bothering you more than just finding the music—"

"You're right."

He sat down again in the chair facing her. "Going back to the night of our victory party," he said; then paused, absorbed in recollection, till the girl said, "Yes?"

He went on: "I've told you I thought Buddy's Grand March was great music. The reason I thought so was that it gave me a feeling I'd had only once in my life before. That was when I was crossing the Channel on D-Day, when I stood on the deck of an American transport and saw with my own eyes the power, the greatness, of our America in action.

"The piece your brother played for us had that same greatness. Except that he seemed to get at the thing behind the ships and the planes and the guns, the thing inside the men, behind them, going back to the factories and the homes, the farms and the streets they'd come from. The thing going back —the spirit, I suppose you'd call it —reaching all the way back to the Hudson River rebellion, to Concord Bridge and Lexington . . ."

He had thought he could never tell it or explain it to anyone, but it did not seem impossible there in the room in the lonely night with Buddy Taylor's sister.

"I don't mean that what we heard was patriotic bragging or even a military march, though it was full of the sound of marching—"

"Oh!" the girl said softly.

"But it seemed closer to the music of your own great spirituals . . . and somehow your brother was using that music as a language to tell the truth about America.

"Because it was the truth, there were discords that hurt your ears to listen to. But even in the discords you could hear the note of power, the people moving forward and the greatness finding itself . . .

"I think that's what impressed the Russians; that, and the fact that they heard in Buddy's masterpiece a revolutionary faith much older and deeper-rooted than their own.

"They'd been taught that Americans were reactionaries, modern barbarians who were out to conquer the world with money and machines. Yet here was an American enlisted man, a member of what they call a minority group, telling them something different. When he'd finished, and we were all crowding around him, I heard their ranking officer say to him in English, 'But this is revolutionary music!' And Buddy said, 'Yes, sir. Every good American is a rebel at heart. Our people got the habit way back in '76, and they've never gotten over it.' Then he looked straight at the Russian and said, 'It takes a free man to be a real revolutionist, sir.' "

Captain Hammond leaned back, put his hands to his face and drew them down slowly across his eyes. "I remember what your brother said, I remember the impression his music made on me, but the feeling I had about it is gone.

"It was strong and clear to me then. Everything was as clear as the sun coming in at the windows. Our victory was real, there was truth and understanding between us and

23

our allies, peace was possible. . . .
"But my faith in these things didn't last. It got lost somewhere between that night and now. So I thought, if I could hear Sergeant Taylor's music again—"

His hands were still. They covered his eyes, and he sat very still, because he was hearing it. There was a sound in the room that he did not identify at once because it seemed an echo suddenly released from his own memory. Then he realized that Lucy was singing, humming, the theme of her brother's American concerto.

"My God, how did you know?"

She did not answer him directly, but then as he dropped his hands to stare at her the low, vibrant voice drifted almost imperceptibly into speech. "I remember now," Lucy said. "It was the summer we were ten years old. Fourth of July . . . and they gave us the little flags and we marched up Lenox Avenue to some hall on 125th Street." Her lips smiled faintly. "It was so hot the asphalt was soft in the street and there must have been hundreds of us kids marching in our Sunday clothes and all our flags waving because we kept fanning ourselves with the flags. . . .

"I was thinking about the ice cream they'd promised us after the celebration, how cool it would taste, but they had a band for us to march to, and when I looked at Buddy I saw he was excited about the band. His eyes were big and shiny the way they always got when he heard music, and he walked so light I knew he felt proud. One of his shoelaces came untied and I told him to stop and fix it, but he wouldn't break the step. I don't know why I should think of that....

"I don't know why we were there at all, except it was election year and they had somebody big, a big man from Albany, going to make a speech. I guess the politicians thought it would be showy to have us children march, or maybe they figured it would help to get the parents out. Anyway, the word was passed down through the precinct captains, and you could go or not, but when I heard about the ice cream I begged Mama to let us go.

"It was hotter than ever in the hall and I felt sorry for the man from Albany. He was a fat man with a fat, red face that he kept mopping all the time. Drinking water and mopping his face all the time, and I guess I got to giggling, because Buddy grabbed my arm and told me hush, and then I saw he was listening to the speech, so I listened too.

"It was all about the first Independence Day and what it meant and what the flags we were carrying stood for. I suppose it was just an ordinary Fourth of July speech, but I remember some things the speaker said. He said the world had never had but two ideas about government: one that it should be master of the people and the other that it should be servant. He said the first meant slavery no matter what name you called it and the second was freedom. He told how America had made its choice for freedom, and how there were some who said it would never work and some who abused it and others who were afraid of it, but it was still the best idea anybody'd ever had, and someday it would lead human beings everywhere out of darkness into the light.

"Then it was over and we got our

ice cream and had to eat it fast before it melted, and then we walked home. When we got to our building I was tired, and wanted to sit on the steps till suppertime, but Buddy said no, we were going to play the marching game.

"I said, 'What game is that?' and he said, 'I just made it up. Come on, I'll show you.' Then he told me to get behind him and we would march up the stairs to the roof, and I said, 'What for?' And he said, 'Because we have to. Because it's part of the game. I'll be the leader because I've got the flag.'

"Well, I'd lost my flag somewhere, but he still had his, so I didn't argue with him. I never did anyway. I just asked him who I was supposed to be. He said, 'You're the people. You're all the people, and you have to follow me because I've got the flag.'

"So then we started up the steps from the street and went through the hall and up the stairs past the door of our flat, with Buddy stomping in front and me marching behind him. It was black as night on the stairs and I heard him singing, 'Dark! Dark! Dark!'—not singing loud but sort of chanting it to himself; and then we came out on the roof.

"It was empty because everybody was down getting supper and I remember there was a breeze blowing and the sky was all red and bright with sunset. We didn't stop but went right on marching around the roof, and Buddy had the little flag held up to catch the breeze, and there was something about the way he looked, and the brightness and the wind blowing on my face, that made me want to cry. I began to think the marching game was won-derful, and then all at once Buddy burst out singing again, really singing this time, at the top of his lungs, like this!"

The girl lifted her head and sang:

"March, march, march, march, march, march, march!
Now all the people are marching in the light!"

The rich, full-throated contralto rose and soared and overflowed the room, triumphant and briefly joyous, repeating in that single phrase, that musical fragment, the great theme that David Hammond remembered, and would always remember now.

Then without any pause or false stillness she was speaking again: "We played the marching game every night for maybe a week or so, and then we didn't play it any more. But I guess Buddy never forgot—"

"No," David said, "I'm sure he never forgot." He leaned toward her, wishing that he could share with her his exultation for something of value saved from the obscene waste of war and death. But all he could think to say was, "Thank you." And again, "Thank you, Lucy Taylor."

Her look was fixed on the open box that rested like a miniature white coffin on her lap. Her hand moved slowly, but with decision, among her brother's childhood treasures.

"I'd like you to have this," she said, and held out to him the gift she'd selected. "Please take it—and keep it . . ."

This time he couldn't thank her. He couldn't say anything at all.

Going down the stairs Captain

25

Hammond did not think about their darkness. Nor did he have now any sense of shadow within himself. The force of his consciousness was directed outward, flowing as a man's strength should flow in calmness and clarity toward the future.

Inevitably he thought of the test he had dreaded, the physical examination that he'd have to take tomorrow. By the time he reached the street, he knew he no longer was worried about it. He was no longer afraid of what the doctors would discover in his mind or in his spirit.

He was no longer afraid.

The night air was cool and good to breathe, it was good to be walking the street of an American city, the muffled, oceanic rhythm of which still came serene and unbroken to his ear. He reached the corner and turned south on Lenox Avenue toward the subway.

He was carrying the gift that Lucy had given him, the small American flag that had once belonged to Buddy Taylor. He carried it upright in his hand, clutching it tightly by its slender stick. He knew he must look ridiculous to the shadowy figures he passed on the sidewalk. But he didn't care. He did not feel ridiculous. He felt as if he were holding on to the one sure thing left in a fearfully shaken and vastly uncertain world.

ON THE SUBJECT OF COURAGE
By ED SULLIVAN

To HEAR Connie Boswell sing, clear, cool notes pouring out of that deep auditorium, you'd hardly think that she was the type of girl who is entitled to all of the medals that they pin on individuals for heroism in action. Yet there are few performers who can match the Boswell record of courage. She is one of the few persons living who has had to whip paralysis twice.

The dread disease first manifested itself in New Orleans when she was three years old, brought on when Connie fell off a speeding kid's wagon. She couldn't speak or move a muscle for months. Just when she was returning to normal health, in 1930, the Boswell Sisters were playing a date at Topeka, Kansas. Connie decided to play a joke on Sisters Martha and "Vet" by disappearing from the hotel room. She thought the ground was only a foot below the window. But she fell ten feet to the concrete floor of a basement well. Both legs were paralyzed by the fall.

She's recovered the partial use of her limbs, but has to sing from a wheel chair. The point is that she kept on singing, refused to be counted out and she's won headline rating.

Herbert Marshall, after the world war, was left with one leg. By every standard of reckoning Marshall could have enjoyed the prestige of a hero, rested on his laurels. He decided that there was no reason he couldn't go on with his acting career. Doctors advised against it; theatrical producers were dubious. Marshall refused to let them douse his enthusiasm. Today he's one of the top performers of the world.

There is no nicer person in Hollywood. He, who had the right to become bitter, became gayer than all the rest and more charming.

Two years ago [1938] we brought out the harvest moon dance champions to make a picture. The plane was to get in at the fairly inconvenient hour of 7 a.m. We wanted a movie star to meet the kids at the airport, to give them the thrill of a real movie star welcome. At 7 a.m. Marshall was at the airport and he made those two youngsters feel that they were the most important persons in the world. In my book, he fits into the Legion of Valor.

Because of its very nature, blindness is a body blow to a professional performer. Managers don't want to engage a performer so afflicted because of the fear that the audience will be depressed by the performer's misfortune. Alec Templeton, however, refused to take the count on his knees. There is only one stipulation in Templeton's act: He is not to be introduced as a blind pianist, and there is to be no reference in advertising or in press agentry to his affliction. He is one of the great acts of show business, a piano virtuoso with a sense of humor so keen that he leaves audiences holding their sides. You've heard performers boast that they "rolled 'em in the aisles." Templeton actually does it.

Nelson Eddy's courage is more responsible for his enormous success than is that of any single actor. Lacking the funds to take lessons, he decided that he'd learn to sing in the only way that was open to him: He bought phonograph records of the great operatic baritones, studied their technique and sang aloud while the records played, to learn where his voice was lacking. If you think that's easy, try it some day on your phonograph—more important, carry it through to the successful conclusion that Eddy achieved. His career was handed to him on a platter, but it was not a silver platter—it was a phonograph platter.

There have been many sensational dancers in vaudeville. One of the greatest is Peg Leg Bates, a Carolina colored boy. I think a train ran over him. A colored boy in the South has a hard enough row to hoe, but a colored boy without a leg has reached a new low in tough sledding. Peg Leg, hopping to school one day, fell in love with a colored girl in the class. His rival was the baseball captain and the one-legged boy, sick at heart because he couldn't show off his prowess on the baseball diamond like his rival, decided he'd triumph over his handicap. He did. Today he is a show stopper of vaudeville and night clubs. His introductory song is a warning to the audience not to give him any sympathy; that he wants to be judged strictly on the merit of his dancing. He performs steps that two-legged dancers can't match.

Raoul Walsh's career as an actor was cut short on a motor trip through Arizona, when a rabbit, frightened by the headlights, leaped through the windshield. The flying glass cost Raoul an eye. He could have folded up. Walsh instead became one of the top flight directors of the business.

Lionel Barrymore, for the last two years, has been compelled to use crutches as an aid to walking. You can assume that at times the veteran has suffered physical agony and that he often thought to himself that he had earned the right to rest. His career was not an insignificant career; he could retire and still remain an important memory. Barrymore, instead of quitting, insisted that he'd continue acting. "You Can't Take It with You" found him on the screen, on crutches. "On Borrowed Time" found him turning in a magnificent performance, in a wheel chair. In the prize ring, they call that sort of fortitude "moxie."

THE FADELESS LIGHT
Nancy Byrd Turner

Oh heart, let's never grow too old
To smile anew, when Christmas comes,
At tassels red and tinsel thread,
And tarlatan bags of sugar-plums;
To catch that unforgotten scent,
Spicy and gay, without a name,
Of pungent orange-peeling blent
With cedar scorched in candle flame;
To draw a well beloved delight
From one dear melody unbound—
While shepherds watched their flocks by night,
A glory shone around.

Let's never grow too old, my heart,
To thrill before the jaunty grace
Of stockings hung with careful art
Beside the chimney's homely face:
Above one rim, a lady doll;
Above the next, a woolly cat;
Topping the third, a rubber ball;
Each stocking knobby-toed and fat.
Pure stuff of magic in the sight,
And one sweet legend with them wound:
While shepherds watched their flocks by night,
A glory shone around.

Oh, heart, let's never be too old
To feel again the yule-log's glow,
To catch the tinkle, keen and cold,
Of silver sleighbells through the snow.
Let's never fail to lean, a space,
Against the frosty window-bar
And mark aloft, in heaven's place,
One solemn, lovely, silent star.
The shadows fall, the dreams take flight,
But every year is Christmas-crowned—
When shepherds watch their flocks by night,
And glory shines around!

A PRAYER

EDWIN MARKHAM

Teach me, Father, how to go
Softly as the grasses grow;
Hush my soul to meet the shock
Of the wild world as a rock;
But my spirit, propt with power,
Make as simple as a flower.
Let the dry heart fill its cup,
Like a poppy looking up;
Let life lightly wear her crown
Like a poppy looking down.

Teach me, Father, how to be
Kind and patient as a tree.
Joyfully the crickets croon
Under shady oak at noon;
Beetle, on his mission bent,
Tarries in that cooling tent.
Let me, also, cheer a spot,
Hidden field or garden grot—
Place where passing souls can rest
On the way and be their best.

SONG

HENRY VAN DYKE

Above the edge of dark appear the lances of the sun;
Along the mountain-ridges clear his rosy heralds run;
    The vapours down the valley go
    Like broken armies, dark and low.
    Look up, my heart, from every hill
    In folds of rose and daffodil
    The sunrise banners flow.

O fly away on silent wing, ye boding owls of night!
O welcome little birds that sing the coming-in of light!
    For new, and new, and ever-new,
    The golden bud within the blue;
    And every morning seems to say:
    "There's something happy on the way,
    And God sends love to you!"

THE MORE a man knows, the more he forgives.—*Anonymous*

WHATSOEVER thy hand findeth to do, do it with thy might.—*The Bible*

BRAVE YOUR STORM with firm endeavor, let your vain repinings go! Hopeful hearts will find forever roses underneath the snow!
—*Cooper*

A HERO is one who knows how to hang on one minute longer.—*Anonymous*

WHAT WEALTH it is to have such friends that we cannot think of them without elevation.—*Thoreau*

WHEN I hear music I fear no danger, I am invulnerable, I see no foe. I am related to the earliest times, and to the latest.—*Thoreau*

I LIKE to praise and reward loudly, to blame quietly.—*Catherine of Russia*

WHY SHOULD THERE NOT be a patient confidence in the ultimate justice of the people? Is there any better or equal hope in the world?—*Abraham Lincoln*

COMMON SENSE, in an uncommon degree, is what the world calls wisdom.—*Coleridge*

TRY FIRST THYSELF, and after call in God; For to the worker God himself lends aid.
—*Euripides*

A THANKFUL HEART is not only the greatest virtue, but the parent of all the other virtues.—*Cicero*

GREAT PEACE have they which love Thy law.—*The Bible*

A NOBLE HEART is a changeless heart.—*Anonymous*

THE WORLD

IT IS more blessed to give than to receive.—*The Bible*

JUSTICE AND TRUTH are the common ties of society.—*John Locke*

I SEE the rainbow in the sky, the dew upon the grass;
I see them, and I ask not why they glimmer or they pass.
With folded arms I linger not to call them back; 'twere vain:
In this, or in some other spot, I know they'll shine again.
                                        —*Landor*

BEGIN; to have begun is half of the work. Let the half still remain; agair
begin this and thou wilt have done all.—*Ausonius*

FLINCH NOT, neither give up nor despair, if the achieving of every ac
in accordance with right principle is not always continuous with thee
—*Marcus Aurelius*

YOUTH, beauty, graceful action seldom fail:
But common interest always will prevail;
And pity never ceases to be shown
To him who makes the people's wrongs his own.
                                        —*Dryden*

GOD who placed me here will do what He pleases with me
hereafter, and He knows best what to do.—*Bolingbrokc*

THREE THINGS return not, even for prayers and tears—
The arrow which the archer shoots at will;
The spoken word, keen-edged and sharp to sting;
The opportunity left unimproved.
If thou would'st speak a word of loving cheer,
Oh, speak it now. This moment is thine own.
                                        —*Richardson*

HIS TENDERNESS in the springing grass,
His beauty in the flowers,
His living love in the sun above—
All here, and near, and ours!
        —*Gilman*

A WORD TO YOUTH
By André Maurois

A QUESTIONNAIRE is, generally speaking, either a nuisance or a bore. But once in a while one comes along that inspires helpful thinking. At such times the interrogated blesses his examiner. That is what I felt one morning recently when I was asked to answer the following:

1. What is the most valuable lesson life has taught you?

2. To a young person in whom you were interested, what advice would you give which would help him to keep his balance in the most difficult experiences of his life?

There we have two beautiful problems. Let us give them a little thought.

Adolescence is the most difficult period of life, because then every defeat seems final. Let the youth live but a little longer and he will learn life's first, most valuable lesson—that nothing is final.

"Things adjust themselves, more or less badly," Disraeli used to say dolefully. Not a very consoling thought, put that way. For it is quite as true that things turn out well. More often still, many actions have no results—they come to naught. A few weeks slip into a few months; and of a situation that seemed at the time to have no possible solution nothing remains but a faint memory, a confused picture, a regret.

The man or woman who has lived through the experience of an unendurable present transformed into a blurred past has more power to face affliction. "A wretched power," the romantic youth will say, "a power made up of indiffer-

ence and skepticism. Rather than that, give me my weakness and my suffering."

The youth is mistaken. Men and women who have reached maturity have not become indifferent. If even in love they know the passion fleeting, that very thought makes the experience more acute, more ardent. "Nothing is sadder than a second love," Goethe said. "But a third comes and soothes the other two."

I speak here not only of personal problems and private sorrows. In political life it is especially true that long-faced prophets of misfortune unsettle inexperienced young men. Now here again a longer life teaches that events straighten themselves out by time and circumstance. And a wise old Italian diplomat used to say to the young men who surrounded him, "Don't ever say, 'This is very serious.' For sixty years I have been hearing that things are very serious."

As a matter of fact, how can a human situation possibly be otherwise than serious? It is very serious to be a man, to live, to carry on. And yet it is also true that, as the Italian minister suggested, life is very simple, very beautiful; and that it has been going on now for some millions of years.

"The hollow optimism of words," some will think. In present sorrow the mere abstract idea of future relief is comfortless. But life itself shows us the way to more active solace. We learn that we can cut loose from its most painful moments. Flee the place of grief and

the ache will heal. Twenty miles
. . . the thought of not seeing for
some time those who have wounded
us . . . and little by little unhappy
memories fade. Better still, even
without stirring from the spot,
escape from torment is possible by
the enjoyment of reading, of music,
and of some form of creation. The
function of Art in life is to substi-
tute for futile and painful con-
centration upon one's self the
serene and selfless contemplation of
Beauty.

Life's second lesson—at least for
me—is that few people are wholly
evil. In his first years of contact
with strangers, the youth who has
known only the mild life of the
family circle is frightened by the
cruelty, selfishness, jealousy, which
he thinks he meets at every turn.
His pessimism is not entirely un-
founded: humanity can be ap-
pallingly base. But as we come to
know people better we find that
they are capable of kindliness, of
enduring tenderness, of great heroism. Then we begin to realize that
what is really fear of life is shield-
ing itself behind the armor of crime.
What seems revenge is really suffering. And, most frequent of all,
ignorance is judging and acting
blindly. The English writer, Charles
Lamb, said one day, "I hate that
man." "But you don't know him,"
a listener objected. "Of course I
don't," said Lamb. "Do you think
I could possibly hate a man I
know?"

"What is the most valuable lesson life has taught me?" A passionate belief in human nature, in
spite of her crimes, in spite of her
madness. For that madness is a result: it is not a cause.

II

We must come to the second question. "What advice would you give
to a young friend which would help
him to keep his balance in the most
difficult experiences of his life?"

That's a question for a book, not
for an essay. I think I should begin
by insisting on the necessity for
discipline. It is not well for a man
or a woman to be ceaselessly seeking the whys and wherefores of
everything. That a life may be
happy, it must be based on fixed
principles. I would almost say that
it is of little importance what those
principles are so long as they are
solid, steady; and that we accept
them without compromise. I am
not speaking here of doctrinal
creeds. "That," says the poet Byron,
"is an affair between a man and his
Maker." I am speaking of action
self-imposed, of building upon solid
base, of living by strict discipline.
The discipline of a religious life,
the discipline of work, of every
kind of sport—those are all sane and
wholesome, provided they are
wholeheartedly believed in.

Another condition making for
mental and moral balance seems to
me to be unity in the plan, con-
tinuity in the pattern. A young
person is tempted by every possibility, and the possibilities are infinite. Limiting himself to a choice
irks him. He wants to have every
kind of friend; to take every possible journey; to embrace all learning; to embark upon every kind of
career. But one of life's conditions
is that he must limit himself; he
has to choose. Then, and only then,
can he live deeply and steadily.

These I think, would be my
answers—if I were to answer.

33

A PRAYER FOR A LITTLE HOME
FLORENCE BONE

God send us a little home
To come back to when we roam—
Low walls and fluted tiles,
Wide windows, a view for miles;
Red firelight and deep chairs;
Small white beds upstairs;
Great talk in little nooks;
Dim colors, rows of books;
One picture on each wall;
Not many things at all.

God send us a little ground—
Tall trees standing round,
Homely flowers in brown sod,
Overhead, the stars, O God!
God bless, when winds blow,
Our home and all we know.

UP A HILL AND A HILL
FANNIE STEARNS DAVIS

Up a hill and a hill there's a sudden orchard slope,
And a little tawny field in the sun,
There's a gray wall that coils like a twist of frayed-out rope,
And grasses nodding news one to one.

Up a hill and a hill there's a windy place to stand,
And between the apple-boughs to find the blue
Of the sleepy summer sea, past the cliffs of orange sand,
And the white charmed ships sliding through.

Up a hill and a hill there's a little house as gray
As a stone that the glaciers scored and stained;
With a red rose by the door, and a tangled garden way,
And a face at the window, checker-paned.

I could climb, I could climb, till the shoes fell off my feet,
Just to find that tawny field above the sea!
Up a hill and a hill,—oh, the honeysuckle's sweet!
And the eyes at the window watch for me!

THE DREAMERS
Theodosia Garrison

The gypsies passed her little gate—
She stopped her wheel to see—
A brown-faced pair who walked the road,
Free as the wind is free;
And suddenly her tidy room
A prison seemed to be.

Her shining plates against the walls,
Her sunlit, sanded floor,
The brass-bound wedding chest that held
Her linen's snowy store,
The very wheel whose humming died,—
Seemed only chains she bore.

She watched the foot-free gypsies pass;
She never knew or guessed
The wistful dream that drew them close
The longing in each breast
Some day to know a home like hers,
Wherein their hearts might rest.

MARRIAGE
A. Warren

I know we loved each other when we walked
So long ago in spring beneath the moon;
When, hand clasped close in hand, we softly talked
Of that new joy our hearts would shelter soon,
Perennially golden and secure
From any change. But O, we could not see
That springtime wonderment would not endure
As first it was but alter blessedly.

We could not know, my dear, we could not guess
How years augment the miracle of love;
How autumn brings a depth of tenderness
That is beyond young April's dreaming of!
How there would burn a richer flame some day
Than that which first threw glory on our way.

35

I Remember the Frandsens

By KATHRYN FORBES

*𝒯*HE SUMMER THAT I was twelve, I vacationed at my uncle's ranch in Santa Clara Valley, California. I was a reluctant visitor. That is, until I met Smithy.

Smithy, who lived on the next ranch, was the most forthright and the most completely adult boy I'd ever known. My aunt said it was because Smithy's parents died before he was eight, and a bachelor uncle had had to rear the boy as best he could. My uncle said that hard-working farm boys were usually old for their years, even at twelve.

Becoming friends with Smithy wasn't easy. I soon learned that the slightest lapse into things either fanciful or childish sent Smithy scurrying. He had an annoying habit of disappearing whenever he got bored or discomfited. My aunt said his real name was Lloyd, but he never admitted it; one called him Smithy, or went unanswered.

When the old Horlick farm was sold, by mail, to an eastern couple named Frandsen, I thought it exciting because I had heard that the new owners were *stage people.* Smithy remained noncommittal, but on the day I chose to happen to walk up the Frandsens' driveway, Smithy was with me. And when, halfway up the walk, we bumped right into Mr. and Mrs. Frandsen and they greeted us with exclamations of joy and welcome, Smithy was too surprised to run away.

The newcomers were, I judged, nearly fifty. Mrs. Frandsen had a beautiful, soft face, and her lovely blond hair was just touched with gray. Mr. Frandsen was shorter than his wife, although he held himself exceedingly straight, and his little brown eyes twinkled with kindness.

We were their very first visitors, they said; we must come out of the hot sun and into the cool of the house. Neither Smithy nor I had ever met grownups like this before. We were not used to sitting in front rooms decorated with spears and masks and signed photographs of costumed ladies and gentlemen, nor to being served tea out of something called a samovar.

Most of all, we were not used to being treated as gay contemporaries. The Frandsens told us exciting anecdotes about New York, about their experiences when they had acted in road companies. We were allowed to glimpse their future plans, the dreams-that-were-going-to-come-true, now that they had retired and settled down.

George—of course we were to call them George and Lisa, were we not their *first* new friends?—George was going to become a real farmer. He had all the Government bulletins. Most wonderful of all, the Frandsens were going to adopt a baby. "A baby girl," Lisa said, "with blue eyes."

George beamed. "For months, now, we have had our request in.

36

When we came through San Francisco we filled out final forms."

"And always," Lisa said, "we'll tell her that we *chose* her." They showed us the books they had about raising babies. Now, as soon as the Agency people sent a lady down to inspect them, the baby would be theirs.

Smithy and I stayed on and on. Never had I felt so welcome, such a distinguished guest. I chattered, and no one said it was time for me to go home, or that my mother wanted me. When Lisa tried to get Smithy to talk, too, and asked his name, I—drunk with social success —blurted out that it was Lloyd Smith. Lisa said Lloyd was a fine name. I expected something to happen, but Smithy just rolled his eyes alarmingly, and looked, for a moment, like my uncle's colt.

When we finally stood up to go, George and Lisa said we were to come back often, *often*, and Lisa kissed my cheek.

I couldn't stay away from the Frandsens. They enchanted me. They called their stove Ophelia, because it was quite, quite mad. They named their bantam rooster Iago; their pig was Falstaff. When we sat on the cool side porch, George and Lisa told me whole plots out of plays, even acted them out. Sometimes I would catch a glimpse of Smithy, out in the orchard, and he would be listening, too.

When my uncle's farm dog, Old Ben, died of age, and no one but me was sad about it, I lugged the poor hound's body over to the Frandsens'. Halfway there, Smithy materialized, and took over my burden. He helped George dig a grave of honor at the foot of the Frand-

sens' pepper tree. After it was all over, Smithy listened quietly while George said the most beautiful words I had ever heard: "Fear no more the heat of the sun, or the furious winter's rages. . . ."

As the days went on I despaired of making Lisa understand that Smithy was not a child. When she baked bread she sent him miniature loaves; when she made cake there was always a tiny one, baked in the lid of the baking powder tin, for Smithy. Obediently, I delivered them; silently, he pocketed them.

On the Saturday that the Agency lady came to inspect the Frandsens I went into the orchard, to be out of the way. I found Smithy there. We each picked a tree, leaned against it, and settled down to wait. I wasn't worried; anyone could see that the Frandsens were remarkable people.

"And the way they do everything," I said, "with—well, with *ceremony*. Smithy, aren't they wonderful?"

Smithy just grunted. I noticed, though, when we heard the Agency lady's car clatter away that he was on his feet as quickly as I. The moment we entered the house, we knew that something was terribly wrong.

Lisa was sitting quietly in a chair. She didn't look gay or young any more. George patted her shoulder, while he told us.

"We are too old. People past forty-five are not permitted to adopt small babies."

I was indignant. "But they must have known—the forms—"

George looked down. "In the theater, one takes off a year here, a year there. Truly, Lisa and I had forgotten—" He shrugged. "Today we told our true ages. The Agency lady is kind, but it is a new rule."

"I can understand," Lisa said bravely. "It is for the child's good. So that—so that a child shall not have old—parents." She began to cry.

I was suddenly aware of being a child, too, without experience or knowledge. I did not know what to say to my friends, how to comfort them. And Smithy was no help. He slipped away without a word.

When, a little later, we heard a thump on the porch, I had the wild hope that it might be the Agency lady coming back. But it was only Smithy. He had his Sunday suit on, and the knickers were too short, and he looked funny. He gave me a terrible frown, and set down three newspaper-wrapped packages and two fishing poles. Standing there in the open doorway, he said matter-of-factly, "People are always adopting children; why can't it be the other way around once in a while?" His voice began to climb. "So I choose you. I asked my uncle, and he doesn't care, because he wants to move to the city anyway. So if you—if you want—"

Lisa ran across the room and put her wet cheek against Smithy's face, and said, "Lloyd! Oh Lloyd!" I was afraid she was going to try to kiss him, and I wished somebody would shut the door. I guess George understood, because he started shaking Smithy's hand manfully, and saying, "Well, now, welcome, welcome."

Smithy seemed to make some tremendous effort. "Isn't there some sort of ceremony?" he asked George. "Shouldn't you—carry me into the house, or something?"

"But that's a ceremony for—" I started to say, but couldn't finish.

I do not think that twelve-year-old girls are particularly aware of poignancy, but I do know that the scene, that day, touched me beyond tears. Vainly trying to swallow the hurting in my throat, I watched George Frandsen stoop and lift the tall, gangly boy, the long, black-stockinged legs awkwardly disposed. Gently, carefully, he carried Smithy over the threshold and into the house.

"Well, now," I heard George say, "well, now, *son* . . ."

DOC BRACKETT

By Damon Runyon

Doc Brackett didn't have black whiskers.

Nonetheless, he was a fine man.

He doctored in Our Town for many years. He doctored more people than any other doctor in Our Town but made less money.

That was because Doc Brackett was always doctoring poor people, who had no money to pay.

He would get up in the middle of the coldest night and ride twenty miles to doctor a sick woman, or child, or to patch up some fellow who got hurt.

Everybody in Our Town knew Doc Brackett's office over Rice's clothing store. It was up a narrow flight of stairs. His office was always filled with people. A sign at the foot of the stairs said: DR.

BRACKETT, OFFICE UPSTAIRS.

Doc Brackett was a bachelor. He was once supposed to marry Miss Elvira Cromwell, the daughter of old Junius Cromwell, the banker, but on the day the wedding was supposed to take place Doc Brackett got a call to go out into the country and doctor a Mexican child.

Miss Elvira got sore at him and called off the wedding. She said that a man who would think more of a Mexican child than of his wedding was no good. Many women in Our Town agreed with Miss Elvira Cromwell, but the parents of the Mexican child were very grateful to Doc Brackett when the child recovered.

For forty years, the lame, and the halt, and the blind of Our Town had climbed up and down the stairs to Doc Brackett's office.

He never turned away anybody. Some said Doc Brackett was a loose character, because he liked to drink whisky and play poker in the back rooms of saloons.

But he lived to be seventy years old, and then one day he keeled over on the sofa in his office and died. By this time his black hair had turned white.

Doc Brackett had one of the biggest funerals ever seen in Our Town. Everybody went to pay their last respects when he was laid out in Gruber's undertaking parlors. He was buried in Riverview Cemetery.

There was talk of raising money to put a nice tombstone on Doc Brackett's grave as a memorial. The talk got as far as arguing about what should be carved on the stone about him. Some thought poetry would be very nice.

Doc Brackett hated poetry.

The matter dragged along and nothing whatever was done.

Then one day George Gruber, the undertaker, said that Doc Brackett's memorial was already over his grave, with an epitaph and all. George Gruber said the Mexican parents of the child Doc Brackett saved years ago had worried about him having no tombstone.

They had no money themselves, so they took the sign from the foot of the stairs at Doc Brackett's office and stuck it over his grave. It read: DR. BRACKETT, OFFICE UPSTAIRS.

ALCHEMY

Sara Teasdale

I lift my heart as spring lifts up
A yellow daisy to the rain;
My heart will be a lovely cup
Altho' it holds but pain.

For I shall learn from flower and leaf
That color every drop they hold,
To change the lifeless wine of grief
To living gold.

39

MEN ARE POLISHED, through act and speech,
Each by each,
As pebbles are smoothed on the rolling beach.
—*Trowbridge*

SELF-TRUST is the first secret of success.—*Emerson*

HE THAT can have patience can have what he will.—*Franklin*

I LOVE to be alone. I never found the companion that was so
companionable as solitude.—*Thoreau*

GOD enters by a private door into every individual.—*Emerson*

AY, we must all hang together, else we shall all hang separately.—*Franklin*

TREAT YOUR FRIENDS for what you know them to be. Regard no surfaces.
Consider not what they did, but what they intended.—*Thoreau*

LIFE is grand, and so are its environments of Past and Future. Would
the face of nature be so serene and beautiful if man's destiny were not
equally so?—*Thoreau*

TO PRODUCE a mighty book, you must choose a mighty theme.—*Melville*

GREAT GOD, I ask thee for no meaner pelf
Than that I may not disappoint myself,
That in my action I may soar as high
As I can now discern with this clear eye.
—*Thoreau*

THE POWER of a man increases steadily by
continuance in one direction.—*Emerson*

THE VIRTUE which we appreciate, we to
some extent appropriate.—*Thoreau*

40

WHAT IS LOVELY never dies,
But passes into other loveliness,
Star-dust, or sea-foam, flower or winged air.
—*Aldrich*

IT IS never too late to give up our prejudices.—*Thoreau*

A GOOD INTENTION clothes itself in sudden power.—*Emerson*

THERE ARE a thousand hacking at the branches of evil, to one
who is striking at the root.—*Thoreau*

NEVER UTTER the truism, but live it among men.—*Emerson*

WHAT I MUST DO is all that concerns me, and not what people think.—*Emerson*

A SENTENCE should read as if its author, had he held a plough instead of
a pen, could have drawn a furrow deep and straight to the end.—*Thoreau*

TRUTH AND SINCERITY have a certain distinguishing native lustre about them
which cannot be perfectly counterfeited; they are like fire and flame, that
cannot be painted.—*Franklin*

BUILD a little fence of trust around to-day,
Fill the space with loving deeds and therein stay;
Look not through the sheltering bars upon to-morrow,
God will help thee bear what comes of joy, or sorrow.
—*Butts*

WHAT YOUR HEART thinks great is great. The soul's
emphasis is always right.—*Emerson*

LIFE is too short to waste ...
'Twill soon be dark;
Up! mind thine own aim, and
God speed the mark!
—*Emerson*

MOTHER OF COMPTONS

By MILTON S. MAYER

HONORARY degrees are supposed to signify achievement. Sometimes they signify the achievement of the recipient in science or the arts. Sometimes they signify (though seldom openly) the achievement of the college in wheedling a new dormitory from a prosperous citizen. A few years ago Ohio's historic Western College for Women bestowed a doctorate of laws for neither of these reasons. The recipient, whose bearing denied that a woman is old at 74, was awarded the LL.D. "for outstanding achievement as wife and mother of Comptons."

Having received this recognition of her contribution to American life, the new doctor hurried back to the welcome obscurity of an old frame house on a quiet street in the little college town of Wooster, Ohio. Otelia Compton doesn't want to be famous, and she isn't. Four of the men to whom she is wife or mother occupy a whole page in "Who's Who in America," but the larger achievement of a middle western farm girl is unrecorded.

Those who extol the virtues of heredity may examine with profit the Compton family tree. For the ancestors of the first family of science were common farmers and unskilled mechanics, and the only one of them associated with scholarship was a carpenter who helped nail together the early buildings of Princeton. True, Elias Compton and Otelia Augspurger both taught school to help support the farms on which they were born, but so had farmers' sons and daughters before them. And there was no reason to predict that the union of two country school teachers would produce a page in "Who's Who."

Nor could the naked eye distinguish in the simple Compton household a special genius in the practice of domestic wisdom. Still, the genius must have been there, for of the four children born to Elias and Otelia Compton, Karl, the oldest, is a distinguished physicist, now [1938] president of the great institution, Massachusetts Institute of Technology; Mary, the second, is principal of a missionary school in India and wife of the president of Allahabad Christian College there; Wilson, the third, is a noted economist and general manager of the U. S. Lumber Manufacturers' Association, and Arthur, the "baby," is, at forty-five, one of the immortals of science—winner of the Nobel Prize in Physics.

How did it happen? The answer of the four famous Comptons is a nod in the direction of the old frame house in Wooster. In the "sitting room" at Wooster I found Elias Compton, beloved elder statesman of Ohio education, who died last May at the age of eighty-one. He taught philosophy at Wooster College for forty-five years. But I did not find the answer to my question in the sitting room, for the father of Comptons explained that he was just one of Otelia's boys and referred me to the kitchen, where the mother of Comptons, at the age of 79, manages the home that gave America one of its most eminent families.

It is characteristic of Otelia Compton's philosophy that she should deny she has a recipe for rearing great men and women. She will admit that her children are "worthy," but what the world calls great has no significance for her. When she heard the news that Arthur had won the world's highest award in science, her first words were. "I hope it doesn't turn his head." In the second place, she refuses to be an expert and has never before permitted herself to be quoted on the secret of successful motherhood. The only way I was able to pry her loose from her reticence was to get her into a good hot argument.

That was the weakness in her armor. For this doctor of laws actually has a set of laws, and to challenge them is to ask for a fight. There is nothing unfair about picking an intellectual quarrel with this woman of almost eighty years; she is more than equal to it. She reads as ardently as any scholar. She thinks as nimbly as any logician. And her youthfulness is such that when, one day this summer, she forgot to take off her wrist-watch before her daily swim, her children kidded her about getting old.

She may disclaim her expertness, but her record is against her. There are her four children, with their total of thirty-one college and university degrees and their memberships in thirty-nine learned societies. They didn't just grow. In addition, there are the hundreds of boys and girls whose lives Otelia Compton shaped during the thirty-five years she spent directing the Presbyterian Church's two homes for the children of its missionaries. Cornered in her kitchen, the mother of Comptons simply had to admit that she knows something about motherhood.

Her recipe is so old it is new, so orthodox it is radical, so commonplace that we have forgotten it and it startles us. "We used the Bible and common sense," she told me. I replied that "the Bible and common sense" was inadequate, since the Bible has been misused by knaves and common sense is an attribute every fool imputes to himself. She looked at me hard through her gold-rimmed glasses. Slowly her gray eyes softened. She smiled, and told me to go ahead and tell her what I wanted to know.

The first thing I wanted to know was, "How important is heredity?"

"That depends on what you mean by heredity."

"Well," I said, "let's say 'blue blood.' "

That was easy for the descendant of Alsatian farmers. "If you mean the principle that worth is handed down in the bloodstream, I don't think much of it. Lincoln's 'heredity' was nil. The dissolute kings of history and the worthless sons and daughters of some of the 'best families' in our own country are pretty good evidence that blood can run awfully thin. No, I've seen too many extraordinary men and women who were children of the common people to put much stock in heredity.

"Don't misunderstand me. There is a kind of heredity that is all-important. That is the heredity of training. A child isn't likely to learn good habits from his parents unless they learned them from their parents. Call that environment if you want to, or environmental heredity. But it is something that is handed down from generation to generation."

In connection with misplaced

43

faith in heredity, the mother of Comptons has something to say about the notion held by so many today that their children "haven't got a chance." It is a notion, she feels, which is becoming entirely too prevalent. "This denial of the American reality of equal opportunity," she said, "suggests a return to the medieval psychology of a permanently degraded peasant class. Once parents have decided their children haven't got a chance, they are not likely to give them one. And the children, in turn, become imbued with this paralyzing attitude of futility."

Certainly the four young Comptons would never have had a chance had their parents regarded economic hardship as insuperable. Elias Compton was earning $1,400 a year as a professor while his wife was rearing four children and maintaining the status a college community demands of faculty households. The children all had their chores, but household duties—and here is an ingredient of the Compton recipe—were never allowed to interfere either with school work or the recreation that develops healthy bodies and sportsmanship.

If heredity is not the answer, I wanted to know, what is?

"The home."

"That's a pleasant platitude," I said, in an effort to draw my "opponent" into the middle of the ring. I succeeded.

"It's a forgotten platitude," she replied sharply. "The tragedy of American life is that the home is becoming incidental at a time when it is needed as never before. Parents forget that neither school nor the world can reform the finished product of a bad home. They forget that their children are their first responsibility.

"Today servants are hired to take care of children. In my day, no matter how many servants a mother could afford she took care of her children herself.

"The first thing parents must remember is that their children are not likely to be any better than they are themselves. Mothers and fathers who wrangle and dissipate need not be surprised if their observant young ones take after them. The next thing is that parents must obtain the confidence of their children in all things if they do not want to make strangers of them and have them go to the boy on the street corner for advice. Number three is that parents must explain to the child every action that affects him, even at the early age when parents believe, usually mistakenly, that the child is incapable of understanding. Only thus will the child mature with the sense that justice has been done him and the impulse to be just himself.

"The mother or father who laughs at a youngster's 'foolish' ideas forgets that those ideas are not foolish to the child. When Arthur was 10 years old he wrote an essay taking issue with other experts on why some elephants were three-toed and others five-toed. He brought it to me to read, and I had a hard time keeping from laughing. But I knew how seriously he took his ideas, so I sat down and worked on them with him."

Arthur—he of the Nobel Prize—was listening to our conversation, and here he interrupted. "Mother," he said, "if you had laughed at me that day, I think you would have killed my interest in research."

44

"The reason why many parents laugh at their children," Mrs. Compton went on, "is that they have no interest in the child's affairs. The mother and father can not retain their influence over their children if their children's life is foreign to them. And it isn't enough to encourage the child; the parents must *participate* in his interests. They must work *with* him, and if his interest turns out to be something about which they know nothing it is their business to educate themselves. If they don't, the child will discover their ignorance and lose his respect for them."

When Karl Compton was twelve, he wrote a "book" on Indian fighting. Mary was absorbed with linguistics. Wilson's devotion to the spitball made him the greatest college pitcher in the Middle West. Arthur, too, was a notable athlete, but his first love was astronomy. The combination of Indian fighting, linguistics, the spitball and astronomy might have driven a lesser woman to despair, but Otelia Compton mastered them all as she did their other diversions. For instance, the summer the Compton family caught 1,120 pounds of fish, mother landed her share.

All the toys the young Comptons had could have been bought for a few dollars, but when the four of them were still under ten years of age their mother packed them up, together with a father who had almost died from pneumonia, and took them to the wilds of northern Michigan, where mother and children hewed a clearing and pitched a tent. There these urban-bred children learned simplicity and hard work. There they found that the things which tempt children

need not be forbidden them when those things are fishing and woodcraft and the stars. There they imbibed, as the mother of Comptons would have every city child imbibe, of the unity and mystery of nature.

The boys all worked summers and in college, gaining priceless experience; and they all had their own bank accounts, "not," their mother explains, "because we wanted them to glorify money but because we wanted them to learn that money, however much or however little, should never be wasted." Would she put hard work first in her lexicon? Mrs. Compton thought a moment. "Yes," she said, "I would. That is, hard work in the right direction. The child who has acquired the habits of work of the right kind does not need anything else."

And what is the "right kind" of hard work?

"The kind of work that is good in itself."

I baited the trap. "What's wrong with working for money?"

The mother of Comptons exploded. "Everything! To teach a child that money-making for the sake of money is worthy is to teach him that the only thing worth while is what the world calls success. That kind of success has nothing to do either with usefulness or happiness. Parents teach it and the schools teach it, and the result is an age that thinks that money means happiness. The man who lives for money never gets enough, and he thinks that that is why he isn't happy. The real reason is that he has had the wrong goal of life set before him."

What did she mean by parents

45

and schools "teaching" that money is happiness?

"I mean all this talk about 'careers' and 'practical' training. Children should be taught how to think, and thinking isn't always practical. Children should be encouraged to develop their natural bents and not forced to choose a 'career.' When our children were still in high school, a friend of ours asked Elias what they were going to be. His answer was, 'I haven't asked them.' Some of our neighbors thought we were silly when we bought Arthur a little telescope and let him sit up all night studying the stars. It wasn't 'practical.'" Yet it was his "impractical" love of the stars that brought him the Nobel Prize and something over $20,000; and in order that he might pursue his cosmic ray research, the University of Chicago equipped a $100,000 laboratory for him.

I thought of the four Comptons and the success that has resulted from their early training, and I wondered if "impractical" parents weren't perhaps the most practical. What could be more tangible than the satisfaction and the honors that have come to them because of their far-flung labors?

❖ ❖ ❖

From *MEDITATIONS*
By Preston Bradley

WE ARE deeply grateful this morning that long ago there was crystallized into the literature of a great religion the ideal that the other word for God was "Love" and on this Sunday it is not the God of theology and the God of the creeds or the God of the churches of which we are thinking, it is the God whose other name is "Love." And of all the moments in the whole history of human-kind when the true and penetrating conception of that ideal would be revealed to our consciousness, it is the moment in which we meet now an ideal which has been disturbed, an ideal which has been attacked and mutilated almost everywhere in the world until such a word as "Love" seems an empty and meaningless thing.

We are so grateful that on this beautiful day it is possible for the heart and the soul of America to unite itself, irrespective of creed or color, of faith or race, into one great effort to bring this ideal of love before our hearts and minds again. The symbol for that love upon the altar of our affections is the precious memory of our mothers. In the quiet contemplation, the stillness and beauty of this moment together, might each of us separate ourselves from all the external influences, difficulties, and problems and just become, for a few seconds, a little child again. Might we recapture some of the joy and some of the enthusiasm of that childhood when mother was so infinitely precious as to be the very center of all of our activities and our functions; the last one to see us at night, and the first to greet us in the morning, standing at the window in the win-

46

tertime waiting for us to come home from school, out at the front gate in the summer watching that the children might come home from their play uninjured and safe.

Somehow, might it not be possible for us to enlarge to such an extent on the protecting, loving care of something which we mean when we say the word "Mother" that in the miracle of Thine own time that ideal of love might once more be the affection of the earth?

We cannot let our Mother's Day meditation come to a close without breathing a prayer, a prayer which comes from a heart burdened and sad with the tragedy of the world, but we could not possibly close our meditation without breathing from the depth of our very inmost soul a prayer for the mothers of the world. God bless Scandinavian mothers today, Russian mothers, German mothers, French mothers, Dutch mothers, British mothers, Italian mothers, O, we could enumerate them all and never leave one out, and now that hate has exploded in all of its virulent form, and the long expected explosion has happened in the world and the saddest Sunday in all history [Pearl Harbor] is now upon us, now that this has come upon civilization, above the din and the carnage might all motherhood be dignified and ennobled, may no hate exist there, for it will finally be the mothers of the earth who will suffer the most and whose hearts will be crushed the oftenest.

We now would dedicate these sacred moments in this service of tribute to the mothers of all the earth, all the mothers everywhere who this moment are having no Mother's Day. No, it is only a day

for Mars and the God of Mars who struts in his pigmylike, little childishness, bedecked with uniform and medals and talking about "Power" and "Superiority." Might that devastation cease, and might the power of Love finally reveal itself as the greatest power of all.

To all mothers who are shut-ins, to all mothers who are ill, to all mothers in hospitals, in institutions, in sanitariums, to all mothers at home in O, perhaps some little lonely farmhouse far removed and lonely today, to all mothers wherever these words are going, might they carry the ardent wish and the deep hope of an appreciation and love, and, perchance, if there is one son or one daughter listening now who has not been in touch with their mothers this day, who did not write that letter, who have not sent that telegram, who have not given Mother evidence that they are thinking of her this day, as a result of this great service here, before this day comes to a close, might they call that mother, if only to say on the telephone "Mother, I love you," might they send that wire, might no one let this day pass who has the opportunity of having their mother with them, without this little remembrance. Might we do that, those who can, and for those of us whose mothers live in our memories, might we find a moment of dedication this day in which once again we will dedicate ourselves to the highest and best ideals which we know our mothers dreamed for us. And then, in the name and in the spirit of the one who loved His mother, and who, through that love and that devotion, was able to love all mankind, we pray His prayer.

LILACS
Amy Lowell

Lilacs,
False blue,
White,
Purple,
Color of lilac,
Your great puffs of flowers
Are everywhere in this my New England.
Among your heart-shaped leaves
Orange orioles hop like music-box birds and sing
Their little weak soft songs;
In the crooks of your branches
The bright eyes of song sparrows sitting on spotted eggs
Peer restlessly through the light and shadow
Of all Springs.
Lilacs in dooryards
Holding quiet conversations with an early moon;
Lilacs watching a deserted house
Settling sideways into the grass of an old road;
Lilacs, wind-beaten, staggering under a lopsided shock of bloom
Above a cellar dug into a hill.
You are everywhere.
You were everywhere.
You tapped the window when the preacher preached his sermon,
And ran along the road beside the boy going to school.
You stood by pasture bars to give the cows good milking;
You persuaded the housewife that her dishpan was of silver
And her husband an image of pure gold.
You flaunted the fragrance of your blossoms
Through the wide doors of Custom Houses—
You, and sandalwood, and tea,
Charging the noses of quill-driving clerks
When a ship was in from China.
You called to them: "Goose-quill men, goose-quill men,
May is a month for flitting,"
Until they writhed on their high stools
And wrote poetry on their letter sheets behind the propped-up ledgers.
Paradoxical New England clerks,
Writing inventories in ledgers, reading the "Song of Solomon" at
    night,
So many verses before bedtime,
Because it was the Bible.

The dead fed you
Amid the slant stones of graveyards.
Pale ghosts who planted you
Came in the nighttime
And let their thin hair blow through your clustered stems.
You are of the green sea,
And of stone hills which reach a long distance. . . .
Cape Cod starts you along the beaches to Rhode Island;
Connecticut takes you from a river to the sea.
You are brighter than apples,
Sweeter than tulips,
You are the great flood of our souls
Bursting above the leaf-shapes of our hearts,
You are the smell of all Summers,
The love of wives and children,
The recollection of the gardens of little children,
And the familiar treading of the foot to and fro on a road it knows.
May is lilac here in New England,
May is a thrush singing "Sun up!" on a tip-top ash tree,
May is white clouds behind pine trees
Puffed out and marching upon a blue sky.
May is a green as no other,
May is much sun through small leaves,
May is soft earth,
And apple blossoms,
And windows open to a south wind.
May is a full light wind of lilac
From Canada to Narragansett Bay.

Lilacs,
False blue,
White,
Purple,
Color of lilac,
Heart-leaves of lilac all over New England,
Roots of lilac under all the soil of New England,
Lilac in me because I am New England,
Because my roots are in it,
Because my leaves are of it,
Because my flowers are for it,
Because it is my country
And I speak to it of itself
And sing of it with my own voice,
Since certainly it is mine.

BE JUST, and fear not; let all the ends thou aimest at be thy country's, thy God's and Truth's.—*Shakespeare*

THE GREATEST ATTRIBUTE of Heaven is mercy.—*Beaumont and Fletcher*

HE THAT loseth his honestie hath nothing else to lose.—*Lyly*

THE GIFT of prayer is not always in our power; in Heaven's sight the wish to pray is prayer.—*Lessing*

THIS ABOVE ALL: to thine own self be true, and it must follow, as the night the day, thou canst not then be false to any man.—*Shakespeare*

JUSTICE—august and pure, the abstract idea of all that would be perfect in the spirits and the inspirations of men!—where the mind rises; where the heart expands; where the countenance is ever placid and benign; where her favorite attitude is to stoop to the unfortunate; to hear their cry and to help them; to rescue and relieve; to succor and save; majestic, from its mercy; venerable, from its utility; uplifted, without pride; firm, without obduracy; beneficent in each preference; lovely, though in her frown!—*Sheridan*

WHAT IS VIRTUE? reason put into practice:—talent? reason expressed with brilliance:—soul? reason delicately put forth; and genius is sublime reason. —*Chenier*

THINGS ARE only worth what one makes them worth.—*Molière*

SONG brings of itself a cheerfulness that wakes the heart of joy.—*Euripides*

THE FRIENDS thou hast, and their adoption tried, Grapple them to thy soul with hoops of steel. —*Shakespeare*

TO GENEROUS SOULS, every task is noble.—*Euripides*

WISE WORDS OF WOMEN

LORD, for tomorrow and its needs,
  I do not pray;
Keep me, my God, from stain of sin,
  Just for today.
            —*Sister Mary Xavier*

THE WORLD does not require so much to be
informed as to be reminded.—*More*

AFTER THE VERB "To Love," "To Help" is the most beautiful verb
in the world!—*Baroness Von Suttner*

WRITE YOUR MASTERPIECES! And do not forget that in your profession there
is no middle state; you must be king—or be only a laborer.—*Mme. Balzac*

I ALWAYS seek the good that is in people and leave the bad to Him who
made mankind and knows how to round off the corners.—*Goethe's Mother*

WHEN AT EVE at the bounding of the landscape the heavens appear to recline so slowly on the earth, imagination pictures beyond the horizon an
asylum of hope,—a native land of love; and nature seems silently to repeat
that man is immortal.—*De Staël*

YOU BETTER live your best and act your best and think your best today;
for today is the sure preparation for tomorrow and all the other to-
morrows that follow.—*Martineau*

WITHOUT DEW AND LIGHT flowers fade. Charity and love are
the dew and light of the human heart.—*De Gentis*

OH, WONDROUS POWER! how little understood,
  Entrusted to the mother's mind alone,
To fashion genius, form the soul for good,
  Inspire a West, or train a Washington.
            —*Hale*

No CHAIN is stronger than its
weakest link.—*Spalding*

The Song of Life

By W. J. LOCKE

$\mathcal{N}$ON CUIVIS HOMINI *contingit adire Corinthum*. It is not everybody's good fortune to go to Corinth. It is also not everybody's good fortune to go to Peckham—still less to live there. But if you were one of the favoured few, and were wont to haunt the Peckham Road and High Street, the bent figure of Angelo Fardetti would have been as familiar to you as the vast frontage of the great Emporium which, in the drapery world, makes Peckham illustrious among London Suburbs. You would have seen him humbly threading his way through the female swarms that clustered at the plate-glass windows —the mere drones of the hive were fooling their frivolous lives away over ledgers in the City—the inquiry of a lost dog in his patient eyes, and an unconscious challenge to Philistia in the wiry bush of white hair that protruded beneath his perky soft felt hat. If he had been short, he might have passed unregarded; but he was very tall—in his heyday he had been six feet two—and very thin. You smile as you recall to mind the black frock-coat, somewhat white at the seams, which, tightly buttoned, had the fit of a garment of corrugated iron. Although he was so tall one never noticed the inconsiderable stretch of trouser below the long skirt. He always appeared to be wearing a truncated cassock. You were inclined to laugh at this queer exotic of the Peckham Road until you looked more keenly at the man himself. Then you saw an old, old face, very swarthy, very lined, very beautiful still in its regularity of feature, maintaining in a little white moustache with waxed ends a pathetic braggadocio of youth; a face in which the sorrows of the world seemed to have their dwelling, but sorrows that on their way thither had passed through the crucible of a simple soul.

Twice a day it was his habit to walk there; shops and faces a meaningless confusion to his eyes, but his ears alert to the many harmonies of the orchestra of the great thoroughfare. For Angelo Fardetti was a musician. Such had he been born; such had he lived. Those aspects of life which could not be interpreted in terms of music were to him unintelligible. During his seventy years empires had crumbled, mighty kingdoms had arisen, bloody wars had been fought, magic conquests been made by man over nature. But none of these convulsive facts had ever stirred Angelo Fardetti's imagination. Even his country he had wellnigh forgotten; it was so many years since he had left it, so much music had passed since then through his being. Yet he had never learned to speak English correctly; and, not having an adequate language (save music) in which to clothe his thoughts, he spoke very little. When addressed he smiled at you sweetly like a pleasant, inarticulate old child.

Though his figure was so familiar to the inhabitants of Peckham, few

52

knew how and where he lived. As a matter of fact, he lived a few hundred yards away from the busy High Street, in Formosa Terrace, at the house of one Anton Kirilov, a musician. He had lodged with the Kirilovs for over twenty years—but not always in the roomy splendour of Formosa Terrace. Once Angelo was first violin in an important orchestra, a man of mark, while Anton fiddled away in the obscurity of a fifth-rate music-hall. Then the famous violinist rented the drawing-room floor of the Kirilovs' little house in Clapham, while the Kirilovs, humble folk, got on as best they could. Now things had changed. Anton Kirilov was musical director of a London theatre, but Angelo, through age and rheumatism and other infirmities, could fiddle in public no more; and so it came to pass that Anton Kirilov and Olga, his wife, and Sonia, their daughter (to whom Angelo had stood godfather twenty years ago), rioted in spaciousness, while the old man lodged in tiny rooms at the top of the house, paying an infinitesimal rent and otherwise living on his scanty savings and such few shillings as he could earn by copying out parts and giving lessons to here and there a snub-nosed little girl in a tradesman's back parlour. Often he might have gone without sufficient nourishment had not Mrs. Kirilov seen to it; and whenever an extra good dish, succulent and strong, appeared at her table, either Sonia or the servant carried a plateful upstairs with homely compliments.

"You are making of me a spoiled child, Olga," he would say sometimes, "and I ought not to eat of the food for which Anton works so hard."

And she would reply with a laugh: "If we did not keep you alive, Signor Fardetti, how should we have our *quatuors* on Sunday afternoons?"

You see, Mrs. Kirilov, like the good Anton, had lived all her life in music too—she was a pianist; and Sonia also was a musician—she played the 'cello in a ladies' orchestra. So they had famous Sunday *quatuors* at Formosa Terrace, in which Fardetti was well content to play second fiddle to Anton's first.

You see, also, that but for these honest souls to whom a musician like Fardetti was a sort of blood-brother, the evening of the old man's days might have been one of tragic sadness. But even their affection and his glad pride in the brilliant success of his old pupil, Geoffrey Chase, could not mitigate the one great sorrow of his life. The violin, yes; he had played it well; he had not aimed at a great soloist's fame, for want of early training, and he had never dreamed such unrealisable dreams; but other dreams had he dreamed with passionate intensity. He had dreamed of being a great composer, and he had beaten his heart out against the bars that shut him from the great mystery. A waltz or two, a few songs, a catchy march, had been published and performed, and had brought him unprized money and a little hateful repute; but the compositions into which he had poured his soul remained in dusty manuscript, despised and rejected of musical men. For many years the artist's imperious craving to create and hope and will kept him serene. Then, in the prime of his days, a tremendous inspiration shook him. He had a divine message to proclaim to the world, a song of life itself, a revelation. It was life, indestructible, eternal. It was the seed that grew into the tree; the tree that flourished lustily, and then grew bare and stark and perished; the seed, again, of the tree that rose unconquerable into the laughing leaf of spring. It was the kiss of lovers that, when they were dead and gone, lived immortal on the lips of grandchildren. It was the endless roll of the seasons, the majestic, triumphant rhythm of existence. It was a cosmic chant, telling of things as only music could tell of them, and as no musician had ever told of them before.

He attempted the impossible, you will say. He did. That was the pity of it. He spent the last drop of his heart's blood over his sonata. He wrote it and rewrote it, wasting years, but never could he imprison within those remorseless ruled lines the elusive sounds that shook his being. An approximation to his dream reached the stage of a completed score. But he knew that it was thin and lifeless. The themes that were to be developed into magic harmonies tinkled into commonplace. The shell of this vast conception was there, but the shell alone. The thing could not live without the unseizable, and that he had not seized. Angelo Fardetti, broken down by toil and misery, fell very sick. Doctors recommended Brighton. Docile as a child, he went to Brighton, and there a pretty lady who admired his playing at the Monday Popular Concerts at St. James's Hall, got hold of him and married him. When she ran away, a year later, with a dashing young stockbroker, he took the score of the sonata that was to be the whole interpretation of life from its half-forgot-ten hiding-place, played it through on the piano, burst into a passion of tears, in the uncontrollable Italian way, sold up his house, and went to lodge with Anton Kirilov. To no son or daughter of man did he ever show a note or play a bar of the sonata. And never again did he write a line of music. Bravely and humbly he faced life, though the tragedy of failure made him prematurely old. And all through the years the sublime message reverberated in his soul and haunted his dreams; and his was the bitter sorrow of knowing that never should that message be delivered for the comforting of the world.

The loss of his position as first violin forced him, at sixty, to take more obscure engagements. That was when he followed the Kirilovs to Peckham. And then he met the joy of his old age—his one pupil of genius, Geoffrey Chase, an untrained lad of fourteen, the son of a well-to-do seed merchant in the High Street.

"His father thinks it waste of time," said Mrs. Chase, a gentle, mild-eyed woman, when she brought the boy to him, "but Geoffrey is so set on it—and so I've persuaded his father to let him have lessons."

"Do you, too, love music?" he asked.

Her eyes grew moist, and she nodded.

"Poor lady! He should not let you starve. Never mind," he said, patting her shoulder. "Take comfort. I will teach your boy to play for you."

And he did. He taught him for three years. He taught him passionately all he knew, for Geoffrey, with music in his blood, had the great gift of the composer. He poured

54

upon the boy all the love of his lonely old heart, and dreamed glorious dreams of his future. The Kirilovs, too, regarded Geoffrey as a prodigy, and welcomed him into their circle, and made much of him. And little Sonia fell in love with him, and he, in his boyish way, fell in love with the dark-haired maiden who played on a 'cello so much bigger than herself. At last the time came when Angelo said:

"My son, I can teach you no more. You must go to Milan."

"My father will never consent," said Geoffrey.

"We will try to arrange that," said Angelo.

So, in their simple ways, Angelo and Mrs. Chase intrigued together until they prevailed upon Mr. Chase to attend one of the Kirilovs' Sunday concerts. He came in church-going clothes, and sat with irreconcilable stiffness on a straight-backed chair. His wife sat close by, much agitated. The others played a concerto arranged as a quintette; Geoffrey first violin, Angelo second, Sonia 'cello, Anton bass, and Mrs. Kirilov at the piano. It was a piece of exquisite tenderness and beauty.

"Very pretty," said Mr. Chase.

"It's beautiful," cried his wife, with tears in her eyes.

"I said so," remarked Mr. Chase.

"And what do you think of my pupil?" Angelo asked excitedly.

"I think he plays very nicely," Mr. Chase admitted.

"But, dear heavens!" cried Angelo. "It is not his playing! One could pick up fifty better violinists in the street. It is the concerto—the composition."

Mr. Chase rose slowly to his feet. "Do you mean to tell me that Geoffrey made up all that himself?"

"Of course. Didn't you know?"

"Will you play it again?"

Gladly they assented. When it was over he took Angelo out into the passage.

"I'm not one of those narrow-minded people who don't believe in art, Mr. Fardetti," said he. "And Geoff has already shown me that he can't sell seeds for toffee. But if he takes up music, will he be able to earn his living at it?"

"Beyond doubt," replied Angelo, with a wide gesture.

"But a good living? You'll forgive me being personal, Mr. Fardetti, but you yourself—"

"I," said the old man humbly, "am only a poor fiddler—but your son is a great musical genius."

"I'll think over it," said Mr. Chase.

Mr. Chase thought over it, and Geoffrey went to Milan, and Angelo Fardetti was once more left desolate. On the day of the lad's departure he and Sonia wept a little in each other's arms, and late that night he once more unearthed the completed score of his sonata, and scanned it through in vain hope of comfort. But as the months passed comfort came. His beloved swan was not a goose, but a wonder among swans. He was a wonder at the Milan Conservatoire, and won prize after prize and medal after medal, and every time he came home he bore his blushing honours thicker upon him. And he remained the same frank, simple youth, always filled with gratitude and reverence for his old master, and though on familiar student terms with all conditions of cosmopolitan damsels, never faithless to the little Anglo-Russian maiden whom he had left at home.

In the course of time his studies were over, and he returned to England. A professorship at the Royal School of Music very soon rendered him financially independent. He began to create. Here and there a piece of his was played at concerts. He wrote incidental music for solemn productions at great London theatres. Critics discovered him, and wrote much about him in the newspapers. Mr. Chase, the seed merchant, though professing to his wife a man-of-the-world's indifference to notoriety, used surreptitiously to cut out the notices and carry them about in his fat pocket-book, and whenever he had a new one he would lie in wait for the lean figure of Angelo Fardetti, and hale him into the shop and make him drink Geoffrey's health in sloe gin, which Angelo abhorred, but gulped down in honour of the prodigy.

One fine October morning Angelo Fardetti missed his walk. He sat instead by his window, and looked unseeingly at the prim row of houses on the opposite side of Formosa Terrace. He had not the heart to go out —and, indeed, he had not the money; for these walks, twice daily, along the High Street and the Peckham Road, took him to and from a queer little Italian restaurant which, with him apparently as its only client, had eked out for years a mysterious and precarious existence. He felt very old—he was seventy-two, very useless, very poor. He had lost his last pupil, a fat, unintelligent girl of thirteen, the daughter of a local chemist, and no one had sent him any copying work for a week. He had nothing to do. He could not even walk to his usual sparrow's meal. It is sad when you are so old that you cannot earn the right to live in a world which wants you no longer.

Looking at unseen bricks through a small window-pane was little consolation. Mechanically he rose and went to a grand piano, his one possession of price, which, with an old horsehair sofa, an oval table covered with a maroon cloth, and a chair or two, congested the tiny room, and, sitting down, began to play one of Stephen Heller's *Nuits Blanches*. You see, Angelo Fardetti was an old-fashioned musician. Suddenly a phrase arrested him. He stopped dead, and remained staring out over the polished plane of the piano. For a few moments he was lost in the chain of associated musical ideas. Then suddenly his swarthy, lined face lit up, and he twirled his little white moustache and began to improvise, striking great majestic chords. Presently he rose, and from a pile of loose music in a corner drew a sheet of ruled paper. He returned to the piano, and began feverishly to pencil down his inspiration. His pulses throbbed. At last he had got the great *andante* movement of his sonata. For an hour he worked intensely; then came the inevitable check. Nothing more would come. He rose and walked about the room, his head swimming. After a quarter of an hour he played over what he had written, and then, with a groan of despair, fell forward, his arms on the keys, his bushy white head on his arms.

The door opened, and Sonia, comely and shapely, entered the room, carrying a tray with food and drink set out on a white cloth. Seeing him bowed over the piano, she put the tray on the table and advanced.

56

"Dear godfather," she said gently, her hand on his shoulder.

He raised his head and smiled. "I did not hear you, my little Sonia."

"You have been composing?"

He sat upright, and tore the pencilled sheets into fragments, which he dropped in a handful on the floor.

"Once, long ago, I had a dream. I lost it. Today I thought that I had found it. But do you know what I did really find?"

"No, godfather," replied Sonia, stooping, with housewifely tidiness, to pick up the litter.

"That I am a poor old fool," said he.

Sonia threw the paper into the grate and again came up behind him.

"It is better to have lost a dream than never to have had one at all. What was your dream?"

"I thought I could write the Song of Life as I heard it—as I hear it still." He smote his forehead lightly. "But no! God has not considered me worthy to sing it. I bow my head to His—to His"—he sought for the word with thin fingers—"to His decree."

She said, with the indulgent wisdom of youth speaking to age:

"He has given you the power to love and to win love."

The old man swung round on the music-stool and put his arm round her waist and smiled into her young face.

"Geoffrey is a very fortunate fellow."

"Because he's a successful composer?"

He looked at her and shook his head, and Sonia, knowing what he meant, blushed very prettily. Then she laughed and broke away.

"Mother has had seventeen partridges sent her as presents this week, and she wants you to help her eat them, and father's offered a bargain in some good Beaujolais, and won't decide until you tell him what you think of it."

Deftly she set out the meal, and drew a chair to the table. Angelo Fardetti rose.

"That I should love you all," said he simply, "is only human, but that you should so much love me is more than I can understand."

You see, he knew that watchful ears had missed his usual outgoing footsteps, and that watchful hearts had divined the reason. To refuse, to hesitate, would be to reject love. So there was no more to be said. He sat down meekly, and Sonia ministered to his wants. As soon as she saw that he was making headway with the partridge and the burgundy, she too sat by the table.

"Godfather," she said, "I've had splendid news this morning."

"Geoffrey?"

"Of course. What other news could be splendid? His Symphony in E flat is going to be given at the Queen's Hall."

"That is indeed beautiful news," said the old man, laying down knife and fork, "but I did not know that he had written a Symphony in E flat."

"That was why he went and buried himself for months in Cornwall—to finish it," she explained.

"I knew nothing about it. Aie! aie!" he sighed. "It is to you, and no longer to me, that he tells things."

"You silly, jealous old dear!" she laughed. "He _had_ to account for deserting me all the summer. But

57

as to what it's all about, I'm as ignorant as you are. I've not heard a note of it. Sometimes Geoff is like that, you know. If he's dead certain sure of himself he won't have any criticism or opinions while the work's in progress. It's only when he's doubtful that he brings one in. And the doubtful things are never anything like the certain ones. You must have noticed it."

"That is true," said Angelo Fardetti, taking up knife and fork again. "He was like that since he was a boy."

"It is going to be given on Saturday fortnight. He'll conduct himself. They've got a splendid programme to send him off. Lembrich's going to play, and Carli's going to sing—just for his sake. Isn't it gorgeous?"

"It is grand. But what does Geoffrey say about it? Come, come, after all he is not the sphinx." He drummed his fingers impatiently on the table.

"Would you really like to know?"

"I am waiting."

"He says it's going to knock 'em!" she laughed.

"Knock 'em?"

"Those were his words."

"But—"

She interpreted into purer English. Geoffrey was confident that his symphony would achieve a sensational success.

"In the meanwhile," said she, "if you don't finish your partridge you'll break mother's heart."

She poured out a glass of burgundy, which the old man drank; but he refused the food.

"No, no," he said, "I cannot eat more. I have a lump there—in my throat. I am too excited. I feel that he is marching to his great triumph.

My little Geoffrey." He rose, knocking his chair over, and strode about the confined space. *"Sacramento!* But I am a wicked old man. I was sorrowful because I was so dull, so stupid that I could not write a sonata. I blamed the good God. *Mea maxima culpa.* And at once he sends me a partridge in a halo of love, and the news of my dear son's glory—"

Sonia stopped him, her plump hands on the front of his old corrugated frock-coat.

"And your glory, too, dear godfather. It if hadn't been for you, where would Geoffrey be? And who realises it more than Geoffrey? Would you like to see a bit of his letter? Only a little bit—for there's a lot of rubbish in it that I would be ashamed of anybody who thinks well of him to read—but just a little bit."

Her hand was at the broad belt joining blouse and skirt. Angelo, towering above her, smiled with an old man's tenderness at the laughing love in her dark eyes, and at the happiness in her young, comely face. Her features were generous, and her mouth frankly large, but her lips were fresh and her teeth white and even, and to the old fellow she looked all that man could dream of the virginal mother-to-be of great sons. She fished the letter from her belt, scanned and folded it carefully.

"There! Read."

And Angelo Fardetti read:

"I've learned my theory and technique, and God knows what—things that only they could teach me—from professors with world-famous names. But for real inspiration, for the fount of music itself, I come back all the time to our dear old

58

maestro, Angelo Fardetti. I can't for the life of me define what it is, but he opened for me a secret chamber behind whose concealed door all these illustrious chaps have walked unsuspectingly. It seems silly to say it because, beyond a few odds and ends, the dear old man has composed nothing, but I am convinced that I owe the *essentials* of everything I do in music to his teaching and influence."

Angelo gave her back the folded letter without a word, and turned and stood again by the window, staring unseeingly at the prim, semi-detached villas opposite. Sonia, having re-hidden her treasure, stole up to him. Feeling her near, he stretched out a hand and laid it on her head.

"God is very wonderful," said he—"very mysterious. Oh, and so good!"

He fumbled, absently and foolishly, with her well-ordered hair, saying nothing more. After a while she freed herself gently and led him back to his partridge.

A day or two afterwards Geoffrey came to Peckham, and mounted with Sonia to Fardetti's rooms, where the old man embraced him tenderly, and expressed his joy in the exuberant foreign way. Geoffrey received the welcome with an Englishman's laughing embarrassment. Perhaps the only fault that Angelo Fardetti could find in the beloved pupil was his uncompromising English manner and appearance. His well-set figure and crisp, short fair hair and fair moustache did not sufficiently express him as a great musician. Angelo had to content himself with the lad's eyes—musician's eyes, as he said, very bright, arresting, dark blue, with depths like sapphires, in which lay

strange thoughts and human laughter.

"I've only run in, dear old *maestro,* to pass the time of day with you, and to give you a ticket for my Queen's Hall show. You'll come, won't you?"

"He asks if I will come! I would get out of my coffin and walk through the streets!"

"I think you'll be pleased," said Geoffrey. "I've been goodness knows how long over it, and I've put into it all I know. If it doesn't come off, I'll—"

He paused.

"You will commit no rashness," cried the old man in alarm.

"I will. I'll marry Sonia the very next day!"

There was laughing talk, and the three spent a happy little quarter of an hour. But Geoffrey went away without giving either of the others an inkling of the nature of his famous symphony. It was Geoffrey's way.

The fateful afternoon arrived. Angelo Fardetti, sitting in the stalls of the Queen's Hall with Sonia and her parents, looked round the great auditorium, and thrilled with pleasure at seeing it full. London had thronged to hear the first performance of his beloved's symphony. As a matter of fact, London had also come to hear the wonderful orchestra give Tchaikowsky's Fourth Symphony, and to hear Lembrich play the violin and Carli sing, which they did once in a blue moon at a symphony concert. But in the old man's eyes these ineffectual fires paled before Geoffrey's genius. So great was his suspense and agitation that he could pay but scant attention to the first two items on the programme. It seemed almost like unmeaning music, far away.

During the interval before the Symphony in E flat his thin hand found Sonia's, and held it tight, and she returned the pressure. She, too, was sick with anxiety. The great orchestra, tier upon tier, was a-flutter with the performers scrambling into their places, and with leaves of scores being turned over, and with a myriad moving bows. Then all having settled into the order of a vast machine, Geoffrey appeared at the conductor's stand. Comforting applause greeted him. Was he not the rising hope of English music? Many others beside those four to whom he was dear, and the mother and father who sat a little way in front of them, felt the same nervous apprehension. The future of English music was at stake. Would it be yet one more disappointment and disillusion, or would it rank the young English composer with the immortals? Geoffrey bowed smilingly at the audience, turned and with his baton gave the signal to begin.

Although only a few years have passed since that memorable first performance, the modestly named Symphony in E flat is now famous and Geoffrey Chase is a great man the wide world over. To every lover of music the symphony is familiar. But only those who were present at the Queen's Hall on that late October afternoon can realise the wild rapture of enthusiasm with which the symphony was greeted. It answered all longings, solved all mysteries. It interpreted, for all who had ears to hear, the fairy dew of love, the burning depths of passion, sorrow and death, and the eternal Triumph of Life. Intensely modern and faultless in technique, it was

new, unexpected, individual, unrelated to any school.

The scene was one of raging tumult; but there was one human being who did not applaud, and that was the old musician, forgotten of the world, Angelo Fardetti. He had fainted.

All through the piece he had sat, bolt upright, his nerves strung to breaking-point, his dark cheeks growing greyer and greyer, and the stare in his eyes growing more and more strange, and the grip on the girl's hand growing more and more vice-like, until she, for sheer agony, had to free herself. And none concerned themselves about him; not even Sonia, for she was enwrapped in the soul of her lover's music. And even between the movements her heart was too full for speech or thought, and when she looked at the old man, she saw him smile wanly and nod his head as one who, like herself, was speechless with emotion. At the end the storm burst. She rose with the shouting, clapping, hand- and handkerchief-waving house, and suddenly, missing him from her side, glanced round and saw him huddled up unconscious in his stall.

The noise and movement were so great that few noticed the long lean old figure being carried out of the hall by one of the side doors fortunately near. In the vestibule, attended by the good Anton and his wife and Sonia, and a commissionaire, he recovered. When he could speak, he looked round and said:

"I am a silly old fellow. I am sorry I have spoiled your happiness. I think I must be too old for happiness, for this is how it has treated me."

There was much discussion between his friends as to what should

60

be done, but good Mrs. Kirilov, once girlishly plump, when Angelo had first known her, now florid and fat and motherly, had her way, and, leaving Anton and Sonia to see the hero of the afternoon, if they could, drove off in a cab to Peckham with the over-wrought old man and put him to bed and gave him homely remedies, invalid food and drink, and commanded him to sleep till morning.

But Angelo Fardetti disobeyed her. For Sonia, although she had found him meekly between the sheets when she went up to see him that evening, heard him later, as she was going to bed—his sitting-room was immediately above her—playing over, on muted strings, various themes of Geoffrey's symphony. At last she went up to his room and put her head in at the door, and saw him, a lank, dilapidated figure in an old, old dressing-gown, fiddle and bow in hand.

"Oh! oh!" she rated. "You are a naughty, naughty old dear. Go to bed at once."

He smiled like a guilty but spoiled child. "I will go," said he.

In the morning she herself took up his simple breakfast and all the newspapers folded at the page on which the notices of the concert were printed. The Press was unanimous in acclamation of the great genius that had raised English music to the spheres. She sat at the foot of the bed and read to him while he sipped his coffee and munched his roll, and, absorbed in her own tremendous happiness, was content to feel the glow of the old man's sympathy. There was little to be said save exclamatory paeans, so overwhelming was the triumph. Tears streamed down his lined cheeks, and between the tears there shone the light of a strange gladness in his eyes. Presently Sonia left him and went about her household duties. An hour or so afterwards she caught the sound of his piano; again he was recalling bits of the great symphony, and she marvelled at his musical memory. Then about half-past eleven she saw him leave the house and stride away, his head in the air, his bent shoulders curiously erect.

Soon came the clatter of a cab stopping at the front door, and Geoffrey Chase, for whom she had been watching from her window, leaped out upon the pavement. She ran down and admitted him. He caught her in his arms and they stood clinging in a long embrace.

"It's too wonderful to talk about," she whispered.

"Then don't let us talk about it," he laughed.

"As if we could help it! I can think of nothing else."

"I can—you," said he, and kissed her again.

Now, in spite of the spaciousness of the house in Formosa Terrace, it had only two reception-rooms, as the house-agents grandiloquently term them, and these, dining-room and drawing-room, were respectively occupied by Anton and Mrs. Kirilov engaged in their morning lessons. The passage where the young people stood was no fit place for lovers' meetings.

"Let us go up to the *maestro's*. He's out," said Sonia.

They did as they had often done in like circumstances. Indeed, the old man, before now, had given up his sitting-room to them, feigning an unconquerable desire to walk abroad. Were they not his children,

61

dearer to him than anyone else in the world? So it was natural that they should make themselves at home in his tiny den. They sat and talked of the great victory, of the playing of the orchestra, of passages that he might take slower or quicker next time, of the ovation, of the mountain of congratulatory telegrams and letters that blocked up his rooms. They talked of Angelo Fardetti and his deep emotion and his pride. And they talked of the future, of their marriage which was to take place very soon. She suggested postponement.

"I want you to be quite sure. This must make a difference."

"Difference!" he cried indignantly.

She waved him off and sat on the music-stool by the piano.

"I must speak sensibly. You are one of the great ones of the musical world, one of the great ones of the world itself. You will go on and on. You will have all sorts of honours heaped on you. You will go about among lords and ladies, what is called Society—oh, I know, you'll not be able to help it. And all the time I remain what I am, just a poor little common girl, a member of a twopenny-halfpenny ladies' band. I'd rather you regretted having taken up with me before than after. So we ought to put it off."

He answered her as a good man who loves deeply can only answer. Her heart was convinced; but she turned her head aside and thought of further argument. Her eye fell on some music open on the rest, and mechanically, with a musician's instinct, she fingered a few bars. The strange familiarity of the theme startled her out of preoccupation. She continued the treble, and suddenly with a cold shiver of wonder, crashed down both hands and played on.

Geoffrey strode up to her.

"What's that you're playing?"

She pointed hastily to the score. He bent over and stared at the faded manuscript.

"Why, good God!" he cried, "it's my symphony."

She stopped, swung round and faced him with fear in her eyes.

"Yes. It's your symphony."

He took the thick manuscript from the rest and looked at the brown-paper cover. On it was written: "The Song of Life. A Sonata by Angelo Fardetti. September, 1878."

There was an amazed silence. Then, in a queer accusing voice, Sonia cried out:

"Geoffrey, what have you done?"

"Heaven knows; but I've never known of this before. My God! Open the thing somewhere else and see."

So Sonia opened the manuscript at random and played, and again it was an echo of Geoffrey's symphony. He sank on a chair like a man crushed by an overwhelming fatality, and held his head in his hands.

"I oughtn't to have done it," he groaned. "But it was more than me. The thing overmastered me, it haunted me so that I couldn't sleep, and the more it haunted me the more it became my own, my very own. It was too big to lose."

Sonia held him with scared eyes.

"What are you talking of?" she asked.

"The way I came to write the Symphony. It's like a nightmare." He rose. "A couple of years ago," said he, "I bought a bundle of old music at a second-hand shop. It

62

contained a collection of eighteenth-century stuff which I wanted. I took the whole lot, and on going through it, found a clump of old, discoloured manuscript partly in faded brown ink, partly in pencil. It was mostly rough notes. I tried it out of curiosity. The composition was feeble and the orchestration childish—I thought it the work of some dead and forgotten amateur—but it was crammed full of ideas, crammed full of beauty. I began tinkering it about, to amuse myself. The more I worked on it the more it fascinated me. It became an obsession. Then I pitched the old score away and started it on my own."

"The *maestro* sold a lot of old music about that time," said Sonia.

The young man threw up his hands. "It's a fatality, an awful fatality. My God," he cried, "to think that I of all men should have stolen Angelo Fardetti's music!"

"No wonder he fainted yesterday," said Sonia.

It was catastrophe. Both regarded it in remorseful silence. Sonia said at last:

"You'll have to explain."

"Of course, of course. But what must the dear old fellow be thinking of me? What else but that I've got hold of this surreptitiously, while he was out of the room? What else but that I'm a mean thief?"

"He loves you, dear, enough to forgive you anything."

"It's the Unforgivable Sin. I'm wiped out. I cease to exist as an honest man. But I had no idea," he cried, with the instinct of self-defence, "that I had come so near him. I thought I had just got a theme here and there. I thought I had recast all the odds and ends according to my own scheme." He

ran his eye over a page or two of the score. "Yes, this is practically the same as the old rough notes. But there was a lot, of course, I couldn't use. Look at that, for instance." He indicated a passage.

"I can't read it like you," said Sonia. "I must play it."

She turned again to the piano, and played the thin, uninspired music that had no relation to the Symphony in E flat, and her eyes filled with tears as she remembered poignantly what the old man had told her of his Song of Life. She went on and on until the music quickened into one of the familiar themes; and the tears fell, for she knew how poorly it was treated.

And then the door burst open. Sonia stopped dead in the middle of a bar, and they both turned round to find Angelo Fardetti standing on the threshold.

"Ah, no!" he cried, waving his thin hands. "Put that away. I did not know I had left it out. You must not play that. Ah, my son! my son!"

He rushed forward and clasped Geoffrey in his arms, and kissed him on the cheeks, and murmured foolish, broken words.

"You have seen it. You have seen the miracle. The miracle of the good God. Oh, I am happy! My son, my son! I am the happiest of old men. Ah!" He shook him tremulously by both shoulders, and looked at him with a magical light in his old eyes. "You are really what our dear Anton calls a prodigy. I have thought and you have executed. Santa Maria!" he cried, raising hands and eyes to heaven. "I thank you for this miracle that has been done!"

He turned away. Geoffrey, in

63

blank bewilderment, made a step forward.

"*Maestro,* I never knew—"

But Sonia, knowledge dawning in her face, clapped her hand over his mouth—and he read her conjecture in her eyes, and drew a great breath. The old man came again and laughed and cried and wrung his hand, and poured out his joy and wonder into the amazed ears of the conscience-stricken young musician. The floodgates of speech were loosened.

"You see what you have done, *figlio mio.* You see the miracle. This—this poor rubbish is of me, Angelo Fardetti. On it I spent my life, my blood, my tears, and it is a thing of nothing, nothing. It is wind and noise; but by the miracle of God I breathed it into your spirit and it grew—and it grew into all that I dreamed—all that I dreamed and could not express. It is my Song of Life sung as I could have sung it if I had been a great genius like you. And you have taken my song from my soul, from my heart, and all the sublime harmonies that could get no farther than this dull head you have put down in immortal music."

He went on exalted, and Sonia and Geoffrey stood pale and silent. To undeceive him was impossible.

"You see it is a miracle?" he asked.

"Yes," replied Geoffrey in a low voice.

"You never saw this before. Ha! ha!" he laughed delightedly. "Not a human soul has seen it or heard it. I kept it locked up there, in my little strong-box. And it was there all the time I was teaching you. And you never suspected."

"No, *maestro,* I did not," said the young man truthfully.

"Now, when did you begin to think of it? How did it come to you—my Song of Life? Did it sing in your brain while you were here and my brain was guiding yours, and then gather form and shape all through the long years?"

"Yes," said Geoffrey. "That was how it came about."

Angelo took Sonia's plump cheeks between his hands and smiled. "Now you understand, my little Sonia, why I was so foolish yesterday. It was emotion, such emotion as a man has never felt before in the world. And now you know why I could not speak this morning. I thought of the letter you showed me. He confessed that old Angelo Fardetti had inspired him, but he did not know how. I know. The little spark flew from the soul of Angelo Fardetti into his soul, and it became a Divine Fire. And my Song of Life is true. The symphony was born in me—it died in me—it is re-born so gloriously in him. The seed is imperishable. It is eternal."

He broke away, laughing through a little sob, and stood by the window, once more gazing unseeingly at the opposite villas of Formosa Terrace. Geoffrey went up to him and fell on his knees—it was a most un-English thing to do—and took the old hand very reverently.

"*Padre mio,*" said he.

"Yes, it is true. I am your father," said the old man in Italian, "and we are bound together by more than human ties." He laid his hand on the young man's head. "May all the blessings of God be upon you."

Geoffrey rose, the humblest man in England. Angelo passed his hand across his forehead, but his face bore a beautiful smile.

"I feel so happy," said he. "So

happy that it is terrible. And I feel so strange. And my heart is full. If you will forgive me, I will lie down for a little." He sank on the horse-hair sofa and smiled up in the face of the young man. "And my head is full of the *andante* movement that I could never write, and you have made it like the harmonies before the Throne of God. Sit down at the piano and play it for me, my son."

So Geoffrey took his seat at the piano, and played, and as he played, he lost himself in his music. And Sonia crept near and stood by him in a dream while the wonderful story of the passing of human things was told. When the sound of the last chords had died away she put her arms round Geoffrey's neck and laid her cheek against his. For a while time stood still. Then they turned and saw the old man sleeping peacefully. She whispered a word, he rose, and they began to tiptoe out of the room. But suddenly instinct caused Sonia to turn her head again. She stopped and gripped Geoffrey's hand. She caught a choking breath. "Is he asleep?"

They went back and bent over him. He was dead.

Angelo Fardetti had died of a happiness too great for mortal man. For to which one of us in a hundred million is it given to behold the utter realisation of his life's dream?

SONG

SARA TEASDALE

You bound strong sandals on my feet.
You gave me bread and wine,
And sent me under sun and stars,
For all the world was mine.

Oh take the sandals off my feet,
You know not what you do;
For all my world is in your arms,
My sun and stars are you.

WINGS

CLARA EDMUNDS-HEMINGWAY

A gull rides the waves, as if
Made for the sea,
A swallow will sail high in air.
Oh let my soul rise, let it
Soar far and free;
Or mount on the high winds of care.

A FRIEND is the half of my life.

CONFIDENCE is the companion of success.

To KNOW how to laugh is to know how to reign.

THE SUPREME LAW of all is the weal of the people.

THE SECRET of success in conversation is to be able to disagree without being disagreeable.

THE THREE PRIMARY PRINCIPLES of wisdom: obedience to the laws of God, concern for the welfare of mankind, and suffering with fortitude all the accidents of life.

IF THERE is righteousness in the heart there will be beauty in the character. If there be beauty in the character, there will be harmony in the home. If there is harmony in the home, there will be order in the nation. When there is order in the nation, there will be peace in the world.

WITH MOST PEOPLE lovability is not absent—it is merely undiscovered.

DISCONTENTS arise from our desires oftener than from our wants.

THE HERITAGE of the past is the seed that brings forth the harvest of the future.

AN OUNCE of loyalty is worth a pound of cleverness.

NOTHING is impossible to a valiant heart.

CLEAR WATER flows from a pure spring.

LOVE YOUR FRIEND with his faults.

66

UNKNOWN THINKERS

HE WHO wills, can.

THE GREATEST MEN are the simplest.

THE GOOD you do is not lost though you forget it.

HE WHO has a thousand friends has not one to spare.

WHERE GOD GIVES, envy cannot harm, and where He gives not, all labour is in vain.

WHAT MAN is there whom contact with a great soul will not exalt? A drop of water upon the petal of a lotus glistens with the splendors of the pearl.

THERE ARE three men that all ought to look upon with affection: he that with affection looks at the face of the earth, that is delighted with rational works of art, and that looks lovingly on little children.

DO WHAT THOU LOVEST; paint or sing or carve. Do what thou lovest, though the body starve! Who works for glory oft may miss the goal. Who works for money merely starves the soul; work for the work's sake, then, and, it may be, these other things'll be added unto thee.

TO KNOW where you can find a thing is in reality the best part of learning.

A MAN'S FORTUNE has its form given to it by his habits.

PATIENCE and perseverance surmount every difficulty.

CONSIDERATION is the parent of wisdom.

THE GIVER makes the gift precious.

WE WERE ON THAT RAFT—
A HUNDRED MILLION OF US—
By Margaret Lee Runbeck

THE Rickenbacker story wasn't the first one that happened. But it was the one that aroused many of us to noticing. Once our eyes were opened to them, we realized that there had been other stories, scattered timidly across the news, which told of men who prayed for rain and had it, who prayed for help and it came.

The Rickenbacker story gave a lot of people courage to tell theirs. Prayers came back into fashion for many people, when Captain Rickenbacker and his men said shamelessly that they had prayed. Some people began praying, experimentally, for the first time in their lives. Others came out into the light and admitted they always *had* prayed. And, what's more, that God had heard them praying.

Captain Rickenbacker and his men have all told of the rescue. They have covered every angle of it.

All but one. They have not told our part of that rescue, ours, the hundred million people who shared that adventure on a raft.

I do not need to tell you how it was, for you know it. It happened to you, just as it happened to me, and to all of us. When Eddie Rickenbacker was lost, we didn't give him up. We read it in our morning papers, and a stab of fear went through us, and then we said, 'No—he can't really be lost. Not Rickenbacker. He'll be back. Something will take care of him. You wait and see.'

Everybody felt that way. Mayor La Guardia asked the whole city of New York to pray for him, and I don't doubt that thousands of them did. Even the ones who didn't know how to pray had a kind of faith about him.

'He'll be back. You wait and see,' they said.

We waited and we did see. Some of us almost gave up. But not the taxi-driver, nor the boy with the shoe-shine box, nor Joe who sells papers, nor Mrs. McGinty. Nor Mrs. Rickenbacker. Nor I.

We weren't very logical about it; but we knew that there was something about Rickenbacker that couldn't be lost at this moment. Not because he was tough or invulnerable, exactly. No, it was something different. Perhaps it was the conviction which all of us had that helped bring him back. Or does that make any sense?

Well, anyway—he came back. You remember the morning. You remember the front page of the Sunday newspaper. You called the news upstairs to the children when you brought in the newspaper; you said, 'Hmmm—that's great, isn't it?' You read down the column.

Four paragraphs down it was, in my newspaper, that that word occurred. 'God.' You don't often meet it in a newspaper. It gave you a funny feeling. And more than that. A strange excited feeling, as if something good had happened to all of us.

You read the words carefully. 'And this part I would hesitate to tell, except that there were six witnesses who saw it with me,' Captain Rickenbacker said. 'A gull came out of nowhere, and lighted upon my head—I reached up my hand very gently—I killed him and then we divided him equally among us. We ate every bit, even the little bones. Never did anything taste so good. . . .'

There was something so moving in those simple words—a sort of Biblical excitement about them—you were still standing in the middle of the floor reading them, and you felt your eyes prickling with a kind of tired tears . . .

You couldn't quite explain the tears. It was as if you'd terribly wanted something to be true which you had never really admitted, and now here it was on the front page of a newspaper. You remembered that dove which Noah had sent out to see if the flood had subsided enough for man to walk upon the earth again—here was the descendant of that dove, this gull which came out of nowhere and landed on a lost man's head in the middle of the Pacific. You hadn't read that story of Noah since you were a child; funny you should think of it now, standing here in the middle of the living-room floor reading a newspaper.

Sunday morning went on. Everybody spoke about it. Everybody had the same irrational feeling as if something good had happened to all of us, as if we had somehow been amplified by Rickenbacker and that gull, and those verses from Matthew read in the bobbing yellow rafts. In the middle of the afternoon, in the midst of the Philharmonic broadcast, suddenly the very air tingled. The music was broken off, and a clipped voice came from the loudspeaker saying that in a moment Captain Ricken-backer was going to speak. Then that curiously vibrant voice came on, not very sure of itself, terribly moving with earnestness, obviously reading the words, obviously stirred almost to the breaking of self-control.

Word for word he said what you had read that morning. You wanted more; you wanted it to go on from there.

If this could happen to those men, out on the Pacific, why couldn't it happen to all of us all the time? If it's true at all, it ought to be true everywhere, you said inside yourself. You wouldn't have said that out loud, of course. But you thought it to yourself.

Secretary Stimson said in the first meeting with the press: 'He has come back. I think more of him came back than went away.' More of us came back, too. More of you; you knew it.

Every little paper picked up the story; ministers preached sermons about it; there probably wasn't a person who didn't mention it to somebody. Everybody, from Eddie Cantor to Thomas Mann, made a public comment.

It wore off in a few days, of course. But those few days showed everybody one thing. Man at this moment is pretty homesick for God; he'd like some news of Him, some kind of sign that He hasn't forgotten.

Then, after a few weeks, full-page advertisements appeared in the newspapers. Eddie Rickenbacker was going to tell the story again. We could hardly wait; we wanted more terribly.

But now something had happened to the story. He hadn't added anything to it. No. Some-

69

thing had been taken away from it. It was written better, much better. It was full of gripping details, and even diagrams of how the men had fitted into those three tiny rubber rafts. But when it came to the Lord's part, it suddenly got very self-conscious.

I wasn't there, of course, when Eddie Rickenbacker was writing his story. I haven't any real way of knowing, but I can imagine what happened. Perhaps it was something like this: Good, experienced, hard-headed editors said, 'Listen, Rick, about that bird—of course there were lots of birds flying around all the time . . .'

'Yes, of course.'

'They'd naturally light on something . . .'

'Yes. But this was different—we had prayed . . .'

'Sure. Well, look—let's sort of tone down that part a little—you were pretty emotional when you came back—anybody would have been, Rick . . .'

I can imagine Captain Rickenbacker protesting, and being embarrassed, and then finally just giving up. He has said he wasn't really a religious man; he was inexpert in finding those strange words to say what had seemed true. He had defended himself by making it clearly understood that he wasn't accustomed. I can imagine how he felt . . .

As he himself says in his *Life* magazine story: 'Men place different values on experiences shared together. What stirred or depressed me may have seemed inconsequential to the others. While I sit in a Rockefeller Center office which I have all to myself, and where a push on a buzzer will summon nearly

anything I need, much of what I went through on that ridiculously small raft now seems almost irrelevant. It is like trying to remember being dead.'

On the contrary, Captain Rickenbacker, I think it must be like trying to remember being *alive*, after you have died again into the conventional banality of everydayness.

In that tragic paragraph, so wry and wistful, lies all human loneliness, the terrifying doubt that what we know and feel can ever really be shared by anyone at all. In a grotesque, frantic way we settle for *anything* just so we can agree between us that it is true.

For of all the things men fear the most, there is no horror like the danger that we may be pushed out on a limb of aloneness, from which we see the thing differently from the rest of the race. Sometimes this human world seems like a fantastic, preposterous dream, but so long as we are certain we are all in the same dream, we do not need to worry too much about ourselves. It is only when we get outside it for a moment of clarity or madness that we are frightened.

We have told each other firsthand experiences about everything on earth. We have bolstered up and reinforced each other with recounted experiences. But the shape of the thing we fear the most we have not been able to form for each other. *For of that one experience we have never had a first-hand account.* Of death we have only the hearsay evidence of bystanders. Nobody has ever said to us, 'Let me tell you about the day I died—it happened like this.'

No, on second thought, there are

70

two experiences we can't testify about. For no one has ever said, 'Did I ever happen to tell you about when I was being born?' But it's too late for us to fear that one; we got through that somehow, and whatever anguish we suffered is forgotten. So we concentrate our fear on the other rumor.

People who want to talk about it—well, they're queer and uncomfortable people. Even heroes who want to tell us how it did *not* happen. That is one of the first tragic cautions a hero must learn; not to talk too truly about it. Eddie Rickenbacker, and his men, learned it quickly.

When they first came back, those men *knew* what had happened to them; I hope they still know unshakably.

When Colonel Hans Christian Adamson was rescued, he wrote to his wife: 'I have found a nearness to our Creator which I have never known before, and I am certain that this new feeling is going to affect both our lives in the future.—While the drifting was a horrible experience, something wonderful has come of it.'

Corporal John F. Bartek said: 'I'm glad that plane fell. It took a lot of nonsense out of my life. I shall like the things I liked before, but there is something now inside me that won't permit me to forget that God stayed right by us out there.'

We must help those men hold on to their story. We must not let rationalization nibble it away. It must not become merely a story of man's heroism, for it was much much more than that. It was a story of God's care.

Man's heroism we are accus-tomed to, this year. That is something we can get our teeth into. But that other thing . . . Well, we must keep holding to that, all of us hundred million people who have been on that raft with Rick.

You see, the reason it is so terribly important to us, why we read every word of it over and over, is that we *know* we're on a raft, each of us alone, when the last truth is told. We don't bother too much about it, but we know it. We know exactly what Captain Rickenbacker meant when he said, 'Let the moment come when nothing is left but life, and you will find that you do not hesitate over the fate of material possessions.' We have felt that, in extreme sickness and in grief, when we came inescapably close to verity. Over the bleak face of this earth rove thousands of refugees who have found that out in the last three years.

But here in America, most of the time we have been able to keep away from that edge of reality; we have amused ourselves and drugged ourselves and exhausted ourselves with our work and our possessions. But underneath we know, all right.

It is not always a desperate raft, of course; sometimes it has been gay and amusing and diverting, skipping over the expanse of nothingness all around us. But it is a raft, nevertheless, and we're not too sure where it's going, or where it came from, and we want with all our hearts to know that Something has us in His care.

And at the same time with wanting to believe it, we want also to disbelieve it. We are relatively safe and rational people living almost customary lives; we are delighted with our mentality because we have logical explanations for everything. If we can't explain it, then it probably didn't happen anyway.

This miracle that Captain Rickenbacker and his men brought back doesn't belong only to him. It belongs to all of us. All of us had it for a little while, even if we individually have lost it somewhere since that Sunday.

And yet, it may be that at the moment when each of us needs it again, it will come alive for us. 'Out of nowhere,' like the gull.

COURAGE
By Sir James Barrie

(From an Address to Students at St. Andrews University, May 3, 1922)

... Do NOT stand aloof, despising, disbelieving, but come in and help—insist on coming in and helping. After all, we have shown a good deal of courage; and your part is to add a greater courage to it. There are glorious years lying ahead of you if you choose to make them glorious. God's in His heaven still. So forward, brave hearts. To what adventures I cannot tell, but I know that your God is watching to see whether you are adventurous. I know that the great partnership is only a first step, but I do not know what are to be the next and the next. The partnership is but a tool; what are you to do with it? Very little, I warn you, if you are merely thinking of yourselves; much if what is at the marrow of your thoughts is a future that even you can scarcely hope to see.

Learn as a beginning how world-shaking situations arise and how they may be countered. Doubt all your betters who would deny you that right of partnership. Begin by doubting all such in high places—except, of course, your professors. But doubt all other professors—yet not conceitedly, as some do, with their noses in the air; avoid all such physical risks. If it necessitates your pushing some of us out of our places, still push; you will find it needs some shoving. But the things courage can do! The things that even incompetence can do if it works with singleness of purpose! The war has done at least one big thing: it has taken spring out of the year. And, this accomplished, our leading people are amazed to find that the other seasons are not conducting themselves as usual. The spring of the year lies buried in the fields of France and elsewhere. By the time the next eruption comes it may be you who are responsible for it and your sons who are in the lava. All, perhaps, because this year you let things slide.

We are a nice and kindly people, but it is already evident that we are stealing back into the old grooves, seeking cushions for our old bones, rather than attempting to build up a fairer future. That is what we mean when we say that the country is settling down. Make haste, or you will become like us, with only the thing we proudly call experience to add to your stock, a poor exchange for the generous feelings that time will take away. We have no intention of giving you your share. Look around and see

72

how much share Youth has now that the war is over. You got a handsome share while it lasted. . . .

If you want an example of courage try Henley. Or Stevenson. I could tell you some stories about these two, but they would not be dull enough for a rectorial address. For courage, again, take Meredith, whose laugh was "as broad as a thousand beaves at pasture." Take, as I think, the greatest figure literature has still left to us, to be added today to the roll of St. Andrews alumni, though it must be in absence. The pomp and circumstance of war will pass, and all others now alive may fade from the scene, but I think the quiet figure of Hardy will live on.

I seem to be taking all my examples from the calling I was lately pretending to despise. I should like to read you some passages of a letter from a man of another calling, which I think will hearten you. I have the little filmy sheets here. I thought you might like to see the actual letter; it has been a long journey; it has been to the South Pole. It is a letter to me from Captain Scott of the Antarctic, and was written in the tent you know of, where it was found long afterwards with his body and those of some other very gallant gentlemen, his comrades. The writing is in pencil, still quite clear, though toward the end some of the words trail away as into the great silence that was waiting for them. It begins: "We are pegging out in a very comfortless spot. Hoping this letter may be found and sent to you, I write you a word of farewell. I want you to think well of me and my end." (After some private instructions too intimate to read, he goes on): "Goodbye—I am not at all afraid of the end, but sad to miss many a simple pleasure which I had planned for the future in our long marches. . . . We are in a desperate state—feet frozen, etc., no fuel, and a long way from food, but it would do your heart good to be in our tent, to hear our songs and our cheery conversation. . . ." Later—(it is here that the words become difficult)—"We are very near the end. . . . We did intend to finish ourselves when things proved like this, but we have decided to die naturally without."

I think it may uplift you all to stand for a moment by that tent and listen, as he says, to their songs and cheery conversation. When I think of Scott I remember the strange Alpine story of the youth who fell down a glacier and was lost, and of how a scientific companion, one of several who accompanied him, all young, computed that the body would again appear at a certain date and place many years afterwards. When that time came round some of the survivors returned to the glacier to see if the prediction would be fulfilled; all old men now; and the body reappeared as young as on the day he left them. So Scott and his comrades emerge out of the white immensities always young.

How comely a thing is affliction borne cheerfully, which is not beyond the reach of the humblest of us. What is beauty? It is these hard-bitten men singing courage to you from their tent; it is the waves of their island home crooning of their deeds to you who are to follow them. Sometimes beauty boils over and then spirits are abroad. Ages

73

may pass as we look or listen, for time is annihilated. There is a very old legend told to me by Nansen the explorer—I like well to be in the company of explorers — the legend of a monk who had wandered into the fields and a lark began to sing. He had never heard a lark before, and he stood there entranced until the bird and its song had become part of the heavens. Then he went back to the monastery and found there a doorkeeper whom he did not know and who did not know him. Other monks came, and they were all strangers to him. He told them he was Father Anselm, but that was no help. Finally they looked through the books of the monastery, and these revealed that there had been a Father Anselm there a hundred or more years before. Time had been blotted out while he listened to the lark. . . .

Courage is the thing. All goes if courage goes. What says our glorious Johnson of courage: "Unless a man has that virtue he has no security for preserving any other." We should thank our Creator three times daily for courage instead of for our bread, which, if we work, is surely the one thing we have a right to claim of Him. This courage is a proof of our immortality, greater even than gardens "when the eve is cool." Pray for it. "Who rises from prayer a better man, his prayer is answered." Be not merely courageous, but light-hearted and gay. . . .

In bidding you goodbye, my last words must be of the lovely virtue. Courage, my children, and "greet the unseen with a cheer." "Fight on, my men," said Sir Andrew Barton. Fight on—you—for the old red gown (of St. Andrews) till the whistle blows.

❖　❖　❖

AS THE MASTER WILLS
By Phillips Brooks

Slowly, through all the universe, the temple of God is being built. Wherever, in any world, a soul, by free-willed obedience, catches the fire of God's likeness, it is set into the growing walls, a living stone. When, in your hard fight, in your tiresome drudgery, or in your terrible temptation, you catch the purpose of your being, and give yourself to God, and so give Him the chance to give Himself to you, your life, a living stone, is taken up and set into that growing wall. Wherever souls are being tried and ripened, in whatever commonplace and homely ways;—there God is hewing out the pillars for His temple. Oh, if the stone can only have some vision of the temple of which it is to be a part forever, what patience must fill it as it feels the blows of the hammer, and knows that success for it is simply to let itself be wrought into what shape the Master wills.

THINGS THAT NEVER DIE
Charles Dickens

The pure, the bright, the beautiful
That stirred our hearts in youth,
The impulses to wordless prayer,
The streams of love and truth,
The longing after something lost,
The spirit's yearning cry,
The striving after better hopes—
These things can never die.

The timid hand stretched forth to aid
A brother in his need;
A kindly word in grief's dark hour
That proves a friend indeed;
The plea for mercy softly breathed,
When justice threatens high,
The sorrow of a contrite heart—
These things shall never die.

Let nothing pass, for every hand
Must find some work to do,
Lose not a chance to waken love—
Be firm and just and true.
So shall a light that cannot fade
Beam on thee from on high,
And angel voices say to thee—
"These things shall never die."

THE SOUL GATHERS FORCE
By W. E. Channing

It is possible, when the future is dim, when our depressed faculties can form no bright ideas of the perfection and happiness of a better world,—it is possible still to cling to the conviction of God's merciful purpose towards His creatures, of His parental goodness even in suffering; still to feel that the path of duty, though trodden with a heavy heart, leads to peace; still to be true to conscience; still to do our work, to resist temptation, to be useful, though with diminished energy, to give up our wills when we cannot rejoice under God's mysterious providence. In this patient, though uncheered obedience, we become prepared for light. The soul gathers force.

75

HOW TO STAY YOUNG

Over General MacArthur's desk
there hangs a message. It will
bring you courage and faith . . .

*Famed War Correspondent Col. Frederick Palmer called on Douglas Mac-
Arthur at his Manila Headquarters. His most vivid memory: three frames
over the General's desk. One, a portrait of Washington. One, a portrait of
Lincoln. One, the framed message which you will read in part below. The
General has had it in sight ever since it was given to him by John W. Lewis,
Jr., in April of 1942, when he was fighting 2,000 miles from Manila:*

YOUTH IS not a time of life—it is a state of mind.

Nobody grows old by merely living a number of years; people grow old only
by deserting their ideals. Years wrinkle the skin, but to give up enthusiasm
wrinkles the soul. Worry, doubt, self-distrust, fear and despair—these are the
long, long years that bow the head and turn the growing spirit back to dust.

Whether seventy or sixteen, there is in every being's heart the love of wonder, the sweet amazement at the stars and the starlike things and thoughts,
the undaunted challenge of events, the unfailing childlike appetite for what
next, and the joy and the game of life.

You are as young as your faith, as old as your doubt; as young as your
self-confidence, as old as your fear; as young as your hope, as old as your
despair.—*Samuel Ullman*

THREE BUILDERS

ANONYMOUS

"WHAT are you doing?" a man asked of three laborers beside a building
under construction.

The first man replied, "Stone-cuttin'."

The second smiled. "Puttin' in time—until a better job comes along."

The third man waited a moment and then said simply, "I'm building a cathedral!"

THE ART OF HAPPINESS

ANONYMOUS

THERE WAS never a time when so much official effort was being expended to
produce happiness, and probably never a time when so little attention was
paid by the individual to creating the personal qualities that make for it.
What one misses most today is the evidence of widespread personal deter-
mination to develop a character that will in itself, given any reasonable odds,
make for happiness. Our whole emphasis is on the reform of living condi-

76

tions, of increased wages, of controls on the economic structure—the government approach—and so little on man improving himself.

The ingredients of happiness are so simple that they can be counted on one hand. Happiness comes from within, and rests most securely on simple goodness and clear conscience. Religion may not be essential to it, but no one is known to have gained it without a philosophy resting on ethical principles. Selfishness is its enemy; to make another happy is to be happy one's self. It is quiet, seldom found for long in crowds, most easily won in moments of solitude and reflection. It cannot be bought; indeed money has very little to do with it.

No one is happy unless he is reasonably well satisfied with himself, so that the quest for tranquillity must of necessity begin with self-examination. We shall not often be content with what we discover in this scrutiny. There is so much to do, and so little done. Upon this searching self-analysis, however, depends the discovery of those qualities that make each man unique, and whose development alone can bring satisfaction.

Of all those who have tried, down the ages, to outline a program for happiness, few have succeeded so well as William Henry Channing, chaplain of the House of Representatives in the middle of the last century:

"To live content with small means; to seek elegance rather than luxury, and refinement rather than fashion; to be worthy, not respectable, and wealthy, not rich; to study hard, think quietly, talk gently, act frankly; to listen to the stars and birds, to babes and sages, with open heart; to bear all cheerfully, do all bravely, await occasions, hurry never; in a word to let the spiritual, unbidden and unconscious, grow up through the common."

It will be noted that no government can do this for you; you must do it for yourself.

A RELIGION THAT DOES THINGS
By SIR WILFRED GRENFELL

... WHY IS IT that the very term "religious life" has come to voice the popular idea that religion is altogether divorced from ordinary life? That conception is the exact opposite of Christ's teachings. Faith, "reason grown courageous," as someone has called it, has become assurance to me now, not because the fight is easy and we are never worsted but because it has made life infinitely worth while, so that I want to get all I can out of it, every hour.

God help us not to neglect the use of a thing—like faith—because we do not know how it works! It would be a criminal offense in a doctor not to use the X ray even if he does not know how barium chloride makes Gamma rays visible. We must know that our opinions are not a matter of very great moment, except in so far as in what they lead us to do. I see no reason whatever to suppose that the Creator lays any stress on them either. Experience answers our problems—experience of faith and common sense. For faith and common sense, taken together, make reasonable service, which ends by giving us the light of life.

THRUSHES
KARLE WILSON BAKER

Through Tanglewood the thrushes trip,
As brown as any clod,
But in their spotted throats are hung
The vesper-bells of God.

And I know little secret truths,
And hidden things of good,
Since I have heard the thrushes sing
At dusk, in Tanglewood.

TOMORROW
JOHN MASEFIELD

Oh yesterday the cutting edge drank thirstily and deep,
The upland outlaws ringed us in and herded us as sheep,
They drove us from the stricken field and bayed us into keep;
    But tomorrow,
  By the living God, we'll try the game again!

Oh yesterday our little troop was ridden through and through,
Our swaying, tattered pennons fled, a broken, beaten few,
And all the summer afternoon they hunted us and slew;
    But tomorrow,
  By the living God, we'll try the game again!

And here upon the turret-top the bale-fire glowers red,
The wake-lights burn and drip about our hacked, disfigured dead,
And many a broken heart is here and many a broken head;
    But tomorrow,
  By the living God, we'll try the game again!

HOLINESS
JOHN DRINKWATER

If all the carts were painted gay
And all the streets swept clean
And all the children came to play
By Hollyhocks with green
Grass to grow between,

If all the houses looked as though
Some heart were in their stone,
If all the people that we know
Were dressed in scarlet gowns
With feathers in their crowns,

I think this gaiety would make
A spiritual land.
I think that holiness would take
This laughter by the hand
Till both should understand.

AFTERNOON ON A HILL
Edna St. Vincent Millay

I will be the gladdest thing
    Under the sun!
I will touch a hundred flowers
    And not pick one.

I will look at cliffs and clouds
    With quiet eyes,
Watch the wind bow down the grass,
    And the grass rise.

And when lights begin to show
    Up from the town,
I will mark which must be mine,
    And then start down!

APRIL
Sara Teasdale

The roofs are shining from the rain,
    The sparrows twitter as they fly,
And with a windy April grace
    The little clouds go by.

Yet the back-yards are bare and brown
    With only one unchanging tree—
I could not be so sure of Spring
    Save that it sings in me.

LIKE SUMMER'S CLOUD—
THE GOSSAMER DREAMS OF BOYHOOD
By MERLE CROWELL

ALL AROUND the Boy in Maine were wonders of which he must find the meaning. The wonder of daybreak, for example. Often he stood at his attic bedroom window, or on the hill back of the barn, and watched dawn come striding over the eastern hills in its flowing crimson robes. As he waited, the first breeze would ruffle the grass, dewdrops would sparkle, and the trills of birds, those minstrels of the morning, would suddenly blend into a chorus. Sometimes the Boy would find himself trembling from ecstasy.

What was back of it all—those magic moments when the heart was lifted out of the rut of life? Who lit the funeral flares in the sky at the death of day? From what cradle of creation came the mystery of a May night with apple blossoms white in the moonlight? Who turned the hills to scarlet in October, wove the lacework of ice on the bare branches and twigs in winter?

Was it God? He would like to believe so. But somehow these miracles did not fit the God of eternal hell-fire, of infant and heathen damnation, whom they preached about in the white meetinghouse on the hill.

The Boy was profoundly puzzled. He craved understanding and found little—for the ways of a boy's mind are hard to fathom. "What are you dreaming about?" the Boy's father would ask.

"Oh, nothing."

He saw men work from dawn to night, plowing and planting. He saw them struggle against weeds and insects. Then would come drought. And hopes of the harvest would shrivel with it.

Life on a rocky New England farm was hard enough anyway. Why must men fight also against wanton fate?

He saw death steal down and carry off those whom the countryside could least afford to lose. And those whom few would miss lived on and on.

He saw the homes of the thrifty struck by lightning, well-kept herds hit by disease, careful folk the victims of accident.

If life was part of a purposeful plan he could find no pattern for it.

And yet in the deepest shadow bloomed the twin flowers of faith and courage. Men whose fields had been laid waste squared their shoulders and looked hopefully ahead to another planting and another harvest. In homes brushed by the wings of the dark angel the battle of living went doggedly on. There was something invincible, indomitable, about the soul of man. Something that could not perish.

In the winter evenings, after the woodbox had been filled and the horses bedded and the cows milked, the Boy curled up in front of the fire with a book, to find things that were lacking in the world he knew. It stirred his imagination to learn what men and women were doing—and had done—far beyond those encircling hills. He dreamed of principalities and powers, of things present and things to come. Out there was a world he did not know. One

80

day he would find out more about its mountains and deserts, rivers and plains. He would go to that great city where men were a milling herd striving for fame and fortune. Other farm boys had gone there before him. There must be room for one more.

The strings of his heart were strummed, too, by the cold fingers of the Maine winter. There was the endless sweep of snow punctuated by pines and firs, the snapping of nails in the roof as he lay in his attic bed at night, the thick white arabesques on the windowpanes when he crawled out of the warm hollow in the featherbed of a January morning. Blizzards might mean a snowbound household, but the howl of the wind along the eaves, the steady swish of the snow, drifts piling up till the windows were half hid, all talked to him of the mighty menace of nature. And when the skies were blue again, and men were breaking the roads with four or five teams of horses a-tandem, he felt a growing conviction that the wild will of the universe could never quite quell the human spirit.

The Boy was acutely sensitive to sights and sounds and smells. In summer, at haying time, the frightened flit of a ground sparrow as the horse rake came close; the fresh swaths in their green geometric patterns; the bulging muscles of the hired man as he tossed titanic forkfuls of hay into the rack; even the clank of ice in the tin pail as he brought water flavored with molasses and ginger to the men at work.

Autumn held for him a special spell. The round harvest moon rising over a field of shocked corn; the drift smoke of burning leaves; trees rustling in the wind; hills and valleys afire with color; in all these there was something eerie, as if ghosts of summer were riding the October air.

The Boy looked forward to Thanksgiving for weeks on end. While rolling pumpkins into a dump-cart, filling the cellar with a hoard of potatoes, and battening the barns against the inevitable onslaught of winter, he was forever anticipating that November day when the end of fall's work would be celebrated with feast and fun.

Yes, it was a good life. From the simplest things—a few toys at Christmas, a trip to the county fair, a husking with its yellow lanterns and kissing games and six kinds of frosted cake—he extracted a succulence that sometimes in later years he was to look back on with envy.

Does youth, with its tremendous trivialities, its gossamer dreams, its fantastic despairs, really transcend the more durable satisfaction of manhood? I suppose not. And yet youth has a special flavor that inevitably is drained dry as a boy or a girl grows up.

Richard Henry Stoddard captured that thought:

There are gains for all our losses,
There are balms for all our pain;
But when youth, the dream, departs,
It takes something from our hearts,
And it never comes again.

FROM A little spark may burst a mighty flame.—*Dante*

WHO FALLS for love of God, shall rise a star.—*Ben Jonson*

WORK without hope draws nectar in a sieve,
And hope without an object can not live.
—*Shelley*

THE GREAT THING in the world is not so much where we stand,
as in what direction we are moving.—*Holmes*

SPEND in all things else, but of old friends be most miserly.—*Lowell*

A GOOD WOMAN is a wondrous creature, cleaving to the right and to the
good under all change: lovely in youthful comeliness, lovely all her life long
in comeliness of heart.—*Tennyson*

IT IS SOMETHING to make two blades of grass grow where only one was growing,
it is much more to have been the occasion of the planting of an oak which
shall defy twenty scores of winters, or of an elm which shall canopy with
its green cloud of foliage half as many generations of mortal immortalities.
—*Holmes*

ONE THORN of experience is worth a whole wilderness of warning.—*Lowell*

POETRY should please by a fine excess and not by singularity.
It should strike the reader as a wording of his own highest
thoughts, and appear almost as a remembrance.—*Keats*

LOVE, HOPE, FEAR, FAITH—these make humanity;
These are its sign, and note and character.
—*Browning*

A MOMENT'S INSIGHT is sometimes worth a life's experience.—*Holmes*

A MOMENT'S THINKING is an hour in words.—*Hood*

OF THE POETS

WHERE THERE is peace, God is.—*Herbert*

NOTHING is impossible to a willing heart.—*Heywood*

DARE TO BE TRUE: nothing can need a lie;
A fault which needs it most, grows two thereby.
—*Herbert*

JUST DEEDS are the best answer to injurious words.—*Milton*

THE BEST of a book is not the thought which it contains, but the thought which it suggests; just as the charm of music dwells not in the tones but in the echoes of our hearts.—*Holmes*

WHATEVER strengthens and purifies the affections, enlarges the imagination, and adds spirit to sense, is useful.—*Shelley*

BOOKS never pall on me. They discourse with us, they take counsel with us, and are united to us by a certain living chatty familiarity. And not only does each book inspire the sense that it belongs to its readers, but it also suggests the name of others, and one begets the desire of the other.—*Petrarch*

MAN IS UNJUST, but God is just; and finally justice triumphs.—*Longfellow*

I SOMETIMES THINK that the most plaintive ditty has brought a fuller joy and of longer duration to its composer than the conquest of Persia to the Macedonian.—*Landor*

ERRORS, like straws, upon the surface flow;
He who would search for pearls must dive below.
—*Dryden*

LOVE is the master key that opens the gates of happiness.—*Holmes*

TIME WASTED is existence; *used* is life.—*Young*

The Littlest Angel

By CHARLES TAZEWELL

$\mathcal{O}$NCE UPON A TIME—oh, many, many years ago as time is calculated by men—but which was only Yesterday in the Celestial Calendar of Heaven—there was, in Paradise, a most miserable, thoroughly unhappy, and utterly dejected cherub who was known throughout Heaven as *The Littlest Angel.*

He was exactly four years, six months, five days, seven hours and forty-two minutes of age when he presented himself to the venerable Gate-Keeper and waited for admittance to the Glorious Kingdom of God.

Standing defiantly, with his short brown legs wide apart, the Littlest Angel tried to pretend that he wasn't at all impressed by such Unearthly Splendor, and that he wasn't at all afraid. But his lower lip trembled, and a tear disgraced him by making a new furrow down his already tear-streaked face—coming to a precipitous halt at the very tip end of his small freckled nose.

But that wasn't all. While the kindly Gate-Keeper was entering the name in his great Book, the Littlest Angel, having left home as usual without a handkerchief, endeavored to hide the tell-tale evidence by snuffing. A most unangelic sound which so unnerved the good Gate-Keeper that he did something he had never done before in all Eternity. He blotted the page!

From that moment on, the Heavenly Peace was never quite the same, and the Littlest Angel soon became the despair of all the Heavenly Host. His shrill, ear-splitting whistle resounded at all hours through the Golden Streets. It startled the Patriarch Prophets and disturbed their meditations. Yes, and on top of that, he inevitably and vociferously sang off-key at the singing practice of the Heavenly Choir, spoiling its ethereal effect.

And, being so small that it seemed to take him just twice as long as anyone else to get to nightly prayers, the Littlest Angel always arrived late, and always knocked everyone's wings askew as he darted into his place.

Although these flaws in behavior might have been overlooked, the general appearance of the Littlest Angel was even more disreputable than his deportment. It was first whispered among the Seraphim and Cherubim, and then said aloud among the Angels and Archangels, that he didn't even look like an angel!

And they were all quite correct. He didn't. His halo was permanently tarnished where he held onto it with one hot little chubby hand when he ran, and he was always running. Furthermore, even when he stood very still, it never behaved like a halo should. It was always slipping down over his right eye.

Or over his left eye.

Or else, just for pure meanness, slipping off the back of his head and rolling away down some

84

Golden Street just so he'd have to chase after it!

Yes, and it must be here recorded that his wings were neither useful nor ornamental. All Paradise held its breath when the Littlest Angel perched himself like an unhappy fledgling sparrow on the very edge of a gilded cloud and prepared to take off. He would teeter this way —and that way—but, after much coaxing and a few false starts, he would shut both of his eyes, hold his freckled nose, count up to three hundred and three, and then hurl himself s l o w l y into space!

However, owing to the regrettable fact that he always forgot to move his wings, the Littlest Angel always fell head over halo!

It was also reported, and never denied, that whenever he was nervous, which was most of the time, he bit his wing-tips!

Now, anyone can easily understand why the Littlest Angel would, soon or late, have to be disciplined. And so, on an Eternal Day of an Eternal Month in the Year Eternal, he was directed to present his small self before an Angel of the Peace.

The Littlest Angel combed his hair, dusted his wings and scrambled into an almost clean robe, and then, with a heavy heart, trudged his way to the place of judgment. He tried to postpone the dreaded ordeal by loitering along the Street of The Guardian Angels, pausing a few timeless moments to minutely pursue the long list of new arrivals, although all Heaven knew he couldn't read a word. And he idled more than several immortal moments to carefully examine a display of aureate harps, although everyone in the Celestial City knew he couldn't tell a crotchet from a semi-quaver. But at length and at last he slowly approached a doorway which was surmounted by a pair of golden scales, signifying that Heavenly Justice was dispensed within. To the Littlest Angel's great surprise, he heard a merry voice, singing!

The Littlest Angel removed his halo and breathed upon it heavily, then polished it upon his robe, a procedure which added nothing to that garment's already untidy appearance, and then t i p - t o e d in!

The Singer, who was known as the Understanding Angel, looked down at the small culprit, and the Littlest Angel instantly tried to make himself invisible by the ingenious process of withdrawing his head into the collar of his robe, very much like a snapping turtle.

At that, the Singer laughed, a jolly, heartwarming sound, and said, "Oh! So you're the one who's been making Heaven so unheavenly! Come here, Cherub, and tell me all about it!" The Littlest Angel ventured a furtive look from beneath his robe.

First one eye.

And then the other eye.

Suddenly, almost before he knew it, he was perched on the lap of the Understanding Angel, and was explaining how very difficult it was for a boy who suddenly finds himself transformed into an angel. Yes, and no matter what the Archangels said, he'd only swung once. Well, twice. Oh, all right, then, he'd swung three times on the Golden Gates. But that was just for something to do!

That was the whole trouble. There wasn't anything for a small angel to do. And he was very

85

homesick. Oh, not that Paradise wasn't beautiful! But the Earth was beautiful, too! Wasn't it created by God, Himself? Why, there were trees to climb, and brooks to fish, and caves to play at pirate chief, the swimming hole, and sun, and rain, and dark, and dawn, and thick brown dust, so soft and warm beneath your feet!

The Understanding Angel smiled, and in his eyes was a long forgotten memory of another small boy in a long ago. Then he asked the Littlest Angel what would make him most happy in Paradise. The Cherub thought for a moment, and whispered in his ear.

"There's a box. I left it under my bed back home. If only I could have that?"

The Understanding Angel nodded his head. "You shall have it," he promised. And a fleet-winged Heavenly messenger was instantly dispatched to bring the box to Paradise.

And then, in all those timeless days that followed, everyone wondered at the great change in the Littlest Angel, for, among all the cherubs in God's Kingdom, he was the most happy. His conduct was above the slightest reproach. His appearance was all that the most fastidious could wish for. And on excursions to Elysian Fields, it could be said, and truly said, that he flew like an angel!

Then it came to pass that Jesus, the Son of God, was to be born of Mary, of Bethlehem, of Judea. And as the glorious tidings spread through Paradise, all the angels rejoiced and their voices were lifted to herald the Miracle of Miracles, the coming of the Christ Child.

The Angels and Archangels, the Seraphim and Cherubim, the Gate-Keeper, the Wingmaker, yes, and even the Halosmith put aside their usual tasks to prepare their gifts for the Blessed Infant. All but the Littlest Angel. He sat himself down on the top-most step of the Golden Stairs and anxiously waited for inspiration.

What could he give that would be most acceptable to the Son of God? At one time, he dreamed of composing a lyric hymn of adoration. But the Littlest Angel was woefully wanting in musical talent.

Then he grew tremendously excited over writing a prayer! A prayer that would live forever in the hearts of men, because it would be the first prayer ever to be heard by the Christ Child. But the Littlest Angel was lamentably lacking in literate skill. "What, oh what, could a small angel give that would please the Holy Infant?"

The time of the Miracle was very close at hand when the Littlest Angel at last decided on his gift. Then, on that Day of Days, he proudly brought it from its hiding place behind a cloud, and humbly, with downcast eyes, placed it before the Throne of God. It was only a small, rough, unsightly box, but inside were all those wonderful things that even a Child of God would treasure!

A small, rough, unsightly box, lying among all those other glorious gifts from all the Angels of Paradise! Gifts of such rare and radiant splendor and breathless beauty that Heaven and all the Universe were lighted by the mere reflection of their glory! And when the Littlest Angel saw this, he suddenly knew that his gift to God's Child was irreverent, and he devoutly wished he might reclaim his shabby gift. It was ugly. It was worthless. If only

86

he could hide it away from the sight of God before it was even noticed!

But it was too late! The Hand of God moved slowly over all that bright array of shining gifts,
then paused,
then dropped,
then came to rest
on the lowly gift of the Littlest Angel!

The Littlest Angel trembled as the box was opened, and there, before the Eyes of God and all His Heavenly Host, was what he offered to the Christ Child.

And what was his gift to the Blessed Infant? Well, there was a butterfly with golden wings, captured one bright summer day on the high hills above Jerusalem, and a sky-blue egg from a bird's nest in the olive tree that stood to shade his mother's kitchen door. Yes, and two white stones, found on a muddy river bank, where he and his friends had played like small brown beavers, and, at the bottom of the box, a limp, tooth-marked leather strap, once worn as a collar by his mongrel dog, who had died as he had lived, in absolute love and infinite devotion.

The Littlest Angel wept hot, bitter tears, for now he knew that instead of honoring the Son of God, he had been most blasphemous.

Why had he ever thought the box was so wonderful?

Why had he dreamed that such utterly useless things would be loved by the Blessed Infant?

In frantic terror, he turned to run and hide from the Divine Wrath of the Heavenly Father, but he stumbled and fell, and with a horrified wail and clatter of halo, rolled in a ball of consummate misery to the very foot of the Heavenly Throne!

There was an ominous and dreadful silence in the Celestial City, a silence complete and undisturbed save for the heart-broken sobbing of the Littlest Angel.

Then, suddenly, The Voice of God, like Divine Music, rose and swelled through Paradise!

And the Voice of God spoke, saying, "Of all the gifts of all the angels, I find that this small box pleases Me most. Its contents are of the Earth and of men, and My Son is born to be King of both. These are the things My Son, too, will know and love and cherish and then, regretful, will leave behind Him when His task is done. I accept this gift in the Name of the Child, Jesus, born of Mary this night in Bethlehem."

There was a breathless pause, and then the rough, unsightly box of the Littlest Angel began to glow with a bright, unearthly light, then the light became a lustrous flame, and the flame became a radiant brilliance that blinded the eyes of all the angels!

None but the Littlest Angel saw it rise from its place before the Throne of God. And he, and only he, watched it arch the firmament to stand and shed its clear, white, beckoning light over a Stable where a Child was Born.

There it shone on that Night of Miracles, and its light was reflected down the centuries deep in the heart of all mankind. Yet, earthly eyes, blinded, too, by its splendor, could never know that the lowly gift of the Littlest Angel was what all men would call forever

"THE SHINING STAR OF

BETHLEHEM!"

TO AN ANXIOUS FRIEND
By WILLIAM ALLEN WHITE

YOU TELL me that law is above freedom of utterance. And I reply that you can have no wise laws nor free enforcement of wise laws unless there is free expression of the wisdom of the people—and, alas, their folly with it. But if there is freedom, folly will die of its own poison, and the wisdom will survive. That is the history of the race. It is the proof of man's kinship with God. You say that freedom of utterance is not for time of stress, and I reply with the sad truth that only in time of stress is freedom of utterance in danger. No one questions it in calm days, because it is not needed. And the reverse is true also; only when free utterance is suppressed is it needed; and when it is needed, it is most vital to justice. Peace is good. But if you are interested in peace through force and without free discussion, that is to say, free utterance decently and in order—your interest in justice is slight. And peace without justice is tyranny, no matter how you may sugar coat it with expediency. The state today is in more danger from suppression than from violence, because in the end, suppression leads to violence. Violence, indeed, is the child of suppression. Whoever pleads for justice helps to keep the peace; and whoever tramples upon the plea for justice, temperately made in the name of peace, only outrages peace and kills something fine in the heart of man which God put there when we got our manhood. When that is killed, brute meets brute on each side of the line.

So, dear friend, put fear out of your heart. This nation will survive, this state will prosper, the orderly business of life will go forward if only men can speak in whatever way given them to utter what their hearts hold—by voice, by posted card, by letter or by press. Reason never has failed men. Only force and repression have made the wrecks in the world.

THE HOPE OF TOMORROW
By JOY ELMER MORGAN

SOMEWHERE in a schoolroom today under the care of an unknown teacher is a child who in his own time, grown to maturity, will lead the world away from war and toward peace. The affection planted in that child's life by wise guidance; the sense of right values with which he is constantly surrounded; the integrity and initiative that are fostered in his unfolding life will come to fruition in a mighty service to the human race. It is a wise providence that no one can tell which of the two million babies born in our country each year is to be this savior of tomorrow. We are done with king-children and their pampered training to maintain a class system. We want the children of the people, of all the people—rich and poor of every race and creed—to have their chance. And when through honest growth, proved merit, and wise leadership the pilots of tomorrow take their places·

at the helm, we want them to be surrounded and supported by their fellows likewise schooled in the simple and abiding principles of democracy. With this purpose and in this faith, the teachers of America carry on. This faith was good enough for the founding fathers who launched this ship of state in even more troubled seas than we now face. This faith has been good enough for the teachers and prophets of all ages who have understood the power of human aspiration and growth. It is the faith of Jesus—the Golden Rule and the brotherhood of man. It is the faith that for 1900 years has held aloft through good times and bad the torch of eternal truth. As we come this year to the Christmas season, let us renew our faith in this destiny of the individual human soul lifted by true teaching through the leavening power of God's grace to nobility and wisdom. This faith of the teacher—your faith and mine as we look into the eager faces of youth—is the hope of tomorrow, a hope that cannot fail. It is bigger than all the fears and partisanships of our time. Let us renew and deepen our faith as we celebrate Christmas.

From *PEACE OF MIND*
By JOSHUA LOTH LIEBMAN

. . . WE KNOW enough now to begin to liberate man. Let us make the attempt upon ourselves; aided by religion, let us engrave upon our hearts the commandments of a new morality:

Thou shalt not be afraid of thy hidden impulses.

Thou shalt learn to respect thyself and then thou wilt love thy neighbor as thyself.

Thou shalt transcend inner anxiety, recognizing thy true competence and courage.

Thou shalt stand undismayed in the presence of grief. Thou shalt not deny the sadness of thy heart. Thou shalt make no detour around sorrow, but shall live through it, and by the aid of human togetherness and comradely sympathy thou shalt win dominion over sorrow.

Thou shalt eternally respect truth and tell it with kindness and also with firmness to all of thy associates, to the young child as well as to thy brother, and through truth shalt thou find healing and salvation.

Thou shalt search thy heart for the traces of immaturity and the temptations of childishness. Thou shalt reject all flight from freedom, all escape from maturity, as unworthy of thy person. Thou shalt turn away from all supine reliance upon authority, all solacing slavery to an omnipotent social father. Thou shalt seek together with thy brothers a kingdom of mature equality.

Thou shalt uproot from thy heart the false doubts and childish petulance which keep thee far from God. Thou shalt not make Him the scapegoat for thy emotional wounds and thy psychic scars. Thou shalt free thyself of the distortions which block thy way to His presence, and by that freedom thou shalt commune at last with Him, the source of truth, the giver of peace.

89

THE HOME AT PEACE
EDGAR A. GUEST

Here is a little world where children play
  And just a few red roses greet July;
  Above it smiles God's stretch of summer sky;
Here laughter rings to mark the close of day;
There is no greater splendor far away.
  Here slumber comes with all her dream supply,
  And friendship visits as the days go by;
Here love and faith keep bitterness at bay.
Should up this walk come wealth or smiling fame,
  Some little treasures might be added here,
But life itself would still remain the same:
  Love is no sweeter in a larger sphere.
This little world of ours wherein we live
Holds now the richest joys which life can give.

THE HOUSE BY THE SIDE OF THE ROAD
SAM WALTER FOSS

There are hermit souls that live withdrawn
In the place of their self-content;
There are souls like stars, that dwell apart,
In a fellowless firmament;
There are pioneer souls that blaze their paths
Where highways never ran—
But let me live by the side of the road
And be a friend to man.

Let me live in a house by the side of the road,
Where the race of men go by—
The men who are good and the men who are bad,
As good and as bad as I.
I would not sit in the scorner's seat,
Or hurl the cynic's ban—
Let me live in a house by the side of the road
And be a friend to man.

I see from my house by the side of the road,
By the side of the highway of life,
The men who press with the ardor of hope,
The men who are faint with the strife.

But I turn not away from their smiles nor their tears,
Both parts of an infinite plan—
Let me live in a house by the side of the road
And be a friend to man.

I know there are brook-gladdened meadows ahead,
And mountains of wearisome height;
That the road passes on through the long afternoon
And stretches away to the night.
But still I rejoice when the travelers rejoice,
And weep with the strangers that moan,
Nor live in my house by the side of the road
Like a man who dwells alone.

Let me live in my house by the side of the road,
Where the race of men go by—
They are good, they are bad, they are weak, they are strong,
Wise, foolish—so am I;
Then why should I sit in the scorner's seat,
Or hurl the cynic's ban?
Let me live in my house by the side of the road
And be a friend to man.

THE JOY OF A GARDEN

Gail Brook Burket

The joy of creation,
A gardener knows,
Holds more than the beauty
Of lily and rose.
For he feels warm blessing,
Like sunshine in May,
Of working together
With God day by day.

The joy of each person
Who shares the glad sight
Of blossoming glory
Is more than delight.
For always in gardens
The soul is aware
Of God's loving presence
And walks with Him there.

DIVINE INSPIRATION

UNTO THE PURE all things are pure.

LET YOUR LIGHT so shine before men that they
may see your good works.

AGAIN THEREFORE Jesus spake unto them, saying, I am the
light of the world: he that followeth me shall not walk in
the darkness, but shall have the light of life.

I AM the resurrection, and the life: he that believeth in me, though
he were dead, yet shall he live: And whosoever liveth and believeth in
me, yet shall he live.

IF IT BE POSSIBLE, as much as lieth in you, live peaceably with all men.

I AM PERSUADED, that neither death, nor life, nor angels, nor principalities, nor things present, nor things to come, nor powers, nor height,
nor depth, nor any other creature, shall be able to separate us from the
love of God, which is in Christ Jesus our Lord.

CONSIDER THE LILIES of the field, how they grow; they toil not, neither
do they spin: yet I say unto you, that even Solomon in all his glory was
not arrayed like one of these. But if God so clothe the grass of the
field, which today is, and tomorrow is cast into the oven, shall he not
much more clothe you, O ye of little faith?

IF YE abide in me, and my words abide in you, ask whatsoever ye
will, and it shall be done unto you.

AND WE KNOW that to them that love God all things work together for
good . . . to them that are called according to His purpose.

GREATER LOVE hath no man than this, that a man lay down his life
for his friend.

Now FAITH is the substance of things hoped for, the
evidence of things not seen.

92

FROM THE BIBLE

RIGHTEOUSNESS exalteth a nation.

REJOICE ALWAYS; pray without ceasing; in everything give thanks: for this is the will of God in Christ Jesus to you.

HE THAT IS slow to anger is better than the mighty; and he that ruleth his spirit than he that taketh a city.

VERILY, verily, I say unto you, He that believeth on me, the works that I do shall he do also; and greater works than these shall he do; because I go unto the Father.

TO GIVE unto them beauty for ashes, the oil of joy for mourning, the garment of praise for the spirit of heaviness.

HE THAT LOOKETH into the perfect law, the law of liberty, and so continueth, being not a hearer that forgetteth but a doer that worketh, this man shall be blessed in his doing.

AND THE WORK of righteousness shall be peace; and the effect of righteousness, quietness and confidence for ever. And my people shall abide in a peaceable habitation, and in safe dwellings, and in quiet resting-places.

THE EFFECTUAL FERVENT PRAYER of a righteous man availeth much.

FOR GOD so loved the world that He gave His only begotten son that whosoever believeth in Him should not perish but have everlasting life.

A GOOD NAME is rather to be chosen than great riches.

THOU HAST loved righteousness, and hated iniquity; therefore God, thy God, hath anointed thee with the oil of gladness above thy fellows.

BEHOLD HOW GOOD and how pleasant it is for brethren to dwell together in unity.

"LISTEN! THE WIND IS RISING"

By Anne Morrow Lindbergh

Listen! the wind is rising,
  and the air is wild with leaves—

I WAS LYING on my bed in Government House, in the middle of the afternoon, learning poetry. There was nothing else to do. Everything was done. My husband was asleep. The plane was in shape. We were packed up, ready to go. And I was resting. We needed the rest for we were going to try again tonight, our last attempt to fly to South America from Bathurst.

"Could we take off tomorrow night?" I had asked my husband in the morning.

"Yes," he had said, doubtfully, "but that's about the last."

"Well, you could still take off at daybreak, couldn't you?" I had pursued.

"No—you see the moon rises later every night. There wouldn't be any moon at all when we reached South America."

I hesitated—that last question, "Could you get off now with no wind?"

"Almost!" he had said.

It was tonight, then, or—well, better not think about it. Rest; sleep; learn poetry. I opened my pocket scrapbook.

Listen! the wind is rising,
  and the air is wild with leaves—

I had copied those lines as we left England, in October; when the last of the dahlias hung clumsy golden heads above their blackened stalks; when leaves rose in gusty flames into the sky, lifting a whole tree before your eyes, bodily, it seemed, into the air. Elm and oak and beech—to think of them here gave me some of the peace of England.

we have had our summer evenings—

(Like long English meadows, rolling out to the sky. There was strength in having them behind your back.)

now for October eves!

It might help, too. Poetry did, sometimes, filling up the mind. I might need it tonight, bobbing up and down under the stars, or even plunging ahead through the dark sky, over the dark ocean—if we got off—

The great beech-trees lean forward,
  and strip like a diver—

(Bright copper leaves, turned up this way and that, burning like coals, under foot.)

and strip like a diver. We—

That was enough, really. The rest was not for us.

                    ... We
had better turn to the fire,
  and shut our minds to the sea—

We couldn't do that—not yet, anyway. We still had work to do.

where the ships of youth are running
  close-hauled on the edge of the wind—

94

Oh—if only we had a wind like that! A wind you could bite into, a wind you could pull hard against, as you could in a boat, heeled over, the sail taut, bowed to the water; the tiller hard against your aching arm; your feet braced on the leeward seat; your cheeks in the wind, warm and tingling underneath but firm and chilled on the surface—like fruit. And the sound of water, rushing, gurgling, racing, tearing under you.

Where the ships of youth are running
    close-hauled on the edge of the wind,
with all adventure before them...*

Yes, but that was the Maine coast I was thinking of. And this was Africa. There was the mosquito net over my head. Here was the white airless room. It was time for tea. And after tea, a drive to the Cape, and after that, supper, and after that—

Listen! the wind is rising—

I got up and dressed. I had tea. My husband went down to the bay. "Is there anything to do?" I asked.
"No," he said. "But I think I'll just go down and look over the plane."
I knew how he felt—anything to fill up the afternoon.

The Governor's wife was taking me for a drive to the gardens where we were the other night. (There, at least, there will be a wind!) We got out and walked in the dusty shade of trees. ("The great beech-

*Humbert Wolfe. "Autumn Resignation."

trees lean forward—") But these were not beech. They were Casuarina, with long whip-like branches spraying above our heads. They were spiny palm and strange gray-leaved trees whose name I did not know. The dry turf crackled under our feet. Spikes of cactus speared the sunshine. There was not a breath of wind, even here. The tangled creepers dripped their yellow flowers, motionless in the still air. Insects rasped out their songs like sawdust. And small metallic-colored birds flicked brightly from one shrub of oleander to another, the only sign of life in that lifeless garden.
I could hardly look at the birds, at the lancet-leaved oleanders, at the trees, strangled with ropes of vine. Like someone in love, all sights, all objects, led back to one thing in my mind. As one might say, "But he is not here to see them," I could only think, "But there is no wind, even here." I could only see that the vines hung listless from their branches. There was not a tremor in the ferns.
We climbed into the car and started back to Government House. Even the artificial breeze from our speed was a relief, although one could tell nothing from that, of course. Out of the window I watched the tops of palms against the sky, and, as we crossed a river, the small boats ("close-hauled on the edge of the wind—"). But they were not close-hauled. Their sails were slack and dimpled untidily, making no headway. There was no wind. The dust on the road, the smoke from distant huts, the ripples in a marsh—everything, I watched. And finally I was looking at the limp flag, wrapped around the pole

outside of Government House. We were back again.

I spoke at last, like a sick person who can no longer control his obsession.

"I am afraid there is very little wind this evening," I said, dry-mouthed.

"Oh, you can't tell from here," said the Governor's wife, anxiously, "we'll go down to the pier and look."

We hurried across the road and walked out over the water. It felt cooler there but the bay was glassy. I held up my hand.

"No, there isn't a breath of wind," I said.

"There is a *little*," said the Governor's wife, "but I can't tell from where." She turned to face the harbor mouth.

I pulled out my handkerchief. "We can see," I said, "if there is any—" The handkerchief hung down limply, swinging slightly from my hand. "No, there isn't enough to lift a handkerchief." And to myself I thought, what a heavy thing a handkerchief is!

We walked back across the road. "You see, it's our last chance tonight," I said, "tomorrow the moon won't be bright enough. If we can't get off tonight—well, we'll just have to change our plans."

"But you can't tell yet," urged the Governor's wife kindly, "the wind may come up after sunset."

"Yes, of course," I said, but I did not feel hopeful. I went up to my room and tried to write, to read, to rest.

Listen! the wind is rising,
    and the air—

But it wasn't rising. It was com-

pletely dead. Why did I learn that poem? I couldn't get it out of my head now. It would taunt me the rest of the evening. It would go on singing inanely in my head no matter what happened. Calm yourself. Learn something else, something quieting. Get out the little scrapbook.

Brave flowers—that I could gallant
    it like you,
And be as little vain!
You come abroad, and make a
    harmless show—*

No, that was too difficult. It would never come to you in a crisis. Only the first line rolled out like a banner:

Brave flowers—that I could gallant
    it like you—

Fifteen minutes, a half-hour, three-quarters passed. It was after sunset. I could stay in no longer. I would go out to the pier again. You couldn't tell, sometimes everything changed in a second and started rolling the right way. It might be happening right now. This might be the very second, the knife edge, when the wind changed. It would do no harm to go and see.

I slipped out of my room quietly and walked in a firm taut step down the stairs and through the halls—the kind of step you used in a dream when you wished to hurry from the person behind, but it would be fatal to run. Down the steps of Government House, out of the driveway. Not in a hurry at all, just a nice brisk walk. Once out in the road, I could clip along

* Henry King, "A Contemplation upon Flowers."

96

faster; it was dark. And when I reached the pier, I was running, my feet clumping down the boardwalk. Yes, it was cooler, definitely cooler, but—("Sister Anne, Sister Anne, do you see anyone coming?" Old fairy tales, old rhymes, raced through my mind. "Flounder, Flounder, in the sea!") was there a wind? I took out my handkerchief, crumpled whiteness in the dark. It hung from my hand; it swayed; it fluttered; it pulled gently away from me. It leaned upon a breath of air. Yes, yes, it had changed! Oh—"Listen! the wind is rising, and the air—"

I ran back to Government House and burst into the room. My husband had just come back from the bay.

"The wind has changed," I panted, out of breath, "I've just been down to the pier. There's enough to lift a handkerchief!"

"Good," he said, "I'll go down with you and see."

We walked down side by side, across the road again, I pushing my steps ahead to keep up with his long ones. Yes, there was a wind. Two handkerchiefs fluttered from the pier. It occurred to me, an aftermath to my excitement, that a wind that could lift a handkerchief might not be able to lift a plane. Still, it was a good sign. There was definitely a change. And there might be more when the moon came up.

We went back to dinner. The Governor toasted our success. I wondered—for the third time—if that would be the last. We said good-bye.

"We'll probably see you at breakfast, though," we laughed in bravado.

The Governor's wife squeezed

both my hands.

"Send us a cable, will you, when you get there?" said the Governor. (Casual, taking it for granted. How British—how grand of him!)

"Yes, we will, good-bye, thank you."

We walked out to the pier again. The moon was up, low and reddish on the horizon, and terribly squashed in, since last night. It looked lopsided and bruised, like a misshapen pear. I was shocked. How fast it changed. This was certainly the last night we could use it. But the wind was a little stronger. That helped.

We went back to the house. There was nothing more to do. Our things, a small handful only, were rolled into the bottom of the white canvas sack. The rest of our clothes lay on the pile of discarded equipment. My husband took only the suit he was wearing. I had, besides my flying clothes, one silk dress, a pair of stockings and a linen hat, wound up in a roll. Altogether we had about twelve ounces in the bottom of the white sack. It was tucked away now. We were ready to go.

But we could not leave until the moon was high; we needed all the light we could get for our take-off. We lay down and waited for the minutes to pass. The house was still. Everyone else had settled for the night. It had not started for us—not yet. Wait, wait, wait—my heart hammered in my throat:

with all adventure before them—with all adventure . . .

At ten-twenty the tall house-boy, Samiker, knocked on the door for our luggage. Luggage? We had none. Only the half-empty white sack, my radio bag, an extra shirt and sweater, and the helmets. He shouldered the limp bag silently and went out. The small open car was at the door. We climbed in the back quietly. Samiker jumped in after us. It wasn't necessary for him to come, but I was glad because I felt he cared. And it was nice to have around you people who cared, even if they said nothing. We started off. Radio bag? Helmets? Lunch? Yes. Samiker sat in front with the white sack. We bumped through the dimly lighted streets. People were closing up for the night. Someone pushed open a shutter above our heads, as we passed, and leaned down out of a lighted window to see what it was. Oh, I thought—looking up for one flashing second at the bright window, at the dark hand stretched out carelessly to draw back the shutters —oh, if only it were as casual as that to us!

The car sighed to a stop in front of the closed gates. The sleepy guard came out and let us through. ("Listen! the wind is rising—" There was not a breath, not a breath on shore.) We climbed into the leaky rowboat. Samiker sat down behind us with the white sack. The water sucked and slopped around our feet. ("—and the air is wild with leaves"—no wind—no wind.) The boy at the oars coughed painfully. We pushed slowly ahead toward the indistinct form of the plane.

There was a fair light from the moon. I could see the captain of the port sitting in a small rowboat near us. There was more wind out here. I turned my head to let it blow back my hair.

"There's as much wind as the morning we tried before, Charles," I said as we touched the side of the plane.

"But not as much as the night?" He climbed out of the boat.

"No—I had on my sweater that night."

We started to arrange the cockpits, to pump out the pontoons, those endless small jobs we had done so many times before. But tonight, it was the last time, they took on an incredible importance. They were lit with an intensity of feeling and stood out like the smallest branches of trees at night in a bright crack of lightning. I knelt on the nose of the pontoon and held the flashlight while my husband pumped. The water sloshed out in regular gasps. "All right, now, the anchor box." Words, too, seemed weighted beyond their usual freight of feeling. He took some putty and worked it with his fingers along the edges of the hatch. "That ought to keep the water out." The circle of light followed his fingers as they moved, deftly and swiftly up and down.

It was very still. I drummed with my fingernails on the light metal under me. *First* in *war—First* in *peace—First* in the *hearts* of his *countree men:*" my fingernails beat out the rhythm in the stillness. Ping, ping, ping; ping, ping, ping. Was there no other sound? Listen, listen, listen—listen, the wind is rising—

My husband looked up from his work. "There's about a five-mile wind right now," he called across the water.

The captain of the port held up his hand in the moonlight. "You air-folk must look at it differently," he drawled back good-naturedly. "Why? What would you call it?" We stopped bolt still, and listened. ("—and the air is wild with leaves—") "Almost a dead calm!" We laughed and bent over the pontoons again. Ping, ping, ping. Ping, ping, ping. *"First* in the *hearts* of his *countree men."* But there *was* more wind, I thought, as I climbed into the cock- pit. There was enough for me to put my sweater on. "Charles, there's enough wind for me to put my sweater on!" But he could not hear. He was untying the lantern, now the bridle.

"If we come back, we'll want these," he said, "otherwise—" The end of his sentence was lost in the moonlight, like the shores, like the trees.

He stood up to say good-bye. "Well, we'll have another try."

He swung up into the cockpit. He started the engine.

I felt under my feet for obstruc- tions; saw that the control wires were free; sat on my extra shirt, stuffed the lunch in the aluminum case; put the radio bag in the seat beside me. There now, fasten the belt. Ready.

We pushed out into the bay. It was not such a strange world to- night. We had been here before. I greeted old landmarks. There were the lights of the town. There was the path of the moon.

(—where the ships of youth are running
close-hauled on the edge of the wind—)

If only there were a wind. There was more out in the bay, but it was not as rough as the other night. Still, we were about two hundred pounds lighter. We taxied over our take-off stretch. We tried out the engine; we throttled down; we swung into the wind. That pause for breath. The last look out: the palms outlined dimly above the town; the moon, a bright path ahead; and the wind—the wind was rising—

"All set?"

"All right."

Here we go. Hold on. The roar, the spray over the wings. Look at your watch. Won't be more than two minutes. Then you'll know. You can stand two minutes. Look at your watch. That's your job. Listen—listen—the spray has stop- ped. We are spanking along. We are up on the step—faster, faster— oh, much faster than before. Sparks from the exhaust. We're going to get off! But how long it takes. Spank, spank—we're off? Not yet— spank— almost. Splutter, choke— the engine? My God—it's coming then—death. He's going on just the same. We're off—no more spanks. Splutter—splutter. What is wrong? Will he turn? Will we land? The wobble pump? Gas? Mixture? Never mind, your job, the watch. Just two, Greenwich. Yes— we're off—we're rising. But why start off with an engine like that?

But it smooths out now, like a long sigh, like a person breathing easily, freely. Like someone sing- ing ecstatically, climbing, soaring— sustained note of power and joy. We turn from the lights of the city; we pivot on a dark wing; we roar over the earth. The plane seems exultant now, even arrogant. We did it, we did it! We're up, above you. We were dependent on you just now, River, prisoners fawning on you for favors, for wind and light. But now, we are free. We are up; we are off. We can toss you aside, you there, way below us, a few lights in the great dark silent world that is ours—for we are above it.

WE JUST LIVE
By DOROTHY CANFIELD

ONE DAY Simple Martin, the half-wit wise man of our sleepy little Vermont village, was asked by one of the summer people: "What do you people in Hillsboro *do* all the time, away off here, so far from everything?" Martin looked around at the lovely, sloping lines of Hemlock Mountain, at Necronsett River singing in the sunlight, at the friendly, familiar faces of people in the street, and answered: *"Do? Why we jes' live!"*

And sometimes it seems to us that we are the only people in America engaged in that wonderful occupation. We know, of course, that there must be countless other Hillsboros, rejoicing as we do in an existence which keeps us responsive to life.

But all we hear from that part of America which is not Hillsboro is the yell of excitement going up from the cities, where people seem to be doing everything except just living. City dwellers make money, make reputations, make with hysteric rapidity more and yet more complications in the labyrinths of their lives, but they never really get to know each other and the pulsing drama of each other's lives.

In Hillsboro we explain the enormous amount of playgoing in cities as due to a perverted form of the natural hunger for life. If people are so situated that they can't get it fresh, they will take it canned. And all novels seem to us badly faded in comparison to the brilliant colors of life on our village street.

Romances, tragedies, farces . . . why, we are the characters of those plots. Every child who runs past the house starts a new story, every old man whom we leave sleeping in the burying ground is the ending of another or perhaps the beginning of a sequel. In the city a hundred more children run past the windows of your apartment, and funeral processions cross your every walk. But they are stories written in a tongue incomprehensible to you. In the city a horrible accident may happen before your eyes. It may shock you, but you do not know enough of what it means to be deeply moved by it. You knew nothing of the victim, you know nothing of his wife and children. You shudder, and hurry along, your heart a little more blunted to the sorrows of others, a little more remote from your fellows even than before.

But all Hillsboro is stirred by the news that Mrs. Brownell has broken her leg, for it means something definite to us, about which we must take action. It means that her sickly oldest daughter will not get the care she needs if somebody doesn't help out; it means that if we do not do something that bright boy of hers will have to leave school, just when he is about to win a scholarship in college; it means a crisis in several human lives, which calls forth active sympathy. In other words, we are not only the characters of our unwritten dramas, but also part authors. Something of the outcome depends upon us.

What dramatic situation on the stage can move you to the sharp throb of sympathy you feel as you see Nelse Pettingrew's mother run down the street, her shawl flung hastily over her head, framing a face of despairing resolve. Somebody has told her that Nelse is drinking again. If she can only coax the burly weakling home till "the fit goes by" he will be saved from a week's debauch. Mrs. Pettingrew takes in sewing for a living. She is quite unlettered, but she is a general in the army of spiritual forces. She stands up to her enemy and fights. She fought the wild beast in Nelse's father, all his life, and he died a better man. Undaunted, she is now fighting it in Nelse; and she generally wins her battles.

Now imagine the excitement in Hillsboro when Nelse begins to look about for a wife. It occurs to us that perhaps the handsome fellow's immense good humor and generosity are as good inheritance as the avarice of priggish young Horace Gallatin, who never drinks a drop. But the main question is, will Nelse find a wife who will carry on his mother's work?

All Hillsboro wonders whether Nelse will marry Ellen Brownell, or Flossie Merton, the girl who came up from Montpelier to wait at the tavern, and who is said to have a taste for drink herself. Old Mrs. Perkins roused herself not long ago from the poverty of her last days and gave Ellen her cherished white silk shawl to wear at village parties; and, racked with rheumatism, the old woman sits up at night to see which girl Nelse is "beauing home." Could the most artfully contrived fiction more blessedly sweep the self-centered complainings of old age into vitalizing interest in the lives of others?

Could Aeschylus himself have plunged us into a more awful desolation of pity than the day we saw old Squire Marvin being taken along the street to the insane asylum? All the self-made miseries of his life were in our minds, the wife he had loved and killed with the violence of a nature he had never learned to control, the children he had adored and spoiled and turned against, the people he had tried to benefit with so much egotistic pride mixed in his kindness that his favors made him hated. At sight of the end of all this there was no heart in Hillsboro that was not wrung.

Nor do we need books to help us feel the meaning of life, the meaning of death. Those in cities, living with feverish haste in the present only, cannot understand the comforting sense we have of belonging also to the past and future. Our own youth is not dead to us, as yours is, from lack of anything to recall it. The people we love do not slip quickly into that bitter oblivion to which the dead are consigned by those too hurried to remember. All their quaint and dear absurdities which make up personality are embalmed in the leisurely talk of the village, still enriched by all that they brought it.

101

WHEN BEFRIENDED, remember it:
When you befriend, forget it.
—*Franklin*

BE NOT simply good; be good for something.—*Thoreau*

GOODNESS is the only investment that never fails.—*Thoreau*

RICHES take wings, comforts vanish, hope withers away, but
love stays with us. Love is God.—*Lew Wallace*

IF YOU have built castles in the air your work need not be lost; that is
where they should be built; now put foundations under them.—*Thoreau*

OUR LIFE is always deeper than we know, is always more divine than it seems,
and hence we are able to survive degradations and despairs which otherwise
must engulf us.—*James*

WASTE NEITHER time nor money, but make the best use of both.—*Franklin*

MUSIC was a thing of the soul—a rose-lipped shell that murmured of the
eternal sea—a strange bird singing the songs of another shore.—*Holland*

THERE WAS NEVER YET a truly great man that was not at the
same time truly virtuous.—*Franklin*

SO HIGH as a tree aspires to grow, so high will it find an atmosphere
suited to it.—*Thoreau*

I HOLD that Christian grace abounds
Where charity is seen; that when
We climb to heaven, 'tis on the rounds
Of love to men.
—*Alice Cary*

A NOBLE DEED is a step toward God.—*Holland*

AMERICAN WRITERS

HE WHO loves best his fellow-man
Is loving God the holiest way he can.
—*Alice Cary*

THE WAY to be happy is to make others so.—*Ingersoll*

IF A MAN constantly aspires, is he not elevated?—*Thoreau*

DRUDGERY is as necessary to call out the treasures of the mind
as harrowing and planting those of the earth.—*Margaret Fuller*

OUR THOUGHTS are the epochs in our lives; all else is but a journal of
the winds that blew while we were here.—*Thoreau*

FAR AWAY there in the sunshine are my highest aspirations. I may not
reach them, but I can look up and see their beauty, believe in them, and
try to follow where they lead.—*Alcott*

THE MOST ACCEPTABLE SERVICE of God is doing good to man.—*Franklin*

THE COST of a thing is the amount of what I will call life which is required to be exchanged for it, immediately or in the long run.—*Thoreau*

EACH YEAR, one bad habit rooted out, in time ought to make
the worst man good.—*Franklin*

EVERY MAN who expresses an honest thought is a soldier in the army of
intellectual liberty.—*Ingersoll*

CONDEMN HER NOT whose hours
  Are not all given to spinning nor to care;
Has God not planted every path with flowers
  Whose end is to be fair?
                    —*Alice Cary*

A GOOD EXAMPLE is the best sermon.—*Franklin*

103

A MOTHER'S PRAYER
ADELAIDE LOVE

Lord Jesus, You who bade the children come
And took them in Your gentle arms and smiled,
Grant me unfailing patience through the days
To understand and help my little child.

I would not only give his body care
And guide his young dependent steps along
The wholesome ways, but I would know his heart,
Attuning mine to childhood's griefs and song.

Oh, give me vision to discern the child
Behind whatever he may do or say,
The wise humility to learn from him
The while I strive to teach him day by day.

A GOD FOR YOU
MARION STROBEL

I am making songs for you,
Soon you will be asking me
With your solemn baby stare—
Soon I'll have to answer you
When you ask me "What is God?"

God is where you want to go
When we reach the river's head
Where the branches are too low—
And we go home instead.

God is everything that you
Have not done and want to do.

God is all those shiny bright
Stories that I say I'll keep
To tell to you another night—
If you will go to sleep.

God is every lovely word
You want to hear and haven't heard.

And if you should want a place,
After searching everywhere,
To hide a secret, or your face—
You could hide it there.

God is much the safest place
To hide a secret—or your face.

BABY FACE
CARL SANDBURG

White Moon comes in on a baby face.
The shafts across her bed are flimmering.

Out on the land White Moon shines,
Shines and glimmers against gnarled shadows,
All silver to slow twisted shadows
Falling across the long road that runs from the house.

Keep a little of your beauty
And some of your flimmering silver
For her by the window to-night
Where you come in, White Moon.

MY MOTHER'S WORDS
ANNA HEMPSTEAD BRANCH

My mother has the prettiest tricks
    Of words and words and words.
Her talk comes out as smooth and sleek
    As breasts of singing birds.

She shapes her speech all silver fine
    Because she loves it so.
And her own eyes begin to shine
    To hear her stories grow.

And if she goes to make a call
    Or out to take a walk,
We leave our work when she returns
    And run to hear her talk.

We had not dreamed these things were so
Of sorrow and of mirth.
Her speech is as a thousand eyes
Through which we see the earth.

God wove a web of loveliness,
Of clouds and stars and birds,
But made not anything at all
So beautiful as words.

They shine around our simple earth
With golden shadowings,
And every common thing they touch
Is exquisite with wings.

There's nothing poor and nothing small
But is made fair with them.
They are the hands of living faith
That touch the garment's hem.

They are as fair as bloom of air,
They shine like any star,
And I am rich who learned from her
How beautiful they are.

❖ ❖ ❖

YOU ARE THE HOPE OF THE WORLD
By Hermann Hagedorn

Girls and boys of *America, you are the hope of the world!*
Not men and women of America, not even young men and young women of America, but girls and boys! You who carry the unblunted swords of ten-to-seventeen, you are the ones who are the hope of the world. Not to die for the world, but to live for it, to think for it, to work for it; to keep sharp and unstained by rust the splendid sword of the spirit!

It is not only because you are yourselves fine and true and upright and daring and free, Young America, that the world finds its hope in you. The world knows the men, the great deeds, and the principles greater than men or deeds, that have made this America of yours and mine. The world knows that in you, whether your ancestors came over in the *Mayflower* three hundred years ago, or in the steerage of a liner twenty years ago, lives

106

the spirit of a great tradition. The world puts its hope in you, but not only in you. It puts its hope in the great ghosts that stand behind you, upholding your arms, whispering wisdom to you, patience, perseverance, courage, crying, "Go on, Young America! We back you up!" Washington, first of all! And around him, Putnam, Warren, Hancock, Samuel Adams, John Adams, Hamilton, Jefferson, Marshall, Greene, Stark! You remember Stark? Stark held the rail fence at Bunker Hill. Morris going from house to house, collecting dollars for the starved Continentals; Ben Franklin, in France, fighting to win friends for the new nation! They are behind you! And there is Marion with his men, living in the wilderness like Robin Hood in Sherwood.

Look behind you, Young America!

Bainbridge, Preble, Decatur!

Hull of the *Constitution* which whipped the *Guerrière;* Perry of Lake Erie; McDonough of Lake Champlain, gallant men all, stand behind you. Jackson is there; Jackson who whipped the troops that whipped Napoleon; that sturdy fighter for free speech, who died with his boots on in the halls of Congress—John Quincy Adams—is behind you!

Union, one and indissoluble!

You remember? Webster said that. Webster is behind you. Clay is behind you! Rogers and Clark are behind you, Fremont, Daniel Boone, Kit Carson, Sam Houston, Davy Crockett. You remember? The frontiersmen, the Indian fighters, the pioneers are behind you, dauntless of spirit; the colonists of Virginia, Massachusetts, Connecti-

cut, the new Netherlands, the Carolinas; the settlers in wild lands, pressing westward to Ohio, to Illinois, to Kansas, to California, men and women, unafraid, clear-eyed; the brave builders of the West are behind you, Young America, upholding your hands! It is a great army of ghosts, Young America, that stands back of you! And there, Sherman, Sheridan, Meade, Thomas, Farragut, Grant, silent, tenacious, magnanimous! Stonewall Jackson, Stuart, Lee! And in the midst of them, the greatest of all, Lincoln, with his hand on your shoulder, Young America, saying, "Sonny, I'm with you. Go on!"

"Captain, my Captain!" Whitman is there, immortal crier of democracy! Longfellow is there, Bryant, Emerson, Whittier, Hawthorne, Poe, Lanier, Moody; the inventors, Fulton, Whitney, Morse; the orators, Garrison, Phillips, Beecher!

There's Patrick Henry! Can't you hear his words echoing down the dark places? "Is life so dear, or peace so sweet as to be purchased at the price of slavery?" Glorious ghost! Thank God, we have proved at last that we have not forgotten him!

Heroes all, Young America, as far as the eye can reach! And beyond them, into the gray distance, the heroes without name—in war, the soldiers, the sailors, the nurses, the women who waited at home; in peace, the school-teachers, the scientists, the parsons, the physicians, the workers in slums; the fighters everywhere for justice, for truth, for light; for clean cities, clean business, clean government!

Heroes are behind you, upholding you, Young America!

107

David's Star of Bethlehem

By CHRISTINE WHITING PARMENTER

$\mathcal{S}$COTT CARSON REACHED HOME in a bad humor. Nancy, slipping a telltale bit of red ribbon into her workbasket, realized this as soon as he came in.

It was the twenty-first of December, and a white Christmas was promised. Snow had been falling for hours, and in most of the houses wreaths were already in the windows. It was what one calls "a Christmasy-feeling day," yet, save for that red ribbon in Nancy's basket, there was no sign in the Carson home of the approaching festival.

Scott said, kissing her absent-mindedly and slumping into a big chair, "This snow is the very limit. If the wind starts blowing there'll be a fierce time with the traffic. My train was twenty minutes late as it is, and— There's the bell. Who can it be at this hour? I want my dinner."

"I'll go to the door," said Nancy hurriedly, as he started up. "Selma's putting dinner on the table now."

Relaxing into his chair Scott heard her open the front door, say something about the storm and, after a moment, wish someone a Merry Christmas.

A Merry Christmas! He wondered that she could say it so calmly. Three years ago on Christmas morning, they had lost their boy—swiftly—terribly—without warning. Meningitis, the doctor said. Only a few hours before the child had seemed a healthy, happy youngster, helping them trim the tree; hoping, with a twinkle in the brown eyes so like his mother's, that Santa Claus would remember the fact that he wanted skis! He had gone happily to bed after Nancy had read them "The Night Before Christmas," a custom of early childhood's days that the eleven-year-old lad still clung to. Later his mother remembered, with a pang, that when she kissed him good night he had said his head felt "kind of funny." But she had left him light-heartedly enough and gone down to help Scott fill the stockings. Santa had not forgotten the skis; but Jimmy never saw them.

Three years—and the memory still hurt so much that the very thought of Christmas was agony to Scott Carson. Jimmy had slipped away just as the carolers stopped innocently beneath his window, their voices rising clear and penetrating on the dawn-sweet air:

"Silent night—holy night. . . ."

Scott arose suddenly. He *must* not live over that time again. "Who was it?" he asked gruffly as Nancy joined him, and understanding the gruffness she answered tactfully, "Only the expressman."

"What'd he bring?"

"Just a—a package."

"One naturally supposes that," replied her husband, with a touch of sarcasm. Then, suspicion gripping him, he burst out, "Look here! If you've been getting a Christmas gift for me, I—I won't have it. I

108

told you I wanted to forget Christmas. I—"

"I know, dear," she broke in hastily. "The package was only from Aunt Mary."

"Didn't you tell her we weren't keeping Christmas?" he demanded irritably.

"Yes, Scott; but—but you know Aunt Mary! Come now, dinner's on and I think it's a good one. You'll feel better after you eat."

But Scott found it unaccountably hard to eat; and later, when Nancy was reading aloud in an effort to soothe him, he could not follow. She had chosen something humorous and diverting; but in the midst of a paragraph he spoke, and she knew that he had not been listening.

"Nancy," he said, "is there any place—any place on God's earth where we can get away from Christmas?"

She looked up, answering with sweet gentleness, "It would be a hard place to find, Scott."

He faced her suddenly: "I feel as if I couldn't stand it—the trees—the carols—the merrymaking, you know. Oh, if I could only sleep this week away! But . . . I've been thinking. . . . Would—would you consider for one moment going up to camp with me for a day or two? I'd go alone, but—"

"Alone!" she echoed. "Up there in the wilderness at Christmas time? Do you think I'd let you?"

"But it would be hard for you, dear, cold and uncomfortable. I'm a brute to ask it, and yet—"

Nancy was thinking rapidly. They could not escape Christmas, of course. No change of locality could make them forget the anniversary of the day that Jimmy went away. But she was worried about Scott, and the change of scene might help him over the difficult hours ahead. The camp, situated on the mountain a mile from any neighbors, would at least be isolated. There was plenty of bedding, and a big fireplace. It was worth trying.

She said, cheerfully, "I'll go with you, dear. Perhaps the change will make things easier for both of us."

This was Tuesday, and on Thursday afternoon they stepped off the north-bound train and stood on the platform watching it vanish into the mountains. The day was crisp and cold. "Two above," the station master told them as they went into the box of a station and moved instinctively toward the red-hot "air-tight" which gave forth grateful warmth.

"I sent a telegram yesterday to Clem Hawkins, over on the mountain road," said Scott. "I know you don't deliver a message so far off; but I took a chance. Do you know if he got it?"

"Yep. Clem don't have a 'phone, but the boy come down for some groceries and I sent it up. If I was you, though, I'd stay to the Central House. Seems as if it would be more cheerful—Christmas time."

"I guess we'll be comfortable enough if Hawkins airs out, and lights a fire," replied Scott, his face hardening at this innocent mention of the holiday. "Is there anyone around here who'll take us up? I'll pay well for it, of course."

"Iry Morse'll go; but you'll have to walk from Hawkinses. The road ain't dug out beyond. . . . There's Iry now. You wait, an' I'll holler to him. Hey, Iry!" he called, going to the door, "Will you carry these

109

folks up to Hawkinses? They'll pay for it."

"Iry," a ruddy-faced young farmer, obligingly appeared, his gray work horse hitched to a one-seated sleigh of ancient and uncomfortable design. "Have to sit three on a seat," he explained cheerfully; "but we'll be all the warmer for it. Tuck the buffalo robe 'round the lady's feet, mister, and you and me'll use the horse blanket. Want to stop to the store for provisions?"

"Yes. I brought some canned stuff, but we'll need other things," said Nancy. "I've made a list."

"Well, you got good courage," grinned the station master. "I hope you don't get froze to death up in the woods. Merry Christmas to yer, anyhow!"

"The same to you!" responded Nancy, smiling; and noted with a stab of pain that her husband's sensitive lips were trembling.

Under Ira's cheerful conversation, however, Scott relaxed. They talked of crops, the neighbors, and local politics—safe subjects all; but as they passed the district school, where a half-dozen sleighs or flivvers were parked, the man explained: "Folks decoratin' the school for the doin's tomorrow afternoon. Christmas tree for the kids, and pieces spoke, and singin'. We got a real live schoolma'am this year, believe me!"

They had reached the road that wound up the mountain toward the Hawkins farm, and as they plodded on, a sudden wind arose that cut their faces. Snow creaked under the runners, and as the sun sank behind the mountain Nancy shivered, not so much with cold as with a sense of loneliness and isolation.

It was Scott's voice that roused her: "Should we have brought snowshoes? I didn't realize that we couldn't be carried all the way."

"Guess you'll get there all right," said Ira. "Snow's packed hard as a drumhead, and it ain't likely to thaw yet a while. Here you are," as he drew up before the weather-beaten, unpainted farmhouse. "You better step inside a minute and warm up."

A shrewish-looking woman was already at the door, opening it but a crack, in order to keep out fresh air and cold.

"I think," said Nancy, with a glance at the deepening shadows, "that we'd better keep right on. I wonder if there's anybody here who'd help carry our bags and provisions.

"There ain't," answered the woman, stepping outside and pulling a faded gray sweater around her shoulders. "Clem's gone to East Conroy with the eggs, and Dave's up to the camp keepin' yer fire goin'. You can take the sled and carry yer stuff on that. There 'tis, by the gate. Dave'll bring it back when he comes. An' tell him to hurry. Like as not, Clem won't get back in time fer milkin'."

"I thought Dave was goin' to help Teacher decorate the school this afternoon," ventured Ira. He was unloading their things as he spoke and roping them to the sled.

"So'd he," responded the woman; "but there wa'n't no one else to light that fire, was they? Guess it won't hurt him none to work for his livin' like other folks. That new schoolma'am, she thinks o' nothin but—"

"Oh, look here!" said the young man, straightening up, a belliger

110

ent light in his blue eyes, "it's Christmas! Can Dave go back with me if I stop and milk for him? They'll be workin' all evenin'—lots o' fun for a kid like him, and—"

"No, he can't!" snapped the woman. "His head's enough turned now with speakin' pieces and singin' silly songs. You better be gettin' on, folks. I can't stand here talkin' till mornin'."

She slammed the door, while Ira glared after her retreating figure, kicked the gate post to relieve his feelings, and then grinned sheepishly.

"Some grouch! Why, she didn't even ask you in to get warm! Well, I wouldn't loiter if I was you. And send that kid right back, or he'll get worse'n a tongue-lashin'. Well, good-bye to you, folks. Hope you have a merry Christmas."

The tramp up the mountain passed almost entirely in silence, for it took their united energy to drag the sled up that steep grade against the wind. Scott drew a breath of relief when they beheld the camp, a spiral of smoke rising from its big stone chimney like a welcome promise of warmth.

"Looks good, doesn't it? But it'll be dark before that boy gets home. I wonder how old—"

They stopped simultaneously as a clear, sweet voice sounded from within the cabin:

"Silent night . . . holy night . . ."

"My God!"

Scott's face went suddenly dead white. He threw out a hand as if to brush something away, but Nancy caught it in hers, pulling it close against her wildly beating heart.

"All is calm . . . all is bright."

The childish treble came weirdly from within, while Nancy cried, "Scott—dearest, don't let go! It's only the little boy singing the carols he's learned in school. Don't you see? Come! Pull yourself together. We must go in."

Even as she spoke the door swung open, and through blurred vision they beheld the figure of a boy standing on the threshold. He was a slim little boy with an old, oddly wistful face, and big brown eyes under a thatch of yellow hair.

"You the city folks that was comin' up? Here, I'll help carry in yer things."

Before either could protest he was down on his knees in the snow, untying Ira's knots with skillful fingers. He would have lifted the heavy suit case himself, had not Scott, jerked back to the present by the boy's action, interfered.

"I'll carry that in." His voice sounded queer and shaky. "You take the basket. We're late, I'm afraid. You'd better hurry home before it gets too dark. Your mother said—"

"I don't mind the dark," said the boy quietly, as they went within. "I'll coast most o' the way down, anyhow. Guess you heard me singin' when you come along." He smiled, a shy, embarrassed smile as he explained: "It was a good chance to practice the Christmas carols. They won't let me, 'round home. We're goin' to have a show at the school tomorrow. I'm one o' the three kings—you know—'We three kings of Orient are.' I sing the first verse all by myself," he added with childish pride.

There followed a moment's si-

111

lence. Nancy was fighting a desire to put her arms about the slim boyish figure, while Scott had turned away, unbuckling the straps of his suit case with fumbling hands. Then Nancy said, "I'm afraid we've kept you from helping at the school this afternoon. I'm so sorry."

The boy drew a resigned breath that struck her as strangely unchildlike.

"You needn't to mind, ma'am. Maybe they wouldn't have let me go anyway; and I've got tomorrow to think about. I—I been reading one o' your books. I like to read."

"What book was it? Would you like to take it home with you for a—" She glanced at Scott, still on his knees by the suit case, and finished hurriedly—"a Christmas gift?"

"Gee! Wouldn't I!" His wistful eyes brightened, then clouded. "Is there a place maybe where I could hide it 'round here? They don't like me to read much to home. They," (a hard look crept into his young eyes), "they burned up the book Teacher gave me a while back. It was 'David Copperfield,' and I hadn't got it finished."

There came a crash as Scott, rising suddenly, upset a chair. The child jumped, and then laughed at himself for being startled.

"Look here, sonny," said Scott huskily, "you must be getting home. Can you bring us some milk tomorrow? I'll find a place to hide your book and tell you about it then. Haven't you got a warmer coat than this?"

He lifted a shabby jacket from the settle and held it out while the boy slipped into it.

"Thanks, mister," he said. "It's hard gettin' it on because it's tore

inside. They's only one button," he added, as Scott groped for them. "She don't get much time to sew 'em on. I'll bring up the milk tomorrow mornin'. I got to hurry now or I'll get fits! Thanks for the book, ma'am. I'd like it better'n anything. Good night."

Standing at the window Nancy watched him start out in the fast descending dusk. It hurt her to think of that lonely walk; but she thrust the thought aside and turned to Scott, who had lighted a fire on the hearth and seemed absorbed in the dancing flames.

"That's good!" she said cheerfully. "I'll get things started for supper, and then make the bed. I'm weary enough to turn in early. You might bring me the canned stuff in your suit case, Scott. A hot soup ought to taste good tonight."

She took an apron from her bag and moved toward the tiny kitchen. Dave evidently knew how to build a fire. The stove lids were almost red, and the kettle was singing. Nancy went about her preparations deftly, tired though she was from the unaccustomed tramp, while Scott opened a can of soup, toasted some bread, and carried their meal on a tray to the settles before the hearthfire. It was all very cozy and "Christmasy," thought Nancy, with the wind blustering outside and the flames leaping up the chimney. But she was strangely quiet. The thought of that lonely little figure trudging off in the gray dusk persisted, despite her efforts to forget. It was Scott who spoke, saying out of a silence, "I wonder how old he is."

"The—the little boy?"

He nodded, and she answered gently, "He seemed no older than—

112

I mean, he seemed very young to be milking cows and doing chores."

Again Scott nodded, and a moment passed before he said, "The work wouldn't hurt him though, if he were strong enough; but—did you notice, Nancy, he didn't look half fed? He is an intelligent little chap, though, and his voice— Good lord!" he broke off suddenly, "how can a shrew like that bring such a child into the world? To burn his book! Nancy, I can't understand how things are ordered. Here's that poor boy struggling for development in an unhappy atmosphere— and our Jimmy, who had love, and understanding, and— Tell me, why is it?"

She stretched out a tender hand; but the question remained unanswered, and the meal was finished in silence.

Dave did not come with the milk next morning. They waited till nearly noon, and then tramped off in the snow-clad, pine-scented woods. It was a glorious day, with diamonds sparkling on every fir tree, and they came back refreshed, and ravenous for their delayed meal. Scott wiped the dishes, whistling as he worked. It struck his wife that he hadn't whistled like that for months. Later, the last kitchen rites accomplished, she went to the window, where he stood gazing down the trail.

"He won't come now, Scott."

"The kid? It's not three yet, Nancy."

"But the party begins at four. I suppose everyone for miles around will be there. I wish—" She was about to add that she wished they could have gone too, but something in Scott's face stopped the words. She said instead, "Do you think we'd better go for the milk ourselves?"

"What's the use? They'll all be at the shindig, even that sour-faced woman, I suppose. But somehow— I feel worried about the boy. If he isn't here bright and early in the morning I'll go down and see what's happened. Looks as if it were clouding up again, doesn't it? Perhaps we'll get snowed in!"

Big, lazy-looking snowflakes were already beginning to drift down. Scott piled more wood on the fire, and stretched out on the settle for a nap. But Nancy was restless. She found herself standing repeatedly at the window looking at the snow. She was there when at last Scott stirred and wakened. He sat up blinking, and asked, noting the twilight, "How long have I been asleep?"

Nancy laughed, relieved to hear his voice after the long stillness.

"It's after five."

"Good thunder!" He arose, putting an arm across her shoulders. "Poor girl! I haven't been much company on this trip! But I didn't sleep well last night, couldn't get that boy out of my mind. Why, look!" Scott was staring out of the window into the growing dusk. "Here he is now! I thought you said—"

He was already at the door, flinging it wide in welcome as he went out to lift the box of milk jars from the sled. It seemed to Nancy, as the child stepped inside, that he looked subtly different—discouraged, she would have said of an older person; and when he raised his eyes she saw the unmistakable signs of recent tears.

"Oh, David!" she exclaimed, "why aren't you at the party?"

113

"I didn't go."

The boy seemed·curiously to have withdrawn into himself. His answer was like a gentle "none of your business"; but Nancy was not without a knowledge of boy nature. She thought, "He's hurt—dreadfully. He's afraid to talk for fear he'll cry; but he'll feel better to get it off his mind." She said, drawing him toward the cheerful hearthfire, "But why not, Dave?"

He swallowed, pulling himself together with an heroic effort.

"I had ter milk. The folks have gone to Conroy to Gramma Hawkins's! I *like* Gramma Hawkins. She told 'em to be sure an' bring me; but there wasn't no one else ter milk, so . . . so . . ."

It was Scott who came to the rescue as David's voice failed suddenly.

"Are you telling us that your people have gone away, for *Christmas,* leaving you home alone?"

The boy nodded, winking back tears as he managed a pathetic smile.

"Oh, I wouldn't ha' minded so much if—if it hadn't been for the doin's at the school. Miss Mary was countin' on me ter sing, and speak a piece. I don't know who they could ha' got to be that wise man." His face hardened in a way not good to see in a little boy, and he burst out angrily, "Oh, I'd have gone—after they got off! *Darn 'em!* But they hung 'round till almost four, and—and when I went for my good suit they—they'd *hid* it—or carried it away! . . . And there was a Christmas tree . . ."

His voice faltered again, while Nancy found herself speechless before what she recognized as a devastating disappointment. She glanced at Scott, and was frightened at the consuming anger in his face; but he came forward calmly, laying a steady hand on the boy's shoulder. He said, and, knowing what the words cost him, Nancy's heart went out to her husband in adoring gratitude, "Buck up, old scout! We'll have a Christmas tree! And we'll have a party too, you and Mother and I—darned if we don't! You can speak your piece and sing your carols for us. And Mother will read us 'The' "—for an appreciable moment Scott's voice faltered, but he went on· gamely— " 'The Night Before Christmas.' Did you ever hear it? And I know some stunts that'll make your eyes shine. We'll have our party tomorrow, Christmas Day, sonny; but now" (he was stooping for his overshoes as he spoke), "now we'll go after that tree before it gets too dark! Come on, Mother. We want you, too!"

Mother! Scott hadn't called her that since Jimmy left them! Through tear-blinded eyes Nancy groped for her coat in the diminutive closet. Darkness was coming swiftly as they went into the snowy forest, but they found their tree, and stopped to cut. fragrant green branches for decoration. Not till the tree stood proudly in its corner did they remember the lack of tinsel trimmings; but Scott brushed this aside as a mere nothing.

"We've got pop corn, and nothing's prettier. Give us a bite of supper, Nancy, and then I'm going to the village."

"The village! At this hour?"

"You take my sled, mister," cried David, and they saw that his eyes were happy once more, and childlike. "You can coast 'most all the way, like lightning! I'll pop the

114

corn. I'd love to! Gee! it's lucky I milked before I come away!"

The hours that followed passed like magic to Nancy Carson. Veritable wonders were wrought in that small cabin; and oh, it was good to be planning and playing again with a little boy! Not till the child, who had been up since dawn, had dropped asleep on the settle from sheer weariness, did she add the finishing touches to the scene.

"It's like a picture of Christmas," she murmured happily. "The tree, so green and slender with its snowy trimmings—the cone-laden pine at the windows—the bulging stocking at the fireplace, and—and the sleeping boy. I wonder—"

She turned, startled by a step on the creaking snow outside, but it was Scott, of course. He came in quietly, not laden with bundles as she'd expected, but empty-handed. There was, she thought, a strange excitement in his manner as he glanced 'round the fire-lit room, his eyes resting for a moment on David's peaceful face. Then he saw the well-filled stocking at the mantel, and his eyes came back unswerving to hers.

"Nancy! Is—is it—?"

She drew nearer, and put her arms about him.

"Yes, dear, it's—Jimmy's—just as we filled it on Christmas Eve three years ago. You see, I couldn't quite bear to leave it behind us when we came away, lying there in his drawer so lonely—at Christmas time. Tell me you don't mind, Scott—won't you? We have our memories, but David—he has so little. That dreadful mother, and—"

Scott cleared his throat; swallowed, and said gently, "He has, I think, the loveliest mother in the world!"

"What do you mean?"

He drew her down onto the settle that faced the sleeping boy, and answered, "Listen, Nancy. I went to the schoolhouse. I thought perhaps they'd give me something to trim the tree. The party was over, but the teacher was there with Ira Morse, clearing things away. I told them about David—why he hadn't shown up; and asked some questions. Nancy—what do you think? That Hawkins woman isn't the child's mother! I *knew* it!

"Nobody around here ever saw her. She died when David was a baby, and his father, half crazed, the natives thought, with grief, brought the child here, and lived like a hermit on the mountain. He died when Dave was about six, and as no one claimed the youngster, and there was no orphan asylum within miles, he was sent to the poor farm, and stayed there until last year, when Clem Hawkins wanted a boy to help do chores, and Dave was the cheapest thing in sight. Guess you wonder where I've been all this time? Well, I've been interviewing the overseer of the poor—destroying red tape by the yard—resorting to bribery and corruption! But— Hello, old man, did I wake you up?"

David, roused suddenly, rubbed his eyes. Then, spying the stocking, he wakened thoroughly and asked, "Say! Is—is it Christmas?"

Scott laughed, and glanced at his watch.

"It will be, in twelve minutes. Come here, sonny."

He drew the boy onto his knee, and went on quietly: "The stores were closed, David, when I reached

115

the village. I couldn't buy you a Christmas gift, you see. But I thought if we gave you a *real mother*, and—and a father—"

"Oh, Scott!"

It was a cry of rapture from Nancy. She had, of course, suspected the ending to his story, but not until that moment had she let herself really believe it. Then, seeing the child's bewilderment, she explained, "He means, dear, that you're our boy now—for always."

David looked up, his brown eyes big with wonder.

"And I needn't go back to Hawkins's? Not *ever?*"

"Not ever," Scott promised, while his throat tightened at the relief in the boy's voice.

"And I'll have folks, same as the other kids?"

"You've guessed right." The new father spoke lightly in an effort to conceal his feeling. "That is, if you think we'll do!" he added, smiling.

"Oh, you'll—"

Suddenly inarticulate, David turned, throwing his thin arms around Scott's neck in a strangling, boylike.hug. Then, a bit ashamed because such things were new to him, he slipped away, standing with his back to them at the window, trying, they saw with understanding hearts, to visualize this unbelievable thing that had come, a miracle, into his starved life. When after a silence they joined him, the candle on the table flared up for a protesting moment, and then went out. Only starlight and firelight lit the cabin now; and Nancy, peering into the night, said gently, "How beautifully it has cleared! I think I never saw the stars so bright."

"Christmas stars," Scott reminded her and, knowing the memory that brought the roughness to his voice, she caught and clasped his hand.

It was David who spoke next. He was leaning close to the window, his elbows resting on the sill, his face cupped in his two hands. He seemed to have forgotten them as he said dreamily, "It's Christmas . . . Silent night . . . holy night . . . like the song. I wonder—" He looked up trustfully into the faces above him— "I wonder if—if maybe one of them stars isn't the Star of Bethlehem!"

❖   ❖   ❖

BALLAD FOR CHRISTMAS
NANCY BYRD TURNER

It's time to welcome Christmas, now.
Off to the woods for wintry vine,
For white and scarlet-berried bough
And patterned fir and frosty pine,
For logs to make the broad hearth shine—
Stout oak, and hickory, dry and hale,
To send a glow across the snow!
The light of Christmas shall not fail.

116

Under the old and arching skies
Clear carols call, by street and hill;
The stars that saw the great Star rise
Are shining still, are shining still.
In all the long years, come what will,
There's nothing new and nothing strange
In one old night of song and light—
The heart of Christmas cannot change!

WINTER MORNING

ROBERT P. TRISTRAM COFFIN

Up, in the coldness of a kitchen where
Heat has been and is no longer there,
And it is colder than the clear outdoors;
Ice must be cracked before the bucket pours.
The farmer coaxes till a small flame stands
Down in the stove between his cupping hands.
Life gets to going very slowly, winters.
The corners of the windowpanes have splinters
Of silver frost the color of the moon.
The farmer hums a melancholy tune
And sees his song around him in the air,
Loch Lomond, or perhaps Robin Adair.
His breathing tags the man round everywhere.
The farmer slices bacon with the knife,
His fingers now start coming back to life,
The cold potatoes have an icy shell.
A winter morning is the best for smell.
The farmer puts the kettle on its place,
The first low sun slants in and strikes his face.
The smoke pours from the cracks across the stove
And it smells warm and makes him think of clove;
He crowds the firewood in up to the covers,
The smoke stays in a bluish sheet and hovers
Just overhead, much like a lower ceiling.
There are tears in onions he is peeling.
He tries the stove top with a moistened finger—
It's hot enough, he feels the smarting linger.
The frying pan goes on. The fragrance spreads
To other rooms, folks stir in their warm beds;
A child pipes up, another and another,
And like a smiling sunrise out comes mother.

DIVINE INSPIRATION

GOD MADE NOT DEATH: neither hath He pleasure in
the destruction of the living.

FOR HE created all things, that they might have their
being: and the generations of the world were healthful;
and there is no poison of destruction in them, nor the
kingdom of death upon the earth.

FOR righteousness is immortal.

FOR GOD created man to be immortal, and made him to be an
image of His own eternity.

BUT THE SOULS of the righteous are in the hand of God, and there shall
no torment touch them.

IN THE SIGHT of the unwise they seemed to die: and their departure
is taken for misery.

AND THEIR GOING from us to be utter destruction: but they
are in peace.

AS GOLD in the furnace hath He tried them, and received them as a burnt offering.

THEY SHALL JUDGE the nations, and have
dominion over the people, and their
Lord shall reign for ever.

THEY THAT PUT their trust in Him shall understand the truth:
and such as be faithful in love shall abide with Him.

LOVE is strong as death . . . many waters cannot quench
love, neither can floods drown it.

WE WALK by faith, not by sight.

118

FROM THE BIBLE

BE SWIFT to hear; and let thy life be sincere;
and with patience give answer.

BE PERFECTED; be comforted; be
of the same mind; live in peace;
and the God of love and peace
shall be with you.

JUDGE NOT, that ye be not judged.

AND BE YE KIND one to another, tender-hearted, forgiving each
other, even as God also in Christ forgave you.

LET ANOTHER MAN praise thee, and not thine own mouth; a stranger, and
not thine own lips.

A NEW COMMANDMENT I give unto you. That ye love one another; as I
have loved you, that ye also love one another.

COME UNTO ME, all ye that labor and are heavy laden, and
I will give you rest. Take my yoke upon you, and learn
of me ... and ye shall find rest unto your souls.

BE NOT FORGETFUL to entertain strangers, for thereby
some have entertained angels unawares.

CAST THY BREAD upon the waters; for thou
shalt find it after many days.

BE NOT OVERCOME of evil, but overcome evil with good.

ALL THINGS whatsoever ye would that men should do
to you, do ye even so to them: for this is the Law
and the Prophets.

BE THOU FAITHFUL unto death.

WHEN THE WISE MAN APPEARED
By WILLIAM ASHLEY ANDERSON

THE battery in the car had gone dead; and it turned out to be a bitterly cold night, vast and empty, a ringing void domed with icy stars. Over Hallet's Hill the evening star danced like tinsel on the tip of a Christmas tree. The still air was resonant as the inside of an iron bell; but within our snug farmhouse it was mellow with the warmth of three cherry-red stoves. The dinner things had been pushed back, and I was feeling relaxed and content, lazily smoking a cigarette, when Bruce came into the room.

He had gone upstairs in heavy boots and flannel cruiser's shirt. He reappeared in a long white nightgown with a purple cloak of tintexed cotton over his shoulders. In one hand he held a tall crown of yellow pasteboard and tinsel. From the other swung an ornate censer. His boots had been replaced by thin flapping sandals.

"What in the world are you supposed to be?" I asked.

My wife looked at him critically. There was both concern and tenderness in the look. Women always look tenderly at Bruce; and then, of course, she had more than a hand in his costuming. She said indignantly:

"He's one of the Wise Men of the East!"

Virginia, my daughter, put both hands to her face, ready to stifle an hysterical shriek because Bruce, who is small for fourteen, likes to be grouped with men, swinging a double-edged axe with the best of them and handling a twelve-gauge as if it were a B B gun. With a tight voice she managed to say:

"Have you got matches for that thing?"

With considerable difficulty Bruce raised his skirts and produced a box from his pants pocket.

"He'll be ready," said my wife, "whatever happens!" She looked at me and I thought again how lovely she is. That did me no good. Her look was an urgent reminder. I felt all the chill of the night air run up my spine, suddenly remembering that I had promised to get the boy to the school-house in town in good time for the Christmas pageant. I shuddered and groaned and went out into the night pulling on a heavy coat.

By one of those freaks of mechanical whimsy that baffle man, its maker, the engine caught at the first turn of the crank, and off we went with a bang, bouncing and roaring across the rough frozen field. That was a trick of the devil.

At the turn by the barn the generator couldn't pick up enough current; and there the engine died. My heart sank with its last long sigh. I looked out the side of my eyes at Bruce, sitting there saying nothing, making me think what a kid he still is, with the crown and censer clasped in his arms, staring down that long endless lane that disappeared in the lonely hills.

It was a moment of deep breathless silence. The hills walled us in from all hope of neighborly assistance. Hallet's place was more than a mile and a half away, and the nearest turn of Route 90, even with the thin chance of a lift, was more than two miles away. Still, what could I do about it? I felt as help-

120

less as a kid myself—and I had promised to get him there on time.

Well, I thought, it's not tragically important. Bruce said nothing, but his eyes were wide, staring now at the big star twinkling just over the ragged edge of the mountain. Then a strange and uneasy feeling stirred in me, because I knew the boy was praying. He had made his promises too!

Before I could move, he dropped his crown and censer and scrambled out of the car, stumbling over his skirts. But all his straining and heaving at the crank was useless. I strained and heaved in turn and was equally impotent. When we weren't sweating we were shivering. The still air cut like knives. The cold metal clung to our hands. Every deep breath rasped my lungs until I sputtered.

Ordinarily we might have pushed the car to the edge of the rise and rolled it down the hill in gear; but the grease stuck like cement, and we couldn't budge it. After a while I straightened my cramped back and guessed I'd smoke a cigarette while I thought it over. When I struck a light with fumbling hands and looked up through the smoke Bruce was scuttling down the lane, one hand holding his skirts, one hand swinging the censer, the high golden crown perched cock-eyed on his head. I hesitated between laughing at him and yelling for him to stop. At the moment it seemed that this was about the only thing he could do. As for me, there wasn't anything I could do. Then I thought of the expression on his face as he prayed, and I felt mean, realizing that a man's view and a boy's view are not necessarily the same.

I threw the cigarette away and began once more to crank.

I don't know how long the struggle lasted, but all at once the engine sneezed. With hands clenched and eyes closed I straightened slowly and held my breath. The engine began to cough throatily. I scrambled frenziedly into the car.

Just about where Fifth Street enters Stroudsburg I overtook Bruce. There was a twist at my innards at sight of that small figure trudging along with the cock-eyed crown on his head and the censer hugged to his stomach. A long sigh went out of me as he turned his face into the lights with a white-lipped grin. His gown was torn and he shivered violently.

"You shouldn't have gone off that way," I growled. "It's too cold. It's terribly cold!"

"I put twigs in the censer," he said, "and made a fire. I kept warm enough."

"But look at your feet! You might have frozen them!"

"It wasn't so bad. I took a bearing on the star and made a short cut across Lasoine's farm. It came out right back there by the new cottage."

After that I was too busy putting on speed to say much. We arrived at the school on time. I stood in back and watched.

A good many years have passed since I last saw the story of Bethlehem and the homage of the Three Wise Men presented by children at Christmastime. It had become so old a story to me that it seemed strange to realize that to them it was new.

When I saw Bruce walking stiff-legged on cut and chilblained feet with his two companions on the

121

stage, kneeling by the crèche, declaiming his studied lines, first I regretted my laughter at the dinner table, then an uneasy awe rose up within me.

Going home we stopped at a garage for anti-freeze and at a soda-counter for hot chocolate, and I said nothing but commonplace things. As we rolled comfortably out Fifth Street Bruce showed me where the short-cut came out.

"That's where the Thompsons lived," I said, "before the place burned down."

"I know," said Bruce; "where the boy was burned to death."

A new house had been built on the old foundations and people were again living there.

"They've got lights burning."

As we passed the Lasoine farm there were lights burning there, too. I thought this was strange, because since George Lasoine had gone off to war the old grandmother, who had lost her youngest son in the first war, had sort of shriveled up, and a gloom lay over the house; but as I slowed down I could see Lou Lasoine through the kitchen window, smoking his pipe and smiling at the two women talking, so I sensed everything was all right.

So far as I knew that was about all there was to the evening; but on Christmas Day the Good Farmer's Wife came by with gifts of mince-meat made from venison and a jug of sassafras cider. She had shaken off her customary pessimism and was full of bounce and high-pitched talk. I heard the laughter and ejaculations in the kitchen where my wife was supervising the Christmas feast; and since I have a weakness for the racy gossip of the countryside, I drifted toward the kitchen too.

"You must hear this!" said my wife, drawing me in.

The Farmer's Wife looked at me with a glittering but wary eye.

"You hain't agoin' to believe it either," she said. "Just the same I'm tellin' you, folks up here in the hills see things and they do believe!"

"What have you been seeing?"

"It was old Mrs. Lasoine. Last Tuesday night when she was a-feelin' awful low she thought she heard something back of the barn and she looked out. Now I'll say this for the old lady—she's got good vision. That she has! Plenty good! There warn't no moonlight, but if you recollect it was a bright starry night. And there she saw, plain as her own husband, one of the Wise Men of the Bible come a-walkin' along the hill with a gold crown on his head, a-swingin' one of them pots with smoke in them—"

My mouth opened and I looked at Rosamunde and Rosamunde looked at me; but before I could say anything, the Farmer's Wife hurried on:

"Now don't you start a-laughin' —not yet!—'cause that hain't the long and short of it! There's other testimony! Them Thompsons. You know the ones whose oldest boy was burned in the fire? Well, there it was the children. First, they heard him. They heard him a-singin' 'Come All Ye Faithful' plain as day. They went runnin' to the window and they seen the Wise Man a-walkin' in the starlight across the lane, gold crown and robes and fire-pot and all! Well, my goodness, they put up such a shoutin' and a yellin' that their parents come a-runnin'. But by then it was too

122

late. He was gone. Just disappeared. Afterward they went out and looked but they couldn't find hide nor hair—"

"Did they see any other signs?" I asked faintly.

The Farmer's Wife scoffed. "Old folks and children see things which maybe we can't. All I can say is this. Lasoines and Thompsons don't even know each other. But old lady Lasoine was heartsick and lonely and a-prayin' about her lost boy, and the Thompsons was heartsick and lonely because this was the first Christmas in the new house without Harry, and you dassent say they wasn't a-prayin' too! Maybe you don't believe that amounts to anythin'—but I'm tellin' you it was a comfort to them to see and believe!"

I swallowed hard, recalling the look on Bruce's face as he stared at the star, when I knew he was praying that he might not fail his friends. Well, not daring to look at my wife, I said with all the sincerity I can feel:

"Yes, I believe God was close that night."

For the first time in her garrulous life the Farmer's Wife was stricken dumb. She looked at me as if an even greater miracle had been performed before her very eyes.

THE LOVE YOU LIBERATE

By GEORGE MATTHEW ADAMS

IF YOU do not love your work there is no plainer fact in this world than this—you can't keep it long.

Liberate your love and it enters into everything you do. It enlarges your soul and strengthens your body.

And the love you liberate is the only love that ever comes back to you.

You can't get anything without giving something.

I have never met an unhappy giver.

We have to do a great many unpleasant things in this world. But if we do them in the spirit of good sports I notice that they aren't so unpleasant after all. This love business you see, works overtime and doesn't mind.

The love you liberate breeds greater love everywhere it goes. It's contagious. In the long run it travels around the world.

If you are working for a concern and you try merely to "just get by," your job itself shrinks and you with it. Success then scampers to the fellow above or below you who puts his heart in his work and so climbs!

Life is a vast business. A part of it is given over to making people happy, and a part to the making of money, building ships, buildings, bridges, and babies' toys. All these pursuits are useful and valuable. But love is the salt that savors the whole and drives away the mists so that the sun may eternally shine.

Love is the greatest thing in the world and the most important ingredient that enters into life and work.

Liberate your love. Spread it out. Keep giving it away. Don't mind if you overflow with it aboard. If there is damage done it is easily repaired!

A MESSAGE TO GARCIA

By ELBERT HUBBARD

IN ALL THIS Cuban business there is one man stands out on the horizon of my memory like Mars at perihelion.

When war broke out between Spain and the United States, it was very necessary to communicate quickly with the leader of the Insurgents. Garcia was somewhere in the mountain fastnesses of Cuba—no one knew where. No mail or telegraph message could reach him. The President must secure his cooperation, and quickly.

What to do!

Someone said to the President, "There is a fellow by the name of Rowan will find Garcia for you, if anybody can."

Rowan was sent for and given a letter to be delivered to Garcia. How the "fellow by the name of Rowan" took the letter, sealed it up in an oilskin pouch, strapped it over his heart, in four days landed by night off the coast of Cuba from an open boat, disappeared into the jungle, and in three weeks came out on the other side of the Island, having traversed a hostile country on foot, and delivered his letter to Garcia—are things I have no special desire now to tell in detail.

The point that I wish to make is this: McKinley gave Rowan a letter to be delivered to Garcia; Rowan took the letter and did not ask, "Where is he at?"

By the Eternal! there is a man whose form should be cast in deathless bronze and the statue placed in every college of the land. It is not book-learning young men need, nor instruction about this and that, but a stiffening of the vertebrae which will cause them to be loyal to a trust, to act promptly, concentrate their energies; do the thing—"Carry a message to Garcia."

General Garcia is dead now, but there are other Garcias. No man who has endeavored to carry out an enterprise where many hands were needed, but has been well nigh appalled at times by the imbecility of the average man—the inability or unwillingness to concentrate on a thing and do it. Slipshod assistance, foolish inattention, dowdy indifference, and half-hearted work seem the rule; and no man succeeds, unless by hook or crook or threat he forces or bribes other men to assist him; or mayhap, God in His goodness performs a miracle, and sends him an Angel of Light for an assistant.

You, reader, put this matter to a test: You are sitting now in your office—six clerks are within call. Summon any one and make this request: "Please look in the encyclopedia and make a brief memorandum for me concerning the life of Correggio."

Will the clerk quietly say, "Yes, sir," and go do the task?

On your life he will not. He will look at you out of a fishy eye and ask one or more of the following questions:

Who was he?

Which encyclopedia?

Where is the encyclopedia?

Was I hired for that?

Don't you mean Bismarck?

What's the matter with Charlie doing it?

Is he dead?

Is there any hurry?

Sha'n't I bring you the book and let you look it up yourself? What do you want to know for? And I will lay you ten to one that after you have answered the questions, and explained how to find the information, and why you want it, the clerk will go off and get one of the other clerks to help him try to find Garcia—and then come back and tell you there is no such man. Of course I may lose my bet, but according to the Law of Average I will not.

Now, if you are wise, you will not bother to explain to your "assistant" that Correggio is indexed under the C's, not in the K's, but you will smile very sweetly and say, "Never mind," and go look it up yourself.

And this incapacity for independent action, this moral stupidity, this infirmity of the will, this unwillingness to cheerfully catch hold and lift—these are the things that put pure Socialism so far into the future. If men will not act for themselves, what will they do when the benefit of their effort is for all?

A first mate with knotted club seems necessary; and the dread of getting "the bounce" Saturday night holds many a worker to his place.

Advertise for a stenographer, and nine out of ten who apply can neither spell nor punctuate—and do not think it necessary to. Can such a one write a letter to Garcia?

"You see that bookkeeper," said the foreman to me in a large factory.

"Yes; what about him?"

"Well, he's a fine accountant, but if I'd send him up town on an errand, he might accomplish the errand all right, and on the other hand, might stop at four saloons on the way, and when he got to Main Street would forget what he had been sent for."

Can such a man be entrusted to carry a message to Garcia?

We have recently been hearing much maudlin sympathy expressed for the "downtrodden denizens of the sweatshop" and the "homeless wanderer searching for honest employment," and with it all often go many hard words for the men in power.

Nothing is said about the employer who grows old before his time in a vain attempt to get frowsy ne'er-do-wells to do intelligent work; and his long, patient striving after "help" that does nothing but loaf when his back is turned. In every store and factory there is a constant weeding-out process going on. The employer is constantly sending away "help" that have shown their incapacity to further the interests of the business, and others are being taken on. No matter how good times are, this sorting continues: only, if times are hard and work is scarce, the sorting is done finer—but out and forever out the incompetent and unworthy go. It is the survival of the fittest. Self-interest prompts every employer to keep the best—those who can carry a message to Garcia.

I know one man of really brilliant parts who has not the ability to manage a business of his own, and yet who is absolutely worthless to anyone else, because he carries with him constantly the insane suspicion that his employer is oppressing, or intending to oppress, him. He cannot give orders, and he will not receive them. Should a message be given him to take to Garcia, his

125

answer would probably be, "Take it yourself!"

Tonight this man walks the streets looking for work, the wind whistling through his threadbare coat. No one who knows him dare employ him, for he is a regular firebrand of discontent. He is impervious to reason, and the only thing that can impress him is the toe of a thick-soled Number Nine boot.

Of course, I know that one so morally deformed is no less to be pitied than a physical cripple; but in our pitying let us drop a tear, too, for the men who are striving to carry on a great enterprise, whose working hours are not limited by the whistle, and whose hair is fast turning white through the struggle to hold in line dowdy indifference, slipshod imbecility, and the heartless ingratitude which, but for their enterprise, would be both hungry and homeless.

Have I put the matter too strongly? Possibly I have; but when all the world has gone a-slumming I wish to speak a word of sympathy for the man who succeeds—the man who, against great odds, has directed the efforts of others, and having succeeded, finds there's nothing in it: nothing but bare board and clothes.

I have carried a dinner-pail and worked for day's wages, and I have also been an employer of labor, and I know there is something to be said on both sides. There is no excellence, *per se*, in poverty; rags are no recommendation; and all employers are not rapacious and highhanded, any more than all poor men are virtuous.

My heart goes out to the man who does his work when the "boss" is away, as well as when he is at home. And the man who, when given a letter for Garcia, quietly takes the missive, without asking any idiotic questions, and with no lurking intention of chucking it into the nearest sewer, or of doing aught else but deliver it, never gets "laid off," nor has to go on a strike for higher wages. Civilization is one long anxious search for just such individuals. Anything such a man asks shall be granted. He is wanted in every city, town, and village—in every office, shop, store and factory. The world cries out for such; he is needed and needed badly—the man who can "Carry a Message to Garcia."

AN AIRMAN'S LETTER

ANONYMOUS

AMONG THE personal belongings of a young R.A.F. pilot in a Bomber Squadron who was recently reported "Missing, believed killed," was a letter to his mother—to be sent to her if he were killed.

"This letter was perhaps the most amazing one I have ever read; simple and direct in its wording but splendid and uplifting in its outlook," says the young officer's station commander. "It was inevitable that I should read it—in fact he must have intended this, for it was left open in order that I might be certain that no prohibited information was disclosed.

"I sent the letter to the bereaved mother, and asked her whether I might publish it anonymously, as I feel its contents may bring comfort to other mothers, and that every one in our country may feel proud to read of the sentiments which support 'an average airman' in the execution of his present arduous duties. I have received the mother's permission, and I hope this letter may be read by the greatest possible number of our countrymen at home and abroad."

DEAREST MOTHER,—Though I feel no premonition at all, events are moving rapidly, and I have instructed that this letter be forwarded to you should I fail to return from one of the raids which we shall shortly be called upon to undertake. You must hope on for a month, but at the end of that time you must accept the fact that I have handed my task over to the extremely capable hands of my comrades of the Royal Air Force, as so many splendid fellows have already done.

First, it will comfort you to know that my role in this war has been of the greatest importance. Our patrols far out over the North Sea have helped to keep the trade routes clear for our convoys and supply ships, and on one occasion our information was instrumental in saving the lives of the men in a crippled lighthouse relief ship. Though it will be difficult for you, you will disappoint me if you do not at least try to accept the facts dispassionately, for I shall have done my duty to the utmost of my ability. No man can do more, and no one calling himself a man could do less.

I have always admired your amazing courage in the face of continual setbacks; in the way you have given me as good an educa-tion and background as anyone in the country; and always kept up appearances without ever losing faith in the future. My death would not mean that your struggle has been in vain. Far from it. It means that your sacrifice is as great as mine. Those who serve England must expect nothing from her; we debase ourselves if we regard our country as merely a place in which to eat and sleep.

History resounds with illustrious names who have given all, yet their sacrifice has resulted in the British Empire, where there is a measure of peace, justice, and freedom for all, and where a higher standard of civilization has evolved, and is still evolving, than anywhere else. But this is not only concerning our own land. Today we are faced with the greatest organized challenge to Christianity and civilization that the world has ever seen, and I count myself lucky and honoured to be the right age and fully trained to throw my full weight into the scale. For this I have to thank you. Yet there is more work for you to do. The home front will still have to stand united for years after the war is won. For all that can be said against it, I still maintain that this war is a very good thing; every individual is having the chance to give and dare all for his principle like the martyrs of old. However long the time may be, one thing can never be altered—I shall have lived and died an Englishman. Nothing else matters one jot nor can anything ever change it.

You must not grieve for me, for if you really believe in religion and all that it entails that would be hypocrisy. I have no fear of death; only a queer elation . . . I would

127

have it no other way. The universe is so vast and so ageless that the life of one man can only be justified by the measure of his sacrifice. We are sent to this world to acquire a personality and a character to take with us that can never be taken from us. Those who just eat and sleep, prosper and procreate, are no better than animals if all their lives they are at peace.

I firmly and absolutely believe that all evil things are sent into the world to try us; they are sent deliberately by our Creator to test our metal because He knows what is good for us. The Bible is full of cases where the easy way out has been discarded for moral principles.

I count myself fortunate in that I have seen the whole country and known men of every calling. But with the final test of war I consider my character fully developed. Thus at my early age my earthly mission is already fulfilled and I am prepared to die with just one regret, and one only—that I could not devote myself to making your declining years more happy by being with you; but you will live in peace and freedom and I shall have directly contributed to that, so here again my life will not have been in vain.

—Your loving Son, . . .

LINCOLN
NANCY BYRD TURNER

There was a boy of other days,
A quiet, awkward, earnest lad,
Who trudged long, weary miles to get
A book on which his heart was set—
And then no candle had!

He was too poor to buy a lamp
But very wise in woodmen's ways.
He gathered seasoned bough, and stem,
And crisping leaf, and kindled them
Into a ruddy blaze.

Then as he lay full length and read,
The firelight flickered on his face,
And etched his shadow on the gloom,
And made a picture in the room,
In that most humble place.

The hard years came, the hard years went,
But gentle, brave, and strong of will,
He met them all. And when today
We see his pictured face, we say,
"There's light upon it still."

GRADATIM

Josiah Gilbert Holland

Heaven is not gained at a single bound;
  But we build the ladder by which we rise
  From the lowly earth to the vaulted skies,
And we mount to its summit round by round.

I count this thing to be grandly true,
  That a noble deed is a step toward God—
  Lifting the soul from the common sod
To a purer air and a broader view.

We rise by things that are 'neath our feet;
  By what we have mastered of good and gain;
  By the pride deposed and the passion slain,
And the vanquished ills that we hourly meet.

We hope, we aspire, we resolve, we trust,
  When the morning calls us to life and light,
  But our hearts grow weary, and, ere the night,
Our lives are trailing the sordid dust.

We hope, we resolve, we aspire, we pray,
  And we think that we mount the air on wings
  Beyond the recall of sensual things,
While our feet still cling to the heavy clay.

Wings for the angels, but feet for men!
  We may borrow the wings to find the way—
  We may hope, and resolve, and aspire, and pray;
But our feet must rise, or we fall again.

Only in dreams is a ladder thrown
  From the weary earth to the sapphire walls;
  But the dream departs, and the vision falls,
And the sleeper wakes on his pillow of stone.

Heaven is not reached at a single bound;
  But we build the ladder by which we rise
  From the lowly earth to the vaulted skies,
And we mount to its summit round by round.

LIFE is too short to be little.—*Disraeli*

A HOUSE without books is like a room without windows.
—*Horace Mann*

RARELY PROMISE. But, if lawful, constantly perform.—*Penn*

THE HEALTH of the people is really the foundation upon which all their happiness and all their powers as a State depend.—*Disraeli*

Do GOOD with what thou hast, or it will do thee no good.—*Penn*

WE HAVE a call to do good, as often as we have the power and occasion.—*Penn*

THE MOST IMPORTANT THOUGHT I ever had was that of my individual responsibility to God.—*Daniel Webster*

WHAT IS DEFEAT? Nothing but education, nothing but the first step to something better.—*Phillips*

WHAT WE obtain too cheap we esteem too lightly; 'tis dearness only that gives everything its value.—*Thomas Paine*

IT IS WISE not to seek a secret; and honest, not to reveal one.—*Penn*

AMERICA has furnished to the world the character of Washington, and if our American institutions had done nothing else, that alone would have entitled them to the respect of mankind.—*Daniel Webster*

KNOWLEDGE is the treasure, but judgment the treasurer, of a wise man.—*Penn*

A WISE MAN'S COUNTRY is the world.—*Garrison*

PATRIOTS AND STATESMEN

DEEDS survive the doers.—*Horace Mann*

THE SECRET of success is constancy of purpose.—*Disraeli*

WISDOM is never dear, provided the article be genuine.—*Greeley*

WE ARE all born for love. It is the principle of existence, and its only end.—*Disraeli*

Do your duty and leave the rest to providence.—*Stonewall Jackson*

PHILOSOPHY becomes poetry, and science imagination, in the enthusiasm of genius.—*Disraeli*

IN PROPORTION as we perceive and embrace the truth do we become just, heroic, magnanimous, divine.—*Garrison*

I INSIST that men shall have the right to work out their lives in their own way, always allowing to others the right to work out their lives in their own way, too.—*Garibaldi*

A GREAT THING is a great book; but a greater thing than all is the talk of a great man.—*Disraeli*

TO THE MEMORY of the man, first in war, first in peace, and first in the hearts of his countrymen.—*General Lee*

I HAVE but one lamp by which my feet are guided, and that is the lamp of experience. I know no way of judging of the future but by the past.—*Patrick Henry*

BE ASHAMED to die until you have won some victory for humanity.—*Horace Mann*

BE SURE you're right, then go ahead.—*Davy Crockett*

131

From *GREAT POSSESSIONS*

By David Grayson

*"I am made immortal by apprehending
my possession of incorruptible goods."*

I HAVE just had one of the pleasant experiences of life. From time to time, these brisk winter days, I like to walk across the fields to Horace's farm. I take a new way each time and make nothing of the snow in the fields or the drifts along the fences.

"Why," asks Harriet, "do you insist on struggling through the snow when there's a good beaten road around?"

"Harriet," I said, "why should anyone take a beaten road when there are new and adventurous ways to travel?"

When I cross the fields, I never know at what moment I may come upon some strange or surprising experience, what new sights I may see, what new sounds I may hear, and I have the further great advantage of appearing unexpectedly at Horace's farm. Sometimes I enter by the cow lane, sometimes by way of the old road through the wood lot, or I appear casually, like a gust of wind, around the corner of the barn, or I let Horace discover me leaning with folded arms upon his cattle fence. I have come to love doing this, for unexpectedness in visitors, as in religion and politics, is disturbing to Horace; and as sand grits in oysters produce pearls, my unexpected appearances have more than once astonished new thoughts in Horace or yielded pearly bits of native humor.

Ever since I have known him, Horace has been rather high-and-mighty with me; but I know he enjoys my visits, for I give him always, I think, a pleasantly renewed sense of his own superiority. When he sees me, his eye lights up with the comfortable knowledge that he can plow so much better than I can, that his corn grows taller than mine, and his hens lay more eggs. He is a wonderfully practical man, is Horace; hard-headed, they call it here. And he never feels so superior, I think, as when he finds me sometimes of a Sunday or an evening walking across the fields where my land joins his, or sitting on a stone fence, or lying on my back in the pasture under a certain friendly thorn-apple tree. This he finds it difficult to understand and thinks it highly undisciplined, impractical, no doubt reprehensible.

One incident of the sort I shall never forget. It was on a June day only a year or so after I came here, and before Horace knew me as well as he does now. I had climbed the hill to look off across his own high-field pasture, where the white daisies, the purple fleabane, and the buttercups made a wild tangle of beauty among the tall herd's-grass. Light airs moved billowing across the field, bobolinks and meadow larks were singing, and all about were the old fences, each with its wild hedgerow of choke cherry, young elms, and black raspberry bushes, and beyond, across miles and miles of sunny green countryside, the mysterious blue of the ever-changing hills. It was a spot I loved then, and have loved more deeply every year since.

Horace found me sitting on the stone fence which there divides our possessions. I think he had been observing me with amusement for some time before I saw him, for when I looked around his face wore a comfortably superior, half-disdainful smile.

"David," said he, "what ye doin' here?"

"Harvesting my crops," I said.

He looked at me sharply to see if I was joking, but I was perfectly sober.

"Harvestin' yer crops?"

"Yes," I said, the fancy growing suddenly upon me, "and just now I've been taking a crop from the field you think you own."

I waved my hand to indicate his high-field pasture.

"Don't I own it?"

"No, Horace, I'm sorry to say, not all of it. To be frank with you, since I came here, I've quietly acquired an undivided interest in that land. I may as well tell you first as last. I'm like you, Horace; I'm reaching out in all directions."

I spoke in as serious a voice as I could command—the tone I use when I sell potatoes. Horace's smile wholly disappeared. A city feller like me was capable of anything!

"How's that?" he exclaimed sharply. "What do you mean? That field came down to me from my Grandfather Jamieson."

I continued to look at Horace with great calmness and gravity.

"Judging from what I now know of your title, Horace," said I, "neither your Grandfather Jamieson nor your father ever owned all of that field. And I've now acquired that part of it, in fee simple, that neither they nor you ever really had."

At this, Horace began to look seriously worried. The idea that anyone could get away from him anything that he possessed, especially without his knowledge, was terrible to him.

"What do you mean, Mr. Grayson?"

He had been calling me David, but he now returned sharply to Mister. In our country when we "Mister" a friend, something serious is about to happen. It's the signal for general mobilization.

I continued to look Horace rather coldly and severely in the eye.

"Yes," said I, "I've acquired a share in that field which I shall not soon surrender."

An unmistakable dogged look came into Horace's face, the look inherited from generations of landowning, home-defending, fighting ancestors. Horace is New England of New England.

"Yes," I said, "I have already had two or three crops from that field."

"Huh!" said Horace. "I've cut the grass and I've cut the rowen every year since you bin here. What's more, I've got the money fer it in the bank."

He tapped his fingers on the top of the wall.

"Nevertheless, Horace," said I, "I've got my crops also from that field, and a steady income too."

"What crops?"

"Well, I've just now been gathering in one of them. What do you think of the value of the fleabane, and the daisies, and the yellow five-

133

finger in that field?"

"Huh!" said Horace.

"Well, I've just been cropping them. And have you observed the wind in the grass—and those shadows along the southern wall? Aren't they valuable?"

"Huh!" said Horace.

"I've rarely seen anything more beautiful," I said, "than this field and the view across it. I'm taking that crop now, and later I shall gather in the rowen of goldenrod and aster, and the red and yellow of the maple trees—and store it all away in *my* bank—to live on next winter."

It was some time before either of us spoke again, but I could see from the corner of my eye that mighty things were going on inside of Horace. Suddenly he broke out into a big laugh and clapped his knee with his hand in a way he has.

"Is that all!" said Horace.

I think it only confirmed him in the light esteem in which he held me. Though I showed him unmeasured wealth in his own fields, ungathered crops of new enjoyment, he was unwilling to take them, but was content with hay. It is a strange thing to me, and a sad one, how many of our farmers (and be it said in a whisper, other people too) own their lands without ever really possessing them, and let the most precious crops of the good earth go to waste.

After that, for a long time, Horace loved to joke me about my crops and his. A joke with Horace is a durable possession.

"S'pose you think that's your field," he'd say.

"The best part of it," I'd return; "but you can have all I've taken, and there'll still be enough for both of us."

"You're a queer one!" he'd say, and then add sometimes dryly, "but there's one crop ye don't git, David," and he'd tap his pocket where he carries his fat, worn, leather pocketbook. "And as fer feelin's, it can't be beat."

So many people have the curious idea that the only thing the world desires enough to pay its hard money for is that which can be seen or eaten or worn. But there never was a greater mistake. While men will haggle to the penny over the price of hay, or fight for a cent more to the bushel of oats, they will turn out their very pockets for strange, intangible joys, hopes, thoughts, or for a moment of peace in a feverish world—the unknown Great Possessions.

So it was that one day, some months afterward, when we had been thus bantering each other with great good humor, I said to him, "Horace, how much did you get for your hay this year?"

"Off that one little piece," he replied, "I figger fifty-two dollars."

"Well, Horace," said I, "I have beaten you. I got more out of it this year than you did."

"Oh, I know what you mean—"

"No, Horace, you don't. This time I mean just what you do: money, cash, dollars."

"How's that, now?"

"Well, I wrote a little piece about your field, and the wind in the grass, and the hedges along the fences, and the weeds among the timothy, and the fragrance of it all in June and sold it last week—" I leaned over toward Horace and whispered behind my hand—in just

134

the way he tells me the price he gets for his pigs.

"What!" he exclaimed. Horace had long known that I was "a kind of literary feller," but his face was now a study in astonishment.

"What?"

Horace scratched his head, as he is accustomed to do when puzzled, with one finger just under the rim of his hat.

"Well, I vum!" said he. Here I have been wandering all around Horace's barn—in the snow—getting at the story I really started to tell, which probably supports Horace's conviction that I am an impractical and unsubstantial person. If I had the true business spirit, I should have gone by the beaten road from my house to Horace's, borrowed the singletree I went for, and hurried straight home. Life is so short when one is after dollars! I should not have wallowed through the snow, nor stopped at the top of the hill to look for a moment across the beautiful wintry earth—gray sky and bare wild trees and frosted farmsteads with homely smoke rising from the chimneys. I should merely have brought home a singletree—and missed the glory of life! As I reflect upon it now, I believe it took me no longer to go by the fields than by the road; and I've got the singletree as securely with me as though I had not looked upon the beauty of the eternal hills, nor reflected, as I tramped, upon the strange ways of man.

Oh, my friend, is it the settled rule of life that we are to accept nothing not expensive? It is not so settled for me. That which is freest, cheapest, seems somehow more valuable than anything I pay for; that which is given, better than that which is bought; that which passes between you and me in the glance of an eye, a touch of the hand, is better than minted money!

EVERY MAN HIS OWN NATURALIST
By DONALD CULROSS PEATTIE

YEARS AGO when I was jobless I walked into a newspaper office and asked to be allowed to write a nature column. The editor, in a welter of next Sunday's pictures, told me wearily that I might try—but he'd have to drop it if readers did not respond.

The day came when I had to have a secretary to battle with their response. I don't attribute this to any popularity of mine, but to the popularity of nature. The column was only a daily jotting of the things I saw that everybody may see. But when the readers began to help me write it, they showed me more than I could show them. They showed me that nature belongs to everyone. That nobody hungers for it like the city dweller. That the young need little help to turn their interest into this widest and healthiest field. That the mature are not too old to want to learn, and find in nature pleasures of which neither years nor adversity can deprive them.

Most of the people who wrote me had never had formal training in natural science. But they heard the beguiling whistles of the birds;

135

they glimpsed from the commuters' train window the fields filling up with wild flowers; they saw the wheeling of the unknown constellations over their suburban roofs. And they saw that human life is short; the years rush down the stream and do not return; and all about is a greater life, zestful, enchanting and deeply significant. And they wanted to learn.

My readers showed me, too, that this vast army of intelligent amateur naturalists can, with their enthusiasm and curiosity, ably assist the professional scientists. A Chicago doctor, for example, who has only a small back yard in the city, has become a leader in bird-banding. To his metropolitan station have come bobwhite and saw-whet owl, Wilson's thrush and Montana junco—ninety kinds of birds and many hundreds of individuals. Every one of these he has banded, and he finds that certain birds return year after year. Birds banded by other workers, in Canada, in South America, come to his harmless trap, and so he helps map their mysterious sky-roads.

A New York businessman, with only his Sundays free, has become an authority on that fascinating bird, the osprey. A Massachusetts judge found that his collection of flowers from all over the world was eagerly studied by scientists. A Pennsylvania mine owner, after thirty years at his desk, began to study fungi and became, when past sixty, an expert consulted by professionals. A Manhattan advertising man has just had a brilliant success with his book of insect photographs, taken in that unknown jungle that is the vacant lot next to yours.

These amateurs all won names for themselves. Some of the greatest naturalists were likewise amateurs. Fabre taught school, Audubon kept a store, Alexander Wilson was a weaver. But a big reputation is not the goal; it is an incidental award. A love and a knowledge of nature can mean in any life a happiness comparable with that which religion brings. If you want to find divinity in nature, you will perceive it there. Or if it is enough for you just to find out something you did not know before, there will be no end to your fun.

And there is no telling what you may turn up that will be new to everybody. A boy of ten who had read the greatest authority on ants in his age discovered, by watching them in his own garden, things that were not in his book. He decided to become the historian of the ants; and while engaged in important medical work during his maturity, he also made himself the greatest formicologist of his time—Auguste Forel.

The wonders of nature exist for everyone, and are found in all places. On the flat roofs of the city, unknown to the sleepers below, nest the nighthawks. To the puddles in an excavation may come flocks of sandpipers, ruddy turnstones and black-bellied plovers. The whole mystery of life is in the inky clouds of frogs' eggs in a ditch, and the riddle of instinct is to be studied in the pavement ants.

People often ask me how to learn —what to look for, and how to understand what they see. Few wish to spend much money on technical equipment, but fortunately no other hobby requires so little outlay. John Muir, when

136

asked how he prepared for an expedition, said: "I put a loaf of bread and a pound of tea in an old sack, and jump over the back fence."

However, I disagree with the logical-sounding maxim that you should study nature, not books. You should study both; a good book will unriddle nature faster than a beginner could hope to do it. As a rule, the books you need are in your public library. Probably you will soon find that some books are so good you want to own them; if so, buy those which look just a little hard, for you will soon catch up with them.

The pocket guide is very helpful in beginning field work, but is usually so general that it doesn't tell enough about the region in which you live. Your state museum or natural history survey has published local studies that are twice as interesting, and are either free or sell at a nominal price.

Every community has in it at least one person who knows a great deal about natural science. High school biology teachers, state and federal foresters and park guides can often help you to just what you need to know. And it is inspiring to see how everyone in this free-masonry of natural science is eager to share his knowledge.

Some people think of nature only as something to collect. Alas for the butterflies, birds' eggs, ferns and orchids! A collection, of course, can be scientifically valuable, but the collecting mania is not related to science or to the enjoyment of nature; the urge to have something nobody else has breaks the first rule of honest science.

Nevertheless, you can make col-lections that museums themselves may envy. Herbaria are overflowing with specimens of flowers, but are weak on fruits and seeds; a correlated collection of the fruits and seeds the local birds eat would be well worth while.

Many beginners sweat needlessly after the rare. Common objects have the widest and deepest significance, and there is never any end to what you can learn about them. Instead of the rare, go after what is new to *you;* you get the same thrill.

Accurate reports of the birds' first coming in the spring are valuable to science. Still more important will your nature diary be if it records the little-known autumn migrations, or the departure dates. The Audubon Society has amateur observers all over the country who count the birds during Christmas week and the nestings in June. Science is also on the lookout for sudden changes in the population of rabbits, field mice, squirrels, chipmunks and tree rats, which give other animals serious trouble.

Not enough has been said about the rapid rise in importance of animal motion pictures, and what the camera fan can do with films of birds and quadrupeds and reptiles living their own private lives.

The men who have traveled most widely are those who have really seen what lies close about them at home. Even a little knowledge puts tremendous new interest into every familiar scene. We behold nature as something more than a beautiful picture. It becomes peopled with friends whom we call by name. And in this newly revealed world we may walk, happy in the mastery that is ours at the price of just a little curiosity and effort.

137

NATURE LOVER'S CREED
Thomas Curtis Clark

My creed is: Stars,
　And wild birds flying,
October winds
　And hills low-lying;

The late March snows
　And April's waking,
With orchard trees
　˙Their pink wealth shaking;

A red-brown road
　From towns far leading
Thru vistas wide—
　Old cares unheeding;

A plain, sweet hut
　By meadows waiting
For hearts grown tired
　Of human hating;

Old fashioned flowers,
　And rains light-tapping;
Wide, sandy shores,
　And bright waves lapping.

So here's my creed—
　And how I love it!—
Beauty in earth,
　And God above it.

WANDERLUST
Gerald Gould

Beyond the East the sunrise, beyond the West the sea,
And East and West the wanderlust that will not let me be;
It works in me like madness, dear, to bid me say good-bye!
For the seas call and the stars call, and oh, the call of the sky!

I know not where the white road runs, nor what the blue hills are,
But man can have the sun for friend, and for his guide a star;

And there's no end of voyaging when once the voice is heard,
For the river calls and the road calls, and oh, the call of a bird!

Yonder the long horizon lies, and there by night and day
The old ships draw me home again, and the young ships sail away;
And come I may, but go I must, and if men ask you why,
You may put the blame on the stars and the sun and the white road
and the sky!

I WANT A PASTURE
Rachel Field

I want a pasture for next door neighbor;
   The sea to be just across the way.
I want to stand at my door for hours
   Talking and passing the time of day
Unhurried, as country people do
Season on season, a whole year through.

I want to give greeting to frost and sun;
   To gossip with thunder and tides and bees;
To mark the doings of wind in boughs;
   Watch apples redden on crookéd trees.
I want to hail each passing thing
That moves, fleet-footed, by fin, or wing.

I want far islands to grow familiar
   As neighbors' faces; clouds be more plain
Than granite boulder; than web of spider
   Patterned with intricate drops of rain.
I want to be wise as the oldest star,
Young as the waves and grasses are.

WINDOWS TOWARD THE GARDEN
Annabelle Merrifield

However torn by tragedy,
Or near to breaking it may be,
My heart can never harden
As long as I have eyes to see—
And windows toward the garden.

THE IDEALS

THEY can conquer who believe they can.

PATIENCE AND FORTITUDE conquer all things.

AND LET HIM GO where he will, he can only find so much beauty or worth as he carries.

FRIENDSHIP is an order of nobility; from its revelations we come more worthily into nature.

ONE OF THE ILLUSIONS of life is that the present hour is not the critical, decisive hour. Write it on your heart that every day is the best day of the year.

DON'T WASTE LIFE in doubts and fears; spend yourself on the work before you, well assured that the right performance of this hour's duties will be the best preparation for the hours or ages that follow it.

ALL I HAVE SEEN teaches me to trust the Creator for all I have not seen.

LOOK SHARPLY after your thoughts. They come unlooked for, like a new bird seen on your trees, and, if you turn to your usual task, disappear; and you shall never find that perception again; never, I say—but perhaps years, ages, and I know not what events and worlds may lie between you and its return.

WHEN A MAN lives with God, his voice shall be as sweet as the murmur of the brook and the rustle of the corn.

CONSIDERATION is the soil in which wisdom may be expected to grow, and strength be given to every up-springing plant of duty.

NOTHING is great but the inexhaustible wealth of nature.

TO MAKE knowledge valuable, you must have the cheerfulness of wisdom.

140

OF EMERSON

SELF-TRUST is the essence of heroism.

THE ONLY WAY to have a friend is to be one.

EVERY GREAT and commanding movement in the annals of the world is the triumph of enthusiasm.

THE WORLD is a divine dream, from which we may presently awake to the glories and certainties of day.

HE WHO KNOWS what sweets and virtues are in the ground, the waters, the plants, the heavens, and how to come at these enchantments, is the rich and royal man.

TO THE ATTENTIVE EYE each moment of the year has its own beauty and in the same field it beholds every hour a picture which was never seen before, and which shall never be seen again.

THE CHIEF WANT in life is somebody who shall make us do the best we can.

"WORK," says Nature to man, "in every hour, paid or unpaid; see only that thou work, and thou canst not escape the reward: whether thy work be fine or coarse, planting corn or writing epics, so only it be honest work, done to thine own approbation, it shall earn a reward to the senses as well as to the thought: no matter how often defeated, you are born to victory. The reward of a thing well done is to have done it."

NOTHING can bring you peace but yourself. Nothing can bring you peace but the triumph of principle.

A FRIEND may well be reckoned the masterpiece of Nature.

MANNERS are the happy ways of doing things.

THE BLAZING EVIDENCE of immortality is our dissatisfaction with any other solution.

141

from Bambi

By FELIX SALTEN

Bambi, a little fawn, lives in the forest with his mother, his aunt Ena, and his cousins Gobo and Faline. The Princes in this tender story are the older male deer.

*A*NOTHER NIGHT PASSED and morning brought an event. It was a cloudless morning, dewy and fresh. All the leaves on the trees and the bushes seemed suddenly to smell sweeter. The meadows sent up great clouds of perfume to the tree-tops.

"Peep!" said the tit-mice when they awoke. They said it very softly. But since it was still gray dawn they said nothing else for a while. For a time it was perfectly still. Then a crow's hoarse, rasping caw sounded far above in the sky. The crows had awakened and were visiting one another in the tree-tops. The magpie answered at once, "Shackarakshak! Did you think I was still asleep?" Then a hundred small voices started in very softly here and there. Peep! peep! tiu! Sleep and the dark were still in these sounds. And they came from far apart.

Suddenly a blackbird flew to the top of a beech. She perched way up on the topmost twig that stuck up thin against the sky and sat there watching how, far away over the trees, the night-weary, pale-gray heavens were glowing in the distant east and coming to life. Then she commenced to sing.

Her little black body seemed only a tiny dark speck at that distance. She looked like a dead leaf. But she poured out her song in a great flood of rejoicing through the whole forest. And everything began to stir. The finches warbled, the little red-throat and the goldfinch were heard. The doves rushed from place to place with a loud clapping and rustling of wings. The pheasants cackled as though their throats would burst. The noise of their wings, as they flew from their roosts to the ground, was soft but powerful. They kept uttering their metallic splintering call with its soft ensuing chuckle. Far above, the falcons cried sharply and joyously, "Yayaya!"

The sun rose.

"Diu diyu!" the yellow bird rejoiced. He flew to and fro among the branches, and his round yellow body flashed in the morning light like a winged ball of gold.

Bambi walked under the great oak on the meadow. It sparkled with dew. It smelled of grass and flowers and moist earth, and whispered of a thousand living things. Friend Hare was there and seemed to be thinking over something important. A haughty pheasant strutted slowly by, nibbling at the grass seeds and peering cautiously in all directions. The dark metallic blue on his neck gleamed in the sun.

One of the Princes was standing

142

close to Bambi. Bambi had never seen any of the fathers so close before. The stag was standing right in front of him next to the hazel bush and was somewhat hidden by the branches. Bambi did not move. He wanted the Prince to come out completely and was wondering whether he dared speak to him. He wanted to ask his mother and looked around for her. But his mother had already gone away and was standing some distance off, beside Aunt Ena. At the same time Gobo and Faline came running out of the woods. Bambi was still thinking it over without stirring. If he went up to his mother and the others now he would have to pass by the Prince. He felt as if he couldn't do it.

"O well," he thought, "I don't have to ask my mother first. The old Prince spoke to me and I didn't tell mother anything about it. I'll say, 'Good-morning, Prince.' He can't be offended at that. But if he does get angry I'll run away fast." Bambi struggled with his resolve which began to waver again.

Presently the Prince walked out from behind the hazel bush onto the meadow.

"Now," thought Bambi.

Then there was a crash like thunder.

Bambi shrank together and didn't know what had happened. He saw the Prince leap into the air under his very nose and watched him rush past him into the forest with one great bound.

Bambi looked around in a daze. The thunder still vibrated. He saw how his mother and Aunt Ena, Gobo and Faline fled into the woods. He saw how Friend Hare scurried away like mad. He saw

the pheasant running with his neck outstretched. He noticed that the forest grew suddenly still. He started and sprang into the thicket. He had made only a few bounds when he saw the Prince lying on the ground in front of him, motionless. Bambi stopped horrified, not understanding what it meant. The Prince lay bleeding from a great wound in his shoulder. He was dead.

"Don't stop!" a voice beside commanded. It was his mother who rushed past at full gallop. "Run," she cried. "Run as fast as you can!" She did not slow up, but raced ahead, and her command brought Bambi after her. He ran with all his might.

"What is it, Mother," he asked. "What is it, Mother?"

His mother answered between gasps, "It—was— He!"

Bambi shuddered and they ran on. At last they stopped for lack of breath.

"What did you say? Tell me, what it was you said?" a soft voice called down from overhead. Bambi looked up. The squirrel came chattering through the branches.

"I ran the whole way with you," he cried. "It was dreadful."

"Were you there?" asked the mother.

"Of course I was there," the squirrel replied. "I am still trembling in every limb." He sat erect, balancing with his splendid tail, displaying his small white chest, and holding his forepaws protestingly against his body. "I'm beside myself with excitement," he said.

"I'm quite weak from fright myself," said the mother. "I don't understand it. Not one of us saw a thing."

142

"Is that so?" the squirrel said pettishly. "I saw Him long before." "So did I," another voice cried. It was the magpie. She flew past and settled on a branch. "So did I," came a croak from above. It was the jay who was sitting on an ash.

A couple of crows in the tree-tops cawed harshly, "We saw Him, too."

They all sat around talking importantly. They were unusually excited and seemed to be full of anger and fear.

"Whom?" Bambi thought. "Whom did they see?"

"I tried my best," the squirrel was saying, pressing his forepaws protestingly against his heart. "I tried my best to warn the poor Prince."

"And I," the jay rasped. "How often did I scream? But he didn't care to hear me."

"He didn't hear me either," the magpie croaked. "I called him at least ten times. I wanted to fly right past him, for, thought I, he hasn't heard me yet; I'll fly to the hazel bush where he's standing. He can't help hearing me there. But at that minute it happened."

"My voice is probably louder than yours, and I warned him as well as I could," the crow said in an impudent tone. "But gentlemen of that stamp pay little attention to the likes of us."

"Much too little, really," the squirrel agreed.

"Well, we did what we could," said the magpie. "We're certainly not to blame when an accident happens."

"Such a handsome Prince," the squirrel lamented. "And in the very prime of life."

"Akh!" croaked the jay. "It would have been better for him if he hadn't been so proud and had paid more attention to us."

"He certainly wasn't proud."

"No more so than the other Princes of his family," the magpie put in.

"Just plain stupid," sneered the jay.

"You're stupid yourself," the crow cried down from over head. "Don't you talk about stupidity. The whole forest knows how stupid you are."

"I!" replied the jay, stiff with astonishment. "Nobody can accuse me of being stupid. I may be forgetful but I'm certainly not stupid."

"O just as you please," said the crow solemnly. "Forget what I said to you but remember that the Prince did not die because he was proud or stupid, but because no one can escape Him."

"Akh!" croaked the jay. "I don't like that kind of talk." He flew away.

The crow went on, "He has already outwitted many of my family. He kills what He wants. Nothing can help us."

"You have to be on your guard against Him," the magpie broke in.

"You certainly do," said the crow sadly. "Good-by." He flew off, his family accompanying him.

Bambi looked around. His mother was no longer there.

"What are they talking about now?" thought Bambi. "I can't understand what they are talking about. Who is this 'He' they talk about? That was He, too, that I saw in the bushes, but He didn't kill me."

Bambi thought of the Prince lying in front of him with his bloody mangled shoulder. He was

144

dead now. Bambi walked along. The forest sang again with a thousand voices, the sun pierced the tree-tops with its broad rays. There was light everywhere. The leaves began to smell. Far above the falcons called, close at hand a woodpecker hammered as if nothing had happened. Bambi was not happy. He felt himself threatened by something dark. He did not understand how the others could be so carefree and happy while life was so difficult and dangerous. Then the desire seized him to go deeper and deeper into the woods. They lured him into their depths. He wanted to find some hiding place where, shielded on all sides by impenetrable thickets, he could never be seen. He never wanted to go to the meadow again.

Something moved very softly in the bushes. Bambi drew back violently. The old stag was standing in front of him.

Bambi trembled. He wanted to run away, but he controlled himself and remained. The old stag looked at him with his great deep eyes and asked, "Were you out there before?"

"Yes," Bambi said softly. His heart was pounding in his throat.

"Where is your mother?" asked the stag.

Bambi answered still very softly, "I don't know."

The old stag kept gazing at him. "And still you're not calling for her?" he said.

Bambi looked into the noble, iron-gray face, looked at the stag's antlers and suddenly felt full of courage. "I can stay by myself, too," he said.

The old stag considered him for a while; then he asked gently, "Aren't you the little one that was crying for his mother not long ago?"

Bambi was somewhat embarrassed, but his courage held. "Yes I am," he confessed.

The old stag looked at him in silence and it seemed to Bambi as if those deep eyes gazed still more mildly. "You scolded me then, Prince," he cried excitedly, "because I was afraid of being left alone. Since then I haven't been."

The stag looked at Bambi appraisingly and smiled a very slight, hardly noticeable smile. Bambi noticed it however. "Noble Prince," he asked confidently, "what has happened? I don't understand it. Who is this 'He' they are all talking about?" He stopped, terrified by the dark glance that bade him be silent.

Another pause ensued. The old stag was gazing past Bambi into the distance. Then he said slowly, "Listen, smell and see for yourself. Find out for yourself." He lifted his antlered head still higher. "Farewell," he said, nothing else. Then he vanished.

Bambi stood transfixed and wanted to cry. But that farewell still rang in his ears and sustained him. Farewell, the old stag had said, so he couldn't have been angry.

Bambi felt himself thrill with pride, felt inspired with a deep earnestness. Yes, life was difficult and full of danger. But come what might he would learn to bear it all.

He walked slowly deeper into the forest.

BEYOND ELECTRONS

ADELAIDE LOVE

The new believers of our age are they,
The men of science, who have come to learn
There is a will that points the cosmic ray,
A power that directs what they discern
In atmosphere, in star and wave and sod;
Beyond electrons they discover—God.

From microscope and tube evolves a faith
Of modern days, sustaining ancient creeds;
It is the scientist who makes a wraith
Of doubt, and finds a God behind His deeds.

THE NEED FOR GOD IN AN AGE OF SCIENCE*

By ARTHUR H. COMPTON

... THE TECHNOLOGY based on science has concentrated its attention upon finding more and better means of living—more abundant and more varied food, more comfortable homes, better clothing, faster means of transportation and of communication. The technical aspects of these problems are being rapidly solved. If not all men enjoy the fruits of these efforts, it is not from any technological failure but because of the unsatisfactory state of our social organization. The means of life are certainly improved. The great problem now facing civilized man is that of learning how to live a satisfying life in the civilization that he has built. This is a question for which our political and economic sages have done as little in finding an answer

as have their technological brothers. ...

Similarly, it is the content of our lives that determines their value. If we limit ourselves to supplying the means of living, in what way have we placed ourselves above the cattle that graze the fields? Cattle can live in comfort. Their every need is amply supplied. Is it not when one exercises his reason, his love of beauty, his desire for friendship, his selection of the good from that which is not so good, that he earns the right to call himself a man? I should be inclined to claim that the person who limits his interests to the means of living without consideration of the content or meaning of his life is defeating God's great purpose when he brought into existence a creature with the intelligence and godlike powers that are found in man. It is in living wisely and fully that one's soul grows. One of life's strange paradoxes is that those who

*Reprinted from THE HUMAN MEANING OF SCIENCE by Arthur H. Compton by permission of THE UNIVERSITY OF NORTH CAROLINA PRESS. Copyright, 1940, by THE UNIVERSITY OF NORTH CAROLINA PRESS.

146

spend great effort in securing the means of living are very apt to lose their appreciation of the values of life. "For what shall it profit a man, if he gain the whole world, and lose his own soul?"

WHEN I HEARD THE LEARN'D ASTRONOMER
WALT WHITMAN

When I heard the learn'd astronomer,
When the proofs, the figures, were ranged in columns before me,
When I was shown the charts and diagrams, to add, divide, and measure them,
When I, sitting, heard the astronomer where he lectured with much applause in the lecture-room,
How soon, unaccountable, I became tired and sick,
Till rising and gliding out I wander'd off by myself
In the mystical moist night-air, and from time to time,
Look'd up in perfect silence at the stars.

From LET US HAVE FAITH
By HELEN KELLER

... FAITH IS a brave look of the soul for new paths to life. It is not dogma. It is a white fire of enthusiasm. Even in its perverted forms it is the strongest motive force we have. In its highest forms it is the kindler of all nobility. It is not confined to any church or institution. Creeds are bodies and die. Faith is immortal.

How vital it is—this hunger that leads people to look for truth in the Bible, the Vedas and the Koran! It is faith—marshaling the most useful and ennobling ideas for all men —that the loftiest thinkers in every age and country have striven and are still striving to impart.

In capturing faith's pure passion and enthusiasm they have abandoned superficial associations with time, number and size. Wherever a courageous soul rises man is invincible. Faith sanctifies any place, renders its climate bracing to weakness, its air luminous to doubt-dimmed eyes. Continents sink; empires disintegrate; but faith and the universe of heroic minds abide forever.

Faith transmutes circumstance, time, condition and mood into vitality. This is why Christ's teaching was momentously effective nineteen centuries ago and still is among those who truly respond to it. Society was regenerated by a race of slaves in the early days of Christianity. To all practical intents and purposes they were chattels and beasts of burden, with eyes that saw not, ears that heard not and wills that were paralyzed by tyranny. Nevertheless, at Jesus' advent

147

they walked erect and whole-hearted and went straight to the fact that life, the Kingdom of God, is within us. From confidence in God they distilled confidence in their fellow men. They kept their souls unmanacled, their minds open to visions and their bodies alert for fulfilment. That was Jesus' miracle for all ages.

Over against a society marked by caste and brute supremacy, throttled by ignorance except for the amazing intellectual activity in a few cities, faith shouldered the issues of life which must be shouldered today. "Bear ye one another's burdens," faith declared, and it went further. It left an inner light as a trust for all human beings. It began remolding the world according to hitherto untried ideas. It made the first purposeful scrutiny of the profundities of the collective soul, and Divine Modesty cried, "Ye shall do mightier things than these."

In days like these to believe that Good is the dominant principle is an ordeal as by fire, but for me it would be much harder to surrender that faith. All too well do I realize that the bitterest fears of modern thinkers did not envisage the ruin into which we are now being hurled. So much more then is faith imperative to pour healing upon blinding anguish and deafening fear. Heaven and earth, it has been affirmed, are mirages rising from the deserts of man's despair. Picturesque indeed would despair be if it could perform such a miracle. But to everyone with faith his own world is real, no matter what it may appear to be to others, and happiness — its fundamental meaning is a free breathing of the soul—has also a share in the mirage. From the delight of young animals in simply being alive, from children at play, from youth risking all for love, from the triumphs that follow long effort—from all these, faith gathers materials for her Temple to form a bulwark against the storm.

I believe in immortality as instinctively as the fruit tree in the seed and quite as growingly, but that is not faith, except as it shines among its aggregate of nerving truths. Without immortality faith would still count it a magnificent vision to look upon God's face a brief while, to hold a beloved mortal's hand, to receive a child's kiss and look through a glass millions of miles to other universes.

. . . Faith . . . has made my limitations ineffectual if not trivial. And since I have the privilege of doing it, I am proud to bear this testimony to the power of faith. If I had not faith to think with and suffer with I could not bear the incessant wrenching at my mind caused by the revival of barbarism and intolerance, the mutilations of mankind by war and persecution and tyranny. Faith is the red blood that braces when all else fails.

. . . Through faith alone can I fulfil the two senses I lack—sight and hearing—and build out from my imperfect speech. Faith has the ingenuity to bring me insight, and I know where I am going. . . .

All men are limited in their service when they fight alone. This is especially true of the severely handicapped, but when they and their normal fellow creatures help one another they have a sure defense, a conquering strength—and it is faith. . . .

148

MY AIN COUNTRIE
MARY DEMAREST

I am far frae my hame an' I'm weary aftenwhiles
For the langed-for hame-bringin' an' my Faither's welcome smiles;
An' I'll ne'er be fu' content until mine een do see
The gowden gates o' heaven an' my ain countrie.

The earth is fleck'd wi' flowers, mony tinted fresh an' gay,
The birdies warble blithely for my Faither made them sae;
But these sichts an' these soun's will as naething be to me,
When I hear the angels singin' in my ain countrie.

I've His gude word o' promise that some gladsome day the King
To His ain royal palace His banished hame will bring;
Wi' een an' wi' hert rinnin' ower, we shall see
The King in His beauty, in oor ain countrie.

My sins hae been mony an' my sorrows hae been sair
But there they'll never vex me nor be remembered mair;
His bluid has made me white,—an' His han' shall dry my e'e
When he brings me hame at last to my ain countrie.

Sae little noo I ken o' yon blessed bonnie place,
I only ken its hame, whaur we shall see His face.
It would surely be eneuch for ever mair to be
In the glory o' His presence in oor ain countrie.

Like a bairn to his mither, a wee birdie to its nest
I wad fain be gangin' noo, unto my Savior's breast;
For He gathers in His bosom witless, worthless lambs like me
An' carries them Himsel', to His ain countrie.

He is faithfu' that hath promised, an' He'll surely come again.
He'll keep His tryst wi' me, at what hour I dinna ken;
But He bids me still to wait, an' ready aye to be
To gang at ony moment to my ain countrie.

Sae I'm watchin' aye an' singin' o' my hame as I wait,
For the soun'ing o' His footfa' this side the gowden gate
God gie His grace to ilka ane wha' listens noo to me,
That we a' may gang in gladness to oor ain countrie.

CONQUER A MAN who never gives by gifts;
Subdue untruthful men by truthfulness;
Vanquish an angry man by gentleness;
And overcome the evil man by goodness.
—*The Maha-Bharata*

ALL HIGHER MOTIVES, ideals, conceptions, sentiments in a man are of no account if they do not come forward to strengthen him for the better discharge of the duties which devolve upon him in the ordinary affairs of life.—*Beecher*

JUDGE NOT thy friend until thou standest in his place.—*Rabbi Hillel*

WHEN I consider what some books have done for the world, and what they are doing, how they keep up our hope, awaken new courage and faith, soothe pain, give an ideal life to those whose hours are cold and hard, bind together distant ages and foreign lands, create new worlds of beauty, bring down truth from heaven; I give eternal blessings for this gift, and thank God for books.—*James Freeman Clarke*

MUSIC is the art of the prophets, the only art that can *calm* the agitations of the soul: it is one of the most magnificent and delightful presents God has given us.—*Luther*

TO THE great tree-loving fraternity we belong. We love trees with universal and unfeigned love, and all things that do grow under them or around them —the whole leaf and root tribe. Not alone when they are in their glory, but in whatever state they are—in leaf, or rimed with frost, or powdered with snow, or crystal-sheathed in ice, or in severe outline stripped and bare against a November sky—we love them.—*Beecher*

A MAN would do nothing, if he waited until he could do it so well that no one would find fault with what he has done.—*Cardinal Newman*

IF THERE'S A JOB to be done, I always ask the busiest man in my parish to take it on and it gets done.—*Beecher*

THE GREATEST ARCHITECT and the one most needed is hope.—*Beecher*

150

RELIGIOUS THINKERS

SINCERITY AND TRUTH are the basis of every virtue.—*Confucius*

A BOOK is a garden, an orchard, a storehouse, a party, a company by the way, a counsellor, a multitude of counsellors.—*Beecher*

A MOTHER HAS, perhaps, the hardest earthly lot; and yet no mother worthy of the name ever gave herself thoroughly for her child who did not feel that, after all, she reaped what she had sown.—*Beecher*

CHRIST is risen! There is life, therefore, after death! His resurrection is the symbol and pledge of universal resurrection!—*Beecher*

IT IS TRUE that we shall not be able to reach perfection, but in our struggle toward it we shall strengthen our characters and give stability to our ideas, so that, whilst ever advancing calmly in the same direction, we shall be rendered capable of applying the faculties with which we have been gifted to the best possible account.—*Confucius*

BAD will be the day for every man when he becomes absolutely contented with the life that he is living, with the thoughts that he is thinking, with the deeds that he is doing, when there is not forever beating at the doors of his soul some great desire to do something larger, which he knows that he was meant and made to do because he is still, in spite of all, the child of God.—*Phillips Brooks*

IF I had but two loaves of bread, I would sell one and buy hyacinths, for they would feed my soul.—*The Koran*

THE GREAT EASTER TRUTH is not that we are to live newly after death—that is not the great thing—but that we are to be new here and now by the power of the resurrection; not so much that we are to live forever as that we are to, and may, live nobly now because we are to live forever.—*Phillips Brooks*

THERE IS in stillness oft a magic power
To calm the breast when struggling passions lower,
Touched by its influence, in the soul arise
Diviner feelings, kindred with the skies.
            —*Cardinal Newman*

151

A Retrieved Reformation

By O. HENRY

A GUARD CAME to the prison shoe-shop, where Jimmy Valentine was assiduously stitching uppers, and escorted him to the front office. There the warden handed Jimmy his pardon, which had been signed that morning by the governor. Jimmy took it in a tired kind of way. He had served nearly ten months of a four-year sentence. He had expected to stay only about three months, at the longest. When a man with as many friends on the outside as Jimmy Valentine had is received in the "stir" it is hardly worth while to cut his hair.

"Now, Valentine," said the warden, "you'll go out in the morning. Brace up, and make a man of yourself. You're not a bad fellow at heart. Stop cracking safes, and live straight."

"Me?" said Jimmy, in surprise. "Why, I never cracked a safe in my life."

"Oh, no," laughed the warden. "Of course not. Let's see, now. How was it you happened to get sent up on that Springfield job? Was it because you wouldn't prove an alibi for fear of compromising somebody in extremely high-toned society? Or was it simply a case of a mean old jury that had it in for you? It's always one or the other with you innocent victims."

"Me?" said Jimmy, still blankly virtuous. "Why, warden, I never was in Springfield in my life!"

"Take him back, Cronin," smiled the warden, "and fix him up with outgoing clothes. Unlock him at seven in the morning, and let him come to the bull-pen. Better think over my advice, Valentine."

At a quarter past seven on the next morning Jimmy stood in the warden's outer office. He had on a suit of the villainously fitting, ready-made clothes and a pair of the stiff, squeaky shoes that the state furnishes to its discharged compulsory guests.

The clerk handed him a railroad ticket and a five-dollar bill with which the law expected him to rehabilitate himself into good citizenship and prosperity. The warden gave him a cigar, and shook hands. Valentine, 9762, was chronicled on the books "Pardoned by Governor," and Mr. James Valentine walked out into the sunshine.

Disregarding the song of the birds, the waving green trees, and the smell of the flowers, Jimmy headed straight for a restaurant. There he tasted the first sweet joys of liberty in the shape of a broiled chicken and a bottle of white wine —followed by a cigar a grade better than the one the warden had given him. From there he proceeded leisurely to the depot. He tossed a quarter into the hat of a blind man sitting by the door, and boarded his train. Three hours set him down in a little town near the state line. He went to the café of one Mike Dolan and shook hands with Mike, who was alone behind the bar.

152

"Sorry we couldn't make it sooner, Jimmy, me boy," said Mike. "But we had that protest from Springfield to buck against, and the governor nearly balked. Feeling all right?"

"Fine," said Jimmy. "Got my key?"

He got his key and went upstairs, unlocking the door of a room at the rear. Everything was just as he had left it. There on the floor was still Ben Price's collar-button that had been torn from that eminent detective's shirtband when they had overpowered Jimmy to arrest him.

Pulling out from the wall a folding-bed, Jimmy slid back a panel in the wall and dragged out a dust-covered suit case. He opened this and gazed fondly at the finest set of burglar's tools in the East. It was a complete set, made of specially tempered steel, the latest designs in drills, punches, braces and bits, jimmies, clamps, and augers, with two or three novelties, invented by Jimmy himself, in which he took pride. Over nine hundred dollars they had cost him to have made at ———, a place where they make such things for the profession.

In half an hour Jimmy went downstairs and through the café. He was now dressed in tasteful and well-fitting clothes, and carried his dusted and cleaned suit case in his hand.

"Got anything on?" asked Mike Dolan, genially.

"Me?" said Jimmy, in a puzzled tone. "I don't understand. I'm representing the New York Amalgamated Short Snap Biscuit Cracker and Frazzled Wheat Company."

This statement delighted Mike to such an extent that Jimmy had to take a seltzer-and-milk on the spot. He never touched "hard" drinks.

A week after the release of Valentine, 9762, there was a neat job of safe-burglary done in Richmond, Indiana, with no clue to the author. A scant eight hundred dollars was all that was secured. Two weeks after that a patented, improved, burglar-proof safe in Logansport was opened like a cheese to the tune of fifteen hundred dollars, currency; securities and silver untouched. That began to interest the rogue-catchers. Then an old-fashioned bank-safe in Jefferson City became active and threw out of its crater an eruption of bank-notes amounting to five thousand dollars. The losses were now high enough to bring the matter up into Ben Price's class of work. By comparing notes, a remarkable similarity in the methods of the burglaries was noticed. Ben Price investigated the scenes of the robberies, and was heard to remark:

"That's Dandy Jim Valentine's autograph. He's resumed business. Look at that combination knob—jerked out as easy as pulling up a radish in wet weather. He's got the only clamps that can do it. And look how clean those tumblers were punched out! Jimmy never has to drill but one hole. Yes, I guess I want Mr. Valentine. He'll do his bit next time without any short-time or clemency foolishness."

Ben Price knew Jimmy's habits. He had learned them while working up the Springfield case. Long jumps, quick get-aways, no confederates, and a taste for good society—these ways had helped Mr. Valentine to become noted as a successful dodger of retribution. It was given out that Ben Price had taken

153

up the trail of the elusive cracksman, and other people with burglar-proof safes felt more at ease.

One afternoon Jimmy Valentine and his suit case climbed out of the mail-hack in Elmore, a little town five miles off the railroad down in the blackjack country of Arkansas. Jimmy, looking like an athletic young senior just home from college, went down the board sidewalk toward the hotel.

A young lady crossed the street, passed him at the corner and entered a door over which was the sign "The Elmore Bank." Jimmy Valentine looked into her eyes, forgot what he was, and became another man. She lowered her eyes and coloured slightly. Young men of Jimmy's style and looks were scarce in Elmore.

Jimmy collared a boy that was loafing on the steps of the bank as if he were one of the stockholders, and began to ask him questions about the town, feeding him dimes at intervals. By and by the young lady came out, looking royally unconscious of the young man with the suit case, and went her way.

"Isn't that young lady Miss Polly Simpson?" asked Jimmy, with specious guile.

"Naw," said the boy. "She's Annabel Adams. Her pa owns this bank. What'd you come to Elmore for? Is that a gold watch chain? I'm going to get a bulldog. Got any more dimes?"

Jimmy went to the Planters' Hotel, registered as Ralph D. Spencer, and engaged a room. He leaned on the desk and declared his platform to the clerk. He said he had come to Elmore to look for a location to go into business. How was the shoe business, now, in the town? He had thought of the shoe business. Was there an opening?

The clerk was impressed by the clothes and manner of Jimmy. He, himself, was something of a pattern of fashion to the thinly gilded youth of Elmore, but he now perceived his shortcomings. While trying to figure out Jimmy's manner of tying his four-in-hand he cordially gave information.

Yes, there ought to be a good opening in the shoe line. There wasn't an exclusive shoe store in the place. The dry-goods and general stores handled them. Business in all lines was fairly good. Hoped Mr. Spencer would decide to locate in Elmore. He would find it a pleasant town to live in, and the people very sociable.

Mr. Spencer thought he would stop over in the town a few days and look over the situation. No, the clerk needn't call the boy. He would carry up his suit case, himself; it was rather heavy.

Mr. Ralph Spencer, the phoenix that arose from Jimmy Valentine's ashes—ashes left by the flame of a sudden and alterative attack of love—remained in Elmore, and prospered. He opened a shoe store and secured a good run of trade.

Socially he was also a success, and made many friends. And he accomplished the wish of his heart. He met Miss Annabel Adams, and became more and more captivated by her charms.

At the end of a year the situation of Mr. Ralph Spencer was this: he had won the respect of the community, his shoe store was flourishing, and he and Annabel were engaged to be married in two weeks. Mr. Adams, the typical, plodding, country banker, approved of Spen-

154

cer. Annabel's pride in him almost equalled her affection. He was as much at home in the family of Mr. Adams and that of Annabel's married sister as if he were already a member.

One day Jimmy sat down in his room and wrote this letter, which he mailed to the safe address of one of his old friends in St. Louis:

Dear Old Pal:

I want you to be at Sullivan's place, in Little Rock, next Wednesday night, at nine o'clock. I want you to wind up some little matters for me. And, also, I want to make you a present of my kit of tools. I know you'll be glad to get them— you couldn't duplicate the lot for a thousand dollars. Say, Billy, I've quit the old business—a year ago. I've got a nice store. I'm making an honest living, and I'm going to marry the finest girl on earth two weeks from now. It's the only life, Billy—the straight one. I wouldn't touch a dollar of another man's money now for a million. After I get married I'm going to sell out and go West, where there won't be so much danger of having old scores brought up against me. I tell you, Billy, she's an angel. She believes in me; and I wouldn't do another crooked thing for the whole world. Be sure to be at Sully's, for I must see you. I'll bring along the tools with me.

Your old friend,
Jimmy.

On the Monday night after Jimmy wrote this letter, Ben Price jogged unobtrusively into Elmore in a livery buggy. He lounged about town in his quiet way until he found out what he wanted to know. From the drug store across the street from Spencer's shoe store he got a good look at Ralph D. Spencer.

"Going to marry the banker's daughter are you, Jimmy?" said Ben to himself, softly. "Well, I don't know!"

The next morning Jimmy took breakfast at the Adamses. He was going to Little Rock that day to order his wedding-suit and buy something nice for Annabel. That would be the first time he had left town since he came to Elmore. It had been more than a year now since those last professional "jobs," and he thought he could safely venture out.

After breakfast quite a family party went downtown together— Mr. Adams, Annabel, Jim, and Annabel's married sister with her two little girls, aged five and nine. They came by the hotel where Jimmy still boarded, and he ran up to his room and brought along his suit case. Then they went on to the bank. There stood Jimmy's horse and buggy and Dolph Gibson, who was going to drive him over to the railroad station.

All went inside the high, carved oak railings into the banking-room —Jimmy included, for Mr. Adams's future son-in-law was welcome anywhere. The clerks were pleased to be greeted by the good-looking, agreeable young man who was going to marry Miss Annabel. Jimmy set his suit case down. Annabel, whose heart was bubbling with happiness and lively youth, put on Jimmy's hat, and picked up the suit case. "Wouldn't I make a nice drummer?" said Annabel. "My! Ralph, how heavy it is! Feels like it was full of gold bricks."

155

"Lot of nickel-plated shoe horns in there," said Jimmy coolly, "that I'm going to return. Thought I'd save express charges by taking them up. I'm getting awfully economical."

The Elmore Bank had just put in a new safe and vault. Mr. Adams was very proud of it, and insisted on an inspection by everyone. The vault was a small one, but it had a new, patented door. It fastened with three solid steel bolts thrown simultaneously with a single handle, and had a time-lock. Mr. Adams beamingly explained its workings to Mr. Spencer, who showed a courteous but not too intelligent interest. The two children, May and Agatha, were delighted by the shining metal and funny clock and knobs.

While they were thus engaged Ben Price sauntered in and leaned on his elbow, looking casually inside between the railings. He told the teller that he didn't want anything; he was just waiting for a man he knew.

Suddenly there was a scream or two from the women, and a commotion. Unperceived by the elders, May, the nine-year-old girl, in a spirit of play, had shut Agatha in the vault. She had then shot the bolts and turned the knob of the combination as she had seen Mr. Adams do.

The old banker sprang to the handle and tugged at it for a moment. "The door can't be opened," he groaned. "The clock hasn't been wound nor the combination set."

Agatha's mother screamed again, hysterically.

"Hush!" said Mr. Adams, raising his trembling hand. "All be quiet for a moment. Agatha!" he called as loudly as he could. "Listen to me." During the following silence they could just hear the faint sound of the child wildly shrieking in the dark vault in a panic of terror.

"My precious darling!" wailed the mother. "She will die of fright! Open the door! Oh, break it open! Can't you men do something?"

"There isn't a man nearer than Little Rock who can open that door," said Mr. Adams, in a shaky voice. "My God! Spencer, what shall we do? That child—she can't stand it long in there. There isn't enough air, and, besides, she'll go into convulsions from fright."

Agatha's mother, frantic now, beat the door of the vault with her hands. Somebody wildly suggested dynamite. Annabel turned to Jimmy, her large eyes full of anguish, but not yet despairing. To a woman nothing seems quite impossible to the powers of the man she worships.

"Can't you do something, Ralph —try, won't you?"

He looked at her with a queer, soft smile on his lips and in his keen eyes.

"Annabel," he said, "give me that rose you are wearing."

Hardly believing that she heard him aright, she unpinned the bud from the bosom of her dress, and placed it in his hand. Jimmy stuffed it into his vest-pocket, threw off his coat and pulled up his shirt-sleeves. With that act Ralph D. Spencer passed away and Jimmy Valentine took his place.

"Get away from the door, all of you," he commanded, shortly.

He set his suit case on the table, and opened it out flat. From that time on he seemed to be unconscious of the presence of anyone

156

else. He laid out the shining, queer implements swiftly and orderly, whistling softly to himself as he always did when at work. In a deep silence and immovable, the others watched him as if under a spell. In a minute Jimmy's pet drill was biting smoothly into the steel door. In ten minutes—breaking his own burglarious record—he threw back the bolts and opened the door.

Agatha, almost collapsed, but safe, was gathered into her mother's arms.

Jimmy Valentine put on his coat, and walked outside the railings toward the front door. As he went he thought he heard a far-away voice that he once knew call "Ralph!" But he never hesitated.

At the door a big man stood somewhat in his way.

"Hello, Ben!" said Jimmy, still with his strange smile. "Got around at last, have you? Well, let's go. I don't know that it makes much difference, now."

And then Ben Price acted rather strangely.

"Guess you're mistaken, Mr. Spencer," he said. "Don't believe I recognize you. Your buggy's waiting for you."

And Ben Price turned and strolled down the street.

FATHER DUFFY

By ALEXANDER WOOLLCOTT

THEY BURIED Father Duffy from St. Patrick's at the end of June in 1932. The huge cathedral might as well have been a tiny chapel for all it could hope to hold those of us who wanted to say good-bye to him. As I waited in the cool, candle-lit dusk of the church for the procession to make its way up the sunny avenue, all around me lips were moving in prayer and gnarled fingers were telling their rosaries. But even the heathen could at least count over their hours with him. There were many of us there, outsiders who, without belonging to his outfit, had nevertheless been attached to him for rations—of the spirit. One had only to stop for a moment and speak to him on the street to go on one's way immensely set up, reassured that there might be a good deal, after all, to this institution called the human race. While we waited, my own wry thoughts jumped back to that desperate October in 1918 when his regiment, the old 69th of New York, was cut to ribbons in the Argonne. Especially I recalled the black day when Colonel Donovan was carried out of the battle on a blanket—Wild Bill, who was the very apple of the Padre's eye. Father Duffy had always scolded him for his gaudy recklessness, and there he was at last with his underpinnings shot from under him. As they carried him into the dressing-station he had just strength enough left to shake a defiant fist. "Ah there, Father," he said, "you thought you'd have the pleasure òf burying me!" Father Duffy shook a fist in reply. "And I will yet," he said. But it was not to be that way. For here, fourteen years later, was Wild Bill and a thousand others of the old regiment coming up the avenue to bury Father Duffy.

157

One by one there came back to me all the times our paths had crossed in France and on the Rhine. He would always have tall tales to tell of his Irish fighters, who, with death all around them, heard only the grace of God purring in their hearts. It delighted him that they spoke of the Ourcq as the O'Rourke, and he enjoyed their wonderment at the French presumption in dignifying so measly a creek by calling it a river. He loved the story of one wounded soldier who waved aside a proffered canteen. "Give it to the Ourcq. It needs it more than I do." And he loved all stories wherein the uppity were discomfited. On the Rhine he relished the spectacle of Pershing vainly trying to unbend a bit and play the little father to his troops. The Commander-in-Chief paused before one Irish doughboy who had three wound stripes on his arm. "Well, my lad," asked the great man in benevolent tones, "and where did you get those?" "From the supply sergeant, Sir," the hero answered, and Father Duffy grinned from ear to ear.

Most often he would talk not of France and the war at all, but of New York. He liked nothing better than to sit in a shell-hole with Clancey and Callahan and Kerrigan and talk about New York. I have stood beside him ankle-deep in the Argonne mud and, above the noise of the rain pattering on our helmets, heard him speculate about the gleam of Fifth Avenue in the October sunshine and say how he would like to see once more that grand actress who called herself Laurette Taylor, but who, mind you, was born a Cooney. And for him the most electric moment in

all the war came on a night of June moonlight in Lorraine when the troops of the old 69th discovered that the shiny new outfit which was relieving them was also from New York. The war had picked them both up by the scruff of the neck, carried them across the world, and dropped them in the French mud, and here they were passing each other on the road. At that time the Rainbow had been in the line only a few weeks, and the Baccarat Sector was a tranquil one. The real slaughter of July and October lay ahead of them but at least they could feel battle-scarred and scornful when compared with these green boys of the 77th, fresh from the transports. Being themselves volunteers, they jeered at the newcomers as conscripts, who retorted, to their surprise, by calling them draft dodgers. There was some excitement as old neighbors would identify each other in the moonlight, and one unforgettable moment when Father Duffy saw two brothers meet. In their emotion they could only take pokes at each other and swear enormously. Then, lest all these ructions draw the attention of the enemy artillery to this relief, order was somehow restored and the march went on, mingling prohibited, speech of any kind forbidden. So these passing regiments just hummed to each other very softly in the darkness. "Give my regards to Broadway." The rhythm staccato, the words unnecessary. "Remember me to Herald Square." The tune said the words for all of them. "Tell all the boys in Forty-second Street that I will soon be there." In the distance the sound grew fainter and fainter. Father Duffy had a lump in his throat.

158

For he was the great New Yorker. Born in Canada, Irish as Irish, schooled in Maynooth, he was surely the first citizen of our town. This city is too large for most of us. But not for Father Duffy. Not too large, I mean, for him to invest it with the homeliness of a neighborhood. When he walked down the street—any street—he was like a *curé* striding through his own village. Everyone knew him. I have walked beside him and thought I had never before seen so many *pleased* faces. The beaming cop would stop all traffic to make a path from curb to curb for Father Duffy. Both the proud-stomached banker who stopped to speak with him on the corner and the checkroom boy who took his hat at the restaurant would grin transcendently at the sight of him. He would call them both by their first names, and you could see how proud they were on that account. Father Duffy was of such dimensions that he made New York into a small town.

No wonder all the sidewalk space as far as one could see was needed for the overflow at his funeral. To my notion, the mute multitude in the June sunlight made the more impressive congregation. To alien ears the Latin passages of the Mass seem as automatic and as passionless as the multiplication table, and at least those who could not get in missed the harangue delivered from the pulpit with the vocal technique of a train announcer. One woman I know saw an unused bit of pavement and asked a huge policeman if she might not stand there. He told her the space was reserved. "But," she explained, as if offering credentials, "I was a personal friend of Father Duffy's." The policeman's answer was an epitaph, "That is true, Ma'am," he said, "of everyone here today."

REACH ME YOUR HAND
RUTH CRARY

Reach down to me Your Hand! The way is steep
That I must go alone; and undefined.
Still blindly, I, who have too long been blind,
Must grope the stony trail and, prostrate, creep
Its weary length. Reach down to me! and keep
My fumbling fingers closely intertwined.
I have been told that earthly shepherds bind
The broken and the wounded of their sheep.

How much more gentle, then, Your touch to form
Anew; to bind the heart and to expand
The soul! And I, though shattered by the storm
That breaks about me now, shall rise—shall stand
Erect, enveloped lovingly and warm;
No more alone. Reach down to me Your Hand!

159

LORD! teach me the way my soul should walk.—*Savonarola*

WE CAN FIX our eyes on perfection, and make almost everything
speed towards it.—*Channing*

A GOOD MAN it is not mine to see. Could I see a man possessed of constancy,
that would satisfy me.—*Confucius*

IF YOU WANT your neighbor to know what the Christ spirit will do for him,
let him see what it has done for you.—*Beecher*

THE GREATEST THING a man can do for his Heavenly Father is to be kind to
some of his other children.—*Drummond*

HE WHO believes in God is not careful for the morrow, but labors joyfully
and with a great heart. "For He giveth His beloved, as in sleep." They
must work and watch, yet never be careful or anxious, but commit all to
Him, and live in serene tranquillity; with a quiet heart, as one who sleeps
safely and quietly.—*Luther*

NOTHING can compare in beauty, and wonder, and admirableness, and divinity
itself, to the silent work in obscure dwellings of faithful women bringing
their children to honour and virtue and piety.—*Beecher*

WE ARE HAUNTED by an ideal life, and it is because we have within
us the beginning and the possibility of it.—*Phillips Brooks*

DESPISE NOT any man, and do not spurn anything; for there is
no man that has not his hour, nor is there anything that has
not its place.—*Rabbi Ben Azai*

DO NOT PRAY for easy lives. Pray to be stronger men! Do not
pray for tasks equal to your powers. Pray for powers equal
to your tasks.—*Phillips Brooks*

IT IS MAN that makes truth great, not truth that makes
man great.—*Confucius*

160

RELIGIOUS THINKERS

TEACH US by your lives.—*Bonar*

THERE IS but one failure, and that is, not to be true to the
very best one knows.—*Canon Farrar*

HOSPITALITY is an expression of divine worship.—*The Talmud*

A MAN who lives right, and is right, has more power in his silence than
another has by his words.—*Phillips Brooks*

WHEN GOD thought of mother, He must have laughed with satisfaction,
and framed it quickly—so rich, so deep, so divine, so full of soul, power,
and beauty, was the conception.—*Beecher*

O LORD, Thou knowest that which is best for us; let this or that be done,
as Thou shalt please. Give what Thou wilt, how much Thou wilt, and when
Thou wilt. Deal with me as Thou thinkest best. Place me where Thou wilt,
and deal with me in all things just as Thou wilt. Behold, I am Thy servant,
prepared for all things: I desire not to live unto myself, but unto Thee;
and oh, that I could do it worthily and perfectly!—*Thomas à Kempis*

CALL YOUR OPINIONS your creed, and you will change it every week. Make
your creed simply and broadly out of the revelation of God, and you may
keep it to the end.—*Phillips Brooks*

A FAITHFUL FRIEND is a strong defence: and he that hath found such an
one hath found a treasure.—*Apocrypha*

THE PRIVATIVE BLESSINGS—the blessings of immunity, safeguard,
liberty, and integrity—which we enjoy deserve the thanksgiving
of a whole life.—*Taylor*

WE ARE JUDGED not by the degree of our light but by
fidelity to the light we have.—*Channing*

IF A WORD spoken in its time is worth one piece of money,
silence in its time is worth two.—*The Talmud*

161

WHEN SHE MUST GO
Margaret Widdemer

When she must go, so much will go with her!
Stories of country summers, far and bright,
Wisdom of berries, flowers and chestnut bur,
And songs to comfort babies in the night;

Old legends and their meanings, half-lost tunes,
Wise craftsmanship in all the household ways,
And roses taught to flower in summer noons,
And children taught the shaping of good days;

A heart still steadfast, stable, that can know
A son's first loss, a daughter's first heartbreak,
And say to them, "This, too, shall pass and go;
This is not all!" while anguished for their sake;

Courage to cling to when the day is lost,
Love to come back to when all love grows cold,
Quiet from tumult; hearth fire from the frost.
Oh, must she ever go, and we be old?

NIGHT THOUGHTS
From The Bible

When thou liest down, thou shalt not be afraid: yea, thou shalt lie down, and thy sleep shall be sweet.

Thou wilt keep him in perfect peace, whose mind is stayed on Thee.

I will both lay me down in peace, and sleep: for Thou, Lord, only makest me dwell in safety.

The Lord is my light and my salvation; whom shall I fear? the Lord is the strength of my life; of whom shall I be afraid?

He will not suffer thy foot to be moved; He that keepeth thee will not slumber. The Lord shall preserve thy going out and thy coming in from this time forth, and even for evermore.

Be careful for nothing; but in every thing by prayer and supplication with thanksgiving let your requests be made known unto God. And the peace of God, which passeth all understanding, shall keep your hearts and minds through Christ Jesus.

162

From *HYMN*
Samuel Taylor Coleridge

Ye ice-falls! ye that from the mountain's brow
Adown enormous ravines slope amain—
Torrents, methinks, that heard a mighty voice,
And stopped at once amid their maddest plunge!
Motionless torrents! silent cataracts!
Who made you glorious as the gates of heaven
Beneath the keen full moon? Who bade the sun
Clothe you with rainbows? Who, with living flowers
Of loveliest blue, spread garlands at your feet?—
God! let the torrents, like a shout of nations,
Answer! and let the ice-plains echo, God!
God! sing, ye meadow-streams, with gladsome voice!
Ye pine-groves, with your soft and soul-like sounds!
And they, too, have a voice, yon piles of snow,
And in their perilous fall shall thunder, God!
Ye living flowers that skirt the eternal frost!
Ye wild goats sporting round the eagle's nest!
Ye eagles, playmates of the mountain-storm!
Ye lightnings, the dread arrows of the clouds!
Ye signs and wonders of the elements!
Utter forth God, and fill the hills with praise!

TO WHOM WILL YE LIKEN GOD
From The Bible

To whom will ye liken God, or what likeness will ye compare unto Him? Have ye not known? Have ye not heard? Hath it not been told you from the beginning? Have ye not understood from the foundations of the earth? It is He that sitteth upon the circle of the earth, and the inhabitants thereof are as grasshoppers; that stretcheth out the heavens as a curtain, and spreadeth them out as a tent to dwell in; that bringeth the princes to nothing: He maketh the judges of the earth as vanity. Yea, they shall not be planted; they shall not be sown; their stock shall not take root in the earth; He shall blow upon them and they shall wither, and the whirlwind shall take them away as stubble.

Hast thou not known, hast thou not heard, that the everlasting God, the Lord, the Creator of the ends of the earth, fainteth not, neither is weary? There is no searching of His understanding. He giveth power to the faint; and to them that have no might He increaseth strength. Even the youths shall faint and be weary, and the young men shall utterly fall, but they that wait upon the Lord shall renew their strength; they shall mount up with wings as eagles, they shall run and not be weary, they shall walk and not faint.

163

THE BOOK THAT CONVERTED ITS AUTHOR

By Elizabeth Rider Montgomery

THE BALCONIES are crowded. Every eye is on the chariots in the great arena below as they speed faster and faster around the course. Will Ben-Hur win? Or will Messala triumph? People are shouting, screaming as the beautiful horses dash into the final stretch. But what has happened? A chariot is overturning. The driver is being dragged along the course! Surely he will be killed!

What a thrilling scene the chariot race in *Ben-Hur* is! In fact, the entire book is an exciting, absorbing story of life in the time of Christ. Though Ben-Hur is the hero, the figure of Christ is always in the background, never forgotten.

Yet *Ben-Hur: A Tale of the Christ* was not written by a religious man. The author, Lew Wallace, had been a soldier, a lawyer, a governor. When he began his famous book, he did not know what he believed about religion. He did not even know whether he believed in Christ. In fact, he began writing the book in an effort to learn for himself the truth about Jesus of Nazareth.

After his active years of service through the Civil War, General Lew Wallace returned to private life and his law practice in Crawfordsville, Indiana. For some time he was restless—the natural reaction from the excitement of war. But at last he settled down to an uneventful life.

Unaccountably, he found himself thinking about religion, although he had no religious convictions whatever. He was particularly haunted by the chapter in the Gospel of St. Matthew which relates the birth of Jesus and the visit of the Wise Men. Who were the Wise Men, he wondered? Where had they come from, and why? He decided to figure out his own conception of the Wise Men from the East.

And so, after much reading and study of the Bible, Wallace wrote an account of the meeting of the Magi in the desert, and their journey to Bethlehem to see the Christchild. When it was finished, he left the manuscript on his desk, undecided what to do with it.

Some time later, on a night in 1876, Wallace was returning home after an evening with friends. He had been listening to a discussion of religion—of God, Jesus, heaven, and eternal life. Wallace had taken little or no part in the argument, for the very good reason that he knew nothing at all about the subject under discussion. Did he believe in God? He did not know. Was Jesus Christ divine? He did not know. Religion had had no place in his active life, and he was totally ignorant about theology.

As he walked home alone in the darkness that evening, Lew Wallace began to regret that ignorance. For the first time in his life he began to feel that religion might be a very important matter. He should believe *something*. But what? How did one find out what to believe? Read sermons? Read theology, on which no two men agreed? No, he would never come to any decision that way. The only thing to do was to read the Bible. As the Bible was the basis for all Christian theology, he would make it the basis for his own religious convictions.

But Wallace knew from experience that he would have to have some definite purpose in studying the Bible—something to keep him at it, to keep him interested. He was not a man to study just for the sake of studying. The search for religious convictions alone would not be enough. He needed something else.

For days Wallace mulled the matter over. Then one day an inspiration came. He went to his wife in great excitement.

"My dear, I'm going to write a book."

"That is splendid," she replied. "I'm glad you are going to start another book. You enjoyed so much your work on *The Fair God*. What will it be this time?"

"A tale of the Christ," Wallace answered. "I shall use what I wrote about the Wise Men as the beginning of the book, and I shall end with the crucifixion. In between—"

"Yes," prompted his wife. "In between—?"

"Well, I hardly know yet. It will be a story which will show the religious and political condition of the world at the time of Christ."

"But will you have Jesus himself in your story?" asked his wife, troubled. "Won't that be dangerous? I'm afraid you will offend many readers who have their own conception of Christ and will not like to see him pictured differently."

Lew Wallace frowned. "That is one of the greatest obstacles I shall have to hurdle," he agreed. "The only solution I can see at present is to have a human hero, who is the central figure in the story. The figure of Christ must be in the background. Yet He must dominate the book. Well, I shan't worry too much about that just yet. I shall be working on this project a long time, no doubt, and many of my difficulties may smooth themselves out before I come to them."

Wallace was right: he worked on his book a long time. More than seven years. Most of the time was taken up with research, rather than writing. He took infinite pains to verify every fact, to substantiate every statement.

And of course, to make his progress even slower, he had to make a living. Writing was merely spare-time work for him. He was in those years, to begin with, a lawyer, busy enough to suit any man. And then, in 1878, with his book far from finished, he was made governor of the territory of New Mexico. Then, indeed, Wallace knew what it was to be busy. Trying simultaneously to manage a legislature of jealous factions, to take care of an Indian war, and to sell some mines which had been located by the Spanish conquistadors, he found it increasingly difficult to finish his book. Sometimes he could not even start to write before midnight. To cap the climax, in the last months of his work on *Ben-Hur*, he knew that his life was in constant danger. "Billy the Kid" had sworn to kill him.

But Lew Wallace was not a man to let either the pressure of work or the fear of death keep him from finishing what he had started. Patiently, tirelessly he labored. And at last his book was completed and carefully copied in purple ink. His work was done. Not only that, he had discovered, himself, what he

165

wanted: religious convictions. Lew Wallace, in writing his book of the Christ, had come to believe in Him.

In 1880, *Ben-Hur: A Tale of the Christ* was published by Harper and Brothers. At first it was not popular. Nearly two years passed before its sales started to grow. But at last it began to be appreciated, and before many more years went by it became one of the most popular books of the century.

✧ ✧ ✧

A Handful of Clay

By HENRY VAN DYKE

*T*HERE WAS A HANDFUL of clay in the bank of a river. It was only common clay, coarse and heavy; but it had high thoughts of its own value, and wonderful dreams of the great place which it was to fill in the world when the time came for its virtues to be discovered.

Overhead, in the spring sunshine, the trees whispered together of the glory which descended upon them when the delicate blossoms and leaves began to expand, and the forest glowed with fair, clear colours, as if the dust of thousands of rubies and emeralds were hanging, in soft clouds, above the earth.

The flowers, surprised with the joy of beauty, bent their heads to one another, as the wind caressed them, and said: "Sisters, how lovely you have become. You make the day bright."

The river, glad of new strength and rejoicing in the unison of all its waters, murmured to the shores in music, telling of its release from icy fetters, its swift flight from the snow-clad mountains, and the mighty work to which it was hurrying—the wheels of many mills to be turned, and great ships to be floated to the sea.

Waiting blindly in its bed, the clay comforted itself with lofty hopes. "My time will come," it said. "I was not made to be hidden forever. Glory and beauty and honour are coming to me in due season."

One day the clay felt itself taken from the place where it had waited so long. A flat blade of iron passed beneath it, and lifted it, and tossed it into a cart with other lumps of clay, and it was carried far away, as it seemed, over a rough and stony road. But it was not afraid, nor discouraged, for it said to itself: "This is necessary. The path to glory is always rugged. Now I am on my way to play a great part in the world."

But the hard journey was nothing compared with the tribulation and distress that came after it. The clay was put into a trough and mixed and beaten and stirred and trampled. It seemed almost unbearable. But there was consolation in the thought that something very fine and noble was certainly coming out

166

of all this trouble. The clay felt sure that, if it could only wait long enough, a wonderful reward was in store for it.

Then it was put upon a swiftly turning wheel, and whirled around until it seemed as if it must fly into a thousand pieces. A strange power pressed it and moulded it, as it revolved, and through all the dizziness and pain it felt that it was taking a new form.

Then an unknown hand put it into an oven, and fires were kindled about it—fierce and penetrating—hotter than all the heats of summer that had ever brooded upon the bank of the river. But through all, the clay held itself together and endured its trials, in the confidence of a great future. "Surely," it thought, "I am intended for something very splendid, since such pains are taken with me. Perhaps I am fashioned for the ornament of a temple, or a precious vase for the table of a king."

At last the baking was finished. The clay was taken from the furnace and set down upon a board, in the cool air, under the blue sky. The tribulation was passed. The reward was at hand.

Close beside the board there was a pool of water, not very deep, nor very clear, but calm enough to reflect, with impartial truth, every image that fell upon it. There, for the first time, as it was lifted from the board, the clay saw its new shape, the reward of all its patience and pain, the consummation of its hopes—a common flowerpot, straight and stiff, red and ugly. And then it felt that it was not destined for a king's house, nor for a palace of art, because it was made without glory or beauty or honour;

and it murmured against the unknown maker, saying, "Why hast thou made me thus?"

Many days it passed in sullen discontent. Then it was filled with earth, and something—it knew not what—but something rough and brown and dead-looking, was thrust into the middle of the earth and covered over. The clay rebelled at this new disgrace. "This is the worst of all that has happened to me, to be filled with dirt and rubbish. Surely I am a failure."

But presently it was set in a greenhouse, where the sunlight fell warm upon it, and water was sprinkled over it, and day by day as it waited, a change began to come to it. Something was stirring within it— a new hope. Still it was ignorant, and knew not what the new hope meant.

One day the clay was lifted again from its place, and carried into a great church. Its dream was coming true after all. It had a fine part to play in the world. Glorious music flowed over it. It was surrounded with flowers. Still it could not understand. So it whispered to another vessel of clay, like itself, close beside it, "Why have they set me here? Why do all the people look toward us?" And the other vessel answered, "Do you not know? You are carrying a royal sceptre of lilies. Their petals are white as snow, and the heart of them is like pure gold. The people look this way because the flower is the most wonderful in the world. And the root of it is in your heart."

Then the clay was content, and silently thanked its maker, because, though an earthen vessel, it held so great a treasure.

167

THE KINDEST and the happiest pair
Will find occasion to forbear;
And something, every day they live,
To pity, and perhaps forgive.
—Cowper

WHO DOES THE BEST his circumstance allows,
Does well, acts nobly—angels could no more.
—Young

THINK NAUGHT A TRIFLE, though it small appear;
Small sands the mountain, moments make the year,
And trifles life.
—Young

No MAN can produce great things who is not thoroughly sincere in dealing
with himself.—*Lowell*

IF GOD made poets for anything, it was to keep alive the traditions of
the pure, the holy, and the beautiful.—*Lowell*

ONLY THE ACTIONS of the just smell sweet and blossom in the dust.
—Shirley

'MID PLEASURES and palaces though we may roam,
Be it ever so humble, there's no place like home.
—Payne

ATTEMPT THE END, and never stand to doubt;
Nothing's so hard but search will find it out.
—Lovelace

NATURE, so far as in her lies, imitates God.
—Tennyson

A MORAL, sensible, and well-bred man
Will not affront me, and no other can.
—Cowper

OF THE POETS

HE IS WISEST, who only gives,
True to himself, the best he can:
Who drifting on the winds of praise,
The inward monitor obeys.
And with the boldness that confuses fear
Takes in the crowded sail, and lets his conscience steer.
                              —*Whittier*

YE THEREFORE who love mercy, teach your sons to love it too.
                              —*Cowper*

NO LONGER FORWARD nor behind I look in hope or fear;
But grateful, take the good I find, the best of now and here.
                              —*Whittier*

HOW MANY undervalue the power of simplicity! But it is the real key to
the heart.—*Wordsworth*

SCIENCE is a first-rate piece of furniture for a man's upper chamber, if
he has common sense on the ground floor.—*Holmes*

FOR MANNERS are not idle, but the fruit of loyal natures and of noble minds.
                              —*Tennyson*

THE TISSUE of the Life to be we weave with colors all our own,
And in the field of Destiny we reap as we have sown.
                              —*Whittier*

EVERY JOY is gain, and gain is gain, however small.
                              —*Browning*

KIND HEARTS are more than coronets,
And simple faith than Norman blood.
                              —*Tennyson*

THE SECRET PLEASURE of a generous act
Is the great mind's great bribe.
                              —*Dryden*

WHEN THERE IS MUSIC
DAVID MORTON

Whenever there is music, it is you
   Who come between me and the sound of strings;
The cloudy portals part to let you through,
   Troubled and strange with long rememberings.
Your nearness gathers ghostwise down the room,
   And through the pleading violins they play,
There drifts the dim and delicate perfume
   That once was you, come dreamily astray.
Behind what thin and shadowy doors you wait
   That such frail things as these should set you free!
When all my need, like armies at a gate,
   Would storm in vain to bring you back to me;
When in this hush of strings you draw more near
Than any sound of music that I hear.

BALLADE OF THE DREAMLAND ROSE
BRIAN HOOKER

Where the waves of burning cloud are rolled
   On the further shore of the sunset sea,
In a land of wonder that none behold,
   There blooms a rose on the Dreamland Tree
That stands in the Garden of Mystery
   Where the River of Slumber softly flows;
And whenever a dream has come to be,
   A petal falls from the Dreamland Rose.

In the heart of the tree, on a branch of gold,
   A silvern bird sings endlessly
A mystic song that is ages old,
   A mournful song in a minor key,
Full of the glamour of faery;
   And whenever a dreamer's ears unclose
To the sound of that distant melody,
   A petal falls from the Dreamland Rose.

Dreams and visions in hosts untold
   Throng around on the moonlit lea:
Dreams of age that are calm and cold,
   Dreams of youth that are fair and free—

Dark with a lone heart's agony,
  Bright with a hope that no one knows—
And whenever a dream and a dream agree,
  A petal falls from the Dreamland Rose.

ENVOI

Princess, you gaze in a reverie
  Where the drowsy firelight redly glows;
Slowly you raise your eyes to me. . . .
  A petal falls from the Dreamland Rose.

WHEN THE WIND IS LOW
CALE YOUNG RICE

When the wind is low, and the sea is soft,
  And the far heat-lightning plays
On the rim of the west where dark clouds nest
  On a darker bank of haze;
When I lean o'er the rail with you that I love
  And gaze to my heart's content;
I know that the heavens are there above—
  But you are my firmament.

When the phosphor-stars are thrown from the bow
  And the watch climbs up the shroud;
When the dim mast dips as the vessel slips
  Through the foam that seethes aloud;
I know that the years of our life are few,
  And fain as a bird to flee,
That time is as brief as a drop of dew—
  But you are Eternity.

JENNY*
JESSE STUART

I know that Jenny loves the whispering corn,
She loves to skip lark-free across the wheat—
I love to watch Jenny on skipping feet
Run out among wind-waves of blowing wheat.
And Jenny loves the smell of morning corn
And morning glories twined around the corn.

*Taken from MAN WITH A BULL-TONGUE PLOW, by Jesse Stuart, published and copyright by E. P. DUTTON & CO., INC., New York. Copyright 1934.

Jenny and I go evenings after cows
And on the grassy hill where cattle browse
We stand to watch the glow of setting sun.
We watch red-evening clouds above green timber
(Red-evening clouds we always shall remember)
Riding at ease above the corn and timber—
Red-evening clouds near setting of the sun.
Jenny cannot forget—I shall remember!

SILHOUETTE
ETHEL JACOBSON

Here is the house
　Where the roof swings low,
And the lilacs against
　The afterglow;

The friendly shadows
　Of elm and yew,
And a ragged space
　Where a star peeps through;

And clear and dear,
　Where the firelight lures,
A form in the doorway
　I know is yours!

From THE GREATEST THING IN THE WORLD
By HENRY DRUMMOND

EVERY ONE has asked himself the great question of antiquity as of the modern world: What is the *summum bonum*—the supreme good? You have life before you. Once only you can live it. What is the noblest object of desire, the supreme gift to covet?

We have been accustomed to be told that the greatest thing in the religious world is Faith. That great word has been the key-note for centuries of the popular religion; and we have easily learned to look upon it as the greatest thing in the world. Well, we are wrong. If we have been told that, we may miss the mark. I have taken you, in the chapter which I have just read, to Christianity at its source; and there we have seen, "The greatest of these is love." It is not an oversight. Paul was speaking of faith just a moment before. He says, "If

172

I have all faith, so that I can remove mountains, and have not love, I am nothing." So far from forgetting, he deliberately contrasts them, "Now abideth Faith, Hope, Love," and without a moment's hesitation, the decision falls, "The greatest of these is Love."

And it is not prejudice. A man is apt to recommend to others his own strong point. Love was not Paul's strong point. The observing student can detect a beautiful tenderness growing and ripening all through his character as Paul gets old; but the hand that wrote, "The greatest of these is love," when we meet it first, is stained with blood.

Nor is this letter to the Corinthians peculiar in singling out love as the *summum bonum*. The masterpieces of Christianity are agreed about it. Peter says, "Above all things have fervent love among yourselves." *Above all things.* And John goes farther, "God is love." And you remember the profound remark which Paul makes elsewhere, "Love is the fulfilling of the law." Did you ever think what he meant by that? In those days men were working their passage to Heaven by keeping the Ten Commandments, and the hundred and ten other commandments which they had manufactured out of them. Christ said, I will show you a more simple way. If you do one thing, you will do these hundred and ten things, without ever thinking about them. If you love, you will unconsciously fulfil the whole law. And you can readily see for yourselves how that must be so. Take any of the commandments. "Thou shalt have no other gods before Me." If a man love God, you will not require to tell him that. Love

is the fulfilling of that law. "Take not His name in vain." Would he ever dream of taking His name in vain if he loved Him? "Remember the Sabbath day to keep it holy." Would he not be too glad to have one day in seven to dedicate more exclusively to the object of his affection? Love would fulfil all these laws regarding God. And so, if he loved Man, you would never think of telling him to honour his father and mother. He could not do anything else. It would be preposterous to tell him not to kill. You could only insult him if you suggested that he should not steal— how could he steal from those he loved? It would be superfluous to beg him not to bear false witness against his neighbour. If he loved him it would be the last thing he would do. And you would never dream of urging him not to covet what his neighbours had. He would rather they possessed it than himself. In this way "Love is the fulfilling of the law." It is the rule for fulfilling all rules, the new commandment for keeping all the old commandments, Christ's one secret of the Christian life.

Now Paul had learned that; and in this noble eulogy he has given us the most wonderful and original account extant of the *summum bonum*. We may divide it into three parts. In the beginning of the short chapter, we have Love *contrasted;* in the heart of it, we have Love analysed; towards the end we have Love defended as the supreme gift.

THE CONTRAST

Paul begins by contrasting Love with other things that men in those days thought much of. I shall not

173

attempt to go over those things in detail. Their inferiority is already obvious.

He contrasts it with eloquence. And what a noble gift it is, the power of playing upon the souls and wills of men, and rousing them to lofty purposes and holy deeds. Paul says, "If I speak with the tongues of men and of angels, and have not love, I am become as sounding brass, or a tinkling cymbal." And we all know why. We have all felt the brazenness of words without emotion, the hollowness, the unaccountable unpersuasiveness, of eloquence behind which lies no Love.

He contrasts it with prophecy. He contrasts it with mysteries. He contrasts it with faith. He contrasts it with charity. Why is Love greater than faith? Because the end is greater than the means. And why is it greater than charity? Because the whole is greater than the part. Love is greater than faith, because the end is greater than the means. What is the use of having faith? It is to connect the soul with God. And what is the object of connecting man with God? That he may become like God. But God is Love. Hence Faith, the means, is in order to Love, the end. Love, therefore, obviously is greater than faith. It is greater than charity, again, because the whole is greater than a part. Charity is only a little bit of Love, one of the innumerable avenues of Love, and there may even be, and there is, a great deal of charity without Love. It is a very easy thing to toss a copper to a beggar in the street; it is generally an easier thing than not to do it. Yet Love is just as often in the withholding. We purchase relief from the sympathetic feeling roused by the spectacle of misery, at the copper's cost. It is too cheap—too cheap for us, and often too dear for the beggar. If we really loved him we would either do more for him, or less.

Then Paul contrasts it with sacrifice and martyrdom. And I beg the little band of would-be missionaries—and I have the honour to call some of you by this name for the first time—to remember that though you give your bodies to be burned, and have not Love, it profits nothing—nothing! You can take nothing greater to the heathen world than the impress and reflection of the Love of God upon your own character. That is the universal language. It will take you years to speak in Chinese, or in the dialects of India. From the day you land, that language of Love, understood by all, will be pouring forth its unconscious eloquence. It is the man who is the missionary, it is not his words. His character is his message. . . . You may take every accomplishment; you may be braced for every sacrifice; but if you give your body to be burned, and have not Love, it will profit you and the cause of Christ *nothing*.

THE DEFENCE

. . . "Love," urges Paul, "never faileth." Then he begins again one of his marvellous lists of the great things of the day, and exposes them one by one. He runs over the things that men thought were going to last, and shows that they are all fleeting, temporary, passing away.

"Whether there be prophecies, they shall fail." It was the mother's ambition for her boy in those days

174

that he should become a prophet. For hundreds of years God had never spoken by means of any prophet, and at that time the prophet was greater than the king. Men waited wistfully for another messenger to come, and hung upon his lips when he appeared as upon the very voice of God. Paul says, "Whether there be prophecies they shall fail." This Book is full of prophecies. One by one they have "failed"; that is, having been fulfilled, their work is finished; they have nothing more to do now in the world except to feed a devout man's faith.

Then Paul talks about tongues. That was another thing that was greatly coveted. "Whether there be tongues, they shall cease." As we all know, many centuries have passed since tongues have been known in this world. They have ceased. Take it in any sense you like. Take it, for illustration merely, as languages in general—a sense which was not in Paul's mind at all, and which though it cannot give us the specific lesson will point the general truth. Consider the words in which these chapters were written—Greek. It has gone. Take the Latin—the other great tongue of those days. It ceased long ago. . . .

Can you tell me anything that is going to last? Many things Paul did not condescend to name. He did not mention money, fortune, fame; but he picked out the great things of his time, the things best men thought had something in them, and brushed them peremptorily aside. Paul had no charge against these things in themselves. All he said about them was that they would not last. They were great things, but not supreme things. There were things beyond them. What we are stretches past what we do, beyond what we possess. . . . There is a great deal in the world that is delightful and beautiful; there is a great deal in it that is great and engrossing; but it will not last. All that is in the world, the lust of the eye, the lust of the flesh, and the pride of life, are but for a little while. Love not the world therefore. Nothing that it contains is worth the life and consecration of an immortal soul. The immortal soul must give itself to something that is immortal. And the only immortal things are these: "Now abideth faith, hope, love, but the greatest of these is love."

Some think the time will come when two of these three things will also pass away—faith into sight, hope into fruition. Paul does not say so. We know but little now about the conditions of the life that is to come. But what is certain is that Love must last. God, the Eternal God, is Love. Covet therefore that everlasting gift, that one thing which it is certain is going to stand, that one coinage which will be current in the Universe when all the other coinages of all the nations of the world shall be useless and unhonoured. You will give yourselves to many things, give yourselves first to Love. Hold things in their proportion. *Hold things in their proportion.* Let at least the first great object of our lives be to achieve the character defended in these words, the character,—and it is the character of Christ—which is built round Love.

I have said this thing is eternal. Did you ever notice how continually John associates love and faith with eternal life? I was not told when I was a boy that "God so loved the world that He gave His only begotten Son, that whosoever believeth in Him should have everlasting life." What I was told, I remember, was that God so loved the world that, if I trusted in Him, I was to have a thing called peace, or I was to have rest, or I was to have joy, or I was to have safety. But I had to find out for myself that whosoever trusteth in Him—that is, whosoever loveth Him, for trust is only the avenue to Love—hath everlasting *life*. The Gospel offers a man life. Never offer men a thimbleful of Gospel. Do not offer them merely joy, or merely peace, or merely rest, or merely safety; tell them how Christ came to give men a more abundant life than they have, a life abundant in love, and therefore abundant in salvation for themselves, and large in enterprise for the alleviation and redemption of the world. Then only can the Gospel take hold of the whole of a man, body, soul, and spirit, and give to each part of his nature its exercise and reward. . . .

To love abundantly is to live abundantly, and to love for ever is to live for ever. Hence, eternal life is inextricably bound up with love. We want to live for ever for the same reason that we want to live tomorrow. Why do you want to live tomorrow? It is because there is some one who loves you, and whom you want to see tomorrow, and be with, and love back. There is no other reason why we should live on than that we love and are beloved. It is when a man has no one to love him that he commits suicide. So long as he has friends, those who love him and whom he loves, he will live; because to live

is to love. Be it but the love of a dog, it will keep him in life; but let that go and he has no contact with life, no reason to live. The "energy of life" has failed. Eternal life also is to know God, and God is love. This is Christ's own definition. Ponder it. "This is life eternal, that they might know Thee the only true God, and Jesus Christ whom Thou hast sent." Love must be eternal. It is what God is. On the last analysis, then, love is Life. Love never faileth, and life never faileth, so long as there is love. That is the philosophy of what Paul is showing us; the reason why in the nature of things Love should be the supreme thing—because it is going to last; because in the nature of things it is an Eternal Life. That Life is a thing that we are living now, not that we get when we die; that we shall have a poor chance of getting when we die unless we are living now. No worse fate can befall a man in this world than to live and grow old alone, unloving and unloved. To be lost is to live in an unregenerate condition, loveless and unloved; and to be saved is to love; and he that dwelleth in love dwelleth already in God. For God is love. . . .

"Love suffereth long, and is kind; love envieth not; love vaunteth not itself." Get these ingredients into your life. Then everything that you do is eternal. It is worth doing. It is worth giving time to. No man can become a saint in his sleep; and to fulfill the condition required demands a certain amount of prayer and meditation and time, just as improvement in any direction, bodily or mental, requires preparation and care. Address yourself to that one thing; at any cost have

176

this transcendent character exchanged for yours. You will find as you look back upon your life that the moments that stand out, the moments when you have really lived, are the moments when you have done things in a spirit of love. As memory scans the past, above and beyond all the transitory pleasures of life, there leap forward those supreme hours when you have been enabled to do unnoticed kindnesses to those around about you, things too trifling to speak about, but which you feel have entered into your eternal life. I have seen almost all the beautiful things that God has made; I have enjoyed almost every pleasure that He has planned for man; and yet as I look back I see, standing out above all the life that has gone, four or five short experiences when the love of God reflected itself in some poor imitation, some small act of love of mine, and these seem to be the things which alone of all one's life abide. Everything else in all our lives is transitory. Every other good is visionary. But the acts of love which no man knows about, or can ever know about—they never fail.

In the Book of Matthew, where the Judgment Day is depicted for us in the imagery of One seated upon a throne and dividing the sheep from the goats, the test of a man then is not, "How have I believed?" but "How have I loved?" The test of religion, the final test of religion, is not religiousness, but Love. I say the final test of religion at that great Day is not religiousness, but Love; not what I have done, not what I have believed, not what I have achieved, but how I have discharged the common charities of life. Sins of commission in that awful indictment are not even referred to. By what we have not done, *by sins of omission,* we are judged. It could not be otherwise. For the withholding of love is the negation of the spirit of Christ, the proof that we never knew Him, that for us He lived in vain. It means that He suggested nothing in all our thoughts, that He inspired nothing in all our lives, that we were not once near enough to Him to be seized with the spell of His compassion for the world. It means that:

"I lived for myself, I thought for
  myself,
For myself, and none beside—
Just as if Jesus had never lived,
As if He had never died."

It is the Son of *Man* before whom the nations of the world shall be gathered. It is in the presence of *Humanity* that we shall be charged. And the spectacle itself, the mere sight of it, will silently judge each one. Those will be there whom we have met and helped; or there, the unpitied multitude whom we neglected or despised. No other Witness need be summoned. No other charge than lovelessness shall be preferred. Be not deceived. The words which all of us shall one Day hear, sound not of theology but of life ... of the hungry and the poor, not of creeds and doctrines but of shelter and clothing, of cups of cold water in the name of Christ. . . . Who is Christ? He who fed the hungry, clothed the naked, visited the sick. And where is Christ? Where?—whoso shall receive a little child in My name receiveth Me. And who are Christ's? Every one that loveth is born of God.

177

THERE IS no power greater than true affection.—*Seneca*

THEY ENHANCE THE VALUE of their favours by the words with which they are accompanied.—*Pliny*

LIVE with men as if God saw you; converse with God as if men heard you.
—*Seneca*

THIS IS MORAL PERFECTION: to live each day as though it were the last; to be tranquil, sincere, yet not indifferent to one's fate.—*Marcus Aurelius*

NATURE has given to us the seeds of knowledge, not knowledge itself.—*Seneca*

AS FOR OLD AGE, embrace and love it. It abounds with pleasure, if you know how to use it The gradually (I do not say rapidly) declining years are amongst the sweetest in a man's life; and, I maintain, that even where they have reached the extreme limit, they have their pleasure still.—*Seneca*

IN NOTHING do men more nearly approach the gods than in doing good to their fellowmen.—*Cicero*

THE GARDENER plants trees, not one berry of which he will ever see: and shall not a public man plant laws, institutions, government, in short, under the same conditions?—*Cicero*

BOOKS are the food of youth, the delight of old age; the ornament of prosperity, the refuge and comfort of adversity; a delight at home, and no hindrance abroad; companions by night, in travelling, in the country.—*Cicero*

LET US say what we feel, and feel what we say; let speech harmonize with life.—*Seneca*

WHATEVER IS to make us better and happy, God has placed either openly before us or close to us.—*Seneca*

IF I can only keep my good name, I shall be rich enough.—*Plautus*

PHILOSOPHERS

TRUTH never perishes.—*Seneca*

MERE LIFE is not a blessing, but to live well.—*Seneca*

WHO NEEDS FORGIVENESS, should the same extend with readiness.—*Seneca*

THE ROAD by precepts is tedious, by example short and efficacious.—*Seneca*

HOW POWERFUL is man! He is able to do all that God wishes him to do. He is able to accept all that God sends upon him.—*Marcus Aurelius*

AS SURGEONS keep their instruments and knives always at hand for cases requiring immediate treatment, so shouldst thou have thy thoughts ready to understand things divine and human, remembering in thy every act, even the smallest, how close is the bond that unites the two.—*Marcus Aurelius*

THE MIND should be allowed some relaxation, that it may return to its work all the better for the rest.—*Seneca*

WHILE ALL OTHER THINGS are uncertain, evanescent, and ephemeral, virtue alone is fixed with deep roots; it can neither be overthrown by any violence or moved from its place.—*Cicero*

WHEN WE consider we are bound to be serviceable to mankind, and bear with their faults, we shall perceive there is a common tie of nature and relation between us.—*Marcus Aurelius*

IT IS a brief period of life that is granted us by nature, but the memory of a well-spent life never dies.—*Cicero*

NOTHING is more praiseworthy, nothing more suited to a great and illustrious man than placability and a merciful disposition.—*Cicero*

A MAN should *be* upright, not be *kept* upright.—*Marcus Aurelius*

179

from The Moon and Sixpence

By W. SOMERSET MAUGHAM

I HAVE AN IDEA that some men are born out of their due place. Accident has cast them amid certain surroundings, but they have always a nostalgia for a home they know not. They are strangers in their birthplace, and the leafy lanes they have known from childhood or the populous streets in which they have played, remain but a place of passage. They may spend their whole lives aliens among their kindred and remain aloof among the only scenes they have ever known. Perhaps it is this sense of strangeness that sends men far and wide in the search for something permanent, to which they may attach themselves. Perhaps some deep-rooted atavism urges the wanderer back to lands which his ancestors left in the dim beginnings of history. Sometimes a man hits upon a place to which he mysteriously feels that he belongs. Here is the home he sought, and he will settle amid scenes that he has never seen before, among men he has never known, as though they were familiar to him from his birth. Here at last he finds rest.

There is the story of a man I had known at St. Thomas's Hospital. He was a Jew named Abraham, a blond, rather stout young man, shy and very unassuming; but he had remarkable gifts. He entered the hospital with a scholarship, and during the five years of the curriculum gained every prize that was open to him. He was made house-physician and house-surgeon. His brilliance was allowed by all. Finally he was elected to a position on the staff, and his career was assured. So far as human things can be pre-dicted, it was certain that he would rise to the greatest heights of his profession. Honours and wealth awaited him. Before he entered upon his new duties he wished to take a holiday, and, having no private means, he went as surgeon on a tramp steamer to the Levant. It did not generally carry a doctor, but one of the senior surgeons at the hospital knew a director of the line, and Abraham was taken as a favour.

In a few weeks the authorities received his resignation of the coveted position on the staff. It created profound astonishment, and wild rumours were current. Whenever a man does anything unexpected, his fellows ascribe it to the most discreditable motives. But there was a man ready to step into Abraham's shoes, and Abraham was forgotten. Nothing more was heard of him. He vanished.

It was perhaps ten years later that one morning on board ship, about to land at Alexandria, I was bidden to line up with the other passengers for the doctor's examination. The doctor was a stout man in shabby clothes, and when he took off his hat I noticed that he was very bald. I had an idea that I had seen him before. Suddenly I remembered.

"Abraham," I said.

180

He turned to me with a puzzled look, and then, recognizing me, seized my hand. After expressions of surprise on either side, hearing that I meant to spend the night in Alexandria, he asked me to dine with him at the English Club. When we met again I declared my astonishment at finding him there. It was a very modest position that he occupied, and there was about him an air of straitened circumstance. Then he told me his story. When he set out on his holiday in the Mediterranean he had every intention of returning to London and his appointment at St. Thomas's. One morning the tramp docked at Alexandria, and from the deck he looked at the city, white in the sunlight, and the crowd on the wharf; he saw the natives in their shabby gabardines, the blacks from the Soudan, the noisy throng of Greeks and Italians, the grave Turks in tarbooshes, the sunshine and the blue sky; and something happened to him. He could not describe it. It was like a thunderclap, he said, and then, dissatisfied with this, he said it was like a revelation. Something seemed to twist his heart, and suddenly he felt an exultation, a sense of wonderful freedom. He felt himself at home, and he made up his mind there and then, in a minute, that he would live the rest of his life in Alexandria. He had no great difficulty in leaving the ship, and in twenty-four hours, with all his belongings, he was on shore.

"The Captain must have thought you as mad as a hatter," I smiled.

"I didn't care what anybody thought. It wasn't I that acted, but something stronger within me. I thought I would go to a little Greek hotel, while I looked about, and I felt I knew where to find one. And do you know, I walked straight there, and when I saw it, I recognized it at once."

"Had you been to Alexandria before?"

"No; I'd never been out of England in my life."

Presently he entered the Government service, and there he had been ever since.

"Have you never regretted it?"

"Never, not for a minute. I earn just enough to live upon, and I'm satisfied. I ask nothing more than to remain as I am till I die. I've had a wonderful life."

I left Alexandria next day, and I forgot about Abraham till a little while ago, when I was dining with another old friend in the profession, Alec Carmichael, who was in England on short leave. I ran across him in the street and congratulated him on the knighthood with which his eminent services during the war had been rewarded. We arranged to spend an evening together for old time's sake, and when I agreed to dine with him, he proposed that he should ask nobody else, so that we could chat without interruption. He had a beautiful old house in Queen Anne Street, and being a man of taste he had furnished it admirably. On the walls of the dining-room I saw a charming Bellotto, and there was a pair of Zoffanys that I envied. When his wife, a tall, lovely creature in cloth of gold, had left us, I remarked laughingly on the change in his present circumstances from those when we had both been medical students. We had looked upon it then as an extravagance to dine in a shabby Italian restaurant in

181

the Westminster Bridge Road. Now Alec Carmichael was on the staff of half a dozen hospitals. I should think he earned ten thousand a year, and his knighthood was but the first of the honours which must inevitably fall to his lot.

"I've done pretty well," he said, "but the strange thing is that I owe it all to one piece of luck."

"What do you mean by that?"

"Well, do you remember Abraham? He was the man who had the future. When we were students he beat me all along the line. He got the prizes and the scholarships that I went in for. I always played second fiddle to him. If he'd kept on he'd be in the position I'm in now. That man had a genius for surgery. No one had a look in with him. When he was appointed Registrar at Thomas's I hadn't a chance of getting on the staff. I should have had to become a G.P., and you know what likelihood there is for a G.P. ever to get out of the common rut. But Abraham fell out, and I got the job. That gave me my opportunity."

"I dare say that's true."

"It was just luck. I suppose there was some kink in Abraham. Poor devil, he's gone to the dogs altogether. He's got some twopenny-halfpenny job in the medical at Alexandria—sanitary officer or something like that. I'm told he lives with an ugly old Greek woman and has half a dozen scrofulous kids. The fact is, I suppose, that it's not enough to have brains. The thing that counts is character. Abraham hadn't got character."

Character? I should have thought it needed a good deal of character to throw up a career after half an hour's meditation, because you saw in another way of living a more intense significance. And it required still more character never to regret the sudden step. But I said nothing, and Alec Carmichael proceeded reflectively:

"Of course it would be hypocritical for me to pretend that I regret what Abraham did. After all, I've scored by it." He puffed luxuriously at the long Corona he was smoking. "But if I weren't personally concerned I should be sorry at the waste. It seems a rotten thing that a man should make such a hash of life."

I wondered if Abraham really had made a hash of life. Is to do what you most want, to live under the conditions that please you, in peace with yourself, to make a hash of life; and is it success to be an eminent surgeon with ten thousand a year and a beautiful wife? I suppose it depends on what meaning you attach to life, the claim which you acknowledge to society, and the claim of the individual. But again I held my tongue, for who am I to argue with a knight?

THE NEW TRINITY

EDWIN MARKHAM

Three things must a man possess if his soul would live,
And know life's perfect good—
Three things would the all-supplying Father give—
Bread, Beauty and Brotherhood.

From *THE BURIED LIFE*
Matthew Arnold

Only—but this is rare—
When a beloved hand is laid in ours,
When, jaded with the rush and glare
Of the interminable hours,
Our eyes can in another's eyes read clear,
When our world-deafen'd ear
Is by the tones of a loved voice caress'd—
A bolt is shot back somewhere in our breast,
And a lost pulse of feeling stirs again.
The eye sinks inward, and the heart lies plain,
And what we mean, we say, and what we would, we know
A man becomes aware of his life's flow,
And hears its winding murmur; and he sees
The meadow where it glides, the sun, the breeze.

And there arrives a lull in the hot race
Wherein he doth forever chase
That flying and elusive shadow, rest.
An air of coolness plays upon his face,
And an unwonted calm pervades his breast
And then he thinks he knows
The hills where his life rose,
And the sea where it goes.

SONNET
John Keats

To one who has been long in city pent
'Tis very sweet to look into the fair
And open face of heaven, to breathe a prayer
Full in the smile of the blue firmament.
Who is more happy, when, with heart's content,
Fatigued he sinks into some pleasant lair
Of wavy grass, and reads a debonair
And gentle tale of love and languishment?
Returning home at evening, with an ear
Catching the notes of Philomel, an eye
Watching the sailing cloudlet's bright career,
He mourns that day so soon has glided by,
Even like the passage of an angel's tear
That falls through the clear ether silently.

183

NOW

LAURA LEE RANDALL

Now is the time to know my full salvation,
Now is the time to welcome Love's control;
Now is the time for deeper consecration
To serve our God with mind and heart and soul.

I have no anxious thought about tomorrow;
No fear of ill; no need to wonder how   •
It will be freed of trouble, pain, or sorrow;
For when tomorrow comes, it will be *now*.

JESUS THE CONQUEROR

LAURA LEE RANDALL

The tender heart of Jesus knew
  The weight of all our human woes,
But Christly courage bore him through
  The tides of error when they rose.
He spoke with sureness of God's power. . . .
  And lo, the angry waves were still.
Today, in trouble's stormy hour,
  The power of Love can heal each ill.

When Jesus spoke to throngs that came
  For help in pain, or sore distress,
He showed them, in his Father's name,
  The healing of Love's tenderness.
He blessed the loaves that were at hand,
  And hungry multitudes were fed.
Today, if we will understand,
  Love freely gives us daily bread.

When Jesus suffered hate and scorn,
  His tender heart they could not reach:
The cruel cross, the piercing thorn,
  But wrought compassion in his speech.
"Forgive them, Father," was his prayer;
  Death and the grave were conquered then.
Today, a ransomed host declare
  God's love is always life to men.

184

From *MEDITATIONS*

By Preston Bradley

Eternal heart, we would have the first word of our prayer and communion on this the very first opportunity of the new year be one of dedication. Might we dedicate these minds and these hearts and these bodies of ours all to the projection of Love and Goodness and Beauty. May we forget and abandon everything of the past which might interfere with this dedication. Might we really begin all over again. These years are getting so short and this something called "time" is so rapid that we cannot waste much more of it; we cannot let life go thoughtlessly and foolishly by much longer; there is not enough of it left to gamble with life like that. So may the consciousness and the sense of need, the evidence of necessity be revealed to our hearts and minds now, and then may the dedication begin. We want of every day, as night deepens and we look back upon what we have said and done and been during that day, we want to be proud of it, we want to be happy over every gesture in life we have made. It is the petition of our hearts that we so order life that we make it a victorious experience day by day and every hour as we pass along.

May we in this spirit of dedication feel the kinship, the relatedness to Thyself, then there will never be another worry, another anxiety, another care, that will be strong enough to alienate us from Thy Love; then we can stand whatever life has to offer, we can face up to it for we will have on our side the principle of undefeatedness that belongs to the permanent triumph of all those who love God and walk in His pathway.

That is our New Year prayer, and as we have prayed it for ourselves might it also be the prayer of those who have sympathetically and harmoniously tarried in the silence with us in prayer. And overshadowing all, above all, and in all, are the words of Him who through every suffering, disillusionment, despair, loss of friends, even the prick of thorns upon His brow and the ghastly gash in His side, above it all He too could pray.

PRAYER

Gail Brook Burket

I do not ask to walk smooth paths
Nor bear an easy load.
I pray for strength and fortitude
To climb the rock strewn road.

Give me such courage I can scale
The hardest peaks alone
And transform every stumbling block
Into a stepping stone.

185

BELIEF IN IMMORTALITY
By PLATO

WHEN SPEAKING of divine perfection, we signify that God is just and true and loving, the author of order, not disorder, of good, not evil. We signify that he is justice, that he is truth, that he is love, that he is order, that he is the very progress of which we were speaking; and that wherever these qualities exist, whether in the human soul or in the order of nature, there God exists. We might still see him everywhere, if we had not been mistakenly seeking for him apart from us, instead of in us; away from the laws of nature, instead of in them. And we become united, not by mystical absorption, but by partaking of that truth and justice and love which He himself is.

Therefore the belief in immortality depends finally upon the belief in God. If there exists a good and wise God, then there also exists a progress of mankind towards perfection; and if there be no progress of men towards perfection, then there cannot be a good and wise God. We cannot suppose that God's moral government, the beginnings of which we see in the world and in ourselves, will cease when we leave this life.

GOODNESS
By PHILLIPS BROOKS

CERTAINLY, in our own little sphere it is not the most active people to whom we owe the most. Among the common people whom we know, it is not necessarily those who are busiest, not those who, meteor-like, are ever on the rush after some visible charge and work. It is the lives, like the stars, which simply pour down on us the calm light of their bright and faithful being, up to which we look and out of which we gather the deepest calm and courage. It seems to me that there is reassurance here for many of us who seem to have no chance for active usefulness. We can do nothing for our fellow-men. But still it is good to know that we can be something for them; to know (and this we may know surely) that no man or woman of the humblest sort can really be strong, gentle, pure, and good, without the world being better for it, without somebody being helped and comforted by the very existence of that goodness.

A HUNDRED YEARS OF STARS AND VIOLETS
By RICHARD JEFFERIES

A COUNTRY girl walks, and the very earth smiles beneath her feet. Something comes with her that is more than mortal—witness the yearning welcome that stretches towards her from all. As the sunshine lights up the aspect of things, so her presence sweetens the very flowers like dew.

A hundred and fifty years at the least, more probably twice that, have passed away, while from all enchanted things of earth and air this preciousness has been drawn.

From the south wind that breathed a century and a half ago over the green wheat; from the perfume of the growing grasses waving over honey-laden clover and laughing veronica, hiding the greenfinches, baffling the bee; from rose-loved hedges, woodbine, and cornflower azure blue, where yellowing wheat-stalks crowd up under the shadow of green firs.

All devious brooklet's sweetness, where the iris stays the sunlight; all the wild woods hold of beauty; all the broad hill's thyme and freedom, thrice a hundred years repeated. A hundred years of cowslips, bluebells, violets; purple spring and golden autumn; sunshine, shower, and dewy mornings; the night immortal, all the rhythm of Time unrolling.

Who shall preserve a record of the petals that fell from the roses a century ago? The swallows to the housetop three hundred times—think a moment of that! Thence she sprang, and the world yearns toward her beauty as to flowers that are past. The loveliness of seventeen is centuries old.

GOD'S WORK

By WILLIAM MAKEPEACE THACKERAY

WHAT WE SEE here of this world is but an expression of God's will, so to speak—a beautiful earth and sky and sea—beautiful affections and sorrows, wonderful changes and developments of creation, suns rising, stars shining, birds singing, clouds and shadows changing and fading, people loving each other, smiling and crying, the multiplied phenomena of Nature, multiplied in fact and fancy, in Art and Science, in every way that a man's intellect or education or imagination can be brought to bear.—And who is to say that we are to ignore all this, or not value them and love them, because there is another unknown world yet to come? Why that unknown future world is but a manifestation of God Almighty's will, and a development of Nature, neither more or less than this in which we are, and an angel glorified or a sparrow on a gutter are equally parts of His creation. The light upon all the saints in Heaven is just as much and no more God's work, as the sun which shall shine tomorrow upon this infinitesimal speck of creation.

POETRY

By LORD DUNSANY

WHAT IS IT to hate poetry? It is to have no little dreams and fancies, no holy memories of golden days, to be unmoved by serene midsummer evenings or dawn over wild lands, singing or sunshine, little tales told by the fire a long while since, glow-worms and briar rose; for of all these things and more is poetry made. It is to be cut off forever from the fellowship of great men that are gone; to see men and women without their halos and the world without its glory; to miss the meaning lurking behind the common things, like elves hiding in flowers; it is to beat one's hands all day against the gates of Fairyland and to find that they are shut and the country empty and its kings gone hence.

187

AN EPIC OF THE NORTH
By Frank M. O'Brien

SCIENCE MADE the antitoxin that is in Nome today, but science could not get it there. All the mechanical transportation marvels of modern times faltered in the presence of the elements. Man has made wonderful machines for speeding on the earth and sea, in the air and under the waters. We have locomotives and motor cars of rare swiftness. We have million-dollar balloons and powerful airplanes. We have steamers, submarines and that gigantic ally of navigation, the icebreaker. None of these could reach Nome from the point, more than 600 miles away, where the healing serum was. Even the plane, which has covered the distance in less than two hours, failed in the hour of need.

But there were two machines that did not fail. Man and his dog, prehistoric companions in struggle, answered the cry of Nome. They, assisted by the crudest of all devices of transport, the sled, went through with the job. Other engines might freeze and choke, but that oldest of all motors, the heart, whose fuel is blood and whose spark is courage, never stalls but once.

The eyes of all this continent were on the contest in which the musher and his huskies were faced by the overwhelming odds of a pitiless North. From Nenana, the last point to which the train could bring the serum, to Nome is 665 miles. That is farther than from New York to Detroit, Michigan. It is a stretch of snow unbroken except for the glaring ice of the rivers. It is a wilderness of blizzard in which winter whips the face with a thousand thongs of ice. It was 60 degrees below zero when Shannon set out with his dogs and his sled and the precious twenty-pound package of antitoxin; set out to make a relay of nearly half the distance between New York and Albany.

There was no rest, for rest meant the stiffening of men and dogs. There was no sleep, for sleep meant death. There was none to guide or encourage, for men were to be seen only at the relay points. The far North has little daylight now and even that daylight was of small use against the blinding storm. Light or dark, there could be no turning back, no halting, nothing but struggle, hour after hour, in a torment of cold and under a cruel burden of fatigue.

What Shannon faced at the outset was what all nine heroic travelers bore—except when their task was even more severe. The great Seppalla mushed forty miles to his relay point and then, without rest, took the serum on the long lap to which he had been assigned! Two other mushers waited for two days without sleep—for sleep in the Arctic is a traitor—until their turn came to carry on with the package.

Gunnar Kasson, whose happy fate it was to make the victorious entry into Nome, missed in the storm the relay that was to relieve him and had to make a double run, but completed his last fifty-four miles in less than eight hours! We can hear the gods in Valhalla crying "*Skoal!*" to this greater Norseman.

Nor shall the glory fade of the dogs who made this race against death in faster time than ever a wolf or a husky sped in the mushing contests for sport. Frozen, hungry, urged to the last ounce of their energy, so flayed by the winds that their lungs were scorched as if by fire, these creatures held the path of torture as if they knew what their errand was; went on in the spirit of Balto, who when Musher Kasson was lost in the blizzard kept his mates headed for Nome and saved the day.

So potent was the combination of man and dog and courage that merciless winter could not prevent it from doing its fine errand. In five and one-half days the relays covered ground that had never before been crossed in less than nine days. Men thought that the limit of speed and endurance had been reached in the famous dog races of Alaska. But a race for sport and money proved to have far less stimulant than this contest in which humanity was the urge and life the prize.

And there again we find science playing a minor part. For there is nothing in science which tells us why one man should imperil his own life to save the life of another, particularly when, as in the race to Nome, the person to be saved is a stranger. No laboratory test can extract the essence of self-sacrifice; no biological formula explain the willingness and the magnificence of the act of these Alaskan heroes.

These men and their dogs have written an epic of the North. Only one other historic episode of the iceland matches their unselfish heroism. That is the story of Captain Oates of the Scott expedition to the Antarctic, who walked out into the storm to die in order that his comrades might have more food. But that was tragedy; this, triumph.

WINGS
GRACE NOLL CROWELL

Within man's heart is ever the longing to fly:
    The inherent upward reaching toward the light,
The eternal call of the heart for the arching sky,
    The tug of invisible wings for a headlong flight—
These have striven within him, and will strive
    As long as one golden eagle, strong and free,
Stretches its sun-tipped wings, alert, alive,
    And climbs to the borderland of eternity.

To be one with the wind in its far-flung heady race,
    To be one with the stars, one with the sun as it swings
Upon its outbound course, to fly with the grace
    Of the wildest bird! For "wings, wings, wings,"
Men have cried, until they found them at last. . . .
    Dear God,
    Steady the wings as they lift these days from the sod.

PROPERLY SPEAKING, all true work is religion.

ALL WORK is as seed sown; it grows and spreads, and
sows itself anew.

IT IS GREAT, and there is no other greatness—to make one nook of
God's creation more fruitful, better, more worthy of God; to make
some human heart a little wiser, manlier, happier—more blessed.

ALL TRUE WORK is sacred. In all true work, were it but true hand
work, there is something of divineness. Labor, wide as the earth,
has its summit in Heaven.

OF ALL THE THINGS which man can do or make here below, by far the most
momentous, wonderful, and worthy are the things we call books.

THERE IS a perennial nobleness, and even sacredness, in work. Were he
never so benighted, forgetful of his high calling, there is always hope
in a man that actually and earnestly works: in idleness alone is there
perpetual despair.

NOTHING that was worthy in the past departs; no truth or goodness realized by man ever dies, or can die; but is all still here, and, recognized or
not, lives and works through endless changes.

HAVING A PURPOSE in life, throw into your work such
strength of mind and muscle as God has given you.

THE MAN who cannot wonder, who does not habitually wonder and
worship, . . . is but a pair of spectacles, behind which there is no eye.

THE COURAGE we desire and prize is not the courage to die
decently, but to live manfully.

FROM THE lowliest depth there is a path to the
loftiest height.

190

ENGLISH WRITERS

THE TRUE UNIVERSITY of these days is a Collection
of Books.—*Carlyle*

THE GREAT LAW of culture is: let each become all that he was
created capable of being.—*Carlyle*

HE THAT GIVES ALL, though but little, gives much; because
God looks not to the quantity of the gift, but to the quality
of the givers.—*Quarles*

HE WHO would write heroic poems should make his whole life a
heroic poem.—*Carlyle*

WE ARE firm believers in the maxim that, for all right judgment of
any man or thing, it is useful, nay, essential, to see his good qualities before pronouncing on his bad.—*Carlyle*

OUR GREAT THOUGHTS, our great affections, the truths of our life, never
leave us. Surely they can not separate from our consciousness, shall
follow it whithersoever that shall go, and are of their nature divine and
immortal.—*Thackeray*

THERE IS NOT a more pleasing exercise of the mind than gratitude.—*Addison*

I DON'T LIKE to talk much with people who always agree with me. It
is amusing to coquette with an echo for a little while, but one soon
tires of it.—*Carlyle*

EVEN in the meanest sorts of Labor, the whole soul of a man is
composed into a kind of real harmony the instant he sets himself
to work.—*Carlyle*

A MAN lives by believing something; not by debating and arguing about many things.—*Carlyle*

BLESSED is he who has found his work; let him ask
no other blessedness.—*Carlyle*

WORK*

By Ida M. Tarbell

THE MOST satisfying interest in my life, books and friends and beauty aside, is work—plain hard steady work. It is for work—books and friends and beauty again aside —that I shall be most grateful on Thanksgiving Day of 1936. As I have been at it for fifty-six of my seventy-nine years, I feel that I have given it a fair trial.

What do I get out of it?

I have no illusions about its nature. If work is to be productive— that is, give the worker something he can exchange for the products of other workers—it is no sinecure. It carries with it fatigue, disappointment, failure, revolt.

I have never in my life undertaken a fresh piece of work that I have not been obliged to take myself by the scruff of the neck and seat myself at my desk and keep my hand on the scruff until my revolt had subsided. That is, I know the difficulties in steady work. If there was nothing in it but the fruits of barter, I would rather trust myself to the road. On the road you can at least go South in winter and North in summer.

But the ability to barter is the least of work's satisfactions, necessary as that may be, great as may be the sense of dignity which a worker gets from being economically independent, joyous as may be the fun of having money to spend, to give, perhaps to waste.

Highest, perhaps, in the satisfactions work gives is the sense that you are keeping in step with the nature of things. That may sound esoteric, but it is plain fact. This is

*Taken from COSMOPOLITAN December 1936.

a working universe. So far as we know, it has been that since the beginning of things. There is no spot in it which stands still. Every star is on the move. Such a reliable universe, too: every planet in its place, doing its task; every eclipse on the minute.

Here on earth everything works —the grain of sand, the oaks, the clouds—works and incessantly changes, passing from one form to another, for nothing dies as a fact. The earth tolerates no dead beats; it keeps everything busy. If it did not it would be out of step in the universe in which it travels year in and out, never behindhand, never off the track—sunrise and sunset, moonrise and moonset always on schedule.

If I am to be happy in this steady-working world I must work, too; otherwise I'll suffer discomfort, uneasiness akin to that which comes to me when in walking I cannot keep step with my companion, when in talking I cannot follow the argument or catch the meaning, when in singing I am off key.

There is a vast unhappiness, inexplicable to those it afflicts, which comes from idleness in a working world. The idle are self-destructive as would be a star which announced that it was going to stand still for an eon or two.

What the idler fails to understand is the beauty of rhythm, the beauty and the excitement of being in his place in the endless chain of creative motion which is the essential nature of this magnificent and incomprehensible universe.

There is no mystification about this. It is as plain a fact as anything we know, and we ignore it to the destruction of our peace of mind, if not to the peril of our lives. It is one of the factors in our situation on earth which must be accepted.

Margaret Fuller Ossoli once announced loftily that she accepted the universe. "She better," commented Ralph Waldo Emerson. We better, or the first thing we know the world will spew us out of its mouth as the universe does a revolting star, breaking it to fragments doomed eternally to cruise through space. Fragments occasionally collide with a planet, burying themselves in its surface—meteorites, we call them. They are pieces (probably!) of a star that tried to get out of work assigned it.

Work means health. The very urges of our bodies show that nature expects action of us if we are to be in health. From the time we kick our heels and try our lungs on being released from our mother's womb we cry for work. Watch the child—never still. It is obeying the order of nature to keep busy.

How defeated and restless the child that is not doing something in which it sees a purpose, a meaning! It is by its self-directed activity that the child, as years pass, finds its work, the thing it wants to do and for which it finally is willing to deny itself pleasure, ease, even sleep and comfort.

In such work comes perhaps the deepest of all work's satisfactions: the consciousness that you are growing, the realization that gradually there is more skill in your fingers and your mind. If you work steadily, persistently, with a conviction of the necessity of effort if you are to be in harmony with the nature of things, you grow.

You do more. By giving yourself freely to your work you become a creator suggesting new techniques, new machines, finding new magic in words, new arrangements of facts and thoughts.

Here lies the worker's salvation when the road he has been following suddenly ends—when the factory, the shop, the office closes. The worker who realizes that he has something to do with the making of new work when the old ends does not sit down by the roadside and cry for someone to take down the barriers. He strikes across the open fields, chops a path through the woods, seizes any odd job he spies, labors to set his own notions in operation.

Thousands of men and women have done that in these last difficult seven years and are coming to Thanksgiving Day blessing the Lord for their larger sense of the nature of work, their obligation to create it, keep it going. Thrown out, they refused to beg it—they set about to make it.

They have learned a fundamental truth—that the creative force in work must be constantly exercised, never checked or tampered with, if work is to be kept abundant, if its wornout forms are to be constantly replaced with those which are higher, finer, more productive.

With growth and creation come satisfactions of new kinds. Your work fits in with the work of others. You know yourself to be finally a part of that working world which produces sound things for sound purposes.

But work does more for you. It is the chief protection you have in suffering, despair, disillusionment, fear. There is no antidote to mental and spiritual uncer-

193

tainty and pain like a regular job.

Here, then, is my philosophy of work—the reasons why after fifty-six years of unbroken trial I thank God for it. It is something which reaches the deepest needs, helps reconcile the baffling mystery of the universe, helps establish order in a disorderly society; which puts despair to sleep, gives experience to offer that youth who is willing to believe you too once were young and had his problems, gives a platter of fruit—small though it may be —to divide with those who for one or another reason have no fruit on their platter.

Blessed work! There will be no finer fruit on our Thanksgiving table.

WORK

A SONG OF TRIUMPH

ANGELA MORGAN

Work!
Thank God for the might of it,
The ardor, the urge, the delight of it—
Work that springs from the heart's desire,
Setting the brain and the soul on fire—
Oh, what is so good as the heat of it,
And what is so glad as the beat of it,
And what is so kind as the stern command,
Challenging brain and heart and hand?

Work!
Thank God for the pride of it,
For the beautiful, conquering tide of it,
Sweeping the life in its furious flood,
Thrilling the arteries, cleansing the blood,
Mastering stupor and dull despair,
Moving the dreamer to do and dare.
Oh, what is so good as the urge of it,
And what is so glad as the surge of it,
And what is so strong as the summons deep,
Rousing the torpid soul from sleep?

Work!
Thank God for the pace of it,
For the terrible, keen, swift race of it;
Fiery steeds in full control,
Nostrils a-quiver to greet the goal.
Work, the Power that drives behind,
Guiding the purposes, taming the mind,
Holding the runaway wishes back,

194

Reining the will to one steady track,
Speeding the energies faster, faster,
Triumphing over disaster.
Oh, what is so good as the pain of it,
And what is so great as the gain of it?
And what is so kind as the cruel goad,
Forcing us on through the rugged road?

Work!
Thank God for the swing of it,
For the clamoring, hammering ring of it,
Passion of labor daily hurled
On the mighty anvils of the world.
Oh, what is so fierce as the flame of it?
And what is so huge as the aim of it?
Thundering on through dearth and doubt,
Calling the plan of the Maker out.
Work, the Titan; Work, the friend,
Shaping the earth to a glorious end,
Draining the swamps and blasting the hills,
Doing whatever the Spirit wills—
Rending a continent apart,
To answer the dream of the Master's heart.
Thank God for a world where none may shirk—
Thank God for the splendor of work!

WORK

HENRY VAN DYKE

Let me but do my work from day to day,
   In field or forest, at the desk or loom,
   In roaring market-place or tranquil room;
Let me but find it in my heart to say,
When vagrant wishes beckon me astray,
   "This is my work; my blessing, not my doom;
   Of all who live, I am the one by whom
This work can best be done in the right way."

Then shall I see it not too great, nor small,
   To suit my spirit and to prove my powers;
   Then shall I cheerful greet the laboring hours,
And cheerful turn, when the long shadows fall
At eventide, to play and love and rest,
Because I know for me my work is best.

FLAMMONDE

EDWIN ARLINGTON ROBINSON

The man Flammonde, from God knows where,
With firm address and foreign air,
With news of nations in his talk
And something royal in his walk,
With glint of iron in his eyes,
But never doubt, nor yet surprise,
Appeared, and stayed, and held his head
As one by kings accredited.

Erect, with his alert repose
About him, and about his clothes,
He pictured all tradition hears
Of what we owe to fifty years.
His cleansing heritage of taste
Paraded neither want nor waste;
And what he needed for his fee
To live, he borrowed graciously.

He never told us what he was,
Or what mischance, or other cause,
Had banished him from better days
To play the Prince of Castaways.
Meanwhile he played surpassing well
A part, for most, unplayable;
In fine, one pauses, half afraid
To say for certain that he played.

For that, one may as well forego
Conviction as to yes or no;
Nor can I say just how intense
Would then have been the difference
To several, who, having striven
In vain to get what he was given,
Would see the stranger taken on
By friends not easy to be won.

Moreover, many a malcontent
He soothed and found munificent;
His courtesy beguiled and foiled
Suspicion that his years were soiled;
His mien distinguished any crowd,

His credit strengthened when he bowed;
And women, young and old, were fond
Of looking at the man Flammonde.

There was a woman in our town
On whom the fashion was to frown;
But while our talk renewed the tinge
Of a long-faded scarlet fringe,
The man Flammonde saw none of that,
And what he saw we wondered at—
That none of us, in her distress,
Could hide or find our littleness.

There was a boy that all agreed
Had shut within him the rare seed
Of learning. We could understand,
But none of us could lift a hand.
The man Flammonde appraised the youth,
And told a few of us the truth;
And thereby, for a little gold,
A flowered future was unrolled.

There were two citizens who fought
For years and years, and over nought;
They made life awkward for their friends,
And shortened their own dividends.
The man Flammonde said what was wrong
Should be made right; nor was it long
Before they were again in line,
And had each other in to dine.

And these I mention are but four
Of many out of many more.
So much for them. But what of him—
So firm in every look and limb?
What small satanic sort of kink
Was in his brain? What broken link
Withheld him from the destinies
That came so near to being his?

What was he, when we came to sift
His meaning, and to note the drift
Of incommunicable ways
That make us ponder while we praise?

Why was it that his charm revealed
Somehow the surface of a shield?
What was it that we never caught?
What was he, and what was he not?

How much it was of him we met
We cannot ever know; nor yet
Shall all he gave us quite atone
For what was his, and his alone;
Nor need we now, since he knew best,
Nourish an ethical unrest:
Rarely at once will nature give
The power to be Flammonde and live.

We cannot know how much we learn
From those who never will return,
Until a flash of unforeseen
Remembrance falls on what has been.
We've each a darkening hill to climb;
And this is why, from time to time
In Tilbury Town, we look beyond
Horizons for the man Flammonde.

IN THE HOSPITAL*

Arthur Guiterman

Because on the branch that is tapping my pane
A sun-wakened leaf-bud uncurled,
Is bursting its rusty brown sheathing in twain,
I known there is Spring in the world.

Because through the sky-patch whose azure and white
My window frames all the day long
A yellow-bird dips for an instant of flight,
I know there is Song.

Because even here in this Mansion of Woe
Where creep the dull hours, leaden-shod,
Compassion and Tenderness aid me, I know
There is God.

*Taken from DEATH AND GENERAL PUTNAM and 101 Other Poems, by Arthur Guiterman, published and copyright by E. P. DUTTON & CO., INC., New York. Copyright 1935.

OF ANCIENT SHACKLES
ADELAIDE LOVE

I am among those unregenerates
Who do not seek "New Freedom," who enjoy
The ancient shackles of old-fashioned love,
Of faith and duty, and would not destroy
All moorings of the spirit that are old.
I like old-fashioned, peaceful firesides,
The steadfastness old homes and gardens knew;
I hold the old belief that love abides,
The old sustaining credences of men
That God must be the nurture of the soul,
That He will lean and listen to a prayer
And watches every man move toward his goal.
I am an unemancipated one
Who wears such fetters with a full content;
I see New Freedom's tortured restlessness
And of my bonds am deeply reverent.

LET US NOW PRAISE FAMOUS MEN
THE APOCRYPHA

LET US now praise famous men, and our fathers that begat us. The Lord hath wrought great glory by them through His great power from the beginning.

Such as did bear rule in their kingdoms, men renowned for their power, giving counsel by their understanding, and declaring prophecies; leaders of the people by their counsels, and by their knowledge of learning meet for the people, wise and eloquent in their instructions; such as found out musical tunes, and recited verses in writing; rich men furnished with ability, living peaceably in their habitations: all these were honoured in their generations, and were the glory of their times.

There be of them that have left a name behind them, that their praises might be reported. And some there be which have no memorial, who are perished, as though they had never been; and are become as though they had never been born; and their children after them. But these were merciful men, whose righteousness hath not been forgotten. With their seed shall continually remain a good inheritance, and their children are within the covenant. Their seed standeth fast, and their children for their sakes.

Their seed shall remain for ever, and their glory shall not be blotted out.

Their bodies are buried in peace; but their name liveth for evermore.

The people will tell of their wisdom and the congregation will show forth their praise.

GENIUS is only patience.—*Leclerc*

NOT IN THE CLAMOR of the crowded street,
Not in the shouts and plaudits of the throng,
But in ourselves are triumph and defeat.
—*Longfellow*

BY THE WORK one knows the workman.—*La Fontaine*

ASSOCIATE REVERENTLY, and as much as you can, with your loftiest thoughts.
—*Thoreau*

A PERFECT LIFE is like that of a ship of war which has its own place in the fleet and can share in its strength and discipline, but can also go forth alone in the solitude of the infinite sea. We ought to belong to society, to have our place in it, and yet be capable of a complete individual existence outside of it.—*Hamerton*

THERE ARE SOULS in this world which have the gift of finding joy everywhere and of leaving it behind them when they go.—*Faber*

THEY SAY. What say they? Let them say.—*Anonymous*

CULTURE is "to know the best that has been said and thought in the world."—*Arnold*

THE HAND that gives, gathers.—*Ray*

LIFE is mostly froth and bubble;
Two things stand like stone:—
Kindness in another's trouble,
Courage in our own.
—*Gordon*

How BEAUTIFUL a day can be
When kindness touches it!
—*Elliston*

THE WORLD

Our doubts are traitors
And make us lose the good we oft might win
By fearing to attempt.
                —*Shakespeare*

AN HONEST HEART possesses a kingdom.—*Seneca*

IF WE can say with Seneca, "This life is only a prelude to eternity,"
then we need not worry so much over the fittings and furnishings of
this ante-room; and more than that, it will give dignity and purpose
to the fleeting days to know they are linked with the eternal things as
prelude and preparation.—*Savage*

MIGHTY is the force of motherhood! It transforms all things by its vital
heat.—*George Eliot*

IT IS DIFFICULT to make a man miserable while he feels he is worthy of himself and claims kindred to the great God who made him.—*Abraham Lincoln*

HE IS not only idle who does nothing, but he is idle who might be better
employed.—*Socrates*

THE IDEAL STATE is that in which an injury done to the least of its
citizens is an injury done to all.—*Solon*

WHATEVER one possesses, becomes of double value, when we have
the opportunity of sharing it with others.—*Bouilly*

THE WISEST MAN could ask no more of fate
Than to be simple, modest, manly, true,
Safe from the many, honored by the few;
Nothing to court in Church, or World, or State,
But inwardly in secret to be great.
                —*Lowell*

IN FRIENDSHIP we find nothing false or in-
sincere; everything is straightforward, and
springs from the heart.—*Cicero*

GENERAL WILLIAM BOOTH ENTERS INTO HEAVEN

Vachel Lindsay

(Bass drum beaten loudly.)
Booth led boldly with his big brass drum—
(Are you washed in the blood of the Lamb?)
The Saints smiled gravely and they said: "He's come."
(Are you washed in the blood of the Lamb?)
Walking lepers followed, rank on rank,
Lurching bravos from the ditches dank,
Drabs from the alleyways and drug fiends pale—
Minds still passion-ridden, soul-powers frail:—
Vermin-eaten saints with moldy breath,
Unwashed legions with the ways of Death—
(Are you washed in the blood of the Lamb?)

(Banjos.)
Every slum had sent its half-a-score
The round world over. (Booth had groaned for more.)
Every banner that the wide world flies
Bloomed with glory and transcendent dyes.
Big-voiced lasses made their banjos bang,
Tranced, fanatical they shrieked and sang:—
"Are you washed in the blood of the Lamb?"
Hallelujah! It was queer to see
Bull-necked convicts with that land make free.
Loons with trumpets blowed a blare, blare, blare
On, on upward thro' the golden air!
(Are you washed in the blood of the Lamb?)

II

(Bass drum slower and softer.)
Booth died blind and still by faith he trod,
Eyes still dazzled by the ways of God.
Booth led boldly, and he looked the chief
Eagle countenance in sharp relief,
Beard a-flying, air of high command
Unabated in that holy land.

(Sweet flute music.)
Jesus came from out the court-house door,
Stretched his hands above the passing poor.

Booth saw not, but led his queer ones there
Round and round the mighty court-house square.
Then, in an instant all that blear review
Marched on spotless, clad in raiment new.
The lame were straightened, withered limbs uncurled
And blind eyes opened on a new, sweet world.

(Bass drum louder.)
Drabs and vixens in a flash made whole!
Gone was the weasel-head, the snout, the jowl!
Sages and sibyls now, and athletes clean,
Rulers of empires, and of forest green!

*(Grand chorus of all instruments. Tambourines to the
foreground.)*
The hosts were sandalled, and their wings were fire!
(Are you washed in the blood of the Lamb?)
But their noise played havoc with the angel-choir.
(Are you washed in the blood of the Lamb?)
Oh, shout Salvation! It was good to see
Kings and Princes by the Lamb set free.
The banjos rattled and the tambourines
Jing-jing-jingled in the hands of Queens.

(Reverently sung, no instruments.)
And when Booth halted by the curb for prayer
He saw his Master thro' the flag-filled air.
Christ came gently with a robe and crown
For Booth the soldier, while the throng knelt down.
He saw King Jesus. They were face to face,
And he knelt a-weeping in that holy place.
Are you washed in the blood of the Lamb?

THE ATHENIAN BOYS' OATH
ANONYMOUS

WE WILL never bring disgrace to this, our city, by any act of dishonesty or cowardice, nor ever desert our suffering comrades in the ranks.

We will fight for the ideals and sacred things of the city, both alone and with many; we will revere and obey the city's laws and do our best to incite a like respect and reverence in those above us who are prone to annul or set them at naught; we will strive unceasingly to quicken the public's sense of civic duty.

Thus in all these ways we will transmit this city not only not less, but greater than it was transmitted to us.

GRATITUDE
By H. E. MANNING

GRATITUDE consists in a watchful, minute attention to the particulars of our state, and to the multitude of God's gifts, taken one by one. It fills us with a consciousness that God loves and cares for us, even to the least event and the smallest need of life. It is a blessed thought, that from our childhood God has been laying His fatherly hands upon us, and always in benediction; that even the strokes of His hands are blessings, and among the chiefest we have ever received. When this feeling is awakened, the heart beats with a pulse of thankfulness. Every gift has its return of praise. It awakens an unceasing daily converse with our Father,—He speaking to us by the descent of blessings, we to Him by the ascent of thanksgiving. And all our whole life is thereby drawn under the light of His countenance, and is filled with a gladness, serenity, and peace which only thankful hearts can know.

THE TIME IS SHORT
By PHILLIPS BROOKS

OH, MY DEAR FRIENDS, you who are letting miserable misunderstandings run on from year to year, meaning to clear them up some day; you who are keeping wretched quarrels alive because you cannot quite make up your mind that now is the day to sacrifice your pride and kill them; you who are passing men sullenly upon the street, not speaking to them out of some silly spite, and yet knowing that it would fill you with shame and remorse if you heard that one of these men were dead to-morrow morning; you who are letting your neighbor starve, till you hear that he is dying of starvation; or letting your friend's heart ache for a word of appreciation or sympathy, which you mean to give him some day,—if you only could know and see and feel, all of a sudden, that "the time is short," how it would break the spell! How you would go instantly and do the thing which you might never have another chance to do.

WALK WITH GOD
From the CHRISTIAN UNION

IS IT possible for any of us in these modern days to so live that we may walk with God? Can we walk with God in the shop, in the office, in the household, and on the street? When men exasperate us, and work wearies us, and the children fret, and the servants annoy, and our best-laid plans fall to pieces, and our castles in the air are dissipated like bubbles that break at a breath, then can we walk with God? That religion which fails us in the every-day trials and experiences of life has somewhere in it a flaw. It should be more than a plank to sustain us in the rushing tide, and land us exhausted and dripping on the other side. It ought, if it come from above, to be always, day by day, to our souls as the wings of a bird, bearing us away from and beyond the impediments which seek to hold us down. If the Divine Love be a conscious presence, an indwelling force with us, it will do this.

From *SAUL*
Robert Browning

XVIII

"I believe it! 'T is thou, God, that givest, 't is I who receive:
In the first is the last, in thy will is my power to believe.
All's one gift: thou canst grant it moreover, as prompt to my prayer
As I breathe out this breath, as I open these arms to the air.
From thy will stream the worlds, life and nature, thy dread Sabaoth:
I will?—the mere atoms despise me! Why am I not loth
To look that, even that in the face too? Why is it I dare
Think but lightly of such impuissance? What stops my despair?
This;—'t is not what man Does which exalts him, but what man Would do!
See the King—I would help him but cannot, the wishes fall through.
Could I wrestle to raise him from sorrow, grow poor to enrich,
To fill up his life, starve my own out, I would—knowing which,
I know that my service is perfect. Oh, speak through me now!
Would I suffer for him that I love? So wouldst thou—so wilt thou!
So shall crown thee the topmost, ineffablest, uttermost crown—
And thy love fill infinitude wholly, nor leave up nor down
One spot for the creature to stand in! It is by no breath,
Turn of eye, wave of hand, that salvation joins issue with death!
As thy Love is discovered almighty, almighty be proved
Thy power, that exists with and for it, of being Beloved!
He who did most, shall bear most; the strongest shall stand the most weak.
'T is the weakness in strength, that I cry for! my flesh, that I seek
In the Godhead! I seek and I find it. O Saul, it shall be
A Face like my face that receives thee; a Man like to me,
Thou shalt love and be loved by, forever: a Hand like this hand
Shall throw open the gates of new life to thee! See the Christ stand!"

THE LIFE OF A HAPPY MAN
By Thomas Dekker

To AWAKEN each morning with a smile brightening my face; to greet the
day with reverence for the opportunities it contains; to approach my work with
a clean mind; to hold ever before me, even in the doing of little things, the
Ultimate Purpose toward which I am working; to meet men and women
with laughter on my lips and love in my heart; to be gentle, kind, and courteous through all the hours; to approach the night with weariness that ever
woos sleep and the joy that comes from work well done—this is how I desire
to waste wisely my days.

Before Gabriel Blows His Horn[*]

By JAMES STREET

*J*UST SEEING Stumpy handle a truck like she was a kiddy-car you'd never think he liked poetry and songs, but a heap of times on the long hauls he's kept me awake by reciting "On the Road to Mandalay" and things like that, and by singing "Alabama Bound" and "The Memphis Blues."

He looks like he ought to sing bass and nothing but honky-tonk songs. He's squat and built like a Diesel job. He's from the Alabama coal country and his hands are as big as hams. His pug nose looks funny because it was knocked cater-cornered in a jackhandle brawl. But he sings baritone and never nothing dirty. Many a time we've been balling the jack and it a-raining and blowing, and ol' Stumpy'd cut down on his favorite hymn—"On Jordan's Stormy Banks I Stand." It makes a fellow feel better. Pushing trucks like me and him shove 'em ain't as safe as sitting in a rocker in front of the fireplace.

Pushers back in Alabama where we usta break a little less than even with our own truck reckoned Stumpy was sort of clutch-drunk, which is how drivers get if they drive themselves as hard as they do their trucks. We were going bust fast, and I was glad when we got a chance to change scenery.

A company in Birmingham opened a truck line in Australia and offered us a job to go down there and help get things going. Stumpy told me, "Peckerwood, let's go."

He always has called me Pecker-

**Taken from* COSMOPOLITAN *July 1941.*

wood since we first buddied up. I'm from Mississippi, and I'm tall and bean-poley. Stumpy can walk under my arm. He's all time telling me that if I grow another inch I'll fork again.

We were doing pretty good in Australia until the war broke out and the guv'ment bought the truck line. That left me and Stumpy without a job and with just a little dough. And there was a bunch of miles between us and Alabama. Our boss man offered to get us a job on a boat, nursemaiding some sheep. Stumpy asked where the boat was heading, and the man said, "Rangoon."

I knew what was coming, and sure 'nuff ol' Stumpy said, "Peckerwood, let's go."

Rangoon is the place in that poetry that Stumpy's all time reciting and I'll admit it does sound pretty—"From Rangoon to Mandalay." But Rangoon ain't nothing to write home about. Stumpy must have liked it, though, because he'd go over to the Irrawaddy River and watch the boats. He said he was looking for flying fish, and I got worried about him, figuring maybe he was clutch-drunk, 'specially when he told me one day that the river was the road to Mandalay. Now, when a man thinks a river's a road, it's time to hit for home.

206

We had to have money to get home on, but white folks over there don't work with their hands if there's any way out of it. 'Sides, wages are so low a man can't reach 'em even if he stoops over. Me and Stumpy said at first that we'd rather starve than rat on the American standard of living, but in Burma nobody gives a hooray if you starve. It's root, hog, or die. So we rooted.

We got a job dock-walloping, and even the coolies snooted us because we were white men and doing hard labor. The only other white man on the job was an Englishman who was on the lam from a jail rap. We got lonesome and down in the mouth. When you're a long ways from home it's the little things you miss most. I missed ketchup and the funny papers, more'n anything. Stumpy said he missed news of the Crimson Tide, which is the Alabama football team.

We were hustling on the wharf one day, unloading a big sister from England. She had fetched over a mess of doodlebugs—them little English trucks. They are fair-to-middling rigs, but alongside our trucks back home they look like starving chicken mites.

Stumpy nudged me and said, "Look at 'em. Back home we'd give 'em to kids for Christmas. They'd do for door-to-door work, but can you picture one of them cockroaches on Highway 11 between Birming-'ygod-ham and New Or'yans?" I was looking at the little trucks, and first thing I knew Stumpy grabbed my arm and said hoarse-like, "Great day in the mawnin'! Looka yonder!"

I glanced up just as they unloaded a big red rig. My eyes got

as big as fried eggs. Maybe I've seen prettier trucks, but I can't remember 'em. She was a donkey-and-trailer job and she looked as big as a barn. She was a fourteen-wheeler. Her running lights were green and her fog lights were yellow, and she looked like she was tired of boats and wanted to do a little rolling on her own. She had "Made in U.S.A." painted on her side. It ain't no use of putting that on trucks like her. Hell, mister! She spoke for herself.

She looked sort of lonesome and out of place, so me and Stumpy walked up to her and he ran his finger along the treads of her tires. Twelve plies. Then we peeped in her cab, and Stumpy said, "I know the breed. Forty tons dead weight. Fast. Stout. Twelve speeds forward. She can run like a rabbit with high life on his tail, and Peckerwood, there's enough horses under that hood to drag that boat up the road to Mandalay."

Some Englishmen and a Chinaman walked up, and the Chinaman pointed at the big rig and said, "That truck is of no use to us."

Stumpy grumbled, "Listen at that Chink runnin' down our truck. I'm gonna write Mama to quit givin' money to the missionary society."

Funny how ol' Stumpy was already calling that rig ours.

One of the Englishmen told the Chinaman, "Some clever American sold a shipment of those lorries to us. We can't use them in England. Too big. They sent that one over for you to try out. If you can use it, you can have the remainder of the shipment for a good price."

The Chinaman said, "A fleet of those things on the Burma Road could carry big cargoes, I'll admit.

207

But it'd be easier to get that steamer through the mountains."

Stumpy stepped right up to the Chinaman and tapped him on the chest. "Listen, Mr. Chop Suey. That rig'll go anywhere and do anything. I can make her skip rope and play hopscotch."

The Englishmen looked at us and stepped back like we had som'n bad, and it was catching. I'll admit we were greasy and dirty.

The Chinaman smiled. "Americans, eh?"

"So what?" Stumpy said, and I started looking for a jack handle.

"Say iron; courthouse; Mary, marry, merry." The Chinaman was grinning.

Stumpy said what he told him, and the Chinaman offered his hand. "From the South, eh? I'd say Alabama or Mississippi, or maybe south Georgia."

He saw we were flabbergasted and introduced himself as Mister Soo Choo, and right then and there we got to calling him "Mister Choo Choo."

"I went to the University of Chicago," he said. "Studied international law until a few guys got to writing a new set of rules with machine guns."

Stumpy said, "Chicago is that school where they ain't got no football team, ain't it? You don't happen to know how Alabama came out last year, huh?"

"Terrible," said Mister Choo Choo. "Tennessee and Mississippi State both beat 'em."

I laughed and asked him how Superman and Joe Palooka were doing. The Englishmen thought we was nuts.

Finally Mister Choo Choo said, "You guys know how to handle these things?" He tapped the truck and talked just like an American.

Stumpy said, "We don't handle 'em. We just whistle and they follow us like pups."

Our pal said, "I'm from Missouri."

Stumpy said, "Then count yourself again, big boy, 'cause you ain't so popeyed many. Get in this rig."

First time I ever saw ol' Stumpy cry. But when he kicked that motor on and heard her growl, he got to sniffing. Mister Choo Choo must have understood how we felt, 'cause he didn't laugh or nothing. Stumpy let her idle low for a few minutes, then juiced her and let her sing. He batted his eyes real fast to run off the tears and whispered to me, "Sounds like she's singing 'Home, Sweet Home.'"

He slipped her all twelve of her forward gears and we went out beyond Rangoon, and Stumpy put her through her paces. Stumpy can thread a needle with a truck. He spun that baby on a dime, put her in a skid and jerked her out.

Mister Choo Choo said, "Pretty good. But what about sand?"

Stumpy said, "You didn't learn much at Chicago, huh? I can run this baby across any sand. Just bleed the tires. Let 'em down almost flat, then high-tail it. Don't give her time to bog."

Mister Choo Choo told him to cut off the motor and we sat there and talked. He asked us if we knew about the Burma Road. Of course we did. It runs from the edge of Burma, 'way into China, and they call it the Chinese life line. The upshot of it was that our pal offered to pay our way home if we'd take that truck up the Burma Road to Kunming and back.

"You'll have to go from Rangoon to Mandalay; then——"
He never finished it. Stumpy cut his eyes over at me, but I beat him to it. "Okay, Stumpy," I said. "Let's go."
We had to paint our truck brown, but before we laid a brush on her Stumpy looked her over. She was big and red.
Stumpy said, "Looks like the Alabama football team. The old Crimson Tide."
I said, "We'll name her that."
The Englishmen and Mister Choo Choo were watching us, and one of the Englishmen said, "I'm aware that America is a remarkable country. But it doesn't have red tides."
Mister Choo Choo winked at us and patted the Englishman on the back. "Skip it, bo."
We loaded the Crimson Tide on a flat car, and that's how we went up the road to Mandalay. Stumpy sure was put out. It was a jerkwater railroad. He got up before daybust the first day. I heard him mumbling, "And the dawn comes up like thunder." It was a right pretty dawn, I reckon, but not like the dawns back home. You don't have to write poetry about the dawns at home. Just seeing one of 'em is all the poetry one man needs.
It's about 400 miles from Rangoon to Mandalay, and we went about 150 miles more to Lashio, where Burma stops and China starts. Mister Choo Choo met us and explained that us and twenty-five of them little doodlebugs would make the haul to Kunming—750 miles through mountains and jungles.
"I'm going along," he said. "We can't take soldiers. Need all the room for cargo. We'll have to stick together. Run at night. No lights. The Japs fly over and bomb us, if they see us."
We were the only white men in the gang. The other drivers were Chinamen, and plenty tough. We got loaded about dark and we rolled at midnight. Mister Choo Choo and his driver were leading.
I caught on pretty quick how come they used small trucks. We hit one grade after another and a mess of hairpin turns. Stumpy had to keep our heavy rig in low-low a heap, and she was panting and groaning and gulping oil. Stumpy was leaning out of the cab, fighting them gears and trying to pick his way.
The truck in front of us showed a little red taillight, and that's all we had to steer by. But the guy behind us was steering by our little light.
I've done some truck driving in my time. I've crossed Lake Pontchartrain when a gale was blowing, and I've mudded through swamps when we had to cut down trees and build our own road. Me and Stumpy have seen some things, but man, you ain't pushed no truck until you've run a rig over the Burma Road. You don't dare take your eyes off the little light in front of you. If you look up, you see nothing but the mountains, and if you look down you see nothing but space.
A hundred times the Crimson Tide lurched, and Stumpy gave her the air. Then he braked her easy and gave her another gear. She chewed that gear, and Stumpy slipped her another one real quick. She was hot and tired out.
Stumpy told me. "Give her a

209

little better dose. Little heavier. She's a big girl, and you can't expect a big girl to get by on skim milk. Give her a little cream."

I regulated the gas flow so she'd get a heavier mixture. She must have appreciated it because she quit whining and growling and got to singing.

Along about dawn we ran off on a spur road that was built for trucks to hide on. The other drivers coiled up in their seats and went to sleep. They slept four hours, then ate a handful of rice and went to work on their rigs, cleaning plugs and such. They didn't worry about nothing. You can kill such folks, I guess, but you can't whip 'em.

Me and Stumpy walked ahead to a village, aiming to buy som'n fit to eat. I don't like rice without chicken gravy. The village never had been much, I reckon, but now it wasn't nothing except a pile of junk. The Japs had flown over the day before and bombed it because it was a stopover on the Burma Road.

I'd never seen anything like it. Men and women were working, trying to rebuild a piece of the road that had been tore up. Some folks had been killed, and their bodies were lying in the sun. Mister Choo Choo walked up to us and said, "They won't bury their dead or rebuild their houses until the road is fixed. Back in America, a road is just a road, but the Burma Road is my country's jugular vein."

Stumpy looked at me and I looked at him. And right then and there me and Stumpy quit driving a truck just for pay and started fighting a war. We went on back to our rig and ate boiled rice.

We rolled again at sundown, and come good dark, we were going downgrade. Stumpy started singing, "Look down, look down that lonesome road, before you travel on." Then I heard him humming, and pretty soon he said, "How does the second verse go? I forgot it."

I didn't know. Ol' Stumpy kept singing the first verse over and over, trying to get the second verse. "I got it right on the end of my tongue," he said. "I'll go nuts till I think of it."

We were dropping down out of some mountains into some level country when the explosion sounded up ahead. The fellow just in front of us blinked his taillight, a signal to stop, and we eased over to the side of the road and Stumpy cut her off. Pretty soon I heard the planes go over. I couldn't see 'em, but I knew they were Japs. The Chinese ain't got nowhere near enough planes to patrol the Burma Road.

The droning died out toward the southeast where Indo-China is, and we started crawling again. Before long the whole line stopped, and me and Stumpy got out and walked up to Mister Choo Choo's truck. He was standing by a sandy gully. There'd been a bridge across it, but it'd been blown to hell and gone. The first thing I thought about was how good them Japs were to be able to hit such a little bridge in the dark.

The other drivers got their tools, crowbars and such, and set in to fix the bridge. Mister Choo Choo said some coolies would be along t'reckly. They stay on the job all night, and as soon as they hear an explosion, they head for it, knowing there's work to be done.

Stumpy looked at the gully and

then climbed down in it. The banks were straight up and down. It wasn't much wider than our truck and about as deep. He got a flashlight and examined the sandy bed, then walked down the gully to where the banks almost evened off. Then he told Mister Choo Choo, "No use waiting for the coolies. Me and my helper will get you across." He poked me in the side. "All right, Peckerwood, let's go."

He backed our truck out of the line and picked his way down to the gully. I took the flash and walked ahead of her, and Stumpy eased her up that gully to where the bridge had been.

We got some timbers from the wrecked bridge and laid 'em across our trailer and made our own bridge, using the trailer for support. The doodlebugs crossed over and Mister Choo Choo was proud of us.

It was coming daybust when we got lined up again, and Mister Choo Choo told his men to rest, and he went back and looked at where the bridge had been. I said som'n about what good bombers the Japs are, and Mister Choo Choo's eyes got narrow.

"That bridge wasn't bombed. It was dynamited."

Then he told us that the planes were transports that bring in dynamiters and machine-gun crews to protect 'em. They dynamite the bridges at night and fly back to their bases.

Mister Choo Choo must have known a heap of things were bothering us, because he said, "There are a hundred valleys around here where planes can land. And hide. Besides, even if the natives saw them land they couldn't fight machine guns with rakes."

We drove on up to a village and hid the trucks as best we could, and Mister Choo Choo got to nosing around. Pretty soon he came up to us and he had a Chinaman with him, a grinning fellow who was dressed better than the other folks in the village. Mister Choo Choo motioned for us to follow, and the grinning Chinaman led us to a hill that sloped off pretty even to a long flat valley, shaped like a meat platter. And down there I saw a big white cross and knew that was where the planes landed.

Mister Choo Choo bowed very politely to the other Chinaman, like he was thanking him for showing us the place, and then he pulled out a pistol and shot the fellow in the head.

I was so taken back I didn't say nothing. Neither did Stumpy. Mister Choo Choo searched the body until he found a purse, and he kept it. I was pretty disgusted and said, "Stealing from the dead is worse than stealing from the blind."

"It's my money." Mister Choo Choo threw some leaves over the body and I knew he aimed to leave it unburied, the worst disgrace a Chinaman can suffer. "That fellow was worse than what you call a Fifth Columnist in America. He took money from the Japs and betrayed us. I paid him more and he betrayed the Japs." That's all he ever said about it. Then he pointed down the valley.

"They land down there about dark. The dynamiters slip up the road and do their dirt while soldiers guard the planes. Then they get away. They landed there yesterday and will again this afternoon."

"How you know?" I asked. "Because the white cross is still there. They'd destroy it if they were moving their emergency field. They'll use this place as long as they think it's safe. The country is so big and wild that you could hide an army in these valleys."

Stumpy hadn't said a word. He was studying the ground, and by and by he asked me, "Reckon we can get the Crimson Tide to the top of this slope?"

I said, "She can make it. Pretty rough, but not too rough."

Then Stumpy looked around until he spotted a patch of ground where there wasn't no trees between the top of the grade and the field—just some brush and a few little shallow ditches. I looked down the clearing too. It was a right smart grade. I knew what Stumpy was thinking and I didn't like it. Not a'*tall!*

He glanced over at Mister Choo Choo and said, "Ever hear of Gen'l Nathan 'ygod Bedford Forrest? My grandpa was with him."

"You mean General Get-there-fustes'-with-the-mostes'-men Forrest?" Mister Choo Choo grinned.

"He said mor'n that. He said, 'Slip up behind 'em when they ain't looking.' He also said, 'Pick out the one thing they figure you can't do, then do it.' Me and my podner will get them planes."

Mister Choo Choo didn't laugh when Stumpy told him what he had up his sleeve. He said, "What'll it cost us?"

"Maybe nothing, if the Lord's with us. If He ain't, it'll cost you our truck."

"But what about you boys?"

"Same's true for us. If the Lord is with us, we'll be okay. If He ain't, then we are gone goslin's any way."

We went back to our truck. We braced our big bumper with some crowbars and fastened some more crowbars from the bumper to the top of our radiator, and some more from the radiator to the top of the cab. It wasn't a fancy job, but it was stout. Then we knocked out our windshield and took the springs from under our seat and put 'em where the windshield had been. We put four crowbars across the springs. It wasn't much protection, but it was som'n.

The Crimson Tide sure did look funny, but she had enough weight, power and steel to bust through a stone wall.

We got the other drivers to take their doodlebugs up the road about a mile, then cut out in the woods amongst some scrub trees. Me and Stumpy took off a couple of the mufflers and loosened some of the others. Then we showed Mister Choo Choo what to do and started back toward our truck, taking a Chinaman with us to act as runner.

Mister Choo Choo called us. "Anything you boys want?"

We said no thanks and started off again, but ol' Stumpy stopped quick and went up to Mister Choo Choo. "Do you happen to know the second verse to 'The Lonesome Road'?"

"Nope," said Mister Choo Choo. "Sorry. I know 'Seafood Mama,' if that'll help."

"It won't help a bit," Stumpy grunted.

We drove our truck across the rolling land, picking our way to the top of the slope. Stumpy drove her just over the hump, aimed her nose at the white cross, cut the motor

212

and pulled up the emergency. We covered her with brush and then climbed in the cab and sat there.

I jumped when Stumpy finally spoke. He said, "Beats all how that verse slipped my mind. I know it good as anything." He got to humming again, figuring the verse would come to him.

It was coming dark when we heard the planes. Then two big babies dropped from 'way up yonder and circled the field. I was popeyed. Stumpy was grinning, and so was the Chinaman. They landed them planes near the cross, and a bunch of Japs jumped out and started piling brush over the planes. Then more Japs got out. There were about thirty of 'em. They mounted two machine guns to guard the planes, while more men kept getting stuff out'n the ships and I knew they were the dynamiters, rigging their charges.

It was dark before we knew it and they were working with flashlights. We could see pretty good. The stars were out, and me and Stumpy can just naturally see at night. You have to if you expect to live and do good in the trucking business. I saw 'em lugging some stuff over to the woods and reckoned they were getting the dynamite a safe piece away from the planes.

Stumpy tapped the Chinaman on the shoulder and nodded. The runner slipped out and shook off through the woods, heading for Mister Choo Choo.

Me and Stumpy just sat there, waiting. We were about three hundred yards from the Japs and could barely see the outlines of the planes. The moon came up full then, and Stumpy looked at it and shook his head. We could've used a few clouds. We could see the Japs plain then. The dynamiters were fixing to go out.

Stumpy grabbed my arm. "I got it," he whispered. He was staring at the sky, and he sang real low:

"Look up, look up and seek yo'
    Maker
'Fore Gabriel blows his horn."

I shivered. It was the second verse, all right, and Stumpy was plum' pleased with himself, but I didn't like the way it sounded.

I said, "How come you to think of it?"

"Just came to me. I was looking up yonder and wondering if the Lord was with us, or if ol' Gabe was fixing to blow his horn. Then I thought of it."

Even though I was ready for it, I cringed when I heard the first explosion from up where the doodlebugs were hiding. It sounded like a big gun, all right. Then there was some sharp explosions, fast and loud. Them Chinamen were doing just like we showed 'em. They were letting the manifolds of them little trucks fill up, then cutting the ignition off and on real quick, and them things were backfiring and popping like rifles.

The Japs must have thought the Chinese Army had 'em. The machine gunners picked up their stuff and ran to the edge of some woods and started setting up their guns again, pointing 'em toward the explosions. Some more fellows started jerking the brush off'n the planes so they could get away in a hurry.

Stumpy let down our emergency brake and said, "Okay, Peckerwood, let's go."

213

We started off real slow down the grade. Stumpy didn't cut on the motor or lights, but let her roll free.

The Japs didn't see us at first. We wasn't making much fuss, and they were excited and busy. By the time that big Tide rolled a hundred yards downgrade, we were going like a bat out of hell.

We took them little ditches like a jack rabbit, but she was bucking and lurching. I'll admit I was a-scared, and I believe Stumpy was too. The cords in his neck were sticking out like ropes, and the muscles in his arms were bunched. It was like trying to hold a locomotive and it off'n the track.

He kept talking to the truck and begging, "Stay on your feet, baby! Don't go back on me now."

There wasn't nothing between us and Gabriel 'cep'n the good Lord who looks after fools like us. We couldn't have stopped if'n we'd tried.

We were mor'n halfway down when the Japs saw us. One of 'em pointed, and I heard him yell above the wind that was whistling around them crowbars and through them springs. Just then Stumpy cut on ever' light we had and bore down on the horn. It was enough to scare anybody—a bolt of lights whistling down a hill from nowhere and a horn bellowing like the devil with a toothache.

A few of the soldiers fired at us from the woods, but they never had time to get their machine guns turned on us. The other Japs never got all the brush off'n them planes, neither. We were on 'em before they could move the planes, and they scattered like quail.

Stumpy yelled, "Duck!"

But he didn't have to tell me.

He cut his wheel and aimed straight for the tail of the first ship. We hit it right behind the rear wheel and cut through the tail like it was tin. A part of it hit the bars and springs in front of us and ripped off. Stumpy hit the second plane a little lower and nipped off the tip of the tail, just enough to keep it on the ground.

I reckoned we were making seventy then and on even ground, but we got to losing headway fast. The Japs were running out of the woods, taking pot shots at us.

Stumpy said, "Okay. We got to get out of here."

He pushed in the clutch and cut on the switch. I found myself pushing against the floorboard, just like I was handling her. It's tough on any machine to give it gears and it rolling fast, but with a big truck like ours it's a plum' dangerous job to give her a gear and her balling the jack. I held my breath. If she refused to take that gear, or if she stripped it, then them Japs would be on us like jay birds on June bugs.

But that Stumpy! A truck-drivin' man from a truck-drivin' lan'. He nursed a high gear into her, eased off the clutch and gunned her. She snatched that gear in her teeth and started getting on down the line. I had my ear cocked, listenin' to the motor. I heard her hum and knew she was heating fast. I nodded to Stumpy. He fed her the highest gear and gave her all the gas she could handle. The wind started singing through them springs again, and Stumpy got to singing too.

We kept our lights on and picked our way back to the highroad, and then, figuring we were safe, I said, "Wonder why them guys didn't chunk some dynamite at us. That would've stopped us."

Stumpy got white around the gills. "Lord a'mercy!" he said. "I never thought about that. Reckon they didn't, either. Else their stuff wasn't rigged so they could chunk it."

I said, "Thought you had ever'thing figured out. How'd you know all the dynamite was out'n them planes? We might've blowed ourselves up."

He got green around the gills then. He said, "You better drive awhile. I ain't feelin' so hot."

Mister Choo Choo was tickled plum' pink. Stumpy told him, "We just cut off their tails. You can get 'em fixed. But how 'bout the Japs? They may get away."

"Not a chance," said Mister Choo Choo. "You know, they haven't got much food and water. They can't stay there, and they can't get word out for help. The natives will take care of them." He looked at Stumpy, and he wasn't smiling when he said, "And by the way, that verse you asked about came to me while I was waiting here, wondering how you guys came out."

Stumpy said, "Thanks. I thought of it, too."

THE WESTERN SKY
Archibald MacLeish

Stand stand against the rising night
O freedom's land, O freedom's air:
Stand steep and keep the fading light
That eastward darkens everywhere.

Hold hold the golden light and lift
Hill after hill-top, one by one—
Lift up America O lift
Green freedom to the evening sun.

Lift up your hills till conquered men
Look westward to their blazing height:
Lift freedom till its fire again
Kindles the countries of the night.

Be proud America to bear
The endless labor of the free—
To strike for freedom everywhere
And everywhere bear liberty.

Lift up O land O land lift clear
The lovely signal of your skies.
If freedom darkens eastward here
Here on the west let freedom rise.

215

LOST ROAD

Frances Frost

The feet which wore this earth to a twisted road
Between two mountains, are halted now and gone
Under the mountains where restless feet are still.
The small green things with blossoms have come back:
Year by year the tangled woods push down
And thicken the shadows above the wagon-track
And cover with fires of blossoming the brown
Wander of dust.

The russet ghosts of lilac-bloom are summer
About a door long opened to the rain.
A locust in a brazen, husky stammer
Stretches tight a yellow afternoon;
And sun and rain fall deeply on this road
Where men with wide, burned shoulders and steady breath
Went, through the ache of days and nights, toward death.

The walls men made in woods . . . beneath the moon
Of summer run forever . . . and by these
Men outlive the hour wherein they die.
Under a sky
Of boughs, the way is lost by which a child
Went laughing from one white house to another,
Scuffling beneath the mounting, golden day.

A road is a message many men wrote down
In dust, of love that listened for the sound
Of footsteps coming home. A road is where
Women, at evening, before the light was gone,
Walked with children living in their flesh
And dreamed of other roads on other mountains
To be carved by strong sons born to wilderness.

A road is a chronicle of loves and years.
A road remembers until the green things take
With blossoms the last faint trace of footsteps going
Between a beginning and an end.
                              O bitter
Growing of woods and sumac, of thorns and fern,
Possess at last
This road which is a word

216

Spoken from darkness, uttered from the years
Abandoned long ago. O wildness, burn
With deep green shadow, the memory of those
Who left this sign between tall grass and grass
As they went past.

UNMANIFEST DESTINY

RICHARD HOVEY

To what new gates, my country, far
　　And unforseen of foe or friend,
Beneath what unexpected star,
　　Compelled to what unchosen end.

Across the sea that knows no beach
　　The Admiral of Nations guides
Thy blind obedient keels to reach
　　The harbor where thy future rides!

The guns that spoke at Lexington
　　Knew not that God was planning then
The trumpet word of Jefferson
　　To bugle forth the rights of men.

To them that wept and cursed Bull Run,
　　What was it but despair and shame?
Who saw behind the cloud the sun?
　　Who knew that God was in the flame?

Had not defeat upon defeat,
　　Disaster on disaster come,
The slave's emancipated feet
　　Had never marched behind the drum.

There is a Hand that bends our deeds
　　To mightier issues than we planned,
Each son that triumphs, each that bleeds,
　　My country, serves Its dark command.

I do not know beneath what sky
　　Nor on what seas shall be thy fate;
I only know it shall be high,
　　I only know it shall be great.

WHERE words fail, music speaks.—*Hans Andersen*

IF I SHOOT at the sun, I may hit a star.—*Barnum*

KINDNESS—a language which the dumb can speak, and the deaf can understand.—*Bovée*

A MAN of intellect without energy added to it is a failure.—*Chamfort*

MUSIC is never stationary; successive forms and styles are only like so many resting-places—like tents pitched and taken down again on the road to the Ideal.—*Liszt*

FROM THE GLOW of enthusiasm I let the melody escape. I pursue it. Breathless I catch up with it. It flies again, it disappears, it plunges into a chaos of diverse emotions. I catch it again, I seize it, I embrace it with delight. I multiply it then by modulations, and at last I triumph in the first theme. There is the whole symphony.—*Beethoven*

EXPERIENCE shows that success is due less to ability than to zeal. The winner is he who gives himself to his work, body and soul.—*Buxton*

THE ROAD TO SUCCESS is not to be run upon by seven-leagued boots. Step by step, little by little, bit by bit—that is the way to wealth, that is the way to wisdom, that is the way to glory.—*Buxton*

I AM FULLY assured that God does not, and therefore that men ought not to require any more of any man than this, to believe the Scripture to be God's word, and to endeavor to find the true sense of it, and to live according to it.—*Chillingworth*

THE WORLD'S A STAGE, where God's omnipotence,
His justice, knowledge, love, and providence
Do act the parts.
   —Du Bartas

TO-DAY is yesterday's pupil.—*Thomas Fuller*

THE WORLD

NOTHING is too high for a man to reach, but he must climb with care and confidence.—*Hans Andersen*

TRUTH is honesty in speech; honesty is truth in action.—*Millard*

HE THAT LOVETH A BOOK, will never want a faithful friend, a wholesome counsellor, a cheerful companion, an effectual comforter.—*Barrow*

THE CRY of the age is more for fraternity than for charity. If one exists the other will follow, or better still, will not be needed.—*Chapin*

WHEN WORDS FAIL to express the exalted sentiments and finer emotions of the human heart, music becomes the sublimated language of the soul, the divine instrumentality for its higher utterance.—*Wendte*

IT IS ONLY to the finest natures that age gives an added beauty and distinction; for the most persistent self has then worked its way to the surface, having modified the expression, and to some extent, the features, to its own likeness.—*Blind*

'TIS WHAT WE DO, not what we say, that makes us worthy of His grace.—*Gilder*

THE ONLY HOPE of preserving what is best, lies in the practice of an immense charity, a wide tolerance, a sincere respect for opinions that are not ours.—*Hamerton*

I AM at peace with God; how then can I be confounded?—*Rumbold*

THOUGHTS are pleasant companions if we choose them as well as we should choose other company.—*Pollock*

SUCCESS OR FAILURE in business is caused more by mental attitude than by mental capacities.—*Walter Dill Scott*

THE BEST LEGACY I can leave my children is free speech, and the example of using it.—*Sidney*

LOUIS PASTEUR, AND LENGTHENED HUMAN LIFE

By OTIS W. CALDWELL

WHEN Louis Pasteur was sixteen years old his father, anxious about his education, decided to send him from the home town of Arbois to Paris. The boy was to have the advantage of instruction in the Ecole Normale, a school in which the father thought there would be an exceptionally good opportunity for his boy since the École Normale had been established to train men for college positions. This was in 1838, when schools were not generally as good in France as they are today. The elder Pasteur did not have the privilege of much schooling but had gained a fair education for his time by personal industry and efforts. Like many a father of recent times, or today for that matter, Louis' hardworking father decided that poverty should not deprive his son of a good education, and thus planned family sacrifices in the name of the boy's education. That parental sacrifice does not guarantee an education was as true of Louis Pasteur as it has proved to be of many another boy or girl. No sooner did the boy find himself at the school in Paris than an old and honourable malady befell the boy—homesickness. It is honourable and eminently respectable to be homesick, even almost disgraceful not to be so on occasion; but succumbing to this worthy emotional illness is not so respectable.

Louis Pasteur's father was a tanner of hides, as had been his grandfather and great-grandfather. His home was near the malodorous tannery yard, and his childhood home street in Dôle before his family moved to Arbois, was known as the "street of the tanners." From his birth in 1822 until he was almost sixteen years of age, his life had been more or less associated with the tannery. And now, as a lonesome boy in a distant school, in a great city one hundred leagues from home, he longed so earnestly "for a whiff of the old tannery" that genuine illness would have been welcome if it could have secured his return to his home. Hours were days to the boy, and he soon decided he could stand it no longer. His work was poor, he was miserable, and so wrote to his father. The father, with much depression, went to Paris and took the boy back to his Arbois home.

The halo over the home and playground is sometimes more easily seen one hundred leagues away than close at hand. It was so with young Pasteur, for the halo evanesced and certain stern realities appeared. He soon announced his readiness to return to Paris, but the wise father replied that the schools of Arbois would suffice for the present. The boy became an outstanding pupil in drawing, so recognized by all. At night he went over all of his day's lessons with his father, not the lessons of the next day, as is so commonly done nowadays to make sure that pupils know their lessons; but the lessons of the preceding morning and afternoon, as the father desired to learn those things with which the son was dealing, and Louis became truly his father's teacher. Two years in the schools of Arbois, then two years in the college at Besançon not far from Arbois, brought to Louis recognition as a successful student and as a tutor of his fellows. Then, at twenty years of age, in 1842, he returned to Paris as a student in the École Normale, soon to be widely recognized as a young man of industry, intellectual integrity, and earnest devotion to his studies.

In addition to other studies, Pasteur attended lectures at the Sorbonne and devoted much time to the study of the structure of crystals. He became widely known and highly respected as a student of chemistry, and on January 15, 1849, began an eight-year period of useful service as professor of chemistry at the University of Strassburg. A characteristic Pasteurism occurred in the early part of his stay at Strassburg. The rector of the University was most cordial to the newly arrived professor of chemistry and took him to his home, where Pasteur was introduced to the rector's wife and daughter. In two weeks Louis addressed a lengthy letter to the rector, serving notice that the elder Pasteur, according to the customs of the times, would soon appear and propose marriage between Louis and the daughter. In this letter Louis informed the rector that, "as to the future, unless my tastes should completely change, I shall give myself up entirely to chemical research." The father came, the proposal was made and duly accepted, the marriage occurred in three months.

At the close of 1854 Pasteur left Strassburg for a professorship at the University of Lille, where he served for two years. Then he went back to Paris, which was the central location of his work for the rest of his life.

When Pasteur went to Lille he fully expected to continue his studies in chemical and physical problems relative to crystals. The brewers and wine makers about Lille were having great difficulty since they could not be certain to secure the kinds of fermentation specifically needed in different cases, in order to produce the different specific results they desired. The wine and beer "went wrong," fermentation could not be controlled, and the industry was suffering great financial losses, said to exceed $20,000,000 yearly in certain years. Pasteur was known as a chemist, and as a manipulator of the crude microscopes of that day. The manufacturers appealed to him to solve their problems, and he reluctantly agreed to the temporary diversion from his chosen studies, for he saw in this study great possibilities of new knowledge. Through the studies of famous German students, much had recently been learned about the yeasts which produce fermentation and about certain bacteria, but application of these studies had not been made in the brewing industries. There was still extended belief that the living organisms of fermentation came into existence spontaneously (spontaneous generation of life, as it was called), and that such organisms spring into existence in the wine and beer because of "a vital force of nature," and thus injure it. Pasteur, and others even more than Pasteur, proved that if nutritive liquids are sterilized and constantly kept from contact with air and other unsterile substances, no organisms will develop within this nutritive liquid no matter how long the experiment is continued. There was recently exhibited in the United

221

States (1922), a flask of beef broth which it is claimed, correctly no doubt, that Pasteur prepared over fifty years ago. The beef broth is still fresh-looking and clear, never having had the stopper removed from the glass flask in which the broth has been constantly kept. Small living things, like the larger ones which we readily see, come only from other living things of their own kind. The process of treating wines as recommended by Pasteur, known as pasteurization, has since been applied to milk in all civilized countries.

With previously gained facts in mind, Pasteur proceeded to separate single living yeast plants under his microscope, and then to grow pure cultures from these organisms thus separated. He not only found that they grew as pure culture, but that each kind of small organism produced its own peculiar kind of fermentative products in the nutritive liquids. He thus taught the brewers and wine manufacturers how to separate, grow, and use the particular kinds of living microscopic organisms which produce the kinds of wine and beer that they desired.

We are not keenly interested in the fact that such discoveries taught people how to save the alcoholic industries of France and Germany. What interests us most is that he isolated the microscopic organisms, grew them in pure cultures, and proved that microscopic living things, like the larger ones we readily see, each produces its own peculiar results as product of its life and growth.

We need to recall that when Pasteur was studying fermentation the human race did not know the causes of human diseases. Causes had been suspected, but not proved. What we know today as the science of public health did not exist. The bacterial origin of diseases was merely suspected, and the idea generally ridiculed. If a person had been bold enough to assert as true even a small part of what we now know to be true, such a person would have been thought insane or foolish. It was then not uncommon to think that persons who became ill had been guilty of some gross wrong-doing, and that illness was sent upon them as punishment for their sins. Or it was sometimes said that the "humours of the body," of which the blood and the bile were two, in some way got into wrong proportions or became deranged and thus caused illness. It is now generally known that most, if not all, common diseases are caused by living microscopic organisms, either bacteria or small animal parasites. Though this knowledge is but a few decades old, it is so common that it is difficult to put ourselves back to the recent date when the human race did not possess this knowledge. It is of such untold importance that Louis Pasteur lived and accomplished what he did, that, as we read this story, we must imagine ourselves for a time moved back a little more than forty years in the history of man's desire and efforts to have better health. Then, as now, most people wished to live instead of to die, and while living wished to have the best possible health. Then, as now, there were some benighted people who would not do the things necessary to produce good health, even if knowledge of how to do them were available.

When Pasteur's yeast and spontaneous generation studies were almost completed, he was urged to go to southern France to try to discover why the silk worms were sick. He tried to decline saying: "I have never touched a silk worm in my life." Why did people urge Pasteur to do this? Why didn't they call a bacteriologist or a student of insect diseases? At that time there were no bacteriologists because there was no bacteriology. Of course there were bacteria, but since no one then knew the laws of bacteria, there was no bacteriology. Likewise there was no science of insect diseases, or science of diseases of men as we now understand those terms.

For many years the silk industry of France had suffered. Often the worms became sick and died, or if they lived, they produced poor cocoons. Poor cocoons, or no cocoons, mean reduction or loss of the desired silk, which means poorer food for the people, poorer education for their children, and all the poorer things which accompany reduction or loss of a fundamental industry. So important was the silk industry in southern France, and so great the anxiety about the health of the silkworms, that one writer says the workers when meeting would salute one another by saying: "Good morning! How are the silk worms this morning?" What they desired was good healthy adult silk moths which laid good moth eggs; that these eggs should hatch into worms which might feed and grow healthily upon their food, the mulberry leaves; that the full-grown worms might spin good cocoons from which the workers could unravel the desired silk; that enough good cocoons should be left to produce adult moths to continue pro-

duction of new supplies of healthy eggs.

Pasteur began this study in 1865. He studied the eggs and found within some of them certain small bodies resembling the smallest animal cells. He called these bodies corpuscles, simply meaning "small bodies." He noted that when eggs which contained the corpuscles hatched, the worms were sickly and usually died. Using his crude microscope, he separated the eggs which contained no corpuscles and caused them to hatch. The worms thus produced seemed to be healthy, and after careful work, Pasteur announced that people could produce healthy worms and good cocoons by selecting eggs which contained no corpuscles. When this was tried and failed, Pasteur patiently returned to his microscopic studies and found another small organism, a facterium, and immediately concluded that the silk worms had two diseases instead of one. One, *pebrine,* was caused by the animal corpuscles; and the other, *flacherie,* caused by bacteria. Through long and careful experiments he discovered that eggs selected so as to be free from corpuscles and bacteria would produce healthy worms; that such worms when grown upon fresh mulberry leaves would mature and produce good silk cocoons; but that even healthy worms when grown were likely to sicken and die. He thus concluded that the corpuscles and bacteria produce the diseases, and that diseases from sick worms may be transmitted to healthy worms by contact with the food in which silk worms have fed. It is not so important that Pasteur taught France how to save her silk

223

industry as it is that he proved that the small organisms produce the diseases; that transmission of the organisms may transmit the disease; and that prevention of transmission prevents disease. We are not likely to overestimate the importance of these discoveries to modern public and individual health.

Meantime the cattle and sheep industry of France and of other countries was suffering from a disease known as anthrax. So deadly was anthrax to human beings that when once it was clear that a person had the disease, it was regarded almost as a death warrant. Fortunately and for reasons then unknown, the disease did not often attack human beings. Its destruction of cattle and sheep was enormous.

Other students had discovered the nature of the bacterium which causes anthrax and had definitely proved the causal relation of the organism. But since no preventive or cure had been discovered, people appealed publicly to Pasteur to attack the problem. No less than 3600 public officers and prominent citizens signed petitions to Pasteur to undertake to find a means of preventing the ravages of this dreaded disease. He responded and began the study. It is interesting and important to know that the so-called anthrax bacteria cause the disease anthrax; but if they cannot be kept from causing the disease what does the knowledge profit us? If cattle and sheep and men must die, there really isn't large comfort in mere knowledge of what caused this wholesale death. That knowledge was essential for the beginning of Pasteur's study, but was merely the beginning.

After many efforts, too many and too intensive to be related in this connection, Pasteur recalled an important discovery made by the Englishman, Jenner, in 1798. Jenner, working in England, noted that persons who milked cows which were ill with cowpox contracted a disease resembling human smallpox, and that thereafter such persons would not contract smallpox from human beings ill with that disease. Jenner devised means, now improved and known to everyone, for giving human beings generally the infection or vaccination which protects against smallpox. In recalling this situation, Pasteur argued that smallpox was caused by a living organism; that the organism when it lived in cattle did not flourish, and that this organism when introduced from cattle into human beings was not vigorous enough to produce a bad case of smallpox; that the case produced was bad enough, however, to leave some kind of protection or immunity against an attack from organisms from persons who have a vigorous case of smallpox. This line of thought is most interesting when we recall that we do not yet possess satisfactory evidence as to just what kind of an organism causes smallpox.

Meantime Pasteur had been carrying on experiments with chicken cholera. He left cultures of chicken cholera germs in his laboratory, and went away for a short vacation. Upon his return he found that these old cultures would no longer produce chicken cholera when some of the cultures were injected into fowls. Most important of all, he found that after the fowls had been treated with these old cultures they would not take chicken cholera even when injected with fresh and virulent germs. Therefore partly by chance came the discovery of the process of vaccinating poultry against cholera by use of depleted cholera germs or possibly by use of the dead products remaining in old cultures of these germs.

Thus Pasteur began his efforts to reduce the vigour of anthrax germs so that perchance they might not produce anthrax of usual destructiveness. Many highly illuminating experiments were performed. Finally, by growing anthrax bacteria in beef broth at high temperatures, it was found that they flourished for a time, then slowly died out. By using some of these cultures when the bacteria were much depleted, it was found that sheep could be given mild attacks of anthrax from which they recovered. After their recovery they were given fully active anthrax germs, from which the sheep promptly developed bad cases of anthrax and died. Pasteur then tried a first vaccination of depleted bacteria, and when the sheep had recovered, gave a second mild attack by use of bacteria much less depleted than those first used, but far from normal vigour. The sheep and cattle upon which this experiment was tried took successive mild attacks of anthrax. Thereafter, fully virulent anthrax bacteria failed to produce the disease, and Pasteur announced his triumph in producing progressive vaccination with successful results.

So important was this discovery that Pasteur was challenged to make a public demonstration of his claims. The Agriculture Society at Melun, France, offered to provide

sheep and cattle for the demonstration. Delegates were invited and came from many interested organizations and countries. Pasteur penned ten sheep to serve as controls to determine whether anthrax was in the food, air, or water given to them and to the other sheep and cattle. Twenty-five sheep and six cows were to be vaccinated, and twenty-three sheep, two goats, and four cows were not to be vaccinated but were to receive fully virulent anthrax bacteria at the same time as the vaccinated sheep and cattle. On May 5, 1881, the first vaccination was given to the twenty-five sheep and six cows. On May 17, 1881, the second vaccination was given to the same animals. On May 31, 1881, fully virulent anthrax germs were given to all vaccinated sheep and cows, to the four remaining cows, and to the twenty-three sheep and the goats. Pasteur told the delegates to return on June 2. This direction was unnecessary as most of them did not leave, so keenly did they appreciate the momentous importance of what was going on. Many were disbelievers and expected Pasteur's downfall. The results were triumphant. On the morning of June 2, all of the non-vaccinated sheep and cows and the goats were dead, dying, or severely ill. Not a vaccinated sheep or cow or a control sheep died as a result of the treatment they had received. Since that day the human race has known how to avoid anthrax, if only it will do what is known as good to do. More than this, the idea of successive vaccination was proved, and this has been the foundation of many subsequent advances in prevention of diseases of several types.

Did Pasteur then retire from active labour, one man's gigantic work having been done? Did he remind his co-workers that since 1868 half-paralysis had made his work very difficult? No! Rather he reminded his closest friends that his part-paralysis which he suffered in 1868 enabled him to make more cautious and effective use of those parts of his body not affected by his malady —a malady for which the answer is not yet at hand. Instead he turned now to his last and most spectacular achievement. For many years the sympathies of this great founder of the science of bacteriology had been sorely tried because of the ravages of the awful disease rabies or hydrophobia. It is doubtless true that the cry of "mad dog" has created human panic since the times of primitive men. No sane person who has witnessed death from hydrophobia will willingly do so a second time, unless he is needed in ministrations of assistance or mercy. For years Pasteur had studied the dreaded disease and performed experiments with rabbits and other animals in efforts to locate the causal organism and to find a preventive or cure. It almost belittles this gigantic task to go directly to results, omitting description of many fruitless efforts, false hopes roused in the man whose heart as well as mind was now devoted to his supreme task. However, one day, after many failures to locate any guiding arrow, Pasteur used for inoculation in a rabbit a piece of old and dry spinal-cord tissue previously taken from a rabbit that had died of rabies. He had previously oftentimes transmitted the disease by use of nerve tissue, but the diseases thus produced were violent and death-producing. This time, however, the desiccated nerve tissue produced a mild attack from which the rabbit recovered. Following this lead, a series of less and less dry nerve tissues were used to produce a cumulative series of mild attacks, after which the bite of a rabid animal failed to produce hydrophobia.

At this juncture one of the most striking events of all science occurred. Frau Meister, of Alsace, had a boy, Joseph, who two days before had been bitten by a rabid dog. Such an attack as that shown by the fourteen bites upon the unfortunate boy had been previously regarded as meaning almost certain death. The mother had heard of Pasteur, and at once started to Paris with her boy. The treatment had not been given to any human being; it was not known whether results would be similar to those obtained in lower animals; it was not known what series or gradation of treatments would be necessary for human beings; it had been proved that the treatment could be applied to animals after a rabid bite, and that protection could be secured. Frau Meister was obdurately insistent. Pasteur's advisers intimated that the boy's death would be upon Pasteur if he refused to treat him and the mother absolved him from responsibility if the treatment were given. Against advice from his friends, Pasteur began the experiment upon the boy, shortening the periods between treatments in efforts to secure cumulative protective results. The ignorant but beautiful confidence of the mother and boy permitted them to sleep and rest between treatments; but the highly intelligent understanding and tremendous responsibility and hope of Pasteur made sleep and rest almost impossible for him until the crisis had passed, and he felt sure that the boy's life had been saved.

Soon Pasteur institutes appeared in available centres throughout the civilized world, and today it is very rarely that a human being need die from hydrophobia. Superstitious and ignorant fear of hydrophobia has given place to the intelligent guidance of modern science.

On Pasteur's seventieth birthday (1892, three years before his death) delegates from the scientific societies and public bodies of the civilized world met in France, in the great theatre room of the Sorbonne. The band of the Republican Guard of France played the triumphal march. The President of the Republic was the escort as down the aisle came one of the greatest heroes and benefactors in human history. Gounod directed a choir which sang his *Ave Maria*. Coquelin recited verses written by him especially for this occasion. The Minister of Public Instruction among other things said:

Who can now say how much human life owes to you and how much more it will owe you in the future? The day will come when another Lucretius will sing, in a new poem on Nature, the immortal Master whose genius engendered such benefits.

Joseph Lister, when called upon said:

Your researches upon fermentations have thrown a powerful light which has illuminated the baleful darkness of surgery and has changed the treatment of wounds from an uncertain and too often disastrous empirical affair into a sure beneficent scientific art. Thanks to you, surgery has undergone a complete revolution which has robbed it of its terrors, and has enlarged almost without limit its efficacious power. Medicine owes not less than surgery to your profound and philosophical studies. You have lifted the veil which had covered infectious diseases during the centuries; you have discovered and demonstrated their microbial nature. Thanks to your initiative and, in many cases, to your own special work, there are already a large number of these pernicious maladies of which we now know the causes.

Then Pasteur rose and spoke quietly and feelingly of his hope that science would save men from their bodily ills; that men will be more useful when free from disease. Then turning to the delegates he said:

And you, delegates from other nations, bring me the deepest joy that can be felt by a man whose invincible belief is that Science and Peace will triumph over Ignorance and War, that nations will unite, not to destroy, but to build, and that the future will belong to those who will have done most for suffering humanity.

The foundations of the science which may remove from man all his bodily ills if only he will turn his mind to them long enough, with sufficient patience and unselfishness—that is the achievement of Louis Pasteur. Human life is now

227

much lengthened because of the work of Pasteur, by the few others of his time, and by the many others since who have been stimulated and whose work has been made possible by him. Those who know and do what modern health science teaches are the ones whose lives are lengthened. It is they who are of most worth to the world. A man at forty has just learned how to work.

To add ten or fifteen or twenty years to his life saves to the world a man who is equipped and ready. His added years may double his service to the world. Surely in an age when great warriors are still extolled, it is supremely important for our young people to appreciate that true heroes help men to live and serve rather than teach them to vanquish and destroy their fellows.

CREDO

ELIAS LIEBERMAN

I believe
That there are greater things in life
Than life itself;
I believe
In climbing upward
Even when the spent and broken thing
I call my body
Cries "Halt!"
I believe
To the last breath
In the truths
Which God permits me to see.
I believe
In fighting for them;
In drawing,
If need be,
Not the bloody sword of man
Brutal with conquest
And drunk with power,
But the white sword of God,
Flaming with His truth
And healing while it slays.

I believe
In my country and her destiny,
In the great dream of her founders,
In her place among the nations,
In her ideals;
I believe
That her democracy must be protected,

Her privileges cherished,
Her freedom defended.
I believe
That, humbly before the Almighty,
But proudly before all mankind,
We must safeguard her standard,
The vision of her Washington,
The martyrdom of her Lincoln,
With the patriotic ardor
Of the minute men
And the boys in blue
Of her glorious past.
I believe
In loyalty to my country
Utter, irrevocable, inviolate.

Thou, in whose sight
A thousand years are but as yesterday
And as a watch in the night,
Help me
In my frailty
To make real
What I believe.

AUTUMN ORACLE
LAURA LEE RANDALL

A sunset sky, and the west wind sighing,
A threat of winter . . . the wild gulls crying;
Swift flocks of birds to the southland winging;
Bare brown boughs in a frenzy flinging
Dying leaves that for long were holden,
Now drifting, dropping, crimson and golden.

The fallen leaves, in uncounted number,
Are warmly quilting the wildflowers' slumber;
There are buds on the bough . . . a springtime
    presage . . .
The birds will return with a lyric message:
The wild gull's cry holds a hint of mating,
To conquer cold is the hearthfire waiting.

The west wind's sighs are of love, not sorrow,
And the sunset sky is the sign for tomorrow.

THE GLOW of inspiration warms us; this holy rapture springs from the seeds of the Divine mind sown in man.—*Ovid*

HE REMOVES the greatest ornament of friendship, who takes away from it respect.—*Cicero*

I THINK the first virtue is to restrain the tongue; he approaches nearest to the gods who knows how to be silent, even though he is in the right.—*Cato*

TEST BY A TRIAL how excellent is the life of the good man—the man who rejoices at the portion given him in the universal lot and abides therein content; just in all his ways and kindly minded toward all men.
—*Marcus Aurelius*

IF THOU workest at that which is before thee, following right reason seriously, vigorously, calmly, without allowing anything else to distract thee, but keeping thy divine part sure, if thou shouldst be bound to give it back immediately; if thou holdest to this, expecting nothing, fearing nothing, but satisfied with thy present activity according to Nature, and with heroic truth in every word and sound which thou utterest, thou wilt live happy. And there is no man who is able to prevent this.
—*Marcus Aurelius*

FRIENDSHIP throws a greater lustre on prosperity, while it lightens adversity by sharing in its griefs and anxieties.—*Cicero*

NEVER esteem anything as of advantage to thee that shall make thee break thy word or lose thy self-respect.—*Marcus Aurelius*

TAKE CARE that the divinity within you has a creditable charge to preside over.—*Marcus Aurelius*

SEARCH THOU thy heart! Therein is the fountain of good! Do thou but dig, and abundantly the stream shall gush forth.—*Marcus Aurelius*

THE TRUE WORTH of a man is to be measured by the objects he pursues.—*Marcus Aurelius*

FRENCH PHILOSOPHERS

WISDOM is to the soul what health
is to the body.—*La Rochefoucauld*

THE FIRST STEP towards philosophy is
incredulity.—*Diderot*

WHEN I am attacked by gloomy thoughts, nothing helps me so
much as running to my books. They quickly absorb me and
banish the clouds from my mind.—*Montaigne*

THE SUPREME HAPPINESS of life is the conviction of being loved for yourself, or, more correctly, being loved in spite of yourself.—*Victor Hugo*

CERTAIN THOUGHTS are prayers. There are moments when, whatever be the
attitude of the body, the soul is on its knees.—*Victor Hugo*

THE MOST evident sign of wisdom is continued cheerfulness.—*Montaigne*

NOTHING is so contagious as example; and we never do any great good or
▸evil which does not produce its like.—*La Rochefoucauld*

THE SUREST PROOF of being endowed with noble qualities, is to be free from
envy.—*La Rochefoucauld*

FAME has only the span of a day they say. But to live in
the hearts of the people—that is worth something.—*Ouida*

INSPIRATION comes of working every day.—*Baudelaire*

IF YOU want a thing done, do it yourself.—*Rousseau*

NO MAN can answer for his courage who has
never been in danger.—*La Rochefoucauld*

COMMON SENSE is not so common.—*Voltaire*

A Day's Pleasure

By HAMLIN GARLAND

$\mathcal{W}$HEN MARKHAM came in from shoveling his last wagonload of corn into the crib he found that his wife had put the children to bed, and was kneading a batch of dough with the dogged action of a tired and sullen woman.

He slipped his soggy boots off his feet, and having laid a piece of wood on top of the stove, put his heels on it comfortably. His chair squeaked as he leaned back on its hinder legs, but he paid no attention; he was used to it, exactly as he was used to his wife's lameness and ceaseless toil.

"That closes up my corn," he said after a silence. "I guess I'll go to town tomorrow to git my horses shod."

"I guess I'll git ready and go along," said his wife, in a sorry attempt to be firm and confident of tone.

"What do you want to go to town fer?" he grumbled.

"What does anybody want to go to town fer?" she burst out, facing him. "I ain't been out o' this house fer six months, while you go an' go!"

"Oh, it ain't six months. You went down that day I got the mower."

"When was that? The tenth of July, and you know it."

"Well, mebbe 'twas. I didn't think it was so long ago. I ain't no objection to your goin', only I'm goin' to take a load of wheat."

"Well, jest leave off a sack, an' that'll balance me an' the baby," she said spiritedly.

"All right," he replied good-naturedly, seeing she was roused.

"Only that wheat ought to be put up tonight if you're goin'. You won't have any time to hold sacks for me in the morning with them young ones to get off to school."

"Well, let's go do it then," she said, sullenly resolute.

"I hate to go out agin; but I s'pose we'd better."

He yawned dismally and began pulling his boots on again, stamping his swollen feet into them with grunts of pain. She put on his coat and one of the boy's caps, and they went out to the granary. The night was cold and clear.

"Don't look so much like snow as it did last night," said Sam. "It may turn warm."

Laying out the sacks in the light of the lantern, they sorted out those which were whole, and Sam climbed into the bin with a tin pail in his hand, and the work began.

He was a sturdy fellow, and he worked desperately fast; the shining tin pail dived deep into the cold wheat and dragged heavily on the woman's tired hands as it came to the mouth of the sack, and she trembled with fatigue, but held on and dragged the sacks away when filled, and brought others, till at last Sam climbed out, puffing and wheezing, to tie them up.

"I guess I'll load 'em in the morning," he said. "You needn't wait

232

fer me. I'll tie 'em up alone."

"Oh, I don't mind," she replied, feeling a little touched by his unexpectedly easy acquiescence to her request. When they went back to the house the moon had risen.

It had scarcely set when they were wakened by the crowing roosters. The man rolled stiffly out of bed and began rattling at the stove in the dark, cold kitchen.

His wife arose lamer and stiffer than usual, and began twisting her thin hair into a knot.

Sam did not stop to wash, but went out to the barn. The woman, however, hastily soused her face into the hard limestone water at the sink, and put the kettle on. Then she called the children. She knew it was early, and they would need several callings. She pushed breakfast forward, running over in her mind the things she must have: two spools of thread, six yards of cotton flannel, a can of coffee, and mittens for Kitty. These she must have—there were oceans of things she needed.

The children soon came scudding down out of the darkness of the upstairs to dress tumultuously at the kitchen stove. They humped and shivered, holding up their bare feet from the cold floor, like chickens in new fallen snow. They were irritable, and snarled and snapped and struck like cats and dogs. Mrs. Markham stood it for a while with mere commands to "hush up," but at last her patience gave out, and she charged down on the struggling mob and cuffed them right and left.

They ate their breakfast by lamplight, and when Sam went back to his work around the barnyard it was scarcely dawn. The children,

left alone with their mother, began to tease her to let them go to town also.

"No, sir—nobody goes but baby. Your father's goin' to take a load of wheat."

She was weak with the worry of it all when she had sent the older children away to school and the kitchen work was finished. She went into the cold bedroom off the little sitting room and put on her best dress. It had never been a good fit, and now she was getting so thin it hung in wrinkled folds everywhere about the shoulders and waist. She lay down on the bed a moment to ease that dull pain in her back. She had a moment's distaste for going out at all. The thought of sleep was more alluring. Then the thought of the long, long day, and the sickening sameness of her life, swept over her again, and she rose and prepared the baby for the journey.

It was but little after sunrise when Sam drove out into the road and started for Belleplaine. His wife sat perched upon the wheat sacks behind him, holding the baby in her lap, a cotton quilt under her, and a cotton horse blanket over her knees.

Sam was disposed to be very good-natured, and he talked back at her occasionally, though she could only understand him when he turned his face toward her. The baby stared out at the passing fence posts, and wiggled his hands out of his mittens at every opportunity. He was merry at least.

It grew warmer as they went on, and a strong south wind arose. The dust settled upon the woman's shawl and hat. Her hair loosened and blew unkemptly about her face. The road which led across the high, level prairie was quite smooth and dry, but still it jolted her, and the pain in her back increased. She had nothing to lean against, and the weight of the child grew greater till she was forced to place him on the sacks beside her, though she could not loose her hold for a moment.

The town drew in sight—a cluster of small frame houses and stores on the dry prairie beside a railway station. There were no trees yet which could be called shade trees. The pitilessly severe light of the sun flooded everything. A few teams were hitched about, and in the lee of the stores a few men could be seen seated comfortably, their broad hat-rims flopping up and down, their faces brown as leather.

Markham put his wife out at one of the grocery stores, and drove off down toward the elevators to sell his wheat.

The grocer greeted Mrs. Markham in a pefunctorily kind manner, and offered her a chair, which she took gratefully. She sat for a quarter of an hour almost without moving, leaning against the back of the high chair. At last the child began to get restless and troublesome, and she spent half an hour helping him amuse himself around the nail kegs.

At length she rose and went out on the walk, carrying the baby. She went into the dry-goods store and took a seat on one of the little revolving stools. A woman was buying some woolen goods for a dress. It was worth twenty-seven cents a yard, the clerk said, but he would knock off two cents if she took ten yards. It looked warm, and Mrs. Markham wished she could afford it for Mary.

A pretty young girl came in and laughed and chatted with the clerk, and bought a pair of gloves. She was the daughter of the grocer. Her happiness made the wife and mother sad. When Sam came back she asked him for some money.

"What you want to do with it?" he asked.

"I want to spend it," she said.

She was not to be trifled with, so he gave her a dollar.

"I need a dollar more."

"Well, I've got to go take up that note at the bank."

"Well, the children's got to have some new underclo'es," she said.

He handed her a two-dollar bill and then went out to pay his note.

She bought her cotton flannel and mittens and thread, and then sat leaning against the counter. It was noon, and she was hungry. She went out to the wagon, got the lunch she had brought, and took it into the grocery to eat it—where she could get a drink of water.

The grocer gave the baby a stick of candy and handed the mother an apple.

"It'll kind o' go down with your doughnuts," he said.

After eating her lunch she got up and went out. She felt ashamed to sit there any longer. She entered another dry-goods store, but when the clerk came toward her saying, "Anything today, Mrs.——?" she answered, "No, I guess not," and turned away with foolish face.

She walked up and down the street, desolately homeless. She did not know what to do with herself. She knew no one except the grocer. She grew bitter as she saw a couple of ladies pass, holding their demi-trains in the latest city fashion.

234

Another woman went by pushing a baby carriage, in which sat a child just about as big as her own. It was bouncing itself up and down on the long slender springs, and laughing and shouting. Its clean round face glowed from its pretty fringed hood. She looked down at the dusty clothes and grimy face of her own little one, and walked on savagely.

She went into the drug store where the soda fountain was, but it made her thirsty to sit there and she went out on the street again. She heard Sam laugh, and saw him in a group of men over by the blacksmith shop. He was having a good time and had forgotten her.

Her back ached so intolerably that she concluded to go in and rest once more in the grocer's chair. The baby was growing cross and fretful. She bought five cents worth of candy to take home to the children, and gave baby a little piece to keep him quiet. She wished Sam would come. It must be getting late. The grocer said it was not much after one. Time seemed terribly long. She felt that she ought to do something while she was in town. She ran over her purchases— yes, that was all she had planned to buy. She fell to figuring on the things she needed. It was terrible. It ran away up into twenty or thirty dollars at the least. Sam, as well as she, needed underwear for the cold winter, but they would have to wear the old ones, even if they were thin and ragged. She would not need a dress, she thought bitterly, because she never went anywhere. She rose and went out on the street once more, and wandered up and down, looking at everything in the hope of enjoying something. A man from Boone Creek backed

a load of apples up to the sidewalk, and as he stood waiting for the grocer he noticed Mrs. Markham and the baby, and gave the baby an apple. This was a pleasure. He had such a hearty way about him. He on his part saw an ordinary farmer's wife with dusty dress, unkempt hair, and tired face. He did not know exactly why she appealed to him, but he tried to cheer her up.

The grocer was familiar with these bedraggled and weary wives. He was accustomed to see them sit for hours in his big wooden chair, and nurse tired and fretful children. Their forlorn, aimless, pathetic wandering up and down the street was a daily occurrence, and had never possessed any special meaning to him.

II

In a cottage around the corner from the grocery store two men and a woman were finishing a dainty luncheon. The woman was dressed in cool, white garments, and she seemed to make the day one of perfect comfort.

The home of the Honorable Mr. Hall was by no means the costliest in the town, but his wife made it the most attractive. He was one of the leading lawyers of the county, and a man of culture and progressive views. He was entertaining a friend who had lectured the night before in the Congregational church.

They were by no means in serious discussion. The talk was rather frivolous. Hall had the ability to caricature men with a few gestures and attitudes, and was giving to his Eastern friend some descriptions of the old-fashioned Western lawyers he had met in his practice. He was very amusing, and his guest laughed heartily for a time.

But suddenly Hall became aware that Otis was not listening. Then he perceived that he was peering out of the window at some one, and that on his face a look of bitter sadness was falling.

Hall stopped. "What do you see, Otis?"

Otis replied, "I see a forlorn, weary woman."

Mrs. Hall rose and went to the window. Mrs. Markham was walking by the house, her baby in her arms. Savage anger and weeping were in her eyes and on her lips, and there was hopeless tragedy in her shambling walk and weak back.

In the silence Otis went on: "I saw the poor, dejected creature twice this morning. I couldn't forget her."

"Who is she?" asked Mrs. Hall, very softly.

"Her name is Markham; she's Sam Markham's wife," said Hall.

The young wife led the way into the sitting room, and the men took seats and lit their cigars. Hall was meditating a diversion when Otis resumed suddenly:

"That woman came to town to-day to get a change, to have a little play-spell, and she's wandering around like a starved and weary cat. I wonder if there is a woman in this town with sympathy enough and courage enough to go out and help that woman? The saloon-keepers, the politicians, and the grocers make it pleasant for the man—so pleasant that he forgets his wife. But the wife is left without a word."

Mrs. Hall's work dropped, and

on her pretty face was a look of pain. The man's harsh words had wounded her—and wakened her. She took up her hat and hurried out on the walk. The men looked at each other, and then the husband said:

"It's going to be a little sultry for the men around these diggings. Suppose we go out for a walk."

Delia felt a hand on her arm as she stood at the corner.

"You look tired, Mrs. Markham; won't you come in a little while? I'm Mrs. Hall."

Mrs. Markham turned with a scowl on her face and a biting word on her tongue, but something in the sweet, round little face of the other woman silenced her, and her brow smoothed out.

"Thank you kindly, but it's most time to go home. I'm looking fer Mr. Markham now."

"Oh, come in a little while, the baby is cross and tired out; please do."

Mrs. Markham yielded to the friendly voice, and together the two women reached the gate just as two men hurriedly turned the other corner.

"Let me relieve you," said Mrs. Hall.

The mother hesitated, "He's so dusty."

"Oh, that won't matter. Oh, what a big fellow he is! I haven't any of my own," said Mrs. Hall, and a look passed like an electric spark between the two women, and Delia was her willing guest from that moment.

They went into the little sitting room, so dainty and lovely to the farmer's wife, and as she sank into an easy chair she was faint and drowsy with the pleasure of it. She

236

submitted to being brushed. She gave the baby into the hands of the Swedish girl, who washed its face and hands and sang it to sleep, while its mother sipped some tea. Through it all she lay back in her easychair, not speaking a word, while the ache passed out of her back, and her hot, swollen head ceased to throb.

But she saw everything—the piano, the pictures, the curtains, the wallpaper, the little tea stand. They were almost as grateful to her as the food and fragrant tea. Such housekeeping as this she had never seen. Her mother had worn her kitchen floor thin as brown paper in keeping a speckless house, and she had been in houses that were larger and costlier, but something of the charm of her hostess was in the arrangement of vases, chairs, or pictures. It was tasteful.

Mrs. Hall did not ask about her affairs. She talked to her about the sturdy little baby, and about the things upon which Delia's eyes dwelt. If she seemed interested in a vase she was told what it was and where it was made. She was shown all the pictures and books. Mrs. Hall seemed to read her visitor's mind. She kept as far from the farm and her guest's affairs as possible, and at last she opened the piano and sang to her—not slow-moving hymns, but catchy love songs full of sentiment, and then played some simple melodies, knowing that Mrs. Markham's eyes were studying her hands, her rings, and the flash of her fingers on the keys—seeing more than she heard—and through it all Mrs. Hall conveyed the impression that she, too, was having a good time.

The rattle of the wagon outside roused them both. Sam was at the gate for her. Mrs. Markham rose hastily. "Oh, it's almost sundown!" she gasped in astonishment as she looked out of the window.

"Oh, that won't kill anybody," replied her hostess. "Don't hurry. Carrie, take the baby out to the wagon for Mrs. Markham while I help her with her things."

"Oh, I've had such a good time," Mrs. Markham said as they went down the little walk.

"So have I," replied Mrs. Hall. She took the baby a moment as her guest climbed in. "Oh, you big, fat fellow!" she cried as she gave him a squeeze. "You must bring your wife in oftener, Mr. Markham," she said, as she handed the baby up.

Sam was staring with amazement.

"Thank you, I will," he finally managed to say.

"Good night," said Mrs. Markham.

"Good night, dear," called Mrs. Hall, and the wagon began to rattle off.

The tenderness and sympathy in her voice brought the tears to Delia's eyes—not hot nor bitter tears, but tears that cooled her eyes and cleared her mind.

The wind had gone down, and the red sunlight fell mistily over the world of corn and stubble. The crickets were still chirping and the feeding cattle were drifting toward the farmyards. The day had been made beautiful by human sympathy.

RAIN IN THE COUNTRY

MARGARET E. SANGSTER

The rain fell like a song of hope on fields that had been dying;
It was a mother's loving kiss upon a wistful face.
Tall trees that had been parched and dry broke into gentle sighing
And happiness lay like a smile upon the garden place.

The house was very snug and sweet; the rain's kind, slender fingers
Made magic on the sloping roof and smoothed the streaming pane.
We lighted candles, slim and white; and, like a dream that lingers,
They painted paths of drifting light against the silver rain.

The house was very sweet and snug—its shadows were caressing—
Yet for a moment we were swept with sudden aching pity
For folk who do not understand that rain may be a blessing,
Who wander, shelterless and sad, across the rain-swept city.

JUST PASSING BY

GLENN WARD DRESBACH

The melting road was long and still
Before I came to the crest of a hill
And saw the lights of a farmhouse glow
Through pines that dropped their weight of snow.
I smelled the wood smoke clinging near
The shadowy roof, then drifting clear.
And I thought of wood still ranked in the shed,
Fragrant and dry, and of horses fed
In the musky barn, on clover hay
And corn, and of cattle sleeping away
The chilly night, but I thought still more
Of the cellar under the farmhouse floor—
The tang of apples in barrel and bin
And vegetables plump and still tucked in
From early Spring moods, and jars, on wide
Shelves, winking with berries and fruit inside,
And of jugs, cobwebbed and smelling of earth,
That gurgle with cider's rustic mirth.
And I thought of the smokehouse mellowed through
With hickory smoke, where hams show dew
Of flavor upon them, in ordered rows,
Upon the beams, and, twitching the nose

With the most tantalizing scent of all,
The russet bacon on pegs in the wall....
No sound I heard but retreat of the snow
And wind in the boughs—but my heart sang low,
Through the damp chill night, a song's reply.
And I was warmed ... just passing by.

TO OUR GUEST
NANCY BYRD TURNER

If you come cheerily,
Here shall be jest for you;
If you come wearily,
Here shall be rest for you.

If you come borrowing,
Gladly we'll loan to you;
If you come sorrowing,
Love shall be shown to you.

Under our thatch, friend,
Place shall abide for you;
Touch but the latch, friend,
The door shall swing wide for you!

RED BRICK COLONIAL
ADELE JORDAN TARR

This house is new, yet shows the gracious line
   That builders loved a hundred years ago.
Simplicity its keynote and design,
   Utility its constant purpose, so
Its every brick and timber tells of home—
   Of shelter warm and safe. No pretense here
Of palace grandeur, nor inutile dome;
   This is a home for love and faith and cheer.

My mother grew to womanhood in one
   In old Virginia, built the self-same way;
Her mother, too, before her. Now my son
   And his, may live here after me, some day.
The love of kin is built into each wall
Their choice is mine—red brick Colonial.

239

FOR DEATH,
Now I know, is that first breath
Which our souls draw when we enter
Life, which is of all life center.
—*Edwin Arnold*

MUSIC is love in search of a word.—*Lanier*

POETRY makes immortal all that is best and most beautiful
in the world.—*Shelley*

BELIEVE ME, every man has his secret sorrows, which the world knows not;
and oftentimes we call a man cold, when he is only sad.—*Longfellow*

THE EVERYDAY CARES AND DUTIES which man call drudgery, are the weights and
counterpoises of the clock of time; giving its pendulum a true vibration
and its hands a regular motion; and when they cease to hang upon its wheels,
the pendulum no longer swings, the hands no longer move, the clock stands
still.—*Longfellow*

ACQUAINT THYSELF with God, if thou wouldst taste His works.—*Cowper*

WHEN MORAL COURAGE feels that it is in the right, there is no
personal daring of which it is incapable.—*Hunt*

MUSIC is the universal language of mankind.—*Longfellow*

BOOKS are yours,
Within whose silent chambers treasure lies
Preserved from age to age; more precious far
Than that accumulated store of gold
And orient gems which, for a day of need,
The Sultan hides deep in ancestral tombs.
These hoards of truth you can unlock at will.
—*Wordsworth*

THE RAYS of happiness, like those of light, are
colorless when unbroken.—*Longfellow*

240

No MAN is born into the world whose work
Is not born with him. There is always work,
And tools to work withal, for those who will;
And blessed are the horny hands of toil.
                                        —Lowell

NOTHING with God can be accidental.*—Longfellow*

I SAY the whole earth and all the stars in the sky are for
religion's sake.*—Whitman*

GOD, You taught me how man can make himself immortal, and it is right that
while I live my tongue should declare the gratitude which I feel.*—Dante*

THE TALENT of success is nothing more than doing what you can do well; and
doing well whatever you do, without a thought of fame.*—Longfellow*

TRULY there is a tide in the affairs of men; but there is no gulf-stream
setting forever in one direction.*—Lowell*

PYGMIES are pygmies still, though percht on Alps;
And pyramids are pyramids in vales.
Each man makes his own stature, builds himself.
Virtue alone outbuilds the Pyramids;
Her monuments shall last when Egypt's fall.
                                        —Young

EVERY MAN feels instinctively that all the beautiful sentiments
in the world weigh less than a single lovely action.*—Lowell*

AN ELEGANT SUFFICIENCY, content,
Retirement, rural quiet, friendship, books,
Ease and alternate labour, useful life,
Progressive virtue, and approving Heaven!
                                —James Thomson

TRUTH is as impossible to be soiled by any outward
touch as the sunbeam.*—Milton*

241

ROOFS
JOYCE KILMER

The road is wide and the stars are out and the breath of the night is sweet,
And this is the time when wanderlust should seize upon my feet.
But I'm glad to turn from the open road and the starlight on my face,
And to leave the splendour of out of doors for a human dwelling place.

I never have seen a vagabond who really liked to roam
All up and down the streets of the world and not to have a home:
The tramp who slept in your barn last night and left at break of day
Will wander only until he finds another place to stay.

A gypsyman will sleep in his cart with canvas overhead;
Or else he'll go into his tent when it is time for bed.
He'll sit on the grass and take his ease so long as the sun is high,
But when it is dark he wants a roof to keep away the sky.

If you call a gypsy a vagabond, I think you do him wrong,
For he never goes a-traveling but he takes his home along.
And the only reason a road is good, as every wanderer knows,
Is just because of the homes, the homes, the homes to which it goes.

They say that life is a highway and its milestones are the years,
And now and then there's a tollgate where you buy your way with tears.
It's a rough road and a steep road and it stretches broad and far,
But at last it leads to a golden town where golden houses are.

LOG SHACKS AND LONESOME WATERS*
By JESSE STUART

WHATEVER I am or ever shall be, school teacher, tiller of the earth, poet, short-story writer, upstart, or not anything—I owe it to my own Kentucky hill-land and to my people who have inhabited these hills for generations. My hills have given me bread. They have put song in my heart to sing. They have made my brain thirst for knowledge so much that I went beyond my own dark hills to get book knowledge. But I got an earthly degree at home from my own dark soil. I got a degree about birds, cornfields, trees, wild-flowers, log shacks, my own people, valleys and rivers and mists in the valleys— scenes of a fairyland childhood that no college under the sun could teach me.

I have learned from walking through the woods in W-Hollow at

Taken from HEAD O' W-HOLLOW, by Jesse Stuart, published and copyright by E. P. DUTTON & CO., INC., New York. 1936.

242

night where the wind soughs through the pine tops, I have learned where the big oak trees and the persimmon trees are; I have learned where the blackberry thickets are; where the wild strawberries grow; where the wild crabapple trees blossom in the spring. I have learned where the large rocks are in the fields; where the crows build their nests; where the groundhogs den; where to find the red fox and the gray fox; where the squirrels keep their young in the hollow tree tops and where the quail hides her nest. I know the little secrets of Nature, of the wild life that leads me to these things. I have tried to write about them in my humble crude fashion. I have enjoyed doing it more than I have eating food, visiting people or cities. My love is with my own soil and my own people and may I truly say the land is a land of log shacks and lonesome waters.

Last night I came home from teaching school. I am teaching school twenty miles away from home on the Ohio River front. Though in the background on the Kentucky side of the river one can see the hills lined back under the Kentucky skies whence cometh the students that make up the majority of our school enrollment. Across the river from where I stay I can see the sky on fire by night and pillars of smoke by day from the mills. The blasting rattles my windowpanes and makes me nervous when I get in bed. I wish that I were far enough away that I could not see fire from the mills. I wish I were back in W-Hollow where the only light I could see would be sunlight, moonlight, starlight; where my windowpanes would be rattled

only by the wind. I wish often that I were back where life is quiet as a floating cloud and where there is poetry in the wind, the skies, the moon and the stars, the people and the good earth. It is true, where I am, I board on a fertile river farm. I eat products direct from the farm. The earth about me supplies the table with food. But the land is a level land. There aren't any hills but the river banks. This river land will produce per acre three times as much as my own rough acres. But that is not it. My land is hill. We have only one hundred and two acres of land. Only two are level and one hundred are rough. I long to return to my own land, because it is my own and I know every foot of it.

Our house is not on a highway where we can hear the drone of motors. It is in the head of W-Hollow and only a rough wagon road leads to it. It is impossible for an automobile to reach us. We have lived hereabout in the Hollow for three generations. The children have gone out beyond the Hollow, but they have come back. There are seven of us children, two of our group sleep eternally out of the Hollow, for there is not a cemetery on the creek. The two married plan to return to the Hollow, the two who have gone out to further their education will return to the Hollow and this one teaching school returns when chances permit.

Last night I returned. The night was dark. I left Riverton, Kentucky, for the Hollow. I had about three miles of mud path to go and carry a load of books, typewriting paper, a small typewriter and my clothes. The mud was yellow and heavy. It stuck to my feet. It was hard to walk through it, but it was good earth mud to me and I didn't care. Sweat trickled down my nose. The white November rain henpecked my face softly and mingled with the sweat. I was happy to get back to the Hollow—back where it was quiet, back where I had roamed the hills at night and had written poetry out alone with the trees, the earth, the stars and cold blue skies and the small gurgling streams. But this night the skies were low and dark. Rain clouds hurried across the sky like long racing greyhounds. I walked up Academy Branch and touched the high hill that led over into the Hollow. I walked up this path, crooked as a snake twisting through a briar thicket. I could smell the storm wind bearing the splashes of rain from the pines. I could smell the ripe shoemake leaves. I could smell the earth. I could see the bare outlines of the leafless twigs etched against the dark racing cloud background. I saw a rabbit dart across my path. I heard the quails calling in one of our desolate winter cornfields. It was a covey getting together after they'd been fired into that day by hunters. They were getting together again to roost in the tall dead crab-grass.

When I reached the top of the hill, I laid my load down and looked into the Valley. I could see an outline where the Ohio River ought to be. I could see below me the bare outlines of hills covered with barren timber—etched against the sky. It made my heart beat fast to be back where I could write poetry, where I had written poetry, where I could live my own life with the trees, the wind, the water, the storms—the night, the day and the

people in the Hollow. I could run wild with the dogs over the old hills now November-desolate and forsaken. I could write poetry. I could live poetry. I could feel poetry in the November wind and hear it in the pine tops. I was back where I could hear the lonesome waters. I could hear the falls at Little Sandy just over the backbone of bony ridge from W-Hollow.

I looked out into the space. I could feel the wind and it seemed with hands tearing at my coat tail. I could feel the cool November wind against my hot face. I picked up my load and crossed the fence onto our own good one hundred and two acres of land. I walked down under the oak trees. There are still bundles of dead leaves clinging to their tops that will not leave regardless of time and tide until next spring when these oak trees put out new buds. Then the dead leaves fall from these oak twigs. I heard the wind pleading for these dead leaves. They resisted the pleas of the wind and they held to their tree of life. I stopped in reverence under the oak trees and uttered my words for reverence for my earth beneath my feet that I would never leave, my earth that feeds me bread from the old stubble fields that are so desolate and wind-swept in late November. I sat on a rock beside the path. I said: "Creator of the Universe: Make me as solid as my hills. Give me the solidness of my stones. Let me still see beauty in the stars that hang above my land. Let me see beauty in the night and hear music in the wind. Let me gather poetry from the wind and from the night. Let me gather poetry from the lonesome waters that I can hear above

244

the wind and rain tonight. Give
me life close to the earth. Let not
my feet stray too far from what is
my own. Let others laugh if they
will. Give me fists big enough to
fight my own battles with, a backbone big as a saw log. Let the white
rain hit my face. Let me feel the
teeth of the wind. Give me the
right to live, the power to live, as
my people have lived before me.
Let me be buried when the power
to live, the right to live is over in
the land that has cradled me. Let
me lie back in the heart of it in the
end. I ask these things, Creator of
the Universe in Your presence, these
and daily bread."

I cannot sing tunes that great men
    have sung.
I cannot follow roads great men
    have gone,

I am not here to sing the songs
    they've sung,
I think I'm here to make a road my
    own.
I shall go forth not knowing where
    I go.
I shall go forth and I shall go alone.
The road I'll travel on is mud, I
    know,
But it's a road that I can call my
    own.
The stars and moon and sun will
    give me light.
The winds will whisper songs I love
    to hear;
Oak leaves will make for me a bed
    at night,
And dawn will break to find me
    lying here.
The winy sunlight of another day
Will find me plodding on my
    muddy way.

PILGRIMAGE

GRACE NOLL CROWELL

I shall plant the seed of this fruit on which I dine,
    By the side of the road. Perhaps some day a tree
Will lift its leafy boughs, and its fruit will shine
    Down a bleak autumn evening goldenly.

I shall place these sticks together, and some gray day
    One following me may see them and pause to start
A quick, bright fire along his lonely way,
    And its wind-blown flame may warm his hands and his
      heart.

I shall pencil a pointing finger where a spring
    Leaps silverly among the rock-strewn grass;
Others will need its clear cold offering,
    And perhaps they might fail to see it as they pass.

At the bend of the road I shall build a wayside shrine.
    Stone by stone I shall rear it and leave it there.
It may be that someone whose need is as great as mine
    May seek it and find new comfort and strength in prayer.

SOLITUDE

By HENRY DAVID THOREAU

THIS IS a delicious evening, when the whole body is one sense, and imbibes delight through every pore. I go and come with a strange liberty in Nature, a part of herself. As I walk along the stony shore of the pond in my shirt-sleeves, though it is cool as well as cloudy and windy, and I see nothing special to attract me, all the elements are unusually congenial to me. The bullfrogs trump to usher in the night, and the note of the whip-poor-will is borne on the rippling wind from over the water. Sympathy with the fluttering alder and poplar leaves almost takes away my breath; yet, like the lake, my serenity is rippled but not ruffled. These small waves raised by the evening wind are as remote from storm as the smooth reflecting surface. Though it is now dark, the wind still blows and roars in the wood, the waves still dash, and some creatures lull the rest with their notes. The repose is never complete. The wildest animals do not repose, but seek their prey now; the fox, and skunk, and rabbit, now roam the fields and woods without fear. They are Nature's watchmen, —links which connect the days of animated life.

When I return to my house I find that visitors have been there and left their cards, either a bunch of flowers, or a wreath of evergreen, or a name in pencil on a yellow walnut leaf or a chip. They who come rarely to the woods take some little piece of the forest into their hands to play with by the way, which they leave, either intentionally or accidentally. One has peeled a willow wand, woven it into a ring, and dropped it on my table. I could always tell if visitors had called in my absence, either by the bended twigs or grass, or the print of their shoes, and generally of what sex or age or quality they were by some slight trace left, as a flower dropped, or a bunch of grass plucked and thrown away, even as far off as the railroad, half a mile distant, or by the lingering odor of a cigar or pipe. Nay, I was frequently notified of the passage of a traveller along the highway sixty rods off by the scent of his pipe.

There is commonly sufficient space about us. Our horizon is never quite at our elbows. The thick woods is not just at our door, nor the pond, but somewhat is always clearing, familiar and worn by us, appropriated and fenced in some way, and reclaimed from Nature. For what reason have I this vast range and circuit, some square miles of unfrequented forest, for my privacy, abandoned to me by men? My nearest neighbor is a mile distant, and no house is visible from any place but the hill-tops within half a mile of my own. I have my horizon bounded by woods all to myself; a distant view of the railroad where it touches the pond on the one hand, and of the fence which skirts the woodland road on the other. But for the most part it is as solitary where I live as on the prairies. It is as much Asia or Africa as New England. I have, as it were, my own sun and moon and stars, and a little world all to myself. At night there was never a traveller passed my house, or

246

knocked at my door, more than if I were the first or last man; unless it were in the spring, when at long intervals some came from the village to fish for pouts,—they plainly fished much more in the Walden Pond of their own natures, and baited their hooks with darkness,—but they soon retreated, usually with light baskets, and left "the world to darkness and to me," and the black kernel of the night was never profaned by any human neighborhood. I believe that men are generally still a little afraid of the dark, though the witches are all hung, and Christianity and candles have been introduced.

Yet I experienced sometimes that the most sweet and tender, the most innocent and encouraging society may be found in any natural object, even for the poor misanthrope and most melancholy man. There can be no very black melancholy to him who lives in the midst of Nature and has his senses still. There was never yet such a storm but it was Aeolian music to a healthy and innocent ear. Nothing can rightly compel a simple and brave man to a vulgar sadness. While I enjoy the friendship of the seasons I trust that nothing can make life a burden to me. The gentle rain which waters my beans and keeps me in the house today is not drear and melancholy, but good for me too. Though it prevents my hoeing them, it is of far more worth than my hoeing. If it should continue so long as to cause the seeds to rot in the ground and destroy the potatoes in the low lands, it would still be good for the grass on the uplands, and, being good for the grass, it would be good for me. Sometimes, when I compare myself with other men, it seems as if I were more favored by the gods than they, beyond any deserts that I am conscious of; as if I had a warrant and surety at their hands which my fellows have not, and were especially guided and guarded. I do not flatter myself, but if it be possible they flatter me. I have never felt lonesome, or in the least oppressed by a sense of solitude, but once, and that was a few weeks after I came to the woods, when, for an hour, I doubted if the near neighborhood of man was not essential to a serene and healthy life. To be alone was something unpleasant. But I was at the same time conscious of a slight insanity in my mood, and seemed to foresee my recovery. In the midst of a gentle rain while these thoughts prevailed, I was suddenly sensible of such sweet and beneficent society in Nature, in the very patter· ing of the drops, and in every sound and sight around my house, an infinite and unaccountable friendliness all at once like an atmosphere sustaining me, as made the fancied advantages of human neighborhood insignificant, and I have never thought of them since. Every little pine needle expanded and swelled with sympathy and befriended me. I was so distinctly made aware of the presence of something kindred to me, even in scenes which we are accustomed to call wild and dreary, and also that the nearest of blood to me and humanest was not a person nor a villager, that I thought no place could ever be strange to me again.—

"Mourning untimely consumes the sad;
Few are their days in the land of the living,
Beautiful daughter of Toscar."

247

Some of my pleasantest hours were during the long rainstorms in the spring or fall, which confined me to the house for the afternoon as well as the forenoon, soothed by their ceaseless roar and pelting; when an early twilight ushered in a long evening in which many thoughts had time to take root and unfold themselves. In those driving northeast rains which tried the village houses so, when the maids stood ready with mop and pail in front entries to keep the deluge out, I sat behind my door in my little house, which was all entry, and thoroughly enjoyed its protection. In one heavy thunder-shower the lightning struck a large pitch pine across the pond, making a very conspicuous and perfectly regular spiral groove from top to bottom, an inch or more deep, and four or five inches wide, as you would groove a walking-stick. I passed it again the other day, and was struck with awe on looking up and beholding that mark, now more distinct than ever, where a terrific and resistless bolt came down out of the harmless sky eight years ago. Men frequently say to me, "I should think you would feel lonesome down there, and want to be nearer to folks, rainy and snowy days and nights especially." I am tempted to reply to such,—This whole earth which we inhabit is but a point in space. How far apart, think you, dwell the two most distant inhabitants of yonder star, the breadth of whose disk cannot be appreciated by our instruments? Why should I feel lonely? Is not our planet in the Milky Way? This which you put seems to me not to be the most important question. What sort of space is that which separates a man from his fellows and makes him solitary? I have found that no exertion of the legs can bring two minds much nearer to one another. What do we want most to dwell near to? Not to many men surely, the depot, the post-office, the bar-room, the meeting-house, the school-house, the grocery, Beacon Hill, or the Five Points, where men most congregate, but to the perennial source of our life, whence in all our experience we have found that to issue, as the willow stands near the water and sends out its roots in that direction. This will vary with different natures, but this is the place where a wise man will dig his cellar. . . . I one evening overtook one of my townsmen, who has accumulated what is called "a handsome property,"—though I never got a *fair* view of it,—on the Walden road, driving a pair of cattle to market, who inquired of me how I could bring my mind to give up so many of the comforts of life. I answered that I was very sure I liked it passably well; I was not joking. And so I went home to my bed, and left him to pick his way through the darkness and mud to Brighton,—or Bright-town,—which place he would reach some time in the morning.

Any prospect of awakening or coming to life to a dead man makes indifferent all times and places. The place where that may occur is always the same, and indecribably pleasant to all our senses. For the most part we allow only outlying and transient circumstances to make our occasions. They are, in fact, the cause of our distraction. Nearest to all things is that power which fashions their being. *Next* to us the grandest laws are continually

248

being executed. *Next* to us is not the workman whom we have hired, with whom we love so well to talk, but the workman whose work we are. "How vast and profound is the influence of the subtile powers of Heaven and of Earth!" "We seek to perceive them, and we do not see them; we seek to hear them, and we do not hear them; identified with the substance of things, they cannot be separated from them."

"They cause that in all the universe men purify and sanctify their hearts, and clothe themselves in their holiday garments to offer sacrifices and oblations to their ancestors. It is an ocean of subtile intelligences. They are everywhere, above us, on our left, on our right; they environ us on all sides."

We are the subjects of an experiment which is not a little interesting to me. Can we not do without the society of our gossips a little while under these circumstances,—have our own thoughts to cheer us? Confucius says truly, "Virtue does not remain as an abandoned orphan; it must of necessity have neighbors."

With thinking we may be beside ourselves in a sane sense. By a conscious effort of the mind we can stand aloof from actions and their consequences; and all things, good and bad, go by us like a torrent. We are not wholly involved in Nature. I may be either the driftwood in the stream, or Indra in the sky looking down on it. I *may* be affected by a theatrical exhibition; on the other hand, I *may not* be affected by an actual event which appears to concern me much more. I only know myself as a human entity; the scene, so to speak, of thoughts and affections; and am sensible of a certain doubleness by which I can stand as remote from myself as from another. However intense my experience, I am conscious of the presence and criticism of a part of me, which, as it were, is not a part of me, but a spectator, sharing no experience, but taking note of it, and that is no more I than it is you. When the play, it may be the tragedy, of life is over, the spectator goes his way. It was a kind of fiction, a work of the imagination only, so far as he was concerned. This doubleness may easily make us poor neighbors and friends sometimes.

I find it wholesome to be alone the greater part of the time. To be in company, even the best, is soon wearisome and dissipating. I love to be alone. I never found the companion that was so companionable as solitude.

RESURGENCE
LAURA LEE RANDALL

Out of the earth, the rose,
Out of the night, the dawn:
Out of my heart, with all its woes,
High courage to press on.

HAPPY is the man that findeth wisdom.—*The Bible*

THE MORE WE KNOW, the better we forgive;
Whoe'er feels deeply, feels for all who live.
—*De Staël*

IT IS the peculiarity of knowledge that those who really thirst
for it always get it.—*Jefferies*

A WRONG-DOER is often a man that has left something undone,
not always he that has done something.—*Marcus Aurelius*

LEARNING is ever in the freshness of its youth, even for the old.—*Aeschylus*

BELIEVE ME when I tell you that thrift of time will repay you in after-life,
with a usury of profit beyond your most sanguine dreams; and that waste
of it will make you dwindle alike in intellectual and moral stature, beyond
your darkest reckoning.—*Gladstone*

FOREWARNED, forearmed; to be prepared is half the victory.—*Cervantes*

MY PRECEPT to all who build is, that the owner should be an
ornament to the house, and not the house to the owner.—*Cicero*

GODS FADE; but God abides and in man's heart
Speaks with the clear unconquerable cry
Of energies and hopes that can not die.
—*Symonds*

A WISE MAN will make more opportunities than he finds.—*Bacon*

DEFER NOT till to-morrow to be wise,
To-morrow's sun to thee may never rise.
—*William Congreve*

SYMPATHY gives us the material for wisdom.—*Anonymous*

THE WORLD

THE USE OF MOTTOES is to indicate something we have not attained, but strive to attain. It is right to keep them always before our eyes.—*Goethe*

INTEND HONESTLY and leave the event to God.—*Aesop*

THE WORLD is my country. All mankind are my brethren. To do good is my religion. I believe in one God and no more.—*Thomas Paine*

DIE WHEN I MAY, I want it said of me by those who knew me best, that I always plucked a thistle and planted a flower where I thought a flower would grow.—*Abraham Lincoln*

I THANK GOD for my mother as for no other gift of His bestowing.—*Willard*

EVERY MAN, however obscure, however far removed from the general recognition, is one of a group of men impressible for good, and impressible for evil, and it is in the nature of things that he can not really improve himself without in some degree improving other men.—*Dickens*

IT IS NOT what he has, nor even what he does, which directly expresses the worth of a man, but what he is.—*Amiel*

THAT SILENCE is one of the great arts of conversation is allowed by Cicero himself, who says there is not only an art, but an eloquence in it.—*More*

IF YOU will observe, it doesn't take a man of giant mould to make
A giant shadow on the wall; and he who in our daily sight
Seems but a figure mean and small, outlined in Fame's illusive light,
May stalk, a silhouette sublime, across the canvas of his time.
                                        —*Trowbridge*

WE CANNOT LIVE pleasantly without living wisely and nobly and righteously.—*Epicurus*

THE WISDOM of the wise and the experience of ages may be preserved by quotations.—*Isaac D'Israeli*

251

from The Story of Dr. Wassell

By JAMES HILTON

The Story of Dr. Wassell *is the simple, heroic story of an American navy doctor who got his wounded men out of Java through the turmoil of the Japanese invasion—and who also got the Navy Cross.*

Our selection begins when the Dutch vessel Janssens *puts out of a little Javanese harbor and heads across perilous waters toward Australia.*

$\mathcal{B}$UT THERE SEEMED no good omen in the moon that rose as the *Janssens* put out of the little harbor. It was a full moon, in a perfect sky, and to the doctor and his seven men it looked the biggest moon they had ever seen. It shone strong and yellow over land and water, marking the hills and the village and the receding beaches almost more clearly than daylight, for then there had been a touch of heat haze above the jungle. But now every line was etched black and clear, and every surface had a pale sheen —especially the cleared decks of a ship as she rode out to sea. And there was not a breath of wind, or more than a ripple stirring, save where the *Janssens's* wake laid a gleaming comet's tail behind her.

Everyone said, fatalistically: "They'll find us—they can't help finding us. We haven't a dog's chance."

But everyone added: "All the same, though, I wouldn't be back on land where those others are."

For the people on the *Janssens* were now a different crowd—they were the hardened gamblers who double their stakes when the timid ones are out of the game.

The *Janssens* was different also. To begin with, there was room on her and the men from the *Marble-* head could have moved into cabins if they had wished. But they were not keen. The cabins were small and stuffy, and the bunks smaller than the mattresses; whereas the decks were cool and wide and accessible. Now that repairs had been made, everyone could be assigned a place in the lifeboats, and to the men from the *Marblehead* one of the advantages of sleeping on deck was that their own lifeboat was only a few paces away. They thought these few paces might be important.

The doctor, however, who had spent the previous night on a chair in the smoke room, accepted the offer of a cabin within easy reach of his men; he would have to share it with two others, one of them a Dutch padre, he was told, but he said: "Sure, I don't mind that—I've known a good many padres in my time."

As the moon rose higher and brighter, the fact that the *Janssens* was no longer crowded made it seem almost empty. Some of the men from the *Marblehead* who could walk actually circumnavigated the whole deck, and in the dining saloon it was now possible to sit down at a table instead of being served cafeteriawise. But the food was late in coming and, for once, badly cooked. The doctor ate a little himself and saw that his men had enough, then he settled them comfortably on their mattresses and advised them to go early to sleep. He was glad to note that all seemed better physically, and he thought that in an emergency he could probably get them into a lifeboat in time.

But planes, of course, would not give one any time.

Everyone knew that, and small knots of people stood about on deck after dinner watching the sky and the horizon. They did not all admit that they were doing this; they said it was such a beautiful night, so cool and fresh and moonlit, it was a pity to go inside. But the fact was, they did not want to go inside. And almost all of them, without comment, had put on life jackets.

The doctor noticed that the girl missionary, McGuffey's friend, was among those who had stayed with the ship, and he told her he was glad.

The doctor also noticed that both the newspaper correspondent and the Dutch boy who was studying to be a naval officer had stayed on the ship, and to each of them also he said he was glad.

Towards ten o'clock a Dutch officer went around amongst the passengers with word that Captain Prass would again like to meet them all in the smoke room immediately.

When the doctor got there he found the Captain scowling down from the platform on which, in happier days, a small orchestra had functioned. He spoke a few sentences in Dutch that sounded ferocious enough; then he switched to his hard-clipped English and began what was evidently both a translation and an amplification. He declared that the *Janssens* was now heading due south, out to sea, and would reach Australia within ten days—barring unforeseen events. At that he glared as if defying them to occur. And he added, with a special glare to the doctor: "I am glad that the wounded American sailors are with us. They show courage. But courage is not enough. We must pull one another together." (The doctor thought he probably meant "pull ourselves together.") "We must work. We are not numerous enough for this ship unless all take a hand. For that reason you must consider yourselves under my orders—passengers and crew alike—no ranks, no exceptions. I shall set watches and duties for all. And the women must work too —we need cooks and helpers in the galley. You understand?" He concentrated himself into a final glare that seemed to convulse his whole body, then shouted as he marched out: "Some of you begin by clearing up this room. Never in all my life at sea have I permitted such a state of affairs on board a ship!" And he pointed with a swift backward fling to the litter of blood and cigarette butts and broken beer bottles that lay on the floor under the portrait of Queen Wilhelmina.

When he had gone everyone felt much better, not only because he had gone, but because he had talked

253

to them like that. It had been tonic, electric, dynamic. The doctor turned to his neighbor, a tall, broad-shouldered Dutchman whom he had not met before, and said cheerfully: "Well, what about it, brother? Shall we set the example?"

The man agreed, so during the next hour, while the *Janssens* rolled gently over the waves, the doctor and this Dutchman fell to with mops and pails and brooms, and by midnight they had the smoke room almost spick-and-span, except for a stain that would not come out of part of the floor. The two men had not talked much, chiefly because they had been too busy, but now it seemed natural for the doctor to invite the man to his cabin for a nightcap. "You see," he added gleefully, "I've got a bottle of Scotch somewhere in my bag. . . ."

"Oh no," protested the other, emphatically. "You must come to *my* cabin. I have some Bols gin—very good. And my name is Van Ryndt."

The doctor responded with his own name, but continued to argue in favor of himself as the host. Presently they tossed a coin that decided in favor of the Dutchman. On the way to his cabin they passed the men from the *Marblehead,* and the doctor, peering to see their faces in the moonlight, spoke some of their names softly to himself.

"You like these men a great deal?" queried the Dutchman.

"Sure, I like them all right—they're my men—*my* men—my job, if you look at it that way. I'd have to like 'em, anyway."

The other mused thoughtfully: "You spoke their names as if—well, it reminded me of saying the beads on a rosary . . . somehow."

The doctor did not see much similarity. "I spoke their names because I wanted to check up if they were all there—and by golly, one of them isn't . . . McGuffey, of course."

"What?"

"I tell you, if there's any place that boy can go where he shouldn't be, you bet he'll find it. . . . Excuse me, but before we do anything else we've got to find him."

They found him some distance away, in the shadow of one of the lifeboats. He was sitting with the girl on a heap of coiled rope.

"Okay," muttered the doctor, checking himself. "I guess we can leave him there."

"You think he is all right?"

"I'm dead sure he's all right. And who wouldn't be?"

"Pardon—I do not fully understand."

"Okay, I say, okay," repeated the doctor, feeling it might be a little indelicate to pass on what exactly was in his mind at that moment. But he smiled and took the Dutchman's arm as they continued on their way to the latter's cabin. Not till they were entering the doorway did the doctor make a belated discovery. "Why, this is *my* cabin!" he exclaimed, staring round and recognizing his own suitcase.

"Then you must be the American doctor?"

"Sure, that's what I am."

There was another man already in one of the bunks, fast asleep and snoring. For some reason the doctor thought this must be the Dutch padre, until his companion said: "You will pardon him—he is

254

one of the ship's officers who is very tired. He was watching for the submarines all day."

The doctor then grasped the inescapable logic of the situation. "Then *you* must be the padre?"

"That is right. Are you surprised?"

"Well, I guess it was the way you knuckled to at that clean-up job. . . . Sort of didn't put the right idea in my mind."

"Oh, but I have often done that in my own church. It is—it was, I mean—a very poor church financially and I do not think there is any shame in physical work."

"You bet there isn't," answered the doctor, and began to remember incidents in his own life during his first medical practice—the way he had chopped wood and cooked his own meals because he couldn't afford help. This led to a pleasant exchange of reminiscence over the drinks, and it was past midnight before the doctor felt the first faint onset of drowsiness. And then he thought of something else. "Just an idea, Padre," he said, "but how'd you feel about us having a prayer tonight before we turn in?"

"Certainly, Doctor. I always do that myself—but in Dutch, of course. If you would like to say your own prayer meanwhile in English . . ."

The doctor thought this was a very reasonable solution of the language problem, so they both knelt by the side of the bunk and prayed in low voices against the deep basso profundo of the third man's snores. The doctor said the Lord's Prayer first of all, but it did not last out the length of the padre's, so he mumbled on: "Oh God, we thank Thee for keeping us safe so far. Oh God, keep on keeping us safe. Give all the boys a quick recovery, and look after Renny, and let's win the war good and proper this time, so all the boys can go home. In Christ's name, Amen."

He did not think it much of a prayer, but then he had never been much good at extempore praying even in Chinese. After waiting awhile for the Dutchman to finish it occurred to him that he hadn't yet touched on his own personal affairs, so he did so now, briefly and simply. Then the Dutchman got to his feet, so the doctor said a quick Amen and followed suit. He felt much better in every possible way, especially when the Dutchman suggested one more nightcap.

"Ah," said the doctor, smiling in anticipation, "that's something I never did turn down. . . ."

The Dutchman poured out a generous allowance, commenting rather quizzically meanwhile: "I didn't know you were a religious man, Doctor."

"Well, I'm not, in a sort of way, but then I am too, in another sort of way."

The padre touched the doctor's arm gently, as with sudden affection. "Perhaps," he said, raising his glass, "the other sort of way is better."

All night the *Janssens* pushed through the light, but towards dawn the moon dipped into the sea, and there was a single hour of darkness before the sky unfurled for another day of blue skies and perfect weather.

But there was now no sight of land, and ten days later the *Jans-*

255

sens nosed into the harbor of Fremantle.

The doctor took the men from the *Marblehead* ashore to an Australian hospital and spent the usual busy time getting them settled. After filling out countless forms, his only remaining problem was that of those lost receipts for the goods he had bought with the Dutch guilders given him by the Navy. He still had about five hundred guilders left, and during the days that followed he made several attempts to get rid of them. The top Navy official at Fremantle Harbor listened to his explanation of their existence and then pushed them gently aside as if they were in some way contaminated. "I can't do anything with these, Doctor—you'll have to hand them in somewhere else."

"But it's Navy money—it doesn't belong to me."

"Well, it doesn't belong to me either. Why don't you try the Paymaster's Office?"

So the doctor went to the Paymaster's Office and was there advised to await word from Washington. "Can't do anything here about it. You see, we wouldn't know how to put it in the books."

The doctor did not think this was a very satisfactory reason, so he trundled his evidently hot money to a third office, where the refusal to accept it was even brusquer. Finally, after worrying about the matter for several days, he had an idea: he would put the bills in an envelope and simply mail them to the Navy Department, Washington, D. C. He reached this decision whilst having a bath, and was just enjoying the sensation of a load lifted from his mind when a message came that the Admiral wanted to see him at once.

Now the doctor's feeling for an admiral was similar to that which as a schoolboy he had felt for a headmaster, as a missionary for a bishop, and as a CCC doctor for some high visiting official. That is to say, he respected them all, but because he began by being shy, he ended as often as not by appearing truculent. Anyhow, the shyness came first, and by the time he had reached the Admiral's house, attired in a clean khaki suit and actually a necktie, he was very shy indeed. The first thing he did on being ushered into the presence was to plank down those five hundred guilders on the desk with a burst of urgent explanation. The Admiral looked rather puzzled as he listened; then he said: "I really don't know anything about this, Doctor. It's not my department, anyhow." ("But that's what they *all* say," thought the doctor.) "What I asked you to come for is something else altogether. . . . By the way, what's the matter? You look worried. . . ."

"Oh no, no, no," said the doctor.

"Well, the point is," continued the Admiral quite sternly, "I have to give you a message, and as I'm not much of a talker, I'll go right at it. You've been awarded the Navy Cross. . . . Congratulations."

The doctor felt his hand seized and could only stammer: "Wh—*what?*"

"I said you've been awarded the Navy Cross. For gallantry in getting your men out of Java. A mighty fine thing to do. You saved their lives—no doubt about it. They say so themselves. They give you all the credit. They say—" "Oh, no ... no ... no ..." said the doctor. And suddenly tears streamed from his eyes. He couldn't help it. It wasn't only being praised by an admiral, but to think that the men from the *Marblehead* thought that much of him ... the *Marblehead* ... those boys ...

A few days later the Admiral gave a dinner and after a certain amount of preliminary festivity the doctor loosened up. It had begun by his merely answering questions put by various officers, but soon he found himself telling them about Three Martini, and the British officer who had seemed at first so aloof but had really been a grand fellow, and Dr. Voorhuys, and the Dutch wireless operator at Tjilatjap. "All those fellows helped us— we couldn't have done *anything* without them. And Captain Prass, of course. That man sure was a man if ever there was one. . . . And then there were the boys themselves. I won't say they're perfect, any of them, but it wouldn't have

been any use me trying to get 'em out if they hadn't had the guts to be got out." He turned more personally to the Admiral. "And finally, sir, there was something I haven't talked to a soul about till now, but I think I ought to mention it. And that's prayer. There was a Dutch padre on board the *Janssens* and every night after that first air attack he and I prayed that those bloody Nips wouldn't find us again. . . . Excuse my language —it's what an English soldier called 'em and it's kinda stuck in my mind. . . . Yes, sir, we prayed hard, and I don't really figger anything else could have got us through."

The Admiral was at first slightly embarrassed by the turn the doctor's remarks had taken, for the power of prayer is not a favorite topic among high-ranking Naval officers; but when he looked across the table and saw the face of a man telling very simply what he very simply believed, he felt he must be equally sincere himself.

So he replied quietly: "You might be right, Dr. Wassell."

THE THINGS I PRIZE

HENRY VAN DYKE

These are the things I prize
And hold of dearest worth:
Light of the sapphire skies,
Peace of the silent hills,
Shelter of the forests, comfort of the grass,
Music of birds, murmur of little rills,
Shadows of cloud that swiftly pass,
And, after showers,
The smell of flowers
And of the good brown earth—
And best of all, along the way, friendship and mirth.

257

BETTER WERE IT to be unborn than to
be ill-bred.—*Sir Walter Raleigh*

OUR ONLY GREATNESS is that we aspire.—*Ingelow*

THERE ARE two freedoms—the false, where a man is free to do
what he likes; the true, where a man is free to do what he
ought.—*Kingsley*

TO BE DISCONTENTED with the divine discontent, and
to be ashamed with the noble shame, is the very germ
of the first upgrowth of all virtue.—*Kingsley*

MUSIC has been called the speech of angels; I will go further, and call
it the speech of God Himself.—*Kingsley*

IT IS RIDICULOUS for any man to criticise the works of another if he has
not distinguished himself by his own performance.—*Addison*

I LIKE NOT only to be loved, but to be told that I am loved; the
realm of silence is large enough beyond the grave.—*George Eliot*

MY FAITH in the people governing is, on the whole, infinitesimal;
my faith in the people governed is, on the whole, illimitable.
—*Dickens*

CHEERFULNESS is the best promoter of health, and is
as friendly to the mind as to the body.—*Addison*

THE BLESSEDNESS of life depends more upon its interests than
upon its comforts.—*Macdonald*

A GREAT DEAL of talent is lost in this world for the want of
a little courage.—*Smith*

SILENCE is one great art of conversation.—*Hazlitt*

258

BRITISH WRITERS

A LOVING HEART is the truest wisdom.—*Dickens*

DOING GOOD is the only certainly happy action of a man's life.—*Sir Philip Sidney*

LOST—somewhere between sunrise and sunset, two golden hours each set with sixty diamond minutes; no reward is offered for they are gone forever.—*Smiles*

No MAN ever sank under the burden of the day. It is when tomorrow's burden is added to the burden of today, that the weight is more than a man can bear.—*Macdonald*

HEALTH is the second blessing that we mortals are capable of,—a blessing that money cannot buy.—*Izaak Walton*

AUTHORITY is derived from reason, and never reason from authority. When authority is not confirmed by reason, it possesses no value.—*Erigena*

THE GRAND ESSENTIALS to happiness in this life are something to do, something to love, and something to hope for.—*Addison*

THERE IS no moment like the present. The man who will not execute his resolutions when they are fresh upon him can have no hope from them afterwards.—*Edgeworth*

LIFE is a mirror: if you frown at it, it frowns back; if you smile, it returns the greeting.—*Thackeray*

WHAT do we live for, if it is not to make life less difficult to each other?—*George Eliot*

TO HAVE what we want, is riches; but to be able to do without, is power.—*Macdonald*

MAKE USE of time if thou lov'st eternity.—*Quarles*

259

THE BALLAD OF EAST AND WEST

RUDYARD KIPLING

Oh, East is East, and West is West, and never the twain shall meet,
Till Earth and Sky stand presently at God's great Judgment Seat;
But there is neither East nor West, Border, nor Breed, nor Birth,
When two strong men stand face to face, though they come from the ends
　　of the earth!

Kamal is out with the twenty men to raise the Border side,
And he has lifted the Colonel's mare that is the Colonel's pride;
He has lifted her out of the stable-door between the dawn and the day
And turned the calkins upon her feet, and ridden her far away.
Then up and spoke the Colonel's son that led a troop of the Guides:
"Is there never a man of all my men can say where Kamal hides?"
Then up and spoke Mohammed Khan, the son of the Ressaldar:
"If ye know the track of the morning mist, ye know where his pickets are.
At dusk he harries the Abazai—at dawn he is into Bonair,
But he must go by Fort Bukloh to his own place to fare,
So if ye gallop to Fort Bukloh as fast as a bird can fly,
By the favor of God ye may cut him off ere he win to the Tongue of Jagai.
But if he be past the Tongue of Jagai, right swiftly turn ye then,
For the length and the breadth of that grisly plain is sown with Kamal's
　　men.
There is rock to the left, and rock to the right, and low lean thorn between.
And ye may hear a breech bolt snick where never a man is seen."
The Colonel's son has taken a horse, and a raw rough dun was he,
With the mouth of a bell and the heart of Hell and the head of a gallows
　　tree.
The Colonel's son to the Fort has won, they bid him stay to eat—
Who rides at the tail of a Border thief, he sits not long at his meat.
He's up and away from Fort Bukloh as fast as he can fly,
Till he was aware of his father's mare in the gut of the Tongue of Jagai,
Till he was aware of his father's mare with Kamal upon her back.
And when he could spy the white of her eye, he made the pistol crack.
He has fired once, he has fired twice, but the whistling ball went wide.
"Ye shot like a soldier," Kamal said. "Show now if ye can ride."
It's up and over the Tongue of Jagai, as blown dust-devils go.
The dun he fled like a stag of ten, but the mare like a barren doe,
The dun he leaned against the bit and slugged his head above,
But the red mare played with the snaffle bars, as a maiden plays with a
　　glove.
There was rock to the left and rock to the right, and low lean thorn
　　between

260

And thrice he heard a breech bolt snick though never a man was seen.
They have ridden the low moon out of the sky, their hoofs drum up the
dawn,
The dun he went like a wounded bull, but the mare like a new-roused
fawn.
The dun he fell at a watercourse—in a woeful heap fell he,
And Kamal has turned the red mare back, and pulled the rider free.
He has knocked the pistol out of his hand—small room was there to strive,
" 'Twas only by favor of mine," quoth he, "ye rode so long alive:
There was not a rock for twenty mile, there was not a clump of tree,
But covered a man of my own men with his rifle cocked on his knee.
If I had raised my bridle hand, as I have held it low,
The little jackals that flee so fast were feasting all in a row:
If I had bowed my head on my breast, as I have held it high,
The kite that whistles above us now were gorged till she could not fly."
Lightly answered the Colonel's son: "Do good to bird and beast,
But count who come for the broken meats before thou makest a feast,
If there should follow a thousand swords to carry my bones away,
Belike the price of a jackal's meal were more than a thief could pay.
They will feed their horse on the standing crop, their men on the garnered
grain.
The thatch of the byres will serve their fires when all the cattle are slain.
But if thou thinkest the price be fair,—thy brethren wait to sup,
The hound is kin to the jackal spawn,—howl, dog, and call them up!
And if thou thinkest the price be high, in steer and gear and stack,
Give me my father's mare again, and I'll fight my own way back!"
Kamal has gripped him by the hand and set him upon his feet.
"No talk shall be of dogs," said he, "when wolf and gray wolf meet.
May I eat dirt if thou hast hurt of me in deed or breath;
What dam of lances brought thee forth to jest at the dawn with Death?"
Lightly answered the Colonel's son: "I hold by the blood of my clan:
Take up the mare for my father's gift—by God, she has carried a man!"
The red mare ran to the Colonel's son, and nuzzled against his breast;
"We be two strong men," said Kamal then, "but she loveth the younger
best.
So she shall go with a lifter's dower, my turquoise-studded rein,
My broidered saddle and saddle-cloth, and silver stirrups twain."
The Colonel's son a pistol drew, and held it muzzle-end,
"Ye have taken the one from a foe," said he; "will ye take the mate from
a friend?"
"A gift for a gift," said Kamal straight; " a limb for the risk of a limb.
Thy father has sent his son to me, I'll send my son to him!"
With that he whistled his only son, that dropped from a mountain crest—
He trod the ling like a buck in spring, and he looked like a lance in rest.

"Now here is thy master," Kamal said, "who leads a troop of the Guides,
And thou must ride at his left side as shield on shoulder rides.
Till Death or I cut loose the tie, at camp and board and bed,
Thy life is his—thy fate it is to guard him with thy head.
So thou must eat the White Queen's meat, and all her foes are thine,
And thou must harry thy father's hold for the peace of the Borderline,
And thou must make a trooper tough and hack thy way to power—
Belike they will raise thee to Ressaldar when I am hanged in Peshawur."
They have looked each other between the eyes, and there they found no
fault,
They have taken the Oath of the Brother-in-Blood on leavened bread and
salt:
They have taken the Oath of the Brother-in-Blood on fire and fresh-cut
sod,
On the hilt and the haft of the Khyber knife, and the Wondrous Names of
God.
The Colonel's son he rides the mare and Kamal's boy the dun,
And two have come back to Fort Bukloh where there went forth but one.
And when they drew to the Quarter-Guard, full twenty swords flew clear—
There was not a man but carried his feud with the blood of the moun-
taineer.
"Ha' done! ha' done!" said the Colonel's son. "Put up the steel at your
sides!
Last night ye had struck at a Border thief—tonight 'tis a man of the
Guides!"
Oh, East is East, and West is West, and never the twain shall meet,
Till Earth and Sky stand presently at God's great Judgment Seat;
But there is neither East nor West, Border, nor Breed, nor Birth,
When two strong men stand face to face, though they come from the ends
of the earth!

MANY LOVE MUSIC
WALTER SAVAGE LANDOR

Many love music but for music's sake,
Many because her touches can awake
Thoughts that repose within the breast half-dead,
And rise to follow where she loves to lead.
What various feelings come from days gone by!
What tears from far-off sources dim the eye!
Few, when light fingers with sweet voices play,
And melodies swell, pause, and melt away,
Mind how at every touch, at every tone,
A spark of life hath glistened and hath gone.

OUR LADY OF THE RED CROSS: CLARA BARTON*
By Mary R. Parkman

"A Christmas baby! Now isn't that the best kind of a Christmas gift for us all?" cried Captain Stephen Barton, who took the interesting flannel bundle from the nurse's arms and held it out proudly to the assembled family.

No longed-for heir to a waiting kingdom could have received a more royal welcome than did that little girl who appeared at the Barton home in Oxford, Massachusetts, on Christmas Day, 1821. Ten years had passed since a child had come to the comfortable farmhouse, and the four big brothers and sisters were very sure that they could not have had a more precious gift than this Christmas baby. No one doubted that she deserved a distinguished name, but it was due to Sister Dorothy, who was a young lady of romantic seventeen and something of a reader, that she was called Clarissa Harlowe, after a well-known heroine of fiction. The name which this heroine of real life actually bore and made famous, however, was Clara Barton; for the Christmas baby proved to be a gift not only to a little group of loving friends, but also to a great nation and to humanity.

The sisters and brothers were teachers rather than playmates for Clara, and her education began so early that she had no recollection of the way they led her toddling steps through the beginnings of book learning. On her first day at

school she announced to the amazed teacher who tried to put a primer into her hands that she could spell the "artichoke words." The teacher had other surprises besides the discovery that this mite of three was acquainted with three-syllabled lore.

Brother Stephen, who was a wizard with figures, had made the sums with which he covered her slate seem a fascinating sort of play at a period when most infants are content with counting the fingers of one hand. All other interests, however, paled before the stories that her father told her of great men and their splendid deeds.

Captain Barton was amused one day at the discovery that his precocious daughter, who always eagerly encored his tales of conquerors and leaders, thought of their greatness in images of quite literal and realistic bigness. A president must, for instance, be as large as a house, and a vice-president as spacious as a barn door at the very least. But these somewhat crude conceptions did not put a check on the epic recitals of the retired officer, who, in the intervals of active service in plowed fields or in pastures where his thoroughbreds grazed with their mettlesome colts, liked to live over the days when he served under "Mad Anthony" Wayne in the Revolutionary War, and had a share in the thrilling adventures of the Western frontier.

Clara was only five years old when Brother David taught her to ride. "Learning to ride is just learning a horse," said this daring youth, who was the "Buffalo Bill" of the

*From HEROINES OF SERVICE by Mary R. Parkman, copyright, 1916, 1917, by the CENTURY COMPANY, 1945, by Lawrence Koenigsberger and Cornelia Whitney, reprinted by permission of D. APPLETON-CENTURY COMPANY, INC.

surrounding country.

"How can I learn a horse, David?" quavered the child, as the high-spirited animals came whinnying to the pasture bars at her brother's call.

"Catch hold of his mane, Clara, and just feel the horse a part of yourself—the big half for the time being," said David, as he put her on the back of a colt that was broken only to bit and halter, and, easily springing on his favorite, held the reins of both in one hand, while he steadied the small sister with the other by seizing hold of one excited foot.

They went over the fields at a gallop that first day, and soon little Clara and her mount understood each other so well that her riding feats became almost as far-famed as those of her brother. The time came when her skill and confidence on horseback—her power to feel the animal she rode a part of herself and keep her place in any sort of saddle through nightlong gallops—meant the saving of many lives.

David taught her many other practical things that helped to make her steady and self-reliant in the face of emergencies. She learned, for instance, to drive a nail straight, and to tie a knot that would hold. Eye and hand were trained to work together with quick decision that made for readiness and efficiency in dealing with a situation, whether it meant the packing of a box, or first-aid measures after an accident on the skating pond.

She was always an outdoor child, with dogs, horses, and ducks for playfellows. The fuzzy ducklings were the best sort of dolls. Sometimes when wild ducks visited the pond and all her waddling favor-ites began to flap their wings ex-citedly, it seemed that her young heart felt, too, the call of large, free spaces.

"The only real fun is to do things," she used to say.

She rode after the cows, helped in the milking and churning, and followed her father about, drop-ping potatoes in their holes or help-ing weed the garden. Once, when the house was being painted, she begged to be allowed to assist in the work, even learning to grind the pigments and mix the colors. The family was at first amused and then amazed at the persistency of her application as day after day she donned her apron and fell to work.

They were not less astonished when she wanted to learn the work of the weavers in her brothers' sat-inet mills. At first, her mother re-fused this extraordinary request; Stephen, who understood the inten-sity of her craving to do things, took her part; and at the end of her first week at the flying shuttle Clara had the satisfaction of finding that her cloth was passed as first-quality goods. Her career as a weaver was of short duration, however, owing to a fire which destroyed the mills.

The young girl was as enthusias-tic in play as at work. Whether it was a canter over the fields on Billy while her dog, Button, dashed along at her side, his curly white tail bob-bing ecstatically, or a coast down the rolling hills in winter, she en-tered into the sport of the moment with her whole heart.

When there was no outlet for her superabundant energy, she was gen-uinely unhappy. Then it was that a self-consciousness and morbid sen-sitiveness became so evident that it

264

was a source of real concern to her friends.

"People say that I must have been born brave," said Clara Barton. "Why, I seem to remember nothing but terrors in my early days. I was a shrinking little bundle of fears—fears of thunder, fears of strange faces, fears of my strange self." It was only when thought and feeling were merged in the zest of some interesting activity that she lost her painful shyness and found herself.

When she was eleven years old she had her first experience as a nurse. A fall which gave David a serious blow on the head, together with the bungling ministrations of doctors, who, when in doubt, had recourse only to the heroic treatment of bleeding and leeches, brought the vigorous brother to a protracted invalidism. For two years Clara was his constant and devoted attendant. She schooled herself to remain calm, cheerful, and resourceful in the presence of suffering and exacting demands. When others gave way to fatigue or "nerves," her wonderful instinct for action kept her, child though she was, at her post. Her sympathy expressed itself in untiring service.

In the years that followed her brother's recovery Clara became a real problem to herself and her friends. The old blighting sensitiveness made her school days restless and unhappy in spite of her alert mind and many interests.

At length her mother, at her wit's end because of this baffling, morbid strain in her remarkable daughter, was advised by a man of sane judgment and considerable understanding of child nature, to throw responsibility upon her and give her a school to teach.

It happened, therefore, that when Clara Barton was fifteen she "put down her skirts, put up her hair," and entered upon her successful career as a teacher. She liked the children and believed in them, entering enthusiastically into their concerns, and opening the way to new interests. When asked how she managed the discipline of the troublesome ones, she said, "The children give no trouble; I never have to discipline at all," quite unconscious of the fact that her vital influence gave her a control that made assertion of authority unnecessary.

"When the boys found that I was as strong as they were and could teach them something on the playground, they thought that perhaps we might discover together a few other worth-while things in school hours," she said.

For eighteen years Clara Barton was a teacher. Always learning herself while teaching others, she decided in 1852 to enter Clinton Liberal Institute in New York as a pupil for graduation, for there was almost no college whose doors were open to women. When she had all that the Institute could give her, she looked about for new fields for effort.

In Bordentown, New Jersey, she found there was a peculiar need for some one who would bring to her task pioneer zeal as well as the passion for teaching. At that time there were no public schools in the town or, indeed, in the State.

"The people who pose as respectable are too proud and too prejudiced to send their boys and girls to a free pauper school, and in the meantime all the children run wild," Miss Barton was told.

265

"We have tried again and again," said a discouraged young pedagogue. "It is impossible to do anything in this place."

"Give me three months, and I will teach free," said Clara Barton. This was just the sort of challenge she loved. There was something to be done. She began with six unpromising gamins in a dilapidated empty building. In a month her quarters proved too narrow. Each youngster became an enthusiastic and effectual advertisement. As always, her success lay in an understanding of her pupils as individuals, and a quickening interest that brought out the latent possibilities of each. The school of six grew in a year to one of six hundred, and the thoroughly converted citizens built an eight-room schoolhouse where Miss Barton remained as principal and teacher until a breakdown of her voice made a complete rest necessary.

The weak throat soon made it evident that her teaching days were over; but she found at the same time in Washington, where she had gone for recuperation, a new work. "Living is doing," she said. "Even while we say there is nothing we can do, we stumble over the opportunities for service that we are passing by in our tear-blinded self-pity."

The over-sensitive girl had learned her lesson well. Life offered moment by moment too many chances for action for a single worker to turn aside to bemoan his own particular condition.

The retired teacher became a confidential secretary in the office of the Commissioner of Patents. Great confusion existed in the Patent Office at that time because some clerks had betrayed the secrets of certain inventions. Miss Barton was the first woman to be employed in a Government department; and while ably handling the critical situation that called for all her energy and resourcefulness, she had to cope not only with the scarcely veiled enmity of those fellow-workers who were guilty or jealous, but also with the open antagonism of the rank and file of the clerks, who were indignant because a woman had been placed in a position of responsibility and influence. She endured covert slander and deliberate disrespect, letting her character and the quality of her work speak for themselves. They spoke so eloquently that when a change in political control caused her removal, she was before long recalled to straighten out the tangle that had ensued.

At the outbreak of the Civil War Miss Barton was, therefore, at the very storm-center.

The early days of the conflict found her binding up the wounds of the Massachusetts boys who had been attacked by a mob while passing through Baltimore, and who for a time were quartered in the Capitol. Some of these recruits were boys from Miss Barton's own town who had been her pupils, and all were dear to her because they were offering their lives for the Union. We find her with other volunteer nurses caring for the injured, feeding groups who gathered about her in the Senate Chamber, and, from the desk of the President of the Senate, reading them the home news from the Worcester papers.

Meeting the needs as they presented themselves in that time of general panic and distress, she sent to the Worcester "Spy" appeals for money and supplies. Other papers took up the work, and soon Miss

266

Barton had to secure space in a large warehouse to hold the provisions that poured in. Not for many days, however, did she remain a steward of supplies. When she met the transports which brought the wounded to the city, her whole nature revolted at the sight of the untold suffering and countless deaths which were resulting from delay in caring for the injured. Her flaming ardor, her rare executive ability, and her tireless persistency won for her the confidence of those in command, and, though it was against all traditions, to say nothing of ironclad army regulations, she obtained permission to go with her stores of food, bandages, and medicines to the firing line, where relief might be given on the battlefield at the time of direst need. The girl who had been a "bundle of fears" had grown into the woman who braved every danger and any suffering to carry help to her fellow-countrymen.

People who spoke of her rare initiative and practical judgment had little comprehension of the absolute simplicity and directness of her methods. She managed the sulky, rebellious drivers of her army wagons, who had little respect for orders that placed a woman in control, in the same way that she had managed children in school. Without relaxing her firmness, she spoke to them courteously, and called them to share the warm dinner she had prepared and spread out in appetizing fashion. When, after clearing away the dishes, she was sitting alone by the fire, the men returned in an awkward, self-conscious group.

"We didn't come to get warm," said their spokesman, as she kindly moved to make room for them at the flames, "we come to tell you we are ashamed. The truth is we didn't want to come. We know there is fighting ahead, and we've seen enough of that for men who don't carry muskets, only whips; and then we've never seen a train under charge of a woman before, and we couldn't understand it. We've been mean and contrary all day, and you've treated us as if we'd been the general and his staff, and given us the best meal we've had in two years. We want to ask your forgiveness, and we sha'n't trouble you again."

She found that a comfortable bed had been arranged for her in her ambulance, a lantern was hanging from the roof, and when next morning she emerged from her shelter, a steaming breakfast awaited her and a devoted corps of assistants stood ready for orders.

"I had cooked my last meal for my drivers," said Clara Barton. "These men remained with me six months through frost and snow and march and camp and battle; they nursed the sick, dressed the wounded, soothed the dying, and buried the dead; and, if possible, they grew kinder and gentler every day."

An incident that occurred at Antietam is typical of her quiet efficiency. According to her directions, the wounded were being fed with bread and crackers moistened in wine, when one of her assistants came to report that the entire supply was exhausted, while many helpless ones lay on the field unfed. Miss Barton's quick eye had noted that the boxes from which the wine was taken had fine Indian meal as packing. Six large kettles were at once unearthed from the farmhouse

267

in which they had taken quarters, and soon her men were carrying buckets of hot gruel for miles over the fields where lay hundreds of wounded and dying. Suddenly, in the midst of her labors, Miss Barton came upon the surgeon in charge sitting alone, gazing at a small piece of tallow candle which flickered uncertainly in the middle of the table.

"Tired, Doctor?" she asked sympathetically.

"Tired indeed!" he replied bitterly; "tired of such heartless neglect and carelessness. What am I to do for my thousand wounded men with night here and that inch of candle all the light I have or can get?"

Miss Barton took him by the arm and led him to the door, where he could see near the barn scores of lanterns gleaming like stars.

"What is that?" he asked amazedly.

"The barn is lighted," she replied, "and the house will be directly."

"Where did you get them?" he gasped.

"Brought them with me."

"How many have you?"

"All you want—four boxes."

The surgeon looked at her for a moment as if he were waking from a dream; and then, as if it were the only answer he could make, fell to work. And so it was invariably that she won her complete command of people as she did of situations, by always proving herself equal to the emergency of the moment.

Though, as she said in explaining the tardiness of a letter, "my hands complain a little of unaccustomed hardships," she never complained of any ill, nor allowed any danger or difficulty to interrupt her work.

"What are my puny ailments beside the agony of our poor shattered boys lying helpless on the field?" she said. And so, while doctors and officers wondered at her unlimited capacity for prompt and effective action, the men who had felt her sympathetic touch and effectual aid loved and revered her as "The Angel of the Battlefield."

One incident well illustrates the characteristic confidence with which she moved about amid scenes of terror and panic. At Fredericksburg, when "every street was a firing line and every house a hospital," she was passing along when she had to step aside to allow a regiment of infantry to sweep by. At that moment General Patrick caught sight of her, and, thinking she was a bewildered resident of the city who had been left behind in the general exodus, leaned from his saddle and said reassuringly:

"You are alone and in great danger, madam. Do you want protection?"

Miss Barton thanked him with a smile, and said, looking about at the ranks, "I believe I am the best-protected woman in the United States."

The soldiers near overheard and cried out, "That's so! that's so!" And the cheer that they gave was echoed by line after line until a mighty shout went up as for a victory.

The courtly old general looked about comprehendingly, and, bowing low, said as he galloped away, "I believe you are right, madam."

Clara Barton was present on sixteen battlefields; she was eight months at the siege of Charleston, and served for a considerable period in the hospitals of Richmond.

When the war was ended and the survivors of the great armies were marching homeward, her heart was touched by the distress in many homes where sons and fathers and brothers were among those listed as "missing." In all, there were 80,000 men of whom no definite report could be given to their friends. She was assisting President Lincoln in answering the hundreds of heartbroken letters, imploring news, which poured in from all over the land when his tragic death left her alone with the task. Then, as no funds were available to finance a thorough investigation of every sort of record of States, hospitals, prisons, and battlefields, she maintained out of her own means a bureau to prosecute the search.

Four years were spent in this great labor, during which time Miss Barton made many public addresses, the proceeds of which were devoted to the cause. One evening in the winter of 1868, while in the midst of a lecture, her voice suddenly left her. This was the beginning of a complete nervous collapse. The hardships and prolonged strain had, in spite of her robust constitution and iron will, told at last on the endurance of that loyal worker.

When able to travel, she went to Geneva, Switzerland, in the hope of winning back her health and strength. Soon after her arrival she was visited by the president and members of the "International Committee for the Relief of the Wounded in War," who came to learn why the United States had refused to sign the Treaty of Geneva, providing for the relief of sick and wounded soldiers. Of all the civilized nations, our great republic alone most unaccountably held aloof.

Miss Barton at once set herself to learn all she could about the ideals and methods of the International Red Cross, and during the Franco-Prussian War she had abundant opportunity to see and experience its practical working on the battlefield.

At the outbreak of the war in 1870 she was urged to go as a leader, taking the same part that she had borne in the Civil War.

"I had not strength to trust for that," said Clara Barton, "and declined with thanks, promising to follow in my own time and way; and I did follow within a week. As I journeyed on," she continued, "I saw the work of these Red Cross societies in the field accomplishing in four months under their systematic organization what we failed to accomplish in four years without it—no mistakes, no needless suffering, no waste, no confusion, but order, plenty, cleanliness, and comfort wherever that little flag made its way—a whole continent marshaled under the banner of the Red Cross. As I saw all this and joined and worked in it, you will not wonder that I said to myself, 'If I live to return to my country, I will try to make my people understand the Red Cross and that treaty.'"

Months of service in caring for the wounded and the helpless victims of siege and famine were followed by a period of nervous exhaustion from which she but slowly crept back to her former hold on health. At last she was able to return to America to devote herself to bringing her country into line with the Red Cross movement.

269

She found that traditionary prejudice against "entangling alliances with other powers," together with a singular failure to comprehend the vital importance of the matter, militated against the great cause. "Why should we make provision for the wounded?" it was said. "We shall never have another war; we have learned our lesson."

It came to Miss Barton then that the work of the Red Cross should be extended to disasters, such as fires, floods, earthquakes, and epidemics — "great public calamities which require, like war, prompt and well-organized help."

Years of devoted missionary work with preoccupied officials and a heedless, shortsighted public at length bore fruit. After the Geneva Treaty received the signature of President Arthur on March 1, 1882, it was promptly ratified by the Senate, and the American National Red Cross came into being, with Clara Barton as its first president. Through her influence, too, the International Congress of Berne adopted the "American Amendment," which dealt with the extension of the Red Cross to relief measures in great calamities occurring in times of peace.

The story of her life from this time on is one with the story of the work of the Red Cross during the stress of such disasters as the Mississippi River floods, the Texas famine in 1885, the Charleston earthquake in 1886, the Johnstown flood in 1899, the Russian famine in 1892, and the Spanish-American War. The prompt, efficient methods followed in the relief of the flood sufferers along the Mississippi in 1884 may serve to illustrate the sane, constructive character of her work.

Supply centers were established, and a steamer chartered to ply back and forth carrying help and hope to the distracted human creatures who stood "wringing their hands on a frozen, fireless shore—with every coalpit filled with water." For three weeks she patrolled the river, distributing food, clothing, and fuel, caring for the sick, and, in order to establish at once normal conditions of life, providing the people with many thousands of dollars' worth of building material, seeds, and farm implements, thus making it possible for them to help themselves and in work find a cure for their benumbing distress.

"Our Lady of the Red Cross" lived past her ninetieth birthday, but her real life is measured by deeds, not days. It was truly a long one, rich in the joy of service. She abundantly proved the truth of the words: "We gain in so far as we give. If we would find our life, we must be willing to lose it."

SANTA FILOMENA

Henry Wadsworth Longfellow

Whene'er a noble deed is wrought,
Whene'er is spoken a noble thought,
Our hearts, in glad surprise,
To higher levels rise.

The tidal wave of deeper souls
Into our inmost being rolls,
  And lifts us unawares
  Out of all meaner cares.

Honor to those whose words or deeds
Thus help us in our daily needs,
  And by their overflow
  Raise us from what is low!

Thus thought I, as by night I read
Of the great army of the dead,
  The trenches cold and damp,
  The starved and frozen camp,—

The wounded from the battle-plain,
In dreary hospitals of pain,
  The cheerless corridors,
  The cold and stony floors.

Lo! in that house of misery
A lady with a lamp I see
  Pass through the glimmering gloom,
  And flit from room to room.

And slow, as in a dream of bliss,
The speechless sufferer turns to kiss
  Her shadow, as it falls
  Upon the darkening walls.

As if a door in heaven should be
Opened and then closed suddenly,
  The vision came and went,
  The light shone and was spent.

On England's annals, through the long
Hereafter of her speech and song,
  That light its rays shall cast
  From portals of the past.

A Lady with a Lamp shall stand
In the great history of the land,
  A noble type of good
  Heroic womanhood.

271

Nor even shall be wanting here
The palm, the lily, and the spear,
The symbols that of yore
Saint Filomena bore.

A LITTLE CHILD SHALL LEAD US
ANONYMOUS

You, little child, with your shining eyes and dimpled cheeks—you can lead us along the pathway to the more abundant life:
We blundering grownups need in our lives the virtues that you have in yours:
The joy and enthusiasm of looking forward to each new day with glorious expectations of wonderful things to come:
The vision that sees the world as a splendid place with good fairies, brave knights, and glistening castles reaching towards the sky:
The radiant curiosity that finds adventure in simple things: the mystery of billowy clouds, the miracle of snowflakes, the magic of growing flowers:
The tolerance that forgets differences as quickly as your childish quarrels are spent; that holds no grudges, that hates never, that loves people for what they are:
The genuineness of being oneself; to be done with sham, pretense, and empty show; to be simple, natural, and sincere:
The courage that rises from defeat and tries again, as you with laughing face rebuild the house of blocks that topples to the floor:
The believing heart that trusts others, knows no fear and has faith in a Divine Father Who watches over His children from the sky:
The contented, trusting mind that, at the close of day woos the blessing of child-like slumber:
Little child, we would become like you, that we may find again the Kingdom of Heaven within our hearts.

RED GERANIUM
(From an "L" Train Window)
ADELE JORDAN TARR

The snow has built a fortress on the hill—
It looms, forbidding in the winter dawn:
The bare trees shiver as the north wind, shrill,
Keens a lament for summer dead and gone.
But in a window where a sunbeam, wan,
Shines for an hour, a splash of crimson bloom
Lightens the shadow, glorifies the room.

SILVER SHIPS
Mildred Plew Meigs

There are trails that a lad may follow
  When the years of his boyhood slip,
But I shall soar like a swallow
  On the wings of a silver ship,
Guiding my bird of metal,
  One with her throbbing frame,
Floating down like a petal,
  Roaring up like a flame;
Winding the wind that scatters
  Smoke from the chimney's lip,
Tearing the clouds to tatters
  With the wings of a silver ship;
Grazing the broad blue skylight
  Up where the falcons fare,
Riding the realms of twilight,
  Brushed by a comet's hair;
Snug in my coat of leather,
  Watching the skyline swing,
Shedding the world like a feather
  From the tip of a tilted wing.
There are trails that a lad may travel
  When the years of his boyhood wane,
But I'll let a rainbow ravel
  Through the wings of my silver plane.

FLIGHT
Clara Edmunds-Hemingway

The flash of sails against the sky,
The glint of seagull winging by,
As airman cleaves the summer sky.

An eagle soars to eyrie, where
His mountain home is cool and fair,
As airman wings his way in air.

To soar above life's sordid things,
Life's failures, or its hurts and stings,
We, too, could rise ... had we the wings.

273

GOD'S GOODNESS hath been great to thee;
Let never day nor night unhallowed pass,
But still remember what the Lord hath done.
—*Shakespeare*

A GOOD NAME is better than a girdle of gold.—*Anonymous*

WHATSOEVER a man soweth, that shall he also reap.—*The Bible*

IF WE ENCOUNTER a man of rare intellect, we should ask him
what books he reads.—*Emerson*

OUR COUNTRY, right or wrong! When right, to be kept right; when wrong,
to be put right!—*Carl Schurz*

WE MEET on the broad pathway of good faith and good will; no advantage
shall be taken on either side, but all shall be openness and love.—*Penn*

MEN are born with two eyes, but with one tongue in order that they should
see twice as much as they say.—*Colton*

IF YOU have knowledge, let others light their candles
at it.—*Margaret Fuller*

BE BRAVE, and rise superior to your sorrows, and maintain
(for you can) a spirit that cannot be broken.—*Ovid*

TIME cannot wither talents' well-earned fame;
True genius has secured a deathless name.
—*Propertius*

A BROAD MARGIN of leisure is as beautiful
in a man's life as in a book.—*Thoreau*

COURAGE is the armed sentinel that guards
liberty, innocence and right.—*Baldwin*

THE WORLD

ERE YOU REMARK another's sin,
Bid thy own conscience look within.
—*Gay*

As HE thinketh in his heart, so is he.—*The Bible*

THAT MAN is idle who does less than he can.—*Anonymous*

MUSIC is a revelation; a revelation loftier than all wisdom
and all philosophy.—*Beethoven*

A HOME is the first necessity of every family; it is indispensable to the
education and qualification of every citizen.—*Seward*

LEND NOT beyond thy ability, nor refuse to lend out of thy ability; especially when it will help others more than it can hurt thee.—*Penn*

THAT IS the best government which desires to make the people happy, and
knows how to make them happy.—*Macaulay*

NOTHING is more simple than greatness; indeed, to be simple
is to be great.—*Emerson*

BY A TRANQUIL MIND I mean nothing else than a mind well
ordered.—*Marcus Aurelius*

AND WHERE we love is home,
Home that our feet may leave, but not our hearts.
The chain may lengthen, but it never parts.
—*Holmes*

COURAGE AND PERSEVERANCE have a magical talisman,
before which difficulties disappear and obstacles vanish
into air.—*John Quincy Adams*

TRUE SINCERITY sends for no witnesses.—*Anonymous*

MY CREED
Edgar A. Guest

To live as gently as I can;
To be, no matter where, a man;
To take what comes of good or ill
And cling to faith and honor still;
To do my best, and let that stand
The record of my brain and hand;
And then, should failure come to me,
Still work and hope for victory.

To have no secret place wherein
I stoop unseen to shame or sin;
To be the same when I'm alone
As when my every deed is known;
To live undaunted, unafraid
Of any step that I have made;
To be without pretense or sham
Exactly what men think I am.

To leave some simple mark behind
To keep my having lived in mind;
If enmity to aught I show,
To be an honest, generous foe,
To play my little part, nor whine
That greater honors are not mine.
This, I believe, is all I need
For my philosophy and creed.

BE STILL
S. Alicia Poole

When you doubt the lovely silence
Of a quiet wooded place,
When you doubt the path of silver
Of some moonlit water space,
When you doubt the winds a'blowing,
Flash of lightning, glistening rain,
Sun or starlit heavens above you
On the land or bounding main,
When you doubt the sleep of loved ones
Deep beneath some precious sod,
Listen to a soft voice saying,
"Be still, and know that I am God."

THIS, TOO, WILL PASS
GRACE NOLL CROWELL

This, too, will pass. O heart, say it over and over,
Out of your deepest sorrow, out of your grief.
No hurt can last forever—perhaps tomorrow
Will bring relief.

This, too, will pass. It will spend itself—its fury
Will die as the wind dies down with the setting sun;
Assuaged and calm, you will rest again, forgetting
A thing that is done.

Repeat it again and again, O heart, for your comfort;
This, too, will pass, as surely as passed before
The old forgotten pain, and the other sorrows
That once you bore.

As certain as stars at night, or dawn after darkness,
Inherent as the lift of the blowing grass,
Whatever your despair or your frustration—
This, too, will pass.

THANKSGIVING SONG
LAURA LEE RANDALL

This is the day the Lord hath made;
    Be glad, give thanks, rejoice;
Stand in his presence, unafraid,
    In praise lift up your voice.
All perfect gifts are from above,
    And all our blessings show
The amplitude of God's dear love
    Which every heart may know.

The Lord will hear before we call,
    And every need supply;
Good things are freely given to all
    Who on His word rely.
We come today to bring Him praise
    Not for such gifts alone,
But for the higher, deeper ways
    In which His love is shown.

For sin destroyed, for sorrow healed,
  For health and peace restored;
For Life and Love by Truth revealed,
  We thank and bless the Lord.
This is the day the Lord hath made,
  In praise lift up your voice.
In shining robes of joy arrayed,
  Be glad, give thanks, rejoice.

THE POET'S PRAYER
JOHN GREENLEAF WHITTIER

If there be some weaker one,
Give me strength to help him on;
If a blinder soul there be,
Let me guide him nearer Thee;
Make my mortal dreams come true
With the work I fain would do;
Clothe with life the weak intent,
Let me be the thing I meant;
Let me find in Thy employ,
Peace that dearer is than joy;
Out of self to love be led,
And to heaven acclimated,
Until all things sweet and good
Seem my natural habitude.

BEAUTIFUL DREAMER
STEPHEN FOSTER

Beautiful dreamer, wake unto me,
Starlight and dewdrops are waiting for thee;
Sounds of the rude world heard in the day,
Lull'd by the moonlight have all pass'd away!
Beautiful dreamer, queen of my song,
List while I woo thee with soft melody;
Gone are the cares of life's busy throng,
Beautiful dreamer, awake unto me!

Beautiful dreamer, out on the sea
Mermaids are chaunting the wild lorelie;

Over the streamlet vapors are borne,
Waiting to fade at the bright coming morn.
Beautiful dreamer, beam on my heart,
E'en as the morn on the streamlet and sea;
Then will all clouds of sorrow depart,
Beautiful dreamer, awake unto me!

OLD HOUSE
WINIFRED WELLES

The house was old and fond of shadow—
  Dappled with grey, it whitely stood,
Squinting across at stream and meadow
  Austerely, as an old house should.

In spring, the apple blossoms drifting
  Left catlike footprints on the air,
Their furred reflections softly shifting
  Across the clapboards bleak and bare.

The maples' starring leaves were stencilled
  Around the roof, and, winter days,
What the wind said was finely pencilled
  By stiff stems in a frigid phrase.

NO SWEETER THING
ADELAIDE LOVE

Life holds no sweeter thing than this—to teach
A little child the tale most loved on earth
And watch the wonder deepen in his eyes
The while you tell him of the Christ Child's birth;

The while you tell of shepherds and a song,
Of gentle drowsy beasts and fragrant hay
On which that starlit night in Bethlehem
God's tiny Son and His young mother lay.

Life holds no sweeter thing than this—to tell
A little child, while Christmas candles glow,
The story of a Babe whose humble birth
Became the loveliest of truths we know.

THE LOVE OF BOOKS, the Golden Key
That opens the Enchanted Door.
—*Andrew Lang*

THE RESPONSIBILITY of tolerance lies with those who
have the wider vision.—*George Eliot*

BOOKS, like proverbs, receive their chief value from the stamp
and esteem of ages through which they passed.—*Temple*

MUSIC RAISES in the mind of the hearer great conceptions: it strengthens and advances praise into rapture.—*Addison*

TRUE FRIENDS visit us in prosperity only when invited, but in adversity
they come without invitation.—*Theophrastus*

BOOK LOVE, my friends, is your pass to the greatest, the purest, and the
most perfect pleasure that God has prepared for His creatures. It lasts
when all other pleasures fade. It will support you when all other recreations
are gone. It will last you until your death. It will make your hours
pleasant to you as long as you live.—*Trollope*

NO SOUL is desolate as long as there is a human being for whom it
can feel trust and reverence.—*George Eliot*

IN ANY EMERGENCY in life there is nothing so strong and
safe as the simple truth.—*Dickens*

EVERY MAN who observes vigilantly and resolves steadfastly,
grows unconsciously into genius.—*Bulwer-Lytton*

AND MUSIC TOO—dear music! that can touch
Beyond all else the soul that loves it much.
—*Moore*

THE FIRST CONDITION of human goodness is something to
love; the second, something to reverence.—*George Eliot*

280

WHERE'ER we turn Thy glories shine,
And all things fair and bright are Thine.
—Moore

WITHOUT CONSTANCY there is neither love, friendship, nor
virtue in the world.—*Addison*

ONE OF THE most important, but one of the most difficult things
for a powerful mind is, to be its own master.—*Addison*

YOUTH will never live to age unless they keep themselves in health
with exercise, and in heart with joyfulness.—*Sir Philip Sidney*

THE PRINTER is a faithful servant. Without him tyrants and humbugs
in all countries would have everything their own way.—*Dickens.*

WHEN I would beget content and increase confidence in the power and wisdom
and providence of Almighty God, I will walk the meadows by some gliding
stream, and there contemplate the lilies that take no care, and those very
many other little living creatures that are not only created, but fed
(man knows not how) by the goodness of the God of Nature, and therefore
trust in Him.—*Izaak Walton*

I LOVE little children, and it is not a slight thing when they,
who are fresh from God, love us.—*Dickens*

No COWARD SOUL is mine,
No trembler in the world's storm-troubled sphere:
I see Heaven's glories shine,
And faith shines equal, arming me from fear.
—Brontë

THE LIVING FOREST with Thy whisper thrills,
And there is holiness in every shade.
—Hemans

WE CAN FINISH nothing in this life; but we may make a
beginning, and bequeath a noble example.—*Smiles*

281

FOR A BIRTHDAY
RUTH CRARY

This would have been your birthday, had you stayed.
You would have been—how old? I cannot think.
I only know that still the golden link
Encircles us. Insatiate years have laid
Relentless hands upon me; have betrayed
The youth that rivaled yours. Now, on the brink
Of every birthday, impotent, I shrink
Before the years I cannot well evade.

But birthdays of the dead may come and go
Without recording; for these, Time stands still.
This is the benison the living know.
And somewhere—somewhere just beyond the chill,
You wait, where all the flowers, unfading, blow—
Forever twenty—on a little hill.

NINETY-FIVE
By JOSEPH FORT NEWTON

SIR WILLIAM MULOCK, Chief Justice of Ontario, is the oldest serving judge in the British Empire today. At a dinner given him on his ninety-fifth birthday recently, he uttered these words:

"I am still at work, with my hand to the plough, and my face to the future. The shadows of evening lengthen about me, but morning is in my heart. I have lived from the forties of one century to the thirties of the next. I have had varied fields of labor, and full contact with men and things, and have warmed both hands before the fire of life.

"The testimony I bear is this: that the Castle of Enchantment is not yet behind me. It is before me still, and daily I catch glimpses of its battlements and towers. The rich spoils of memory are mine. Mine, too, are the precious things of today—books, flowers, pictures, nature, and sport. The first of May is still an enchanted day to me. The best thing of all is friends. The best of life is always farther on. Its real lure is hidden from our eyes, some-where behind the hills of time."

To add any word is needless—nay, it is almost impertinent; but one may be allowed to say that a finer piece of English prose it would be hard to name, or even to imagine. Also, such a testimony, by its dignity, simplicity and serenity, does give one a wistful moment of quiet, deep down and far back in his heart, the while he wonders about his own adventure in living, and whether life is not something richer and more rewarding than what he by his haste, his fretting doubt and fevered dreaming, and

282

the mists of dismay, has found it to be.

If only we can hold the treasures of memory untarnished, carry the glow of morning through the long day, despite its clouds, keep a mind clear and unafraid, doing the work appointed without haste and without confusion, live simply with the grace to forgive and the humility to be forgiven, responsive, expectant, looking forward, and above all keep faith with life, enjoying the beautiful things God has given and the hand of man has made—we, too, may really live!

DEATH IS A DOOR
Nancy Byrd Turner

Death is only an old door
　　Set in a garden wall.
On quiet hinges it gives at dusk,
　　When the thrushes call.

Along the lintel are green leaves,
　　Beyond, the light lies still;
Very weary and willing feet
　　Go over that sill.

There is nothing to trouble any heart,
　　Nothing to hurt at all.
Death is only an old door
　　In a garden wall.

I THINK THAT GOD IS PROUD
Grace Noll Crowell

I think that God is proud of those who bear
　　A sorrow bravely—proud indeed of them
Who walk straight through the dark to find Him there,
　　And kneel in faith to touch His garment's hem.
Oh, proud of them who lifts their heads to shake
　　Away the tears from eyes that have grown dim,
Who tighten quivering lips and turn to take
　　The only road they know that leads to Him.

How proud He must be of them—He who knows
　　All sorrows, and how hard grief is to bear!
I think He sees them coming, and He goes
　　With outstretched arms and hands to meet them there.
And with a look, a touch on hand or head,
Each finds his hurt heart strangely comforted.

283

BY THE SAME LAW
ADELAIDE LOVE

I saw one day a straight young pear tree bound
With thongs of leather to a garden wall
And, both amazed and troubled to have found
Such slim, green loveliness in helpless thrall,
I sought the gardener, asking why he tied
The pliant tree to obdurate brick and stone.
"To make it bear its fruits, ma'am," he replied,
"When left to spread, it ran to leaves alone."

With this for answer and rebuke, I saw
How well the Husbandman supreme contrives
By virtue of a strange, impartial law
To gather ampler fruit from human lives.
How often have I seen a spirit know
Restraint of bonds before its fruits would grow.

AT LAST
JOHN GREENLEAF WHITTIER

When on my day of life the night is falling,
    And, in the winds from unsunned spaces blown,
I hear far voices out of darkness calling
    My feet to paths unknown.

Thou who hast made my home of life so pleasant,
    Leave not its tenant when its walls decay;
O Love divine, O Helper ever present,
    Be Thou my strength and stay!

Be near me when all else is from me drifting:
    Earth, sky, home's pictures, days of shade and shine,
And kindly faces to my own uplifting
    The love which answers mine.

I have but Thee, my Father! let Thy spirit
    Be with me then to comfort and uphold;
No gate of pearl, no branch of palm I merit,
    Nor street of shining gold.

Suffice it if—my good and ill unreckoned,
    And both forgiven through Thy abounding grace—

284

I find myself by hands familiar beckoned
   Unto my fitting place.

Some humble door among Thy many mansions,
   Some sheltering shade where sin and striving cease,
And flows for ever through heaven's green expansions
   The river of Thy peace.

There, from the music round about me stealing,
   I fain would learn the new and holy song,
And find at last, beneath Thy trees of healing,
   The life for which I long.

TO A YOUNG GIRL
HESTER SUTHERS

Your laughter is a fount of radiance
Which thrills the vivid air as you lilt by;
Your feet are sandaled like the April wind's,
That lovely wayward daughter of the sky.

Your brow is bright with dreams, your lips upcurved
With sweetness of your thought; in your clear eyes
That still hold shining wonder in their deeps
The unspent glory of the morning lies.

AT DAY'S END
ADELAIDE LOVE

I hold you in my arms before the fire
And tell the fairy tale you love the best,
While winter twilight deepens and the first
White star comes forth to glitter in the west.

So softly do you lie against my heart
I scarcely know if it be child or flower
I cradle, till you stir and draw a breath
Of wonder at the tale. O, blessed hour

That every mother knows when at day's end
She holds her little child, a wistful ache
Commingling with her joy, and dreams a dream
For him and breathes a prayer for his dear sake!

NOTHING is so strong as gentleness,
Nothing is so gentle as real strength.
—*De Sales*

LOVE the truth but pardon error.—*Voltaire*

THERE ARE three things difficult: to keep a secret,
to suffer an injury, to use leisure.—*Voltaire*

HAPPINESS lies in the taste, and not in things; and it is from having
what we desire that we are happy—not from having what others think
desirable.—*La Rochefoucauld*

YOU ONLY HOLD THE CROWN from God, sire. Deign to remember that God
only crowns kings in order to procure for his subjects security of life, personal
liberty, and peaceful enjoyment of prosperity.—*Malesherbes*

ALL OUR DIGNITY consists in thought. Let us labor, then, to think well.
That is the principle of morality.—*Pascal*

LITTLE MINDS are too much hurt by little things; great minds are quite
conscious of them, and despise them.—*La Rochefoucauld*

THE COIN of wisdom is its great thoughts, its eloquent flights,
its proverbs and pithy sentences.—*Joubert*

DOING EASILY what others find difficult is talent; doing what
is impossible *for talent* is genius.—*Amiel*

GREAT THOUGHTS come from the heart.—*De Musset*

GREAT MEN are the true men, the men in whom
nature has succeeded.—*Amiel*

IF THERE were no God, it would be necessary
to invent him.—*Voltaire*

PHILOSOPHERS

FRIENDSHIP is the highest degree of
perfection in society.—*Montaigne*

SORROW is a fruit: God does not make it grow on limbs
too weak to bear it.—*Victor Hugo*

IN ORDER to do great things, one must be enthusiastic.—*De Rouvroy*

WHEN A BOOK raises your spirit and inspires you with noble and manly
thoughts, seek for no other test of its excellence. It is good and made by
a good workman.—*La Bruyère*

MARCUS AURELIUS produces such an effect upon our minds that we think better
of ourselves, because he inspires us with a better opinion of mankind.
—*Montesquieu*

THE MOST disastrous times have produced the greatest minds. The purest
metal comes of the most ardent furnace, the most brilliant lightning comes
of the darkest clouds.—*Chateaubriand*

IT IS in a certain degree to be a sharer in noble deeds when we praise
them with all our heart.—*La Rochefoucauld*

VIRTUE as much as happiness comes from heaven.—*Voltaire*

WE SHOULD NOT JUDGE of a man's merit by his good qualities,
but by the use he can make of them.—*La Rochefoucauld*

WHEN WE cannot find contentment in ourselves, it is
useless to seek it elsewhere.—*La Rochefoucauld*

WHO DOES NOT in some sort live to others,
does not live much to himself.—*Montaigne*

THE BEAUTIFUL is as useful
as the useful.—*Victor Hugo*

A Mother in Mannville

By MARJORIE KINNAN RAWLINGS

*T*HE ORPHANAGE is high in the Carolina mountains. Sometimes in winter the snowdrifts are so deep that the institution is cut off from the village below, from all the world. Fog hides the mountain peaks, the snow swirls down the valleys, and a wind blows so bitterly that the orphanage boys who take the milk twice daily to the baby cottage reach the door with fingers stiff in an agony of numbness.

"Or when we carry trays from the cookhouse for the ones that are sick," Jerry said, "we get our faces frostbit, because we can't put our hands over them. I have gloves," he added. "Some of the boys don't have any."

He liked the late spring, he said. The rhododendron was in bloom, a carpet of color, across the mountainsides, soft as the May winds that stirred the hemlocks. He called it laurel.

"It's pretty when the laurel blooms," he said. "Some of it's pink and some of it's white."

I was there in the autumn. I wanted quiet, isolation, to do some troublesome writing. I wanted mountain air to blow out the malaria from too long a time in the subtropics. I was homesick, too, for the flaming of maples in October, and for corn shocks and pumpkins and black-walnut trees and the lift of hills. I found them all, living in a cabin that belonged to the orphanage, half a mile beyond the orphanage farm. When I took the cabin, I asked for a boy or man to come and chop wood for the fireplace. The first few days were warm. I found what wood I needed about the cabin, no one came, and I forgot the order.

I looked up from my typewriter one late afternoon, a little startled. A boy stood at the door, and my pointer dog, my companion, was at his side and had not barked to warn me. The boy was probably twelve years old, but undersized. He wore overalls and a torn shirt, and was barefooted.

He said, "I can chop some wood today."

I said, "But I have a boy coming from the orphanage."

"I'm the boy."

"You? But you're small."

"Size don't matter, chopping wood," he said. "Some of the big boys don't chop good. I've been chopping wood at the orphanage a long time."

I visualized mangled and inadequate branches for my fires. I was well into my work and not inclined to conversation. I was a little blunt.

"Very well. There's the ax. Go ahead and see what you can do."

I went back to work, closing the door. At first the sound of the boy dragging brush annoyed me. Then he began to chop. The blows were rhythmic and steady, and shortly I had forgotten him, the sound no more of an interruption than a consistent rain. I suppose an hour and a half passed, for when I stopped

288

and stretched, and heard the boy's steps on the cabin stoop, the sun was dropping behind the farthest mountain, and the valleys were purple with something deeper than the asters.

The boy said, "I have to go to supper now. I can come again tomorrow evening."

I said, "I'll pay you now for what you've done," thinking I should probably have to insist on an older boy. "Ten cents an hour?"

"Anything is all right."

We went together back of the cabin. An astonishing amount of solid wood had been cut. There were cherry logs and heavy roots of rhododendron, and blocks from the waste pine and oak left from the building of the cabin.

"But you've done as much as a man," I said. "This is a splendid pile."

I looked at him, actually, for the first time. His hair was the color of the corn shocks and his eyes, very direct, were like the mountain sky when rain is pending—gray, with a shadowing of that miraculous blue. As I spoke, a light came over him, as though the setting sun had touched him with the same suffused glory with which it touched the mountains. I gave him a quarter.

"You may come tomorrow," I said, "and thank you very much."

He looked at me, and at the coin, and seemed to want to speak, but could not, and turned away.

"I'll split kindling tomorrow," he said over his thin ragged shoulder. "You'll need kindling and medium wood and logs and backlogs."

At daylight I was half wakened by the sound of chopping. Again it was so even in texture that I went back to sleep. When I left my bed in the cool morning, the boy had come and gone, and a stack of kindling was neat against the cabin wall. He came again after school in the afternoon and worked until time to return to the orphanage. His name was Jerry; he was twelve years old, and he had been at the orphanage since he was four. I could picture him at four, with the same grave gray, blue eyes and the same—independence? No, the word that comes to me is "integrity."

The word means something very special to me, and the quality for which I use it is a rare one. My father had it—there is another of whom I am almost sure—but almost no man of my acquaintance possesses it with the clarity, the purity, the simplicity of a mountain stream. But the boy Jerry had it. It is bedded on courage, but it is more than brave. It is honest, but it is more than honesty. The ax handle broke one day. Jerry said the woodshop at the orphanage would repair it. I brought money to pay for the job and he refused it.

"I'll pay for it," he said. "I broke it. I brought the ax down careless."

"But no one hits accurately every time," I told him. "The fault was in the wood of the handle. I'll see the man from whom I bought it."

It was only then that he would take the money. He was standing back of his own carelessness. He was a free-will agent and he chose to do careful work, and if he failed, he took the responsibility without subterfuge.

And he did for me the unnecessary thing, the gracious thing, that we find done only by the great of heart. Things no training can

289

teach, for they are done on the instant, with no predicated experience. He found a cubbyhole beside the fireplace that I had not noticed. There, of his own accord, he put kindling and "medium" wood, so that I might always have dry fire material ready in case of sudden wet weather. A stone was loose in the rough walk to the cabin. He dug a deeper hole and steadied it, although he came, himself, by a short cut over the bank. I found that when I tried to return his thoughtfulness with such things as candy and apples, he was wordless. "Thank you" was, perhaps, an expression for which he had had no use, for his courtesy was instinctive. He only looked at the gift and at me, and a curtain lifted, so that I saw deep into the clear well of his eyes, and gratitude was there, and affection, soft over the firm granite of his character.

He made simple excuses to come and sit with me. I could no more have turned him away than if he had been physically hungry. I suggested once that the best time for us to visit was just before supper, when I left off my writing. After that, he waited always until my typewriter had been some time quiet. One day I worked until nearly dark. I went outside the cabin, having forgotten him. I saw him going up over the hill in the twilight toward the orphanage. When I sat down on my stoop, a place was warm from his body where he had been sitting.

He became intimate, of course, with my pointer, Pat. There is a strange communion between a boy and a dog. Perhaps they possess the same singleness of spirit, the same kind of wisdom. It is difficult to explain, but it exists. When I went across the state for a week end, I left the dog in Jerry's charge. I gave him the dog whistle and the key to the cabin, and left sufficient food. He was to come two or three times a day and let out the dog, and feed and exercise him. I should return Sunday night, and Jerry would take out the dog for the last time Sunday afternoon and then leave the key under an agreed hiding place.

My return was belated and fog filled the mountain passes so treacherously that I dared not drive at night. The fog held the next morning, and it was Monday noon before I reached the cabin. The dog had been fed and cared for that morning. Jerry came early in the afternoon, anxious.

"The superintendent said nobody would drive in the fog," he said. "I came just before bedtime last night and you hadn't come. So I brought Pat some of my breakfast this morning. I wouldn't have let anything happen to him."

"I was sure of that. I didn't worry."

"When I heard about the fog, I thought you'd know."

He was needed for work at the orphanage and he had to return at once. I gave him a dollar in payment, and he looked at it and went away. But that night he came in the darkness and knocked at the door.

"Come in, Jerry," I said, "if you're allowed to be away this late."

"I told maybe a story," he said. "I told them I thought you would want to see me."

"That's true," I assured him, and I saw his relief. "I want to hear

290

about how you managed with the dog."

He sat by the fire with me, with no other light, and told me of their two days together. The dog lay close to him, and found a comfort there that I did not have for him. And it seemed to me that being with my dog, and caring for him, had brought the boy and me, too, together, so that he felt that he belonged to me as well as to the animal.

"He stayed right with me," he told me, "except when he ran in the laurel. He likes the laurel. I took him up over the hill and we both ran fast. There was a place where the grass was high and I lay down in it and hid. I could hear Pat hunting for me. He found my trail and he barked. When he found me, he acted crazy, and he ran around and around me, in circles."

We watched the flames.

"That's an apple log," he said. "It burns the prettiest of any wood."

We were very close.

He was suddenly impelled to speak of things he had not spoken of before, nor had I cared to ask him.

"You look a little bit like my mother," he said. "Especially in the dark, by the fire."

"But you were only four, Jerry, when you came here. You have remembered how she looked, all these years?"

"My mother lives in Mannville," he said.

For a moment, finding that he had a mother shocked me as greatly as anything in my life has ever done, and I did not know why it disturbed me. Then I understood my distress. I was filled with a passionate resentment that any woman should go away and leave her son. A fresh anger added itself. A son like this one— The orphanage was a wholesome place, the executives were kind, good people, the food was more than adequate, the boys were healthy, a ragged shirt was no hardship, nor the doing of clean labor. Granted, perhaps, that the boy felt no lack, what blood fed the bowels of a woman who did not yearn over this child's lean body that had come in parturition out of her own? At four he would have looked the same as now. Nothing, I thought, nothing in life could change those eyes. His quality must be apparent to an idiot, a fool. I burned with questions I could not ask. In any, I was afraid, there would be pain.

"Have you seen her, Jerry—lately?"

"I see her every summer. She sends for me."

I wanted to cry out, "Why are you not with her? How can she let you go away again?"

He said, "She comes up here from Mannville whenever she can. She doesn't have a job now."

His face shone in the firelight.

"She wanted to give me a puppy, but they can't let any one boy keep a puppy. You remember the suit I had on last Sunday?" He was plainly proud. "She sent me that for Christmas. The Christmas before that"—he drew a long breath, savoring the memory—"she sent me a pair of skates."

"Roller skates?"

My mind was busy, making pictures of her, trying to understand her. She had not, then, entirely deserted or forgotten him. But

291

why, then—— I thought, "I must not condemn her without knowing."

"Roller skates. I let the other boys use them. They're always borrowing them. But they're careful of them."

What circumstance other than poverty——

"I'm going to take the dollar you gave me for taking care of Pat," he said, "and buy her a pair of gloves."

I could only say, "That will be nice. Do you know her size?"

"I think it's 8½," he said.

He looked at my hands.

"Do you wear 8½?" he asked.

"No. I wear a smaller size, a 6."

"Oh! Then I guess her hands are bigger than yours."

I hated her. Poverty or no, there was other food than bread, and the soul could starve as quickly as the body. He was taking his dollar to buy gloves for her big stupid hands, and she lived away from him, in Mannville, and contented herself with sending him skates.

"She likes white gloves," he said. "Do you think I can get them for a dollar?"

"I think so," I said.

I decided that I should not leave the mountains without seeing her and knowing for myself why she had done this thing.

The human mind scatters its interests as though made of thistledown, and every wind stirs and moves it. I finished my work. It did not please me, and I gave my thoughts to another field. I should need some Mexican material. I made arrangements to close my Florida place. Mexico immediately, and doing the writing there, if conditions were favorable. Then, Alaska with my brother. After that, heaven knew what or where.

I did not take time to go to Mannville to see Jerry's mother, nor even to talk with the orphanage officials about her. I was a trifle abstracted about the boy, because of my work and plans. And after my first fury at her—we did not speak of her again—his having a mother, any sort at all, not far away, in Mannville, relieved me of the ache I had had about him. He did not question the anomalous relation. He was not lonely. It was none of my concern.

He came every day and cut my wood and did small helpful favors and stayed to talk. The days had become cold, and often I let him come inside the cabin. He would lie on the floor in front of the fire, with one arm across the pointer, and they would both doze and wait quietly for me. Other days they ran with a common ecstasy through the laurel, and since the asters were now gone, he brought me back vermilion maple leaves, and chestnut boughs dripping with imperial yellow. I was ready to go.

I said to him, "You have been my good friend, Jerry. I shall often think of you and miss you. Pat will miss you too. I am leaving tomorrow."

He did not answer. When he went away, I remember that a new moon hung over the mountains, and I watched him go in silence up the hill. I expected him the next day, but he did not come. The details of packing my personal belongings, loading my car, arranging the bed over the seat, where the dog would ride, occupied me until late in the day. I closed the cabin and started the car, noticing that the

292

sun was in the west and I should do well to be out of the mountains by nightfall. I stopped by the orphanage and left the cabin key and money for my light bill with Miss Clark.

"And will you call Jerry for me to say good-bye to him?"

"I don't know where he is," she said. "I'm afraid he's not well. He didn't eaʳ his dinner this noon. One of the other boys saw him going over the hill into the laurel. He was supposed to fire the boiler this afternoon. It's not like him; he's unusually reliable."

I was almost relieved, for I knew I should never see him again, and it would be easier not to say good-bye to him.

I said, "I wanted to talk with you about his mother—why he's here—but I'm in more of a hurry than I expected to be. It's out of the question for me to see her now too. But here's some money I'd like to leave with you to buy things for him at Christmas and on his birthday. It will be better than for me to try to send him things. I could so easily duplicate—skates, for instance."

She blinked her honest spinster's eyes.

"There's not much use for skates here," she said.

Her stupidity annoyed me.

"What I mean," I said, "is that I don't want to duplicate things his mother sends him. I might have chosen skates if I didn't know she had already given them to him."

She stared at me.

"I don't understand," she said. "He has no mother. He has no skates."

SKY-BORN MUSIC

RALPH WALDO EMERSON

Let me go where'er I will
I hear a sky-born music still:
It sounds from all things old,
It sounds from all things young,
From all that's fair. . . .
Peals out a cheerful song.
It is not only in the rose,
It is not only in the bird,
Not only where the rainbow glows,
Nor in the song of woman heard,
But in the darkest, meanest things
There always, always something sings.
'Tis not in the high stars alone,
Nor in the cups of budding flowers,
Nor in the redbreast's mellow tone,
Nor in the bow that smiles in showers,
But in the mud and scum of things
There always, always something sings.

THE REFLECTIONS

WHATEVER YOU cannot understand,
you cannot possess.

FAITH is private capital, kept in one's own house.

THERE ARE PEOPLE who make no mistakes because they never try
to do anything worth doing.

WHICH IS the best government? That which teaches us to govern ourselves.

THOSE FROM WHOM we are always learning are rightly called our masters;
but not every one who teaches us deserves this title.

IT IS much easier to recognise error than to find truth; for error lies on the
surface and may be overcome; but truth lies in the depths, and to search for it
is not given to every one.

IF A MAN knows where to get good advice, it is as though he could supply
it himself.

THERE IS no outward sign of courtesy that does not rest on a
deep moral foundation.

To LIVE in a great idea means to treat the impossible
as though it were possible. It is just the same with a
strong character; and when an idea and a character meet,
things arise which fill the world with wonder for
thousands of years.

THE DEED is everything: the fame is nothing.

No ONE who cannot master himself is worthy to rule.
and only he can rule.

To APPRECIATE what is noble is a gain
that can never be taken from us.

294

ART LITTLE? Do thy little well,
  And for thy comfort know
Great men can do their greatest work
  No better than just so.

LOVE AND DESIRE are the spirit's wings to great deeds.

EVERY MAN has enough power left to carry out that of which
he is convinced.

THE FIRST AND LAST THING that is required of genius is love of truth.

IN CONTEMPLATION as in action, we must distinguish between what may be
attained and what is unattainable. Without this, little can be achieved,
either in life or in knowledge.

THE USEFUL may be trusted to further itself, for many produce it and no
one can do without it; but the beautiful must be specially encouraged, for
few can present it, while yet all have need of it.

To BE and remain true to oneself and others is to possess the noblest
attribute of the greatest talents.

HE IS happiest, be he king or peasant, who finds peace in his home,

LOVE of truth shows itself in this, that a man knows how to
find and value the good in everything.

MAKE THE MOST of time, it flies away so fast; yet method
will teach you to win time.

WOULD'ST SHAPE a noble life? Then cast
No backward glances toward the past,
  And though somewhat be lost and gone,
  Yet do thou act as one new-born;
What each day needs, that shalt thou ask,
Each day will set its proper task.

CHARACTER calls forth character.

ENTHUSIASM is of the greatest value, so long as we are not carried away by it.

THE WORK of life alone teaches us to value the good of life.

IT IS only men of practical ability, knowing their powers and using them with moderation and prudence, who will be successful in worldly affairs.

THAT THERE ARE so many spiritual capacities in man which he cannot develop in this life, points to a better and more harmonious future.

BE GENUINE AND STRENUOUS; earn for yourself, and look for grace from those in high places; from the powerful, favour; from the active and the good, advancement; from the many, affection; from the individual, love.

GENEROSITY wins favour for every one, especially when it is accompanied by modesty.

How CAN A MAN come to know himself? Never by thinking, but by doing. Try to do your duty, and you will know at once what you are worth.

I AM NOT DREAMING. I am not deluded. Nearer to the grave new light streams for me. We shall continue to exist. We shall see each other again.

INGRATITUDE is always a kind of weakness. I have never known men of ability to be ungrateful.

WE ARE shaped and fashioned by what we love.

NOTHING is more highly to be prized than the value of each day.

GERMAN PHILOSOPHERS

LOVE is the reward of Love.—*Schiller*

A MAN must seek his happiness and inward peace from objects which cannot be taken away from him.—*Humboldt*

COURAGE consists not in blindly overlooking danger, but in seeing it and conquering it.—*Richter*

IS THY FRIEND angry with thee? Then provide him an opportunity of showing thee a great favor. Over that his heart must needs melt, and he will love thee again.—*Richter*

HUMANITY is never so beautiful as when praying for forgiveness, or else forgiving another.—*Richter*

OUR PLANS AND DESIGNS should be so perfect in truth and beauty, that in touching them the world could only mar. We should thus have the advantage of setting right what is wrong, and restoring what is destroyed.—*Goethe*

IT IS a great error to take oneself for more than one is, or for less than one is worth.—*Goethe*

To LOVE is to find pleasure in the happiness of the person loved.—*Leibnitz*

ORDINARY PEOPLE think merely how they shall *spend* their time; a man of intellect tries to *use* it.—*Schopenhauer*

I CAN PROMISE to be sincere, but not to be impartial.—*Goethe*

IT IS a gain to find a beautiful human soul.—*Herder*

THERE IS only one true Religion, but there may be many forms of belief.—*Kant*

GREAT SOULS suffer in silence.—*Schiller*

TO MAKE THIS LIFE WORTH WHILE
GEORGE ELIOT

May every soul that touches mine—
Be it the slightest contact—
Get therefrom some good;
Some little grace; one kindly thought;
One aspiration yet unfelt;
One bit of courage
For the darkening sky;
One gleam of faith
To brave the thickening ills of life;
One glimpse of brighter skies
Beyond the gathering mists—
To make this life worth while . . .

THE BUILDERS
HENRY WADSWORTH LONGFELLOW

All are architects of Fate,
    Working in these walls of Time;
Some with massive deeds and great,
    Some with ornaments of rhyme.

Nothing useless is, or low;
    Each thing in its place is best;
And what seems but idle show
    Strengthens and supports the rest.

For the structure that we raise,
    Time is with materials filled;
Our todays and yesterdays
    Are the blocks with which we build.

Truly shape and fashion these;
    Leave no yawning gaps between;
Think not, because no man sees,
    Such things will remain unseen.

In the elder days of Art,
    Builders wrought with greatest care
Each minute and unseen part;
    For the gods see everywhere.

Let us do our work as well,
  Both the unseen and the seen;
Make the house where gods may dwell
  Beautiful, entire, and clean,

Else our lives are incomplete,
  Standing in these walls of Time,
Broken stairways, where the feet
  Stumble, as they seek to climb.

Build today, then, strong and sure,
  With a firm and ample base;
And ascending and secure
  Shall tomorrow find its place.

Thus alone can we attain
  To those turrets, where the eye
Sees the world as one vast plain,
  And one boundless reach of sky.

FORGIVE

John Greenleaf Whittier

Forgive, O Lord, our severing ways,
The rival altars that we raise,
The wrangling tongues that mar thy praise!

Thy grace impart! In time to be
Shall one great temple rise to Thee—
Thy Church our broad humanity.

White flowers of love its wall shall climb,
Soft bells of peace shall ring its chime,
Its days shall all be holy time.

A sweeter song shall then be heard,
Confessing, in a world's accord,
The inward Christ, the living Word.

That song shall swell from shore to shore.
One hope, one faith, one love restore
The seamless robe that Jesus wore.

GOD GIVE ME JOY

Thomas Curtis Clark

God give me joy in the common things:
In the dawn that lures, the eve that sings.

In the new grass sparkling after rain,
In the late wind's wild and weird refrain;

In the springtime's spacious field of gold,
In the precious light by winter doled.

God give me joy in the love of friends,
In their dear home talk as summer ends;

In the songs of children, unrestrained;
In the sober wisdom age has gained.

God give me joy in the tasks that press,
In the memories that burn and bless;

In the thought that life has love to spend,
In the faith that God's at journey's end.

God give me hope for each day that springs,
God give me joy in the common things!

SO FAITH IS STRONG

George Eliot

So faith is strong
Only when we are strong, shrinks when we shrink.
It comes when music stirs us, and the chords,
Moving on some grand climax, shake our souls
With influx new that makes new energies.
It comes in swellings of the heart and tears
That rise at noble and at gentle deeds.
It comes in moments of heroic love,
Unjealous joy in joy not made for us;
In conscious triumph of the good within,
Making us worship goodness that rebukes.
Even our failures are a prophecy,
Even our yearnings and our bitter tears

After that fair and true we cannot grasp.
Presentiment of better things on earth
Sweeps in with every force that stirs our souls
To admiration, self-renouncing love.

USE WELL THE MOMENT
Johann Wolfgang von Goethe

Use well the moment; what the hour
Brings for thy use is in thy power;
And what thou best canst understand
Is just the thing lies nearest to thy hand.

EASTER
Thomas Curtis Clark

Say not that death is king, that night is lord,
That loveliness is passing, beauty dies;
Nor tell me hope's a vain, deceptive dream
Fate lends to life, a pleasing, luring gleam
To light awhile the earth's despondent skies,
Till death brings swift and sure its dread reward.
Say not that youth deceives, but age is true,
That roses quickly pass, while cypress bides,
That happiness is foolish, grief is wise,
That stubborn dust shall choke our human cries.
Death tells new worlds, and life immortal hides
Beyond the veil, which shall all wrongs undo.
This was the tale God breathed to me at dawn
When flooding sunrise told the night was gone.

LIFE
John Greenleaf Whittier

Alas for him who never sees
The stars shine through his cypress-trees!
Who, hopeless, lays his dead away,
Nor looks to see the breaking day
Across the mournful marbles play!
Who hath not learned, in hours of faith,
The truth to flesh and sense unknown,
That Life is ever Lord of Death,
And Love can never lose its own!

301

THE PRICE of wisdom is above rubies.

DAYS SHOULD SPEAK and multitude of years should
teach wisdom.

BE YE DOERS of the word and not hearers only.

TRAIN UP a child in the way he should go; and when he is
old he will not depart from it.

REMEMBER NOW thy Creator in the days of thy youth.

THEREFORE all things whatsoever ye would that men should do to you,
do ye even so to them.

INASMUCH AS ye did it unto one of these my brethren, even these least,
ye did it unto me.

BUT THERE IS a spirit in man: and the inspiration of the Almighty giveth
them understanding.

Now THE GOD of hope fill you with all joy and peace in believing, that
ye may abound in hope, in the power of the Holy Spirit.

WE KNOW in part, and we prophesy in part; but when that which
is perfect is come, that which is in part shall be done away.

WHEN THOU doest alms, let not thy left hand know
what thy right hand doeth.

BELOVED, let us love one another:
for love is of God.

PROVE all things; hold fast that
which is good.

I DON'T THINK MUCH of a man who is not wiser today than he was yesterday.—*Abraham Lincoln*

ALL THAT I AM my mother made me.—*John Quincy Adams*

THE WILL of the people is the best law.—*Ulysses S. Grant*

I HAVE SWORN upon the altar of God hostility against every form of tyranny over the mind of man.—*Thomas Jefferson*

PUBLIC OFFICERS are the servants and agents of the people, to execute the laws which the people have made.—*Grover Cleveland*

LABOUR to keep alive in your breast that little spark of celestial fire,—conscience.—*George Washington*

IT IS of more importance to the community that innocence should be protected than it is that guilt should be punished.—*John Adams*

I CONCEIVE that a knowledge of books is the basis on which all other knowledge rests.—*George Washington*

HE serves his party best who serves his country best.
—*Rutherford B. Hayes*

NEXT IN IMPORTANCE to freedom and justice is popular education, without which neither freedom nor justice can be permanently maintained.—*James Abram Garfield*

THE SECOND, sober thought of the people is seldom wrong, and always efficient.—*Martin Van Buren*

No MAN is poor who has had a godly mother.—*Abraham Lincoln*

LET the people rule.—*Andrew Jackson*

The Wind Fighters

By KEENE ABBOTT

𝒥N ANXIOUS HASTE the settler had begun chopping down the two bone-dry, scraggy trees in front of the sod house. And his wife, hearing the stroke of the ax, came promptly to see what he was about.

"It's a heartless thing," she protested—"a heartless thing you're doing, Jim Dara!"

In quality and accent and deep modulation her voice was unmistakably Irish, as was also the voice of the man. But he did not reply at once. It was not until the first of the trees, the maple, had crashed upon the ground that he answered quietly:

"It's no heartless thing I'm doing. It would be morbidness only to keep them standing."

The woman said, looking at a white chip she had picked up:

"There would be sap enough, maybe, for new leaves this year."

"I know, dear, what you want of the trees. If they would live and come green again! The one of them, the maple, we planted when the little girl was born, and the elm was for the boy. But they couldn't grow, dear." His toilworn hand gently patted her shoulder. "Last year I knew they couldn't, only I hadn't the heart to be cutting them down."

That evening, with the chores all done and the sun gone down, Dara sat with his wife on the doorstep and would have played a while on his flute, for the tunes of their sweetheart time had come singing back to him as they were wont to do in the spring of the year. But the three parts of the instrument,

once they had been taken out of the grooves of purple velvet in the leather case, were too shrunken at the joints for them to fit together.

"Never mind," he said. "I'll have to soak them up before they're any good." As he closed the leather case, he added, "We'll just listen to the flute notes of the meadowlarks calling. They know how so much better, anyhow, than I do."

As they hearkened a while, the woman gazed afar at some upfloating wraiths—thin plumes, gray and violet, that lifted themselves above the horizon, a vast bluish line, sharp-cut as if done by the colossal sweep of a scythe. It was smoke she was looking at, the burning of cornstalks cleared away from fields where the soil was being prepared for yet another seed planting. For, though a great number of people had moved back East, deserting their homesteads, many settlers still remained; and now Dara's wife could see that this spring, as in other springs, they were courageously doing their work.

"Do you think, Jim boy," she musefully asked, "it will be a good year, this one?"

He said decisively:

"There were snows aplenty; the rains have come; the soil is black and rich. It will be a good year for crops, this one."

He looked across a field at the

plow standing at the end of a furrow. The shovel, scoured bright, was like a mirror stuck in the ground—was like a clear looking glass reflecting the red of the west. "A good year," Dara repeated. "A fine year for crops."

His wife, reflecting upon winds and drought and hard times, presently observed:

"We've done real well, considering. We're not like them that had to take aid."

"No, and what's owing Martin Byrne"—he was referring to his good friend the storekeeper in the prairie town—"what's owing him," Dara repeated, "we'll wipe it all out, every cent, in one year or two."

"Charity," his wife proudly asserted, "we have not had to take."

Dara sighed a little as he said:

"You never got the lace, dear, to put on the dress of the little girl."

"They were sweet dresses the baby had," she replied. "You said so yourself. You said there was nobody could tell they were made of flour sacks."

"Fine dresses, Nora; they were that—they were, for a fact."

The twilight faded out, and now that the bluish, lukewarm night was come, pale stars began to quiver in the tender sky as if they were fire drops trembling. The woman, as she sat looking at them, heard her name spoken.

"Nora?"

"What is it, Jim boy?"

"I didn't like to cut down the trees."

"They couldn't grow," she told him.

"No, dear, they couldn't."

Before long he was saying with mild self-contempt:

"It was a senseless thing not to plant cottonwoods; for such trees, Nora, do be easy growers."

"Yes, they do be easy growers, the cottonwoods."

"It would be a grand thing to have them, the green trees!"

And his wife said courageously:

"I do have my house plants. There be the two geraniums, dear—both growing fine in tin cans, and the one of them coming into bloom."

By and by she was whispering, as she rested her head against his shoulder:

"We have had two little babies."

Her husband boastfully replied:

"There is Martin Byrne—he never had any babies at all."

"Poor Martin Byrne!" sighed the woman, and her husband went on:

"It's the like of us, Nora, can pity him. He's the same, almost, as a widower; his woman leaving him, and all, and going back to her folks. Fond of him, too, I'm thinking. Only she couldn't stand it out here. She was that lonesome and sorry on account of the winds blowing always."

"He did what he could to make her easy and contented," said the woman. "He even got her the fine piano I told him to get."

"Yes, Nora; and now—he would be selling the piano, to get rid of it, and not have it standing like a tombstone in the house."

"Think of that!" said Nora, as if she did not know what Jim was coming to. In the fear of what he was about to propose she clasped her hands, and the dry palms of them made a raspy sound before they stiffly slunk away into hiding in the sag of her skirt between her knees.

"If we were to take the thing off

his hands, as a kindness. . . . What do you say, Nora?"

"A fine thing to have, Jim boy. Would look too grand in the room."

"We could practice up some of the old tunes," he went on.

"The old tunes," she repeated, and he did not know she was wringing her knuckly hands in the sag of her skirt.

"Sometimes," her husband added, "we could have the neighbors for a bit of music, to cheer them up."

Neighbors! And the nearest of them living five miles away!

"It's a cheerful thing, is music," said Nora.

"A grand thing," Dara called out.

"A grand thing," said Nora, his wife.

Only there was no time, neither this week nor the next, for bringing the piano to the farm. It must wait. There was the spring work to be done: the plowing, the harrowing, the planting. He was in the field when the sun rose; in the evening also, after the sun went down, until darkness came, he held to his labor in the field.

All was going well. On the doorstep, beside his wife, before they went to bed, he played his flute in the starshine, while slumbrous odors out of the darkness, good, grassy odors—"the smell of bigness," Nora called it—came breathing in upon them. Sometimes, in a hushed voice, the woman sang to the playing of the flute, sang those pensive little ballads of Ireland that are not mournful and yet have tears in them.

"It's going to be a fine year, this one," said Dara. And the barking of the little prairie wolves, coming from afar, was like friendly voices

out yonder in the night. "We'll pay off everything, the piano included!"

"Yes," said Nora. But by and by she was humbly adding, "Say, Jim boy . . ."

"Well?"

"Don't get it, that piano."

"Don't get! What's that you're saying?"

"I want no piano."

"You want—Look here, Nora, is it plum daft you are?"

"I am not, and won't be, God help us; for I work outdoors, doing a man's work when I'm able. You've been all for shutting me up in the house and protecting me from hard labor. But if them that have gone queer in their heads had done the same as me—had worked in the fields the way they wouldn't hear the winds whining—"

Abruptly she held out to him her stiffened hands, and she said, not bitterly, but with kindness, "Understand, James Dara, you will be getting me no piano."

The husband clasped one of those hands in his. He felt of it wonderingly. How very curious it could have come to this, and he never have noticed!

Now he clung to that hand. He began rocking back and forth; he fondled the knuckly thing against his cheek, against his lips, but there came out of him neither groan nor cry. Quiet words only he spoke.

"It was soft once," he was saying. "It was limber and white. The fingers could touch the notes that lightly I couldn't mind my flute playing for watching them, the curve of them, and they touching the keys that gently."

"Get the piano!" his wife said.

"You couldn't play it, dear."

306

"I could play it."

"We will not hear the old tunes again," he went on, "never any more, never, never!"

"We *will* play them, Jim boy. I'll learn them again, all of them. Get the piano. The stiffness will come out of my hands. Lard will soften them. We will have the neighbors in for a bit of music to cheer them up. Will you get me the piano, Jim?"

"No," he said.

But in May he brought it home; and, a neighbor helping him, the instrument was set in place, against the wall of the front room, beneath the crayon portraits of two children. Then, as soon as he was in the field, distantly guiding the cultivator up and down the golden green of the corn rows, she began her practicing. And she tried to play softly, that he might not hear how clumsily her fingers stumbled over the keys.

Each day, indefatigably, she toiled at her exercises, the simple ones, the rudimentary and tiresome scales. Then, at the end of a week, he said to her at suppertime:

"We'll have a try at it tonight, Nora—flute and piano together."

"Not tonight, Jim," she replied.

On the doorstep, in the dusk of a June evening, they sat listening to the quiet wash and soothing sibilance of the pale-green lake aripple under the stars.

"It's a fine stand of corn, that one," said Dara.

"Yes," Nora replied.

"Will go sixty bushels to the acre."

"Will it, Jim?"

"Or maybe seventy. Shouldn't wonder a bit if she would come seventy bushels to the acre."

"It's fine growing weather," Nora declared.

"It is, by the grace of God; it is that—fine growing weather."

So June passed, and now July was passing. By day, all day long, there was the amazing sun fire, an enormous white light, quivering. By night no cooling of the earth. Heat rising continuously from the soil—black heat, moist and powerful.

"Good corn weather," people say, and sometimes they say it with the hush of fear in their voices. For there are winds that blow. Winds come up out of the south—dry winds, dust-choked and terrifying. They are a flameless burning of the air. In a day, a half day, an hour's time, they shrivel green fields and meadow grass to parched and brittle mockeries.

In the afternoon, on the fourteenth day of August, something ominous appeared. Now and again, in a swooning cornfield, a gray and vaporous streak lifted itself. It rose like a spinning plume of smoke, and, having trailed skyward, it whirled away and vanished—a scarf of dust abruptly sucked up by a mysterious air current, and as suddenly dissolved. Corn leaves, violently agitated, stirred with a papery rustle for a time, then hung stiffly motionless, weighed down once more by the overpressure of heat.

Throughout the afternoon, intermittently, the phenomenon continued; and again, the following day, the dust whirls were seen. Then, by noon, when the earth was stripped of its purplish shadows, there came something even more sinister.

Dara's wife, standing in the doorway of the sod house, felt an acrid sultriness—felt it as if she were testing the heat of a flatiron by raising it near her cheek. She looked out upon the tasseled cornfield, immense, blue-green, opulent—a field of vast acreage, representing so much toil, so many hopes, so brave a fight!

But what cares nature for courage, or for hopes, or for human aspiration? Wind had begun to blow. Viewless fire, enormously puffing, ran in repeated whiffs across the prairie.

"It's blowing up a rain," said Dara. He spoke cheerfully as he came clumping into the house for his dinner.

A shudder passed through the great field. The woman, still gazing out yonder at the billowing of the glossy leaves, whispered with husky dryness in her voice:

"The corn is firing."

It was true. Unfailingly, each year, ever since this homestead was new to the plow, the same sinister forecast of drought had appeared—the yellow crispening of short leaves, close to the earth, at the base of the cornstalks.

But Dara said to his wife:

"We're going to have rain."

To humor him, she anxiously agreed:

"Yes, Jim, the rain's coming."

"The range cattle sense it," he added. "They sense it. They're restless; they're on the move. A sure sign!"

"A sure sign," said Nora, his wife.

Then she shut the door, shut the windows, sealed up her house against the whining of the wind.

Heat, dry heat, thinned the air with a burning acridity. A smell of dust became more penetrating.

"Look here, Nora! Look!" Dara excitedly called out, peering through the window. "There's a rain cloud bulging up."

"Dust!" said Nora.

Both were wrong. It was the gray swell of a wagon sheet showing above a ridge, beyond the twin cottonwoods. After the first there came a second prairie van, then a third.

"Only look at that, now!" Dara said contemptuously. "Deserting their homesteads!"

"Don't be scornful, Jim boy. Maybe it's the winds they're going from. Maybe they can't get used to the winds grieving always, come summer, come winter, snow winds and dust winds, ice and fire forever!"

"Yes, dear; the winds do be grieving in lean times. But come fat times, and our corn all cribbed, and the gold of it looking through the cracks, then will the winds be changing their tune. They will sing *then*, I'm telling you. They will, so they will!"

Mad rejoicing was in Dara's face. He took down his flute; he fitted its parts together. Nothing could be stranger than his boyish exultation as he hurriedly added:

"We'll hold those people, Nora. We'll stop them; we'll play for them. If they've lost their nerve, it's music will be giving it back to them."

Dumbly hearkening for a time to the slow clack and creak of the three wagons drawing nearer and nearer, the woman huskily whispered:

"Let them not be stopping here, James Dara. If green trees do be calling them, and the gurgle of clear water over mossy stones, and

308

bees humming in the pink clover, let those people not be stopping here."

But stop them he did. Bareheaded, the jointed flute in his hand, he ran out to the barbed-wire fence and hailed the emigrants.

"Better take a nooning," he insisted. "You'll be wanting to feed your teams and rest them a spell, and they dripping sweat from their fetlocks in the hot sun. Come in, neighbors; come right in!"

A bristle-faced man, driver of the first wagon, leaned forward, a wisp of hay caught in his shaggy beard.

Dara added earnestly:

"There's a piano in the house. Nora will play for you, and me with my flute knocking out tunes beside it if you would care for a bit of music."

Con Lewis, the bearded man, laughed raucously.

"Music! There's the hot wind will make music for us!"

But the frail woman on the seat with him, a baby in her arms, nudged him in the side with her elbow.

"It's the piano you got off Martin Byrne," said she to Dara. "We've heard tell your woman can finger it just grand."

From the second wagon, with the curve of the bows showing through the gray canvas like the ribs of a starved elephant, a man's voice called out:

"Better load up your stuff, Jimmy, and throw in with us."

The woman with the baby added:

"We could easy get overhet if we was to dance on a day like this; but it would be nice, all the same, to hear some tunes played on the piano and the flute."

Almost jovially the man in the second wagon called out:

"In three weeks or four we'll land you all hunky-dory in God's country if you throw in with us. Then you won't have to see your corn burning up the same as last year and every year."

Dara said impatiently:

"Fetch in some of the chairs you have roped to the tail of your wagon when you get your horses watered and fed."

The flute player had his way with these people from homesteads newly abandoned. The company assembled in the house for the concert; three men, four women, eight children, including the baby.

When the music began, the little folks grew quiet, the baby stopped fretting, and, mildly interested, the men condescended to listen.

As for the women, they leaned forward, forgetting the suffocation of the heat. They drank in the simple melodies—drank of that music as if they were thirst-famished things come upon a rill of clear water.

Flute and piano may have sung together in a poor performance. No matter! Familiar tunes pulsed graciously through the house: first "The Wearing of the Green," next "Swanee River," then "The Minstrel Boy," then "The Harp That Once through Tara's Halls."

In the pauses after each duet a silence of growing sultriness made itself felt in the two crowded rooms. In the garden plot, seen from the window, yellow sunflowers stared into the ominous hush, each bloom and leaf listlessly hanging.

Long the heat torpor held. The flat, sick land lay in a stupefaction, stunned, naked to the enormous glare. Once the whir of a harvest fly half a mile away in the twin cottonwoods wearily rasped the silence, and stopped, and began again. The two ragged tree shapes, far off, crouched together, sulkily waiting for something. For what?

"Rain is coming," said Dara.

Nobody believed him.

"Play something else, please," a frail-voiced woman requested.

He would have called attention to dark blotches flitting along the ground, light, transparent shadows rapidly herding together across the prairie; but the Confederate veteran Con Lewis, the bearded man, said peremptorily:

"Yes, tear loose again. Something lively!"

He frowned. He did not like waiting here so long.

But Dara did not begin at once. He shut his eyes, wiped the mouthpiece of his flute upon his sleeve; then, getting to his feet, he reached across his wife's shoulder and struck a sounding chord upon the piano. She understood. Looking up at her husband, as he took a deep breath with the flute to his mouth, her hands suddenly leaped upon the keys.

Carefree and swift, a rousing melody was evoked. The wind instrument lost its crooning mellowness. Now it was like a fire. Its breath was martial, gay, exultant. It shrilled with a mad, frolicking, rollicking triumph.

"Dixie" was the tune. The shaggy head of Lewis swayed in time to the music. His feet began shuffling. He hummed in an undertone. His fists were beating upon the wooden arms of his chair. And he could not remain seated. Abruptly he stood up; he waved his hat; he stamped and shouted.

"That's it!" Dara called out. "There's a charge and a yell and a big fight in that tune. *Well* you know that, Con Lewis. You were a soldier once for your Dixie Land. You didn't run from bullets, I'm thinking. But will you now be running from the land?"

The enthusiasm of the bearded man was quenched at once.

"Why *not* pull out?" he sullenly questioned. "What's to stay for? Don't you know, you Irish son of a gun, when you're clean licked? You can't fight the winds," he added. "Nobody can."

"They did it in Iowa," said Dara. "They did it in Illinois. They made a corn empire of it, the richest in all the world. Cultivation of the soil brought the rains. Trees grew; climate changed. God's country, you call it."

"Was never the same as this," said Lewis, stubbornly shaking his head. "Could *grow* something, that country could—something besides sage and soapweed and buffalo grass. Me, I won't stay to see my crop burn up."

"There's something grows here better than corn."

"In God's name, what?"

"I'll tell you what!" said Dara. "There's Mrs. Arnold sitting yonder; she who came to us when darkness was in our house and our little children dying. She stayed with us. She gave us comfort. We had no money for her. We had no money for the doctor; but he came, too. He did what he could for us. Coal and groceries and clothes we needed, and there was Martin Byrne, in town, let us have them. And he's done the like of that for the rest of you, I'm thinking. So, will you tell me, Con Lewis, is there any country, anywhere, can produce a bigger crop of kindness?"

Dumbly unwilling to reply, Lewis sat down and looked at the floor between his two dusty boots. And Dara suddenly called out:

"There, see that?"

A bluish light, abrupt and livid, had twitched in the room. It was followed by a low grumble, as if an empty wagon might be rumbling far off. Distantly, against the blue-black storm gloom of the sky, the two cottonwoods, cowering above the horizon, had begun to shudder. Their glossy leaves were all aripple as if a shiver of cool wind had passed through them. And suddenly the cornfield broke into billows, as of green flames dancing.

As swiftly their whispering was hushed. Silence once again, expectancy! Something clicked on the window glass. With a sounding spat a silver needle, a big water blob, had flattened itself against the pane. Then, as scraggy fire slit the sky with a branching quiver, a winking brightness jiggled in, bluishly flaring upon tense faces.

A horse neighed; thunder broke. Prodigiously it exploded, and the quake of it jarred the house, shook the windows, cavernously rumbled and tumbled down the sky, in prolonged reverberations.

Rain began to fall. On came the rush of it—tumultuous rain; panic-whirling films of the silvery, racing rain; the green ocean of corn heaved and streamed. Down plumped the water. It roared on the roof, spouted from the eaves, slapped in great splashes against the window.

A damp, dusty odor penetrated the house, and people drank of it—that wet, good smell! They watched the storm, enormously swishing. Sunflowers bobbed and throbbed. The drenching waste blurred the twin cottonwoods into gray phantoms that seemed trying to skip and leap and dance.

Men whacked each other, laughed, hopped about, yelled like prankish boys. Then they flung wide the doors. They plunged out into the downpour, shot off their guns, chased to and fro, shouted themselves hoarse. Children followed, prancing and skipping, adding their cries to the common din.

Women kissed each other, clung to each other. One laughed, one sobbed. And the rain continuously fell.

It was a good year, that one.

THY PRESENCE

SAMUEL LONGFELLOW

Thy calmness bends serene above
My restlessness to still;
Around me flows Thy quickening life,
To nerve my faltering will;
Thy presence fills my solitude;
Thy providence turns all to good.

GENIUS is eternal patience.—*Michaelangelo*

LIFE is beautiful when one sees beyond it.—*Bonnat*

IF PEOPLE knew how hard I have had to work to gain my mastery, it wouldn't seem wonderful at all.—*Michaelangelo*

EVERY DUTY we omit, obscures some truth we should have known.—*Ruskin*

IT IS not written, blessed is he that *feedeth* the poor, but he that *considereth* the poor. A little thought and a little kindness are often worth more than a great deal of money.—*Ruskin*

YOU WILL FIND it less easy to uproot faults than to choke them by gaining virtues. Do not think of your faults; still less of others' faults. In every person who comes near you look for what is good and strong; honor that; rejoice in it; as you can, try to imitate it, and your faults will drop off, like dead leaves, when their time comes.—*Ruskin*

IF YOU have genius, industry will improve it; if you have none, industry will supply its place.—*Sir Joshua Reynolds*

IT IS a good and safe rule to sojourn in every place, as if you meant to spend your life there, never omitting an opportunity of doing a kindness, or speaking a true word, or making a friend.—*Ruskin*

THE WEAKEST AMONG US has a gift, however seemingly trivial, which is peculiar to him, and which worthily used, will be a gift also to his race.—*Ruskin*

YOU WERE MADE for enjoyment, and the world was filled with things which you will enjoy, unless you are too proud to be pleased with them, or too grasping to care for what you can not turn to other account than mere delight.—*Ruskin*

WHEN LOVE AND SKILL work together expect a masterpiece.—*Ruskin*

312

THE ARTISTS

Do NOT THINK it wasted time to submit yourself to any influence which may bring upon you any noble feeling.—*Ruskin*

HE ONLY is advancing in life whose heart is getting softer, whose blood warmer, whose brain quicker, whose spirit is entering into living peace.—*Ruskin*

IN RIVERS the water that you touch is the last of what has passed and the first of that which comes: so with present time.—*Da Vinci*

IF YOU accept art, it must be part of your daily lives, and the daily life of every man. It will be with us wherever we go, in the ancient city full of traditions of past time, in the newly cleared farm in America or the colonies, where no man has dwelt for tradition to gather around him; in the quiet countryside, as in the busy town, no place shall be without it. You will have it with you in your sorrow as in your joy, in your work-a-day as in your leisure. It shall be no respecter of persons, but be shared by gentle and simple, learned and unlearned, and be as a language that all can understand.—*William Morris*

TRY TO PUT well in practice what you already know; in so doing you will, in good time, discover the hidden things which you now inquire about.
—*Rembrandt*

THE TREE which moves some to tears of joy is in the eyes of others only a green thing which stands in the way. Some see Nature all ridicule and deformity, and by these I shall not regulate my proportions; and some scarce see Nature at all. But to the eyes of the man of imagination Nature is Imagination itself. As a man is, so he sees.—*Blake*

WHAT WE *like* determines what we *are*, and is the sign of what we are; and to teach taste is inevitably to form character.—*Ruskin*

IRON RUSTS from disuse, stagnant water loses its purity and in cold weather becomes frozen; even so does inaction sap the vigors of the mind.—*Da Vinci*

A ROOM hung with pictures is a room hung with thoughts.
—*Sir Joshua Reynolds*

313

ON HEARING A SYMPHONY OF BEETHOVEN
Edna St. Vincent Millay

Sweet sounds, oh, beautiful music, do not cease!
Reject me not into the world again.
With you alone is excellence and peace,
Mankind made plausible, his purpose plain.
Enchanted in your air benign and shrewd,
With limbs a-sprawl and empty faces pale,
The spiteful and the stingy and the rude
Sleep like the scullions in the fairy-tale.
This moment is the best the world can give:
The tranquil blossom on the tortured stem.
Reject me not, sweet sounds! oh, let me live,
Till Doom espy my towers and scatter them,
A city spell-bound under the aging sun.
Music my rampart, and my only one.

LOST
Maurice Lesemann

The light was gone, and there wasn't a sound
But the roar of wind through the pines and firs.
I came to a clearing at last and found
That I'd lost my way in the universe.

It wasn't alone that I'd lost my way
In the timber land I was plunging through:
Somehow I'd circled and lost the lay
Of the sky; there wasn't a star I knew.

The wind lashed down at the wintry grass,
And the dark was scattered high and far
With glints of fire and dust of glass.
I stared in panic to find a star

That burned familiar in its place.
It seemed the earth had strayed for once,
And now was running amuck through space
Among a swarm of hostile suns.

Then, like a name thrown suddenly out,
Perseus appeared, and over the trees

314

Lyra, and then as if with a shout
Orion came, and the Pleiades,

And all the others, score on score.
Again the galaxy was right,
The planet in place, and I once more
Was a man on the earth, at home in the night.

THICK IS THE DARKNESS
William Ernest Henley

Thick is the darkness—
  Sunward, O, sunward!
Rough is the highway—
  Onward, still onward!

Dawn harbors surely
  East of the shadows.
Facing us somewhere
  Spread the sweet meadows.

Upward and forward!
  Time will restore us:
Light is above us,
  Rest is before us.

MORNING SONG
Karle Wilson Baker

There's a mellower light just over the hill,
And somewhere a yellower daffodil,
And honey, somewhere, that's sweeter still.

And some were meant to stay like a stone,
Knowing the things they have always known,
Sinking down deeper into their own.

But some must follow the wind and me,
Who like to be starting and like to be free,
Never so glad as we're going to be!

315

A MOTHER'S SONG

HESTER SUTHERS

My little unborn child, I carry you
Without your yes or no to life and light.
Would you consent, I wonder, to be born,
If you could choose and know each grief, each plight
We all endure who walk the mortal road?
Would you consent to share the human load?

I think you would; you are so close, so close
These many months to one rejoicing heart
You cannot help but feel how strong, how sweet
A joy can be, and long to claim your part
In such a heritage which life bestows
To more than compensate for all the woes.

I know you would; for I can promise you
The wonder of the stars, the seas, the hills,
The miracle of love and comradeship,
The breathless sum of loveliness which fills
Our world. O small, new soul that looks toward birth,
I bring you to a good, a glorious earth.

FAITH MUST STAND

CLARA EDMUNDS-HEMINGWAY

I wish that I might tower, like a tree;
    As straight as any pine, with strength to stand
Alive and green in winter, though there be
    Deep blanketings of snow upon the land.
Though all the trees in sight may shed their leaves
    Of faith; and winds among the branches moan;
Though every helpless bush about me grieves,
    My faith in God shall let me stand—alone.

I would not be a clinging, twisted vine,
    To drag my weight upon another's heart;
        But be erect, whenever tempests hurled
Their javelins: when elements combine
    To wrench my clinging roots and earth apart.
        My faith must stand, in our bewildered world.

316

THE JOYS OF THE ROAD
Bliss Carman

Now the joys of the road are chiefly these:
A crimson touch on the hard-wood trees;

A vagrant's morning wide and blue,
In early fall, when the wind walks, too;

A shadowy highway cool and brown,
Alluring up and enticing down

From rippled water to dappled swamp,
From purple glory to scarlet pomp;

The outward eye, the quiet will,
And the striding hart from hill to hill;

The tempter apple over the fence;
The cobweb bloom on the yellow quince;

The palish asters along the wood,
A lyric touch of the solitude;

An open hand, an easy shoe,
And a hope to make the day go through,—

Another to sleep with, and a third
To wake me up at the voice of a bird;

The resonant, far-listening morn,
And the hoarse whisper of the corn;

The crickets mourning their comrades lost,
In the night's retreat from the gathering frost;

(Or is it their slogan, plaintive and shrill,
As they beat on their corselets, valiant still?)

A hunger fit for the kings of the sea,
And a loaf of bread for Dickon and me;

A thirst like that of the Thirsty Sword,
And a jug of cider on the board;

An idle noon, a bubbling spring,
The sea in the pine-tops murmuring;

A scrap of gossip at the ferry;
A comrade neither glum nor merry,

Asking nothing, revealing naught,
But minting his words from a fund of thought,

A keeper of silence eloquent,
Needy, yet royally well content,

Of the mettled breed, yet abhorring strife,
And full of the mellow juice of life,

No fidget and no reformer, just
A calm observer of ought and must,

A lover of books, but a reader of man,
No cynic and no charlatan,

Who never defers and never demands,
But, smiling, takes the world in his hands,—

Seeing it good as when God first saw
And gave it the weight of His will for law.

And O the joy that is never won,
But follows and follows the journeying sun,

By marsh and tide, by meadow and stream,
A will-o'-the-wind, a light-o'-dream,

Delusion afar, delight anear,
From morrow to morrow, from year to year,

A jack-o'-lantern, a fairy fire,
A dare, a bliss, and a desire!

The racy smell of the forest loam,
When the stealthy, sad-heart leaves go home;

(O leaves, O leaves, I am one with you,
Of the mould and the sun and the wind and the dew!)

The broad gold wake of the afternoon;
The silent fleck of the cold new moon;

The sound of the hollow sea's release
From stormy tumult to starry peace;

With only another league to wend;
And two brown arms at the journey's end!

These are the joys of the open road—
For him who travels without a load.

Three Stockings

By JAN STRUTHER

*H*OWEVER MUCH one groaned about it beforehand, however much one hated making arrangements and doing up parcels and ordering several days' meals in advance—when it actually happened Christmas Day was always fun.

It began in the same way every year: the handle of her bedroom door being turned just loudly enough to wake her up, but softly enough not to count as waking her up on purpose; Toby glimmering like a moth in the dark doorway, clutching a nobbly Christmas stocking in one hand and holding up his pyjama trousers with the other. (He insisted upon pyjamas, but he had not yet outgrown his sleeping-suit figure.)

"Toby! It's only just after six. I did say not till seven."

"But, Mummy, I can't tell the time." He was barefoot and shivering, and his eyes were like stars.

"Come here and get warm, you little *goat*." He was into her bed in a flash, stocking and all. The tail of a clockwork dog scratched her shoulder. A few moments later another head appeared round the door, a little higher up.

"Judy, darling, it's *too* early, honestly."

"I know, but I heard Toby come in, so I knew you must be awake."

"All right, you can come into bed, but you've got to keep quiet for a bit. Daddy's still asleep."

And then a third head, higher up still, and Vin's voice, even deeper than it had been at Long Leave.

"I say, are the others in here? I thought I heard them."

He curled himself up on the foot of his father's bed. And by that time, of course, Clem was awake too. The old transparent stratagem had worked to perfection once more: there was nothing for it but to switch on the lights, shut the windows, and admit that Christmas Day had insidiously but definitely begun.

319

The three right hands—Vin's strong and broad, Judy's thin and flexible, Toby's still a star-fish— plunged in and out of the three distorted stockings, until there was nothing left but the time-hallowed tangerine in the toe. (It was curious how that tradition lingered, even nowadays when children had a good supply of fruit all the year round.) Their methods were as different as their hands. Vin, with little grunts of approval, examined each object carefully as he drew it out, exploring all its possibilities before he went on to the next. Judy, talking the whole time, pulled all her treasures out in a heap, took a quick glance at them and went straight for the one she liked best— a minikin black baby in a wicker cradle. Toby pulled all his out, too, but he arranged them in a neat pattern on the eiderdown and looked at them for a long time in complete silence. Then he picked up one of them—a big glass marble with coloured squirls inside—and put it by itself a little way off. After that he played with the other toys, appreciatively enough; but from time to time his eyes would stray towards the glass marble, as though to make sure it was still waiting for him.

Mrs. Miniver watched him with a mixture of delight and misgiving. It was her own favourite approach to life: but the trouble was that sometimes the marble rolled away. Judy's was safer; Vin's, on the whole, the wisest of the three.

To the banquet of real presents which was waiting downstairs, covered with a red and white dust-sheet, the stocking-toys, of course, were only an *apéritif;* but they had a special and exciting quality of their own. Perhaps it was the atmosphere in which they were opened—the chill, the black window-panes, the unfamiliar hour; perhaps it was the powerful charm of the miniature, of toy toys, of smallness squared; perhaps it was the sense of limitation within a strict form, which gives to both the filler and the emptier of a Christmas stocking something of the same enjoyment which is experienced by the writer and the reader of a sonnet; or perhaps it was merely that the spell of the old legend still persisted, even though for everybody in the room except Toby the legend itself was outworn.

There were cross-currents of pleasure, too: smiling glances exchanged by her and Vin about the two younger children (she remembered suddenly, having been an eldest child, the unsurpassable sense of grandeur that such glances gave one); and by her and Clem, because they were both grown-ups; and by her and Judy, because they were both women; and by her and Toby, because they were both the kind that leaves the glass marble till the end. The room was laced with an invisible network of affectionate understanding.

This was one of the moments, thought Mrs. Miniver, which paid off at a single stroke all the accumulations on the debit side of parenthood: the morning sickness and the quite astonishing pain; the pram in the passage, the cold mulish glint in the cook's eye; the holiday nurse who had been in the best families; the pungent white mice, the shriveled caterpillars; the plasticine on the door-handles, the face-flannels in the bathroom, the nameless horrors down the crevices of armchairs;

320

the alarms and emergencies, the swallowed button, the inexplicable earache, the ominous rash appearing on the eve of a journey; the school bills and the dentists' bills; the shortened step, the tempered pace, the emotional compromises, the divided loyalties, the adventures continually forsworn.

And now Vin was eating his tangerine, pig by pig: Judy had undressed the baby doll and was putting on its frock again back to front;

Toby was turning the glass marble round and round against the light, trying to count the squirls. There were sounds of movement in the house; they were within measurable distance of the blessed chink of early morning tea. Mrs. Miniver looked towards the window. The dark sky had already paled a little in its frame of cherry-pink chintz. Eternity framed in domesticity. Never mind. One had to frame it in something, to see it at all.

✧ ✧ ✧

ROADSIDE FLOWERS
Bliss Carman

We are the roadside flowers,
  Straying from garden grounds;
Lovers of idle hours,
  Breakers of ordered bounds.

If only the earth will feed us,
  If only the wind be kind,
We blossom for those who need us,
  The stragglers left behind.

And lo, the Lord of the Garden,
  He makes His sun to rise,
And His rain to fall like pardon
  On our dusty paradise.

On us He has laid the duty—
  The task of the wandering breed—
To better the world with beauty,
  Wherever the way may lead.

Who shall inquire of the season,
  Or question the wind where it blows?
We blossom and ask no reason,
  The Lord of the Garden knows.

321

LEARN to stand in awe of thyself.—*Democritus*

AS SOON AS laws are necessary for men, they are no longer fit for freedom.—*Pythagoras*

AS FOR THE FUTURE, it is not to be treated lightly nor with fear, but we must approach it with a calm reason.—*Plato*

NO ONE is free who has not obtained the empire of himself.—*Pythagoras*

COURAGE consists not in hazarding without fear, but being resolutely minded in a just cause.—*Plutarch*

CALL NO MAN HAPPY till you know the nature of his death. He who possesses the most advantages, and afterwards leaves the world with composure, he alone, O Croesus, is entitled to our admiration.—*Solon*

EACH HUMAN BEING is in the first instance a citizen of his own nation or commonwealth; but he is also a member of the great city of gods and men.
—*Epictetus*

NO GREAT THING is created suddenly, any more than a bunch of grapes or a fig. If you tell me that you desire a fig, I answer you that there must be time. Let it first blossom, then bear fruit, then ripen.—*Epictetus*

IF YOU have a mind to adorn your city by consecrated monuments first consecrate in yourself the most beautiful monument of gentleness and justice and benevolence.—*Epictetus*

MEN are taught by virtue and a love of independence, by living in the country.—*Menander*

THINKING is the talking of the soul with itself.—*Plato*

FOR, according to the proverb, the beginning is half the whole business.—*Plato*

GREEK PHILOSOPHERS

KNOW thyself.—*Socrates*

GOD is truth and light his shadow.—*Plato*

SELF-CONQUEST is the greatest of victories.—*Plato*

THAT CITY is well fortified which has a wall of men
instead of brick.—*Lycurgus*

To THE MAN who himself strives earnestly, God also lends
a helping hand.—*Aeschylus*

GOD HAS DELIVERED yourself to your care, and says: I had no one fitter
to trust than you. Preserve this person for me such as he is by nature:
modest, beautiful, faithful, noble, tranquil.—*Epictetus*

WHEN YOU have closed your doors, and darkened your room, remember never
to say that you are alone, for you are not alone; God is within, and
your genius is within,—and what need have they of light to see what
you are doing?—*Epictetus*

Do THAT which you judge to be beautiful and honest, though you should
acquire no glory from the performance.—*Pythagoras*

HE IS a wise man who does not grieve for the things which he has not,
but rejoices for those which he has.—*Epictetus*

THE BEST WAY of training the young is to train yourself at the
same time; not to admonish them, but to be seen never doing
that of which you would admonish them.—*Plato*

BEAUTY of style and harmony and grace and good rhythm
depend on simplicity.—*Plato*

BE CONTENT with your lot; one cannot be first
in everything.—*Aesop*

The Passing of the
Third Floor Back

By JEROME K. JEROME

*T*HE NEIGHBOURHOOD of Blooms-bury Square towards four o'clock of a November afternoon is not so crowded as to secure to the stranger, of appearance anything out of the common, immunity from observation. Tibb's boy, screaming at the top of his voice that *she* was his honey, stopped suddenly, stepped backwards on to the toes of a voluble young lady wheeling a perambulator, and remained deaf, apparently, to the somewhat personal remarks of the voluble young lady. Not until he had reached the next corner—and then more as a soliloquy than as information to the street —did Tibb's boy recover sufficient interest in his own affairs to remark that *he* was her bee. The voluble young lady herself, following some half-a-dozen yards behind, forgot her wrongs in contemplation of the stranger's back. There was this that was peculiar about the stranger's back: that instead of being flat it presented a decided curve. "It ain't a 'ump, and it don't look like ker-vitcher of the spine," observed the voluble young lady to herself. "Blimy if I don't believe 'e's taking 'ome 'is washing up his back."

The constable at the corner, trying to seem busy doing nothing, noticed the stranger's approach with gathering interest. "That's an odd sort of a walk of yours, young man," thought the constable. "You take care you don't fall down and tumble over yourself."

"Thought he was a young man," murmured the constable, the stranger having passed him. "He had a young face right enough."

The daylight was fading. The stranger, finding it impossible to read the name of the street upon the corner house, turned back. "Why, 'tis a young man," the constable told himself; "a mere boy."

"I beg your pardon," said the stranger; "but would you mind telling me my way to Bloomsbury Square."

"This is Bloomsbury Square," exclaimed the constable; "leastways round the corner is. What number might you be wanting?"

The stranger took from the ticket pocket of his tightly buttoned overcoat a piece of paper, unfolded it and read it out: "Mrs. Pennycherry. Number forty-eight."

"Round to the left," instructed him the constable; "fourth house. Been recommended there?"

"By—by a friend," replied the stranger. " Thank you very much."

"Ah," muttered the constable to himself; "guess you won't be calling him that by the end of the week, young——

"Funny," added the constable, gazing after the retreating figure of the stranger. "Seen plenty of the other sex as looked young behind and old in front. This cove looks young in front and old behind. Guess he'll look old all round if he stops long at Mother Pennycherry's: stingy old cat."

Constables whose beat included Bloomsbury Square had their reasons for not liking Mrs. Pennycherry. Indeed, it might have been difficult to discover any human being with reasons for liking that sharp-featured lady. Maybe the keeping of second-rate boarding houses in the neighbourhood of Bloomsbury does not tend to develop the virtues of generosity and amiability.

Meanwhile, the stranger, proceeding upon his way, had rung the bell of Number Forty-eight. Mrs. Pennycherry, peeping from the area and catching a glimpse, above the railings, of a handsome if somewhat effeminate masculine face, hastened to readjust her widow's cap before the looking-glass while directing Mary Jane to show the stranger, should he prove a problematical boarder, into the dining-room, and to light the gas.

"And don't stop gossiping, and don't you take it upon yourself to answer questions. Say I'll be up in a minute," were Mrs. Pennycherry's further instructions, "and mind you hide your hands as much as you can."

"What are you grinning at?" demanded Mrs. Pennycherry, a couple of minutes later, of the dingy Mary Jane.

"Wasn't grinning," explained the meek Mary Jane, "was only smiling to myself."

"What at?"

"Dunno," admitted Mary Jane.

But still she went on smiling.

"What's he like, then?" demanded Mrs. Pennycherry.

"'E ain't the usual sort," was Mary Jane's opinion.

"Thank God for that," ejaculated Mrs. Pennycherry piously.

"Says 'e's been recommended, by a friend."

"By whom?"

"By a friend. 'E didn't say no name."

Mrs. Pennycherry pondered. "He's not the funny sort, is he?"

Not that sort at all. Mary Jane was sure of it.

Mrs. Pennycherry ascended the stairs still pondering. As she entered the room the stranger rose and bowed. Nothing could have been simpler than the stranger's bow, yet there came with it to Mrs. Pennycherry a rush of old sensations long forgotten. For one brief moment Mrs. Pennycherry saw herself an amiable well-bred lady, widow of a solicitor: a visitor had called to see her. It was but a momentary fancy. The next instant Reality reasserted itself. Mrs. Pennycherry, a lodging-house keeper, existing precariously upon a daily round of petty meannesses, was prepared for contest with a possible new boarder, who fortunately looked an inexperienced young gentleman.

"Someone has recommended me to you," began Mrs. Pennycherry; "may I ask who?"

But the stranger waved the question aside as immaterial.

"You might not remember—him," he smiled. "He thought that I should do well to pass the few months I am given—that I have to be in London, here. You can take me in?"

Mrs. Pennycherry thought that she would be able to take the stranger in.

"A room to sleep in," explained the stranger, "—any room will do—with food and drink sufficient for a man, is all that I require."

"For breakfast," began Mrs. Pennycherry, "I always give——"

"What is right and proper, I am convinced," interrupted the stranger. "Pray do not trouble to go into detail, Mrs. Pennycherry. With whatever it is I shall be content."

Mrs. Pennycherry, puzzled, shot a quick glance at the stranger, but his face, though the gentle eyes were smiling, was frank and serious.

"At all events, you will see the room," suggested Mrs. Pennycherry, "before we discuss terms."

"Certainly," agreed the stranger. "I am a little tired and shall be glad to rest there."

Mrs. Pennycherry led the way upward; on the landing of the third floor, paused a moment undecided, then opened the door of the back bedroom.

"It is very comfortable," commented the stranger.

"For this room," stated Mrs. Pennycherry, "together with full board, consisting of——"

"Of everything needful. It goes without saying," again interrupted the stranger with his quiet, grave smile.

"I have generally asked," continued Mrs. Pennycherry, "four pounds a week. To you—" Mrs. Pennycherry's voice, unknown to her, took to itself the note of aggressive generosity—"seeing you have been recommended here, say three pounds ten."

"Dear lady," said the stranger, "that is kind of you. As you have divined, I am not a rich man. If it be not imposing upon you I accept your reduction with gratitude."

Again Mrs. Pennycherry, familiar with the satirical method, shot a suspicious glance upon the stranger, but not a line was there, upon that smooth fair face, to which a sneer could for a moment have clung. Clearly he was as simple as he looked.

"Gas, of course, extra."

"Of course," agreed the stranger.

"Coals——"

"We shall not quarrel," for a third time the stranger interrupted. "You have been very considerate to me as it is. I feel, Mrs. Pennycherry, I can leave myself entirely in your hands."

The stranger appeared anxious to be alone. Mrs. Pennycherry, having put a match to the stranger's fire, turned to depart. And at this point it was that Mrs. Pennycherry, the holder hitherto of an unbroken record for sanity, behaved in a manner she herself, five minutes earlier in her career, would have deemed impossible—that no living soul who had ever known her would have believed, even had Mrs. Pennycherry gone down upon her knees and sworn it to them.

"Did I say three pound ten?" demanded Mrs. Pennycherry of the stranger, her hand upon the door. She spoke crossly. She was feeling cross, with the stranger, with herself—particularly with herself.

"You were kind enough to reduce it to that amount," replied the stranger; "but if upon reflection you find yourself unable——"

"I was making a mistake," said Mrs. Pennycherry, "it should have been two pound ten."

"I cannot—I will not accept such

sacrifice," exlaimed the stranger; "the three pound ten I can well afford."

"Two pound ten are my terms," snapped Mrs. Pennycherry. "If you are bent on paying more, you can go elsewhere. You'll find plenty to oblige you."

Her vehemence must have impressed the stranger. "We will not contend further," he smiled. "I was merely afraid that in the goodness of your heart——"

"Oh, it isn't as good as all that," growled Mrs. Pennycherry.

"I am not so sure," returned the stranger. "I am somewhat suspicious of you. But wilful woman must, I suppose, have her way."

The stranger held out his hand, and to Mrs. Pennycherry, at that moment, it seemed the most natural thing in the world to take it as if it had been the hand of an old friend and to end the interview with a pleasant laugh—though laughing was an exercise not often indulged in by Mrs. Pennycherry.

Mary Jane was standing by the window, her hands folded in front of her, when Mrs. Pennycherry re-entered the kitchen. By standing close to the window one caught a glimpse of the trees in Bloomsbury Square, and, through their bare branches, of the sky beyond.

"There's nothing much to do for the next half hour, till cook comes back. I'll see to the door if you'd like to run out?" suggested Mrs. Pennycherry.

"It would be nice," agreed the girl so soon as she had recovered power of speech; "it's just the time of day I like."

"Don't be longer than the half hour," added Mrs. Pennycherry.

Forty-eight Bloomsbury Square, assembled after dinner in the drawing-room, discussed the stranger with that freedom and frankness characteristic of Forty-eight Bloomsbury Square toward the absent.

"Not what I call a smart young man," was the opinion of Augustus Longcord, who was something in the City.

"Thpeaking for mythelf," commented his partner Isidore, "hav'-n'th any uthe for the thmart young man. Too many of him, ath it ith."

"Must be pretty smart if he's one too many for you," laughed his partner. There was this to be said for the repartee of Forty-eight Bloomsbury Square: it was simple of construction and easy of comprehension.

"Well, it made me feel good just looking at him," declared Miss Kite, the highly coloured. "It was his clothes, I suppose—made me think of Noah and the ark—all that sort of thing."

"It would be clothes that would make you think—if anything," drawled the languid Miss Devine. She was a tall, handsome girl, engaged at the moment in futile efforts to recline with elegance and comfort combined upon a horse-hair sofa. Miss Kite, by reason of having secured the only easy-chair, was unpopular that evening; so that Miss Devine's remark received from the rest of the company more approbation than perhaps it merited.

"Is that intended to be clever, dear, or only rude?" Miss Kite requested to be informed.

"Both," claimed Miss Devine.

"Myself, I must confess," shouted the tall young lady's father, commonly called the Colonel, "I found him a fool."

"I noticed you seemed to be get-

327

ting on very well together," purred his wife, a plump, smiling little lady.

"Possibly we were," retorted the Colonel. "Fate has accustomed me to the society of fools."

"Isn't it a pity to start quarreling immediately after dinner, you two?" suggested their thoughtful daughter from the sofa. "You'll have nothing left to amuse you for the rest of the evening."

"He didn't strike me as a conversationalist," said the lady who was cousin to a baronet; "but he did pass the vegetables before he helped himself. A little thing like that shows breeding."

"Or that he didn't know you and thought maybe you'd leave him half a spoonful," laughed Augustus the wit.

"What I can't make out about him—" shouted the Colonel.

The stranger entered the room.

The Colonel, securing the evening paper, retired into a corner. The highly coloured Kite, reaching down from the mantelpiece a paper fan, held it coyly before her face. Miss Devine sat upright on the horse-hair sofa, and rearranged her skirts.

"Know anything?" demanded Augustus of the stranger, breaking the somewhat remarkable silence.

The stranger evidently did not understand. It was necessary for Augustus, the witty, to advance further into that odd silence.

"What's going to pull off the Lincoln handicap? Tell me, and I'll go out straight and put my shirt upon it."

"I think you would act unwisely," smiled the stranger; "I am not an authority upon the subject."

"Not! Why, they told me you were Captain Spy of the *Sporting Life*—in disguise."

It would have been difficult for a joke to fall more flat. Nobody laughed, though why, Mr. Augustus Longcord could not understand, and maybe none of his audience could have told him, for at Forty-eight Bloomsbury Square Mr. Augustus Longcord passed as a humourist. The stranger himself appeared unaware that he was being made fun of.

"You have been misinformed," the stranger assured him.

"I beg your pardon," said Mr. Augustus Longcord.

"It is nothing," replied the stranger in his sweet low voice, and passed on.

"Well, what about this theatre," demanded Mr. Longcord of his friend and partner; "do you want to go or don't you?" Mr. Longcord was feeling irritable.

"Goth the ticketh—may ath well," thought Isidore.

"Damn stupid piece, I'm told."

"Motht of them thupid, more or leth. Pity to wathte the ticketh," argued Isidore, and the pair went out.

"Are you staying long in London?" asked Miss Kite, raising her practised eyes toward the stranger.

"Not long," answered the stranger. "At least, I do not know. It depends."

An unusual quiet had invaded the drawing-room of Forty-eight Bloomsbury Square, generally noisy with strident voices about this hour. The Colonel remained engrossed in his paper. Mrs. Devine sat with her plump white hands folded on her lap, whether asleep or not it was impossible to say. The lady who was cousin to a baronet had shifted her

328

chair beneath the gasolier, her eyes bent on her everlasting crochet work. The languid Miss Devine had crossed to the piano, where she sat fingering softly the tuneless keys, her back to the cold, barely furnished room.

"Sit down," commanded saucily Miss Kite, indicating with her fan the vacant seat beside her. "Tell me about yourself. You interest me." Miss Kite adopted a pretty authoritative air toward all youthful-looking members of the opposite sex. It harmonized with the peach complexion and the golden hair, and fitted her about as well.

"I am glad of that," answered the stranger, taking the chair suggested. "I so wish to interest you."

"You're a very bold boy." Miss Kite lowered her fan, for the purpose of glancing archly over the edge of it, and for the first time encountered the eyes of the stranger looking into hers. And then it was that Miss Kite experienced precisely the same curious sensation that an hour or so ago had troubled Mrs. Pennycherry when the stranger had first bowed to her. It seemed to Miss Kite that she was no longer the Miss Kite that, had she risen and looked into it, the fly-blown mirror over the marble mantelpiece would, she knew, have presented to her view; but quite another Miss Kite—a cheerful, bright-eyed lady verging on middle-age, yet still good-looking in spite of her faded complexion and somewhat thin brown locks. Miss Kite felt a pang of jealousy shoot through her; this middle-aged Miss Kite seemed, on the whole, a more attractive lady. There was a wholesomeness, a broadmindedness about her that instinctively drew one toward her. Not hampered, as

Miss Kite herself was, by the necessity of appearing to be somewhere between eighteen and twenty-two, this other Miss Kite could talk sensibly, even brilliantly: one felt it. A thoroughly "nice" woman, this other Miss Kite; the real Miss Kite, though envious, was bound to admit it. Miss Kite wished to goodness she had never seen the woman. The glimpse of her had rendered Miss Kite dissatisfied with herself.

"I am not a boy," explained the stranger; "and I had no intention of being bold."

"I know," replied Miss Kite. "It was a silly remark. Whatever induced me to make it, I can't think. Getting foolish in my old age, I suppose."

The stranger laughed. "Surely you are not old."

"I'm thirty-nine," snapped out Miss Kite. "You don't call it young?"

"I think it a beautiful age," insisted the stranger: "young enough not to have lost the joy of youth, old enough to have learnt sympathy."

"Oh, I daresay," returned Miss Kite, "any age you'd think beautiful. I'm going to bed." Miss Kite rose. The paper fan had somehow got itself broken. She threw the fragments into the fire.

"It is early yet," pleaded the stranger. "I was looking forward to a talk with you."

"Well, you'll be able to look forward to it," retorted Miss Kite. "Good-night."

The truth was, Miss Kite was impatient to have a look at herself in the glass, in her own room with the door shut. The vision of that other Miss Kite—the clean-looking lady of the pale face and the brown hair had been so vivid, Miss Kite wondered whether temporary forgetfulness might not have fallen upon her while dressing for dinner that evening.

The stranger, left to his own devices, strolled toward the low table, seeking something to read.

"You seem to have frightened away Miss Kite," remarked the lady who was cousin to a baronet.

"It seems so," admitted the stranger.

"My cousin, Sir William Bosster," observed the crocheting lady, "who married old Lord Egham's niece—you never met the Eghams?"

"Hitherto," replied the stranger, "I have not had that pleasure."

"A charming family. Cannot understand—my cousin Sir William, I mean, cannot understand my remaining here. 'My dear Emily'—he says the same thing every time he sees me: 'My dear Emily, how can you exist among the sort of people one meets with in a boarding-house.' But they amuse me."

A sense of humour, agreed the stranger, was always of advantage.

"Our family on my mother's side," continued Sir William's cousin in her placid monotone, "was connected with the Tatton-Joneses, who, when King George the Fourth—" Sir William's cousin, needing another reel of cotton, glanced up, and met the stranger's gaze.

"I'm sure I don't know why I'm telling you all this," said Sir William's cousin in an irritable tone. "It can't possibly interest you."

"Everything connected with you interests me," gravely the stranger assured her.

"It is very kind of you to say so," sighed Sir William's cousin, but without conviction; "I am afraid sometimes I bore people."

The polite stranger refrained from contradiction.

"You see," continued the poor lady, "I really am of good family."

"Dear lady," said the stranger, "your gentle face, your gentle voice, your gentle bearing, all proclaim it."

She looked without flinching into the stranger's eyes, and gradually a smile banished the reigning dulness of her features.

"How foolish of me." She spoke rather to herself than to the stranger. "Why, of course, people—people whose opinion is worth troubling about—judge of you by what you are, not by what you go about saying you are."

The stranger remained silent.

"I am the widow of a provincial doctor, with an income of just two hundred and thirty pounds per annum," she argued. "The sensible thing for me to do is to make the best of it, and to worry myself about these high and mighty relations of mine as little as they have ever worried themselves about me."

The stranger appeared unable to think of anything worth saying.

"I have other connections," remembered Sir William's cousin; "those of my poor husband, to whom instead of being the 'poor relation' I could be the fairy god-mama. They are my people—or would be," added Sir William's cousin tartly, "if I wasn't a vulgar snob."

She flushed the instant she had said the words and, rising, commenced preparations for a hurried departure.

"Now it seems I am driving you away," sighed the stranger.

"Having been called a 'vulgar snob,' " retorted the lady with some heat, "I think it about time I went."

"The words were your own," the stranger reminded her.

"Whatever I may have thought," remarked the indignant dame, "no lady—least of all in the presence of a total stranger—would have called herself—" The poor dame paused, bewildered. "There is something very curious the matter with me this evening, that I cannot understand," she explained. "I seem quite unable to avoid insulting myself."

Still surrounded by bewilderment, she wished the stranger good-night, hoping that when next they met she would be more herself. The stranger, hoping so also, opened the door and closed it again behind her.

"Tell me," laughed Miss Devine, who by sheer force of talent was contriving to wring harmony from the reluctant piano, "how did you manage to do it? I should like to know."

"How did I do what?" inquired the stranger.

"Contrive to get rid so quickly of those two old frumps?"

"How well you play!" observed the stranger. "I knew you had genius for music the moment I saw you."

"How could you tell?"

"It is written so clearly in your face."

The girl laughed, well pleased. "You seem to have lost no time in studying my face."

"It is a beautiful and interesting face," observed the stranger.

She swung around sharply on the stool and their eyes met.

"You can read faces?"

"Yes."

"Tell me, what else do you read in mine?"

"Frankness, courage——"

"Ah, yes, all the virtues. Perhaps. We will take them for granted." It was odd how serious the girl had suddenly become. "Tell me the reverse side."

"I see no reverse side," replied the stranger. "I see but a fair girl, bursting into noble womanhood."

"And nothing else? You read no trace of greed, of vanity, of sordidness, of—" An angry laugh escaped her lips. "And you are a reader of faces!"

"A reader of faces." The stranger smiled. "Do you know what is written upon yours at this very moment? A love of truth that is almost fierce, scorn of lies, scorn of hypocrisy, the desire for all things pure, contempt of all things that are contemptible—especially of such things as are contemptible in woman. Tell me, do I not read aright?"

I wonder, thought the girl, is that why those two others both hurried from the room? Does everyone feel ashamed of the littleness that is in them when looked at by those clear, believing eyes of yours?

The idea occurred to her: "Papa seemed to have a good deal to say to you during dinner. Tell me, what were you talking about?"

"The military looking gentleman upon my left? We talked about your mother principally."

"I am sorry," returned the girl, wishful now she had not asked the question. "I was hoping he might have chosen another topic for the first evening!"

"He did try one or two," admitted the stranger; "but I have been about the world so little, I was glad when he talked to me about himself. I feel we shall be friends. He spoke so nicely, too, about Mrs. Devine."

"Indeed," commented the girl.

"He told me he had been married

for twenty years and had never regretted it but once!"

Her black eyes flashed upon him, but meeting his, the suspicion died from them. She turned aside to hide her smile.

"So he regretted it—once."

"Only once," explained the stranger, "a passing irritable mood. It was so frank of him to admit it. He told me—I think he has taken a liking to me. Indeed, he hinted as much. He said he did not often get an opportunity of talking to a man like myself—he told me that he and your mother, when they travel together, are always mistaken for a honeymoon couple. Some of the experiences he related to me were really quite amusing." The stranger laughed at recollection of them—"that even here, in this place, they are generally referred to as 'Darby and Joan.'"

"Yes," said the girl, "that is true. Mr. Longcord gave them that name, the second evening after our arrival. It was considered clever—but rather obvious, I thought myself."

"Nothing—so it seems to me," said the stranger, "is more beautiful than the love that has weathered the storms of life. The sweet, tender blossom that flowers in the heart of the young—in hearts such as yours—that, too, is beautiful. The love of the young for the young, that is the beginning of life. But the love of the old for the old, that is the beginning of—of things longer."

"You seem to find all things beautiful," the girl grumbled.

"But are not all things beautiful?" demanded the stranger.

The Colonel had finished his paper.

"You two are engaged in a very absorbing conversation," observed the Colonel, approaching them.

"We were discussing Darbies and Joans," explained his daughter. "How beautiful is the love that has weathered the storms of life!"

"Ah!" smiled the Colonel, "that is hardly fair. My friend has been repeating to cynical youth the confessions of an amorous husband's affection for his middle-aged and somewhat—" The Colonel in playful mood laid his hand upon the stranger's shoulder, an action that necessitated his looking straight into the stranger's eyes. The Colonel drew himself up stiffly and turned scarlet.

Somebody was calling the Colonel a cad. Not only that, but was explaining quite clearly, so that the Colonel could see it for himself, why he was a cad.

"That you and your wife lead a cat and dog existence is a disgrace to both of you. At least you might have the decency to try and hide it from the world—not make a jest of your shame to every passing stranger. You are a cad, sir, a cad!"

Who was daring to say these things? Not the stranger, his lips had not moved. Besides, it was not his voice. Indeed it sounded much more like the voice of the Colonel himself. The Colonel looked from the stranger to his daughter, from his daughter back to the stranger. Clearly they had not heard the voice—a mere hallucination. The Colonel breathed again.

Yet the impression remaining was not to be shaken off. Undoubtedly it was bad taste to have joked to the stranger upon such a subject. No gentleman would have done so.

But then no gentleman would have permitted such a jest to be possible. No gentleman would be forever wrangling with his wife—cer-

332

tainly never in public. However irritating the woman, a gentleman would have exercised self-control.

Mrs. Devine had risen, was coming slowly across the room. Fear laid hold of the Colonel. She was going to address some aggravating remark to him—he could see it in her eye—which would irritate him into savage retort. Even this prize idiot of a stranger would understand why boarding-house wits had dubbed them "Darby and Joan," would grasp the fact that the gallant Colonel had thought it amusing, in conversation with a table acquaintance, to hold his own wife up to ridicule.

"My dear," cried the Colonel, hurrying to speak first, "does not this room strike you as cold? Let me fetch you a shawl."

It was useless: the Colonel felt it. It had been too long the custom of both of them to preface with politeness their deadliest insults to each other. She came on, thinking of a suitable reply: suitable from her point of view, that is. In another moment the truth would be out. A wild, fantastic possibility flashed through the Colonel's brain: If to him, why not to her?

"Letitia," cried the Colonel, and the tone of his voice surprised her into silence, "I want you to look closely at our friend. Does he not remind you of someone?"

Mrs. Devine, so urged, looked at the stranger long and hard. "Yes," she murmured, turning to her husband, "he does; who is it?"

"I cannot fix it," replied the Colonel; "I thought that maybe you would remember."

"It will come to me," mused Mrs. Devine. "It is someone—years ago, when I was a girl—in Devonshire. Thank you, if it isn't troubling you,

Harry. I left it in the dining-room."

It was, as Mr. Augustus Longcord explained to his partner Isidore, the colossal foolishness of the stranger that was the cause of all the trouble. "Give me a man who can take care of himself—or thinks he can," declared Augustus Longcord, "and I am prepared to give a good account of myself. But when a helpless baby refuses even to look at what you call your figures, tells you that your mere word is sufficient for him, and hands you over his cheque-book to fill up for yourself—well, it isn't playing the game."

"Auguthuth," was the curt comment of his partner, "you're a fool."

"All right, my boy, you try," suggested Augustus.

"Jutht what I mean to do," asserted his partner.

"Well," demanded Augustus one evening later, meeting Isidore ascending the stairs after a long talk with the stranger in the dining-room with the door shut.

"Oh, don't arth me," retorted Isidore, "thilly ath, thath what he ith."

"What did he say?"

"What did he thay! talked about the Jewth: what a grand rathe they were—how people mithjudged them. "Thaid thome of the motht honourable men he had ever met had been Jewth. Thought I wath one of 'em!"

"Well, did you get anything out of him?"

"Get anything out of him? Of courthe not! Couldn't very well thell the whole rathe, ath it were, for a couple of hundred poundth, after that. Didn't theem worth it."

There were many things Forty-eight Bloomsbury Square came gradually to the conclusion were not worth the doing:—Snatching at the

333

gravy; pouncing out of one's turn upon the vegetables and helping oneself to more than one's fair share; maneuvering for the easy-chair; sitting on the evening paper while pretending not to have seen it—all such-like tiresome bits of business. For the little one made out of it, really was not worth the bother. Grumbling everlastingly at one's food; grumbling everlastingly at most things; abusing Pennycherry behind her back; abusing, for a change, one's fellow-boarders; squabbling with one's fellow-boarders about nothing in particular; sneering at one's fellow-boarders; talking scandal of one's fellow-boarders; making senseless jokes about one's fellow-boarders; talking big about oneself, nobody believing one—all such-like vulgarities. Other boarding-houses might indulge in them: Forty-eight Bloomsbury Square had its dignity to consider.

The truth is, Forty-eight Bloomsbury Square was coming to a very good opinion of itself: for the which not Bloomsbury Square so much as the stranger must be blamed. The stranger had arrived at Forty-eight Bloomsbury Square with the preconceived idea—where obtained from, Heaven knows—that its seemingly commonplace, mean-minded, coarse-fibered occupants were in reality ladies and gentlemen of the first water; and time and observation had apparently only strengthened this absurd idea. The natural result was, Forty-eight Bloomsbury Square was coming round to the stranger's opinion of itself.

Mrs. Pennycherry, the stranger would persist in regarding as a lady born and bred, compelled by circumstances over which she had no control to fill an arduous but honourable position of middle-class society—a sort of foster-mother, to whom were due the thanks and gratitude of her promiscuous family; and this view of herself Mrs. Pennycherry now clung to with obstinate conviction. There were disadvantages attaching, but these Mrs. Pennycherry appeared prepared to suffer cheerfully. A lady born and bred can not charge other ladies and gentlemen for coals and candles they have never burnt; a foster-mother can not palm off upon her children New Zealand mutton for Southdown. A mere lodging-house-keeper can play these tricks, and pocket the profits. But a lady feels she can not: Mrs. Pennycherry felt she no longer could.

To the stranger Miss Kite was a witty and delightful conversationalist of most attractive personality. Miss Kite had one failing: it was lack of vanity. She was unaware of her own delicate and refined beauty. If Miss Kite could only see herself with his, the stranger's eyes, the modesty that rendered her distrustful of her natural charms would fall from her. The stranger was so sure of it Miss Kite determined to put it to the test. One evening, an hour before dinner, there entered the drawing-room, when the stranger only was there and before the gas was lighted, a pleasant, good-looking lady, somewhat pale, with neatly arranged brown hair, who demanded of the stranger if he knew her. All her body was trembling, and her voice seemed inclined to run away from her and become a sob. But when the stranger, looking straight into her eyes, told her that from the likeness he thought she must be Miss Kite's younger sister, but much prettier, it became a laugh instead: and that evening the golden-haired Miss Kite disappeared never to show her high-coloured face again; and, what perhaps, more than all else, might have impressed some former habitué of Forty-eight Bloomsbury Square with awe, it was that no one in the house made even a passing inquiry concerning her.

Sir William's cousin the stranger thought an acquisition to any boarding-house. A lady of high-class family! There was nothing outward or visible perhaps to tell you that she was of high-class family. She herself, naturally, would not mention the fact, yet somehow you felt it. Unconsciously she set a high-class tone, diffused an atmosphere of gentle manners. Not that the stranger had said this in so many words; Sir William's cousin gathered that he thought it, and felt herself in agreement with him.

For Mr. Longcord and his partner, as representatives of the best type of business men, the stranger had a great respect, with what unfortunate results to themselves has been noted. The curious thing is that the firm appeared content with the price they had paid for the stranger's good opinion—had even, it was rumoured, acquired a taste for honest men's respect—that in the long run was likely to cost them dear. But we all have our pet extravagance.

The Colonel and Mrs. Devine both suffered a good deal at first from the necessity imposed upon them of learning, somewhat late in life, new tricks. In the privacy of their own apartment they condoled with one another.

"Tomfool nonsense," grumbled the Colonel, "you and I starting billing and cooing at our age!"

"What I object to," said Mrs. De-

vine, "is the feeling that somehow I am being made to do it."

"The idea that a man and his wife can not have their little joke together for fear of what some impertinent jackanapes may think of them! it's damned ridiculous," the Colonel exploded.

"Even when he isn't there," said Mrs. Devine, "I seem to see him looking at me with those vexing eyes of his. Really, the man quite haunts me."

"I have met him somewhere," mused the Colonel, "I'll swear I've met him somewhere. I wish to goodness he would go."

A hundred things a day the Colonel wanted to say to Mrs. Devine, a hundred things a day Mrs. Devine would have liked to observe to the Colonel. But by the time the opportunity occurred—when nobody else was by to hear—all interest in saying them was gone.

"Women will be women," was the sentiment with which the Colonel consoled himself. "A man must bear with them—must never forget that he is a gentleman."

"Oh well, I suppose they're all alike," laughed Mrs. Devine to herself, having arrived at that stage of despair when one seeks refuge in cheerfulness. "What's the use of putting oneself out—it does no good, and only upsets one."

There is a certain satisfaction in feeling you are bearing with heroic resignation the irritating follies of others. Colonel and Mrs. Devine came to enjoy the luxury of much self-approbation.

But the person seriously annoyed by the stranger's bigoted belief in the innate goodness of everyone he came across was the languid, handsome Miss Devine. The stranger

335

would have it that Miss Devine was a noble-souled, high-minded young woman, something midway between a Flora Macdonald and a Joan of Arc. Miss Devine, on the contrary, knew herself to be a sleek, luxury-loving animal, quite willing to sell herself to the bidder who could offer her the finest clothes, the richest foods, the most sumptuous surroundings. Such a bidder was to hand in the person of a retired bookmaker, a somewhat greasy old gentleman, but exceedingly rich and undoubtedly fond of her.

Miss Devine, having made up her mind that the thing had got to be done, was anxious that it should be done quickly. And here it was that the stranger's ridiculous opinion of her not only irritated but inconvenienced her. Under the very eyes of a person—however foolish—convinced that you are possessed of all the highest attributes of your sex, it is difficult to behave as though actuated by only the basest motives. A dozen times had Miss Devine determined to end the matter by formal acceptance of her elderly admirer's large and flabby hand, and a dozen times—the vision intervening of the stranger's grave, believing eyes—had Miss Devine refused decided answer. The stranger would one day depart. Indeed, he had told her himself, he was but a passing traveler. When he was gone it would be easier. So she thought at the time.

One afternoon the stranger entered the room where she was standing by the window, looking out upon the bare branches of the trees in Bloomsbury Square. She remembered afterwards, it was just such another foggy afternoon as the afternoon of the stranger's arrival three months before. No one else was in

the room. The stranger closed the door, and came toward her with that curious, quick-leaping step of his. His long coat was tightly buttoned, and in his hands he carried his old felt hat and the massive knotted stick that was almost a staff.

"I have come to say good-bye," explained the stranger. "I am going."

"I shall not see you again?" asked the girl.

"I can not say," replied the stranger. "But you will think of me?"

"Yes," she answered with a smile, "I can promise that."

"And I shall always remember you," promised the stranger, "and I wish you every joy—the joy of love, the joy of a happy marriage."

The girl winced. "Love and marriage are not always the same thing," she said.

"Not always," agreed the stranger, "but in your case they will be one."

She looked at him.

"Do you think I have not noticed?" smiled the stranger. "A gallant, handsome lad, and clever. You love him and he loves you. I could not have gone away without knowing it was well with you."

Her gaze wandered toward the fading light.

"Ah, yes, I love him," she answered petulantly. "Your eyes can see clearly enough, when they want to. But one does not live on love, in our world. I will tell you the man I am going to marry, if you care to know." She would not meet his eyes. She kept her gaze still fixed upon the dingy trees, the mist beyond, and spoke rapidly and vehemently: "The man who can give me all my soul's desire—money and the things that money can buy. You think me a woman; I'm only a pig. He is moist, and breathes like a porpoise; with

336

cunning in place of a brain, and the rest of him mere stomach. But he is good enough for me."

She hoped this would shock the stranger and that now, perhaps, he would go. It irritated her to hear him only laugh.

"No," he said, "you will not marry him."

"Who will stop me?" she cried angrily.

"Your Better Self."

His voice had a strange ring of authority, compelling her to turn and look upon his face. Yes, it was true, the fancy that from the very first had haunted her. She had met him, talked to him—in silent country roads, in crowded city streets, where was it? And always in talking with him her spirit had been lifted up, she had been—what he had always thought her.

"There are those," continued the stranger (and for the first time she saw that he was of a noble presence, that his gentle, childlike eyes could also command), "whose Better Self lies slain by their own hand and troubles them no more. But yours, my child, you have let grow too strong; it will ever be your master. You must obey. Flee from it and it will follow you; you cannot escape it. Insult it and it will chastise you with burning shame, with stinging self-reproach from day to day." The sternness faded from the beautiful face, the tenderness crept back. He laid his hand upon the young girl's shoulder. "You will marry your lover," he smiled. "With him you will walk the way of sunlight and of shadow."

And the girl, looking up into the strong, calm face, knew that it would be so, that the power of resisting her Better Self had passed away from her forever.

"Now," said the stranger, "come to the door with me. Leave-takings are but wasted sadness. Let me pass out quietly. Close the door softly behind me."

She thought that perhaps he would turn his face again, but she saw no more of him than the odd roundness of his back under the tightly buttoned coat, before he faded into the gathering fog.

Then softly she closed the door.

❖   ❖   ❖

THE ETERNAL GOODNESS
John Greenleaf Whittier

O friends! with whom my feet have trod
   The quiet aisles of prayer,
Glad witness to your zeal for God
   And love of man I bear.

I trace your lines of argument;
   Your logic linked and strong
I weigh as one who dreads dissent,
   And fears a doubt as wrong.

But still my human hands are weak
To hold your iron creeds;
Against the words ye bid me speak
My heart within me pleads.

Who fathoms the Eternal Thought?
Who talks of scheme and plan?
The Lord is God! He needeth not
The poor device of man.

I walk with bare, hushed feet the ground
Ye tread with boldness shod;
I dare not fix with mete and bound
The love and power of God.

Ye praise his justice; even such
His pitying love I deem:
Ye seek a king; I fain would touch
The robe that hath no seam.

Ye see the curse which overbroods
A world of pain and loss;
I hear our Lord's beatitudes
And prayer upon the cross . . .

I bow my forehead to the dust,
I veil mine eyes for shame,
And urge, in trembling self-distrust,
A prayer without a claim.

I see the wrong that round me lies,
I feel the guilt within;
I hear, with groan and travail-cries,
The world confess its sin.

Yet, in the maddening maze of things,
And tossed by storm and flood,
To one fixed trust my spirit clings;
I know that God is good . . .

The wrong that pains my soul below
I dare not throne above,
I know not of his hate,—I know
His goodness and his love.

I dimly guess from blessings known
  Of greater out of sight,
And, with the chastened Psalmist, own
  His judgments too are right.

I long for household voices gone,
  For vanished smiles I long,
But God hath led my dear ones on,
  And he can do no wrong.

I know not what the future hath
  Of marvel or surprise,
Assured alone that life and death
  His mercy underlies.

And if my heart and flesh are weak
  To bear an untried pain,
The bruised reed he will not break,
  But strengthen and sustain.

No offering of my own I have,
  Nor works my faith to prove;
I can but give the gifts he gave,
  And plead his love for love.

And so beside the Silent Sea
  I wait the muffled oar;
No harm from him can come to me
  On ocean or on shore.

I know not where his islands lift
  Their fronded palms in air;
I only know I cannot drift
  Beyond his love and care.

O brothers! if my faith is vain,
  If hopes like these betray,
Pray for me that my feet may gain
  The sure and safer way.

And Thou, O Lord! by whom are seen
  Thy creatures as they be,
Forgive me if too close I lean
  My human heart on thee!

FROM THE ROMAN

IF THOU wishest to be loved, love.—*Seneca*

WHEN YOU have set yourself a task finish it.—*Ovid*

LET THE WELFARE of the people be the supreme law.—*Cicero*

IF THOU art a man, admire those who attempt great enterprises, even though they fail.—*Seneca*

YOU SHOULD FORGIVE many things in others, nothing in yourself.—*Ausonius*

IF THOU live according to nature, thou wilt never be poor; if according to the opinions of the world, thou wilt never be rich.—*Seneca*

OBJECTS which are usually the motives of our travels by land and by sea are often overlooked and neglected if they lie under our eye. . . . We put off from time to time going and seeing what we know we have an opportunity of seeing when we please.—*Pliny the Younger*

WHEN A MAN has done thee any wrong, immediately consider with what opinion about good or evil he has done wrong. For when thou hast seen this, thou wilt pity him, and wilt neither wonder nor be angry. . . . —*Marcus Aurelius*

MEN ARE CREATED that they may live for each other.—*Marcus Aurelius*

CONSCIOUSNESS of an honourable intention is the greatest consolation in troubles.—*Cicero*

CONFIDENCE placed in another often compels confidence in return.—*Livy*

ACTS OF KINDNESS shown to good men are never thrown away.—*Plautus*

THE NOBLEST MOTIVE is the public good.—*Virgil*

340

rHILOSOPHERS

WORTHY THINGS happen to the worthy.—*Plautus*

REAL FRIENDS are best known by adversity.—*Ennius*

FIRE is the test of gold; adversity, of strong men.—*Seneca*

IT IS the property of a generous and noble mind to aid and do good to others.—*Seneca*

HOPE ever urges us on, and tells us tomorrow will be better.—*Tibullus*

EVERY MAN'S LIFE lies within the present; for the past is spent and done with, and the future is uncertain.—*Marcus Aurelius*

LIFE is to be considered happy, not in the absence of evil, but in the acquisition of good: and this we should seek for, not in inactivity, enjoyment, or freedom from trouble, but by employment of some kind, or by reflection.—*Cicero*

THE BEAUTY of the world and the orderly arrangement of everything celestial makes us confess that there is an excellent and eternal nature, which ought to be worshipped and admired by all mankind.—*Cicero*

IT SUFFICES to do well what remains to be done.—*Marcus Aurelius*

A GRATEFUL MIND is not only the greatest of virtues, but the parent of all the other virtues.—*Cicero*

ENVY assails the noblest; the wind howls round the highest peaks.—*Ovid*

HE WHO is not prepared today will be less so tomorrow.—*Ovid*

COURAGE in danger is half the battle.—*Plautus*

341

Last Day on Earth

By CYNTHIA HOPE and FRANCES ANCKER

$\mathcal{D}$OCTOR CARLYLE KNEW, a moment after he inserted the needle and watched the fluid drain slowly into his arm, that something had gone wrong.

It came to him, in a slow crystallization of horror, that the test tubes were not in their right order. And when he checked the numbers again, with an almost desperate precision, he saw what he had done.

He, Doctor William Roy Carlyle, at the peak of a great career in research, had injected himself with almost certain death.

He stared at the needle on the table, and while he watched, a strange light crept over it. Dawn! He raised his eyes and saw the day come through the high windows of his laboratory; gentle and golden, like a woman with her arms outstretched. His last dawn?

He pushed himself up from the table and crossed the room on stiff, trembling legs. The sky was flushed with a spreading light, and the east sides of all the great buildings of the city had turned gold in the rising sun. He stared at it, like an exile about to be banished from a loved country. And he knew in that bitter moment that though forty-three years of his life were spent, he had never really *seen* the dawn before.

Too often it had merely meant a time to stop work, after some laboratory experiment carried on far into the night; a symbol that he must admit another grueling failure to find his way through the pathless forest of science.

But now, in this quickened instant, he saw the dawn for what it was. Bright, gilded, promising; offering its twelve daylight hours without favor or prejudice to all on earth to do with as they pleased.

He turned away from it, passing a hand across his eyes and down over the short stubble of beard which grew along his jaw. His arm had begun to swell slowly, almost imperceptibly, in the area of the injection.

This was the way it worked—763X—slow as a drowsing rattlesnake, just as deadly when it struck. The white mice they'd tested had appeared normal for six hours after the injections. Then, just when it seemed the experiment would succeed, death had struck through both cages; violent, irrevocable.

Carlyle thrust the memory from his mind. He had tried this experiment on himself against the advice of his co-workers and his own better judgment—tried it in a moment of exhaustion, when fatigue stood at his elbow, fogging his vision, clouding his mind.

Reaching for 764X, he had taken up the old 763X, the very serum that had already been tested and proved fatal!

Now, too late, he saw what his error would cost him. There was no known antidote. He must see this day through with the cool de-

342

tachment science had ingrained in him. For it would be his last experiment. His last day on earth.

He took up his pencil and began to jot the necessary data in his notebook in a quick, jerky scrawl. There was a slim chance that he could still be of some use. Science might learn through his error.

Semler came in before he'd quite finished, and with a brief nod set about his work. It gave Carlyle a strange feeling—like a spy almost—to watch young Semler, so sure of life, frowning over his test tubes. He wanted to warn the younger man; to tell him that life was only a loan and a brief loan at that—and that he must spend it well, spend it now!

"Semler—" he began. But the fierce discipline which the laboratory forced upon them, made the words come hard. He rose restlessly and crossed the room to the window.

Spring had laid her first magic across the city in a pale web of green. Between the bricks and masonry, in empty lots and neglected back yards, the earth had come alive again—resurgent and triumphant.

"How long," Carlyle wondered aloud, "how long, Semler, since you've taken a real vacation and gotten into the country, where there's fresh earth and open sky overhead and plenty of air to fill your lungs with?"

Semler was staring at him strangely through his heavy-lensed glasses. And there was something about the young scientist both confused and childlike; as if he had become lost in the world of test tubes and could not find his way out again.

How gaunt he was, Carlyle thought! No color in his lean face; and even his blue eyes, strained and weak from search, seemed to have faded to a paler blue than they'd been when he first came here.

"Vacation?" Semler said. "Why, not in a good while, sir. My wife went away—" he dreamed over it for a moment. "She went to Cape Cod for two weeks last summer. She told me about it—the surf and the sand dunes. I meant to get up for a week end"—he glanced down at the glass slide in the palm of his gloved hand—"but you know how it is—"

Yes, Carlyle knew. But a feeling of guilt so poignant that it seemed almost too much to bear, seemed to take his heart and twist it. For he had never known until today that Semler had a wife. He didn't know where the man lived, where he had been born, who his parents were; what fears or doubts or dreams lived with him in his private world. He had never, in the three years they'd worked together, even asked after Semler's health.

If Semler was ill, it meant lost time on an experiment. Little more. But oh, how much he had looked past in this young assistant of his! How vulnerable Semler was—how lost and life-hungry!

"I'm arranging for you to leave for a month's vacation," Carlyle said now. "You must put your work aside and take time off. You'll come back with a fresh viewpoint, Semler. You'll see."

Semler set the slide down. His fingers in the gleaming rubber gloves trembled a bit: "But we're so close to the serum we're looking for," he protested. "Another week —another month, and we'll have it!

343

764X, sir, may even be the one—"

Carlyle's arm had begun to throb a little, and the swelling, though still scarcely perceptible, had fanned out now in a slightly larger area. He smiled at Semler—a strange dry smile.

"Haven't we always been close to the answer, Semler? Hasn't it always been another week? Another month? Another year—while life slipped by and all the things we promised ourselves slipped by with it? Don't wait! Take your vacation while you're young and there's still time." He turned his back to conceal the emotion he knew must show in his face.

When he'd regained control of his voice again, he said evenly, "I've some business to attend. I'm taking the day off. Tomorrow—" he chose the words carefully—"tomorrow I may be called away. All my latest findings are there, Semler, if you need to refer to them. On the last page of my notebook."

He held out his hand briefly, and shook Semler's gloved one: "Carry on!" his soul whispered. Then he turned and hurried down the dark, soundless corridor.

Outside, the spring sun shone warmly on his back, and as he made his way along the crowded street, the very air seemed to seduce him.

Had spring ever been so gentle, so endearing before? Had every little scene, every shop window, every face he passed ever been so wonderfully interesting? Yes, there was a time . . . He struggled to remember. And he knew suddenly when it had been . . . the year he'd fallen in love. That gave him the answer. Now that he must leave it, he had fallen in love with life.

At Sixty-second Street he hailed a cab and gave the driver his home address. It would take a little explaining; coming home this way when he'd planned just to take a short nap in the laboratory and work the rest of the day. But he'd figure it out some way. Spring fever, he'd call it. He smiled. Life-fever, that's what it came closer to being.

He stared out the cab window all the way home, pressed forward in the seat, so that when the cab stopped suddenly, he was jolted against the door. Had the forsythia bloomed this morning? Why hadn't he seen it? And the grass along the drive—it couldn't have gotten green in a single day!

Almost, it seemed, fate was mocking him. And yet he knew that was not true. His blind past was mocking this brief stretch of present.

When she heard his ring at the door, his wife came running. "Roy," she called out, "Roy is anything wrong?"

He stood on the threshold and watched her open the door to him. Mary, his wife. Just so, she had opened her life to him ten years ago. Mary, with her soft hair—like a wreath of golden sunlight—and her blue eyes which still could look at him as if he contained her world.

He caught her against him, soundlessly, wordlessly, and rocked her for a moment.

She struggled in his arms: "Roy, Roy," she cried, "something's gone wrong—terribly wrong! My darling, what is it?"

He felt the trembling deep inside him, the terrible trembling. For of all the bonds which held him to life, this was the strongest, the deepest.

How could he kiss her for the last

time—knowing it was the last?

"Nothing's wrong," he managed. "Only that it's spring, and I decided to take a day off. I promised Felice I'd take her to the park. Where's Felice?"

At the mention of her name, his little girl bounded in from the back room.

"Daddy!" she cried and flung herself upon him. "Daddy-daddy-daddy!"

Was that how it had always sounded, the funny little music of her voice, the sound of his name when she said it? Had her hair always been this way to his touch—silken and smelling of soap?

He caught her under her arms and swung her high in the air, so that her starched dress fanned out behind her. "How's my big girl?" he asked, searching her dancing gray eyes. She hung around his neck, kicking and laughing—overjoyed at this surprise visit at the start of a routine day.

"We're going to the park," he announced. "Remember, Felice—I promised I'd take you—oh, a long time ago?"

Three years ago? Yes, three long springs ago, when Semler had first come to him to work on 124X and they'd thought they would have the answer with 125X.

"We'll buy you a balloon," he'd promised Felice, "any color you want, and we'll have lunch outside, under the big umbrellas. How will you like that?"

She'd sobbed with joy and sung that wonderful song—that wonderful, wonderful song that went: "Oh, Daddy-daddy-daddy!"

And he'd let three years slip by. 124X, 125X—like stones around his neck, they'd weighted his whole life.

Why hadn't he stolen a day—an hour of all that time? He never would have missed it!

"Hurry now," he told Felice. "Put on your hat and button your pink coat. We're all three going. You and Mother and I—"

Hurry now, hurry now. Only a few more hours were left to him.

Hurry downstairs, hurry into the cab. Hurry down bright Fifth Avenue, where the sun glints on taxicab-roofs, and the nursemaids are pushing little pink-blanketed bundles with rattles swinging above them and a whole life to spend. Hurry now, hurry now. But see everything. Love everything. Taste and enjoy and exult in everything.

Oh, this is the way he should always have felt; through all the drab, weighted days when he had worried over the rent, his work, a rude word from a cabbie—when he had wasted time. Time, which was life's elixir.

He took Mary's hand in his. He must remember, remember like a lesson he'd learned, not to press her hand too hard. Not to say anything that would let her know. She would know soon—much too soon, anyway.

They took one of the rowboats and sailed across the lagoon, Felice in one end and Mary in the other. It was so calm that all the buildings of Manhattan looked down and preened themselves in the water, and the proud white swans seemed to slip by on glass.

Felice had a lollipop, and she hung off the back of the rowboat, trailing her hand in the water, laughing and showing her starched white petticoat. Oh, it was a beautiful ride!

But the sun was climbing, climb-

345

ing. And his arm had swollen so that very often now, he would have to rest the oars.

Mary moved back in the boat and put her head on his shoulder. He did not tell her that his shoulder had begun to ache, or that he felt tired. Because the weariness was a symptom and he knew it. The more tired he felt, the less time there was left to him.

And he did not tell Felice that the merry-go-round was a terrible effort, and when he climbed up on the child-sized black horse, he felt he had climbed a mountain.

And when three o'clock drew near, and he knew that he must go home, must make them take him home—he tried to sit straight in the cab. He tried to forget about the white mice and how they had died in their cages, and to concentrate, instead, on this day—this golden day of spring which had been the best of his whole life.

He thought he was doing well at it, even in the elevator. . . . And then, just as Mary put her key in the lock, he heard her scream his name, and he felt his head strike the door. . . .

The lost thread of time came back to him slowly, and with it came consciousness, heavy and smothering. Something was reaching for him—black, formless, awful. He sank again. Then he saw the white blur of a room and heard someone's name being called. It was a moment before he knew it

was his own name . . . Mary's voice calling him.

When he forced open his eyes, he saw Semler, bending over him, breathing heavily—his eyes pale behind his thick-lensed glasses. "You're going to be all right, sir," Semler managed. "They told us so —this morning."

This morning? What morning? And suddenly, startlingly, while he struggled to remember, Semler fell on his knees beside the bed. "763X," he gasped, "Doctor Carlyle, it's fatal to the test animals, but it can be used on human beings. Do you know what that means, sir? It means we're on the brink—on the brink of our great discovery!"

Carlyle endeavored to piece the words together; slowly, with a great effort. 763X! Like a key in a lock, it swung back the door of memory. The terrible moment after the injection when he realized what he'd done . . . the dawn . . . and the way the sky had looked . . . Semler, that new Semler he had never quite known before . . . the street . . . the sweet smell of spring and life . . . Mary . . . Felice . . . the lagoon . . . and now . . . perhaps, the great discovery!

He smiled, a wan smile, and motioned Semler closer. "Tell them—" he began, and then shook his head and fell silent. For the world would not be interested in his greatest discovery. The one he'd made yesterday. That every day should be lived as if it were the last day—the last day on earth.

SPORTSMANSHIP
William Makepeace Thackeray

And in the world as in the school,
  You know how Fate may turn and shift;
The prize be sometimes to the fool,
  The race not always to the swift.
Who misses or who gains the prize,
  Go, lose or conquer as you can;
But if you fall or if you rise,
  Be each, pray God, a gentleman.

THE BEST ROAD OF ALL
Charles Hanson Towne

I like a road that leads away to prospects white and fair,
A road that is an ordered road, like a nun's evening prayer;
But, best of all, I love a road that leads to God knows where.

You come upon it suddenly—you cannot seek it out;
It's like a secret still unheard and never noised about;
But when you see it, gone at once is every lurking doubt.

It winds beside some rushing stream where aspens lightly quiver;
It follows many a broken field by many a shining river;
It seems to lead you on and on, forever and forever!

You tramp along its dusty way, beneath its shadowy trees,
And hear beside you chattering birds or happy booming bees,
And all around you golden sounds, the green leaves' litanies.

And here's a hedge, and there's a cot; and then—strange, sudden
    turns—
A dip, a rise, a little glimpse where the red sunset burns;
A bit of sky at evening time, the scent of hidden ferns.

A winding road, a loitering road, a finger-mark of God
Traced when the Maker of the world leaned over ways untrod.
See! Here He smiled His glowing smile, and lo, the goldenrod!

I like a road that wanders straight; the King's highway is fair,
And lovely are the sheltered lanes that take you here and there;
But, best of all, I love a road that leads to God knows where.

347

REFUGE

LEW SARETT

When stars ride in on the wings of dusk,
  Out on the silent plain,
After the fevered fret of day,
  I find my strength again.

Under the million friendly eyes
  That smile in the lonely night,
Close to the rolling prairie's heart,
  I find my heart for the fight.

Out where the cool long winds blow free,
  I fling myself on the sod;
And there in the tranquil solitude
  I find my soul—and God.

IN THE NIGHT

STEPHEN CRANE

In the night
Grey heavy clouds muffled the valleys,
And the peaks looked toward God alone.
  'O Master, that movest the wind with a finger,
Humble, idle, futile peaks are we.
Grant that we may run swiftly across the world
To huddle in worship at Thy feet.'

In the morning
A noise of men at work came the clear blue miles,
And the little black cities were apparent.
  'O Master, that knowest the meaning of raindrops,
Humble, idle, futile peaks are we.
Give voice to us, we pray, O Lord,
That we may sing Thy goodness to the sun.'

In the evening
The far valleys were sprinkled with tiny lights.
  'O Master,
Thou that knowest the value of kings and birds,
Thou hast made us humble, idle, futile peaks.
Thou only needst eternal patience;

348

We bow to Thy wisdom, O Lord—
Humble, idle, futile peaks.'

In the night
Grey heavy clouds muffled the valleys,
And the peaks looked toward God alone.

EARTH LOVER
Harold Vinal

Old loveliness has such a way with me,
   That I am close to tears when petals fall
   And needs must hide my face behind a wall,
When autumn trees burn red with ecstasy.
For I am haunted by a hundred things
   And more than I have seen in April days;
   I have worn stars above my head in praise,
I have worn beauty as two costly rings.

Alas, how short a state does beauty keep,
   Then let me clasp it wildly to my heart
   And hurt myself until I am a part
Of all its rapture, then turn back to sleep.
   Remembering through all the dusty years
   What sudden wonder brought me close to tears.

RULES FOR THE ROAD
Edwin Markham

Stand straight;
Step firmly, throw your weight:
The heaven is high above your head
And the good gray road is faithful to your tread.

Be strong:
Sing to your heart a battle song:
Though hidden foemen lie in wait,
Something is in you that can smile at Fate.

Press through:
Nothing can harm if you are true.
And when the night comes, rest:
The earth is friendly as a mother's breast.

FROM THE ENGLISH

NATURE is the art of God.—*Sir Thomas Browne*

CHIEFLY, the mould of a man's fortune is in his own hands.
—*Bacon*

CENSURE is the tax man pays to the public for being eminent.—*Swift*

ASK COUNSEL of both times: of the ancient time what is best; and of the latter time what is fittest.—*Bacon*

TRUE POLITENESS is perfect ease and freedom. It simply consists in treating others just as you love to be treated yourself.—*Chesterfield*

ONE CAN NOT eat one's cake and have it too. Those who elect to be free in thought and deed must not hanker after the rewards, if they are to be so called, which the world offers to those who put up with its fetters.
—*Thomas H. Huxley*

IF THOU believest a thing impossible, thy despondency shall make it so; but he that persevereth, shall overcome all difficulties.—*Chesterfield*

IF WE begin with certainties, we shall end in doubts; but if we begin with doubts, and are patient in them, we shall end in certainties.
—*Bacon*

IT IS thy duty therefore to be a friend to mankind, as it is thy interest that man should be friendly to thee.—*Chesterfield*

THEY BUILD NOT castles in the air who would build churches on earth: and though they leave no such structures here, may lay good foundations in Heaven.—*Sir Thomas Browne*

EXAMPLE is the school of mankind, and they will learn at no other.
—*Burke*

GOOD ORDER is the foundation of all good things.—*Burke*

PHILOSOPHERS

THE FIRST STEP to greatness is to be honest.—*Johnson*

YOU MUST LOOK into people as well as at them.—*Chesterfield*

GOOD MANNERS is the art of making those people easy with whom we converse.—*Swift*

A NOBLE SPIRIT disdaineth the malice of fortune; his greatness of soul is not cast down.—*Chesterfield*

EVERYTHING that enlarges the sphere of human powers, that shows man he can do what he thought he could not do, is valuable.—*Johnson*

WE CANNOT LOOK, however imperfectly, upon a great man without gaining something by him. He is the living light-fountain, which it is good and pleasant to be near.—*Carlyle*

THE MOST ILLITERATE MAN who is touched with devotion, and uses frequent exercises of it, contracts a certain greatness of mind, mingled with a noble simplicity, that raises him above others of the same condition. By this, a man in the lowest condition will not appear mean, or in the most splendid fortune insolent.—*Johnson*

FROM THE EXPERIENCE of others, do thou learn wisdom: and from their failings, correct thine own faults.—*Chesterfield*

IT IS in men as in soils where sometimes there is a vein of gold which the owner knows not of.—*Swift*

IF A MAN be gracious and courteous to strangers, it shows he is a citizen of the world.—*Bacon*

IF I have done the public any service, it is due to patient thought.—*Newton*

FEW THINGS are impossible to diligence and skill.—*Johnson*

The Deep-Sea Doctor*

By MARY R. PARKMAN

$\mathcal{W}$HEN PEOPLE MEET Dr. Grenfell, the good doctor who braves the storms of the most dangerous of all seacoasts and endures the hardships of arctic winters to care for the lonely fisherfolk of Labrador, they often ask, with pitying wonder:

"How do you manage it, Doctor, day in and day out through all the long months? It seems too much for any man to sacrifice himself as you do."

"Don't think for a moment that I'm a martyr," replies Dr. Grenfell, a bit impatiently. "Why, I have a jolly good time of it! There's nothing like a really good scrimmage to make a fellow sure that he's alive, and glad of it. I learned that in my football days, and Labrador gives even better chances to know the joy of winning out in a tingling good tussle."

Dr. Grenfell's face, with the warm color glowing through the tan, his clear, steady eyes, and erect, vigorous form, all testify to his keen zest in the adventure of life. Ever since he could remember, he had, he told us, been in love with the thrill of strenuous action. When a small boy, he looked at the tiger-skin and other trophies of the hunt which his soldier uncles had sent from India, and dreamed of the time when he should learn the ways of the jungle at first hand.

He comes of a race of strong men. One uncle was a general who bore himself with distinguished gallantry in the Indian Mutiny at Lucknow when the little garrison of seventeen hundred men held the city for twelve weeks against a besieging force ten times as great. One of his father's ancestors was Sir Richard Grenville, the hero of the *Revenge*, who, desperately struggling to save his wounded men, fought with his one ship against the whole Spanish fleet of fifty-three. Perhaps you remember Tennyson's thrilling lines:

And the stately Spanish men to their
    flagship bore him then,
Where they laid him by the mast,
    old Sir Richard caught at last,
And they praised him to his face
    with their courtly foreign
    grace;
But he rose upon their decks, and
    he cried:
"I have fought for Queen and Faith
    like a valiant man and true;
I have only done my duty as a
    man is bound to do;
With a joyful spirit I, Sir Richard
    Grenville, die!"

How .these lines sang in his memory! Is it any wonder that the lad who heard this story as one among many thrilling tales of his own people should have felt that life was a splendid adventure?

As a boy in his home at Parkgate,

*From HEROES OF TODAY by Mary R. Parkman, copyright, 1916, 1917, by the CENTURY COMPANY, 1945, by Lawrence Koenigsberger and Cornelia Whitney, reprinted by permission of D. APPLETON-CENTURY COMPANY, INC.

near Chester, England, he was early accustomed to strenuous days in the open. He knew the stretches of sand-banks,—the famous "Sands of Dee,"—with their deep, intersecting "gutters" where many curlews, mallards, and other water-birds sought hiding. In his rocking home-made boat he explored from end to end the estuary into which the River Dee flowed, now and again hailing a fishing-smack for a tow home, if evening fell too soon, and sharing with the crew their supper of boiled shrimps. He seemed to know as by instinct the moods of the tides and storm-vexed waves, which little boats must learn to watch and circumvent. He became a lover, also, of wild nature—birds, animals, and plants—and of simple, vigorous men who lived rough, wholesome lives in the open.

Though he went from the boys' school at Parkgate to Marlborough College, and later to Oxford, he had at this time no hint of the splendid adventures that life offers in the realm of mental and spiritual activities. Rugby football, in which he did his share to uphold the credit of the university, certainly made the most vital part of this chapter of his life. It was not until he took up the study of medicine at the London Hospital that he began to appreciate the value of knowledge "because it enables one to do things."

There was one day of this study-time in London that made a change in the young doctor's whole life. Partly out of curiosity, he followed a crowd in the poorer part of the city, into a large tent, where a religious meeting was being held. In a moment he came to realize that his religion had been just a matter of believing as he was taught, of conducting himself as did those about him, and of going to church on Sunday. It seemed that here, however, were men to whom religion was as real and practical a thing as the rudder is to a boat. All at once he saw what it would mean to have a strong guiding power in one's life.

His mind seemed wonderfully set free. There were no longer conflicting aims, ideals, uncertainties, and misgivings. There was one purpose, one desire—to enter "the service that is perfect freedom," the service of the King of Kings. Life was indeed a glorious adventure, whose meaning was plain and whose end sure.

How he enjoyed his class of unruly boys from the slums! Most people would have considered them hopeless "toughs." He saw that they were just active boys, eager for life, who had been made what they were by unwholesome surroundings. "All they need is to get hold of the rudder and to feel the breath of healthy living in their faces," he said. He fitted up one of his rooms with gymnasium material and taught the boys to box. He took them for outings into the country. When he saw the way they responded to this little chance for happy activity, he became one of the founders of the Lads' Brigades and Lads' Camps, which have done the same sort of good in England that the Boy Scouts organization has done in this country.

When he completed his medical course, the young doctor looked about for a field that would give chance for adventure and for service where a physician was really needed.

353

"I feel there is something for me besides hanging out my sign in a city where there are already doctors and to spare," he said.

"Why don't you see what can be done with a hospital ship among the North Sea fishermen?" said Sir Frederick Treves, who was a great surgeon and a master mariner as well.

When Dr. Grenfell heard about how sick and injured men suffered for lack of care when on their long fishing expeditions, he decided to fall in with this suggestion. He joined the staff of the Mission to Deep Sea Fishermen, and fitted out the first hospital ship to the North Sea fisheries, which cruised about from the Bay of Biscay to Iceland, giving medical aid where it was often desperately needed.

When this work was well established, and other volunteers offered to take it up, Dr. Grenfell sought a new world of adventure. Hearing of the forlorn condition of the English-speaking settlers and natives on the remote shores of wind-swept Labrador, he resolved to fit out a hospital ship and bring them what help he could. So began in 1892 Dr. Grenfell's great work with his schooner *Albert*, in which he cruised about for three months and ministered to nine hundred patients, who, but for him, would have had no intelligent care.

Can you picture Labrador as something more than a pink patch on the cold part of the map? That strip of coast northwest of Newfoundland is a land of sheer cliffs broken by deep fiords, like much of Norway. Rocky islands and hidden reefs make the shores dangerous to ships in the terrific gales that are of frequent occurrence. But this for-bidding, wreck-strewn land of wild, jutting crags has a weird beauty of its own. Picture it in winter when the deep snow has effaced all inequalities of surface and the dark spruces alone stand out against the gleaming whiteness. The fiords and streams are bound in an icy silence which holds the sea itself in thrall. Think of the colors of the moonlight on the ice, and the flaming splendor of the northern lights. Then picture it when summer has unloosed the land from the frozen spell. Mosses, brilliant lichens, and bright berries cover the rocky ground, the evergreens stand in unrivaled freshness, and gleaming trout and salmon dart out of the water, where great icebergs go floating by like monster fragments of the crystal city of the frost giants, borne along now by the arctic current to tell the world about the victory of the sun over the powers of cold in the far North.

When Dr. Grenfell sailed about in the *Albert* that first summer, the people thought he was some strange, big-hearted madman, who bore a charmed life. He seemed to know nothing and care nothing about foamy reefs, unfamiliar tides and currents, and treacherous winds. When it was impossible to put out in the schooner, he went in a whaleboat, which was worn out—honorably discharged from service —after a single season. The people who guarded the lives of their watercraft with jealous care shook their heads. Truly, the man must be mad. His boat was capsized, swamped, blown on the rocks, and once driven out to sea by a gale that terrified the crew of the solidly built mailboat. This time he was reported lost, but after a few days he appeared in the harbor of St. John's, face aglow, and eyes fairly snapping with the zest of the conflict.

"Sure, the Lord must kape an eye on that man," said an old skipper, devoutly.

It was often said of a gale on the Labrador coast, "That's a wind that'll bring Grenfell." The doctor, impatient of delays, and feeling the same exhilaration in a good stiff breeze that a lover of horses feels in managing a spirited thoroughbred, never failed to make use of a wind that might help send him on his way.

What sort of people are these to whom Dr. Grenfell ministers? They are, as you might think, simple, hardy men, in whom ceaseless struggle against bleak conditions of life has developed strength of character, and capacity to endure. Besides the scattered groups of Eskimos in the north, who live by hunting seal and walrus, and the Indians who roam the interior in search of furs, there are some seven or eight thousand English-speaking inhabitants widely scattered along the coast. In summer as many as thirty thousand fishermen are drawn from Newfoundland and Nova Scotia to share in the profit of the cod and salmon fisheries. All of these people were practically without medical care before Dr. Grenfell came. Can you imagine what this meant? This is the story of one fisherman in his own words:

"I had a poisoned finger. It rose up and got very bad. I did not know what to do, so I took a passage on a schooner and went to Halifax. It was nine months before I was able to get back, as there was no boat going back before the winter. It cost me seventy-five dollars, and my hand was the same as useless, as it was so long before it was treated."

Another told of having to wait nine days after "shooting his hand" before he could reach a doctor; and he had made the necessary journey in remarkably good time at that. He did not know if he ought to thank the doctor for saving his life when it was too late to save his hand. What can a poor fisherman do without a hand?

The chief sources of danger to these people who live by the food of the sea are the uncertain winds and the treacherous ice floes. When the ice begins to break in spring, the swift currents move great masses along with terrific force. Then woe betide the rash schooner that ventures into the path of these ice rafts! For a moment she pushes her way among the floating "pans" or cakes of ice. All at once the terrible jam comes. The schooner is caught like a rat in a trap. The jaws of the ice monster never relax, while the timbers of the vessel crack and splinter and the solid deck-beams arch up, bow fashion, and snap like so many straws. Then, perhaps, the pressure changes. With a sudden shift of the wind a rift comes between the huge ice masses, and the sea swallows its prey.

It is a strange thing that but few of the fishermen know how to swim. "You see, we has enough o' the water without goin' to bother wi' it when we *are* ashore," one old skipper told the doctor in explanation.

The only means of rescue when one finds himself in the water is a line or a pole held by friends until a boat can be brought to the scene. Many stories might be told of the bravery of these people and their instant willingness to serve each other. Once a girl, who saw her brother fall through a hole in the ice, ran swiftly to the spot, while the men who were trying to reach the place with their boat shouted to her to go back. Stretching full length, however, on the gradually sinking ice, she held on to her brother till the boat forced its way to them.

Perhaps the most terrible experience that has come to the brave doctor was caused by the ice floes. It was on Easter Sunday in 1908 when word came to the hospital that a boy was very ill in a little village sixty miles away. The doctor at once got his "komatik," or dog sledge, in readiness and his splendid team of eight dogs, who had often carried him through many tight places. Brin, the leader, was the one who could be trusted to keep the trail when all signs and landmarks were covered by snow and ice. There were also Doc, Spy, Jack, Sue, Jerry, Watch, and Moody—each no less beloved for his own strong points and faithful service.

It was while crossing an arm of the sea, a ten-mile run on salt-water ice, that the accident occurred. An unusually heavy sea had left great openings between enormous blocks or "pans" of ice a little to seaward. It seemed, however, that the doctor could be sure of a safe passage on an ice bridge, that though rough, was firmly packed, while the stiff sea-breeze was making it stronger moment by moment through driving the floating pans toward the shore. But all at once there came a sudden change in the wind. It began to blow from the land, and in a moment the doctor realized that his ice bridge had broken asunder and the portion on which he found himself was separated by a widening chasm from the rest. He was adrift on an ice pan.

It all happened so quickly that he was unable to do anything but cut the harness of the dogs to keep them from being tangled in the traces and dragged down after the sled. He found himself soaking wet, his sledge, with his extra clothing, gone, and only the remotest chance of being seen from the lonely shore and rescued. If only water had separated him from the bank, he might have tried swimming, but, for the most part, between the floating pans was "slob ice," that is, ice broken into tiny bits by the grinding together of the huge masses.

Night came, and with it such intense cold that he was obliged to sacrifice three of his dogs and clothe himself in their skins to keep from freezing, for coat, hat, and gloves had been lost in the first struggle to gain a place on the largest available "pan" of ice. Then, curled up among the remaining dogs, and so, somewhat protected from the bitter wind, he fell asleep.

When daylight came, he took off his gaily-colored shirt, which was a relic of his football days, and, with the leg bones of the slain dogs as a pole, constructed a flag of distress. The warmth of the sun brought cheer; and so, even though his reason told him that there was but the smallest chance of being seen, he stood up and waved his flag steadily until too weary to make another move. Every time he sat down for a moment of rest, "Doc" came and licked his face and then went to the edge of the ice, as if to suggest it was high time to start.

At last Dr. Grenfell thought he saw the gleam of an oar. He could hardly believe his eyes, which were, indeed, almost snow-blinded, as his dark glasses had been lost with all his other things. Then—yes—surely there was the keel of a boat, and a man waving to him! In a moment came the blessed sound of a friendly voice.

Now that the struggle was over, he felt himself lifted into the boat as in a dream. In the same way he swallowed the hot tea which they had brought in a bottle. This is what one of the rescuers said, in telling about it afterward:

"When we got near un, it didn't seem like 't was the doctor. 'E looked so old an' 'is face such a queer color. 'E was very solemn-like when us took un an' the dogs in th' boat. Th' first thing 'e said was how wonderfu' sorry 'e was o' gettin' into such a mess an' givin' we th' trouble o' comin' out for un. Then 'e fretted about the b'y 'e was goin' to see, it bein' too late to reach un, and us to' un 'is life was worth more 'n the b'y, fur 'e could save others. But 'e still fretted."

They had an exciting time of it, reaching the shore. Sometimes they had to jump out and force the ice pans apart; again, when the wind packed the blocks together too close, they had to drag the boat over.

When the bank was gained at last and the doctor dressed in the warm clothes that the fishermen wear, they got a sledge ready to take him to the hospital, where his frozen hands and feet could be treated. There, too, the next day the sick boy was brought, and his life saved.

Afterward, in telling of his experience, the thing which moved the doctor most was the sacrifice of his dogs. In his hallway a bronze tablet was placed with this inscription:

TO THE MEMORY OF
THREE NOBLE DOGS
MOODY
WATCH
SPY
WHOSE LIVES WERE GIVEN
FOR MINE ON THE ICE
APRIL 21ST, 1908
WILFRED GRENFELL

In his old home in England his brother put up a similar tablet, adding these words, "Not one of them is forgotten before your Father which is in heaven."

Besides caring for the people himself, Dr. Grenfell won the interest of other workers — doctors, nurses, and teachers. Through his efforts, hospitals, schools, and orphan-asylums have been built. Of all the problems, however, with which this large-hearted, practical friend of the deep-sea fishermen has had to deal in his Labrador work, perhaps the chief was that of the dire poverty of the people. It seemed idle to try to cure men of ills which were the direct result of conditions under which they lived.

When the doctor began his work in 1892 he found that the poverty-stricken people were practically at the mercy of unprincipled, scheming storekeepers who charged two or three prices for flour, salt, and other necessaries of life. The men, as a result, were always in debt, mortgaging their next summer's catch of fish long before the winter was over. To cure this evil, Grenfell opened co-operative stores, run solely for the benefit of the fishermen, and established industries that would give a chance of employment during the cold months. A grant of timberland was obtained from the government and a lumbermill opened. A schooner-building yard, and a cooperage for making kegs and barrels to hold the fish exported, were next installed.

This made it possible to gather together the people, who were formerly widely scattered because dependent on food gained through hunting and trapping. This made it possible, too, to carry out plans for general improvement—schools for the children and some social life. Two small jails, no longer needed in this capacity, were converted into clubs, with libraries and games. Realizing the general need for healthful recreation, the doctor introduced rubber footballs, which might be used in the snow. The supply of imported articles could not keep pace with the demand, however. All along the coast, young and old joined in the game. Even the Eskimo women, with wee babies in their hoods, played with their brown-faced boys and girls, using sealskin balls stuffed with dry grass.

Knowing that Labrador can never hope to do much in agriculture, as even the cabbages and potatoes frequently suffer through summer frosts, the doctor tried to add to the resources of the country by introducing a herd of reindeer from Lapland, together with three families of Lapps to teach the people how to care for them. Reindeer milk is rich and makes good cheese. Moreover, the supply of meat and leather they provide is helping to make up for the falling-off in the number of seals, due to unrestricted hunting. The trans-portation afforded by the reindeer is also important in a land where rapid transit consists of dog sledges.

Dr. Grenfell has himself financed his various schemes, using, in addition to gifts from those whom he can interest, the entire income gained from his books and lectures. He keeps nothing for himself but the small salary as mission doctor to pay actual living expenses. All of the industrial enterprises—cooperative stores, sawmills, reindeer, fox-farms, are deeded to the Deep-Sea Mission, and become its property as soon as they begin to be profitable.

Would you like to spend a day with Dr. Grenfell in summer, when he cruises about in his hospital ship three or four thousand miles back and forth, from St. John's all along the Labrador coast? You would see what a wonderful pilot the doctor is as he faces the perils of hidden reefs, icebergs, fogs, and storms. You would see that he can doctor his ship, should it leak or the propeller go lame, as well as the numbers of people who come to him with every sort of ill from aching teeth to broken bones.

Perhaps, though, you might prefer a fine, crisp day in winter. Then you could drive forty or fifty miles in the komatik, getting off to run when you feel a bit stiff with the cold, especially if it happens to be uphill. You might be tempted to coast down the hills, but you find that dogs can't stand that any more than horses could, so you let down the "drug" (a piece of iron chain) to block the runners. There is no sound except the lone twitter of a venturesome tomtit who decided to risk the winter in a particularly thick spruce tree. Sometimes you

358

go bumpity-bump over fallen trees, with pitfalls between, lightly covered with snow. Sometimes the dogs bound ahead eagerly over smooth ground where the only signs of the times are the occasional tracks of a rabbit, partridge, fox, or caribou. Then how you will enjoy the dinner of hot toasted pork cakes before the open fire, after the excitement of feeding the ravenous dogs with huge pieces of frozen seal-meat and seeing them burrow down under the snow for their night's sleep. If there is no pressing need of his services next morning, the doctor may take you skiing, or show you how to catch trout through a hole in the ice.

Winter or summer, perhaps you might come to agree with Dr. Grenfell that one may have "a jolly good time" while doing a man's work in rough, out-of-the-way Labrador. You would, at any rate, have a chance to discover that life may be a splendid adventure.

❖ ❖ ❖

A LEGACY

JOHN GREENLEAF WHITTIER

Friend of my many years!
When the great silence falls, at last, on me,
Let me not leave, to pain and sadden thee,
 A memory of tears,

But pleasant thoughts alone
Of one who was thy friendship's honored guest
And drank the wine of consolation pressed
 From sorrows of thy own.

I leave with thee a sense
Of hands upheld and trials rendered less—
The unselfish joy which is to helpfulness
 Its own great recompense;

The knowledge that from thine,
As from the garments of the Master, stole
Calmness and strength, the virtue which makes whole
 And heals without a sign;

Yea more, the assurance strong
That love, which fails of perfect utterance here,
Lives on to fill the heavenly atmosphere
 With its immortal song.

AS TREES
GAIL BROOK BURKET

Let me grow old as trees grow old, dear Lord,
With pliant boughs, made resolute and strong
By wrestling storms, extended to afford
The welcome shade which shelters woodland song.
As trees are harps for every breeze, keep me
Attuned to life. As trees are havens, give
My days the joy of constant ministry
To human need so long as I shall live.
As trees put forth green leaves for every spring,
Let me renew my hope throughout the years.
As trees become more stalwart, let age bring
Adversity unmarred by sapling fears.
Let me greet death, when it is time to die,
With valiant head uplifted to the sky.

THE FAITH OF A GRANDMOTHER
A. WARREN

She was so comforted to die
Because she knew
That she would be with him;
That, if he had attained a lofty sky,
He would come back for her and raise her too;
Because she knew, as life grew dim,
They would not grope in strange worlds, mystified,
But find each other soon—though Death prove wide!

TESTAMENT
JOHN HOLMES

There are too many poems with the word
Death, death, death, tolling among the rhyme.
Let us remember death, a soaring bird
Whose wing will shadow all of us in time.

Let us remember death, an accident
Of darkness fallen far away and near.
But, being mortal, be most eloquent
Of daylight and the moment now and here.

Not to the name of death over and over,
But the prouder name of life, is poetry sworn.
The living man has words that rediscover
Even the dust from whence the man was born,

And words that may be water, food, and fire,
Of love and pity and perfection wrought,
Or swords or roses, as we may require,
Or sudden towers for the climbing thought.

Out of the beating heart the words that beat
Sing of the fountain that is never spent.
Let us remember life, the salt, the sweet,
And make of that our tireless testament.

SUNDOWN

BERT LESTON TAYLOR (B.L.T.)

When my sun of life is low,
   When the dewy shadows creep,
Say for me before I go,
   "Now I lay me down to sleep."

I am at the journey's end,
   I have sown and I must reap;
There are no more ways to mend—
   Now I lay me down to sleep,

Nothing more to doubt or dare,
   Nothing more to give or keep:
Say for me the children's prayer,
   "Now I lay me down to sleep."

Who has learned along the way—
   Primrose path or stony steep—
More of wisdom than to say,
   "Now I lay me down to sleep"?

What have you more wise to tell
   When the shadows round me creep? ...
All is over, all is well ...
   Now I lay me down to sleep.

Is HE DEAD whose glorious mind
Lifts thine on high?
To live in hearts we leave behind
Is not to die.
—Campbell

TO BE TRUSTED is a greater compliment than
to be loved.*—Macdonald*

As YOU GROW ready for it, somewhere or other you will find what
is needful for you, in a book, or a friend, or, best of all, in
your own thoughts, the eternal thought speaking in your thought.
—Macdonald

WHEN HE understood it, he called for his friends, and told them of it.
Then said he, 'I am going to my Father's; and though with great difficulty
I have got hither, yet now I do not regret me of all the trouble I have
been at to arrive where I am. My sword I give to him that shall succeed me in
my pilgrimage, and my courage and skill to him that can get it. My marks and
scars I carry with me, to be a witness for me that I have fought His battle
who will now be my rewarder.' When the day that he must go hence was
come, many accompanied him to the river-side, into which as he went, he said,
'Death, where is thy sting?' And as he went down deeper, he said,
'Grave, where is thy victory?' So he passed over, and all the trumpets sounded
for him on the other side.*—Bunyan*

THE FIRST TIME I read an excellent book, it is to me just as if
I had gained a new friend. When I read over a book I have perused
before, it resembles the meeting with an old one.*—Goldsmith*

THEY'RE only truly great who are truly good.*—Chapman*

CHARMS strike the sight, but merit wins the soul.*—Pope*

HE FEARLESS STANDS; he knows whom he doth trust:
Strange strength resideth in the soul that's just.
—Drayton

MAN'S RANK is his power to uplift.*—Macdonald*

Do IT that very moment!
Don't put it off—don't wait.
There's no use in doing a kindness
If you do it a day too late!
    —Kingsley

LIFE must be measured by thought and action,
not by time.*—Lubbock*

WHAT SUNSHINE is to flowers, smiles are to humanity. They are
but trifles, to be sure; but, scattered along life's pathway, the good
they do is inconceivable.*—Addison*

OH, BE at least able to say in that day,—Lord, I am no hero. I have
been careless, cowardly, sometimes all but mutinous. Punishment I have
deserved, I deny it not. But a traitor I have never been; a deserter
I have never been. I have tried to fight on Thy side in Thy battle
against evil. I have tried to do the duty which lay nearest me; and to
leave whatever Thou didst commit to my charge a little better than I
found it. I have not been good, but I have at least tried to be good.
Take the will for the deed, good Lord. Strike not my unworthy name off
the roll-call of the noble and victorious army, which is the blessed
company of all faithful people; and let me, too, be found written in
the Book of Life; even though I stand the lowest and last upon its list.
Amen.*—Kingsley*

GOOD INTENTIONS are, at least, the seed of good actions; and
every one ought to sow them, and leave it to the soil and the
seasons whether he or any other gather the fruit.*—Temple*

GROWING THOUGHT makes growing revelation.*—George Eliot*

HEALTH AND CHEERFULNESS mutually beget each other.*—Addison*

UNLESS above himself he can
Erect himself, how poor a thing is man!
    —Daniel

THERE IS a majesty in simplicity.*—Pope*

from Good-bye, Mr. Chips

By JAMES HILTON

"GOOD-BYE, MR. CHIPS *was written more quickly, more easily, and with fewer subsequent alterations than anything I had ever written before, or have ever written since," writes James Hilton.*

This tender, inspired story of the English schoolmaster, Mr. Chips, his beloved wife Katherine, and the boys at the Brookfield school has charmed and stirred the hearts of all. Our selections begin with Chips, a young man of 68, about to end his retirement and resume teaching Latin to "his boys" during war years. So . . . hello, again, Mr. Chips!

1916 . . . THE SOMME BATTLE.

Twenty-three names read out one Sunday evening.

Toward the close of that catastrophic July, Chatteris talked to Chips one afternoon at Mrs. Wickett's. He was overworked and over-worried and looked very ill. "To tell you the truth, Chipping, I'm not having too easy a time here. I'm thirty-nine, you know, and unmarried, and lots of people seem to think they know what I ought to do. Also, I happen to be diabetic, and couldn't pass the blindest M.O., but I don't see why I should pin a medical certificate on my front door."

Chips hadn't known anything about this; it was a shock to him, for he liked Chatteris.

The latter continued: "You see how it is. Ralston filled the place up with young men—all very good, of course—but now most of them have joined up and the substitutes are pretty dreadful, on the whole. They poured ink down a man's neck in prep one night last week— silly fool—got hysterical. I have to take classes myself, take prep for fools like that, work till midnight every night, and get cold-shouldered as a slacker on top of everything. I can't stand it much longer. If things don't improve next term I shall have a breakdown."

"I do sympathize with you," Chips said.

"I hoped you would. And that brings me to what I came here to ask you. Briefly, my suggestion is that—if you felt equal to it and would care to—how about coming back here for a while? You look pretty fit, and, of course, you know all the ropes. I don't mean a lot of hard work for you—you needn't take anything strenuously—just a few odd jobs here and there, as you choose. What I'd like you for more than anything else is not for the actual work you'd do—though that, naturally, would be very valuable— but for your help in other ways—in just *belonging* here. There's no-body ever been more popular than you were, and are still—you'd help to hold things together if there were any danger of them flying to bits.

364

And perhaps there *is* that danger. . . ."

Chips answered, breathlessly and with a holy joy in his heart: "I'll come. . . ."

He still kept on his rooms with Mrs. Wickett; indeed, he still lived there; but every morning, about half-past ten, he put on his coat and muffler and crossed the road to the School. He felt very fit, and the actual work was not taxing. Just a few forms in Latin and Roman History—the old lessons—even the old pronunciation. The same joke about the Lex Canuleia—there was a new generation that had not heard it, and he was absurdly gratified by the success it achieved. He felt a little like a music-hall favorite returning to the boards after a positively last appearance.

They all said how marvelous it was that he knew every boy's name and face so quickly. They did not guess how closely he had kept in touch from across the road.

He was a grand success altogether. In some strange way he did, and they all knew and felt it, help things. For the first time in his life he felt *necessary*—and necessary to something that was nearest his heart. There is no sublimer feeling in the world, and it was his at last.

He made new jokes, too—about the O.T.C. and the food-rationing system and the anti-air-raid blinds that had to be fitted on all the windows. There was a mysterious kind of rissole that began to appear on the School menu on Mondays, and Chips called it *abhorrendum*— "meat to be abhorred." The story went round—heard Chip's latest?

Chatteris fell ill during the win-ter of '17, and again, for the second time in his life, Chips became Acting Head of Brookfield. Then in April Chatteris died, and the Governors asked Chips if he would carry on "for the duration." He said he would, if they would refrain from appointing him officially. From that last honor, within his reach at last, he shrank instinctively, feeling himself in so many ways unequal to it. He said to Rivers: "You see, I'm not a young man and I don't want people to— um—expect a lot from me. I'm like all these new colonels and majors you see everywhere—just a war-time fluke. A ranker—that's all I am really."

1917. 1918. Chips lived through it all. He sat in the headmaster's study every morning, handling problems, dealing with plaints and requests. Out of vast experience had emerged a kindly, gentle confidence in himself. To keep a sense of proportion, that was the main thing. So much of the world was losing it; as well keep it where it had, or ought to have, a congenial home.

On Sundays in Chapel it was he who now read out the tragic list, and sometimes it was seen and heard that he was in tears over it. Well, why not, the School said; he was an old man; they might have despised anyone else for the weakness.

One day he got a letter from Switzerland, from friends there; it was heavily censored, but conveyed some news. On the following Sunday, after the names and biographies of old boys, he paused a moment and then added:—

"Those few of you who were here before the War will remember Max

Staefel, the German master. He was in Germany, visiting his home, when war broke out. He was popular while he was here, and made many friends. Those who knew him will be sorry to hear that he was killed last week, on the Western Front."

He was a little pale when he sat down afterward, aware that he had done something unusual. He had consulted nobody about it, anyhow; no one else could be blamed. Later, outside the Chapel, he heard an argument:—

"On the Western Front, Chips said. Does that mean he was fighting for the Germans?"

"I suppose it does."

"Seems funny, then, to read his name out with all the others. After all, he was an *enemy.*"

"Oh, just one of Chip's ideas, I expect. The old boy still has 'em."

Chips, in his room again, was not displeased by the comment. Yes, he still had 'em—those ideas of dignity and generosity that were becoming increasingly rare in a frantic world. And he thought: Brookfield will take them, too, from me; but it wouldn't from anyone else.

Once, asked for his opinion of bayonet practice being carried on near the cricket pavilion, he answered, with that lazy, slightly asthmatic intonation that had been so often and so extravagantly imitated: "It seems—to me—umph—a very vulgar way of killing people."

The yarn was passed on and joyously appreciated—how Chips had told some big brass hat from the War Office that bayonet fighting was vulgar. Just like Chips. And they found an adjective for him—an adjective just beginning to be used: he was pre-War.

And once, on a night of full moonlight, the air-raid warning was given while Chips was taking his lower fourth in Latin. The guns began almost instantly, and, as there was plenty of shrapnel falling about outside, it seemed to Chips that they might just as well stay where they were, on the ground floor of School House. It was pretty solidly built and made as good a dugout as Brookfield could offer; and as for a direct hit, well, they could not expect to survive that, wherever they were.

So he went on with his Latin, speaking a little louder amid the reverberating crashes of the guns and the shrill whine of anti-aircraft shells. Some of the boys were nervous; few were able to be attentive. He said, gently: "It may possibly seem to you, Robertson—at this particular moment in the world's history—umph—that the affairs of Caesar in Gaul some two thousand years ago—are—umph—of somewhat secondary importance—and that—umph—the irregular conjugation of the verb *tollo* is—umph—even less important still. But believe me—umph—my dear Robertson—that is not really the case." Just then there came a particularly loud explosion—quite near. "You cannot—umph—judge the importance of things—umph—by the noise they make. Oh dear me, no." A little chuckle. "And these things—umph—that have mattered—for thousands of years—are not going to be—snuffed out—because some stink merchant—in his laboratory—invents a new kind of mischief." Titters of nervous laughter; for Buffles, the pale, lean, and medically unfit science master, was nicknamed the Stink Merchant. Another explosion—

366

nearer still. "Let us—um—resume our work. If it is fate that we are soon to be—umph—interrupted, let us be found employing ourselves in something—umph—really appropriate. Is there anyone who will volunteer to construe?"

Maynard, chubby, dauntless, clever, and impudent, said: "I will, sir."

"Very good. Turn to page forty and begin at the bottom line."

The explosions still continued deafeningly; the whole building shook as if it were being lifted off its foundations. Maynard found the page, which was some way ahead, and began, shrilly:—

"*Genus hoc erat pugnae*—this was the kind of fight—*quo se Germani exercuerant*—in which the Germans busied themselves. Oh, sir, that's good—that's really very funny indeed, sir—one of your very best—"

Laughing began, and Chips added: "Well—umph—you can see—now—that these dead languages—umph—can come to life again—sometimes—eh? Eh?"

Afterward they learned that five bombs had fallen in and around Brookfield, the nearest of them just outside the School grounds. Nine persons had been killed.

The story was told, retold, embellished. "The dear old boy never turned a hair. Even found some old tag to illustrate what was going on. Something in Caesar about the way the Germans fought. You wouldn't think there were things like that in Caesar, would you? And the way Chips laughed . . . you know the way he *does* laugh . . . the tears all running down his face . . . never seen him laugh so much. . . ."

He was a legend.

With his old and tattered gown,

his walk that was just beginning to break into a stumble, his mild eyes peering over the steel-rimmed spectacles, and his quaintly humorous sayings, Brookfield would not have had an atom of him different.

November 11, 1918.

News came through in the morning; a whole holiday was decreed for the School, and the kitchen staff were implored to provide as cheerful a spread as war-time rationing permitted. There was much cheering and singing, and a bread fight across the Dining Hall. When Chips entered in the midst of the uproar there was an instant hush, and then wave upon wave of cheering; everyone gazed on him with eager, shining eyes, as on a symbol of victory. He walked to the dais, seeming as if he wished to speak; they made silence for him, but he shook his head after a moment, smiled, and walked away again.

It had been a damp, foggy day, and the walk across the quadrangle to the Dining Hall had given him a chill. The next day he was in bed with bronchitis, and stayed there till after Christmas. But already, on that night of November 11, after his visit to the Dining Hall, he had sent in his resignation to the Board of Governors.

When school reassembled after the holidays he was back at Mrs. Wickett's. At his own request there were no more farewells or presentations, nothing but a handshake with his successor and the word "acting" crossed out on official stationery. The "duration" was over.

He sat in his front parlor at Mrs. Wickett's on a November afternoon in thirty-three. It was cold and

367

foggy, and he dare not go out. He had not felt too well since Armistice Day; he fancied he might have caught a slight chill during the Chapel service. Merivale had been that morning for his usual fortnightly chat. "Everything all right? Feeling hearty? That's the style—keep indoors this weather—there's a lot of flu about. Wish I could have your life for a day or two."

His life . . . and what a life it had been! The whole pageant of it swung before him as he sat by the fire that afternoon. The things he had done and seen: Cambridge in the sixties; Great Gable on an August morning; Brookfield at all times and seasons throughout the years. And, for that matter, the things he had *not* done, and would never do now that he had left them too late —he had never traveled by air, for instance, and he had never been to a talkie-show. So that he was both more and less experienced than the youngest new boy at the School might well be; and that, that paradox of age and youth, was what the world called progress.

Mrs. Wickett had gone out, visiting relatives in a neighbourly village; she had left the tea things ready on the table, with bread and butter and extra cups laid out in case anybody called. On such a day, however, visitors were not very likely; with the fog thickening hourly outside, he would probably be alone.

But no. About a quarter to four a ring came, and Chips, answering the front door himself (which he oughtn't to have done), encountered a rather small boy wearing a Brookfield cap and an expression of anxious timidity. "Please, sir," he began, "does Mr. Chips live here?"

"Umph—you'd better come inside," Chips answered. And in his room a moment later he added: "I am—umph—the person you want. Now what can I—umph—do for you?"

"I was told you wanted me, sir."

Chips smiled. An old joke—an old leg-pull, and he, of all people, having made so many old jokes in his time, ought not to complain. And it amused him to cap their joke, as it were, with one of his own; to let them see that he could keep his end up, even yet. So he said, with eyes twinkling: "Quite right, my boy. I wanted you to take tea with me. Will you—umph —sit down by the fire? Umph—I don't think I have seen your face before. How is that?"

"I've only just come out of the sanitorium, sir—I've been there since the beginning of term with measles."

"Ah, that accounts for it."

Chips began his usual ritualistic blending of tea from the different caddies; luckily there was half a walnut cake with pink icing in the cupboard He found out that the boy's name was Linford, that he lived in Shropshire, and that he was the first of his family at Brookfield.

"You know—umph—Linford— you'll like Brookfield—when you get used to it. It's not half such an awful place—as you imagine. You're a bit afraid of it—um, yes—eh? So was I, my dear boy—at first. But that was—um—a long time ago. Sixty-three years ago—umph—to be precise. When I—um—first went into Big Hall and—um—I saw all those boys—I tell you—I was quite scared. Indeed—umph—I don't think I've ever been so scared in my life. Not even when—umph—the Germans bombed us—during the War. But—umph—it didn't last long—the scared feeling, I mean. I soon made myself—um—at home."

"Were there a lot of other new boys that term, sir?" asked Linford shyly.

"Eh? But—God bless my soul—I wasn't a boy at all—I was a man—a young man of twenty-two! And the next time you see a young man—a new master—taking his first prep in Big Hall—umph—just think—what it feels like!"

"But if you were twenty-two then, sir—"

"Yes? Eh?"

"You must be—very old—now, sir."

Chips laughed quietly and steadily to himself. It was a good joke. "Well—umph—I'm certainly—umph—no chicken."

He laughed quietly to himself for a long time.

Then he talked of other matters, of Shropshire, of schools and school life in general, of the news in that day's papers. "You're growing up into—umph—a very cross sort of world, Linford. Maybe it will have got over some of its—umph—crossness—by the time you're ready for it. Let's hope so—umph—at any rate. . . . Well . . ." And with a glance at the clock he delivered himself of his old familiar formula. "I'm—umph—sorry—you can't stay . . ."

At the front door he shook hands. "Good-bye, my boy."

And the answer came, in a shrill treble: "Good-bye, Mr. Chips. . . ."

Chips sat by the fire again, with those words echoing along the corridors of his mind. "Good-bye, Mr. Chips. . . ." An old leg-pull, to make new boys think that his name was really Chips; the joke was almost traditional. He did not mind. "Good-bye, Mr. Chips. . . ." He remembered that on the eve of his wedding day Kathie had used that same phrase, mocking him gently for the seriousness he had had in those days. He thought: Nobody would call me serious today, that's very certain. . . .

Suddenly the tears began to roll down his cheeks—an old man's failing; silly, perhaps, but he couldn't help it. He felt very tired; talking to Linford like that had quite exhausted him. But he was glad he had met Linford. Nice boy. Would do well.

Over the fog-laden air came the bell for call-over, tremulous and muffled. Chips looked at the window, graying into twilight; it was time to light up. But as soon as he began to move he felt that he couldn't; he was too tired; and, anyhow, it didn't matter. He leaned back in his chair. No chicken—eh, well—that was true enough. And it had been amusing about Linford. A neat score off the jokers who had sent the boy over. Good-bye, Mr. Chips . . . odd, though, that he should have said it just like that. . . .

When he awoke, for he seemed to have been asleep, he found himself in bed; and Merivale was there, stooping over him and smiling. "Well, you old ruffian—feeling all right? That was a fine shock you gave us!"

369

Chips murmured, after a pause, and in a voice that surprised him by its weakness: "Why—um—what —what has happened?"

"Merely that you threw a faint. Mrs. Wickett came in and found you—lucky she did. You're all right now. Take it easy. Sleep again if you feel inclined."

He was glad someone had suggested such a good idea. He felt so weak that he wasn't even puzzled by the details of the business—how they had got him upstairs, what Mrs. Wickett had said, and so on. But then, suddenly, at the other side of the bed, he saw Mrs. Wickett. She was smiling. He thought: God bless my soul, what's she doing up here? And then, in the shadows behind Merivale, he saw Cartwright, the new Head (he thought of him as "new," even though he had been at Brookfield since 1919), and old Buffles, commonly called "Roddy." Funny, the way they were all here. He felt: Anyhow, I can't be bothered to wonder why about anything. I'm going to go to sleep.

But it wasn't sleep, and it wasn't quite wakefulness, either; it was a sort of in-between state, full of dreams and faces and voices. Old scenes and old scraps of tunes: a Mozart trio that Kathie had once played in—cheers and laughter and the sound of guns—and, over it all, Brookfield bells, Brookfield bells. "So you see, if Miss Plebs wanted Mr. Patrician to marry her . . . yes, you can, you liar. . . ." Joke . . . Meat to be abhorred. . . . Joke . . . That you, Max? Yes, come in. What's the news from the Fatherland? . . . *O mihi praeteritos* . . . Ralston said I was slack and inefficient—but they couldn't manage without me. . . . *Obile heres ago fortibus es in aro* . . . Can you translate that, any of you? . . . It's a joke. . . .

Once he heard them talking about him in the room.

Cartwright was whispering to Merivale. "Poor old chap—must have lived a lonely sort of life, all by himself."

Merivale answered: "Not always by himself. He married, you know."

"Oh, did he? I never knew about that."

"She died. It must have been—oh, quite thirty years ago. More, possibly."

"Pity. Pity he never had any children."

And at that, Chips opened his eyes as wide as he could and sought to attract their attention. It was hard for him to speak out loud, but he managed to murmur something, and they all looked round and came nearer to him.

He struggled, slowly, with his words. "What—was that—um—you were saying—about me—just now?"

Old Buffles smiled and said: "Nothing at all, old chap—nothing at all—we were just wondering when you were going to wake out of your beauty sleep."

"But—umph—I heard you—you *were* talking about me—"

"Absolutely nothing of any consequence, my dear fellow—really, I give you my word. . . ."

"I thought I heard you—one of you—saying it was a pity—umph—a pity I never had—any children . . . eh? . . . But I have, you know . . . I have . . ."

The others smiled without answering, and after a pause Chips began a faint and palpitating chuckle.

"Yes—umph—I have," he added, with quavering merriment. "Thousands of 'em . . . thousands of 'em . . . and all boys."

And then the chorus sang in his ears in final harmony, more grandly and sweetly than he had ever heard it before, and more comfortingly too. . . . Pettifer, Pollett, Porson, Potts, Pullman, Purvis, Pym-Wilson, Radlett, Rapson, Reade, Reaper, Reddy Primus . . . come round me now, all of you, for a last word and a joke. . . . Harper, Haslett, Hatfield, Hatherley . . . my last joke . . . did you hear it? Did it make you laugh? . . . Bone, Boston, Bovey, Bradford, Bradley, Bramhall-Anderson . . . wherever you are, whatever has happened, give me this moment with you . . . this last moment . . . my boys . . .

And soon Chips was asleep.

He seemed so peaceful that they did not disturb him to say goodnight; but in the morning, as the School bell sounded for breakfast, Brookfield had the news. "Brookfield will never forget his lovableness," said Cartwright, in a speech to the School. Which was absurd, because all things are forgotten in the end. But Linford, at any rate, will remember and tell the tale: "I said good-bye to Chips the night before he died. . . ."

CANTICLE OF THE SUN

St. Francis of Assisi

Translation of Matthew Arnold

O most high, almighty, good Lord God, to Thee belong praise, glory, honour, and all blessing!

Praised be my Lord God with all His creatures; and specially our brother the sun, who brings us the day, and who brings us the light; fair is he, and shining with a very great splendour: O Lord, he signifies to us Thee!

Praised be my Lord for our sister the moon, and for the stars, the which He has set clear and lovely in heaven.

Praised be my Lord for our brother the wind, and for air and cloud, calms and all weather, by the which Thou upholdest life in all creatures.

Praised be my Lord for our sister water, who is very serviceable unto us, and humble, and precious, and clean.

Praised be my Lord for our brother fire, through whom Thou givest us light in the darkness; and he is bright, and pleasant, and very mighty, and strong.

Praised be my Lord for our mother the earth, the which doth sustain us and keep us, and bringeth forth divers fruits, and flowers of many colours, and grass.

* * * *

Praise ye, and bless ye the Lord, and give thanks unto Him, and serve Him with great humility.

371

MANY LITTLE LEAKS may sink a ship.—*Thomas Fuller*

WHOEVER makes home seem to the young dearer and more happy, is a public benefactor.—*Beecher*

ONLY IN THE LOVES we have for others than ourselves, can we truly live—or die.—*Phillips Brooks*

SOCRATES trusted still in the raft his soul had built and with a brave farewell to the few true friends who had stood by him on the shore he put out into the darkness, a moral Columbus, trusting in his haven on the faith of an idea.—*King*

TO SEE what is right and not to do it, is want of courage.—*Confucius*

IT IS DEFEAT that turns bone to flint, and gristle to muscle, and makes men invincible, and formed those heroic natures that are now in ascendency in the world. Do not then be afraid of defeat. You are never so near to victory as when defeated in a good cause.—*Beecher*

TRUTH never yet fell dead in the streets; it has such affinity with the soul of man, the seed however broadcast will catch somewhere and produce its hundredfold.—*Theodore Parker*

A GOOD MAN is the best friend, and therefore soonest to be chosen, longer to be retained; and indeed, never to be parted with.—*Taylor*

TAKING THE FIRST FOOTSTEP with a good thought, the second with a good word, and the third with a good deed, I entered Paradise.—*Zoroaster*

IF ALL THE TREES on earth were pens, and if there were seven oceans full of ink, they would not suffice to describe the wonders of the Almighty.—*Mohammed*

THERE HAS NEVER BEEN a great or beautiful character which has not become so by filling well the ordinary and smaller offices appointed by God.—*Bushnell*

372

RELIGIOUS THINKERS

THOSE who are not touched by music, I hold
to be like sticks and stones.—*Luther*

GOD is more truly imagined than expressed, and He exists more
truly than He is imagined.—*St. Augustine*

IT IS love that asks, that seeks, that knocks, that finds, and that is faithful
to what it finds.—*St. Augustine*

A MAN may set forth his own learning and eloquence in a fine sermon, but
the true sign of success is when his words induce people to leave off
bad habits.—*St. Francis of Sales*

GRATITUDE is the fairest blossom which springs from the soul.—*Ballou*

STAND UP, on this Thanksgiving Day, stand upon your feet. Believe in
man. Soberly and with clear eyes, believe in your own time and place.
There is not, and there never has been a better time, or a better place
to live in.—*Phillips Brooks*

WE ALL have need of that prayer of the British mariner: "Save us, O God,
Thine ocean is so large, and our little boat so small."—*Canon Farrar*

EVERY CHARITABLE ACT is a stepping stone towards heaven.—*Beecher*

A GRINDSTONE that had not grit in it how long would it take
to sharpen an axe? And affairs that had not grit in them how
long would they take to make a man?—*Beecher*

THE TRUEST self-respect is not to think of self.—*Beecher*

INTO THE WELL which supplies thee with water,
cast no stones.—*The Talmud*

GOD is like us to this extent, that whatever
in us is good is like God.—*Beecher*

373

POSSIBILITIES

By Mary Elizabeth Bain

Despite the fact that the age in which we live is the freest, and our civilization is the richest in the world's history, there are everywhere malcontents and Jeremiahs who magnify the past, who proclaim that the golden age has passed, and that today there are no battles to be fought, no triumphs to be gained. Blind to the new possibilities of life, their ears closed to the voice of action, they fold their hands and journey down to their graves with nothing attempted and nothing achieved. "Impossible," is their cry, and yet all the luminous deeds of this world have been done against the voice of this cry.

It is true that science has revealed many wondrous secrets. She has read the stories upon the rocks, laid hold upon the stars, and penetrated nature's mysteries. But even now, for the aspiring man, she has still greater mysteries to divulge.

True, the fundamental principles of law have been expounded, but with our complex civilization, new questions clamor forth for answers, more wrongs cry to be righted, and more crimes need to be condemned.

True another Caesar may not win his fame or with iron hand rule the world, yet, here in the palace, in the hovel of the poor, with king or peasant, everywhere is opportunity for the man of will, nerve and soul to write his name among the stars. There may never be another Washington, but there are opportunities for true-hearted men to catch inspiration from his noble life, and drive from our shores the tyrant wrong, and place God's banner triumphant over the walls of sin.

Beneficent age, when every man may become a king, every woman a queen and yet none wear a crown! To those who are really seeking an opportunity to develop the best there is in them, who wish to declare a dividend on their heart powers and on their mind powers, let me say in the words of Hillis, "That you dwell in a glass dome and the world is open on every side."

To him who seeks possibilities, opportunities rise in every wind, sing in every breeze, smile in every atom, and are locked in every cell. For him, every dewdrop is a force to turn his spindle, every breath of air an energy to drive his ship, every sunbeam a power to energize his machine. To the hopeful, ambitious man, every day is a chance to demonstrate his worth, every hour an opportunity to show his power, every second a time in which rise to him ultimate possibilities.

It is true that some doors have been closed. There are yet others unlocked, behind which are hidden treasures. Diamonds have been found in mother earth, but there are still brighter gems. Waterloos have been won on fields of blood, but greater battles are yet to be won on fields of peace. The earth has been girdled with electric wires, but it is yet unrimmed by Christian civilization.

There are latent, in every heart, songs as yet unsung, anthems as yet unheard, chords which, if but struck, would fill this old world of ours with music, thrill the soul of man with joy, string his heart and nerves with strength, exalt his life with hope, sweeten it with gladness, and set his whole being atingle with nobleness and love.

There are fruits as yet un-plucked, sweeter than the honey of Hybea, and more beautiful than the sight of sun-kissed clusters of purpling grapes. There are books yet unread, and leaves yet un-cut in the life of every man. There are chaplets awaiting the brows of every man who conquers difficulties, uti-lizes his talents and invests his un-told worth.

For all who but strive, who will but use untried forces, unknown energies, there are un-gathered riches, un-heard harmonies, un-won crowns, yea, an unrevealed heaven.

❖ ❖ ❖

IN THE HOUR OF DARKNESS
By CHARLES KINGSLEY

. . . AM I and my misery alone together in the universe? Is my misery without any meaning, and I without hope? If there be no God, then all that is left for me is despair and death. But if there be, then I can hope that there is a meaning in my misery; that it comes to me not without cause, even though that cause be my own fault. I can plead with God like poor Job of old, even though in wild words like Job; and ask—What is the meaning of this sorrow? What have I done? What should I do? "I will say unto God, Do not condemn me; shew me wherefore thou contendest with me. Surely I would speak unto the Almighty, and desire to reason with God."

"I would speak unto the Al-mighty, and desire to reason with God." Oh my friends, a man, I believe, can gain courage and wis-dom to say that, only by the inspir-ation of the Spirit of God.

But when once he has said that from his heart, he begins to be justified by faith. For he has had faith in God; he has trusted God enough to speak to God who made him; and so he has put himself, so far at least, into his just and right place, as a spiritual and rational being, made in the image of God.

But more, he has justified God. He has confessed that God is not a mere force or law of nature; nor a mere tyrant and tormenter: but a reasonable being, who will hear reason, and a just being, who will do justice by the creatures whom He has made.

And so the very act of prayer justifies God, and honours God, and gives glory to God; for it con-fesses that God is what He is, a good God, to whom the humblest and the most fallen of His creatures dare speak out the depths of their abasement, and acknowledge that His glory is this—That in spite of all His majesty, He is one who heareth prayer; a being as magnifi-cent in His justice as He is mag-nificent in His Majesty and His might.

FRIENDS

Thomas Curtis Clark

If all the sorrows of the weary earth,
The pains and heartaches of humanity—
If all were gathered up and given me,
I still should have my share of wealth and worth
Who have you, Friend of Old, to be my cheer
Through life's uncertain fortunes, year by year.

Thank God for friends, more prized as years increase,
Who, as possessions fail our hearts and hands,
Become the boon supreme, than gold and lands
More precious. Let all else, if must be, cease;
But, Lord of Life, I pray on me bestow
The gift of Friends to share the way I go.

FOR ALL OF TROUBLED HEART

A. Warren

The snow is falling softly on the earth,
Grown hushed beneath its covering of white;
O Father, let another peace descend
On all of troubled heart this winter night.

Look down upon them in their anxious dark,
On those who sleep not for their fear and care,
On those with tremulous prayers on their lips,
The prayers that stand between them and despair.

Let fall Thy comfort as this soundless snow;
Make troubled hearts aware in Thine own way
Of Love beside them in this quiet hour,
Of Strength with which to meet the coming day.

ON FRIENDSHIP

By Henry David Thoreau

MY FRIEND is that one whom I can associate with my choicest thought. I always assign to him a nobler employment in my absence than I ever find him engaged in; and I imagine that the hours which he devotes to me were snatched from a higher society.

Our actual friends are but distant relations of those to whom we

376

are pledged. We never exchange more than three words with a Friend in our lives on that level to which our thoughts and feelings almost habitually rise. — O my Friend, may it come to pass once, that when you are my Friend, I may be yours.

A Friend is one who incessantly pays us the compliment of expecting from us all the virtues, and who can appreciate them in us.

The Friend asks no return but that his Friend will religiously accept and wear and not disgrace his apotheosis of him. They cherish each other's hopes. They are kind to each other's dreams.

That kindness which has so good a reputation elsewhere can least of all consist with this relation, and no such affront can be offered to a Friend, as a conscious good-will, a friendliness which is not a necessity of the Friend's nature.

Friendship is never established as an understood relation.—It is a miracle which requires constant proofs. It is an exercise of the purest imagination and of the rarest faith.

We do not wish for Friends to feed and clothe our bodies,—neighbors are kind enough for that,—but to do the like office to our spirit. For this, few are rich enough, however well disposed they may be.

Of what use the friendliest disposition even, if there are no hours given to Friendship, if it is forever postponed to unimportant duties and relations? Friendship is first, Friendship last.

The Friend is a *necessarius,* and meets his Friend on homely ground; not on carpets and cushions, but on the ground and rocks they will sit, obeying natural and primitive laws.

The language of Friendship is not words, but meanings. It is an intelligence above language.

Silence is the ambrosial night in the intercourse of Friends, in which their sincerity is recruited and takes deeper root.

A base Friendship is of a narrowing and exclusive tendency, but a noble one is not exclusive; its very superfluity and dispersed love is the humanity which sweetens society, and sympathizes with foreign nations; for though its foundations are private, it is, in effect, a public affair and a public advantage....

A CREED
EDWIN MARKHAM

There is a destiny that makes us brothers;
  None goes his way alone:
All that we send into the lives of others
  Comes back into our own.

I care not what his temples or his creeds,
  One thing holds firm and fast—
That into his fateful heap of days and deeds
  The soul of man is cast.

377

OLD FRIENDSHIP

Eunice Tietjens

Beautiful and rich is an old friendship,
Grateful to the touch as ancient ivory,
Smooth as aged wine, or sheen of tapestry
Where light has lingered, intimate and long.

Full of tears and warm is an old friendship.
That asks no longer deeds of gallantry,
Or any deed at all—save that the friend shall be
Alive and breathing somewhere, like a song.

AT THE CROSSROADS

Richard Hovey

You to the left and I to the right,
For the ways of men must sever—
And it well may be for a day and a night,
And it well may be forever.
But whether we meet or whether we part
(For our ways are past our knowing),
A pledge from the heart to its fellow heart
On the ways we all are going!
Here's luck!
For we know not where we are going.

Whether we win or whether we lose
With the hands that life is dealing,
It is not we nor the ways we choose
But the fall of the cards that's sealing.
There's a fate in love and a fate in fight,
And the best of us all go under—
And whether we're wrong or whether we're right,
We win, sometimes, to our wonder.
Here's luck!
That we may not yet go under!

With a steady swing and an open brow
We have tramped the ways together,
But we're clasping hands at the crossroads now
In the Fiend's own night for weather;
And whether we bleed or whether we smile

In the leagues that lie before us
The ways of life are many a mile
And the dark of Fate is o'er us.
Here's luck!
And a cheer for the dark before us!

You to the left and I to the right,
For the ways of men must sever,
And it well may be for a day and a night
And it well may be forever!
But whether we live or whether we die
(For the end is past our knowing),
Here's two frank hearts and the open sky,
Be a fair or an ill wind blowing!
Here's luck!
In the teeth of all winds blowing.

OLD LETTERS

ADELE JORDAN TARR

I keep your letters for a rainy day;
    Then take them out and read them all again.
So, reading, I forget that skies are gray,
    And pathways sodden under falling rain.

They are so full of simple friendliness,—
    Of understanding of the things I love.
No phrase obscure or vague, to make me guess,—
    No deep philosophy my soul to move.

And though your eyes are "lifted to the hills"
    You still keep faith with earth, and earthy things;
Prosaic duty all your hour fills
    The while you listen for the beat of wings.

You have read deeply in the book of life,
    And you have added lines that I shall keep
To be a shield against the petty strife
    Until such time as I shall fall asleep.

So when I would forget that skies are gray
I read your letters on a rainy day.

THE TRULY GENEROUS is the truly wise;
He who loves not others lives unblest.
—*Home*

GLORY makes us live forever in posterity; love,
for an instant in the infinite.—*Weiss*

A FRIEND in the market is better than money in the chest.—*Thomas Fuller*

AFTER WE COME to mature years, there is nothing of which we are so vividly conscious as of the swiftness of time. Its brevity and littleness are the theme of poets, moralists and preachers. Yet there is nothing of which there is so much—nor day nor night, ocean nor sky, winter nor summer equal it. It is a perpetual flow from the inexhaustible fountains of eternity:—And we have no adequate conception of our earthly life until we think of it and live in it as a part of forever. *Now* is eternity, and will be, to-morrow and next day, through the endless years of God.—*Stebbins*

CULTURE is the power which makes a man capable of appreciating the life around him, and the power of making that life worth appreciating.—*Mallock*

A LITTLE LEARNING is not a dangerous thing to one who does not
mistake it for a great deal.—*White*

THE FIRE-FLY only shines when on the wing. So it is with man; when once
we rest we darken.—*Bailey*

ACTIONS, LOOKS, WORDS,—steps from the alphabet by which you
spell character.—*Lavater*

BODY AND MIND are like two clocks which act together, because
at each instant they are adjusted by God.—*Geulincx*

No METAPHYSICIAN ever felt the deficiency of
language so much as the grateful.—*Colton*

IT IS BETTER to wear out than to rust out.—*Cumberland*

380

THE WORLD

DOUBT whom you will, but never yourself.—*Bovée*

SOME PEOPLE are always grumbling because roses have thorns.
I am thankful that thorns have roses.—*Karr*

WE ARE all part of an eternal scheme of things, happy workers on a
pyramid that grows ever nearer the stars.—*Pollock*

THE WORLD rests upon three things: doctrine, the service of God,
and benevolence.—*Simon the Just*

REVERENCE THE HIGHEST, have patience with the lowest. Are the stars too
distant, pick up the pebble that lies at thy feet.—*Margaret Fuller*

WHATEVER ELSE may be shaken, there are some facts established beyond war-
ring; for virtue is better than vice, truth is better than falsehood, kindness
than brutality. These, like love, never fail.—*Hogg*

As OLD WOOD is best to burn, old horse to ride, old books to read, and
old wine to drink, so are old friends always most trusty to use.—*Wright*

HOPE awakens courage. He who can implant courage in the human soul is
the best physician.—*Von Knebel*

YOU, O Books, are the golden vessels of the temple, . . . burning lamps to be
held ever in the hand.—*De Bury*

EVEN IN ordinary life, contact with nobler natures arouses
the feeling of unused power and quickens the consciousness
of responsibility.—*Canon Westcott*

To TEACH the way of life and peace,
It is the Christ-like thing.
        —*How*

NEW THOUGHT is new life.—*Mulford*

381

Happy Land

By MACKINLAY KANTOR

*T*HE SIGN ABOVE THE DRUGSTORE windows had been there a long time—gold and black letters, a scabby gilt mortar-and-pestle. . . . It said simply, "Marsh's," and that meant a great deal to everybody in Hartfield.

It meant gleaming old mirrors, and white-topped, wire-legged tables at which three generations of Hartfield people had eaten strawberry sundaes. It meant prescriptions faithfully filled—a place to lounge and joke and smoke and gossip—to read magazines on the rack free—or to play victrola records in the back room at the side, also free.

"I saw him in at Marsh's last night and—"

"All right, dearie; you and Jenny take this dime and go down to Marsh's and get two big ice-cream cones."

"Mrs. Johnson, I think these capsules ought to fix you up. Just drop in at Marsh's and give this prescription to Lew; he'll fill it while you're getting your groceries next door..."

Miss Emmy, the old maid who worked at Marsh's—Miss Emmy went home to dinner at 11:30 and got back at 12:30; and then Lew Marsh could go home to his own dinner. The only bad thing about it was that there was no registered pharmacist in the store from 12:30 until 1:30; but if any emergency ever came up (that happened seldom) Lew would leave his dinner and hurry back downtown.

Miss Emmy couldn't fill prescriptions, and neither could Chris, the lame youth who was "helping out" since young Rusty Marsh went into

the navy. Rusty was barely twenty-one when he enlisted.

Lew thought that not many boys of Rusty's age could achieve the rating of a First-class Pharmacist's Mate as readily as Rusty had done.

Rusty's picture, taken in uniform with his rating showing on his sleeve, looked down from among the calendars and drug charts and doctors' telephone numbers that adorned the wall beside the prescription booth.

Lew Marsh saw the picture, now, as he closed the big drug register in which he had been making some notations.

Miss Emmy was back, so Lew could go and have his own midday dinner. He yelled good-bye to Miss Emmy and Chris; he warned Chris to be sure to fill the chocolate syrup tank at the fountain, if that new bottle of syrup arrived from the wholesalers. . . . Lew hurried down Second Street.

At the corner of Second and Willson Avenue, Lew turned right past the post office and hastened toward meat balls and escalloped potatoes and sliced tomatoes, skillfully prepared in abundance by his wife, Agnes.

Lew was forty-six years old, but he didn't think that he looked it. His hair was getting quite gray and thinner, and he had had to wear

382

glasses all the time for the past ten years, but he didn't think that he looked forty-six and neither did the loyal and admiring Agnes.

Beneath arching elms and maple trees Lew passed briskly along, until he reached the slight hill which marked the end of Willson Avenue, and the pleasant, shabby white house surrounded by peonies and lilac bushes which was his home, and had been the home of his grandparents before.

Lew was raised in that house through most of his childhood, and Rusty had been raised there too. . . . Each in his own generation had climbed that Whitney tree a hundred times and surfeited himself with fragrant red apples, nourished by roots anchored deep in the black soil of the Middle West.

Lew and Agnes chatted about the events of their respective mornings, while they ate at the round old-fashioned table in the dining room. . . . You don't talk about the war very much—not when you have a son who has been gone with the Pacific Fleet for nearly two years, and when you haven't heard from him for six weeks or more.

They did talk about Rusty a little, though. Old Biff came scratching at the screen, and they let him in, and he wandered around the table working his black nose and sniffing and begging in accustomed style; and Agnes pretended not to see when Lew slipped Biff the last bite of his fifth meat ball.

"Let's see," said Agnes. "How old is Biff now?"

Lew figured it out—Biff was going on twelve. "Pretty old for a dog."

"Remember the first stray that Rusty ever brought home?" asked Agnes.

And as she spoke the words, a girl was pedaling a bicycle along Willson Avenue—coming their way, coming very close—and they hadn't seen or heard her.

"Remember that puppy, all shaggy and full of burs? Rusty insisted that it must be a fine hunting dog. He couldn't have been more than four or five then, I guess."

Then came the ringing of the squeaky doorbell, and Lew's answering journey to the door. Then came the little telegraph girl who had ridden the bicycle, with her pale face and staring eyes . . . then came a yellow envelope and the queer lines of type which were so hard to understand.

THE NAVY DEPARTMENT DEEPLY REGRETS TO INFORM YOU THAT YOUR SON WAS KILLED IN ACTION IN THE PERFORMANCE OF HIS DUTY AND IN THE SERVICE OF HIS COUNTRY. THE DEPARTMENT EXTENDS TO YOU ITS SINCEREST SYMPATHY IN YOUR GREAT LOSS.

For several weeks after that, Lew Marsh didn't stay at the store any more than he could help. He sent down to Des Moines and managed to hire a draft-exempt pharmacist to take charge of prescriptions. . . . Miss Emmy and Chris, with affectionate sympathy and devotion, could run the rest of the store well enough.

Lew and Agnes just stayed around home. Tires on their old Chev were worn thin and smooth, or they might have saved up their gas ration to go on a short motor trip. Things being as they were, they just stayed home.

383

Sometimes Lew would go down to the store late in the evening, when there weren't many folks around, and try to keep his eye on things—the books, and the drug stock, and the general inventory. Agnes seemed to snap out of it sooner than he. She tried to plan little things for his pleasure. She suggested two-handed pinochle, and iced tea under the grape arbor out in the back yard, and things like that. They went to church the first Sunday, but that was the only public appearance they made.

Friends and neighbors came in . . . there was the very bad picture of Rusty, reproduced not exactly to their liking in the Hartfield *Citizen and Express,* and the next week even in the Des Moines *Register.*

Lew sat around . . . he couldn't seem to shake himself out of it. In his mind was one big WHY? Why, why, why?

It wasn't fair, it wasn't right; this wasn't the world he had always believed in. Death could happen so blankly, so relentlessly, so needlessly to Rusty. . . .

It wasn't right.

Chinese could be killed, and Japs, and Germans, and English boys, too—and, of course, a lot of American boys had been killed—but those were always anonymous thousands and hundreds and dozens. You read about them vaguely, and heard about them over the radio. . . .

It wasn't fair for Rusty to be killed. Marshes fought in wars; they didn't get killed in them. Lew's grandfather had fought for years in the Army of the Tennessee. Third Iowa Volunteer Infantry: that was his regiment. And Lew's own father had gone to Chickamauga with the National Guards in 1898. He

hadn't been killed, or even shot at, in the Spanish-American War, though, possibly the fever that he suffered down there in camp had in some way brought on his weakness and eventual vanishment, when Lew was just a little boy.

Lew Marsh, himself, had gone all through the last business with Company C, 168th Infantry, 42nd Division. He had seen a lot of shooting and had dodged a lot of shells all the way from the Marne to the Meuse-Argonne offensive. But he hadn't been killed.

Now it had happened. A Marsh had been killed, in 1943, fighting for his country.

What was Rusty Marsh's country, anyway? What was Rusty's world? He didn't know life and he didn't know the world—he hadn't had a chance to live. He hadn't ever eaten at the Ritz, or watched the Brooklyn Dodgers play. He hadn't ever seen Hollywood or Radio City or any of those wonderful places you read about—he hadn't ever paid his own rent, or made a scooter for his little boy. . . . There hadn't been a chance for him to taste the complete riches of existence. He was only a young fellow living at home, going to school, working for his Dad, going out on a mild date, having his dreams. And then the war —and then the Pacific Fleet—far-removed, unlisted breadth of water— and arduous work, and maybe seasickness . . . and then, death.

Where was any personal world, any wonderful and worth-while world, for which Rusty Marsh had fought and died?

Some of these things were in Lew's mind (they seemed to be in his mind all the time). He was lying there on the living-room davenport, staring at a couple of cracks in the ceiling wallpaper, when there came a ring of the doorbell.

At first Lew didn't go to the door, but the bell kept on ringing. He thought that Agnes would go, but it turned out that she had gone into the back yard to pick petunias. So at last Lew got up and went to the door, not caring, not wanting to go —weakly and remotely dreading the attention of some neighbor or the brash spiel of some salesman. . . .

He opened the door and looked out on the porch.

"Grampa."

Everything went filmy, and tried to flow away from Lew Marsh. All he could do was stare, and try to whisper the word again.

But Grampa was there, just the same. He looked as Lew remembered him: smiling, screwed-up face with a shaggy gray mustache, grimy little glasses with bent gilt rims, the shabby gray pants, the slight powdery discoloration of drugs on his sagging vest, the old scuffed black shoes never shined, and the Grand Army hat with its crumby cord, which Gramp always insisted on wearing after he grew older.

"Well, Lew," said Grampa, "aren't you going to ask me to come in and set down?"

Lew told him that it wasn't right or sane; people didn't ever come back like that; and no self-respecting Marsh should try to astonish Eternity.

"You died just after Rusty was born, and that's over twenty-two years ago," said Lew accusingly.

"I know, I know," conceded Grampa. "But I couldn't stand it any longer, the way things are with you. You were grieving so hard and so long that I kind of felt that I should do something. So I told the Authorities that I would like to come and take a walk with you; and they finally consented. Come on, Lew, let's take a little stroll."

Lew Marsh was stubborn. He said that he didn't want to take a little stroll—not even with a well-loved grandfather who had raised him from a pup—a grandfather who had come sauntering up from a generation in the grave.

"It's the least you can do, seeing as how I went to such great lengths to get permission," said Grampa Marsh.

"I tell you," cried Lew spitefully, "that I don't want to take a walk with you or anybody else!" And he slammed the door.

Well, you couldn't keep Grampa out that way—not as he was situated. . . . He made a face, and chuckled, and walked right through the wall, following Lew Marsh into the living room.

Lew sat down on the couch and stared resentfully when Grampa ambled to the window and looked out at the shady lawns of Willson Avenue.

"I see that young Cecil Weeks has put up a new fence along the back side of their property," said Grampa, peering through the curtain. "Looks a lot better than the place did when the old lady was still running it. Did she ever pay you for all that perfume she bought, Lew—the time she broke the bottles, and then claimed she had never taken them out of the store, or that we hadn't sent them up to her house, or something?"

"Ed paid for them after the old lady died," said Lew, and then Agnes came in with a bowl of fresh petunias.

385

Lew was open-mouthed, wondering what Agnes would say when she saw Grampa, but she walked right past him.

"Aren't these pretty, Lew?" said Agnes. "We've got so many. Now I'm going to pick a big basketful and take them over to Aunt Sally Ross; she's been bed-ridden all week . . ."

While she was saying these things, Agnes stood so close to Grampa that she almost touched his sleeve; then she turned around and went back out to the garden.

Old Biff came in as she banged the back door; and when Biff entered the living room Lew was certain that the dog, at least, would notice Grampa.

But Biff didn't growl or anything —just walked right past the old man, and sniffed around his favorite chair, and then jumped up on the hollow cushion. Biff thudded his tail a couple of times, looked reassuringly at Lew, and prepared to take a nap.

"You see how it is," said Grampa. "You won't get any help from them. How are they to argue against me? Go get your hat, and come for that walk we're going to take."

They went down the street past the box-elder trees by the Andrews' house; and by this time, Lew was beginning to get used to Gramp a little bit.

He looked to see whether Mrs. Andrews and her daughter-in-law would recognize Grampa when they passed the corner of the property, but they didn't even speak to the old man. Mrs. Andrews told Lew brightly, "Well, it's a nice day for a walk, Mr. Marsh," and that was all.

Lew and Grampa went on down, past the public library and the Congregational and Baptist churches. When they got near the post office, they seemed to be hearing a band.

"I didn't know there was a parade in town today," said Lew.

"How could you know what was going on?" countered Grampa. "You just set at home all the time, grieving about Rusty. You just say 'Why was Rusty killed?' and then you ask yourself if it was worth while for you to lose him, and then you answer yourself, and say 'No.' Well, I'll show you a thing or two. . . ."

They turned the corner by Bossert's store at Second and Willson; and there they saw the parade coming down the street.

The funny thing about it was that Lew Marsh was in the parade.

But the Lew Marsh in the parade was only about twenty-two years old, and he was wearing a well-fitting O.D. uniform, and he had a tin hat and he carried a Springfield rifle, and had a full pack on his back, and the Rainbow Division insignia on his left shoulder. He was a corporal, too.

"Well, look at that!" said Gramp. "Corporal Lew Marsh and a lot of the other boys from the local militia company, coming home in 1919 from service overseas. And there I am, with the rest of the G.A.R.'s, forming a guard of welcome or something. I must have just stepped out of the store—I see I'm still wearing my old white coat. . . ."

That was the way it was. That was the first thing Lew and Grampa saw as they walked around town.

386

Ever since he went overseas, young Lew had been dreaming about a girl who lived out on West Walnut Street. She hadn't written much the past few months, but mail always had a hard time catching up with the 168th Infantry.

The first minute Lew could break away from his grandfather and the welcoming friends, he hustled out there to West Walnut Street.

Nobody in sight, on the porch. He ran up the steps and knocked at the screen door; and while he was waiting he stood and looked at the old, familiar canvas porch-swing, and remembered the times he had sat there with Velma.

A guy about his age—a young fellow in a gyrene uniform with the Indian head of the Second Division on the shoulder of his blouse—this fellow suddenly showed up inside the screen.

"Yes?" and he stood looking out at Lew.

Lew stared at the marine, wondering who he was. "Where's Velma?"

"She's here. Who wants to know?"

Lew Marsh felt himself getting sore. "Listen, I want to know. Tell her that Lew Marsh is here and—"

The gyrene began to grin. "Velma's tied up, Jack."

"Tied up? Say, what—"

"Tied up," the marine repeated. "That's what I said: bound and tied—to me. The marines have landed and have the situation well in hand."

Lew stammered and blinked. He tried to say things—

"Forget it, Jack." The marine came outside and shook Lew's flabby hand. "Glad you're back safe and—But here's the story. I'm Andy Jacobson—from up in Mason City where Velma used to live when she was in high school. I got sent back with a casual outfit a while ago and —Well, Velma and I were married last month. Hope you don't mind!"

Lew was still groggy when he got back to the drugstore.

He felt pretty low, naturally, and Grampa tried to cheer him up without much success.

Anyway, it was good to get behind a counter in the store again; and good to take off his army blouse. He found one of his old drugstore coats in a rear closet, and put it on, and decided to straighten up things behind the fountain.

He was painstakingly constructing a pyramid of glasses in front of the mirror, when a cozy voice spoke from the other side of the fountain:

"May I have a peanut sundae, please?"

Lew looked at her in the mirror, and then turned slowly and saw her in the flesh. She was small, chubby, round-bosomed, with a sparkle in her eye.

He had always liked girls in blue middy-blouse suits, especially when they wore sailor hats with long, streaming ribbons.

"I don't think we've got any peanuts. For sundaes, I mean. . . . Here's some chopped walnut meats. . . . Do you mean a peanut-dope sundae?"

She laughed. "What on earth is a peanut-dope sundae?"

"Grampa invented it. Let's see, it ought to be in this jar. . . . Yes, here it is. See, all nice and creamy. . . . He makes it out of peanut butter and marshmallow cream and stuff. Say, you must be a stranger

387

in Hartfield—not to know about Marsh's peanut-dope—"

. . . She thought the peanut-dope sundae was wonderful; and Lew kept talking to her eagerly, and he neglected to wait on trade at some of the other counters, and Mrs. Billings squawked at him angrily, and said, "Young man, please wait on me—I want a bottle of Father Tom's Magic Emulsion—"

Maybe the peanut-dope was a kind of magic emulsion, too.

. . . Her name was Agnes Dickens. She was the new Methodist minister's daughter. And while she still lingered at the fountain—while Lew kept her lingering there—Paul Nickerson walked in, still wearing his uniform, and Paul reminded Lew about that picnic they had been planning all along . . . all through those other grim picnics in the mud of France, Paul and Lew and a couple of other boys had planned just what they would do as soon as they got home.

They would go out to Briggs' Woods in an old car; and they'd take a lot of potato salad and deviled eggs and stuff, and steaks to cook over an open fire, and sandwiches. And girls. Oh, yes, they'd take girls.

There weren't many flowers growing in the woods at that season, but Agnes thought that they might find some anyway. She and Lew wandered away from the others (who were perfectly willing to be wandered away from) and kept on through warm and friendly woods, until they reached a wire fence.

Cows lay in the shade, in the pasture beyond. "Oo," Agnes said, "I'm afraid of cows."

"They won't hurt you," Lew told

her boldly. He held down the bottom strand of barbed wire with one hand and lifted the next strand with the other, making a place for Agnes to crawl through. . . . She wrapped her skirts around her legs (real pretty legs) and slipped through, bending her auburn head to avoid the wire.

(Barbed wire. The wire in France was coarser, heavier, sharper. Lew shook his head.)

Well, Agnes put her heel in a gopher hole, and tripped and fell in the long grass; and somehow Lew fell beside her. They lay there, feeling secret and deliciously sinful in their green nest, giggling at each other.

Agnes plucked a piece of sorrel and tried to tickle Lew's nose. He bit the sorrel instead.

"Oh, don't eat it! Silly, it'll poison you—"

"Nope. Good to eat. Like salad or something. Come on—try some."

"No, Lew, I won't—"

"Yes, you *will*—"

"Lew, stop! Now, please. Lew—"

The cows watched them solemnly as they laughed and struggled.

(Lew Marsh, forty-six years old, stood with Grampa and looked at the church across the street. "That's where you and Agnes were married, Lew," said Grampa. "And her own father performed the ceremony. Remember? I got to sneezing when you walked down the aisle. Flowers in the church—autumn flowers. Gave me a kind of hay fever, I guess.")

Grampa didn't insist on their living with him. He invited them, of course—but not as if they had to do it. He knew that young folks ought to be by themselves. So Lew rented a little house over on Webster Street, and he and Agnes moved in there after a wedding trip to the Wisconsin Dells.

Rusty was born in 1920; and Agnes had a rather bad time of it (they never had any more children afterward); so that was the reason Lew was at the hospital all night that night; and also, that was the reason Grampa Marsh left them soon afterward.

It was about two in the morning, and the telephone kept ringing and ringing. Grampa came downstairs in his long nightshirt and answered. The call wasn't from Lew—it was from Mrs. Billings. Her husband had just suffered another bad spell, and the prescription ordered by Doc Hammond earlier that week was all used up.

The prescription needed to be refilled immediately. Mr. Billings was suffering agonies; and Mrs. Billings wailed tearfully that she couldn't get hold of Doc Hammond on the phone. If Lew wouldn't mind going down to the drugstore right away, she'd send her nephew for the medicine and—

"Lew's not here," said Grampa. "He's up at the hospital, and I reckon that's where Doc Hammond is, too. Now don't fret, Mrs. Billings. I'll hustle right down there to the store my own self, and refill that prescription for Walter. You send your nephew in an hour and it'll be all ready."

It was nearly three-quarters of a mile, down to Marsh's. And raining—a cold, steady, raw rain. Grampa's round shoulders were soaked by the time he reached the store, and his feet were wet. He turned on the light behind the prescription desk, and opened the file. . . . All the time, he kept shivering.

He was seventy-eight years old.

Grampa got to see young Russell before he went. Pneumonia isn't that quick, even with the old.

He whispered, "Mighty red of face, isn't he? And reddish hair— guess you ought to call him Rusty." And, more feebly, "Hello there, Rusty. . . ."

They always took Rusty with them on the morning of each Decoration Day, when they went to the cemetery to fix up the lot—to put big bunches of iris and snowballs and late lilacs on the graves.

Some few of the stores remained open in Hartfield, on Decoration Day, but not Marsh's.

Rusty wanted to know why there were all those flags around.

"That's where the soldiers are sleeping, Rusty. Each one of those graves is where a soldier is buried."

"We got two," said Russell T. Marsh, pointing proudly.

"Yes. That's Grampa. Your great-grandfather. He was a soldier in the Civil War. . . . And this one over here is your grandfather—my own dad. He was in the army at the time of the Spanish-American War."

"Will you have a flag, Pop, when you get died?"

"Sure! You bet I will. I'll have a dandy."

Rusty said, "I want one."

"No telling," said Lew, frowning over his grass-shears, "you might have one by that time."

Agnes cried, "Why, Lew. Don't tell him such things!"

"Well, he might."

Agnes told Rusty, "No, honey. We hope you never have to have a

389

flag. We all hope there'll never, never be another dreadful war—not as long as any of us is alive. Now, here—bring Mamma that big bunch of bleeding-hearts from the basket. . . ."

Lew could remember how she said that . . . all the time they stood listening to the outdoor services—all the time the fife-and-drum corps played, and while the chaplain prayed and the quartet sang and the shaggy line of old soldiers stared and listened, and while all of Hartfield watched reverently . . . no more war. That was right. That was the way an American kid should be brought up—not to dream of gaudy conquests and campaigns.

But to dream of the homely green world in which he lived—a world where the corn grew tall.

In this tall corn, when it was drying in the first coolness of early September, Rusty ran and played Indian. Followed by another little boy and a girl, he whooped his way through the long straight rows that stretched down a hill behind the old Marsh house—the house where Grampa had lived, where Lew and Agnes and Rusty lived now.

It was after supper . . . pale blue mists came up from the Boone River; it was time for children to be in bed. But in those same mists the Sauks had ridden . . . this was dark ground on which Sioux and Pottawatomies had built their fires.

("That's one thing," said Grampa to the modern Lew Marsh, as they stood in ghostly corn and watched the ghostly children. "Kids could always do that in America. They could always play Indian. War clubs, Daniel Boone, Sitting Bull, Buffalo Bill . . . oh yes, I reckon it wouldn't have been proper for kids in other countries to really play Indian. It wouldn't have looked natural. . . . You know, Lew, that's one thing God intended in America, forever. Kids have got to play Indian—always. Nobody must be allowed to make them stop. . . .")

Maybe he didn't have young Agnes Marsh in mind, but at that very moment she came out of the yard. "Hoo-hoo," she kept calling, as she walked through the corn. "Rusty—Rusty—it's bedtime. Hey, where are you? Answer me."

Rusty got up from concealment in the cornstalks, followed by his fellow tribesmen. He held up one grubby hand in a gesture of friendship. "Me no Rusty, woman. Me big chief. Ugh!"

Agnes looked pretty, standing there with sunset on her hair. "Ugh," she said, "me squaw. You come with squaw to wigwam—maybe lie on blanket. Great White Father send for you. Other Indians maybe go to their home villages. Ugh!"

In this way she lured him to the house, and up to his high old bed in the little room next to hers and Lew's.

She lay beside him after he was in bed.

". . . And, just think: day-after-tomorrow my big boy will go to school for the first time!"

"Why do I have to go to school, Mamma?"

"It's kindergarten. That's where you start to school, at first."

"Why do they call it that? That's a funny word—"

"Kindergarten? It's a German word."

"What's German?"

"There's a country, far across the sea, where Germans live. And they speak another language, different from ours."

Rusty whispered drowsily, "Oh, yes, Daddy fought Germans in the war. When I get big I'm going to kill a lot of Germans."

"Oh, no," said Agnes decisively, "you are not! Because we are friends of the Germans again. They had a bad old king, dear, called the Kaiser, who wanted to make war against the whole world. But now the Kaiser is gone from Germany, and we are at peace, and probably we always will be."

"What do Germans look like, Mamma?"

"Well, you know nice old Mr. Gerber, over on Cedar Street? Patsy's grandfather? Well, Patsy's grandfather is a German—he used to be a German, he came all the way from Germany long ago, but now he is an American. And little Mrs. Rasch—and Mr. and Mrs. Ziehl —they all came from Germany. . . . You know, Rusty, in Germany there are fine teachers and wonderful, wonderful schools. And great doctors, and men who make beautiful music; oh yes, many of the Germans are splendid, kind people. . . . And one time, some of the teachers decided that it was hard for little children to have their first learning from big dull books and maps, in dark rooms. So they made a wonderful place for children to start to school in—bright sunshine, and pretty colored papers, and scissors to cut things out, and colored crayons to make pretty pictures— And they called it 'kindergarten,' which means in our language 'child's garden.' Now they have places like that all over the civilized world— and that means almost everywhere, you see. And we have a kindergar-

ten right here in Hartfield, just like the Germans have—a place for children to learn in, and sing in—to learn to make things, and to play new games—that's the way school begins. You'll love it when you start day-after-tomorrow."

There were Miss Belle and Miss Margie. Miss Belle was old and jolly, and Miss Margie was young— she seemed just like a little girl herself, and Rusty thought she was beautiful when she took his hand and led him around the circle.

The children all sat in red chairs arranged in a large circle. They sang, "Good morning to you, good morning to you, good morning, dear teachers, good morning to you. . . ."

("Better'n the school I first started to," whispered Grampa Marsh to Lew. "I tell you, Lew, the world is getting better in spite of everything. Why, the first day I started to school—nearly a hundred years ago, now—the master basted my bottom with a hickory stick because I accidentally upset the water bucket. . . .")

There were two little boys sitting next to Rusty: new boys in the public kindergarten, like himself. But whereas Rusty had a crisp new blouse and neat blue pants, these boys were dressed in ragged old overalls, and their hair wasn't even combed; and they smelled funny, too.

Their names were Jacky and Tod, they told him.

"Where do you live?"

"Oh, we live in an old house out by the fairgrounds. We just moved here from Dakota."

They had pinched faces—pale, eager faces . . . you could see that, after Miss Belle took them out in

391

the hall and gently washed off the dirt that had covered them.

"Do you like ice-cream?" asked Rusty.

"I had some once," said Jacky. "Tod—he's littler than me—he never had none."

Rusty gasped, "What? Never had any?"

"Once I had a Hershey bar," Tod told him proudly.

Rusty boasted, "My father—he's got a store just full of ice-cream and stuff. I bet he's got a thousand old Hershey bars and a million thousand tons of ice-cream. All kinds: my father's got chocolate and strawberry and vanilla and maple-pecan and orange and—"

Well, they couldn't believe that, naturally; though their eyes stuck out and their pinched noses quivered at the very idea.

Kindergarten hadn't "let out" more than ten minutes when there was a light scuffling of six small feet in the back room of Marsh's, and Lew looked down in astonishment at three faces—one beaming with satisfaction, the other two white with fear and anticipation.

"Papa," said Rusty, "this is Jacky and Tod. Jacky only had ice-cream once, and Tod never had any."

. . . It was remarkable how much ice-cream those two ragged kids could eat, sitting there at the fountain, and how catholic were their tastes. Maple, chocolate, cherry: all was grist that came to their mill—until Lew was actually afraid to give them any more.

He let Rusty help them select some candy bars, while he announced over the phone, to Agnes, the result of his judicious questioning.

"Yes, I guess maybe you'd better take the car and run out there. It must be that old shack beyond the Halton place; they say their father's a ditcher, but hasn't been able to work lately, and I guess their mother's got a new baby too. . . . They look at least three-quarters starved. Better take a lot of clean rags and things . . . got any of that stew left from yesterday? A whole kettleful? Good . . . you stop at Sheldon's grocery, and I'll call him and tell him to have a basket of stuff waiting: you know—flour and bacon and eggs and milk and stuff—"

He didn't know that Rusty was there beside him. He didn't know that Jacky and Tod were gone—until he felt a small hand twisting his trouser leg, and looked down to see his son.

"Papa. . . ."

"Yes?"

"Was that for those poor kids?"

"Was what for the poor kids? Are they gone, Rusty?"

"Yes, they went home now. I mean—those things you were talking about with Mamma: stew and bacon and things—"

Lew felt a little shy as the big, solemn eyes looked up at him. "You know, Rus, sometimes people have to do that. Because they want to, I mean. When you see a fellow that hasn't got anything—and you've got things—why, you just give some of your things to him. Some folks call it charity. Me—I don't like the word so well. . . . Maybe's it's just being friendly. You ought to be friendly with folks, Rusty. That's what my Gramp always taught me."

Rusty said, "Can I help?"

"Do what?"

"Just help you, Pop—I mean, be friendly with you. Can I, Pop? You have to work real hard, I think, and I want to help you."

Lew laughed, though his eyes felt

a little wet suddenly. "O.K. You grab that broom, and begin to sweep. You can help me sweep out the back room."

Rusty took the big broom and began to sweep furiously, eagerly. He was helping Dad.

He helped Dad for a real long time. (As Lew Marsh and Grampa looked on, Rusty grew taller and longer—his clothes changed, and the shape of his head and face changed a little, too.)

He was at least twelve years old, or thereabouts. And Lew, as now observed behind the cigar counter, had lost some hair and put on specs.

Marsh's looked much the same, though there were fewer magazines on the racks and fewer drugs on the shelves. This was the rock bottom of the Depression, now; and the Depression started a lot earlier in the farming states than it did farther east.

It had been a long pull; business was still as slow as molasses in January; but Marsh's drugstore managed to hang on.

The store wasn't the only place where Rusty worked. The store wasn't fetching in very much money in those days, with collections slow and the farm people unable to come to town and buy much. From the start, Lew had paid Rusty a small wage for things he did around the store on Saturdays, and before and after school during the week; but at this ripe age of twelve Rusty had developed a certain economic consciousness as, perforce, millions of other American little boys had to do. He staunchly refused to take any extra money from his father, as his duties and responsibilities increased.

Rus had a bicycle, so during the after-school hours he would deliver the Hartfield *Citizen and Express* to a route of subscribers. He got two dollars a week for this chore, and, by mutual family consent, one dollar of his wage was turned into the family exchequer. That way Rusty considered that he was helping out at home. Lew felt badly about it, although he recognized the necessity; but sometimes Agnes thought that it was a pretty good thing. She told Lew so. She said that it would give Rusty a sense of family responsibility, and probably she was right.

This particular day was to be a big day in Rusty's life. On this evening he was to be formally sworn in as a member of the Owl Patrol, Troop One, Boy Scouts of America.

The ceremony took place on the third floor of the primary-school building which had served as the town's Boy Scout headquarters for nearly twenty years. It was an open meeting. They held these twice a year, once in the spring and once in the fall so that the parents of the boys could see.

The Scout hall was a barn-like place which would have been gloomy but for the pennants and home-framed snapshots and colorful charts fastened over the walls. Along one side of the room was a row of glass cases made by the Scouts themselves, and filled with their nature collection. Autumn leaves, pressed wildflowers, chunks of glacial rock, snakes in glass jars —the fauna and mineralogy of mid-America were represented there— together with arrowheads and broken pieces of prehistoric implements which the boys had found.

Lew Marsh and Agnes examined the collection. Vaguely Lew sensed that by accumulating and studying

393

and loving such things, all of the Scouts might realize that America was a much older and more important place than Hartfield civilization sometimes made it seem.

And there was the service flag from the World War, hanging in dusty pride above an alcove: all those blue stars represented former Scouts who had served in the war.· Lew was a little old to be in the Scouts when they organized the first bunch there in town, but some of the younger fellows in Company C had been members of the troop. . . . Lew knew who those three gold stars were, too.

He told Rusty about them as they examined the flag before the meeting officially opened.

"Three of them, Rusty. One would be for Myron Hahne. He died with the flu, down there at Ames. And that next one might be for Benny Billings—he got drowned in the navy—washed off a minesweeper or something like that. And the third one: that's Morton Blitzstein."

Rusty stood very straight and solemn, looking at the flag. "Do you mean Blitzstein's Notions and Men's Apparel? Did old Mister Blitzstein have a boy that got killed in the war?"

"He sure did. Mort was with me. We were in the same company—same platoon, as a matter of fact."

There was something in the way Lew Marsh said the words that kept even twelve-year-old Rusty from asking any more questions—and trying to imagine, after all these years, the chill and noise of the Champagne Sector when Company C went up to the front.

Lew and Agnes took their places with other parents, far back on the crowded benches. There were even

quite a few people standing. Lew told Agnes later that he really got a big kick out of the ceremony . . . there was the flag, and the arrowheads, and the sudden hush, and all that. . . . Of course, it was just kid stuff; but sometimes Lew thought there might be more to the Boy Scouts than appeared on the surface.

All those little kids in their sweaters and shirts, lined up before the Scoutmaster (he was Mr. McMurray who ran the big chicken hatchery, and he was proud and eager to be Scoutmaster) . . . holding up their hands with three fingers extended in the Scout salute . . . the other boys who were full-fledged Scouts, some of them tall brawny youths already playing football in high school, standing at attention in full uniform, watching the Tenderfeet being sworn in. . . .

"On my honor, I will do my best to do my duty to God and my country, and to obey the Scout law; to help other people at all times; and to keep myself physically strong, mentally awake, and morally straight."

Contests, afterward; and then the awarding of some honors, and two teams of the new boys demonstrating some of the tests which they had passed; and games; and finally refreshments which the Scouts had prepared themselves.

Everybody standing and singing:

"My country, 'tis of thee,
Sweet land of liberty,
Of thee I sing—"

After the meeting, Lew walked through the courthouse park with Agnes and Rusty, leaving them to turn toward Willson Avenue and go home alone while he went down

394

to the store to check up and close things for the night.

All that Rusty could talk about was a Scout axe. He was bound and determined to have one. "Didn't you notice them, Pop? They're not a required thing—I mean, you don't *have* to have them —But they're swell . . . and a little leather case and everything, that fastens on your belt."

Lew said, doubtfully: "Well, I don't know. How much does a Scout axe cost?"

"The one I want costs two-eighty-five," said Rusty glibly.

Lew looked at him in the gloom. "Think you can save that much, very easily?"

Rusty swallowed. "I don't know. I'll try."

He did try, too. He had a hoard of pennies and nickels and dimes; he saved them in an empty baby-powder can hidden at the back of a shelf in the pharmacy chamber. The drugstore was just about as much home to Rusty as the house was.

Lew used to watch him, time and again, getting down that can to count over the money and see how close he was to attaining his axe. Rus went without a lot of things in order to get that little hoard together. Finally after a number of weeks, the total had reached two-forty-seven.

"Not very far to go now!" chortled Rusty, as he banged the can back up on the shelf.

It was early morning when he said this.

"Rusty," said his father, "will you be here awhile?"

"Sure. I don't have to leave for school for about another fifteen minutes."

Lew told him, "If Miss Emmy is busy waiting on trade out front, and I'm not yet back from the post office, you deliver that prescription there on the desk, if the customer comes in for it. It's all made up, and the amount's written on the package. I don't know the customer—Doctor McKee gave me the prescription—so be sure you get the cash."

Lew went to the post office and got his morning mail out of the box. On the way back up the alley he was reading letters, and one of them made him sore as a boil.

The Apex Supply Company had deliberately misinterpreted his order with regard to the refund, and so on. Well, he remembered he had kept a copy of that letter he wrote to them. . . .

He entered his store through the back door; and he was up on the little balcony above the rear room, looking through his office files, when he heard steps approaching that end of the store. He looked down.

Rusty came into the prescription room and took a professional stance inside the window, though he could barely see over the top.

"Yes, sir," he said to the customer. "I believe the prescription's here all right. What's the name, please?"

It was fun to stand there unobserved, and look down and see your own son being such a man about things.

Lew could see through the window, even from that angle. He could see the customer: a flat-chested, round-shouldered man of sixty-five, with a haunted, stubbly face.

The customer said, "Watson, sonny. Sam Watson's my name. That there medicine is what the

doctor said my wife was to have"
Rusty examined the little box.
"That's right. 'S. Watson.' Two
dollars and a quarter, Mr. Watson."

The man gulped, and put his
hands on the broad sill. "I wonder, sonny," he asked, in a mild
voice, "if maybe I could speak to
the manager?"

Lew was about to sing out from
his place on the balcony, but something kept him from it.

"Sorry, Mr. Watson," said Rusty.
"My father isn't in right now. He
told me to deliver the prescription
when the customer called. And—
and he said I was to get cash."

"Sonny." Old Watson's voice was
a desperate whisper. "I ain't only
got but—thirty-five cents. That's all
I got to my name. I tell you, sonny,
Mrs. Watson—She's having quite a
little pain and—Well, now, I've
heard of your father, and I guess
he's an upstanding citizen. Well,
do you suppose he'd mind trusting
me for the other dollar-ninety? I'll
maybe get some work next week,
and—"

There was silence, during which
Lew stood there and listened, and
he heard two girls laughing up front
by the magazine stand. Far away,
the bell in the schoolhouse steeple
was beginning to ring. Rusty would
have to leave in a minute.

Rusty made a smothered sound.
He reached out and drew in the
thirty-five cents which Mr. Watson
offered through the window.

"I guess," said Rusty, "that that'll
be—all right with the manager."

The old man muttered something
which sounded like, "God bless you,
sonny," and went away weakly with
the package grasped in his hand.

A board cracked under Lew's

foot just then, but Rus never heard
it. He was getting down the baby-
powder can and slowly counting
out one dollar and ninety cents,
which he put with Mr. Watson's
quarter and dime in the cash
drawer.

Lew didn't say a word; just stood
there and watched him do it, and
saw him hurry away to school.

No, Lew didn't even mention it
to Agnes. But that night, when
Rusty went to crawl into bed, he
turned back the sheet because he
felt a big lump underneath. And
there was a lump, all right. It was
the Scout axe.

Rusty used that axe a long time.
In memory now, Lew Marsh and
Grampa could see the blade flashing through the years, and could
hear its solid *chop, chop, chop.*

There was firewood to be cut, on
overnight hikes where the Boy
Scouts went ... times when the boys
sat in a cross-legged ring around the
campfire and sang everything from
"Sweet Genevieve" through "Down
by the Old Mill Stream," up to and
including that grim Depression
ditty of modern times, "Brother,
Can You Spare a Dime?" And the
glorified campaign shout of 1936,
when Rusty was an Eagle Scout,
and the boys all sang, "Happy Days
Are Here Again"...

The axe was used to split kindling for the old fireplace at home,
too, on nights when there were parties. High school kids coming in
... the battered golden-oak victrola
squawking, or the old piano bang-
ing under its tasseled cover in the
hall ... again the kids were picking
up Big Apple and jitterbug tunes
out of some evening broadcast.

The axe was used to break ice

for fruit punch, and to pound up windows when they stuck, and to tap against a wheel of the old car when Rusty was changing tires. Eventually the axe found its way down to the store; and there in the back room Rusty pried open the wooden packing-cases which came from wholesale houses . . . A strong axe—a good little axe. It seemed that the handle would never break.

"No, I suppose you wouldn't call him a religious boy," whispered Grampa to Lew Marsh, "but after all, what ordinary and normal American boy is extremely religious? When he was a Scout, he did his duty to God and his country just as he promised to do. It didn't mean that he had to grow up to be a missionary. Not necessarily."

Lew said: "One thing I do remember; he was treasurer of his Sunday-school class for a while."

"That's right," nodded Grampa. "I guess he made a good treasurer, if a reluctant one. And then, he always went to the young people's meetings a lot—Epworth League, and things like that."

"For a very good reason, too," said Lew.

They both giggled, and stood in shadows and watched a tall lean Rusty and a lot of other boys, hanging around on an early Sunday evening, watching to see which girls went into the church to young people's meeting; and then skulking in after them and joining, somewhat shame-faced and embarrassed, in all the talk about living worth-while lives and making their parents proud of them.

When the meeting broke up, that was the important thing. The boys got outside first, and lined up and waited for the girls. If you were already hooked up, through preference and habit, to some certain girl, you simply stepped up and took her arm and went away laughing with her.

But, on the other hand, if there were a new girl in town—say a remarkably pretty one, with long pale yellow hair, like Gretchen Porter—you had to nerve yourself to the ordeal. You stepped up and shuffled your feet, and were suddenly at a loss for words, and then said something about its being a nice night. And if Gretchen agreed that it was a nice night, and lingered to talk about it for a moment—why then, pretty soon you found yourself moving west through the chilly shadows of Bank Street with her. You may have been stepping in autumn leaves, but you thought you were really walking on the clouds.

It was a pretty good year, all in all—that last year of high school. Sometimes, generally speaking, it didn't seem as if there was a lot to do—for young people, that is—in a town like Hartfield. Of course there was always work at the store; and there were always lessons to prepare; and Rusty was taking a double dose of science at high school, so that meant a lot of extra work for him. He was trying to read some big pharmaceutical books, too, between times, down at the store.

He had an awful lot of interference with his reading.

Sure as he opened a book, there was bound to come a lot of giggling and wise-cracking and laughter: the front door of Marsh's would bang, and girls or boys would be ganged up around the soda fountain and around the record cabinets at the back of the store, and around Rusty always. . . . They called him "Doc" whenever they saw him with those big pharmaceutical books.

He wasn't heavy enough for football, though he tried out for the team, and they made a scrub out of him. He got to play two quarters in the game with Iowa Falls; then he hurt his shoulder and had to go around in a cast for about ten days, so that effectually stopped his football career.

Rusty did better in the spring when track season opened. The two-twenty hurdles: that was Rusty's dish. He got first in the sub-district, and later on managed to squeeze out a victory in the district meet, but was roundly beaten when Hartfield sent its track team to the state meet.

("I was proud of him," Lew whispered to Grampa. "I guess I was even prouder of him when he lost. He lost so damn well."

"Person's got to learn to lose well, just the same as win well," said Grampa, taking an emphatic bite out of his highly-seasoned tobacco plug.

"Wish I could have done more for him, though. . . ."

Grampa chewed serenely. "Don't see where you could have done any better. If an American small town isn't a good place for young folks to grow up in, then I'm suffering from delusions. We hear a lot of news, up there where I've been. But I never heard tell that MacArthur came from a big city. Admiral King was a small-town boy, and so was Wendell Willkie, and so was Eisenhower, and so was Harry Hopkins; and Henry Wallace came from Iowa. Lew, I guess you gave Rusty just about the best there was.")

Well, he gave him love and potato salad in Briggs' Woods, just as Lew himself had had them . . . and there was Rusty, holding fence wires so that a girl could crawl through and wander in the pasture with him.

Rus had some fishing in the Boone River, and the family Chev to drive sometimes on dates after he was big enough, and he had the free public library and the county fair, and street carnivals; and almost every year of his life he got to go to the big Lions' Club picnic—the Tri-County one, over at Fort Dodge—for Lew was a Lion, and the Tri-County picnic was one of the most important Roars of the year, and all the Lionesses and Cubs were invited along, too.

Lew and Agnes gave Rusty a thousand hours in which to dream and plan and plot his personal ambitions. They and their world offered him the bob-rides, on cold winter nights when snow was so deep that you would never have thought there was any pavement in town . . . when sleigh bells sang on the harness, and girls squealed and whispered in the straw of the bob-sled; and there was a chance to hold hands, to feel the warm and affectionate presence of another creature (a creature like yourself, but still bewitchingly different) underneath the blankets. The bob-rides ended up invariably with oyster stew somewhere, and hot chocolate, too; plenty of times those oyster stews were served over the marble fountain at Marsh's.

The store was a modern store now. That was the winter of early 1938, and Lew had installed a lot of shiny chromium steam-table equipment,

Yes, Rusty had his work, and his private thoughts, and his ordinary falls from grace, and his decent acts of tenderness or superiority. He had his girl, too. She was still the yellow-haired Gretchen, though Lew privately didn't approve of her very much because she was getting to be such a flibberty-gibbet. She put on too much make-up, and she dressed more expensively than her family could really afford. Lew and Agnes shook their heads about it, though naturally they never let on to Rusty.

There came the end of the school year, and the baccalaureate sermon at the church. It was a fairly good sermon, such as should be delivered to a high school class graduating into a world where the name *Hitler* rang with shrill menace.

Privately, Agnes didn't feel that the sermon was as good as the one her own father might have delivered; but she was prejudiced.

They sat together, Lew and Agnes, and held hands like a couple of kids themselves, and watched the fifty-four members of the class file into the auditorium, singing.

But Rusty himself looked sober when he came down to the store about ten-thirty. Agnes had driven Lew downtown after the baccalaureate exercises were over, and had then gone on home. But naturally, Rusty had important business of his own. He had to take Gretchen home from the church.

He came into the store slowly, and Lew looked at him with pride through the prescription window, because Rusty had a new suit that he had earned himself—purchased it out of his own salary for part-time work at the store.

He wore the new shoes and neck-tie and hat which had been his father's graduation present.

"Going to close up soon, Pop?"

Lew glanced at the clock. "Any time now. You know I sort of make a habit of staying open until eleven on Fridays, just in case. . . . Those were pretty good exercises up at the church, Rusty."

"Yes," said Rusty, and that was all he would say; and pretty soon when Lew turned around he found Rus had pulled on an old overall suit over his good clothes and was preparing to open a packing case.

Lew remonstrated. Said that it wasn't necessary.

"Oh," said Rusty, "I'd just as soon, while you're getting ready to close up. This box has got all those new bath salts in, and you know I wanted to make a big display early tomorrow, out there in the center for the Saturday trade."

For a while there wasn't much sound in the store except the crack and prying as Rusty worked with the little Boy Scout axe.

Lew cleared his throat. "Anything go wrong tonight, son?"

"Oh," said Rusty, "it was just Gretchen," and Lew's heart jumped.

"What happened?" He tried to make his question seem casual.

"It was just—about Sunday." After a while Rusty added: "I had a date with her for Sunday afternoon. We thought we'd go with some of the others down to Briggs' Woods, but—well, there's a guy works for her father, salesman or something, fellow about twenty-four, named Cliff Jeffers."

Lew said, "Yes, I know him. He's a customer here at the store," and his tone told much. After all, a druggist is something like ⌐ doctor;

he knows a lot about the personal habits of people.

Rusty said: "This fellow Jeffers—he's got a real sweet car and he wanted to take Gretchen all the way down to Des Moines . . . I don't know, have supper and go to a movie or something. . . ."

Lew said, after a moment, "Rusty, Mother and I won't be needing the Chev. If you'd like to drive to Des Moines—"

"Hell, no," said Rusty decisively. "Didn't I tell you we were planning a picnic? Well, if that's the way she feels about it, she can damn well go to Des Moines! And she can damn well keep on going with Cliff Jeffers, for all I care."

Lew wanted to cheer. But just at that moment Rusty gave a vengeful pry to the last board of the box, and the handle of the little axe snapped and shivered.

Rusty looked at the slivery fragments. "Well, Pop, I guess that axe will have to have a new handle. Remember the day you gave it to me?"

"I sure do," said Lew.

A few minutes later they were walking home together through the warm night, and it seemed as if Rusty were another man and not just a boy. Lew offered him a cigarette and Rusty said, "No, thanks. Mind if I smoke my pipe?"

The pipe and the cigarette glowed like flowers along the darkness of Willson Avenue.

When they got home, while Rusty was sampling oatmeal cookies (Agnes always left something out on the table when they came in late), Lew went down cellar and pretty soon he came back with a bottle of home-made loganberry wine. An old lady made it, there in Hartfield, and sometimes she gave Lew a few bottles when she wasn't able to pay her little bill at the store.

Lew filled two sherbet cups—Agnes got those from her aunt for a wedding present, he remembered. He filled them solemnly with the sweet dark wine, and he and Rusty drank in silence and in pride.

After Lew got into bed beside Agnes it took him a long while to go to sleep. He didn't hear a sound from Rusty's room, but he had a hunch that Rus wasn't asleep either. Maybe in this sudden maturity, Rusty was just as proud of being a man as Lew was to have him be one.

Now that he had become a man he didn't necessarily put away all the childish things he once had loved.

"Funny thing," said Grampa, nodding through mists of recollection to Lew, as together they watched Rusty packing ice-cream into a dry-pack container to carry along on his inevitable Sunday picnic. "Funny thing—but the man who makes a clean sweep and puts all childish things away forever—somehow he becomes less a man than the one who always remains a little childish in some ways."

Certainly Rusty still enjoyed picnics, though he didn't take Gretchen to any more of them. He sort of shopped around among girls there in town; and he was always the eligible boy who gets asked for a blind date when there comes a visiting niece from Omaha, or a new young teacher in the kindergarten.

It took him about a year to settle his affections in any particular direction, and then he settled them right next door.

400

The Prentiss family lived there, long-time neighbors of Agnes and Lew; and they had a daughter whom Rusty never noticed except with loathing, when he was in high school. . . . If he wanted to make an invidious comparison he'd say: "Gosh! She looks just about as bad as Lenore Prentiss," or, "Lenore Prentiss and a lot of awful girls like that. . . ."

But by the fall of 1938, Lenore Prentiss herself was an upperclassman in high school. And the next thing anyone knew, Charley Prentiss made a good chunk of money and got a fine promotion in his insurance organization, and to the amazement of the neighborhood he sent Lenore off to a fancy junior college, a regular girls' school in Missouri. It was something like an Eastern finishing school, people said.

When Lenore came back she was quite a different person; at least Rusty thought so. She wasn't beautiful: just the regular type of American girl with a good-looking body and a full, laughing mouth and level gray-green eyes. She wasn't pretty, but she was young, and her hair shone.

Rusty took her out a good deal that summer. Of course, he went with other girls when Lenore wasn't in Hartfield; they weren't engaged or anything like that; they were just young people having a good time. Rusty saved up and bought a croquet set—a heavy, modern set—with a rubber face on one end of every mallet-head. Rusty worked early Sunday mornings, leveling the ground in the back yard until it was as smooth as a pool table; he and his mother planted a special grass there and tended the new sod

carefully. The resulting croquet ground was the delight of youthful Hartfield.

Mallets clacked all summer long, and heavy balls whistled through the thick steel wickets—or bounced disappointingly off the edges. A portable radio chanted under the grape arbor. Agnes made chicken and bologna sandwiches in the kitchen, until Rusty rebelled and carried Agnes outside, squealing and struggling like a young girl herself; and he threw her into the hammock and tied the edges to imprison her. He said that hereafter he and the gang would make their own sandwiches. . . .

Croquet balls pounded across the turf, evenings and holidays, and catbirds meowed under the gooseberry bushes. Then suddenly the radio songs were stilled. Men's taut voices filled the ether.

Hitler had gone crushing into Poland.

A few nights later, at the store, Rusty spoke with Lew in the back room. He said that a lot of the boys were talking about going up to Canada and getting into this thing. Arch Birmingham, for instance: he was quite an intellectual, for all that he was a good amateur welterweight, too. Sometimes when he and Rusty were younger, and momentarily mad at their little world, they had talked about running away to Spain and joining the fight there. But Arch wasn't a kid any longer. And he was bound and determined to get into this war.

Bud Flanagan and Peter Orcutt both had their private pilot's licenses . . . they said that they thought they would go up to Winnipeg or somewhere and join the Canadian flying corps.

401

"I suppose that means you've got a notion you want to go with them, Rusty?" asked Lew.

Rus shook his head. "Not exactly. But you know, a lot of us were talking last night, and we've got a hunch that this thing is going to go a lot further and last a lot longer than most people around here think. No, I'm no pilot, and maybe I wouldn't even be very good with a gun."

He laughed. "You know, I never shot anything but a .22. Rats and tin cans and things. . . ."

Lew carefully dampened a poison label and put it on a little bottle which he had just filled with white capsules. "Yes," he said easily, "wars are an unsettling business."

Rusty muttered, "It makes a guy feel like he wants to do something . . . kind of get straightened around and head for somewhere."

Lew told him: "We talked about college last year. I offered to help you down at Ames or Iowa U. or anywhere else. But you said you didn't want to."

Rusty snapped a rubber band at his father, and Lew ducked.

Rus said, "We talked about medicine, but I don't feel any ambition to be a doctor. I'd waste your investment and my own energy. Perhaps I'd be frittering away half my time, all because I didn't have any business in medical school. It makes me sick the way some guys go down there and spend a lot of dough and then come back, after a year or two, just where they left off. I guess I was some help to you in the store, wasn't I?"

Lew shrugged. "Well, maybe, just a little! Say, I'd have had to pay two extra people at least a hundred dollars a month apiece to do what

you've done around here this year. I didn't pay you anything like that."

"O.K.," said Rusty. "Now look, Pop, I'm pretty well up in my pharmacopoeia. If you can get along without me for a while, I'll go down to the Des Moines School of Pharmacy and get busy. Eventually I'll qualify for my license. If the war's over and the world is running smoothly, I'll be set to do some real good for the store and myself too. We might even buy old Granville's grocery building next door, and make one side of this place into a high-class luncheonette and confectionery place, and the other side all drugs and sundries, the way you've talked about doing sometimes."

Lew wrapped the bottle, and put a rubber band around it. "If the world isn't at peace and running smoothly, what about that?"

Rusty was silent for a moment. Then he said: "I guess I'll be a lot more good to the army or navy or marines or somebody—I guess I'll be worth more to them as a skilled technician, even in pharmacy, than as an unskilled recruit. What do you say, Pop?"

Lew felt warm and valiant. He felt something like he did the first day he saw Agnes . . . or farther back, the day he was made a corporal in the infantry long ago.

"I say," he cried, "that you'd better plan to go down to Des Moines to the College of Pharmacy."

When he and Rusty got home that night they drank some loganberry wine.

In 1941 the world wasn't at peace, and it wasn't running smoothly.

When Rusty was at home, working in the store that summer, Lew mentioned having made some conversation with old man Granville about the grocery building next door; not an actual proposition, not in so many words—but he edged around the subject a little. That was just bait. He wanted to see how Rus would react to it.

Rusty reacted, all right. He came out in the yard on Sunday evening in the twilight, as Lew was finishing watering the flowers with the hose.

"Pop, maybe you'd better not talk any more to Mr. Granville."

"Why not? Don't you think that would be a good proposition?"

"In ordinary times, yes. But these aren't ordinary times."

"I guess not," muttered Lew. "Not when you look at the papers, or listen to the radio and hear what's happening in Russia and places like that."

"Don't forget the Pacific," said Rusty.

Lew squirted a fine spray from the hose toward old Biff—not getting him wet, just teasing him—and Biff dodged and made a challenging sound.

Lew asked, "Why do you mention the Pacific?"

"Little brown men no like Amelicans," said Rusty, making a queer face and pretending that he was a Japanese, although he had never actually seen a Japanese.

Then he burst out: "What's the use of waiting to be drafted? Maybe if everybody keeps on waiting we'll find we've waited too long!"

His father went up to the house and turned off the hydrant. He unscrewed the hose, and Rusty began to reel it up on its little wooden cart.

"O.K.," Lew told him. "What's

it going to be, big boy; army, navy or marines?"

"You sound kind of resentful about the marines," said Rusty. looking at him. "How come?"

"Never mind," said Lew, and he couldn't help grinning to himself. "What's it going to be? Maybe the air corps?"

"Sure," laughed Rusty. "Pharmacy ought to help a lot, there! No, Pop, I'll tell you. It's kind of silly, but—Well, I always did want to see the ocean."

It was getting dark. Lew watched Rusty wheeling the hose reel into the tool-shed next to the garage. After Rusty came to meet him by the grape arbor, and as they walked to the house together, Lew said, "Go ahead! Join the navy, and see a lot of oceans!"

"Wonder if I'll get seasick?" meditated Rusty.

"I know I did, in the last war!" said Lew. Already unconsciously people were calling it that. "Twice. I got sick as a dog going over, and coming back."

They walked into the house. Lew went to hunt for the loganberry wine, but it was all gone.

"Looked real good in his uniform," whispered Grampa.

"Yes. . . ."

"Sailors' uniforms," said Grampa, "haven't changed as much since the Civil War as the army has. 'Course, I never saw many sailors, not where I was—with the Third Iowa. But after the war, sometimes, at G. A. R. encampments—"

Lew put his hand on Grampa's sleeve. "Look," he said, "look at Lenore Prentiss, will you? She's saying that his uniform is cute; isn't that just like a girl? They go for a sailor every time, if you give them half a chance."

"Do you reckon he and Lenore were engaged, Lew?"

Lew shook his head.

"Or maybe in love," pursued Grampa, "or—"

Lew said, "Maybe Agnes would know more about that than I would. I'd hazard a guess that they liked each other a lot but—I don't know. If he had come back, why maybe—You can't tell about such things."

Grampa rolled his tobacco in his mouth. "It's a kind of wisdom, Lew," he said, "when a man admits ignorance in such a case."

The bus pulled out, the bus bound for Des Moines, and Rusty waved a freckled hand at the window. And then he was gone, and that was the end of Rusty (wailed Lew to himself, clenching his fists) and that was the end of everything.

Grampa walked so silently beside Lew now, strolling back toward the old house, that Lew wondered if Grampa might not be reading his thoughts.

". . . As long as kids can play Indian in the corn," whispered Grampa.

Lew stopped and looked at him. "What did you say?"

Grampa kept walking. He stopped to poke among the clovers at a certain place along the parking, with the tip of his cane. Lew remembered that: a little weakness of the old man. He used to stop there, almost square in front of the Andrews house, every day when he went past. He would spend a minute or two looking for four-leaf clovers. Sometimes he found one, and put it in his little pocket note-

book. There were many such four-leaf clovers, drying and brown, staining the pages of the old drug register down at the store.

Lew kept plaguing Grampa. . . . "What's that about playing Indian in the corn?"

"Did I talk about corn?" asked Grampa mildly. "Must have been thinking out loud. . . . Remember this, Lew: as long as American boys can be Boy Scouts, as long as they can eat ice-cream, as long as they can do a good turn daily, as long as they can go to high school, or play football, or have a picnic in Briggs' Woods . . . as long as they can feel impelled to take a hard-saved dollar-and-ninety-cents out of a baby-powder box—"

Lew was puzzled. "As long as all those things, then—what?"

"It'll be worth while," said Grampa.

"What'll be worth while?"

"A guy named Rusty," said Grampa. "A lot of kids like that, with a lot of names."

Lew Marsh felt all choked up inside. He wanted to shout and say, "What are you trying to do? Tell me I ought to be glad because my own son was killed in the war?"

. . . Sometimes he and Grampa used to have arguments, pretty spicy ones; though Grampa hadn't licked him after he was ten or eleven. Maybe he hadn't needed to be licked, but—

Well, there was no sense in offending the old man—especially since he said he had gone to so much trouble to get permission from the Authorities, and all that. And since he had been so nice about taking Lew for a stroll around town.

It was a stroll that had lasted

404

twenty-odd years, though by modern Hartfield time it consumed only a few hours.

Here they were now, back where they started, lingering in front of the kind old house, halting for a moment to listen to a mourning-dove up in that big maple somewhere.

Lew cleared his throat. "Gramp, it's getting on toward suppertime. It's kind of an awkward situation. I don't know quite how to handle it, with Agnes not able to notice you and—But if you wanted to stay, and sit down to supper with us, why—"

Grampa laughed. "You forget, Lew," he said, "you forget my peculiar condition."

Lew felt embarrassed. To cover his confusion he said, "Well, anyway, let's go round in back. I imagine Agnes is out there watering her flowers. It takes quite a while, now that we haven't got any hose; but she says she thinks that old-time watering-can is pretty picturesque, anyway."

They went round the corner of the house, out past the syringa bushes and the bird bath and Biff's kennel; and sure enough, there was Agnes, wearing a pair of old tennis shoes and a pink apron and managing to look pretty picturesque herself.

"Why, Lew Marsh," scolded Agnes (but in some delight, as if she were pleased that he had gotten out and taken a good long walk). "Where on earth have you been? Aren't you all tired out?"

Lew smiled at her slowly. "Not at all. Fact is, I feel better than I've felt in some weeks."

He cleared his throat again. "Fact is, after supper I thought I might go down to the store and get busy."

He turned to see how Grampa would take this, because Agnes was obviously so tickled at his change of heart. But Grampa wasn't there.

Old Biff came and rubbed against Lew's legs . . . Grampa wasn't anywhere around.

Lew looked all over, and then he saw him. Grampa was going up the long slope past the Mansfield house. He stopped, with bright orange sunset light around him, and when he saw Lew looking, he waved his cane. Then he turned and kept on going, away up to the head of Prospect Street, up to a wide park-like hill. That was where he was going —under old elms and black pines, up there where little flags flapped and whistled on their staffs above the soldiers' graves.

It was after ten o'clock that night when Lew had to admit frankly that he was tired. Except for bookkeeping work, he hadn't really done anything much in weeks—and only a few hours of books.

But something struck him tonight, the moment he entered the store. He saw immediately a dozen things he wanted to change. He saw a hundred frayed edges that had developed during his reclusion . . . a kind of fringe on the abstract structure of the store, which needed his skill for the clipping.

Scarcely could he feel the friendly pressure of hands that reached for his across the counter. . . . Old Judge Colvin: they had quarreled, he and Lew, over the extension of the gas main out on Willson Avenue, and Judge Colvin hadn't shaken hands with him in years, though he always brought his business to that store because it was the best. . . . Now the judge let his bright black eyes soften under their tufted brows, and he reached his fat soft hand across the counter past a big pile of Kleenex, and he said: "Well, Lew, how're you doing?" and then nodded again before he went away with his purchases. Lew felt a warmth toward Judge Colvin. Suddenly, as his spirit embraced this petulant old enemy, he found that it was embracing all of Hartfield with new eagerness.

Still, he scarcely felt the physical touch of these people upon him. He was inspired, rather than depressed, by the trivia of his own existence. He wanted to get that cracked glass fixed, at the end of the perfume counter; and the electric ventilating fan in the rear wall was clicking again and needed oiling. Those patent medicines looked ugly, there so close to the toilet soaps and face powder, and why hadn't he ever thought to change them over to the shadowy shelves on the opposite side? Chris could do it just as well the next morning, but it seemed to Lew Marsh that the task should be performed now.

So he was working there . . . the night watchman came in and bought cigarettes, and Doc McKee stopped by to pick up some codeine. It was after ten o'clock. Lew sold two sodas and a hot fudge sundae and a chocolate malt to some kids homeward bound from the movies; then he rubbed off the top of the fountain and washed the few dishes and glasses.

He heard the ten-thirteen train come in, over on the I.C., and he remembered the two or three times that he and Rusty had escorted Agnes to that very train, when she went to visit her folks in Rockford, Illinois.

Lew pressed a switch: the whole front of Marsh's went dark. That was the go-to-bed signal . . . when people saw those lights out, over the fountain and cigar and magazine counters, they knew that Marsh's was officially closed for the evening. The door was always left unlocked until Lew actually went home, just in case, so he wouldn't have to go and unfasten it to let in a doctor or somebody. He was perfectly willing to wait on stray customers, too—even gum-buying customers, right up to the last minute —just so they didn't want any sodas.

Now he would finish putting those ugly patent medicine packages —the ugly labels, the phoney panaceas which he hated to sell, though people eternally demanded them— he would finish installing them in their new home on the high dark shelves, and then he would go home himself.

Mounted on a step-ladder and holding a basket on his arm for convenience as he worked, Lew carefully placed the orange-and-black boxes of Father Tom's Magic Emulsion in front of each other.

He heard the front door open, but he couldn't turn around and crane his neck past the pipe display without endangering his perch on the ladder. . . . Lew Marsh thought he knew the step of half the people who came in the store, and he wondered whose step this was. Sounded like Tommy Glenn or Dave Boylston; he wasn't sure which.

He was just about to sing out, "Hey, Tommy," or, "Hey, Dave," when someone halted behind him.

An unfamiliar voice, and rather strained, asked: "Is this Marsh's?"

Lew turned around on the ladder

406

and he got a brief shock. The young fellow who addressed him wore the uniform of the United States Navy, and that in itself was a real wallop for Lew just then.

He put his hand on the shelf. He knocked off one bottle of Father Tom's, but it only fell as far as the counter ledge and didn't break.

The young fellow took off his cap; there was a manner of salute in the way he did it. He was a steady-faced youth with a strong thick neck and round gray eyes that fairly looked a hole through Lew Marsh. His face was extremely sunburnt, and you could see where he had had a recent haircut, because the close-cropped area around his temples wasn't tanned at all.

"Evening," said Lew. "Yes, this is Marsh's."

The sailor looked at him a while. Then he said, "I guess you're Rusty's father, aren't you?"

Lew got down off the ladder blindly. He stood there with the package of patent medicine in his hands. "What do you know about Rusty?"

The boy had two little bars of ribbon on his left breast; Lew didn't know it then, but he found out later: one of those was the ribbon of the Navy Cross.

"I'm Anton Cavrek," and the name meant nothing to the buzzing ears of Lew Marsh.

He looked down through the top and side glass of the counter, and he could see the shiny black shoes that the stranger wore below his blue uniform pants.

There was a little zipper bag on the floor beside him.

"Any friend of—Are you—?"

The round gray eyes blinked two or three times. "I'm Tony. I thought maybe Rusty had said something about me in his letters and—"

. . . All the way back to the time when Rusty was at the recruit depot.

Got acquainted with a pretty nice guy this week, from Chicago. His name is Tony. When we got liberty, night before last, we . . .

I wish you could enjoy the view from that big hotel in San Francisco like I did. It's certainly beautiful. Tony and I were up there Sunday afternoon, and had some beer in the bar on the roof, and just looked out of the windows. . . .

At the U. S. O. dance last week, Tony and I met a couple of real nice girls. We had liberty ashore on Sunday again, and went out to one of the girls' houses. She had a remarkable collection of records, and we surely—

Lew said flatly, "So you're Tony."

"Yes, sir."

"For goodness' sake."

They shook hands among the Kleenex, but this was different from shaking hands with Judge Colvin. . . . Lew didn't want to let go of Tony Cavrek's hand.

"Let's see," he said, "seems to me Rusty said your home was in Chicago?"

The boy nodded. "Yes sir." His voice was smooth and low, but still strong and alert. "Such a home as I've got, I mean to say, sir. See, I've been an orphan since I was sixteen; but of course I kept on living in Chicago until I joined the navy."

He glanced around the store and Lew thought that he saw approval in Tony's gaze, or at least some kind of satisfaction. "I don't know

407

whether Rusty told you," said Tony Cavrek, "but you know I used to jerk sodas in Chicago. This does seem familiar. You got a nice fountain there, Mr. Marsh."

It didn't seem right somehow to stay behind the counter any longer. But there were the bottles of patent medicine—

Tony understood at once, when Lew glanced up at the shelves. Then he was around the counter before you could wink, and up on the stepladder.

"Here, just hand them up to me," and in a few moments the job was done.

Lew Marsh thanked him. "Want a cigar?"

"I wouldn't mind."

Lew started toward the cigar counter. But the sailor said: "Where do you keep this ladder?" and Lew pointed out the back room.

He went on up to the cigar counter and got out the best cigars he could find. They were three-for-fifty-cent coronas; Judge Colvin and Dave Boylston and a very few other men in Hartfield smoked cigars like that.

Lew got out two cigars, and when Tony joined him they lit up.

"Gee," said Tony, "this is a swell cigar! I don't very often smoke cigars, sir. You know how it is: cigarettes usually. But this is sure swell."

"Look here," said Lew, "are you bound for Chicago? When do you have to leave?"

Tony said that he didn't have to leave at any special time. . . . He had a trick of dropping his eyes for a moment and then they'd come up clear and strong, and you'd feel them going through you again.

"You see, Mr. Marsh, it was like this: Rusty and I used to talk about —about what might happen and— See, I haven't got any folks or anything; but Rusty always said that if anything happened—I mean, to him —he said I ought to come when I got a chance and—call on you and his mother—"

There was a misty silence. It wasn't the silence of an empty store, but a place populated with many people, all of whom seemed to be holding their breaths and waiting for something.

"You came in on the ten-thirteen from the west?"

"Yes, sir. I came from a Pacific port; sorry I can't tell you the name. But I still got the better part of two weeks ahead of me before I have to go back."

Lew said, "Well." Then he thought of the telephone. "I guess maybe I'd better call up—Rusty's mother—before we leave the store here. And tell her we're coming...."

"Yes, sir," said Tony.

Lew made the call, and then the store was locked. In a few minutes he and Tony were moving south along the dark woodsy tunnel of Willson Avenue.

Lew pointed out the Congregational and Baptist churches, and he told Tony that the Methodist church, where they belonged, was a block over west.

"I was raised a Catholic, kind of," said Tony Cavrek.

"Oh, yes," said Lew, quickly. "You know, Father Frein here in Hartfield is one of my best friends and customers."

When they approached the house Agnes had lights turned on in the living room and in the kitchen; probably she was fixing something to eat.

Lew halted, just before they turned up the walk, and pointed out the big maple tree on the parking. "Rusty used to tap that," and Tony wanted to know what *tap* was. "You bore a hole," said Lew. "Then the sap comes out. The kids used to call it sugar-water, and they liked to drink it."

"I bet it's good," said Tony Cavrek. "You know how it is in Chicago, on the west side. We didn't have any such sugar-water things."

Lew asked him: "You like to play croquet? I mean the modern kind, with great big mallets and heavy balls? We've got a swell set here . . . hasn't been used much lately."

They reached the steps. "I guess it would be swell," Tony said. "I would have to have somebody show me, though. I used to box some at the *Sokol*—that's a kind of club—and I play handball. That's about the only games I know much about."

"Well," said Lew, opening the screen door, "I guess Lenore Prentiss—she's a girl lives next door—I guess maybe she could show you."

They went into the house. Agnes began to cry; then she kissed Tony Cavrek. Lew went into the front room by the bay window and cried a little himself, just for a moment.

He came back, blowing his nose heartily and saying: "Well, well, well! Mother, where we going to put this big tramp of a sailor?"

Agnes wiped her eyes and smiled. "I guess you know where." She looked at Lew. "If he wants to . . ."

Tony's strong gray eyes were blinking rapidly. "It is O.K. by me, Mrs. Marsh," he said, and his mild voice seemed to ring through the rooms.

"I was just getting some lunch," said Agnes.

They followed her out into the kitchen and stood watching as she sliced the cold meat-loaf.

Lew said, "I wonder . . . maybe we'd better discuss it now. Is there anything you ought to tell us, Tony?"

The sailor stood very straight before them, and they watched his chest moving in its strong, easy breath behind the bright slabs of medal ribbon. He said, "You understand that I can't tell you where it was. I guess you know the date, maybe. When you got your telegram . . . ?"

Lew nodded. Somehow he didn't feel like crying any more.

"They came over awfully fast," said Tony. "We weren't surprised, but they had more planes than us; and a lot of them got through and began pounding us—our boat, I mean—pretty hard. Rusty and I were both topside to begin with, but he was ordered down to the sick bay right away. I saw him once, about twenty minutes later, when I had to go down there for a minute. . . . He was working hard, helping the doctors. They had a lot of wounded coming in, and I think Rusty saved quite a few lives. He was real good at his job."

Tony Cavrek looked at the kitchen stove, and seemed to be counting the little handles of the gas switches. Then he repeated slowly, "Rusty was real good—at any job he had to do."

He went on and told them: "An aerial torpedo came in on that side.

409

It exploded through a couple of decks. They said Rusty was helping carry out some of the guys that were hurt, when he got it. I guess there isn't very much more I can tell you, except that I thought quite a lot of Rusty."

He stopped abruptly. . . . Finally Lew went over, and made a fist out of his hand, and hit Tony lightly two or three times on the shoulder. "You like loganberry wine?" he asked. "There's an old lady here in town makes it, and she gave me a couple of bottles last week."

"I guess I never had any loganberry wine," said Tony Cavrek, "but I bet it sure would be swell."

IMMORTALITY
FRANCESCA FALK MILLER

And there shall come a day . . . in Spring
When death and winter
Loose their chill, white hold
Quite suddenly. A day of sunlit air
When winging birds return,
And earth her gentle bosoms bare
So that new, thirsty life
May nurture there.
That breathless hour . . .
So filled with warm, soft miracles
That faith is born anew.
On such a day . . .
I shall return to you!

You may not touch me . . . no,
For you have thought of me as dead.
But in the silence lift believing eyes
Toward the dear infinity
Of skies. And listen . . .
With your very soul held still . . .
For you will hear me on some little hill,
Advancing with the coming of the year.
Not far away . . . Not dead . . .
Not even gone.
The day will suddenly be filled
With immortality and song,
And without stirring from your quiet place,
Your love will welcome mine . . .
Across the little space,
And we will talk of every lovely thing . . .
When I return . . . in Spring!

STARS
SARA TEASDALE

Alone in the night
On a dark hill
With pines around me
Spicy and still,

And a heaven full of stars
Over my head,
White and topaz
And misty red;

Myriads with beating
Hearts of fire
That aeons
Cannot vex or tire;

Up the dome of heaven
Like a great hill,
I watch them marching
Stately and still,

And I know that I
Am honored to be
Witness
Of so much majesty.

GOD IS AT THE ANVIL
LEW SARETT

God is at the anvil, beating out the sun;
  Where the molten metal spills,
  At his forge among the hills
He has hammered out the glory of a day that's done.

God is at the anvil, welding golden bars;
  In the scarlet-streaming flame
  He is fashioning a frame
For the shimmering silver beauty of the evening stars.

411

Author Index

413

414

415

416

418

419

Title Index

423

426

Subject Index

AMBITION

Builders, The,
Henry Wadsworth Longfellow 298
Quotations
Adams, J. Q.	275
Alcott	103
Andersen	219
Anonymous	66, 67
Aurelius	230
Bacon	250, 350
Beecher	372, 373
Brooks	151, 160
Bulwer-Lytton	280
Chamfort	218
Channing	160
Chesterfield	350
Confucius	151
Congreve	250
Daniel	362
De Rouvroy	287
Disraeli	131
Dryden	83
Emerson	140, 141
Franklin	103
Gladstone	250
Goethe	251, 294, 296
Heywood	83
Holmes, O. W.	82
Ingelow	258
Jefferies	250
Johnson	351
Lovelace	168
Seneca	340
Shakespeare	50
Smith	258
Thoreau	40, 102, 103, 200
Whittier	169

Silver Ships, Mildred Plew Meigs 273

BEAUTY

Alchemy, Sara Teasdale 39
Baby Face, Carl Sandburg 105
Ballad for Christmas,
Nancy Byrd Turner 116
Earth Lover, Harold Vinal 349
Hold Fast Your Dreams, Louise Driscoll 1
Holiness, John Drinkwater 78
Hundred Years of Stars and Violets, A,
Richard Jefferies 186
Many Love Music,
Walter Savage Landor 262
Old House, Winifred Welles 279

On Hearing a Symphony of Beethoven,
Edna St. Vincent Millay 314
Pilgrimage, Grace Noll Crowell 245
Poetry, Lord Dunsany 187
Quotations
Addison	280
Andersen	218
Beethoven	218, 275
Bonnat	312
Disraeli	131
Emerson	140, 141
Goethe	294, 297
Herder	297
Holland	102
Hugo	287
Keats	82
Kingsley	258
Koran	151
Landor	83
Lanier	240
Liszt	218
Longfellow	240
Lowell, J. R.	168
Luther	150, 373
Moore	280
Morris	313
Plato	323
Reynolds	313
Shelley	240
Thoreau	30
Wendte	219

Roadside Flowers, Bliss Carman 321

BOOKS

Quotations
Barrow	219
Beecher	151
Carlyle	190, 191
Cicero	178
Clarke	150
De Bury	381
Emerson	274
Frederick the Great	12
Goldsmith	362
Holmes, O. W.	83
La Bruyère	287
Lang	280
Melville	40
Montaigne	231
Petrarch	83
Temple	280
Thoreau	41
Trollope	280

428

430

431

LOVE OF NATURE

NOBILITY OF CHARACTER

WISE WORDS

SYMPATHY

WORK